Daughters of the People
Omnibus One
Books 1-3

LUCY VARNA

Daughters of the People
Omnibus One
Books 1-3

LUCY VARNA

Bone Diggers Press
www.bonediggerspress.com

Published by Bone Diggers Press, Clayton, Georgia.

ISBN 978-1-943465-04-0

TITLES BY LUCY VARNA

THE DAUGHTERS OF THE PEOPLE SERIES
Book 1: *The Prophecy*
Book 2: *Light's Bane*
Book 3: *The Enemy Within*
Book 3.5: *Tempered*
Book 4: *In All Things, Balance*

THE SONS OF THE PEOPLE SERIES
Book 1: *Say Yes*

THE PRUXNÆ SERIES
Book 1: *The Choosing*

THE CULLOWHEE HERITAGE SERIES
Book 1: *A Higher Purpose*
Book 2: *A Wicked Love*

COMING SOON
Sanctuary (Daughters of the People, Book 5)

Table of Contents

Notes from the Fab Four

Notes on the People compiled by Tom Fairfax, Phil Walters, George Howe, and James Terhune, known at the IECS unofficially as the Fab Four.

Aenkanien. A tattoo inked into the left-hand shoulder blade of a Son who becomes the husband of a Daughter. Once approval has been granted by the mothers of both parties and the tattoo is in place, a formal marriage ceremony is unnecessary; the two are considered married in the eyes of the People, though many couples choose to undergo a civil or, less frequently, traditional ceremony.

Amaetien. The tattoo Sons receive on their sixteenth birthday (the day they become men under the traditions and laws of the People) to indicate their maternal lineage. Usually inked onto the upper left arm, the *amaetien* is a symbol of the mother's eternal protection and devotion, and a warning to any who would harm the Son.

Ankana. Woman. Also refers to the Woman with No Face.

Council of Seven. The People's ruling body, consisting of seven women, one representing the line of each of the Seven Sisters.

Daughter. A direct descendant of one of the Seven Sisters, Daughters may be either immortal (if they have not yet broken their own curse) or mortal (if they have broken their own curse or are the daughter of a mortal Daughter).

Eknon. Student.

Eternal Order. A supposedly mythical group devoted to undermining the ultimate goal of the People, to break the curse of immortality for every Daughter through the fulfillment of the Prophecy of Light.

High Guard. Seven Daughters devoted to eradicating the Eternal Order.

A highly secret and deadly group.

Institute of Early Cultural Studies (IECS). Located in Tellowee, Georgia, USA, the IECS is the main historical research branch of the People and serves as a repository for much of its history.

Kaetyrm. Sister, usually used in a formal situation, though not always.

Maetyrm. Mother, usually used as a term of respect for an elder Daughter and not necessarily as a reference to one's own mother. Teachers, for example, are referred to as Maetyrm.

People, The. The name used by the descendants of the Seven Sisters to describe themselves. The People include all immortal and mortal Daughters, Sons, and the mortal descendants of all submitted Daughters to the second degree (i.e. through the grandchildren of Daughters who have submitted their wills and become mortal). Other descendants are not counted among the numbers of the People.

Prophecy of Light. Issued by an unknown person at some distant point in the past, the Prophecy of Light portends a way for the curse of immortality to be lifted from all of the People, and not solely the Daughters who submit their wills and become mortal. (See the Daughters of the People website.)

Seven Sisters. The progenitors of the modern People. The seven women, all sisters, avenged the deaths of their parents by killing the men of the People (the original band) and were cursed by the god An to live immortal lives without the ability to bear sons. The curse was tempered by the goddess Ki, who decreed that the curse could be broken by each one if she would submit her will, in whatever way (except sexually), to the man she loved. (See the Legend of Beginnings on the Daughters of the People website.)

Shadow Enemy. The traditional enemy of the People.

Son. Usually refers to the child of a Daughter who has broken the curse and become mortal, but may also reference the child of a Son or another male descendant of a Daughter.

Tellowee, Georgia, USA. One of the centers of the People, located in rural northeast Georgia.

Book 1
The Prophecy

PROLOGUE

Circa 7,500 B.C.E.

A HARD MOON shone down upon four hands worth of seasonal shelters. Kiya, eldest daughter of the First Seer in her union with the Warrior Chief, leaned her spear against a boulder and settled into her shift of the watch on top of a flat stretch of dirt. She squinted at the moon, so round and full above her. Its light was as pure as anything she'd ever seen. Maybe this would be the night the Lady Ki would grant her a vision, the way Mother always said She would. Kiya's bleeding time had come upon her two moons past. She was a woman now and ready to fulfill her duty to the gods, but without that first vision, she was relegated to the watch, a position anybody with two eyes and working ears could fill. Would she ever be able to begin her training as the People's next Seer or would the Lady find another of her sisters more worthy?

A pebble bounded across the rocks behind her and Kiya sighed. "Come out, Abragni. I know you're there."

Kiya's youngest sister crawled out of the shadows and sat down an arm's span away. "How come you always know it's me?"

"Because you're the noisiest of the Seven." Kiya held her arm out, beckoning Abragni closer. "You should be sleeping. We break camp tomorrow. Who knows how long it'll take us to reach the next one."

Abragni leaned her head against Kiya's scrawny chest and snuggled into her sister's embrace. "Marnan keeps poking me and Bagda won't make her stop."

"I'll speak to them."

"They won't listen to you either."

"Then I'll speak to Mother."

"Speak to the Lady, Kiya. *She'll* make them stop."

Kiya pressed her lips together. How could she tell her sweet sister that the Lady refused to share the future, guarding it as closely as Father did the People's safety? "I'll pray to An. How's that?"

Abragni's voice dropped to a whisper. "But He's grumpy."

"And He hears all," Kiya teased. "Here, little one. Rest your head on my leg. I'll protect you."

"I know you will." Abragni yawned and curled up on the ground beside Kiya, one hand on Kiya's leg under her head. "Forever and ever."

"Forever and ever," Kiya echoed.

The moon moved steadily across the sky, sliding through the stars along its nightly path. Kiya smoothed her hand over Abragni's dark hair, soothing her sister into sleep. The camp was still and quiet, the fires banked, the People resting with their families. Weariness crept over her. She shook it away, sharpening her gaze, tuning her ears to the slightest noise.

The guard wouldn't have been necessary if they weren't camped so close to another settlement, a walled city half a day's journey away. Father had refused to share his reasoning, but there had been rumors, ugly whispers among the women that their men grew tired of the People's nomadic life and wished to join their fortunes to those dwelling behind the high walls.

Nonsense, of course. The People were happy and hale, their children hearty, and though they had no wall to protect them from predators and war, they did well enough.

A shadow flitted across the encampment. Kiya sucked in a quick breath and scanned the valley floor around the People's shelters. The shadow moved again, shifting from one side of the camp to the other, zigzagging toward the tent on the far side where Mother and Father rested with Kiya's five other sisters.

Another shadow joined the first and a third, and Kiya's heart thudded hard in her chest. She pressed one hand over her sister's mouth and shook her awake with the other. Abragni's wide, dark eyes blinked open. Kiya leaned down and whispered, "Something's wrong. We need to wake everybody. Can you help me?"

Abragni nodded slowly.

Kiya removed her hand and grabbed her spear. "If we get separated, make your way to the edge of the waters next to the cave Ganenda likes to hide in and wait for me there."

"I will," Abragni whispered. "You won't leave me there, will you?"

"I'd never do that."

They made their way around the perimeter of the camp, searching for the other men and women who were supposed to be on watch, and found no one. With each step, Kiya's chest grew a little tighter, her skin a little more prickly. She grasped Abragni's hand and urged her forward. They were halfway between the last watch position and the encampment when a scream rent the air, shattering the night's quiet.

Kiya's breath froze in her throat. "Mother."

Abragni's face crumpled. A tear slid down her round cheek. "I'm scared, Kiya."

Me, too. Kiya swallowed her fear and knelt in front of her sister. "Go to the cave now, little one. I'll wake our sisters and meet you there. Stick to the shadows."

Abragni sniffed and swiped the back of her hand across her face, smearing dirt through the tears. "I hate the shadows."

"Don't. You've nothing to fear among them. Now go."

Abragni slipped away and Kiya stood, spear in hand. An unnatural hush settled over the People's shelters. Nothing moved. She sniffed, testing the air, and found no scent that shouldn't be there.

Kiya approached Mother and Father's shelter cautiously. Her footsteps were

4

silent as she moved over the hard earth and her eyes never still. Three spear lengths away, a soft sob drifted to her and a female voice spoke, the words too faint for Kiya to make out. She eased up to the back of the shelter and dropped to her haunches in the sparse shadows lingering there. The voice came again, scarcely louder than it had been, and Kiya strained her ears, hoping to discern meaning in the quietly spoken words.

No, the voice was still too soft.

She crept around the edge of the shelter toward the opening and halted. In the clearing between the shelters, a handful of men stood over two limp forms lying prone on the ground.

"It's done, then," a man said, and Kiya's eyes widened. That had sounded like Dunan, Belara's man.

"A shame they had to be killed." That voice belonged to Tem'n, a young warrior just into his manhood, barely two seasons older than Kiya. "Especially the Seer. Her visions were useful."

An odd pressure filled her chest. *The Seer.* Her mother, the revered conduit between the People and the gods. Could she truly be dead?

"Are the women bound?"

Kiya frowned. She couldn't place that voice. It had to be a male of the People. Who else would be in their camp at night?

"It's been done," Dunan said. "We're missing two, the eldest and youngest of the Seven."

"The Seven?" the unfamiliar man said.

"The Seer's daughters," Tem'n said. "Five are inside. They're strong girls, brave. They'll make good slaves."

Kiya's heart skipped a beat. Kind Tem'n had never had a cross word to say to any woman, and now he wished to enslave her and her sisters? Such a life would be intolerable for any among the People. They were free, roaming where they willed, their only limits their need for food, shelter, and protection from the wild beasts and other people. How could anybody wish to deprive her and her sisters of that freedom, and why?

The men moved away, their conversation dwindling into murmurs too low for Kiya to understand. She waited and watched, biding her time. The men disappeared into a shelter on the far side of the camp. The moon's light dimmed, throwing the area around her into shadow. She glanced up. A cloud, a large, dark one, fully covered the bright moon. It would give her just enough time.

She crawled forward as quietly as she could along the hard-packed earth, her eyes scanning the darkness, and stopped beside the two still forms. Mother's eyes stared blindly into the sky. Something dark covered one side of her head, her life force, surely. Beside her, Father rested on his stomach. Kiya edged her fingers along the back of his head and encountered a dent the size of her fist among the sticky strands of his dark hair.

A whimper alerted her to another person's presence. Kiya crouched low, scanning the encampment. It came again, and this time she pinpointed it precisely. The whimpers were coming from her, from her own mouth. She bit into the side of her hand and closed her eyes, and a storm of sorrow whirled through her. Mother and

Father, dead. The women of the People bound by their men. Five of her sisters enslaved, and one alone in the dark.

And she, barely fourteen seasons, had no guidance, no voice in her heart, no vision sent by the Lady illuminating the path Kiya must take.

Tears leaked down her face over her hand. She sat there for long moments, rocking slowly to and fro, her heart pounding and her breaths uneven. She couldn't do anything about Mother and Father. Their spirits were long gone now, lost to the Seven as surely as if they'd been taken by An. There were too many men to free all the women, too many for one lone woman to counter, but she could at least try to free her sisters.

She released her hand and ignored the throb of teeth marks imprinted into the skin. Her spear. She'd need that if the men had left a guard. She grasped it firmly and inched across the ground toward Mother and Father's shelter.

A sliver of light peeked out from under the edge of the opening flap, barely enough to see by. Kiya shifted onto her haunches beside the flap and lifted it aside a scant hand's breadth. A fire crackled in the center, its edges delineated by stacked stones. Her sisters huddled together on the far side, their eyes wide. Kiya squinted and eased upright slightly. Their hands were in front of them, maybe bound, maybe not.

A solitary man passed between them and the fire. Thin, white scars marred his sun-darkened skin, formed under the claws of the animals the People hunted, and under the hands of their enemies. Kiya dropped the flap and put her back to the shelter. Young Mol'k, one the fiercest warriors among the People. He was brutal and hard, and so skilled, none could take him, not even the great beasts. She pressed trembling fingers over her mouth and breathed a prayer to the Lady. She'd never been to battle before, never faced man or beast except in practice, but her sisters were in there, relegated to a fate as harsh as death. How could she leave them?

Kiya inhaled through her nose and exhaled through her mouth, again and again in slow draws, willing her heart to calm and her mind to clear. Mol'k had her sisters. They needed to be freed. Kiya was the only one left to help them. Whatever she must do, so it must be.

She stood slowly and gripped her spear, then slid into the shelter. In a single glance, she took in her sisters' frightened faces, their hands and feet bound in front of them, and the man standing between her and them.

Mol'k turned, facing her. His lower body was clad in leather breeches, his feet were bare under the hem, and the muscles of his upper body rippled as he moved. "We've been looking for you, Kiya."

"I was on watch." She rolled her shoulders. "Why are my sisters bound?"

His eyes glittered in the firelight. A small smile twisted his lips. "I think you know why."

"Maybe."

"You should join them."

Kiya bared her teeth. "I think not."

He laughed and edged around the fire toward her, hands held out to his sides. "I always liked your spirit. Come quietly, little one, and I'll make sure your sisters go to good men."

"Will you?" she murmured. "And what of me?"

His smile widened. "I've already claimed you."

"Have you?"

"No one will challenge me. Who would dare?" He inched his way forward, drawing ever closer, and Kiya's hand tightened around the shaft of the spear. He wiggled his fingers. "Give me the spear, little one. Think of your sisters. Think of the life you could have with me. I'll protect you and the children we make, this I swear."

Behind him, Lilleni shook her head slowly, barely moving it from side to side.

Kiya focused on Mol'k, on his size and strength, on his unwavering smile. She lowered the spear and loosened her grip. "You're a good man, Mol'k."

"Kiya, no!" Eleni cried, and Bagda rammed her shoulder into her sister's arm.

"Father respected you," Kiya continued, and gathered her courage for what must be done. "If I give myself to you, can you guarantee my sisters' safety?"

Ganenda lowered her head, hiding the tears streaming down her face, her shoulders heaving in silent sobs. Kiya's sisters leaned their heads together, Bagda with her dark, steady eyes on Kiya. She lifted her hand, flashing a stone-bladed knife, and Kiya jerked her attention to Mol'k.

"I'll do everything I can." He stepped forward, closing the distance between them, and held a hand out. "Give me the spear, Kiya. Let me help you."

"I'll give you the spear in exchange for a kiss. I've never..." She cleared her throat and shoved down the nerves biting her insides. "I've never lain with a man."

"I know." Mol'k placed a hand on the spear's shaft behind the point, pushing it to the side, and slid a hard arm around her waist. "A kiss, then, so you'll know I can be more than the hardened warrior your father trusted."

Kiya bowed her head. "Did you kill him?"

"I had no hand in that, little one, nor in your mother's death." He brushed his cheek along her temple and lowered his voice. "I went to her after your first bleeding time and asked for you."

Her heart leapt into her throat. "What of Rila?"

"Barren. She wishes to return to her people at the next gathering. I've already freed her." Mol'k's sigh feathered across Kiya's skin. "Your mother asked me to wait for you, said I'd know when the time was right to claim you, and when I saw her body on the ground..."

"She's dead."

"I know."

"Do my sisters know?"

"They suspect." He laughed, soft and short. "The Seer said even after I claimed you, you'd make me wait to have you. I can't believe she was so wrong."

"She never was," Kiya said softly. And wouldn't be this time. She had only to delay. Surely the six of them together could take down this one warrior, even with his strength and cunning. She dropped her hold on the spear and gripped his narrow hips. "You promised me a kiss."

Mol'k tossed the spear aside and cupped her face. His mouth lowered to hers, claiming her gently, and she forced herself to relax under his unfamiliar touch. A little longer. Bagda had to've freed herself by now. She had to be working on freeing their sisters.

Mol'k's hand slid down her face and cupped her nape, holding her close to him as his mouth moved across hers. A scuff sounded behind him and he jerked back, breaking the kiss.

Kiya wrapped her arms around his lean torso and stood on tiptoe. "Teach me how to please you."

"I will, Kiya," he murmured. "We'll please each other."

His hands tightened on her skin and his mouth met hers, hard and demanding, and Kiya pressed into him, desperate to buy more time for her sisters. A little longer. A little more.

A thud shuddered through him and his hold loosened. He swayed and crumpled to the ground, taking Kiya with him, and she bit back a sob as they fell into the dirt. Soft hands tugged her away from him into the embrace of her sisters.

She pushed herself away from them and knelt beside Mol'k, running her hands over the lump one of her sisters had knocked into his head. He groaned and stirred, and she backed away.

"We have to hurry," she whispered. "Abragni's waiting for us by Ganenda's cave."

Bagda lifted Kiya's spear and jerked her head at Mol'k. "What of him?"

Kiya stood. "Leave him."

"He'll come after us," Lilleni murmured.

Kiya shook her head. "Mother told him he'd have to wait to claim me. He won't go against her vision."

She shushed their questions and ushered them out of the shelter one by one. They traveled on quiet feet to the edge of the water, accompanied by the moon's cold light. Abragni was waiting for them, huddled inside the cave's entrance, her tiny body shivering, her face streaked with tears. Kiya lifted the youngest into her arms, holding her close, and told her sisters what she'd observed, of Mother and Father's deaths, of the men's treachery, and of the vision Mol'k had shared. They sat in silence for long moments, listening to the water lapping against the shore and the breeze blowing through the brush.

Lilleni lifted her face to the moon. "What will we do, Kiya?"

"We wait. We learn. We prepare." Kiya stood and stared down at her sisters, meeting their gazes one by one. "And when the time is right, we strike, avenging the wrongs done to the People tonight. Tomorrow, we seek shelter away from those who harmed Mother and Father. For now, we rest. Get some sleep, my sisters. We have a long journey ahead of us."

"Blessed be Ki," Eleni said.

"Blessed be Ki," Kiya murmured.

The soft cry echoed through the cave's interior, bouncing against its stone walls, embedded there as surely as if it had been carved. From that night on, the Seven Sisters hardened their hearts, and they never, ever forgot the fate delivered upon them by the envy of men.

ONE

The present

MAYA BELLEGARDE stepped off the private jet and breathed in the sweet air of late spring, bracing herself against the heat boiling up from the tarmac. The flight from the States to Stockholm hadn't been bad. Long, but not bad, and it had given her plenty of time to think.

Dani Nehring halted beside her, yawned, and pulled her body into a bone-popping stretch. "So, Swedish men or Swedish food?"

Maya didn't bother with exasperation. The younger Daughter was irrepressible, her sunny personality a reflection of her bright looks. Dani's blonde curls, crystal green eyes, and easy-going smile drew stares wherever she went. In many ways, she was an ideal companion, optimistic and always quick on the uptake, and maybe that was her biggest flaw. Very little came between her and a good joke, the bigger the better. Maya had learned early on to never drop her guard around Dani, unless she wanted to fall victim to a good-natured prank.

A trim woman approached from the hangar, her ebony hair pulled into a high ponytail, her pale face set in an impassive gaze. She was an inch taller than Maya's own five foot seven inch frame, slender and graceful, her body fit beneath a loose white cotton shirt and olive green cargo pants. The woman bowed and her ponytail swung forward, brushing the ends over one shoulder.

Maya returned the bow. "How have you been, Indigo?"

Indigo's sapphire eyes glinted in the bright sunlight. "Very well, Maetyrm. How was your flight?"

"Largely uneventful, even with Dani cracking jokes from takeoff to landing."

"Hey, now," Dani said, and Maya shot her a quick grin.

A slight smile tilted Indigo's serious features into soft humor. "I've already made arrangements for your stay. Two rooms inland close to Sandby borg and a late model Volvo sedan, exactly as Director Upton requested."

"And the dig?"

"As soon as you've settled into your cabins."

"So, no men, then?" Dani asked.

Maya rolled her eyes skyward. "Business before pleasure."

Dani grinned and flipped her blonde curls back. "I have to brush up on my Swedish first, anyway."

As soon as the luggage was loaded, Indigo slid into the driver's seat of the Volvo. Maya slipped into the back, leaving a chattering Dani to the front. During the drive southeast from Stockholm, Maya tuned one ear to Indigo and Dani's conversation as they shared gossip old and new, and focused on their destination, an archaeological dig at Sandby borg, the site of a fifth century land fort that had been abandoned after a brutal massacre.

When Indigo had contacted Rebecca Upton, head of the Institute for Early Cultural Studies, to report a promising gravesite at the borg, Maya had volunteered to visit and examine the skeleton and any artifacts. She'd tried not to get her hopes up. Over the years, she'd visited a lot of archaeological sites only to come away disappointed. This one was different, though. There was something here, something the People could use. She could feel it in her bones, and a Daughter's instincts never lied.

THEY CROSSED ÖLAND BRIDGE, a six kilometer road connecting Öland Island to the Swedish mainland. Maya brought her attention back to the conversation as Indigo pointed out landmarks in the small villages they passed through. They took the perimeter highway north, then a series of smaller roads inland. Within twenty minutes, a small group of rental cabins appeared on the side of the road. Indigo pulled up beside one and parked.

Dani stepped out of the rental and wrinkled her slim, straight nose. "I thought Sweden was, like, old. This looks like downtown back home."

"Not everybody can live in medieval castles, Dani," Indigo said.

They checked in at the main cabin, dropped their luggage off in their separate units, and freshened up in Maya's room. The cabins weren't air conditioned. The June heat had driven the interior temperatures to a nearly unbearable level, in spite of the efforts of a single desktop fan placed in each room.

Dani tugged the neckline of her t-shirt away from her chest. "Man, tonight's gonna be miserable. How do you stand it?"

Indigo smiled, flashing dimples. "We have air conditioning."

"Spoiled," Maya said.

Dani groaned. "You're not gonna tell us one of those 'good ol' days' tales, are you?"

"Maybe later, if you're really bored," Maya said drily. "If it makes you feel better, you'll be spending part of the night watching the camp instead of here sweltering in the heat."

"She may not need to be at the dig tonight." Indigo dropped onto the edge of the room's only bed. "Looters have hit a couple of nearby digs, so we've been taking turns staying on site at night. It's my turn tonight."

Maya nodded. "Still, I may have Dani do a little recon after dark."

"She can keep me company, then."

"Sure," Dani said. "Soon as I have a good look-see."

The dig was a short drive from the cabin. Indigo slowed on approach, allowing plenty of time for Maya and Dani to study the outer ring of Sandby borg's ruins. The crumbling foundations of ancient walls rose from the grass, a long-unneeded protection for the interior buildings. A handful of tents covered tables stacked with tools, plastic and cardboard storage boxes, and computers. A trailer was located on the opposite end of the site, near a small storage shed. Only a handful of people were on site, some engaged in fine digging, others apparently sorting and cataloguing. One young woman sat alone about fifty yards from the main dig in an open, rectangular pit, her bent head and shoulders visible above the earth.

Indigo brought the Volvo to a halt in the graveled parking area next to a handful of other vehicles. The three women got out, and Maya and Dani followed Indigo into the main part of the dig toward the tents. As they approached, two men looked up from their work at one of the tables, one ancient and stooped, the other on the upside of middle age.

The older man retrieved a wooden cane from its resting place against the table and leaned into it as he faced the women. "Indigo, my dear," he said, his English heavily accented, his sagging features animated under a mop of silver hair. "You've brought us quite the treat today."

"Dr. Lindberg, this is Dr. Maya Bellegarde from the Institute for Early Cultural Studies and her assistant, Daniella Nehring. They're here to examine the anomalous burial."

"Of course. I remember. So much excitement here now. The days run together." Dr. Lindberg gestured to the younger man by his side. "This is my colleague, Dr. James Terhune. I brought him in to consult on that burial."

"Pleased to meet you." James grasped Maya's hand, his own calloused and firm. The warmth of their grip spread up Maya's arm. Her heart skipped and her skin tightened, and a delicious flutter of nerves tingled in her abdomen.

The heat generated by the simple touch intrigued her. She studied James from beneath lowered lashes, assessing him carefully. He was taller than her by about four inches, slim and athletic. Intense chocolate brown eyes peered at her out of a thin face with high cheekbones, an aristocratic nose, and a mouth that wasn't quite wide enough to overpower his other features. He hadn't shaved in a day or so and his rich brown hair was slightly unkempt. The ends brushed over the collar of an untucked, blue cotton shirt worn over jeans and hiking boots. His hand slid away from hers, creating a warm friction along her palm, and her stomach jumped.

"Likewise." Maya tucked her hands into the pockets of her cargo pants, curling her fingers around the heat lingering on her palm. "We're anxious to see the site."

Dr. Lindberg pointed the end of his cane toward the grave. "Come, then. James and I shall escort you. Indigo, would you be a dear and set up refreshments for our guests?"

"Certainly, Dr. Lindberg."

"Supper tonight," Maya said.

Indigo nodded and bowed. "Yes, Maetyrm. Dani, gentlemen." She pivoted and strode toward the trailer, her movements efficient and precise.

Dr. Lindberg smiled fondly after Indigo. "Such a good girl, always so helpful.

Very bright, too."

"I've found her to be so myself," Maya agreed mildly. The *girl* he'd just sent on errands was twice his age, though Maya had a feeling that wouldn't matter one whit to Dr. Lindberg, even if she could tell him. His fondness would undoubtedly color his opinion and he'd still think of Indigo as a young woman and not the century-and-a-half years old warrior she was.

Dani tucked her hand into the crook of Dr. Lindberg's elbow. "Well, now that the competition's out of the way, I can flirt with the handsomest man here."

Dr. Lindberg laughed and patted her hand with gnarled fingers. "Tell that to my wife, please. She thinks I've become crotchety in my old age."

As the unlikely pair strolled across the site, Maya fell into step beside Dr. Terhune. They walked for a few moments in silence, listening to the cadence of the conversation between Dani and Dr. Lindberg.

"I read your paper on female divinities in sedentary hunter-gather bands. Fascinating perspective." James stuffed his fingers into the front pockets of his jeans. "Now that I've met you, though, I can't believe somebody as young as you are could write something like that. The research alone must've taken years and you..."

Maya glanced at him. "I what?"

He cleared his throat, his gaze focused on the couple in front of them. "You barely look old enough to be out of college."

"Just what every woman wants to hear."

He smiled and the corners of his eyes crinkled along faint laugh lines. Their arms brushed as they walked, shooting a spark of warmth down Maya's arm.

"You take the IECS' *Journal,* then?" she asked.

"Who doesn't?" He hesitated, cleared his throat again. "I applied for a pass to the IECS Archives a few years back. They turned me down flat."

Maya pursed her lips together. So he wanted access to the Archives, did he? And just when the People needed him to be there. "I'm sure Director Upton could be persuaded to grant you a pass if you're still interested. I'd be happy to put in a good word for you."

"Just like that, no strings attached, for a man you just met?"

"Oh, there are always strings, and we have just met, but your reputation precedes you. You're part of the reason we're here."

"Do tell." His mouth twitched into a crooked grin, flashing white, even teeth. "Is that my professional reputation or the reputation I gained in my misspent youth?"

She laughed. "We're hoping to lure you to the IECS to work with a new collection we've acquired."

"So, my professional reputation, then."

"It's a good one."

Maya slowed to a stop. Ahead of them, Dani and Dr. Lindberg had reached the pit, and whatever was in it must've been something. Dani loped away from it, crossing the open ground quickly, and bounced to a stop in front of Maya and James, her green eyes sparkling. "Maetyrm, you have *got* to see this." She spun and bounded back to the pit.

James eyed Dani's receding figure. "Does she always bounce like that?"

Maya sighed. "I'm afraid so."

They approached the pit at a quicker pace. The young woman Maya had spotted earlier was hunched over a sketchpad next to a single skeleton turned partially on its side. Over time, dirt had filled in the space between the bones, holding the remains in place, allowing the archaeological team to examine it *in situ*. Wisps of what could've been fabric clung to some of the bones. Aside from an armband encircling the humerus of the top-facing arm, the only other items resting near the body were the remains of a long, fire-hardened wooden spear with a rusted metal point, still partially submerged in the dirt.

Maya inhaled deeply, willing her racing heart to calm. "Female?"

Dani tilted her head in a slight nod.

"Quite exciting. Burials from that time period are very rare. Immolation." Dr. Lindberg leaned against his cane, both hands pressing into its top. "Pyres were very popular in the fifth century. Good for the soul, but bad for archaeologists, eh?"

"Have you definitively dated the burial?" Maya asked.

"Still waiting for the lab to settle that." James shifted into a wide-legged stance and crossed his arms over his chest. "Some of the artifacts appear to be centuries older than others. It's made dating the burial itself a little tricky, but the team here believes she was buried at the same time as the massacre."

A tendril of excitement wound through Maya. Dani caught her eye and inclined her head toward the skeleton, her eyebrows raised.

"Dr. Lindberg, would you mind if I took a closer look?" Maya asked.

"Certainly not." A gentle smile lifted Dr. Lindberg's expression. "We welcome your good opinion."

The sketch artist gathered her material and climbed out of the pit, heading toward the main encampment. "Be back when you're done."

"Thanks." Maya maneuvered herself carefully into the pit and examined the skeleton's upper torso as she picked her way around the remains. "Strange that this one body was buried when the others were left laying where they fell."

"She must have been quite significant," Dr. Lindberg said. "Perhaps a courier or a diplomat of some sort."

Maya paused in mid-step. "What makes you say that?"

"That's the reason I'm here." James waggled his eyebrows. "Late last week, the team found a small stash of documents sealed in a metal box that was buried with our mysterious female."

Indigo had reported that cylinder seals had been found with the body, possibly worn as jewelry, but not documents. Maya filtered through her knowledge of Iron Age Scandinavia. "Documents, in northern Europe during the fifth century? Maybe Roman in origin?"

"Only one." James' smile exuded the same excitement clawing at Maya. "But it wasn't produced in northern Europe, best I can tell. There were at least three languages written on a variety of media buried here. Some pictographs as well." His smile stretched into the grin of an academic with a rare treasure on his hands. "One item was a small clay tablet written in Linear A."

Maya blinked, clamping her jaws together against a disbelieving gape. "No."

"Oh, yes." He rocked forward onto the balls of his feet and back again. "So far, we've uncovered the clay tablet, animal skin, papyrus, half a dozen cylinder seals.

13

Some of it just fragments, but still."

She sucked in a breath. The smell of freshly turned dirt seeped through her, comforting in its familiarity. "A regular library, then."

Dani cleared her throat. "Maetyrm, *the armband.*"

Maya knelt in the dirt beside the skeleton, carefully balancing herself above it. The armband glittered dully in the late afternoon sunlight, and a small chill went up Maya's spine. It was crafted of hammered copper, greening with age and exposure to the elements and the dirt it had been buried in. In the dimming light, she could just make out a symbol stamped into it, a single eye staring at her from across at least fifteen centuries. It was a symbol she knew well and it raised her hopes higher than she'd ever allowed them to soar.

She stood and brushed her hands off against the loose cotton of her cargo pants. Dani's grin held smug satisfaction, an emotion Maya could hardly deny the younger Daughter. It was welling up in her own chest, even as she tried to tamp it down. Hope could do funny things to a Daughter, and here was hope in its highest form, a possible clue to the lost prophecy contained in one of the most ancient symbols of the People, a symbol associated specifically with that prophecy.

Maya glanced from Dr. Lindberg's weathered face to James' smiling one. "Take me to the artifacts," she said, and crawled out of the pit.

THREE HOURS LATER, Maya stood in front of the bathroom's mirror towel-drying her hair. As soon as they'd arrived back from the dig, still burning with excitement, she and Dani had retreated to their separate rooms to clean up. Jet lag would kick in soon, but for now, adrenaline kept them going.

Moisture fogged the mirror. Maya swiped a hand towel over it and cleared a space big enough to work, preparing for the night ahead. She smoothed an anti-frizz product through her hair. The tightly coiled curls relaxed slightly then sprang into shape. As a young woman, she'd wished for any kind of hair other than the slightly coarse, kinky brown headful she'd inherited from her mother. Long silky hair like Indigo's or wavy curls like Dani's. Anything. Nostalgia plucked at her. Young girls always wanted to be different, no matter the era.

Maya leaned forward and applied eyeliner to her almond shaped eyes, then brushed mascara over the thick, black lashes. She'd inherited those features from her mother, along with the high, arching eyebrows, the wide, full lips, and pixie face. The aristocratic nose came from her father and seemed out of place covered by her *café au lait* skin. A sharp pang hit her, regret mingling with sorrow. She'd had them for such a short time. What she wouldn't give to have known them better.

She paused, gazing at herself in the mirror. Her mind rarely drifted to her parents. They were both long dead and, except for the night of their brutal murders, she remembered very little about them. Sometimes a smell reminded her of her mother's embrace or she'd hear her father's voice in the timbre of another man's. Their kindness, their love; those were the things she'd clung to during the long, lonely years of her childhood.

She shook the memories away and checked her watch, set to local time as soon as they landed. After a quick mental calculation of the time difference between

Sweden and the IECS, she called Director Upton. The director's receptionist answered on the second ring, then patched Maya through.

"Maya." The voice was smooth, cultured, and well-modulated. Rebecca Upton appeared to be in her early fifties, but she was much, much older, and had the political and business savvy to prove it. Maya closed her eyes and imagined the director as she usually was in the middle of the afternoon on a workday, wearing a tailored power suit, bold but tasteful, with spike-heeled shoes in a matching color, and just the right touch of accessories. Her ash blonde hair would be twisted into a chignon, not a strand out of place, and her delicate features would be artfully enhanced with barely-there makeup.

To the world, Rebecca Upton was a successful business woman who ran the Institute for Early Cultural Studies with the precision and strategy of a battlefield general. Few knew that she was in reality a centuries-old warrior and had once literally been the equivalent of a battlefield general. Few among the Daughters were as canny, or as powerful.

"Director Upton." Maya wandered to the lone window and flicked the curtains closed as she briefly outlined the status of their trip and relayed the information they'd gathered on the dig: The condition of the other skeletons, unmoved after the massacre; the discovery of jewelry and other artifacts, also left by the marauders; and the threat of looting that had pushed Lund University, one of the dig's sponsors, to take protective measures.

"What about the burial Indigo reported?" Director Upton asked.

"More than promising, Director. The skeleton was female. She was buried with a spear and a small cache of writing."

The creak of a chair drifted over the line. "Fragments?"

"Primarily, some in remarkable condition. Dr. Terhune believes at least three separate written languages are represented, but there could be more."

"I'd like to see those myself, if it can be arranged."

"I'll discuss that with Dr. Lindberg tonight."

"Do that." The chair creaked again. "And Dr. Terhune?"

Maya paused, considered. "I can think of no one better suited to deal with these artifacts."

"You'll make the arrangements?"

"Tonight, if possible."

"I'll look forward to seeing you in a few days, then."

"One more thing, Director." Maya inhaled a deep, steadying breath. "The skeleton was wearing the symbol of Marnan."

"The eye." The director breathed the word out, her voice soft and reverent. "I never thought we'd find it again."

"None of us did."

"Finally, we have hope." Rebecca laughed, the wondrous, brilliant laugh of someone discovering light after years of living in darkness. "After all this time."

"Yes, Director, I believe we do."

"There's no question then that this is a Daughter." Another sigh, a slight creak. "Make the arrangements, Maya. I'll contact the Council of Seven immediately. They'll want a full report on your return."

They ended the call not long after. Maya checked her watch again, wished briefly that Dierdre wasn't in school right then, and promised herself a call to her youngest daughter after supper. Business before pleasure, she reminded herself, and left her room in search of Dani.

TWO

J AMES TERHUNE sat at the bar of a hotel in Borgholm where the dig crew had gathered after Maya had treated them all to a meal. He sipped a local brew and watched Dani charm Olaf Lindberg's wife, Helene. The young woman had latched on to the elderly couple at dinner and appeared to be delighted with their company. The three shared a love of old movies, something they'd discovered when Dani had shared a childhood wish to *be* Audrey Hepburn when she grew up.

Strange young woman, that one. James couldn't quite put his finger on what was off about her. On the surface, she appeared to be a typical blonde co-ed, friendly, vapid, and working toward a Mrs. degree. After observing her for a while, though, he realized that the ditzy act was just that. Dani blended in wherever she went, as at ease chatting with the students as she was discussing classic film stars with the Lindbergs. She was astute, observant, and a lot more intelligent than he'd first thought, and that surprised him. Usually, he was a better judge of character.

His gaze drifted to Maya, deep in conversation with Dr. Lindberg. Now, *there* was a mystery and another woman he suspected possessed hidden depths. Maya Bellegarde appeared to be no older than Dani, yet she commanded the respect of the other woman with an ease hinting at a far greater depth of experience. Where Dani was a sunflower basking in the warmth of the light, Maya was reserved and occasionally somber. During dinner, she'd maneuvered the conversation with little effort, directing it from topic to topic in order, it seemed, to achieve a specific goal without saying much herself. He suspected that goal had something to do with the anomalous burial, but her manipulation was so subtle, sometimes he thought he'd imagined it.

He also suspected he was attracted to her, and that touched off an emotion he couldn't quite pinpoint. Concern? Dismay? He shrugged it off. She was an attractive woman. Ergo, it wasn't unusual for him, a red-blooded man in his prime, to be attracted to her.

Maya smiled at Dr. Lindberg, drawing the older man out. She didn't flirt and charm as Dani might. Instead, she met Olaf on an intellectual level. That intellect was damn appealing, especially when coupled with serene features and a compact, athletic body. Apparently, he was drawn to women who wore their power well. Who knew?

Since his divorce two years before, he'd hidden himself away from the dating world. His and his wife's parting had been amicable, or amicable enough. He and Linda had both wanted to protect their daughter, Amelia, the center of their world, or so he'd thought. When Linda had told him she wanted a divorce, he'd been stunned. In her view, they were two moons on different orbital trajectories independently circling a planet named Amelia.

He'd thought they were a family and she'd thought they were a planetary system. That's what he got for marrying an astrophysicist.

He wasn't ready to go through that again. Hell, he wasn't even ready to date yet. Thankfully, none of his friends were stupid enough to try setting him up on a blind date, or any date for that matter. Between work and Amelia, he'd managed to fill his free time and ignore the loneliness that had moved into his apartment with him.

He frowned down at his glass. One beer and he was as morose as a man deep in his cups. If that's all it took to push him into that kind of contemplation, he really needed to get out more.

"May I join you?"

James glanced up. Maya stood beside him, hands in the pockets of loose cargo pants, one eyebrow arched.

"Sure," he said.

She perched on a stool beside him and waved away the bartender, then swiveled, facing the room. The noise of the crowd ebbed and flowed around them. Laughter rang out, drawing his eye to the Lindbergs' table. Dani rose and pulled Helene up from her chair, tilting her head toward the stage, speaking softly to the older woman. Finally, Helene smiled shyly and nodded, and the two women threaded their way across the bar to a karaoke machine. They chose a song and a moment later, the opening measures of an old doo-wop rang through the bar. The two hopped up on the small stage, Dani leading the way, and began to sing, hamming it up for the crowd egging them on.

"She's something else." James pointed toward the stage. "Your assistant."

Maya's lips twitched into a small smile. "Yes, she is."

"You've known her a while?"

"Since she was a little girl."

"So, the two of you grew up together."

Her smile widened. "Not exactly."

He sipped his beer, eyeing that smile. "What exactly, then?"

"She was my student for a while, a long time ago."

He huffed out a laugh. "You can't be more than a year or two older than her, not nearly old enough to be her teacher."

"You're very kind." She dipped her head toward him, her eyes sparkling. They were almond shaped and an odd golden brown in the low light of the bar. "But I'm a good deal older than I appear."

"You know, men don't really care about a woman's age."

"I know," she said, grinning. "That's why we torment you with it."

He laughed and his earlier mood slipped away. "So, you were her teacher, then. And Indigo? Did you teach her, too?"

Maya nodded. "She was an excellent student, as was Dani."

"Is that why they call you... What was the word they used?"

"Maetyrm."

He tried the word out, letting the syllables roll across his tongue as he analyzed them. "A Latin derivative?"

Maya turned her gaze to Dani and Helene's extravagant bows. "Not quite."

He couldn't tell if she was ignoring him or simply didn't want to answer the question. "What does it mean?"

She hesitated, smiled as Dani raised her hands in a cheer while she bounced back to the Lindbergs' table. "It's a term of respect, usually meaning mother or even revered mother. At the school, it's reserved for teachers. And yes, I'm certain it isn't a Latin derivative."

His brow furrowed as he mentally sifted through the roots of the many languages he'd studied, searching for a match.

"It's not from a language you've ever studied."

Her voice startled him. "What, are you a mind-reader now?"

She laughed and her golden-brown eyes glimmered. "You're one of the world's foremost experts on archaic languages. I'd expect you to pick apart an unfamiliar word and trace it back to its origins."

He slid back on the stool, nonplussed. "Am I that easy to read?"

"Your occupation is. If you weren't curious about word origins, I doubt you'd be such a success in your chosen field."

He lifted his glass in a simple salute. "You've got me there."

"Speaking of which." Maya scooted around on her stool, facing him. "Were you serious about researching at the IECS?"

"Absolutely."

Her eyes met his, and his heart jumped in his chest. Damn attraction.

"Dr. Lindberg will probably release the artifacts from the burial to the IECS for conservation. We have facilities there that can't be matched in Sweden."

"To deal with the writing fragments?" The noise in the bar escalated. Without thinking, he leaned closer to Maya. "Will they be allowed out of the country?"

"We'll eventually be returning them to Sweden, so yes, I believe so."

"What if they're not released to the IECS?"

"Then we'll find another way to handle the matter."

He studied her, admiring her steady gaze and calm composure. "Do I want to know how?"

"Only if you want a detailed account of wrangling with politicians."

James mulled that over. If politicians were involved, he really didn't want to know. Her, though, he wanted to know more about, and he damn sure wanted to figure out how to get a crack at the IECS' Archives. "What does my interest in the Archives have to do with the Sandby borg artifacts?"

"We want you to come work for the IECS on a temporary basis, deciphering and translating the documents found in the anomalous burial. If you have time after that to work with our other collections, all the better." She tilted her head to one side and her lips twitched into a knowing smile. "Of course, you'll have plenty of free time to work on any special projects you might bring with you."

What an offer. The very thing he'd been working toward on his own, handed to him on a silver platter. It couldn't be that easy. "What's the catch?"

"No catch. You'll receive on-site housing and a salary while you're there. We won't claim any of your work product other than any translations you make for items held in our possession. It's a beautiful work environment."

"It feels like there should be a catch."

"No catch," she insisted. "You'll have your own office and a separate laboratory, full access to a library, the dining hall, and the gym. The campus is lovely and has miles of running, biking, and horse-riding trails, camping and picnic areas. We do have schools on-site, so teachers, students, and even other staff members may drop by on occasion to chat with you."

"I knew there was a catch."

She laughed, full-throated, beautiful, and a wave of heat washed over him. Damn attraction.

"Set office hours and you'll be fine," she assured him.

"It sounds idyllic."

"In a lot of ways, it is, but not all. Summer in Georgia makes Sweden feel like Antarctica. Humidity is always a problem and the mosquitoes are relentless."

"Another catch."

"I'll make sure you have plenty of bug repellent."

He grinned. When was the last time he'd had a conversation this interesting? Hell, when was the last time he'd had anything close to an interesting conversation with a woman?

His grin faded. That woman was giving him an opportunity to follow a dream, of going to the IECS and working with those artifacts, of having the chance to pursue his own research in the archives there. Either opportunity alone was worth the hassle of finding somebody to sublet his apartment and take over his classes. It was so difficult to gain access to the IECS' holdings, this might be his only shot. If he passed it up, could he live with himself afterwards?

Then again, a move like that would be hard on Amelia. Linda loved their daughter, but sometimes, she got distracted to the point of neglect. That wasn't a problem when he was a stone's throw away, but if he moved several states south, how would his daughter fare?

He released a slow breath. "I'll have to think about it."

"I expected as much."

"You're taking that awfully well. I expected you to argue or, I don't know, cajole."

She smiled in that enigmatic way she had, as if she knew something he didn't and wasn't about to share. "Everything will work out exactly the way it should."

Dani bounced up to them, her step light in spite of the late hour. "I'm heading back to the site now."

"Indigo said it was her turn to stand guard tonight," Maya explained. "Dani's keeping her company for a while."

"Let me guess," James said. "You went to school together."

Dani cocked her head to the side. "Nope. We're just friends in a friendly way, playing catch up."

Maya groaned. "Please, Dani. Not the ketchup gag."

Dani green eyes widened. "Would I do that?"

"You absolutely would." She turned to James. "I've been the victim of that one myself. Don't let her draw you in with that innocent face or she'll pull it on you, too." To Dani, she said, "Give me a minute and I'll ride with you as far as the cabin."

"Yes, Maetyrm." Dani bowed slightly, then pivoted on her heel and left.

James watched her go, amused in spite of himself. "She's something, isn't she?"

"She absolutely is," Maya agreed. She stood and caught Olaf's eye. "We'll be here for a few days if you have any questions about my proposal."

"I appreciate that. Thanks for considering me."

"Oh, you're very welcome. We could use someone at the IECS with your particular skill set. I hope you'll decide to join us."

"It would be hard to turn you down," he admitted.

"That's the idea. See you on-site tomorrow?"

James nodded, shook her hand, and for the umpteenth time, cursed the attraction flowing between them. It was distracting and would be a damn nuisance if he accepted her offer.

She picked her way through the crowd, said farewell to the Lindbergs, then waved at other members of the group who called out goodbyes as she left. Without meaning to, he imagined working with her on a daily basis, feeling the nascent attraction bloom into something stronger, and maybe even acting on it.

He cut the thought off abruptly. Too much, too soon. He wasn't ready for that kind of entanglement. Still, it had been a good long while since he'd thought about a woman that way. He just didn't know if doing so was such a good idea, particularly when the woman in question was as attractive and mysterious as Maya Bellegarde.

THE SHRILL RING of her phone woke Maya from a deep sleep. She groped her way to the nightstand, picked it up, and glanced at the small bedside clock. 2:47 a.m. Alarm shot through her. "Hello."

"It's Dani. Come to the site now. There's been a break-in."

Maya scrambled out of bed and grabbed clothes, dressing one-handed. "Are you and Indigo ok?"

"I'm fine." Dani sucked in a breath. When she spoke again, her voice was tight and thin. "Indi, not so much, but she'll live."

"Does Dr. Lindberg know?"

"Yeah. Indi called him and Dr. Terhune."

"Any damage?"

"Yeah." Bitterness crept into the younger Daughter's tone. "Everything's a mess, but at least a couple of the documents were taken."

Maya closed her eyes, a deep dread creeping through her. "I'll be there as soon as I can."

As she finished dressing, her mind flashed rapidly through the situation. Dani still had the rented Volvo out at the borg, leaving Maya temporarily stranded. There was no way around it. She'd have to run the five-odd miles from the cabin to the borg. She yanked the laces of her boots tight, grabbed a flashlight out of her suitcase, and exited the cabin, locking it behind her.

"Maya!"

She swung around, searching for the speaker. James was standing half in and half out of his rental car, waving her over.

"C'mon," he said. "Indigo said you needed a ride."

The next few minutes were tense. The streets were empty and James took advantage, whipping the car along the roads winding through open farmland at a breakneck speed. Maya gripped the car's door with one hand and the edge of her seat with the other, questions jostling around in her mind. Who was behind the theft? What exactly had been taken? And why had the dig been targeted right after she and Dani had arrived, or was that a coincidence? As much as Maya would like to believe that, she couldn't quite bring herself to, not given the potential importance of the anomalous burial to the People.

They arrived at the site within minutes and tumbled out of the car as soon as it was safely parked. A cluster of flashlights huddled near the trailer. From the number of voices, Maya guessed most of the students had already arrived. She clicked her flashlight on and hurried toward them, James close behind her.

Her steps slowed as she neared the trailer. Indigo sat on the steps leading into it, an ice pack pressed to the back of her head, a bruise spreading across her jaw. Helene leaned over the other Daughter, gently patting her back. Dr. Lindberg and two of the students were standing close by, in deep conversation. They turned toward her and James as they approached, Olaf shaking his head.

Maya knelt on the lowest step in front of Indigo and gently grasped her chin, turning her bruised face into what little light there was. "Are you all right?"

"Maetyrm." Indigo winced and touched her fingers to the bruise along her jaw. "Whoever it was got the jump on me. Knocked me out cold. I didn't even hear them coming."

Apprehension tightened the skin on the back of Maya's neck. Not many people could move quietly enough to elude a Daughter's keen hearing.

"I've failed." Indigo dropped her head into one hand. "Failed Dr. Lindberg, failed the People. I'm so sorry."

"Oh, bosh," Helene said in her thickly accented English. "These hoodlums, they did this to you. Steal the artifacts, loot the dig, and then hit this poor girl on the head as she tried to do her work."

"Can you tell me what happened?" Maya asked.

Indigo nodded, then winced and held her head still. "Dani was still here. We lost track of time talking and were a little late making our last round. I stopped to wash my hands. Popcorn. Hate having dirty hands." Her shoulders rose and fell on a deep sigh. "Anyway, Dani said she wanted to stretch her legs, so she went out ahead of me. She hadn't been gone two minutes when the lights went out. I came out of the bathroom and took a blow to the jaw, then one to the head. It must've knocked me out for a minute. When I woke up, Dani was hovering over me assessing my wounds."

"Where is she?"

Indigo hesitated and cut her eyes toward Helene. "I think she's trying to restore power to the trailer."

Dani jogged around the end of the trailer, flashlight in hand. Her gaze zeroed in on Maya. "Around back," she said, then pivoted and disappeared into the dark behind the trailer.

Maya stood and studied Indigo's wan features. "I'll be right back. Try not to move too much until we can have a doctor look you over."

"Yes, Maetyrm."

James appeared at Maya's elbow. "I'm coming with you."

She looked him square in the face, saw the suspicion blooming there, and nodded. "Yes, that would be best."

Dani was standing under the power lines, her flashlight playing over the spot where they intersected with the trailer. She flicked her flashlight at Maya and James, then fixed it back on a spot on the trailer's exterior. "Power was cut here, probably with bolt cutters. Stupid."

Maya nodded. Cutting a live power line like that was bound to cause sparks, maybe even a fire, if it didn't electrocute the person cutting it first.

"From the roof or the ground?" James asked.

"Definitely the ground." Dani stepped back and played her flashlight over a block and the ground around it. "Somebody used this as a boost. There's a footprint here."

Maya knelt beside the print. "Any thoughts?"

"Yeah, lots, and none of them good." She crouched beside Maya and pointed at the print, her finger well above the ground. "By the size and shape of the print and the use of a block, I'd say it was somebody small and lightweight. Probably a woman. Possibly a man with really narrow feet, but I'm thinking a woman, maybe five seven, a hundred and thirty pounds. Small but strong."

Maya stood and brushed dirt off the knees of her pants. "Any other damage?"

"Lots. The bolt's broken on the storage shed."

"Hence the use of bolt cutters here," James said.

Dani pushed herself into a stand. "Looks like. I only took a quick peek in there, but it's pretty messy. Same with the storage containers under the tent. I'd say the looter started there..."

"Looter?" Maya asked sharply.

"Oh, yeah," Dani said, nodding. "Just the one. She, or he, started with the easy stuff under the tents, then hit the storage shed, and finally the trailer. I can't be sure because I don't know what's supposed to be here, but it doesn't look like a lot was taken. I mean, a lot of the boxes in storage were dumped out. Stuff is everywhere, but there's an awful lot of it, so I'd guess not much was taken."

"So the looter, singular, was looking for something in particular and kept looking until he found it," James said.

Maya glanced at him. "When Dani called, she told me some of the items taken were linked to the gravesite."

"That's a big coincidence, you showing up the day before a looter breaks in and takes the very thing you're here to see."

Dani stiffened. Maya laid a hand on her arm and shook her head slightly. "Yes, it is, but we aren't responsible, not directly at any rate."

"You have to admit it looks bad."

Dani's eyes turned frigid. "If you think we're responsible, just say so."

Maya tightened her grip around Dani's arm. "Stay calm, Dani. Anyone else would think the same thing. It's best to clear those suspicions up now before they take root and distract everyone from finding the real culprit."

"Yes, Maetyrm." Dani relaxed slightly, though her gaze remained cold. "If you don't mind, I'd like to check on Indigo."

"Of course."

As soon as Dani was out of earshot, James said, "She's got a short fuse."

"Not usually. I'd suggest not provoking her further, though."

He shot her a startled look.

Maya tucked her hands into the pockets of her cargo pants and shrugged. "People look at Dani and see only the surface, a bright, energetic young woman who charms and flirts her way through life, much to the detriment of anyone who crosses her. I assure you, Daniella makes a formidable enemy."

James crossed his arms over his chest and scowled. "Is that a threat?"

"Merely a friendly warning. Stay on her good side." Maya smiled, mischief getting the better of her. "Chocolate usually helps."

"I'll remember that."

"If it helps, keep in mind that it takes a lot to anger her. The looting and Indigo's injury have upset her. This dig is as important to Dani as it is to anyone else here. Once she's able to take a positive action to resolve the situation, she'll find her calm."

"Right."

James' voice betrayed his doubt, but Maya let it go. Better for him to be at least a little wary of the young warrior.

They walked around the trailer and joined the main group. The students were chattering quietly among themselves. Olaf, Helene, and Dani hovered over Indigo, who was still holding an ice pack to the back of her head.

While Maya was checking on Indigo, a lone police officer arrived and cordoned off the areas with the worst damage. Very little of the site had remained untouched, with the exception of the pits themselves. Helene finally convinced Indigo to go to the hospital to check for a concussion. Dani insisted on driving, and Helene tagged along as the navigator.

Maya spoke briefly with Dr. Lindberg and offered her assistance in sorting through the artifacts. Restoring order to the dig would give her a chance to assess what had been taken, but it would also give her a chance to covertly monitor the police's investigation and begin her own. The students gave statements to the officer and, with Olaf's encouragement, wandered back to their lodgings for a few hours' rest, leaving Olaf, James, and Maya to guard the site.

As daylight broke in the eastern sky, Maya found herself drawn to the undisturbed anomalous grave. The skeleton still wore the ancient copper armband, the symbol of Marnan just visible through the patina. Maya was certain the burial was of a Daughter, but questions circled endlessly in her head. Had the Daughter really been buried around the time of the massacre? If so, why had she been buried when all the other victims had been left where they'd fallen, at a time when it was more common to consecrate the dead with fire? Would the fragments contain an as yet unknown part of the Daughters' history? Or would the writings the Daughter carried contain a dire warning for their future?

Most of all, Maya considered the who. Who was this Daughter and how had she ended up in Scandinavia? And who was behind the looting? Was it simply local artifact hunters looking for a quick money-making scheme, or was it someone, or something, more deadly?

Dread settled low in Maya's gut. Their ancient enemy had been silent for decades. She fervently hoped they'd stay that way, but if her suspicions were correct, *they* were behind the looting. Her mind buzzed with the consequences of their reappearance, to the Daughters and the IECS, to herself and her own daughters, and to the people they loved.

Maya checked her watch and calculated the time difference for the third time since her arrival in Sweden less than twenty-four hours before. She called Director Upton and caught her just after the other Daughter had gone to bed. In spite of the late hour, the director's voice was crisp, calm, and cool. Maya outlined the situation with the artifacts, including Indigo's injury, and assured the director that she'd remain on site as long as she needed to.

She'd just hung up when a scuffed footfall alerted her to someone else's presence. She glanced over her shoulder. James was ambling slowly toward her. In the distance, Dr. Lindberg sat in a chair, head in hands, talking to the police officer.

Maya tilted her head toward Olaf. "How's he holding up?"

James halted beside her, his gaze drawn to the partially uncovered skeleton at the bottom of the pit. "He's fine. Tired, worried. The usual."

She nodded. Looting at an active dig was heartbreaking, especially when you were in charge.

"Listen." He exhaled sharply and stuffed his hands into the pockets of his jeans. "About earlier. I don't really suspect you or Dani or the IECS of being behind this, and I apologize for implying that."

Maya slashed a hand through the air. "Don't worry about it. It's natural to suspect us. If I were in your shoes, I'd do the same."

"Yeah, maybe." He jerked his chin toward the skeleton. "What was she carrying that was so important?"

"I was just asking myself the same thing."

"And if those artifacts were the target, how did the looter know what to take? Is there a spy here at the dig? Has somebody been feeding information to an outsider?"

"That's unlikely. All of the students are loyal to Dr. Lindberg, which leaves only me, Dani, and you." Maya slid a sly glance toward him. "I can vouch for me and Dani. What about you?"

He laughed softly. "Touché."

"On the other hand, if data were being transmitted electronically, it would be easy to spy on the dig without being on site, simply by listening in on phone calls or tracking e-mails. How did Dr. Lindberg convince you to visit?"

James grimaced. "By e-mail and in great detail."

"It's not that difficult, if you know what to do."

"Yeah, but it's illegal."

"Only if you get caught."

"Good point."

They stood for a few moments more, until the sun had fully risen and the police officer finished his conversation with Dr. Lindberg. Another officer arrived and, by mutual consent, Maya and James walked across the site to meet her.

THREE

THE FIRST FULL DAY after the looting was long and tedious. Maya convinced James to scrounge breakfast for them from a nearby restaurant while Dr. Lindberg dealt with the police. The students drifted back on site, though the police refused to allow anyone inside the taped off areas.

James returned with breakfast for Maya and Dr. Lindberg. Behind him came the County Police Commissioner and the head of the County Administrative Board, the local authority charged with protecting and overseeing cultural heritage sites like Sandby borg. James retreated to the less onerous task of overseeing the students, leaving Maya to help Dr. Lindberg handle the politicians. More officers arrived to process the scene and created as much of a mess as the looter had. A crew from a Stockholm television station arrived and made a polite nuisance of themselves.

Helene, Dani, and Indigo returned not long after, joining the growing crowd mingling around the site. At midmorning, James drove Maya to her cabin and dropped her off there to shower and change clothes while he did the same in his own cabin. They grabbed food for the students and, by the time they returned to Sandby borg, the police had finished their work and cleared the students to begin clean-up. A single officer stayed behind to serve as a guard and a liaison. He promptly chased the television crew away.

Maya and James cleared one of the tables and set out a variety of sandwich fixings and sides. Everyone except the Lindbergs ate standing up, huddled into a group. Once lunch was done and cleaned up, duties were assigned and the real work began.

The students were divided between the tents and the storage shed. Paper inventories were printed out so that item tags could be compared against box labels and artifacts checked off as they were sorted and repacked.

Maya and James volunteered to sort out the trailer. Dani's assessment of the looter's path through the site had been spot-on, surprising Maya not at all. The younger Daughter had told Maya in an odd moment that she'd been away from the trailer less than five minutes total while the looter was on site. She'd started on the normal rounds around the perimeter, familiar after the previous two rounds she'd made with Indigo, and hadn't gone far when the power was cut. She'd immediately returned to the trailer and found the door wide open and Indigo bleeding on the floor, and had started after the looter only after making sure Indigo was conscious.

The looter had escaped into the shadows, leaving very little of himself behind. The police had dusted for prints, but Maya suspected they'd find none that shouldn't be there.

After straightening up and cleaning away fingerprint dust as best they could, James began sorting the photographs while Maya searched for any fragments or photos that might've slid under furniture. Indigo entered the trailer just as they finished sorting everything out. She sat down on a cushy, worn-out upholstered chair and nodded to both of them.

"How are you feeling?" Maya asked.

"Better." Indigo's gaze slid from Maya to James and back again. "A few days resting should do the trick."

"See that you actually rest," James said.

Indigo smiled wanly. "I'll be fine. I promised Dr. Lindberg I'd help you sort through this mess. Dani and I removed some of the document fragments from storage last night so we could take more photographs and study the writing."

"Thank God you did," James said, "or the looter might've gotten the whole lot."

"As it is, the darkness that confounded me also confounded the looter, at least in here. He must've rushed after taking me out. Maybe he knew Dani was on the grounds and his time was limited." She shrugged and her mouth twisted into a thoughtful frown. "He grabbed mostly print copies of some of the photographs taken when the items were catalogued. A few original textual fragments, yes, but mostly photos, and he completely missed the storage boxes under the coffee table."

"Hmm. I saw these." Maya knelt and pulled one of the boxes out. "What's in them?"

"Documents that are too fragile to handle. We only brought them in to use as a comparison. See?" Indigo opened one of the boxes. Inside were three small pieces of parchment, each rolled up and tied with thin twine. The parchment had been burned, but some text was still visible. Indigo pointed to a symbol on one. "I remembered seeing this symbol on several of the fragments, but couldn't find it on the photographs."

"So you decided to pull the boxes out of storage and photograph them again," James said.

"Sort of. We were going to compare the photos against the parchment tonight and have one of the other students photograph them again tomorrow morning when the light's better."

"Have any other items been discovered missing?" Maya asked.

"No, not yet. There's just so much to go through. Part of the artifacts have already been sent to the University, including the metal box we found the documents in. Anything with writing of any kind was left here in anticipation of Dr. Terhune's arrival."

James scrubbed a hand over his hair. "So if it weren't for me, the entire contents of the grave might already have been put into more secure storage."

"We don't know that." Maya laid her hand on his arm. His skin was warm through his shirt and a little too tempting for her peace of mind. She allowed her hand to slide away and faced Indigo. "Has Dr. Lindberg called the University to check on the status of items sent ahead for storage?"

"Not yet, but he will."

Indigo and Maya shared a long look. What he might find was anybody's guess. A looter here, maybe another there, and no one the wiser as to the whys, not yet anyway. As soon as they knew exactly what had been taken, Maya would set Dani on the looter's trail. If anyone could hunt down the thief, she could.

The three began cross-checking the few fragments Indigo had brought to the trailer against a copy of the inventory, storing each item as soon as it was accounted for. Indigo remembered only two items she'd removed from storage that were missing from the lot, a small piece of papyrus no bigger than her hand and a larger piece of parchment.

Once they'd gone through the inventory, they sorted the photographs and placed them back into their respective folders, one for each object. Several appeared to be missing, but Indigo waved that problem away. "These are print copies of digital images. Even if the looter knew which computer they were stored on, it wouldn't matter. They're also on an external hard drive and in cloud storage."

James stacked the folders into a carefully constructed pile. "Dr. Lindberg sent some of the images to me so I could begin working on deciphering and translation."

"So there are digital copies everywhere," Maya confirmed. "But the looter still has some of the photographs. He can begin deciphering and translating the way you have, depending on which photos were taken."

"Is that important?" James asked.

Maya glanced at Indigo, the other Daughter's frown a twin to her own. "It could be."

"Let's hope not," Indigo said, and Maya silently agreed. Everyday looters wouldn't care what information those documents contained. They'd simply be looking for a payout. But plenty of people might be interested in the contents, and it was those individuals Maya suspected might've stolen them. It wasn't something she liked to consider, but it wasn't something she could rightly ignore, not for the sake of a thorough investigation.

THAT POSSIBILITY stayed in the back of Maya's mind throughout the afternoon as the site was reorganized. While she, James, and Indigo cleaned the trailer and sorted out its contents, Dr. Lindberg called in an electrician to restore power.

He'd also called Lund University and been met with bad news. The artifacts in storage there had been pilfered. Any artifact found with the anomalous burial had been stolen, including the metal box that had once housed the Daughter's cache of documents. It hadn't been scheduled for study yet, but the drawings and photographs of it were still available. Those would come in handy, if she could persuade Dr. Lindberg to share copies.

Maya's resolution hardened into grim purpose as the sun crept westward on its daily voyage. Supper was eaten on site amid hushed whispers and quiet speculation. After, the group gathered together under one of the tents to hear the final count. All of the artifacts stored in the shed related to the Daughter's burial had been taken. An external hard drive was also missing and two computers had been sabotaged, but beyond that, the only other items not accounted for was a sign-out sheet for items stored in the shed and three cylinder seals.

"Whoops," James said. "I signed those seals out last night so I could begin working with them. When we went out for lunch today, I boxed them back up and put them in the trunk of the car. I forgot about them in all the fuss."

Dani held out her hand, her expression flat. "Keys."

James dug them out of his pocket and handed them over, his shoulders hunched, and Maya bit back a laugh. The poor man had a lot of work ahead of him where Dani was concerned.

Dani grabbed one of the students, a strapping young archaeology major named Lars with shaggy blond hair and a friendly smile. Maya shook her head. Trust Dani to pick out the handsome one.

The two returned shortly and compared the contents of the storage box James had signed out against the inventory. A collective sigh of relief filtered through the group when all the items were accounted for.

"Some good news, then, thanks to my friend." Dr. Lindberg set the end of his cane against the earth and pushed himself into a stand. "And so, we have lost some items, but have found some, too. Now, I think it's time we all get some rest. Tomorrow, we must continue our work."

The students drifted off, heading toward the parking lot. The University and the Kalmer Läns Museum had each chipped in money towards private security until the dig's season ended. None of the students would have to stay overnight while the looter remained at large.

As the students were leaving, Maya caught Dani's eye and nodded toward the trailer. The two slipped quietly away, leaving Indigo to distract James and Dr. Lindberg.

When she and Dani were out of earshot, Maya asked, "Did you find any other signs of the looter today?"

Dani rubbed a narrow hand over the nape of her neck. "None."

"You know what to do, then."

"Yes, Maetyrm."

"Get some rest before you start."

Dani glanced at the trio still gathered near the array of tents sheltering the dig's equipment. "I'd like to say goodbye to Dr. Lindberg first."

"Of course." Maya cupped Dani's shoulders and squeezed lightly. Dani had been a beautiful child, as bright as the sun, full of laughter and warmth. It was the child looking at her now out of the young Daughter's eyes, and so it was the child Maya addressed. "This wasn't your fault, Daniella."

Dani's head bowed. "I feel responsible."

"You did what you could and that's all that can be asked of you. Don't take on the burdens of the world, eknon."

Dani's mouth tipped into a slight smile. "I haven't been called a student in a long time."

"Yet you continue to call me teacher."

"I still have a lot to learn from you."

Maya slid her hands down Dani's arms and gripped her elbows. "No, Dani," Maya corrected gently. "We have many things yet to learn from one another."

Dani touched her forehead to Maya's. "I won't fail you, kaetyrm."

"Nor I you."

Dani bounced off with some of her normal vigor. Maya gave her a few moments to say her farewells, then trailed behind her and said her own goodbyes for the night.

FOUR

JAMES LEFT two days after the looting. He would've liked to stay longer, but duty called him back to the States. As it was, he'd made not even a small dent in identifying all of the scripts used in the fragments Dr. Lindberg had been so anxious for him to see, but he had digital copies of the photographs to work with and a few prints. Indigo's keen eye for detail had not only saved some of the texts from the looter. It had also made the photographic evidence more complete.

He'd fully intended to work from the physical prints during the flight home. His thoughts were caught instead by the three women so tightly bound to one another. What were the real relationships between Maya, Dani, and Indigo? They seemed too close, too respectful even, to be teacher and students. The fact that the three women appeared nearly identical in age was also a puzzler, yet there was no question that Maya was older than Dani and Indigo. The deference both paid her was obvious, and Maya's poise was well beyond that of a woman in her early to mid-twenties, as he'd assumed her to be.

Maya commanded respect with little effort, regardless of the people she interacted with. Even the Lindbergs had deferred to her judgment. James had no doubt that right at that moment, she was sweet-talking Olaf into handing all of the remaining burial-related artifacts over to the IECS. The permits needed to get them out of the country would be a piece of cake by comparison.

On the other hand, the IECS was undoubtedly the best place for the artifacts to be. Their facilities were, by reputation, some of the best in the world, and their campus was rumored to be one of the most secure. Somebody had targeted those artifacts. Even if the IECS wasn't the best facility for conservation or restoration, the level of security they had would at least deter further attempts at theft.

He hoped so, anyway.

With the artifacts almost certainly on their way to the IECS in the next few weeks, the only question remaining was whether or not he'd join them. He could easily continue working on identifying the scripts and possibly translating the texts from photographs during his free time back home, but would he be satisfied with that, knowing the documents could literally be in his grasp if he'd only accept Maya's offer?

He shifted in his seat, stirring the forgotten photographs resting on his lap, and stared blankly at the seat in front of him. Thinking of Maya led him to a completely different set of problems. She was an attractive woman. He closed his eyes and an image popped into his head, of her at the bar the night they'd met. The dim lighting had turned her hair into a dark halo of wild curls and her eyes had glowed with the mysterious secrets only women knew.

He wanted to get to know her better, maybe spend time with her and see if the attraction was mutual. The thought surprised him. Had another woman ever tempted him this much? Of course, he could never act on that temptation. His life was in Connecticut with Amelia and his job, hers was in Georgia at the IECS, and ne'er the twain shall meet.

Unless he took Maya up on her offer.

James blew out a sigh. His mind was going around in unproductive circles, like a puppy chasing its tail. That's about what he felt like right then, a puppy with an intriguing new toy dangling just out of its reach.

The realization that he might want the toy didn't really help bring it into his grasp.

He shook his head clear and focused on the photographs in his lap. This, at least, he understood. Women? Never. Dead languages in forgotten scripts were far easier to deal with.

MAYA SPENT nearly three frustrating weeks gaining permission to take the artifacts out of Sweden. The attempted theft of all, and the actual theft of some, had set the entire heritage bureaucracy on its collective ear. It seemed every bureaucrat and politician in the country wanted a say in how the remaining artifacts would be handled. She certainly felt as if she'd spoken to all of them, personally or by phone, or if not them, then a myriad array of receptionists, secretaries, assistants, and junior bureaucrats.

With Dr. Lindberg's backing and the sterling reputation of the IECS behind her, it was difficult for resistance to her request to linger, even among those insisting the artifacts should remain in Sweden. With permission gained at last, she personally oversaw packaging and ensured that the whole was shipped directly to the IECS via a trusted private courier. No chances would be taken with those precious items.

The Lindbergs were sorry to see her go, they assured her, and made her promise to visit again, with "that lovely girl, Dani." Maya had grown fond of them as well and made a note in her calendar to plan a future trip with Dierdre. Her daughter would love the countryside, and maybe they could spend time exploring and just hanging out.

Maya's plane touched down in Atlanta on what felt like the most sweltering day of the year. She pushed her way through security, avoided the groping hands of a lothario disguised as a TSA agent, and climbed gratefully into her garaged car for the trip home.

It wasn't a bad drive in spite of the heavy traffic, all of which seemed to be going northeast with her. Halfway home, the sky opened up and a thunderstorm burst out. The rain slowed the traffic down only slightly. Cars continued to whiz by her at upwards of eighty miles per hour, weaving in and out of traffic without the use of turn signals or apparently any concern for the proximity to other vehicles.

Driving in the Greater Atlanta area wasn't for sissies.

The IECS compound was located more than two hours from the airport by car.

The Daughters had settled in the area during the French and Indian War, living among the native tribes in relative harmony and even fighting alongside them on occasion. No one loved a good fight like the Daughters.

The natives had eventually been driven out. Most of the Daughters had remained on the land, gaining legal title to it under new governments as they rose, and adopting an outward face that was compatible with the social mores of each passing era. Underneath, though, they were still the proud, fierce warrior women the Cherokees had befriended.

The compound itself had been built over time. What had begun as a pre-Revolutionary War village had developed into a small town serving as a gateway to the IECS campus. The inhabitants were largely Daughters and Sons, with exceptions granted rarely. Property was never sold or bequeathed to anyone outside of family. Outsiders posed too big of a security risk, for one, and too many immortal Daughters lived and worked in or around the compound. Mortal humans tended to notice when someone didn't age as she should. The Daughters had learned how to deal with that long ago, but it was nice to have a place where it wasn't such a worry.

The thunderstorm petered out during the drive and ended completely by the time Maya rolled past the city limit sign for Tellowee and parked in the still-damp driveway of her two-and-a-half story American Queen Anne style home. The previous owners had maintained it in close to its original condition, expanding and modernizing it over time, sticking to the original style whenever possible. She'd fallen in love with the intricate design, with the two round towers, the sweeping staircase leading to a rounded side porch, and the crenellated eaves, and with the interior rooms that were by turns spacious or cramped, depending on the function and exterior design. The house had an almost haphazard feel to it that most people never associated with her reserved personality, but it suited her family's needs well. When she'd bought it a few months prior to Dierdre's birth, it had seemed like the perfect home. She still felt that way, even after a grueling month overseas dealing with red tape.

Maya spotted a section of loose shingling and cursed inwardly. Well, it was *mostly* perfect.

Dierdre ran out of the house, all gangly arms and legs. Maya opened the car door and stepped into a full-bodied hug, holding her youngest daughter close for a long moment.

At last Dierdre stepped back. Maya caught her hands and held them out so she could look her fill. "You've grown. Again! Look at you." She smoothed a hand over her daughter's curls, far tamer than her own kinky brown mass.

"Well, geez, Mom. You were gone forever."

"Hardly, sweet girl." Maya squeezed Dierdre's hands and turned toward the trunk of her car. "It feels like it, though, doesn't it?"

"Yeah." Dierdre heaved the kind of heartfelt sigh only a fourteen-year-old girl could make. "I hate it when you have to leave."

"Me, too, Squiggles."

They emptied Maya's baggage out of the trunk and walked slowly into the house and up the stairs to Maya's bedroom where they dropped the entire load. Dierdre chattered on about all the latest happenings, who was dating whom, which teachers were on the outs with the students, the A+ she'd received on her end-of-year history essay.

The fact that Johnny Linton had tried to sneak a kiss from her after their mixed martial arts class.

Maya made a mental note to speak to Johnny's parents. Her eyes narrowed to slits. No, she'd speak to Johnny himself. Nothing like a centuries-old warrior to dampen a young man's hormones.

Her daughter had plopped onto the bed and was still chatting away. Maya realized she'd lost part of the conversation with her motherly thoughts. "I'm sorry, what?"

Dierdre rolled her eyes skyward. "I said, then I put him on his hiney 'cause he didn't ask."

"Johnny?"

"Yes, Johnny," Dierdre repeated patiently. "Honestly."

Maya leveled a steady look on her daughter. "Be respectful of the old woman."

Dierdre hid her grin behind one hand. "Yes, ma'am."

"So you took him down for kissing you. Then what?"

Dierdre casually buffed her nails against her shirt, then flicked her fingers outward. "I hauled him back up and laid a big one on him."

Maya scowled. "Whatever for?"

"'Cause I wanted to. Why else do you kiss a boy? Geez, Mom, are you feeling ok? Like, maybe you left part of your brain in Sweden or something?"

"Very funny, young lady."

Dierdre grinned, bounced off the bed, and threw her arms around Maya. "I just love you, Mom."

"I love you, too." Maya drew back and slid her hands over her daughter's shoulders. "Movie night later or do you have homework?"

"Just a little. Should I start supper?"

"Homework first."

Dierdre nodded, not questioning the priority. Self-discipline was taught at an early age to the children of Daughters, usually by necessity. It rarely failed to blossom.

"I have to talk with Director Upton first, but that shouldn't take long," Maya said. "Will you stay the night here or at the dorm?"

Dierdre grimaced. "At the dorm. We've got a hike first thing in the morning and I don't want to miss it, not with the exhibition coming up."

Maya stifled her disappointment. A month-long absence wasn't enough to justify skipping planned activities no matter how much she'd missed her daughter. "An early night, then. Maybe we can make up for it with a little extra family time this weekend."

Dierdre lightly hit the side of her head and cupped a hand behind one ear. "I'm sorry. Maybe I didn't hear you right. What was that you said about taking me to the mall on Sunday?"

Maya laughed and shooed the giggling teenager into her bedroom and the homework awaiting her daughter's attention.

HALF AN HOUR LATER, Maya knocked on the door leading into Director Upton's office.

"Come in," a muffled voice called.

Maya entered and closed the door behind herself. Rebecca was seated behind her desk talking on the phone. Maya looked politely away, giving the director at least the appearance of privacy.

The room was spacious and richly appointed, a testament to the wealth and power the Daughters had accumulated over time. An antique settee and two matching chairs were artfully arranged on top of an antique rug to one side. Rumor had it the rug had been gifted to a previous director by an infatuated foreign dignitary, and that the man had pursued the Daughter over the ends of the Earth.

The truth was probably far less romantic, but even the most pragmatic Daughter sighed over the tale, true or not. Maya preferred the romance, even as she chastised her soft heart.

Late afternoon sunlight filtered through the curtained windows, showcasing the sitting area. She'd be out in the sunshine tomorrow, maybe on a nice winding trip through the forest surrounding the IECS along one of the dedicated bike trails. The chain on her bicycle had probably rusted from disuse. She could do a thorough check on it that night after the movie, unless Dierdre changed her mind about staying home.

Maya rolled her shoulders, easing her disappointment, and shifted her gaze. The opposite side of the room held glass cases filled with Director Upton's personal collection of antique weapons and memorabilia, including her first sword, Silverthorn, earned during the Battle of Hastings when the director was very young. Many Daughters had similar collections, though most put theirs to the uses they'd been created for. Rebecca had retired her weaponry when she'd fallen in love with her husband nearly thirty years before, but she still kept her hand in. To do otherwise would be suicide. Even if *they* hadn't made an appearance in a long while, it was never wise to allow one's defensive skills to wither. No Daughter worth her salt would be so unwise.

The phone clicked into its cradle, and the director rose and crossed the room. "Maya. It's so good to see you."

"And you, Director." Maya bowed as Rebecca stepped lightly across the wooden floor, dressed in one of her signature power suits, this one carnelian red paired with matching heels. Maya preferred the freedom of her loose cargo pants and camp shirt, but had to admit the director looked lovely in her tailored outfit.

Rebecca perched elegantly on the settee. "How was your flight?"

Maya dropped into one of the chairs and crossed an ankle over one knee. "As expected."

"And Dierdre?"

Maya smiled. "Also as expected."

"I saw her a few days ago. I couldn't quite resist checking up on her during your absence."

"I appreciate that."

"She's getting so tall now." A wistful note entered the director's voice. "They do grow up quickly, don't they?"

"Much too quickly," Maya agreed, and bit back her own nostalgia. Dierdre *had* grown an inch or so over the past month, and Maya had missed seeing it.

"Down to business then, so you can get back to your reunion with her. The artifacts' delivery is on schedule, I take it."

"Yes, Director. I spoke with our courier just before leaving Sweden. They should be here tomorrow afternoon."

"Good. I'll rest better once they're here."

"We all will."

"And the pictures?"

Maya pulled a flash drive and a photograph out of a side pocket of her pants and handed both to the director. "Digital images of all the artifacts are on the thumb drive, but I thought you'd like a hard copy of this particular one."

Rebecca laid the flash drive aside, her eyes riveted to the photograph. "The Eye," she breathed. She traced a finger lightly over the glyph captured within the photo. "Surely the Daughter buried at Sandby borg was of the line of Marnan."

"We might be able to know that for certain."

Rebecca glanced up. "Oh?"

"The students finished excavating the skeleton before I left. Her skull was bashed in, by the way, but her head was turned during the burial so the damage was hidden. It was probably the blow that killed her."

"So she might've died in the massacre?"

"It's possible. We'll know more once the artifacts are dated. In the meantime, Dr. Lindberg hopes we'll be able to extract DNA from the bones."

"Will we be allowed to examine them?"

A spurt of triumph shot through Maya. "Dr. Lindberg agreed to release the skeleton to us. I slid it in under the same permit as the artifacts. It'll arrive by courier next week."

Rebecca laughed and grasped Maya's hand. "Well done, kaetyrm."

"I can't take all of the credit. Dani's charm softened the Lindbergs to our cause and Dr. Terhune spoke on our behalf. The IECS does have a certain reputation."

"Yes, it does, with many thanks to people like you. Will Dr. Terhune be joining us?"

Maya shifted in the chair. She'd managed to put the attractive-but-not-quite-handsome language expert out of her mind for a few days. "He was undecided when he left Sweden, but I believe his hesitation will give way once he fully considers the situation."

"I'm sure you sweetened the pot."

"Of course. He could be a valuable asset."

"Agreed. Let me know what I can do to help."

Maya nodded. "A letter from you might go a long way toward convincing him. He knows how difficult it is to gain access to our archives, though he doesn't know why."

Rebecca tapped the edge of the photograph against her palm. "He wants access? How badly?"

"I don't know. He has a pet project he implied would depend on accessing our holdings, but he never elaborated on it. There simply wasn't time. But, I believe his wish to fulfill this personal project is quite strong."

"Reminding him of that desire could tip the cards in our favor. I'll compose a letter to him as soon as I can, reiterating your offer."

"Thank you." Maya pursed her lips, containing her relief. "I thought it would be harder to convince you."

"Am I that difficult to manipulate?"

Maya's eyes widened as a breath wheezed out of her. "I'd never do that, Director."

Rebecca threw her head back and laughed. "Oh, Maya. You mustn't let me tease you so. After all that time with Dani, and you're still so literal." She placed a light hand on Maya's arm. "You must promise me you'll work on that."

Maya inhaled deeply, willing her heart to calm. Imagine, the director teasing. What had the world come to? "I will."

"I imagine you'd like to spend some time with your lovely daughter, now that you're home." Rebecca rose gracefully. "I've arranged a meeting with the Council of Seven for next week. They'll want your full report. I'd like to have a copy ahead of time, if possible."

Maya stood. "Of course, Director. I'll have it on your desk first thing Monday morning."

"Make it Tuesday, and take the weekend for yourself. You've earned some rest."

"Thank you, Director."

Rebecca shook her head. "Always so formal."

"It sets a good example," Maya said with a small smile.

"Go on then. I'll see you Tuesday morning and not a moment earlier."

Maya bowed and left the room, her heart still skittering over the director's little joke. She must be mellowing, Maya thought as she made her way out of the building. A hundred years ago, the slightest hint of someone manipulating her would've had the director reaching for a weapon. Maya shook her head and bounded down the outside steps. Must be the husband's influence.

She fell into a jog and tucked the incident away for another day's worry. Right then, she wanted to spend some q.t. with her daughter and catch up on the exact nature of Dierdre's relationship with young Johnny Linton.

AFTER MAYA LEFT, Rebecca resumed her seat behind her desk and lost herself in thought. Shadows lengthened across the room as the sun slipped behind the surrounding hills, cloaking the office in a deepening darkness.

She'd propped the photograph of the armband up against a framed picture of her family. It was one of her favorite portraits, taken weeks after her son turned five years old and a mere eight years after she'd surrendered her immortality by trusting Robert. No, that wasn't quite right. She'd loved him enough to trust him, and that had been the key she'd needed to finally break the curse of immortality.

Her gaze lingered on the portrait. In it, she sat facing her husband with their son between them and her youngest natural daughter standing behind them. It had been a happy day, though she'd forgotten exactly why, and they were all smiling, even Jerusha. Four of her daughters yet lived with the curse, including her youngest. Rebecca leaned forward and picked up the photograph of the armband. Would the texts found with this innocuous adornment lead them to a way to break the curse for all of the Daughters?

There were rumors that there was a way, always rumors. The Daughters had been chasing them for millennia. For nearly thirty years, the task of heading that search had fallen to her. Was there hope at last or were they following yet another dead end?

"You have found her."

The voice startled Rebecca out of her reverie. She hadn't heard anyone enter her office. A figure stepped from the shadows into the light cast by her desk lamp and Rebecca's heart skittered and sank. The woman in front of her wore a hooded, knee-length leather jacket over a plain cotton tank top tucked into jeans, with lineman's boots laced up to her knees. Her face was fully hidden behind a mask, save for eyes as black and cold as midnight. A thin, white scar circled her neck, the only skin showing on the woman's entire body.

To the People, she was the Woman with No Face, an almost mythical figure of doom and death. Most people, mortals included, believed she was an assassin. Very few saw her and lived to tell the tale, but she was known widely by the mark she carved into her victims, a triangle set on one point with a half circle hanging from the top line. No one knew her true identity. None was brave enough to pursue such information, though whispered tales found their way into plenty of ears.

Rebecca had met her once before, in 1939. Fear had etched the incident into her memory with a clarity few other emotions had the power to convey.

She had never wished to see the Woman again.

The fear rose, clogging her throat, stultifying her breath. Rebecca gathered her will and shoved the emotion aside. "Who have I found?"

The Woman raised one gloved hand and pointed at the photo of the armband. "Her."

"Who is she?"

The hand dropped and the figure stared at Rebecca, eyes unblinking behind the mask.

Silence stretched between them. After a moment, Rebecca cleared her throat and tried again. "Is she important?"

"You will see."

The mask muffled the Woman's voice, unnerving Rebecca. She stifled a shudder and trained her gaze carefully on the assassin. "Why have you come?"

"I bring a warning, Rebecca of the Blade. Your enemy approaches and is aided from within. Strengthen your gates and arm the People, for the time draws near."

"The time for what?"

The Woman pointed again to the photo. Rebecca placed it carefully onto her desk and spread her trembling hands flat against its surface.

The Woman stepped forward, one step, then two, until she was barely an arm's length away. Cold chills broke out along Rebecca's skin.

"Is the child well?"

Rebecca searched her mind frantically for a moment before memory caught. "She's doing very well."

"You named her for her father."

A breathy laugh sputtered out of Rebecca. "I could hardly name her for her mother."

The Woman nodded. "You have done well by her. For this, you have my gratitude."

The sentiment was so unexpected, it caught Rebecca by surprise. Not knowing what else to say, she settled for, "Thank you."

"Her task approaches. She must complete it without hesitation. The fate of the People depends upon it."

"I'll warn her."

"No." The word snapped through the air between them, hard and flat and terse. "She must do this on her own. I have foreseen it."

"As you wish."

"As the Lady Goddess wishes," the Woman corrected.

"Of course."

The Woman's expressionless eyes bore into hers. Rebecca found herself drawn into them. She leaned forward and, as quickly as a striking cobra, the Woman snatched Rebecca's hand into a painful grip, squeezing hard enough to draw an involuntary gasp from Rebecca. Blackness swam in front of her eyes. Gradually, a scene appeared, of seven women sitting around a campfire, laughing. They were replaced by the chaos of battle, the screams of the dying. A woman holding another who'd been mortally wounded, then pain and more death before the campfire scene returned. One by one, the women faded into shadow. The Woman let go and Rebecca collapsed against her desk, her breaths panting audibly out of her lungs, her vision swimming.

"The One who Sleeps. Is she well?"

Rebecca drew herself up by sheer dint of will. "I'm sorry. What?"

"I believe you call her the Oracle."

"Oh, yes. Of course." Rebecca inhaled a deep, stuttering breath. "She still sleeps."

"Protect her, Rebecca of the Blade. She may yet be your salvation, or perhaps your doom. This I have yet to foresee."

Rebecca nodded and swallowed the questions crowding into the back of her mouth. She closed her eyes and rubbed them, trying to clear her vision.

Find the traitor, child, a voice whispered in her mind.

Rebecca glanced up, certain she'd imagined the soft words. The Woman with No Face was gone. A breeze stirred through an open window, wafting the summer night into Rebecca's office.

She looked down, expecting to find the photo of the armband, but it was gone. In its place was a small, thin piece of homemade paper containing a rough charcoal drawing of an upside down triangle with a half circle dropping from the top line.

FIVE

THE ROOF'S GRAVELED SURFACE bit into Dani's skin through the tough leather pants she'd chosen for that night's recon. She shifted and wished for the dozenth time that she'd chosen a better surveillance position.

Of course, then she wouldn't have been able to observe the muscled spectacle in front of her. Correction, the *shirtless* muscled spectacle. Definitely a two hubba sight, maybe even three. She pondered it for a minute and decided to split the difference, placing Shirtless Wonder at a solid two point five on the Hubba Meter.

She'd seen a three point fiver once, but she didn't like to think about him. He'd gotten her all hot and bothered, and then, bad boy that he was, she'd had to give him the smack down, totally ruining it for her. A grown man pleading for mercy was not a turn on, especially when she hadn't even shown him her A game.

"Oh, yeah, baby," she murmured. "Lift that box. Mmm. Make 'em ripple for me."

She set the binoculars down and reviewed her notes as Shirtless Wonder hefted a box to Muscled Nitwit, who, yup, dropped the box. Again.

Geez. Didn't Nitwit know he was handling precious cargo?

Tonight was her first night staking out this warehouse. It showed real promise as one of the last resting places of the artifacts she was tracking. After saying goodbye to Dr. Lindberg, she'd scouted the area around the dig, checking rooms for rent, restaurants, shops, anywhere a visitor to the island would've been.

When it became clear that the looter had zeroed in on artifacts from the Daughter's burial site, Dani had known they were dealing with a stranger and not a local. She wasn't sure why or how, she just *knew*. Knowing that had tailored her plan of action. The island of Öland had been relatively easy to case. She'd done a thorough job there, even though her gut screamed that the looter had already left the island.

She'd hit Stockholm next, visiting dives that would've given anybody the heebies, she assured herself. Then London, and ditto, because where else would a gal find out what was going on in an area except in the lowest of the low? And finally here, back in the States in a warehouse near the docks in New York City. The looter was long gone. Dani hadn't been able to turn up a single, solid description, but at least she'd been able to figure out that the artifacts were in the Big Apple. She intended to find them before they went any farther.

Dani picked the binoculars back up, fitted them to her eyes, and blew out a soft whistle. "Well, hello there, big boy."

A new player had arrived. Six two, maybe six three, two hundred twenty-five pounds of solid muscle encased in a plain black t-shirt and faded jeans. His face was obscured by a battered Chicago Cubs baseball cap.

"Ouch," she murmured. "No taste, dude."

New Guy was obviously a member of this team. Shirtless and Nitwit both stopped unloading boxes from the truck trailer they'd been emptying to talk to him. Body language said it was a serious convo. New Guy pulled his cap off, ran a hand over his hair. She got the impression of strong features before he yanked the cap back on. He turned and stalked off, and as he did, Dani's stomach jumped and urgency grabbed hold of her. *This one*, her gut said. She stuffed her gear into her backpack and did exactly what instinct demanded.

A WEEK PASSED QUICKLY as Maya settled back into her normal routine. As promised, she'd had her report on the director's desk the Tuesday after she'd arrived, then presented the report in person to the Council of Seven. She'd tried to convey the amazing promise the artifacts presented, particularly the texts, without giving undue hope. As it usually did, meeting with the Council had drained her.

The next day, bad news arrived from Dr. Lindberg via Lars. Someone had hacked into their computer system and systematically destroyed the digital images taken of the stolen artifacts. E-mails that had pictures attached were gone on both ends and the cloud storage where the pictures were being held had also come under attack. Some of the images had previously been printed, but not all. Between the missing inventories, the damage to the on-site computer and hard drive, and the electronic attacks, Dr. Lindberg feared that some artifacts from the Daughter's burial were bound to be overlooked and would thus never be found. A computer expert had been called in to try to beef up their electronic security, but it was probably too little too late. Indigo had called separately and told Maya that they were compiling a handwritten list of the artifacts based on everyone's memories of the burial, and Maya promised to contribute as well.

She talked to James only once, and that not long after her talk with Indigo. He didn't mention whether or not he'd made a decision on working at the IECS, and she didn't push him. She did make sure Director Upton had mailed a personal letter to him.

Maya tried very hard not to linger on thoughts of Dr. James Terhune. Her lab needed a good cleaning before the artifacts arrived, so she settled her mind there instead of on him. Sometimes it was easy, others not so much. If anything, the avoidance made her uncomfortable. It felt like a lie, hiding from her interest in him. That was what she was doing, she admitted to herself, hiding like a child who'd broken a rule and couldn't face the punishment.

She was knee deep in boxes and packing materials when she realized that. The courier had come with the first shipment of artifacts, a delivery she'd personally overseen, and now she'd taken on the task of making sure that everything shipped had also arrived.

Sitting in the middle of near chaos, with the possibility of finding answers, of uncovering enough of the People's past to make a difference to their future, and she was avoiding thinking about the possibility of a relationship holding that same potential, simply on an individual scale. Maya threw down the pen she'd been using to check off artifacts against inventories and pushed her hands through her hair. Honesty. It was something she'd always promised herself, so now she'd be brutally honest.

She blew out a breath and leaned back in her chair. The bright lights of her lab illuminated every corner, from the gleaming countertops to the high-backed barstools she preferred to all of her equipment. This was as much home as her house was. She felt comfortable there surrounded by history, in a way she'd never been comfortable inside her own head, particularly in matters of the heart.

But history was also the problem here. She'd lost her parents so young, then more recently Dierdre's father, and in between was a long line of people who'd hurt or betrayed her, whether intentionally or not. Trust was always an issue for Daughters. It was part of their nature. For her, the inability to trust had been built over a long, long time. She rubbed grubby fingers over tired eyes. Yes, she'd lost the ability to trust, so gradually she seldom thought about it anymore.

She had people she trusted, at least to an extent. Her daughters, the director, a handful of other Daughters she called friends, but trusting a man and particularly with her heart? Her mind immediately recoiled from the idea, so swiftly she realized another emotion must be at play here. It took her a moment to recognize fear, something she so seldom acknowledged. The thought of actually opening herself up to a man as something other than a friend or colleague shriveled her insides, and that made her a little angry. Fear was the first thing a Daughter learned how to conquer, yet it had been driving her for weeks now. That couldn't be allowed, not for any reason.

No, she *wouldn't* allow it. She was a Daughter, a proud warrior of the People, respected in her own right for the gifts and abilities she'd cultivated through years of hard work and sacrifice. She'd be damned if a mere man caused her to act like a child cowering from the dark. Maybe she'd never be able to trust a man again, but she certainly *could* control her fear.

JUNE TURNED TO JULY without James making a decision. The pictures of the documents found in the Sandby borg grave languished on his desk, neglected while he vacillated between going to the IECS or not.

It wasn't work holding him back. He'd already spoken with his department chair and knew he'd be able to take an indefinite leave, given where he'd be going. Though he tried to quell the rumors, word spread rapidly through the department that he'd be taking an assignment at the IECS. The number of requests he'd already received from colleagues to pull records in the IECS Archives was astounding. He'd promised nothing, but that hadn't stopped anybody from slipping notes under his door containing scrawled pleas for access.

No, the problem here wasn't work. It was Amelia. As much as he wanted to seize the opportunity, he simply couldn't abandon his daughter to her mother's loving but occasionally neglectful care. For only the second time in his life, he was torn between what he wanted to do and what he needed to do. Both times had involved his beautiful child.

The window of opportunity for accepting Maya's offer was closing, and quickly. He'd received a letter from Director Rebecca Upton just two days before, restating the job offer and personally extending an invitation to him to access the IECS Archives. While Director Upton hadn't said so outright, he'd inferred that access was contingent upon his acceptance of that offer.

He sat in his car outside his former residence, the house he and Linda had tried and failed to turn into a home. Since the divorce, they'd continued to have family night once a month, more often if their schedules allowed. At first, it had hurt being there not as a husband and father, but as a guest. Now, he relied on these evenings with his daughter in a normal setting where they could be a family without the bickering and hatefulness he'd witnessed after some of his friends had divorced.

Director Upton's letter burned a hole in his pants pocket where he'd stuck it on his way out of his office. Tonight he'd have to make a decision, but first, he had to tell Amelia and Linda.

He got out and slammed the car door shut. Almost immediately, the front door burst open and his daughter ran out, her elven face wreathed in smiles, her mahogany hair glimmering in the late evening sun. James held out his arms and grabbed her as she bounded down the sidewalk and into a hug. He held her close, breathing in the perfume he'd gotten her for her thirteenth birthday. His heart expanded with the joy of holding her, and ached, too. Soon, she wouldn't be his little girl anymore, and he dreaded the day she finally grew up on him.

Amelia drew away and beamed at him. "You're late. We've been waiting forever."

James made a show of checking his watch and nodded solemnly. "Yes, I see I'm all of three minutes late. I'll have to do better next time."

"See that you do," Amelia replied, her chin tilted at a pert angle. She abandoned her reprimand and tugged on his hand. "C'mon. Mom let me make supper."

They walked hand in hand to the door, Amelia chattering about school, James teasing her into blushes. He followed her into the kitchen, where Linda was peering into a large pot, slowly stirring the contents.

Linda looked up when he and Amelia walked in and smiled, then offered her cheek for a perfunctory kiss. Except for a strand or two of silver in her strawberry blonde hair, the years had been very kind to his ex-wife. Maybe a laugh line or two had been added since they'd met eighteen years before as freshmen at the University of Connecticut, but otherwise she looked very much like the young woman he'd fallen in love with.

Amelia sidled up to Linda and the two bent their heads together, one dark, the other light, identical smiles on their faces. They looked more like sisters than mother and daughter. Every time he looked at Amelia, Linda's gray-green eyes stared back, and maybe that was a good thing. His heart lightened. Yeah, maybe it was better Amelia resembled her beautiful mother instead of her scruffy old dad.

He leaned a hip against the counter. "Smells good."

"Oh, well, we've been having a little fun," Linda said, her voice light. "No promises on edibility."

James grinned. "Isn't that usually the case?"

Linda smacked his arm and Amelia laughed.

"Go on then, you two," Linda said. "For that you can set the table."

Not long after, they ate at the small, square kitchen table. The meal was more than edible, a simple red sauce over pasta accompanied by salad and bread. James listened as Linda and Amelia chatted about school and work and everything in between, and he settled in, comfortable and happy for the first time in days.

After they'd cleaned the table and sat down again for healthy slices of his favorite cake from a local bakery, James cleared his throat. "I have some news."

Linda's brow furrowed. "Nothing bad, I hope."

"No, nothing bad. I've been offered a temporary job at the Institute for Early Cultural Studies in Georgia. They want me to work with some of the documents found at the Sandby borg site."

"Oh," Linda said. "I heard you might be going there."

James stifled a grin. God bless the college rumor mill.

Amelia set her fork on her plate. "What'll you be doing?"

"I'll be translating some documents found in that dig, maybe help conserve them, and while I'm there, I can work on some personal projects."

Linda leaned forward, her eyes bright, and peppered him with questions. Amelia tilted her head. A small frown pulled her lips into a downward curve. The more questions he answered, the deeper her frown got.

When Linda wound down, Amelia said, "How long will you be gone?"

James sighed and leaned back in his chair. "I don't know, honey. Anywhere from a few weeks to several months or maybe longer."

"Will you come back home at all?"

"Sure." He gripped her smaller hand, squeezing lightly. "If I go, I'll come back as often as I can, and you can visit, if your mom says it's ok. I've heard the IECS campus has all kinds of biking and hiking trails we can explore."

Amelia nodded, her brow furrowed. "I'll miss you is all."

"I haven't made a decision yet. It may be that I can't go."

Linda rose and stacked their plates into a pile. "This is a good opportunity for you, James. You should take advantage of it while you can."

He glanced toward Amelia. "There are still some things I have to take into consideration."

Linda set the plates down in the sink, then turned and rested her back against the counter with her arms crossed over her chest. "Amelia, darling, why don't you go get your fall school schedule so your father can look it over?"

Amelia rolled her eyes. "Geez, Mom. That wasn't obvious at all. If you want to talk to Dad in private, why don't you just say so?"

"Ok, then," Linda said evenly. "I want to talk to your father in private, but I'm sure he'll want to see your schedule, too."

"Yes, ma'am." Amelia rose and left the room, her stride just short of flouncing.

"When did she grow up on us?"

Linda sighed and faced the dirty dishes piled in the sink. "When we weren't looking, I promise."

James rose and joined her. He rummaged for a dish towel and slung it over his shoulder. "What did you want to talk about?"

Linda waited until the sink was full of sudsy water to reply. "I know you're worried about leaving Amelia here with me. I'm not the irresponsible parent you make me out to be, James."

"I never said you were irresponsible."

"Right." She laughed, the sound rough and bitter. "I forget to pick her up from school one time and suddenly I'm a monster."

James gripped the edge of the sink, tamping down the slow burn of anger rising in him. "It's more than forgetting to pick her up from school, Linda, and you know it. You get so wrapped up in work you forget she's there."

"I do not."

"Yes, you do," he insisted. "You used to do the same thing to me. You'd shut me out while your mind was filled with some project you were working on and it drove me crazy. It's one thing to do that to your husband and something else to do it to your kid."

"I never shut you out," Linda said flatly. "You stopped listening to me. You stopped caring, James."

James reared back. "No. I always cared."

"If you did, you didn't show it." Linda slumped against the counter. "I thought you were having an affair."

"I never cheated on you. Never."

"But you didn't come home, either."

"God, Linda. I was working."

She nodded. "I know. You took on extra classes, extra projects, more students, anything to keep you away from home."

"I was giving you the space I thought you needed."

"I needed my husband."

"Jesus." He barked out a short, humorless laugh. "Why didn't you tell me that before we got divorced?"

The tension drained out of Linda's shoulders and a half smile curved her beautiful mouth. "Stubbornness?"

"Hunh. Maybe some on my part, too." God, wasn't that the truth. Both of them were too stubborn for their own good, and it was well past time they got over it. James shook his head. That wasn't a wound he wanted to prod again. "I don't want to leave you and Amelia alone."

"You won't be." She slid her arms around his waist and rested her head on his shoulder. "If we need help, you'll be just a phone call away."

He wrapped his arms around her and rested his chin on top of her head. "Sure. It's just..."

"No." Linda pulled away and met his gaze evenly. "No buts. You're going, and while you're gone, you'll call every night or two, and you'll come up or Amelia will come down. It'll all work out."

"I can have Jena drop in to help out."

She shuddered. "No, thank you. Your sister hates me, and I can't see her willingly stooping to helping me out, not even for Amelia."

James acknowledged that with a shrug. Linda and Jena had never gotten along, though he'd always put it down to differences in personality. That and his sister didn't like anyone, not even herself.

Amelia flounced in, schedule in hand, and James let the conversation slide. He settled in and watched a movie with them, and was pleasantly surprised by how smoothly the rest of the evening went. Linda had set some of his fears to rest, enough that by the time he left to go home, he'd made the decision to take Maya up on her offer to work at the IECS. He'd make the arrangements the next day and by the end of the week, he'd be on his way.

Seeing Maya Bellegarde again had nothing to do with the excitement pinging through him, nothing at all.

SIX

REBECCA STUDIED the final draft of the notes she'd made detailing her encounter with the Woman with No Face. It had taken days to finish the report, first to calm down, and then to tease all the nuances of the meeting from her memory.

She'd started locking her office windows at night, though she suspected it would do nothing to keep the Woman *out* should she wish to be *in*.

Rebecca read the report a final time, then placed the typed notes into a file folder along with the piece of paper the Woman had left on her desk. The morning after the encounter, she'd called down to the Archives and had them gather every scrap of information on file about the Woman, several linear feet of material dating back at least three millennia, as far as Naomi Spillfeite, the archivist, could tell.

So much information, yet no one knew the Woman's true identity.

Surely she was a Daughter. Her skills and age attested to that, assuming the mask hadn't been taken up by several successive individuals. Rebecca was certain, at least, that the one who'd brought the infant to her in 1939 was the same woman who'd visited her office just days ago. Beyond that, who knew?

A quick phone call to the Archives ensured that an intern was on the way to drop off the first box of material and simultaneously pick up Rebecca's notes to add to the collection. She'd waited until her report was finished to begin reviewing the files they maintained on the Woman, quite deliberately. It wouldn't do to taint her memory with the recollections of others.

Still, she was anxious to begin and was grateful, not for the first time, that the People had gone to the trouble to collect and maintain such an extensive database on themselves, their allies, and their enemies. Or, in the case of the Woman with No Face, a person of an indeterminate relationship.

A hard knock rapped on the office door and Rebecca smiled. The second phone call she'd made after the Woman's visit had been to someone she trusted nearly as much as she trusted herself. As the door opened, she rose and studied her youngest natural daughter.

Jerusha had grown from a laughing child into a solemn adult, but that was to be expected. The lives the People led were somewhat easier now than they had been when Rebecca was a child, but it was still difficult, particularly for the youngest daughters. Those were the ones who witnessed their mother's happiness, if such was fated, and the birth of the long-awaited first son. Some daughters grew jealous of their younger male sibling. Thankfully, not her own.

"Jerusha, love," Rebecca gestured for her daughter and the two met in a hug. In spite of her heels, the top of Rebecca's head was inches shorter than her daughter's. Thank the Goddess Jerusha had gained her father's height instead of her own. "It's been too long. How's London?"

"Decadent," Jerusha replied, a hint of sarcasm tingeing her voice. Her crystalline blue eyes sparkled, adding a mischievous hint to her expression. "Digging in the dirt, reconstructing skeletons, guarding the loot. I'm constantly overwhelmed by the excitement."

Rebecca smiled and led her daughter to the sitting area. "I'm sorry to have to pull you away from your work, especially now."

Jerusha shrugged and dropped into an overstuffed chair. "It'll be there when I go back."

"Hopefully." Rebecca settled onto the settee. "Have you heard about the Öland Island dig?"

"Yeah. I ran into Dani in London while she was tracking the artifacts. We had a high time on the town searching for clues."

"The two of you must be mellowing. The last time you and Dani painted a town red, I had to send in the cavalry."

Jerusha snorted. "We've aged a little since then."

"Yes, you have. I'm quite proud of the both of you. A mother couldn't ask for finer daughters."

"Nor could we have asked for a finer mother."

Tears welling up in Rebecca's eyes at the standard, formal exchange, said so often between Mother and Daughter. She quickly sniffed them back, appalled at both the overflow of emotion and the lack of control. Truly, being mortal had its drawbacks. "Well. I'm sure you're wondering why I asked you to drop everything and come home."

Jerusha arched a black eyebrow and leaned back in the chair. "I did wonder a time or two what was so important."

"I have a job that needs doing and I need someone I can trust to help me. You mustn't tell anyone, not a single soul," Rebecca cautioned. "This mission depends upon your utmost discretion. Will you help me?"

"Of course. What do you need?"

Rebecca took a deep breath. She'd thought long and hard about telling Jerusha of her meeting with the Woman with No Face and had decided against it. Only a handful of individuals needed to know of that incident, and knowing might hinder Jerusha's work. "I've received intelligence that our enemy grows strong. I need you to confirm this."

"They've been quiet for decades now. Do you have any specifics?"

"Unfortunately, no, but it shouldn't be hard to assess their strength."

Jerusha pushed herself off the chair. "I'll get on it right away."

"There's more." Rebecca hesitated as Jerusha sat back down on the edge of the chair. "My intelligence says we've been betrayed."

"By who?" Jerusha asked, a hard edge to her voice.

"By a Daughter."

"You're certain?"

"As certain as I can be without hard evidence."

They shared a moment of silence. Some Daughters opposed the majority's goal to overcome the curse for them all. A few clung to their immortality, using it as a shield against love, against trust. Others simply had no wish to ever become mortal. Still, all were more or less open about their feelings on the subject, or pretended to be. Very few would ever stoop to such an insidious act as betraying the larger cause, but determining who would've done so might be difficult depending on a number of factors Rebecca refused to consider. She was no longer in the loop where efforts to contain the Eternal Order were concerned, but they were rumored to have been forcibly disbanded long ago. Surely this wasn't their handiwork.

"I'll get that proof for you."

A weight lifted off of Rebecca's chest. "Good. Now, Robert and Bobby will want to see you while you're in town."

"I'll stop by tonight after I've visited the Archives."

"I put in a request a few days ago for the files you'll need. They should be waiting for you, but please don't hesitate to request additional information."

"I won't." Jerusha smiled and the mischief returned to her expression. "My mother, the director. Always so on top of things."

Rebecca laughed and settled in for a little girl talk with her daughter.

NIGHT HAD FALLEN by the time James reached the IECS compound. Once he'd gotten the ball rolling with a call to Maya, it hadn't taken long to make arrangements for an extended leave from work and find somebody to take over his classes.

Saying goodbye to Amelia had been the hardest part. Even the promise of frequent calls and her visit during the Labor Day holiday before school started hadn't been enough to dampen her tears. When he'd stopped by to see her the night before he'd left, she'd clung to him, and the guilt of leaving her had nearly overwhelmed him. Linda had reassured him they'd be ok a dozen times, but it hadn't assuaged his worry.

Because his time at the IECS was likely to be long, he'd opted to drive down over two days. The long journey had left too much room for second thoughts. Several times, he caught himself searching for exits so he could turn around and head back home. Each time, he forced himself to remember that Amelia would be fine, his work was important. He'd see her soon.

He called Maya when he crossed the South Carolina-Georgia line and let her know he was near. An hour later, he entered Tellowee, the small town bordering the IECS. He pulled over twice and checked the directions Maya had e-mailed him, and finally found the main gate.

James stared at it, glanced around and glimpsed the IECS sign, then stared again. From where he sat, a ten-foot high brick wall extended to either side, bright lights scattered evenly along it. Two guard shacks flanked the main entrance on the outside. A sturdy iron gate blocked the road into the compound. In the distance, he could just make out guard towers, adorned with what he could've sworn were machine guns pointed toward the peaceful town.

Surely not. He blinked, shook his head, and put the vision down to two days of hard driving.

Maya stepped into the beams of his headlights, startling him. She waved, then came around to the passenger's side and slid inside. "Hey. The guards need to do a vehicle check, and then we're good to go. Pop the trunk and the hood, would you?"

What followed was surely the most bizarre security check James had ever been through. Four guards stepped out of the guard shacks, two from each one. A fifth approached from the side holding the leash of a German Shepherd. All were dressed completely in black, with Kevlar vests visibly thickening their torsos and handguns strapped onto their waists. Each carried a machine gun slung over a shoulder. The dog handler was the only male. The rest were tall, well-built Amazons, their expressions so neutral and flat, their faces might as well have been made out of stone.

One guard stepped to the back of James' car and rummaged through the trunk. Another walked around the car holding a long-handled mirror to the ground. A third inspected the engine.

James glanced helplessly at Maya.

Her mouth twitched into a slight smile. "Sorry. I forgot to warn you about security."

"What are they doing?"

"Checking for bombs."

He did a double take, eyes wide, and clamped his teeth shut over his astonishment.

"It's routine," she said. "No one expects you to actually have a bomb."

"Well, that's a relief."

"Roll down the window and I'll introduce you."

"I don't know. I think that one's got it in for me." He nodded toward one guard, a pretty blue-eyed brunette. She'd stood to the side the entire time his vehicle was being inspected, staring intently at him, her rifle held crosswise over her body. James was pretty sure she was itching to use it on him.

Maya shot him an exasperated look. He obligingly rolled the window down.

"Y'all knock it off," she said. "You're scaring our guest."

The pretty brunette slumped and slung her gun back over her shoulder. "We were just having a little fun."

"I know. That's why I let you go so long." Maya winked at her. "I remember what guard duty's like."

James closed his eyes, unsure whether to laugh or bang his head against the steering wheel.

The guards dropped all pretense of searching his car and crowded around his open window, neutral expressions replaced by sheepish grins. Maya introduced them one by one, and James shook their hands, trying to keep names with faces. After a few minutes of chatting, during which each one called him "Dr. T.," the brunette (Andrea, maybe?) jogged into one of the guard shacks and triggered the gate open.

He drove slowly through it and followed Maya's directions around the IECS campus. To the left, a standard-sized oval track with bleachers on both sides dominated the open field. The landscape rose behind it, dotted with other buildings whose functions he couldn't quite figure out.

The other side of the road seemed more familiar. Maya pointed out each feature in calm, even tones. The first building they passed held classrooms, offices, the library, and a small museum. The road branched and Maya gestured to the right. He turned off and drove past the main administrative building, a small cafeteria, a building devoted to labs, and finally, the building containing quarters for guests and interns. The entire compound was lit by security lights and was bright enough that he could clearly make out people exercising or walking around the grounds.

After he parked, Maya led him up two flights of stairs to rooms used, she explained, specifically for visitors to the Archives. "Elevator's out. Should be fixed in a few days."

She opened the door into a great room with a small kitchen on the left and a sitting area to the middle. Two doors on the right led from the main room into what looked like bedrooms. What captured his gaze, though, were the windows framing a view across a good portion of the compound. Maya caught his stare, crossed to one window, and pulled down a shade. "Sorry about the light. It can get annoying, but if you pull the shades down and close the curtains, it should be dark enough to get some sleep at night."

James nodded, a little dazed from the long drive or the lack of sleep, or maybe reality was setting in and it was just different enough from the way he'd envisioned it to throw him off. "Is all that security really necessary?"

"It's not just the IECS we're protecting." She tugged on the shade. It slid upward, revealing the view. "We have a school on the other side of campus, plus the Archives."

"Ah," James said, though he certainly didn't understand. He'd never seen a campus with such high security. The White House, maybe, but not an institute devoted to studying the past, and though he'd heard rumors of the IECS' high security, the reality was a long way from what he'd imagined.

Maya crossed to a round table situated near the kitchen and picked up a folder. She wiggled it at him before setting it back down. "Your welcome packet. There's a map to campus, keys and directions to your office and lab, and so on. You'll likely need it for a few days. Just stick to the IECS side of the campus and you'll be fine." She walked toward the door and put her hand on the knob. "Oh, and the running trails and such. There's a town business directory in the packet, but if you have questions, just call. Do you need help getting your bags in?"

"I'll get them, thanks."

Maya smiled. "All right, then. I'll come by in the morning and give you the tour."

James nodded and showed her out, then flopped into one of the chairs in the sitting area. It was surprisingly comfortable and after a while, he nodded off. In his dreams, Maya chased him, German Shepherd in tow, the Guard Pack hot on her heels gleefully waving paintball guns at each other.

SEVEN

MAYA KNOCKED on the door of James' suite early the next morning. He'd looked tired the night before, security's prank on him notwithstanding. Hopefully, he'd gotten a good night's rest.

For her sake, she'd hoped the attraction she felt for him would've dimmed by the time he arrived in Tellowee. No such luck. He'd been so cute the previous evening, gawking at the guards as if he'd never been through a security check point before. They'd been a little rough on him, all in the name of good-natured fun. Poor kids.

And he'd been so *cute*, though he probably wouldn't appreciate that particular description.

A grin still lingered on her features when James opened the door, alert and apparently well-rested. He was sharply dressed in a sky blue button-down shirt and khaki slacks and he'd even taken the time to shave.

She eyed his clean-shaven jaw, a steady sinking sensation filling her gut. How could she possibly prefer his lean face covered in stubble? She didn't even like men with facial hair.

"Hey." He stepped aside and gestured her in. "Just a minute more. Briefcase? Ah, there it is."

"No rush."

He nodded absent-mindedly, shoved his welcome packet in the briefcase, and slammed it shut. "All set then. So, what's on the agenda today?"

Maya waited until he closed and locked the suite's door. "Not much. I thought you'd appreciate a day to settle in before we get to work on the artifacts. Breakfast first at the cafeteria, then I'll show you around."

Sunlight bathed the campus in early morning heat as Maya led James from his suite to the cafeteria. There, they joined a growing line of teachers, professors, interns, students, and other campus residents. Maya helped him juggle his briefcase and a tray of food as they worked their way through the line and to a table.

As they sat down to eat, James leaned forward and quietly asked, "Is it just me or is everybody staring?"

"It's not just you. We don't have many visitors here. The word's already out on who you are and why you're here. Office hours." She waggled her spoon at him. "Trust me."

Dierdre bounced up to them, tray in hand, a huge smile on her face. She set her tray on the table and plopped into a chair. "So, this is the famous Dr. T., huh, Mom?"

James swung his head toward Maya and mouthed, *Mom?*

Maya introduced James to her daughter, adding, "Dierdre attends school here."

"Pleased to meet you," James said, nodding.

Dierdre nodded back solemnly, then turned in her chair and held up two fingers. A group of girls at a nearby table broke into giggles and gave her two thumbs up all around.

Maya bit the inside of her cheek and glanced at James. He appeared to be completely engrossed in his bacon except for a faint tinge of red creeping up his cheeks.

"What brings you by, Squiggles?" Maya asked.

Dierdre feigned an innocent look. "Gee, Mom. Can't a daughter have breakfast with her only mother without it being a big deal?"

Maya stared steadily at her daughter.

"Ok, all right. Geez. Everybody wanted to know what Dr. T. was like, so I volunteered to come check him out." She waggled her eyebrows. "And I have to say, he is *hawt.*"

James dropped his head into a hand and muttered something under his breath that sounded suspiciously like, *God save me from teenage girls.* Maya stifled a laugh.

"But the mother-daughter thing was totally true, too," Dierdre said, her brown eyes wide.

Maya had pity on James and changed the subject. "How are plans for the Labor Day camping trip coming along?"

Dierdre perked up. "It's gonna be totally awesome. Except, you know, not many of us are going. But Maetyrm Holly said some of the interns might go, too, which would be *sweet* 'cause they know all the good ghost stories and stuff."

"How long will you be gone?" James asked.

Dierdre lifted one shoulder in an off-hand shrug. "Just two nights so we can be back for the Labor Day stuff in town."

"There'll be a parade, then fireworks," Maya said. "Most people bring a supper picnic and sit out in their yards or on the athletic field here on campus for the light show."

"Sounds like fun. My daughter Amelia's coming down the week before Labor Day, so maybe we'll go." In an aside to Dierdre, he said, "School doesn't start back home until mid-September."

"Oh, well, Fall Term hasn't started here yet either."

"Many of the students choose to attend a summer session where they can work on particular skills," Maya explained. "Dierdre is taking classes in martial arts and horseback riding."

"And outdoor survival skills," Dierdre added.

"Hence the camping trip," James guessed.

"You bet." Dierdre beamed at him, then screwed her face into a thoughtful frown. "Your daughter can go camping with us, if she wants to."

"That's a generous offer. I'll ask her, but she'll probably want to spend most of her time here with me, since we won't see each other again until Thanksgiving."

"Aw." Dierdre wrinkled her nose. "She's not a girly girl, is she?"

James laughed. "Only when she wants to be. She used to be more of a tomboy, and then she discovered the magical land of shopping."

"Woot!" Dierdre shot a triumphant look at Maya. "Mall of Georgia, here we come!"

Maya sighed. "Don't encourage her, please."

He crossed a finger over his chest and held up a hand, palm out. "No more. You have my word as the Payer of Shopping Bills."

Maya laughed as Dierdre giggled and clutched her stomach.

"Whew! You're a riot, Dr. T." The table of girls Dierdre had signed to earlier rose and gathered their breakfast trays. One of them called Dierdre's name, and she looked around. "Time to go." She rose hastily, dropped a smacking kiss on her mother's upturned cheek, and said, "Laters!" She held up two fingers to Maya and grinned, then bounded off, joining her friends as they emptied their trays and pushed their way outside. The cafeteria was noticeably quieter after the girls left.

Maya picked up her spoon and stirred her oatmeal. "Sorry about that. If I'd known she was stopping by, I would've warned you ahead of time."

"No problem. Just two questions, though. First, Mom?"

"She's my youngest daughter."

James' eyebrows shot up. "What were you, twelve when she was born?"

"Hardly. I told you, I'm older than I look."

He eyed her critically. "Are you sure she's not adopted?"

Warmth pooled low in Maya's abdomen, curling through her in insidious tendrils. She reined it in and cleared her throat. "Positive. Your other question?"

"What's with the peace sign?"

"Dierdre's been hanging around Dani too much. Two fingers means you're a two hubba guy."

"Hubba?"

"You know, *hubba, hubba.*" Maya sipped her coffee and peered at him over the cup's rim. "She's got good taste. You're definitely at least two hubbas."

James leaned closer. His eyes bored into hers and the warmth in Maya's middle morphed into breathlessness need.

"So, does that mean you think I'm *hawt*, too?" he asked.

Maya laughed and the spell was broken. "I'm so sorry. She's not normally that bad."

"It's ok. Amelia's about the same age, and she and her friends do the same thing. You'd think I'd be used to it by now."

"I don't think anybody can ever get used to teenagers," Maya said wryly.

After breakfast, Maya took him by the office he'd use during his time at the IECS, then by a small room in the lab building where he could work with the artifacts. She showed him where her office and lab were, then took him to meet Director Upton, who graciously welcomed him to the IECS.

In between, she filled him in on the history of the area, the town, and the IECS in particular. Some of the buildings dated back to the Civil War era, including the main administrative building where Director Upton's office was located.

"This structure," she explained as they left the director's office, "was built just after the war to replace an earlier one destroyed by fire."

"Sherman?"

Maya shook her head. "That's what everyone thinks. The truth is much less glamorous. At that time, the building was used primarily as a school for girls. The local Sheriff heard rumors of a large Federal force nearby and took it upon himself to come by and check on the students, and one teacher in particular who, rumor has it, he was sweet on. Unfortunately, he was a bit tipsy at the time and not quite steady on his feet."

"I can see where that might be a problem."

"Oh, yes," Maya agreed. "He tripped over a chair, knocked over a lantern, and managed to spill his flask full of corn liquor into the fire. The building went up in flames too fast for it to be saved. Fortunately, everyone was evacuated before it was fully engulfed, including the Sheriff."

"Lucky save, then, but what about the budding romance?"

"Those seeds never bore fruition," Maya said, mildly and with a straight face. The poor man had chased after her for months. After the fire, he'd been too embarrassed to approach her again and had eventually married a local girl and raised a large family.

She and James chatted comfortably as she guided him back to their offices. Had she imagined the heat she'd felt earlier when he'd teased her over breakfast? He was so at ease, so laid back, she simply couldn't tell if he felt anything in return.

And she wasn't a teenaged girl, so why was she obsessing about it? Yes, he was *hawt* from his lean, athletic build to the keen intelligence hidden behind his rich, gray eyes. She itched to explore him, to learn every curve of muscle and the exact feel of his skin under her fingers, but he was just a man. Nothing to be afraid of, nothing to fret over.

He held the door open for her, and she entered the air conditioned interior of the building that held their offices, the library, and several classrooms. Her arm brushed his as she passed and a spark jumped over her skin.

She sucked in a breath. Maybe there was something to fret over after all.

Their footsteps echoed in the hallway as they walked to his office. When they arrived, James groaned. Half a dozen notes were tacked to the corkboard affixed to a wall beside his door. "This is like being back home. I've not even been here a full day, and look at this." He pulled down two separate requests for consultations on doctoral dissertations and shook his head, then took down a third note and held it out to her. "Is Dr. Upton who I think he is?"

"That's the director's husband. He's our resident genealogist."

He glanced at the note. "Hmm. Wonder what he wants."

"I'd guess he wants help translating something written in an obscure archaic language."

"Har." James pinned the notes back onto the board. "Tomorrow."

"Post office hours," Maya reminded him. "You're the only language expert in residence right now, so do yourself a favor and set limits while you still can."

"I'll do that." He turned his back on the corkboard and leaned casually against the wall, his mouth tilted in a grin, his gaze warm. "So, what does a beautiful woman like you do for supper around here?"

Maya eyed that grin and cursed the answering heat rising within her. "Are you asking me for a date or trying to weasel the names of the best local restaurants out of me?"

"Both," he admitted. "I can't take you out for a thank you meal if I don't know where you like to eat."

"You don't have to take me out."

"Oh, I insist."

He brushed his hand over her shoulder. The fleeting touch heated Maya's skin through the barrier of her cotton shirt and she shivered. One touch from him, one charming offer for a meal, and she was ready to yank him close and discover how his mouth would fit against hers.

"After all, you protected me from the vicious security guards and a gaggle of teenaged girls. A meal's the least I can do to thank you." His voice dropped a notch as he leaned closer. "Is it so awful, spending time with a man who thinks you're attractive?"

Maya narrowed her eyes. "Are you flirting with me?"

He straightened away from the wall and lifted both hands in a shrug. "I must be rustier than I thought if you have to ask."

"Not that rusty."

Two female students walked by, chatting quietly with each other, both surreptitiously studying James. One held up two fingers to Maya and winked broadly, and Maya heaved a sigh. Dierdre had been busy that morning.

"Does everybody know about the two hubba thing?" James asked.

"Probably."

"But it'll blow over, right?"

"Eventually, if you're lucky." Maya bit back a grin and tapped the notes tacked to the corkboard, then turned toward her own office. "You have bigger problems right now and I'm late for my own office hours. We can set a schedule for lab work tomorrow, if you like."

"Sure. How's Thursday sound?"

She turned back to him, puzzled. "For what?"

"Supper."

Maya paused and really looked at him. "You're serious."

"Is that so hard to believe?"

She shook her head. "I'll think about it."

His smile was slow and sexy, as if he knew thoughts of him had already kept her up at night.

Damn him.

She turned on her heel and left, ignoring the skip in her heartbeat and the charming man watching her walk away.

JAMES CALLED AMELIA the next night. He'd spent his first afternoon at the IECS setting his office up and familiarizing himself with the campus. True to her word, Maya had stopped by earlier that morning and scheduled lab time with him. Apparently, Linear A was a hobby of hers. She'd been trying to crack it for years.

James snorted. So had every other language geek in the world, including himself.

The phone rang three times before Amelia picked up. She squealed when she heard his voice, then chatted with him about shopping, boys, Linda, boys, summer camp, and boys, in that order.

For some reason, Dierdre's face popped into his head.

After the fourth time she mentioned a boy named Mark, James interrupted, purely for her own good and not because he already wanted to strangle the young man his precious baby apparently had a crush on. "Has your mom bought your plane ticket yet?"

"Geez, Dad, no. I did that with the credit card you gave me."

"Ah." He made a mental note to have somebody pick up his mail and forward it to him, now that he had an address, so he could pay the credit card off when the bill came in. Because he knew he'd forget, he searched through his briefcase for a scrap piece of paper and a pen. "You're going to love it here. I've got a suite with a spare bedroom and there's a school on campus with lots of kids your age."

He hesitated for a moment, unsure whether or not to mention Maya, and decided *why not*. Amelia had to know that he and Linda would eventually begin dating again. "The woman I'm working with. Maya? She has a daughter around your age. You're invited to go camping with her when you come down."

"Oh?" Amelia's voice was as carefully casual as his own. He could picture her winding a strand of hair around one finger, a habit she'd developed as a child. "What's she like?"

"Dierdre?"

"No, Maya."

"Ah, well." He searched for something innocuous to say, sure his thirteen-year-old daughter wouldn't want to hear how compelling and sexy he found Maya, and that he spent entirely too much time daydreaming about kissing her. "She's pretty and smart."

Amelia's sigh distorted the phone's signal. "So's Mom."

James winced. "Er, yes, she is."

Please don't ask why we divorced if I still think she's pretty and smart, he thought.

The phone gods had mercy on him, or maybe Amelia didn't want to talk about that either. "What about Dierdre? Is she, like, cool or what?"

James exhaled a relieved sigh and sent a silent thank you to the god of phone conversations. "I've only met her once, but she seems nice. She's in summer school here taking martial arts and horseback riding. She mentioned taking you to the mall."

"The Mall of Georgia? That's, like, the biggest mall in the South."

Imaginary credit card bills danced through his mind. He grimaced and rubbed a hand over his eyes. "I don't know if we'll be able to go yet. There's a picnic on Labor Day and fireworks and an awful lot of interesting things to do around here."

"Dad, the Mall of Georgia is a historical landmark or something. Just think of what an enriching experience it would be to go there."

"Har."

"Please?"

"We'll see," he promised.

A knock came at the door and he rolled his eyes, hoping it wasn't another student dropping by to meet him or a teacher needing advice on curriculum planning. After the third interruption the day before, he'd finally done as Maya suggested and posted office hours on the corkboard outside his office door. The knocks petered off, but when he left for lunch, his corkboard had been covered with notes.

He opened the suite's door. Three men of various ages and builds stood in the hallway, all strangers. He held up a finger, then pushed the door nearly shut.

"Amelia, I have to go now. Somebody's at the door."

"Sure, Dad. You're just trying to avoid the mall talk."

"No, I promise. We'll talk about that later, ok?"

"Ok. Call soon!"

"I will. Love you."

"Love you, too, Dad."

He hung up and opened the door. The men were looking at each other, their expressions puzzled. One gestured to the phone. "Wife?"

"Ah, no," James said. "Daughter. Why?"

The men grinned and high-fived each other. One, a burly young man in his mid-twenties with wide shoulders and sandy blond hair, said, "Tom's got a hypothesis. Long story. I'm Phil Walters, this is Tom Fairfax." Phil pointed to a tall, lanky man with a touch of gray in his dark hair. "And that's George Howe." George was a stocky young man with a slight pooch and stylishly cut golden hair. "We're the other three visiting professors."

He shook each man's hand in turn. He'd known there were other visitors, just not who. "James Terhune."

"We know," said George. "You're the talk of the campus."

"Two hubbas." Tom shook his head. "Dani only gave me a one point seven five."

James leaned a shoulder on the doorframe. "You know Dani?"

Phil crossed his arms and rocked back on his heels. "Who doesn't? It's a small community. You'll find that out soon enough."

Tom hitched a thumb over his shoulder. "We're going out to The Omega, a local sports bar. Thought you might like to tag along."

"Sure." James patted his pockets. Crap. He still had on his office clothes. He motioned for the men to enter and shut the door behind them. "Sorry about the mess. I'm still getting settled in. I, ah, need to change. Be just a minute."

The men wandered around the suite, chatting amiably. James changed into jeans and a t-shirt emblazoned with a UConn basketball logo, then followed the men outside to Phil's car.

THE OMEGA was located a short ten minute drive away in Tellowee's tiny downtown business district. It was crowded for a Wednesday night and seemed to be less of a sports bar than a local watering hole, judging by the large age range of the people wandering around the interior. The staring guard from his first night was in one corner, playing darts with an older man James didn't recognize. A group crowded around the bar, fixated on the baseball game showing on a large flat screen TV mounted to the wall. Several bar-height tables with high-backed stools took up the middle space, while a small stage with a dance floor in front of it occupied a large space in another corner.

Through a large, arched doorway, James spied pool tables. Several women clustered around one, watching silently as a young woman with a very fine rear bent over to make a shot. She stood and turned, and recognition hit. Maya. He rocked onto the balls of his feet and stuffed his hands in his pockets. Suddenly, the evening looked a lot more promising.

James followed George to an empty table away from most of the crowd while Phil and Tom made the rounds, greeting people they knew, just about everybody as far as James could tell. He took a seat where he had a clear view of Maya's game. As if she could feel her eyes on him, she glanced around and raised an eyebrow, and he grinned. Yup, very promising.

When all four of the men were settled at the table, a waitress came by and took their drink orders, smiling flirtatiously with the other three men.

As soon as she whirled away, James said, "Is it just me or did the waitress give me the cold shoulder?"

Phil barked out a laugh. "Word is, you're as good as taken, my friend. The women here don't poach, if you know what I mean."

"No, I really don't."

"Oh, come on," George said, his expression as skeptical as the tone of his voice. "Don't tell me you're not in a relationship with Dr. Bellegarde."

The waitress came back and set their drinks on the table in front of them. She was friendly to James, but no more than that. He took in the men's knowing glances and a light went off in his head. Dierdre and her two hubbas.

The waitress whirled away again, her tray held high. James focused on the three men staring at him with thinly disguised curiosity. "I barely know her."

Tom waggled his eyebrows. "But you'd like to, right?"

"She's a beautiful woman."

"Understatement," Tom said.

Phil tilted his bottle of beer toward the crowd. "Here's to the beautiful women of Tellowee, Georgia."

George raised his glass of coke. "I'll second that."

James clinked his beer against the other men's drinks. "Speaking of, what's with all the women? Everywhere I turn, there's another young, athletic female. It's kinda weird."

"Ah." Tom leaned back and scratched his lean torso. "You've noticed the low male-to-female ratio."

"Here it comes," George muttered into his glass.

Tom ignored him. "But you've not been here long enough to notice that most of the younger men seem to be relatives."

"Can't say that I have," James confirmed.

"And most of the older men are married," Phil added.

George's pudgy face sagged. He glanced toward one corner of the bar. "Regrettably."

James followed George's gaze toward where the staring guard and the older man were playing darts. He really needed to learn her name. "She doesn't look old enough to be married."

"She's not," Phil said. "That's her step-father."

George's round shoulders slumped. "He's got a shotgun and he's not afraid to use it."

Tom leaned close to James and muttered, "George found that out the hard way."

"No shots were fired," George said, "but I got the picture."

James reassessed the couple playing darts. "I don't know. She looks like she can take care of herself."

Phil snickered. "George found that out the hard way, too."

"If one of 'em offers to teach you a little hand to hand, don't do it," Tom offered. "Fight like wildcats."

"Skilled wildcats," Phil said. "But man, oh, man, what a sight."

"Gotcha." James filed the advice away in the corner of his mind. Truth be told, he wouldn't mind Maya putting her hands all over him, hand to hand combat or not. He glanced casually at the pool table and caught her watching him. He saluted her with his beer and she nodded back.

Phil glanced around, saw Maya, and turned back to the table with a low whistle. "You sure you're not seeing her? 'Cause the look she just gave you was *scorchin'*."

"There was a definite heat factor," George said.

Tom's thin lips twitched. "Or a *hawt* factor."

James sank lower in his chair.

Phil's mouth stretched into a knowing grin. "Yeah, we heard about that, too."

"Jesus. Does anybody here do anything but gossip?"

"Sure." Tom pointed to George, then Phil. "Shorty there is a genius with genetics, Phil's doing his doctoral dissertation. Don't ask or you'll never hear the end of it."

"Hey, now," Phil said.

Tom waved away the protest. "And I'm working with the Archives to upgrade their procedures for storage and conservation. We all work hard."

George raised his glass. "That we do."

"But at the end of the day, we're visitors to a very small, tight-knit community. Everybody here's curious, so we've gotten to know a lot of the permanent staff, the locals, hell, even the school kids."

"And a lot of that community consists of good-looking, eligible women," Phil added.

Tom leaned back in his chair. "Which brings me back to my hypothesis. It's a definite possibility that with the shortage of eligible men around here..."

Phil interrupted. "Who aren't relatives."

"Right, who aren't relatives," Tom said, "that we were deliberately brought here to widen the gene pool."

"Though some of the relatives date, just not their own family," George said.

Phil gave George a *well, duh* look. "Tom's been here the longest. He's had time to study on this."

"How long have you been here?" James asked.

Tom ruffled his hands over his dark hair. "A year and a half, and in all that time, only a handful of women have been invited to study at the IECS."

"Far as we can tell, most of those were relatives of people who live or work here," Phil pointed out.

"True," Tom acknowledged, "which makes my case even stronger. The men invited here are, without a doubt, some of the top minds in the world in their field. So, they're strongly intellectual and, more importantly, they're all single."

James stared at Tom across the width of the table. "Are you serious?"

"Absolutely." Phil slapped his hand against a muscled thigh. "And the women, the eligible ones, are very straightforward. Not many game players here, if you know what I mean."

Tom nodded. "If they want you, they say so, though I wouldn't call any of the ones I've gone out with promiscuous."

"Nope," Phil agreed. "But there's no hesitation. It's like a meat market and we're prime rib, baby. Even George managed to snag a date or two before he got caught by Lady Love."

"It's not like that, guys," George said softly.

"But you." Tom tilted the neck of his beer bottle toward James. "You're already spoken for, so rumor mill has it. The ladies might look, but they'll never touch, not while you and Maya are an item."

"We're not an item," James said evenly. He was beginning to wish they were, but that was a far cry from actually being in a relationship with her.

"Poor, delusional sap." Phil slapped his back in sympathy, or maybe pity. James couldn't tell which, and maybe that was a good thing. Wasn't it bad enough everybody thought he and Maya had a thing going? Any more protests would only add fuel to the fire.

A slow song came on the jukebox, drowning out the baseball game. A few couples drifted onto the dance floor. The staring guard appeared at George's shoulder and tugged him out of his seat. Two women James didn't recognize claimed Phil and Tom, leaving him sitting alone.

He glanced up, searching for Maya. She was watching him, her expression impassive. She was surrounded by women, and even as long as he'd been out of the game, he knew a lone man didn't approach a crowd of women in a bar. That was a sure path to an ego's quick and untimely demise.

Their gazes caught and held, and the rest of the room faded away. Without a word, she handed her pool cue off and glided across the room toward him.

EIGHT

MAYA WENDED her way across the bar toward James and called herself all kinds of fool for doing so. She wanted him, yes, more and more each time they met, but actually entering into a relationship with him seemed too much like tempting fate. Hadn't she learned her lesson already, more than once?

He sat calmly at the table, watching her walk, and stood when she reached his chair. Maya took his hand and led him to the small dance floor, hesitating on the edge as a shaft of fear pierced her heart. She took a deep breath and willed herself to overcome it.

I'm not afraid of this. I refuse to give in to fear.

James' hand slid to the small of her back. He guided her gently the rest of the way onto the floor, as if he knew she needed an encouraging push. Maya steeled herself, then slipped into his embrace. He took her right hand and held it against his chest over his heartbeat, steady and strong. It filled her with courage, enough to run her other hand down his shoulder and grasp his triceps. She admired the firm muscle under her fingers, then slid her hand to the back of his shoulder and stepped fractionally closer.

He was warm against her, steady, and in his arms, she felt safe and comfortable and a hundred other things she'd never expected to experience again with a man. Need swirled inside her, hot and strong. She tried to tamp it down, to rein it in and regain her reason, and failed miserably.

Other couples moved by, talking softly or swaying to the music. James leaned down. His lips brushed her ear and she shuddered as desire stabbed at her. She closed her eyes and leaned into him a little more. Their legs brushed as they moved slowly in time to the singer's lyrical voice.

"So, what's a pretty girl like you doing in a gin joint like this?"

A startled laugh erupted from her. "Girls' night out. You?"

"Boys' night out. Phil, Tom, and George showed up on my doorstep an hour ago and shanghaied me."

"Mmm."

He brushed his chin against her cheek. His late day stubble scratched along her skin and liquid heat swirled through her. Oh, yes. She preferred him a little scruffy.

"I have a confession to make," he said.

"Oh?"

"I've wanted to hold you like this since that night at the bar in Borgholm."

She drew away and pinned a narrow-eyed stare on him. "Really?"

"Absolutely. James, I said to myself, there's a beautiful woman. You should make it a priority to dance with her."

"Do you always have conversations with yourself?"

"Often, particularly where beautiful women are concerned."

"I'm flattered."

"Funny." James relaxed his hold and met her gaze, an odd expression on his face. "You don't sound flattered."

Maya drifted to a halt. What had she been thinking? It really had been wrong of her to dance with him, so horribly wrong to lead him on that way. "I'm sorry. I don't think it's a good idea for us to get involved."

"Who said we had to get involved?" James pulled her back into the dance, cradling her body against his at a distance that wasn't quite decent. "We're just two colleagues with a lot in common who happen to be attracted to one another and are expressing that attraction with a dance. That's not involved. That's exploring an opportunity."

Maya breathed out a laugh and relaxed against him. "And how far would you like to explore that opportunity, Dr. Terhune?"

"Oh, as far as you'll let me, Dr. Bellegarde." His grin was wicked and sharp, and held the heat of a man enjoying his view. "I am a man."

One song melded into another. Couples left the dance floor, others entered it. It was so easy to lose herself in his kindness, his calm. As they swayed to the music, she felt as if she'd stepped out of the storm and into the deceptive safety of its eye. "So this counts as a date, then?"

"A date is where I pick you up and take you out to a nice restaurant, maybe a movie afterward. We sit and talk and get to know each other, and then I take you back home and try to sneak a kiss when I walk you to your door."

She hid a smile against his shoulder. "So that was your plan when you asked me out."

"Yup. Dinner, a movie, and a kiss. Sounds like a perfect night in my book." He pulled her closer and maneuvered them into a less crowded spot on the dance floor. "Unless you're into sports. We could have hotdogs and a game, and then a kiss. Hey, whatever makes you happy."

Maya snickered, couldn't help it. "What if I like opera?"

"That might be pushing it. We manly men can't be seen at such places."

She shook her head, amused by the banter. He seemed so shy, even reserved at times. It was easy to overlook his sly sense of humor, easy to overlook how attractive that humor was.

And she was attracted, more so every day. In spite of that, Maya didn't want to rush into anything with him. She could *feel* that they were headed into something, something she couldn't quite make out. It was leading her, maybe leading them both. She wanted desperately to not be afraid of that pull, but that didn't mean she had to give in to it completely.

They swayed through several more songs, all slow and romantic, and they talked quietly about nothing in particular, their bodies syncing to the music's rhythm.

At nine o'clock, Maya reluctantly pulled away, feeling for all the world like a young lover facing the dawn and her parents' stern disapproval. In this case, a fourteen-year-old had set the curfew, not in disapproval, but so they could have their ritual mother-daughter chat before bedtime. It wasn't something Maya easily surrendered, not when her job forced her away from Dierdre so often.

"Tomorrow's Thursday," James said. "Any chance you're going to take me up on my offer?"

Maya slid her hand down the back of his arm. "I need to think about it, just a little more."

"All right." He hesitated, then bent down and pressed his lips lightly to her cheek. "I'll see you tomorrow, then."

Maya nodded and left. Her thoughts lingered on him through the rest of the evening. She fell asleep and dreamed of holding him under a moonless sky, their bodies entwined in passion, their hearts beating to the rhythm of the music they'd danced to.

NEW YORK CITY might be a Yankee town, but its summers were just as sweltering as any Southern town Dani had ever visited. Night had fallen an hour ago and still the humidity lingered. She eyed the low, thick clouds hanging overhead and hoped for rain, even if it would ruin the outfit she'd chosen for that night's work, black leather pants, a matching lace-up tank top, and thick-heeled motorcycle boots, also black and adorned with crisscrossing straps and shineless buckles.

A woman could never have too many buckles.

And there was her target, the man she'd followed a few nights earlier. He jogged toward her, his long, muscled build a well-oiled machine, his attention on the path ahead of him as if he had no idea she was waiting for him.

Well, how could the dear man expect somebody to follow him, spend a week figuring out who and what he was, and show up on one of his carefully randomized running routes, waiting to ambush him with his secret?

And it was a very big secret. Naughty boy.

He slowed to a stop and bent over, his breaths panting out in regular huffs. Even in ragged running clothes dampened with sweat, he caught her interest, though she couldn't pinpoint exactly why. His clean-shaven features were attractive in an ordinary way, his dishwater blond hair cut close, his clothes chosen for their plainness. He blended, deliberately so, just your average underworld stooge working his way up the ladder of criminal success.

Not.

Dani stepped out of the shadows. He glanced at her, his expression blandly curious, no more, no less. Did he practice that look in a mirror or what?

"Hello, G-Man."

He stood, hands on hips, and inspected her from head to toe. "Do I know you?"

She shrugged. "How could you? We've never met."

"Ok." He appeared completely unruffled, as if he had conversations with strangers in the middle of the night in a deserted park all the time. "Can I help you?"

"Oh, yes," Dani purred. She stepped closer, pleased when wariness flickering through his expression. "So glad you asked. I need an inside man, Davy boy. You've got a lot of practice at being an inside man, don't you?"

His expression went flat. "I have no idea what you're talking about."

"Don't be coy." She took another step and another, and planted herself inches away from him. She caught the collar of his t-shirt between two fingers and twisted it playfully as she leaned against him. "I need information and you're gonna give it to me."

His hands came up, grasping her elbows lightly. "Or what?"

She stood on tip-toe and whispered, "Or I'm gonna spill your little secret into the wrong ear and blow your cover."

His fingers tightened on her elbows and he hustled her into the shadows of the tree she'd been using for cover. As soon as they were out of sight of the path, she twisted her arm, loosening his hold. She brought her other arm across his body and slammed it into his chest in a blow that would've knocked a less sturdy man off his feet.

He grunted, dodged a blow she aimed at his jaw, then swung her around and shoved her against the tree, holding her there with the full weight and length of his body. Her short staff dug into her spine where she'd anchored it earlier and she wiggled, trying to ease the ache. He shot her a droll look and leaned harder into her, bracing his forearms against the trunk above her head.

His head bent toward hers. "What do you know?" he demanded in a low voice.

In the low light from a distance, they'd look like lovers, if anybody was watching, which they weren't. She and her handy-dandy short staff had taken care of the little problem of Feebi tails and criminal watch dogs alike.

Some days, she loved her job, usually on the days when she got to crack skulls.

But she had to wonder why Davy boy was being watched so heavily. That was something she hadn't dug up. Yet.

"I know who you are." She breathed deeply, inhaling the masculine scent of sweat and soap. Too bad the dark masked the color of his eyes. Were they as deliberately bland as the rest of him, or would they give her a different picture of him all together? She shook her curiosity off and focused on the reason they were there. "I know what you're doing and I know why."

"I doubt that."

"Oh, Davy. Don't be naïve. An informant here, a computer hack there, and I know everything about you from where you were born to the size of your shoe."

"Jesus," he breathed.

"Hardly," Dani said drily. "Just money applied to the right person at the right time."

"I want names." His voice was hard, uncompromising, and his body firm against hers.

Naturally, she obliged, though probably not in the way he intended. Why make it easy for him? "David Allen Winstead, twenty-nine years old. A Taurus, born and raised in a little town outside Kansas City to a farmer and his wife. Graduated from Notre Dame with honors and a degree in criminal justice, a minor in psychology." She hesitated, giving him time to understand that she really *had* found out everything about him. "Were you deliberately aiming for a government law enforcement job or were you just tired of growing wheat?"

"Oh, my God." He closed his eyes and beat his forehead twice against the tree's trunk. "I've been working on this case for two years and a castoff from a Goth vampire porn novel blows my cover on a damn whim."

Dani gaped, torn between outrage and amusement, then remembered her outfit. Her lips curled into a snarky smile.

Dave's eyebrows veed over an angry glare.

"Your cover is perfectly intact, Davy. You'd be no good to me if it weren't."

He hissed out a breath and pushed away from her, stepping back into a wide-legged stance with his arms crossed over his chest. "Ok, you've got my attention."

Dani allowed a hint of triumph to creep into her smile. "I knew you'd come around," she said, and then she explained exactly what she needed him for.

THE FIRST FULL DAY in his lab, James devoted his time to deciphering the half dozen cylinder seals unearthed in the anomalous burial at Sandby borg. Each one was between one and one and a half inches in height, though they were made of different materials. They were meant to be rolled over clay as a signatory, so that's exactly what he did.

The flat impressions were much easier to work with than the seals. After taking additional pictures of the tiny cylinders, he packed them away and sent them to the Archives for storage. He snapped more images of the flat impressions, then set them out of the way where they could dry and harden for later use.

The previous day, before his adventure with Phil, George, and Tom at the bar, James had taken the time to sort through the pictures taken at Sandby borg and pin them up onto the corkboard taking up an entire wall in his lab. As a decorating scheme, it left a lot to be desired, but it was handy for his purposes and probably why he'd been assigned that particular room.

Now, the photographs were arranged chronologically, with earlier writing systems on the left and later ones on the right. There was a pattern there, he was sure. It just hadn't jumped out at him yet.

He'd started working with the cylinder seals first since their inscriptions, rendered as images partnered with a smattering of cuneiform, represented some of the oldest inscriptions found in the Sandby borg grave. The language was Sumerian or maybe Akkadian, but he wasn't quite sure. In spite of his reputation as an archaic language expert, the ancient Near Eastern languages weren't his specialty and he was a little rusty there. He'd often wondered if he'd spent too much time on the Classical languages, their origins, and derivatives, and now he was absolutely sure of it.

But he had a book that might help. He peered around at the lab's fixtures and ran a frustrated hand through his hair. The book was in his office in a box he hadn't unpacked yet. He uttered a mild oath and set out, bringing copies of the photographed impressions with him. Now that he had those, he could just as easily work in his office.

Maya had been right about the weather in Tellowee, he reflected during the short walk between buildings. It was miserably humid during the day. The frequent afternoon squalls rarely helped. The days would grow warmer as summer progressed and the humidity with it, and he was confined to a business casual dress code. What he wouldn't give to be able to work in shorts and a t-shirt. On the other hand, walking around in only his running shorts might not be such a good idea, given the number of women on campus.

The previous evening popped into his mind, bringing with it an image of Maya swaying with him to some slow jazzy number, her eyes half-closed, her body relaxed against his. He'd taken liberties there that he wouldn't normally, but had figured at the time that, given her standoffish attitude, the opportunity to dance with her might not come again for a long time, if ever. So he'd held her a little closer than propriety deemed correct and for a little longer, too.

It had felt good, holding her, and somehow right.

Now, if he could just convince her to go out on a date with him.

He laughed quietly as he opened the door to the building housing his temporary office. He'd never been the hound dog some of his friends were. He didn't date a lot, but in the past, when he'd been interested in a woman, nobody had turned him down. Of course, the last time he'd dated seriously, he'd ended up married to her, and hadn't dated since their divorce. Maybe he was a little rusty there, too.

The building was cool and dim compared to the bright summer heat. His footsteps echoed in the empty hallway, eliciting an odd nostalgia. That sound always reminded him of his father, a professor at UConn when James was young. His father had often taken him to work on the weekends at his office on campus. It had been a happy time for both of them. Those childhood memories had spurred James into academia as an adult, a place he'd grown comfortable with long before he decided on a career.

He rounded the corner and pulled up short. Dierdre dawdled casually outside his office. She wore a black tank top and calf-length Yoga tights, each embroidered with the high school's logo. Her dark hair was braided into thin plaits that were pulled back into a loose pony tail. The outfit emphasized her lean, toned figure. James stifled the urge to find a shirt for her to wear over the revealing clothing.

She pushed away from the wall, her shoulders stiff. "Hey, Dr. T."

"Hello, Dierdre." He unlocked the door and opened it. "What brings you by?"

"Oh, you know, just checking to see how you're doing."

James studied her carefully. Her words didn't sound like a lie, but they didn't quite ring true either. He tilted his head toward the door. "Come on in."

She followed him into his office and plopped into one of the chairs placed in front of his desk. The room had come furnished, as had his lab and the suite he was using. Maya had told him to take what he needed from basement storage, but he'd been satisfied with the simple furniture already gracing this room. The walnut desk was a little dinged, but it was sturdy and functional. The bookcases lining the walls were mostly bare. He'd only had room to bring four boxes of books on the trip down and already missed the rest of his home library.

A loveseat was shoved into a corner across from his desk. It was covered in a hideous floral print, but it was comfortable. A small desk lamp sat near the edge of his desktop. The only other furnishings were three chairs, one behind the desk and two for visitors. It wasn't much, but it would serve him well during his time at the IECS.

James dropped into the chair behind his desk and set the pictures aside. Dierdre pulled the ends of her hair over her shoulder and twirled one thin braid around a finger. Her wide-eyed stare was fixed on him. She opened her mouth, closed it again, and frowned.

"Yes?" he prompted.

"I know you're interested in my mom," she blurted out in a rush.

Her words caught him off guard. He searched for a polite way of agreeing and came up blank. How did a man even begin to discuss his interest in a woman with her daughter?

"I'm ok with that," she continued, her voice a little firmer.

"I'm glad?" he ventured cautiously.

Dierdre nodded, as if he'd said exactly the right thing. She dropped the ends of her hair and drummed her fingers on the chair's arms. "You should be, 'cause I could make your life real difficult if I weren't."

"I'm sure you could," he said with as much sincerity as he could muster.

"I know what you're thinking." Her gaze was steady and calm, reminding him eerily of her mother. "You think I don't know what's going on, but I do."

"Er," he said, confused. "What's going on?"

"Duh, Dr. T." She crossed her arms over her chest. "I know about the birds and the bees. I know you want to have sex with Mom."

Heat flooded his cheeks. "Jesus, Dierdre. We haven't even been on a date, yet."

"Yeah, but that's what comes after. I'm not stupid, you know."

James stifled a curse and rubbed a hand over his eyes. "If we did do...that, it wouldn't be anything you'd need to know about."

"Yeah, ok, whatever." Dierdre rolled her eyes. "The important thing is that you want to snag Mom. You're not gonna get her if you play all shy and stuff. I mean, it's sexy and cute and all, but it ain't gonna work, you know?"

He groaned and buried his head in his hands. "Dierdre, stop. Please."

"I'm sorry, Dr. T."

James looked up and caught an unguarded yearning cross the teenager's features, so fleeting he thought he'd imagined it.

"It's just, I want my mom to be happy and stuff, and she likes you, she really does." Dierdre leaned forward, her voice earnest. "But she's got this hang up about dating and I think she's scared to try again, and if you don't do something, she'll never go out with you and then we'll be all alone again, like after Dad died, and I don't want that."

Her lips trembled and tears welled up in her eyes, and his heart ripped just a little.

"Hey," he said softly. He stood and walked around the desk, intending to pat her arm and maybe reassure her, and never got the chance. Dierdre launched herself at him, wrapping her arms around his waist, clinging to him with a muffled sob.

He froze. God, a crying female. He'd never been good at dealing with them, never been good at comforting women, and this one baffled him completely, poised as she was between the maturity of womanhood and the longing of a child for her father. Another sob hit his chest, so he did the only thing he could. He wrapped his arms around her and patted her hair and hoped for the best.

"When did your Dad die?" he asked.

Dierdre sniffled and pulled away, her cheeks flushed pink, her eyes wet. She ran a careless hand over her face, dashing away her tears. "I was, I don't know, four maybe? I remember him, though, and I miss him, so much."

His heart nosedived. Is this what Amelia had gone through since the divorce? He hadn't died, but still. Living apart from him might've felt like it to her. Familiar guilt stabbed at him and he shoved it down. There was nothing he could do about the situation with Amelia that he wasn't already doing.

"He must've loved you a lot."

"That's what Mom says. I think she misses him, too, but probably not the same way."

"Probably not," he said softly.

"It's been a long time since he left. Like, forever, you know? And she hasn't dated or been interested in a guy or anything, not 'til you."

He perked up, interested in spite of himself. "Oh, really?"

Dierdre tilted her head and peeked at him from the corners of her eyes. "And she really likes you."

"Hmm."

She huffed out a sigh. "Any other guy would be pumping me for information right now."

"Been through this before, have you?"

"Dude, guys, like, fall all over the women here. It's embarrassing."

He lifted one eyebrow. "Is it, now?"

"Yeah, but Mom's not interested, no matter how many guys throw themselves at her."

"Maybe they're going about it the wrong way." When she narrowed her eyes at him, he shrugged and added, "Just a thought."

"Maybe," she conceded. "But I know for sure she'll put you off forever if you don't make a move on her or something. Like last night at the bar. I heard you had some smooth moves, Dr. T."

He didn't even wonder how she knew about that. Small town rumor mill. He was getting used to it.

"So, I came up with a plan."

"Er, I've got my own plans, Dierdre."

"Yeah, but too slow, dude. I'm in a hurry here." She sat back down in her chair and crossed her legs, her demeanor that of a general strategizing a war. "Now, I know you asked her out and she wouldn't go, so here's what I'm thinking. There's an exhibition coming up next week. Lots of us are competing. You know, demonstrating our skills with weapons and hand to hand and stuff. You'll come, right?"

He nodded slowly. "Sure."

"'Cause I'm competing and I want you to be there, ok?"

"Ok."

"Also, Mom will be, too, and..."

He sat bolt upright. "Wait. Maya's competing?"

"Um, yeah, 'cause she was a teacher here, like, ages ago, and since she's in town, she'll be put on the roster."

"She won't by any chance be wearing that outfit, will she?"

Dierdre looked at her own outfit, then grinned broadly. "Oh, yeah, Dr. T. She will be."

"Hmm." Visions of Maya in tight exercise clothes flitted through his head and heat throbbed through him. He casually turned and sat down behind his desk. Some things a daughter didn't need to see, no matter how worldly she thought she was.

"Anyhow, after the exhibition, you'll say how you were impressed and all, and then you'll, like, ask her to teach you how to fight."

"What?" James snapped abruptly out of his daydream. "Oh, no. No, no, no. I've been warned about that already. No fighting, absolutely not."

"Aw, c'mon," Dierdre wheedled. "She won't hurt you."

She said that as if it were a given that Maya was the better fighter, which she probably was. What did he know about fighting?

"But I've heard the older girls talk about how, you know." She gestured helplessly. "Fighting leads to other stuff."

"Stuff?"

"Don't be dense, Dr. T. *Stuff.*"

A light dawned. "Right. *Stuff.*"

"But you'll tell Mom you won't do that *stuff* with her unless she'll go out with you first." She brushed her hands together and relaxed confidently into the chair. "Easy, peasy."

He somehow thought it wouldn't be all that easy. "How about if I reserve the fighting lesson as a backup in case my plan falls through?"

Her expression turned doubtful. "I dunno, Dr. T. Guys never come up with good plans."

"Thanks a lot, kiddo."

"Ok, fine. So, here's another one. After the exhibition, I'll invite you over for movie night. We'll grab a pizza for supper and have popcorn and stuff. It'll be fun."

"And you think Maya won't see through that."

"Oh, she'll see right through it," she assured him. "But once you get there and snuggle with her on the couch, you can wear her down and talk her into a date."

Not for one second did he believe Maya would allow any of that to happen. "We'll see."

"Trust me, Dr. T. It'll work." Dierdre glanced at her watch. "Whoops! Gotta run. Class starts in ten. Don't wanna be late." She jumped up and rushed over, hugged him hard, and hustled toward the door. "Don't forget the plan, Dr. T. I'm counting on you."

She shut the door behind herself. James slouched into his chair, torn between amusement and exasperation. How sad was it that a fourteen-year-old girl thought he needed her help getting a date with her mother?

Pretty damn sad and probably true. Maya hadn't caved after The Dance, and while he wasn't in a hurry to start a relationship with her, he'd at least like to see where this attraction would lead. To do that, he had to talk her into a date or at least find a way to spend time with her outside of work.

The fighting lesson Dierdre had suggested was out of the question and having Maya's daughter invite him over was just pathetic. Surely no man could ever be that desperate. Nope, he'd stick to his own plan and hope for the best.

God help him.

NINE

MAYA SPENT a week avoiding James outside of work. No more girls' nights out, no more running on the track on campus, just in case. Meals were a little trickier, since they saw each other every day as the translations steadily progressed, but she'd managed to avoid him there as often as not.

He hadn't asked her out again.

She threw her pen down in a huff. What was wrong with the man? One minute he was giving her the shy man's version of a full court press, and the next, he barely gave her the time of day. Fickle man.

Grimly, she shoved him out of her mind and stared at the photographs in front of her, trying to concentrate on the text she had to translate into English. The urgency to decipher the texts found in the unknown Daughter's grave pushed at her each day. While James had started on the older scripts, she was tackling the easiest, a scroll written in Latin dating possibly from the third century C.E.

She'd chosen this particular document not to horn in on James' territory, but because it was one language she was very familiar with. Unlike most schools in the U.S., schools for Daughters and Sons still taught Latin and ancient Greek, for the same reason their children learned to read and write cursive handwriting, to preserve their history. The IECS Archives and its counterparts around the world held documents written in a variety of languages, including the Classical languages. It would be foolish to let them die out and thus lose the ability to read their own history.

Five more minutes of futile effort, then ten, and Maya realized her concentration was shot. With a discouraged sigh, she rubbed her hands over her face, tugging her fingers through her hair in frustration.

Maybe she needed more sleep. Her nights over the past week had been restless. Pushing her body to the breaking point night after night hadn't kept her from reliving that evening at the bar in her sleep, or, as she usually thought of it, The Foolishness. What had she been thinking?

It was useless to dwell on it. She knew this. There was no changing the past and no point wasting time with regrets.

Except, a small, secret part of her didn't regret the evening spent in James' arms. She'd tried very hard to quell that part of herself, without success.

Would it be so bad to go out with him? She folded her arms on her work table and rested her head on them, eyes closed as she imagined a date with James. She'd wear the dress Dierdre had talked her into buying on their last shopping trip, a filmy little black number with a fluid skirt that swirled to a stop just above her knees. He'd be in slacks and that shirt she liked, the sky blue one that was slightly fitted, with a tie and jacket. They could go to Mama G's, have something fabulously decadent, and listen to a good live band. And at the end of the evening, after they'd laughed and talked and danced until the wee hours of the morning, he'd bring her home and pull her into his arms and press his lips against hers...

A knock rapped against the door, startling Maya awake. She scrubbed her hands over her face and bit back a curse. How sad was it that she'd fallen asleep daydreaming about James?

Dierdre popped her head around the door. "Come on, Mom. We're gonna be late."

Right. The exhibition. She'd almost forgotten. Maya checked her watch. If she hurried, she had just enough time to change. "Sorry, Squiggles. I dozed off for a minute."

"I knew it! You've not been getting enough sleep."

"No biggie," Maya said, smiling softly. "Just a lot on my mind."

Dierdre cocked her head, her own smile sly. "Like a certain Dr. T.?"

"Knock it off, shorty, or I'll rearrange the roster so I can spank your little bottom tonight."

"Bring it, Big Mama."

Maya grabbed her gym bag and slung it over her shoulder. "Speaking of, who did I pull in the draw?"

Dierdre grimaced. "India Furia."

"Great." To be matched against that particular Daughter on top of everything else. Maya pursed her lips, quelling a sigh, and shared a commiserating glance with her daughter as they locked up Maya's on-campus lab.

The walk across campus relaxed Maya, enough for her to shunt aside her unease over fighting India. She and Dierdre joined the steady stream of Daughters, mortal and immortal alike, making their way into the gym's dressing rooms.

The youngest students were marching onto the gym floor by the time Maya finished dressing. She hurried through the final touches so she could watch them. It was always her favorite part of these events, seeing the happiness on their cherubic faces, before time and reality had a chance to dull it.

Dierdre spotted her training coach and jogged off to join her group, shouting goodbyes over her shoulder as she went. Maya tugged a jacket on over her athletic clothes and hurried into the gym, settling herself into the bleachers on the opposite side of the crowd.

Just as all Daughters and Sons learned certain academic subjects, they also all spent a lot of time on physical development and training. Gymnastics and martial arts were started at young ages, training the mind and body to be flexible and disciplined.

As the children began their routines on the mats scattered across the gym's floor, a tiny tingle shivered up Maya's spine. She glanced up and spotted James on the opposite side of the gym. He was leaning against the railing at the top of the bleachers chatting with Robert Upton, but his eyes were fixed on her.

The strangest feeling shuddered through her. Her muscles clenched and butterflies fluttered in her stomach. It took Maya a moment to figure out that those butterflies were her nerves setting up a ruckus. She closed her eyes and groaned. How could a nearly three hundred-year-old woman skilled in the warrior arts possibly be nervous about a simple exhibition fight?

James was still watching her, and it hit her then that she was nervous because *he* was there.

When he looked away, she slipped into the dressing room to warm up and unwind. She'd need all of her focus tonight and simply couldn't afford to have anything distracting her, not even the increasingly attractive James Terhune.

THE GYM was nearly full by the time James arrived. He pushed through the crowded foyer into an empty spot against the railing overlooking the gym floor, painted in standard lines for basketball and volleyball. The bleachers were jam packed, so he leaned against the railing instead, his eyes scanning the crowd. An older man in a wheelchair rolled up beside him. James scooted over, making room.

"Good crowd," the man said, his lined face set in a friendly smile.

James nodded. The number of people in attendance had surprised him until a group of four and five year old children had walked onto the floor. The exhibition must feature a large variety of age groups. Looked like the whole neighboring town might be in attendance. "Do you have a child competing?"

"Oh, no. My children are too old for this." The man stuck his hand out. "Robert Upton."

James shook Robert's hand. "Director Upton's husband."

"Right on the first try. You must be our new language expert. I've been meaning to catch up with you."

"You and everybody else," James said, his smile wry.

"New kid on the block. It'll wear off in a couple of months, once everyone's had a chance to pick your brains."

"Don't think I'll have anything left once this crowd gets through with me."

Robert laughed, a hearty, infectious boom.

Across the gym, people trickled in and out of dressing rooms. Dierdre came out with a group of people her age, giggling and cutting up. A few minutes later, Maya entered the gym floor and found a seat in the bleachers across from him. Disappointment twisted through him. She wore a coat over athletic wear similar to the outfit Dierdre had worn to his office the week before. He'd been waiting a whole week to see Maya dressed that way and had hoped reality came close to his imagination. Heat spilled into his gut, strong and steady, and he shifted against the railing. Maybe not too close to reality, not in public anyway.

The youngest group of children finished their set of gymnastics and martial arts forms to enthusiastic applause, their young faces beaming. After, two successively older groups performed ever more complex maneuvers. A break was called and the mats were rearranged across the hardwood floor, leaving four behind.

James chatted off and on with Robert, surprised to discover the other man had known James' father during their early days as professors at UConn.

"I was teaching history at the time to large groups of students who were more interested in dating than studying," Robert said. "Then I came here to do some research, fell in love with Rebecca, and that was that."

A group of middle-school students ran out and divided into four groups of nearly equal size. Two students from each of the groups stepped onto one of the four mats and faced each other, bowed, and assumed fighting stances. The other students sat down out of the way as referees stepped up to the mats. A bell sounded and the students on the mats sprang into action, attacking each other with fierce punches and kicks.

The crowd went wild, cheering the students on. Robert managed a shouted explanation over the noise. Each pair was given five minutes to score three points or knock their opponent completely off the mat. Two of the fighting couples were composed of a male and a female each instead of the students being paired by sex. James made a mental note to ask Maya about that later, then patted his pockets absent-mindedly for a piece of paper to write the reminder on.

Another bell dinged and the competitions immediately stopped. The spectators broke into applause. The students bowed to one another and, without fail, walked off the mats grinning, their arms slung around each other's shoulders. Two more students settled themselves onto each mat and the competitions began again, cycling through all the students waiting on the sidelines.

Dierdre's group came out next carrying wooden sticks.

James nodded toward the floor. "Should I be worried?"

"Ah, yes. I heard you were stepping out with Maya."

James didn't bother denying it. What was one voice against the community grape vine?

Robert threaded his fingers together at his waist. "As far as worrying, there's no need. These young people can take of themselves. You'll see."

And James did. Dierdre stepped onto one of the mats, her body relaxed, her face a picture of intense focus. A young man stepped onto the mat facing her. The two bowed and assumed ready positions.

"Who's her opponent?" James asked.

"Johnny Linton. I hear he has a crush on her."

James frowned as the bell dinged and the students began sparring. He soon saw that Robert was right. Dierdre could certainly take care of herself. She scored her first point by coming in under Johnny's swing, sweeping him off his feet with her staff, and tapping him lightly on the chest with the staff's end. Johnny took the next point on the rebound, catching Dierdre off guard as she stepped away and gave him room to regain his footing. Her face hardened and she went into a controlled attack that would've been brutally vicious if not for the fact that when it came time to score points, the hits were lightly made.

The bell dinged a moment after she scored her third point. She and Johnny bowed to one another, slung casual arms around each other's shoulders, and walked off grinning. As she sat down, Dierdre shared her grin with James and waved at him.

He waved back, ignoring the curious stares and whispers directed his way.

After Dierdre's group finished, another break was called and the floor was rearranged again. This time, a single mat slightly larger than the others was pulled out into the center of the floor.

"Ah." Robert leaned back in his wheelchair and rubbed his hands together, a huge smile wrinkling his face. "Now the real sport begins."

Two women entered the mat, each carrying a sturdy, yard-long stick similar to the ones Dierdre and her crew had used. One of the women was older and looked vaguely familiar, though James couldn't quite pin down why. Like most of the people he'd seen in his time at the IECS, she was trim and fit. Her light blonde hair was pulled into a ponytail high on the back of her head. He searched his memory, trying to put a name with her face, and came up blank.

The women fell into ready stances, the bell dinged, and they circled one another. The younger woman said something, the older woman smile, and then the attacks began. They used the sticks as if they were swords, slashing and stabbing at one another, blocking and dodging when needed. The younger woman swung her staff in a waist high, back-handed arc. The older woman jumped back and blocked the cut with her own staff. The younger woman did a three sixty and swung her staff around her body into a back-handed upper cut at the torso of the older woman. She calmly blocked again, then twisted her staff around the other woman's, disarming her.

"Atta girl!" Robert shouted.

"Eh," James said. "You know her?"

"My wife, Rebecca. You've already met her, I believe."

"Briefly."

James turned his attention back to the competition. Rebecca had stepped back, allowing the younger woman time to pick up her staff. James tried to reconcile the two images he had of the director, on the one hand, the powerful middle-aged woman who ran the IECS with a velvet-gloved iron fist, and on the other, the woman who expertly wielded a weapon as if it were an extension of herself.

Robert leaned toward James. "Rebecca the Blade, they called her."

"Excuse me?"

"Before we were married. They called her Rebecca the Blade because of her skill with the sword. She stopped teaching and fighting when our son was born, but she still keeps sharp. Practices every day."

The bell dinged, ending the round, and the women bowed and hustled off the mat. Two more women assumed stances on the mat, each carrying a staff, and the round began. When they finished, a third pair of women with no weapons stepped onto the mat. After their bout, a fourth pair entered the mat holding two short sticks each, one per hand, and wielded them with dizzying speed.

James watched the competitions, fascinated by the women's grace, strength, and obvious skill. The matches often ended with only one point being scored, sometimes none.

His parents had never allowed or condoned fighting, not even for competition. In spite of James' strong desire to learn a martial art or maybe boxing, his parents were firm pacifists and had discouraged his interest. He and his sister hadn't even been allowed to watch fighting as a sport, a restriction James had broken as an adult. He'd long since realized that violence didn't beget violence, as his parents feared, and that there was a large difference between healthy competition and war.

Still, when Amelia had wanted to enroll in a Kung Fu class, he'd automatically dismissed her wish out of hand. It was one of the few things he and Linda had fought about. She'd insisted that a woman should be able to defend herself, but he had, in a rare burst of shortsightedness, never envisioned his daughter growing up enough to leave the house. He seldom acknowledged the fact that she *would* grow up. Deep down, he wanted her to stay his little girl forever, but now, here she was a teenager within a few years of dating, and he was beginning to worry about how she'd handle herself when she was, God help him, alone with a boy. After watching Dierdre take down a young man a full head taller and at least thirty pounds heavier, maybe he should reconsider his opposition.

The crowd's furtive whispers drew James' attention back to the exhibition. Maya walked onto the mat carrying a short staff in her left hand, swinging it around in slow, testing circles. James took a closer look at the other woman and frowned. "I thought Indigo was still in Sweden."

"She is." Robert's mouth thinned. "That's her twin, India. They're nearly identical in looks, but their personalities couldn't be more different."

The crowd hushed. Even the younger children grew still and quiet.

The bell dinged and India attacked. Maya calmly countered, quelling the onslaught of India's fury with steady, even strokes of her staff.

And it was fury, unlike in the other matches where even the youngest participant exhibited an amazing degree of control. India wore her anger like a shield, attacking in short bursts of speed that would've left another opponent winded and likely seriously injured. Horror crept slowly over him as Maya broke into a light sweat, her body moving continually into a defensive position, never an offensive one. What was she waiting for?

India attacked again and again, her fury seeming to mount at Maya's steadfast refusal to attack and at her inability to break through Maya's defense. She screamed. The sound echoed eerily through the tense silence. The bell dinged, signaling the end of the round, and the fight continued, Maya circling away, India pursuing in short, brutal attacks. James glanced around. Why was nobody stepping in to stop the fight?

Several minutes after the bell rang, Maya shifted the stick to her right hand and went on the offensive. India's fury never dimmed, her strength never waned. Maya, on the other hand, looked as if her second wind had hit. She swung her stick up under India's guard and bashed the other woman's ribcage twice in short succession, *thud, thud,* each blow hard enough to crack a rib. India skittered away and rebounded, popping her staff around one-handed. Maya ducked under the swing and thrust the end of her staff into India's abdomen. India gasped and staggered back, nearly losing her balance. Maya waited, her body loose and ready. India's shoulders heaved as she sucked in breath after breath, her beautiful features pulled into a furious glare. Maya murmured something too low to carry and India laughed, harsh and bitter. She leapt forward and lashed out, apparently unfazed, and Maya countered, graceful and calm.

Just when James was ready to go down there and break up the round himself, injury be damned, Maya crouched and swept a leg around, hitting the back of India's legs above her ankles. India crashed back first into the mat. Maya popped up and calmly tapped the end of her staff lightly against India's cheek.

"Yield," Maya said, her clear voice ringing through the gymnasium.

"Never," India declared. She snaked one hand toward Maya's bare ankle. Maya twirled her staff down, cracking it against India's forearm, sweeping the limb aside, then dropped to one knee and punched India's jaw with a balled up fist. India's face jerked to the side and her body went slack.

Maya rose and stood over the limp figure of her opponent, her expression oddly dispassionate. Director Upton walked over and spoke quietly to Maya, then directed two of the women standing on the sidelines to remove India from the floor. They weren't gentle about it, either, dragging the unconscious woman out in by her ankles, leaving her head to bounce against the floor and anything else in their path.

The crowd began murmuring, softly at first, the noise building into a normal volume as Maya and Director Upton left the gym floor and another pair of women approached the mat.

James pushed himself away from the railing, torn between his need to check on her and the urge to respect her privacy.

Robert's hand shot out and latched around James' forearm. "Give her some time. Trust me, she needs it."

James sighed. If anybody knew how to handle a woman like Maya, it would be Robert. After all, the older man had a woman like that for his own. "Sure," James said, but he couldn't bring himself to relax against the railing again. He watched the final few matches while worry niggled at him, and counted down the minutes until he could break away from the crowd and find Maya and Dierdre.

ONCE THE MATCHES ENDED, the crowd spilled onto the gym's floor. Maya pushed her way through the crush of people, searching for Dierdre, greeting friends and acquaintances as she went.

No one mentioned her bout with India.

The match had drained her, not physically, no, but emotionally. India had once been a shining star of potential, destined to be one of the greats, but her spirit had been corrupted by envy and a twisted hatred fueled by a crushing need to conquer, to grind her enemies into the dust.

That was not the way of the People.

India was tolerated because the People were so few. Their numbers needed to be preserved. And India rarely allowed her anger to burn in such a reckless display. Maya feared the younger Daughter might've gone too far this time.

Guilt swamped her, bringing anger in its wake. India had once been her student. Maya had had the chance then to help her find redemption, and had failed. For a Daughter, such failure was intolerable. It had taken a long time for Maya to understand that the failure was not her own and never had been. India simply didn't recognize the difference between friend and foe. Still, the guilt chased Maya and, inevitably, the anger.

James was still standing at the railing talking to Director Upton and her husband. Maya had caught the exchange between him and her daughter and had puzzled over it. Now, she wondered why he hadn't made his way down to the floor to find them, to find her.

Had he even noticed her outfit?

Maya bit back a groan, embarrassed at her own thoughts. Of course, he had. She was wearing skin tight Lycra that left little to the imagination. Any man with half a brain and a working penis would notice. By the Goddess, what was wrong with her? Here she was covered in sweat, not a stitch of make-up on, her hair frizzed into a rat's nest, and she was worried that a man might not have noticed her. As if any woman in her right mind would want to be noticed in such a state.

Which just proved she wasn't in her right mind.

He peered down, his eyes homing in on her as if he'd known where she was all along, yet he made no move to join her.

Was he playing hard to get? No, that wasn't right. *He* was chasing *her*. She just hadn't decided yet whether or not she wanted to be caught.

She was leaning more toward getting caught every day, but only if he pursued her.

With a frustrated *hmph*, she turned her back on him and finally spotted Dierdre plowing her way across the crowded floor, Johnny Linton in tow. When they reached her, Dierdre asked, "Where's Dr. T.? I thought he'd be down here by now."

Maya shrugged and affected an innocent look, as if she didn't know exactly where he was right at that very minute.

Dierdre narrowed her eyes. "Did you chase him away? Geez, Mom. What is that, like, a record?"

"I did no such thing."

"Uh-huh. Well, let's go find him. I want him to meet Johnny."

"Why don't I meet the two of you outside? I could use a little fresh air."

That last was the truth, at least. The gym had grown stifling over the evening. After the confrontation with India, all Maya really wanted was the cool breeze on her face and an hour of silence.

Dierdre snagged Maya's arm in an iron grip. "Oh, no, you don't. I know you're interested in Dr. T., and he's interested in you, and we're gonna go up and meet him and invite him over for pizza and a movie, and you're gonna like it and that's that, young lady."

Maya pursed her lips, trying and failing to suppress a smile. "Oh, really?"

"Really." Dierdre's sternness melted away. She slung her arm around Maya's shoulders and squeezed. "Come on, Mom. It'll be fun."

And it was.

There was no awkwardness as Maya extended the invitation to James, nor at the pizza parlor where many of the Daughters gathered after the exhibition, nor during the movie when she, James, Dierdre, and Johnny all slumped into on the overlarge sofa Maya had purchased when it became evident that her daughter enjoyed having people around her.

They sat shoulder to shoulder during the movie with Maya and Dierdre in the middle and "their fellers," as Dierdre insisted on calling James and Johnny, sitting on the outside. Dierdre had picked an old favorite, an adventurous, fantastical romp with a pirate, a giant, and a Spaniard facing the forces of the evil prince to gain the heart of the princess.

After the scene where the pirate and the Spaniard fought a duel on the cliffs, James tilted his head toward Maya and whispered, "You're not left-handed either, are you?"

She shook her head, her heart melting a little. He'd noticed her switch during the fight. The move had been intended to incite India into rash behavior. Any Daughter would've understand that Maya was insulting her by using her weaker hand to defend, but India, with her hair-trigger temper and wavering control, would take it doubly so, and it had worked. India had burned through her energy and lost focus, allowing Maya to control the fight from start to finish.

Later, James reached behind her to tease Dierdre by pulling at one of her braids and left his arm across Maya's shoulder.

And she didn't mind.

He didn't ask about India or the oddness of their match. He didn't push her to go out with him or try to take advantage of the situation. He just waited, his presence firm and strong and reassuring.

It was exactly the right tactic to take.

Maya allowed her head to fall against his shoulder during the final scenes, when the Spaniard was searching for his father's murderer and the pirate overcame the dastardly prince. She sighed as his arm tightened around her, engulfing her in the safety and warmth she'd reveled in the night they'd danced.

She'd have to go out with him. He was wearing her down just by being himself, an intelligent, reserved man with deep wells of compassion and humor. If she didn't act soon, the attraction between them would spiral out of control, and then where would she be?

As the credits rolled across the TV screen, she leaned her head back and whispered, "Ok."

"Ok, what?"

"I'll go out with you."

He smiled down at her, the corners of his eyes crinkling. "Next Friday?"

"Sure."

He laid his cheek against the top of her head, and she closed her eyes, hoping she'd made the right decision.

TEN

The translations progressed nicely. The cylinder seals, the first items James had tackled, had presented less of a problem once he'd remembered that the symbols engraved on them could be symbolic representations other than language. Scenes of worship, maybe, or historically significant events.

If he hadn't been so distracted by his growing attraction for Maya and his worry over Amelia, he would've realized that a lot sooner, a fact that nagged at him. To effectively do the job he'd been hired to do, he'd have to find his focus sooner rather than later.

He checked his watch. Maya would be at the lab any minute now to go with him to present their findings to Director Upton. He finished packing the small impressions of the seals and stuffed the reports he'd prepared in his briefcase, eager to get through the meeting.

Tonight was the Big Night, his date with Maya. He'd taken the entire week to plan this one evening. He scrubbed his hands down his thighs and exhaled a shaky breath. Had he ever been this anxious over a date before or so worried about its outcome?

Maya was still a tantalizing mystery to him. She'd been more open since the exhibition. God knows why, but that night seemed to have been some kind of turning point for her. Curiosity over the match she'd fought with Indigo's sister ate at him, but he refused to bring it up. It had obviously been a difficult night for her, and if she wanted to talk about it, she would. His nagging would only push her away. Still, the whole incident tugged at him. Maybe she'd open up once she felt more comfortable around him.

On the other hand, maybe she'd never trust him enough to open up. He had no end game in mind with her except to, as he'd told her during The Dance, explore the possibilities. What was wrong with two intelligent, unattached adults who were attracted to each other trying to find common ground?

When he'd presented that question to the Three Professorteers, Phil had leveled a pitying look on James and said, "You're overthinking it, man. Just go with the flow."

Maybe Phil was right.

A hard rap on the door startled him back to the present. He jerked his gaze around. Maya leaned against the doorframe, her mouth curled into a smile. "You looked like you were a million miles away."

"Yeah. Sorry. Just, ah, thinking."

Not in a million years would he tell her what he'd been thinking about.

The walk to Director Upton's office went quickly. She was waiting for them in a small sitting area set up on one side of her office. "Punctual as usual, Maya. Dr. Terhune, would you like something to drink before we begin?"

James settled onto the overstuffed chair to Rebecca's left. "Thanks, no."

"I'll start, then." Maya perched on the loveseat next to the director and launched into an explanation of her progress translating one of the texts from the burial. "One of the problems I've had is that the text seems to be written in a strange dialect of Latin, possibly one that was in the early stages of becoming its own language. If so, it's not a dialect I've encountered before."

James nodded. "It's possible the account was rendered in Latin as a translation of another, quite different language. Normally, that wouldn't make a difference, but if the text's author wasn't a native Latin speaker, it could account for some of the oddities Maya's encountered."

"How far along are you?" Rebecca asked.

"About halfway through." Maya pursed her lips and shrugged. "It seems to be an account of an event that must've had some importance to the woman in the grave, though it's not an event I'm personally familiar with. There were a few names and places mentioned that I'd like to research in the Archives, once I'm finished translating the whole. "

"A sound approach," Rebecca said. "I'd like to read the account myself. I wouldn't mind helping with additional research, if you need a hand."

"Of course, Director."

Rebecca turned her pale gaze on James. "How is your work coming, Dr. Terhune?"

"Steadily. I've been working with the cylinder seals. They seem to be the oldest textual artifacts." James opened his briefcase and pulled out the reports he'd printed. He handed one to each of the women and kept one for himself, then placed the box of impressions on the table, opening the top so that they were displayed against the foam holding them in place. "The seal in the first picture of the report corresponds to this impression."

One by one, James took the director through an explanation of the cylinder seals, describing the materials they were made of, the time period they might've been created during, and linking each to a possible place of origin.

Rebecca scanned through the report, lingering over the images embedded into it. "The carvings on these are incredibly intricate. What was their function?"

"Anything from a scene of worship to the equivalent of a notary's seal or a signature. I haven't yet determined that for most of these." He flipped to an image of a limestone cylinder seal and pointed out the corresponding impression. "This one for example. The image begins here on the left with seven figures, two groups of three stacked on top of each other with the seventh rendered twice as large as the others. Next is what could be a grove of trees, and finally a four-legged creature of some sort. That section is too worn to really lend itself to a solid identification."

Rebecca leaned forward, studying the impression. "What does it mean?"

"I'm not sure," James admitted, "but there are a couple of observations I've made that might be important to determining the meaning. These figures are clearly female. It's difficult to make out in the smaller figures, but the larger one has definite breasts. Usually, cylinder seals depict men or possibly goddesses, but ordinary women aren't often portrayed."

"Are these goddesses, then?"

"I don't think so. They're carrying weapons, specifically quivers for arrows, not unheard of for a goddess. But, normally when gods are portrayed on these seals, it's during an act of worship or the god-figure is accompanied by a name or symbol. That isn't the case here."

Rebecca and Maya exchanged a look James couldn't decipher. He glanced between them. "What?"

"Seven women, a grove of trees, and a four-legged creature," Maya murmured. "Sounds familiar, doesn't it."

"Indeed," Rebecca said.

James raised his hand. "Mind cluing me in?"

Maya ignored him. "I thought so, too, when I first saw the seal, but..."

"You didn't want to get your hopes up." Rebecca ran one finger lightly over the impression of the scene. "It may be time, Maya."

Maya's gaze pierced through him as if he were paper thin. "Not yet, Director."

"Soon, then," Rebecca said firmly.

James huffed out a breath. "What are the two of you talking about?"

Rebecca set her copy of the report on the table. "We have some documents here that might have bearing on your work with these seals. I'd like the two of you to finish the translations or as much of them as you can before you have a look at those."

"Context is everything when interpreting images like these." James exhaled sharply and rubbed his hands down his thighs. "Part of the reason I can't tell you what these mean is because they're isolated from their time period and the locality where they were created."

"The fact that they're part of a collection is just as important and probably an overriding factor to other possible contexts," Maya pointed out.

"Yes, of course," James agreed. "But if you have relevant information that could shed light on the original context..."

"All in good time, Dr. Terhune," Rebecca said. "You have my word."

James slumped into his chair. They were holding back something important, that much was clear. On the other hand, he wasn't willing to risk his removal from the project. If they wanted him to wait, he would, but it rankled. "As you wish."

Maya shot him an exasperated glare.

Rebecca flipped to images of two seals James had deliberately included on the same page. "These look as if they were made of the same material."

"They're lapis lazuli." James pointed out the appropriate impressions. "These appear to represent two different individuals. Notice the mixture of symbols and similar cuneiform. It's possible they were made at the same time or in the same locality."

James continued his explanation of the possible meanings and origins of each seal. He concluded by pointing out the holes drilled into the top back side of each one. "It was fairly common for cylinder seals to be strung and worn as a necklace or in some other fashion."

"Is there any possibility the woman from the grave wore all of these on the same necklace?" Rebecca asked.

James mulled the idea over. "It's possible. Of course, it's equally possible they were carried in a pouch. At this point, it'd be unwise to rule out any possibility. We simply don't know enough yet."

"Mmm." Director Upton studied the impressions, her fingers brushing over each one. "Well, I've kept you long enough. The two of you have made excellent progress. I hope you'll have more news for me soon."

After packing the impressions away and saying goodbye, Maya and James left the director's office. When they were outside under the hot Southern sun, he said, "I can do a better job if you share whatever it is you're holding back."

"I'm not holding anything back."

He snagged Maya's elbow and pulled her onto the grass, earning a startled look from a passing student. "Except whatever documents the IECS has that might be related to the seven figures seal."

Maya shook his hold off. "It's not important, not yet, anyway."

He scrubbed his hands over his hair and glared at her. "How do I know that if you won't show it to me, whatever it is?"

"Because I'm telling you it's not important right now."

"So you want me to trust you, is that it?"

"Yes, I do."

He glanced away. "But you don't trust me."

Maya edged closer and laid a gentle hand on his arm. "Where these artifacts are concerned, yes, of course I do."

"But not enough to share important information with me."

Maya exhaled a heavy sigh. "It's not really my decision."

"Director Upton didn't seem to think so."

"Ok, it's partly my decision, but you have to understand that there's a lot at stake here. I'm not the only one..." Her voice trailed off. "There are things here you don't understand."

"Because you won't tell me," he gritted out.

Maya leaned her head back, closing her eyes against the sun's brightness. "People could be hurt."

"It's just a cylinder seal, Maya."

"No, it's not." Something close to sadness flitted across her normally tranquil features. "It's potentially something much greater."

"Then let me help. Tell me what's going on."

"I can't, not yet." She squeezed his arm lightly and warmth spread through him, rippling away from her simple touch. "Have a little patience and trust me, ok?"

She seemed so anxious and a little tired, as if a heavy weight had settled on her and she was the only person available to carry the load.

He clenched his hands into fists, relaxed them. "You have to show it to me eventually."

"Soon, I promise."

He walked her back to her office and left her there with a reminder that he'd pick her up that evening at six thirty sharp. As he returned to his own office, the conversation whirled through his head. How deep did Maya's secrets run? And what was so sacred she couldn't share it with him?

MAYA STUDIED her reflection in the mirror, examining her appearance. She'd deliberately chosen the apricot sheath because it was *not* a dress she'd dreamed of wearing on a date with James. It was simple and sleeveless, cut high at the neck, and dipped to a few inches above her waist in the back. The fabric clung to her figure, accentuating her flat stomach and the curve of her breasts and hips, and stopped just below mid-thigh. She'd paired it with a simple two-stranded, gold necklace and a matching bracelet, and a shawl, heels, and purse all in black.

She twisted to and fro, examining her three-inch heels in the mirror. They'd put her nearly eye to eye with James. A thread of uncertainty worried at her. She straightened her shoulders and pushed it away. He didn't seem the type to care about a woman's height, and if he was, better to find out now so she could usher him right back out of her life.

Dierdre whistled softly and flopped crosswise onto Maya's bed. "You're totally rockin' that outfit, Mom."

Maya smoothed a hand down her stomach, eyeing her reflection critically. "You're just saying that because I'm your mother."

"No, I'm totally serious. Dr. T. is gonna, like, go wild over that dress."

"You think?"

"Oh, yeah." Dierdre's eyes widened and she nodded emphatically. "He totally digs your bod."

"Dierdre, honestly." Maya paused and glanced at her daughter. "Really?"

"Yup. He got all hot and bothered when I told him what you were gonna wear to the exhibition."

"And you talked to him about that when, young lady?"

"Oh, er, you know." Dierdre flipped over and stared at the ceiling. "When I went to his office and invited him to come."

Maya shook her head. Curls bounced around her face and she whirled toward the mirror in a panic. She and Dierdre had spent half an hour taming her hair into a chignon, leaving some curls pulled out in strategic places to achieve a *sexy mama* look.

Dierdre certainly had a way with words.

Maya brushed her fingers over the stray curls and exhaled. Everything was in place, right where it was supposed to be, but if she didn't get ahold of herself, she'd never make it through the evening in one piece.

"Besides," Dierdre said. "He doesn't mind. I stop by all the time to chat with him."

"Define all the time."

"Well, not, like, every day or anything."

"Dierdre, honey, James is here to work."

"I know." Dierdre rolled onto her stomach and rested her chin on her folded hands. "It's just, he's nice and everything, and he likes to talk to me."

The words were soft spoken, her daughter's voice small and thin. Dierdre was so independent, so self-assured, it was easy to forget she was still young. Maya joined her daughter on the bed and stroked a hand over the teenager's braids. "Just don't make a nuisance of yourself. Now, what time are you going to the movies?"

They discussed Dierdre's plans for a night out with friends, and Maya reiterated the rules. Home by ten or as soon as the movie let out if they went to a late show, no friends inside the house, and cell phone set to vibrate or ring at all times. Dierdre was a Daughter, true, but she was a *teenaged* Daughter. Not setting firm limits tempted fate.

The doorbell rang. Dierdre bounced off the bed and loped down the stairs. Maya followed at a more leisurely pace, taking her time navigating the wooden steps. It had been a while since she'd worn heels. She pressed a hand to the nerves dancing in her stomach. It had been a while since she'd been on a date, too.

She was a few steps away from the foyer when James glanced up and saw her. His gaze drifted slowly down her body and up again, scorching a trail of heat along her skin. His eyes met hers, his so hot, a thrill shot through her. Dierdre had been right. James *was* attracted to her, more than a little. How could Maya have missed that?

He glanced away and cleared his throat, and a hint of pink tinged his cheeks. He turned to Dierdre and handed her a small, elaborately wrapped box. "For you."

Dierdre's eyes widened. "Wow. Really?" She tore the wrapping off, revealing a box of expensive chocolates. "Thanks, Dr. T."

"You're welcome, kiddo." James took Maya's hand and helped her down the last few steps, then handed her a bouquet of wildflowers. "These reminded me of you."

Maya buried her nose in the flowers, hiding a pleased smile. "Maybe I wanted the chocolates."

He grinned and tucked his hands into his pants pockets. "You're teasing."

"I am."

"You do it so rarely, sometimes it's hard to tell."

"I'll have to do it more often, then. Let me put these in water."

"Take your time."

Maya walked into the kitchen, one ear on Dierdre and James' conversation. They seemed so familiar with one another, casual even. She scrounged for a vase and filled it with water. She'd have to ask him about that later, make sure Dierdre really wasn't bothering him. Her youngest could be a bit too persistent sometimes, especially when she really wanted something. Maya set the flowers on the kitchen table where the blooms would greet her each morning at breakfast and worried on her lower lip. What could Dierdre possibly want from James?

BEFORE SHE AND JAMES LEFT, Maya restated the rules for Dierdre's night out one last time.

Dierdre rolled her eyes. "Yeah, yeah, I got it, Mom. Just give me a hug already."

Maya tsked and kissed her daughter's cheek. "We won't be late."

"Geez, Mom. Be late." Dierdre hopped onto tiptoes and kissed James' cheek. "But, you know, let me know if you can't make it home before bedtime."

James grinned and tugged one of Dierdre's braids. "Ok, Mom."

Dierdre shooed them out, grinning madly as she shut the front door behind Maya and James.

He was dressed exactly as she'd pictured him, in the sky blue shirt she liked with khaki slacks and a navy blue sports jacket, the epitome of a college professor out for a night on the town. He was clean shaven, his hair slightly damp from the shower. As they settled into his car, she caught a whiff of woodsy cologne and smiled. *Mmm.* A scent to get closer to.

He started the car and pulled out onto the street. His radio was on, the volume low as the DJ wound up a commercial and played a classic rock ballad. Maya crossed her legs and folded her hands in her lap. "Where are we going?"

His eyes were fixed on the road as they cruised through Tellowee, but the corner of his lips turned upward into a grin. "It's a surprise."

"No hints?"

"Not a one," he said cheerfully. "I love your house."

"I'll give you the grand tour later."

"I'd love that. How did you find it?"

"When I was pregnant with Dierdre," she explained. "I wanted to put down roots, at least while she was young. Director Upton heard I was looking to settle and offered me a job at the IECS. This house came up for sale right after that. It seemed like serendipity."

"I love it when a plan comes together. When was it built?"

"About 1893. It had been in the same family since then, and they took wonderful care of it."

They chatted off and on during the half hour drive, though Maya had trouble keeping her full attention on the conversation. Once she discovered that James' eyes followed her legs each time she shifted, she couldn't help wiggling a little more than was strictly necessary.

The desire to tease him into a physical reaction surprised her. She'd played plenty of games before with men, becoming shy and coy or bold and reckless to fit the situation, but she'd never been a tease. It had always struck her as somehow dishonest. Too many women enticed men into lust without following through and it was wrong.

James brought out the temptress in her, with his shy sidelong glances and hesitant touch. The look he'd given her earlier, as if he were imagining exactly what she looked like underneath her dress, had been so unlike him. Even after Dierdre had told her that James wanted her, Maya hadn't quite believed it, in spite of their dance at the bar, in spite of Dierdre's insistence. That look had convinced her, and now, she wanted to see it again, even if it meant teasing him.

The restaurant he'd chosen was in a neighboring town, a good half hour's drive from Maya's home. It was also one of her favorites, especially during summer weekends when local bands played in the outside eating area. How had he known?

Dierdre, she guessed. The rat.

James placed his hand on the small of her back as they waited. It should've been polite, would've been if he'd placed his hand a little lower. His fingers brushed over the bare skin of her back, warming her, and inched upward along her spine. He leaned close and whispered, "Are you wearing a bra?"

She arched an eyebrow. "What do you think?"

He groaned softly. "I was trying to be good, Maya."

She grinned. "Yes, but I wasn't."

The restaurant's service was slow, the food excellent. Over salads, homemade rolls, and fresh pasta, their conversation roved from movies and books to parenting, and even to the forbidden first-date topics of politics and religion. Surprisingly, they agreed more than they disagreed, given his reserved Yankee upbringing and the gypsy-like lifestyle of the People.

The sun slipped behind the mountains, bringing a slight chill to the air. A singer-songwriter stepped onto the raised platform serving as a stage, guitar in hand. Maya and James fell into a companionable silence as the performer sang one bluesy original after another. His hand crept to the back of her chair, to the ends of her hair, to her bare shoulder, and she shivered.

Wherever he touched her, heat rose, delicious and sweet, and a fine tension spooled between them. It tugged at her, distracting her from the songwriter's performance and the hefty slice of white chocolate cheesecake their server brought them. Anticipation. How long had it been since she'd anticipated the end of an evening and the kiss that was sure to follow? Everything else, the dinner, the music, the conversation, was merely leading to that one moment when he'd draw her close and lower his lips to her own.

She sucked in a breath and pressed her hand over the desire pooling within her. She wanted that kiss, needed to feel his mouth on hers. Did he want that, too, or had he only mentioned it as a matter of course?

After the performer's second set, James paid the bill and they left. He helped her with her shawl, his hands lingering on her nearly bare shoulders, and rested his hand on her waist as they left the restaurant. His heat seared her through the thin fabric of her dress. Blessed Ki, why did he have to be such a gentleman?

The drive home seemed twice as long as the drive into town. Maya crossed her legs, tapped one foot nervously to the rhythm of the radio, then stilled. What was she doing? Daughters never got nervous. It wasn't in their nature, yet here she was, fidgeting, her mind tangled in knots over the possibility of a kiss, her fingers twisted together at her waist. What must he think of her?

She glanced at James. He stared straight ahead, his attention seemingly focused solely on the road, and her heart sank. Why didn't he say something, anything to break the silence?

Maybe he was waiting for her to speak.

She bit her lower lip and searched for an appropriate topic. The only thing that came to mind was the kiss, his mouth on hers, his hands gripping her waist and skimming over her back. She swallowed and leaned her head against the cool glass of the passenger's side window.

Maybe he was nervous, too.

At last, they arrived, and Maya bit back a relieved sigh. James helped her politely out of the car and walked with her to the front door, holding her hand lightly in his.

At the top of the steps, she said, "Thank you. I had a lovely time."

His eyes crinkled at the corners in a gentle smile. "Me, too."

Still, he made no move to leave.

She grasped her purse with both hands and gnawed on the inside of her cheek. "Would you like some coffee?"

"Thanks, no." He stuffed his hands into the pockets of his slacks. "I should probably head home now."

"Ok. Well." At a loss, Maya turned and walked to the door, hesitating with her hand on the doorknob. His hands cupped her shoulders, strong and warm, and she turned and met his gaze with her own, that sweet gaze, so intense and hot. Her heart flipped over and her breath shallowed, and she stepped back, bumping into the solid wood of the door.

"You're so beautiful," he said. His hands slipped to her waist and he leaned into her, his face inches from her own. He brushed his lips over hers, once, twice, lightly as if giving her a chance to say no.

The feathering touches set butterflies loose in her stomach. She dropped her purse and gripped his shoulders, urging him into a deeper response. His lips pressed firmly against her own, and she shuddered. It felt so good, his kiss. Her skin tightened and heat pooled within her as he explored her mouth, slowly and thoroughly, his hands tightening against her waist, drawing her firmly against him. The solid length of his body aligned perfectly with her own. He leaned into her, pressing her into the door, and his hardening need pushed into the juncture of her thighs, inches from the center of her own desire.

She twined her fingers into his hair, clutching the cool, silky strands. He groaned and rocked against her, and his mouth left hers and trailed hot kisses down her neck. He bit her gently, and she gasped as fire raced through her.

"James," she whispered. "Please."

He soothed the sting with another kiss and murmured, "Please what? Please more, please stop, please don't ever let you go?"

The porch light flickered violently off and on, and Maya sagged against the door. Dierdre. What perfectly awful timing.

James' soft moan whispered against her ear, sending shivers over her skin. "Saved by a teenager."

"Soon to be a grounded teenager," Maya muttered.

He laughed softly and kissed her, slow and easy, and slid his hands up her arms to her neck. "I've mussed your hair."

Maya bit her lip, hiding a smile. "You're the only man I know who'd put it that way."

"It's the truth." He wound one of her curls around his finger, tugging gently. "When can I see you again?"

"When do you want to see me again?"

Heat reignited in his eyes. He nuzzled her neck, licked her pulse. "I don't think you want to know the answer to that question."

"Fair enough." Though, secretly, she already did, and was glad that he, at least, had enough restraint to pull away. Five more minutes, ten tops, and she would've yanked him inside the house and had him in the foyer.

Thank the Goddess for Dierdre.

"Tomorrow?"

"Movie night with Dierdre." She hesitated, weighing one need against the other.

"Would you like to come?"

"It won't be an intrusion?"

"No," she said firmly. "As long as you don't mind the movie. It's Dierdre's turn to pick."

"Ok. Just one more," he murmured, and kissed her again, claiming her with a need equal to her own.

One turned to two before James left, and Maya couldn't blame him, not for the kisses, not for the reluctance to leave. She had just enough control left to keep herself from staggering inside. She locked the door, against temptation as much as anything. *Mmm.* Who would've thought James' reserve hid such passion? And boy, did he know how to use it. Hidden depths were the best finds, always.

Dierdre had retreated to the couch and was watching a movie. Maya stuck her head in the living room and said goodnight, then climbed the steps to her room, her gait not quite steady. She undressed slowly, her mind caught on the night she'd shared with James, and his kiss. She fell into bed smiling and slept soundly through the night.

ELEVEN

The early morning light illuminated the practice room in Rebecca's home. Every morning, she rose early and went through her routine, stretching, exercising, and training. Achieving mortality hadn't been enough to overcome centuries of habits.

This morning, she eschewed weapons practice in favor of yogic stretches. Her body was aging and needed more work to stay limber and flexible, something she hadn't had to worry about as an immortal, or not as much. She emptied her mind and flowed through several forms, holding each pose before easing into the next, breathing through the stretches.

Here in her home, she felt safe enough to relax, but not so much that she lost awareness of her surroundings. The door to her home gym opened, disrupting the meditative rhythm of her exercise. Jerusha entered, murmuring a hello and an apology in one breath.

Rebecca rose from her final pose and greeted her daughter, examining her from head to toe. Dark circles marred the skin under Jerusha's eyes and her shoulders were slumped. "When did you get in?"

Jerusha rubbed a hand over her nape and yawned. "Just now. I have some info. Thought you'd want it as soon as I could get it to you."

Rebecca exhaled slowly. Whatever news Jerusha carried, whatever she'd dug up, it must be bad. "Why don't you take some time to freshen up? I'll make you some breakfast and then we can talk."

Jerusha nodded and headed upstairs, her steps slow and even. Rebecca threw a track suit on over her workout clothes and bustled into the kitchen, her thoughts buzzing over Jerusha's news. Good or bad, and it must be truly gut-wrenching, it would be easier for Jerusha to deliver it on a full stomach, and easier for Rebecca to absorb and act on it. Breakfast, then, a hearty one. She pulled bacon and fixings out of the fridge and tucked her worry away as she prepared a meal.

Half an hour later, Jerusha bounced down the stairs wearing clean clothes, her expression alert. Robert followed her into the kitchen and maneuvered his wheelchair over to Rebecca. "Look who I found wandering around upstairs."

"The prodigal daughter has returned." Rebecca bent down and planted a firm kiss on his mouth. Three decades had failed to dim the sweetness of his touch. "We'll kill the fatted calf tonight and have a feast fit for the Seven."

Robert waggled his bushy eyebrows and grinned. "That we will. Nothing's too good for my girls."

Bobby stomped down the stairs whistling and ducked into the kitchen. His handsome face stretched into a mischievous smile. "Jerusha, hey. I thought I heard an elephant clomping around."

"You're the elephant. I'm the gazelle." Jerusha held her arms out and laughed as he grabbed her up and swung her around. "Put me down, you oaf. We can wrestle later."

Bobby set her down and settled his hands on her waist. "I like wrestling now. Thought we wouldn't see you 'til Thanksgiving."

Jerusha's dark eyes slid to Rebecca. "Got some stuff for Mom."

"Stuff, huh. Is that what we're calling it now?" He shook his head and eased away from her. "How come you get all the good stuff?"

Jerusha stuck her tongue in her cheek. "Maybe because you're the baby and I'm the grown up."

Rebecca plated the bacon and set it on the kitchen counter. "Children, can we please eat before the two of you launch into a full-scale war?"

"No chance," Robert muttered. "We can still make a run for it."

Rebecca tutted and shooed him and her children to the table. The meal passed in a noisy exchange of barbs between Jerusha and Bobby. When they'd run out of ammunition, the conversation turned to Jerusha's work in London at an archaeological dig and Bobby's work at his security firm.

In the middle of one of Bobby's tales of childhood pranks, Robert slid his hand over Rebecca's. "Everything ok?"

She'd never been able to fool him. No matter what was going on, he always knew when something was bothering her. "Everything's fine, darling. I'm a little distracted by some business Jerusha and I have to deal with this morning."

"If you're sure," he said, and she squeezed his hand gently.

When breakfast was done, the men took over kitchen clean-up while Rebecca and Jerusha retreated to the library. It was one of her favorite rooms, with its book-lined walls and leather furnishings. She and Robert had spent many hours in here over the years, immersed in their mutual love for the written word.

Jerusha settled onto one end of the couch across from the fireplace, one leg folded beneath her.

Rebecca took the other end, mirroring her daughter's pose. "What have you found?"

"The Shadow Enemy hasn't been dormant for the past few decades, as we thought. They've just been underground, rebuilding."

"But Alexiou was so young..." Rebecca pursed her lips together. Rumor had it, Lukas Alexiou, the Shadow Enemy's current head, had killed his father at the tender age of thirteen some twenty-five years before. All of the intelligence she'd received since then indicated that most of his energy had been devoted to keeping that organization and his family together, every single scrap. "Specifics?"

Jerusha knuckled the furrow between her eyebrows. "On the surface, Alexiou is a charming, generous man, known for his philanthropy. He runs a small auction house specializing in rare antiquities, but that's just the surface. His business connections run much deeper. He also owns antiquity dealers, an import-export business, a treasure-hunting venture, but the layers he's put between himself and those interests are deep. It took a lot of digging to find them."

"Interesting that his businesses deal primarily with antiques."

"That's not the worrying part. At the same time that Alexiou's been building his business, he's also been gathering followers to his ultimate cause, the same cause that his father pursued, destroying the People. I couldn't pin down the number of people directly associated with this aspect of the younger Alexiou's movements, but it's easily double the number his father controlled."

"By the Lady Ki, how has this slipped past us? I've personally had people following key members of the Shadow Enemy since I took over the directorship, and not a one has reported any of this to me." A slow burn twisted through Rebecca. She sucked in a breath and pinned her daughter with a hard stare. "Are you saying they've all betrayed me, and through me, the People?"

"No." Jerusha shifted and pulled a piece of paper out of her pants pocket. "I believe they're being manipulated by two or possibly three of these individuals. I just can't figure out which ones."

Rebecca took the paper with stiff fingers and examined the names. The list was headed by two members of the Council of Seven, one of whom Rebecca had always thought was a firm supporter of her leadership. Her heart thudded in her chest, booming so hard she was certain Jerusha could hear it. "This can't be right."

"I'm sorry, Mom, but everything I've learned leads me to those people."

There were more than a half dozen other names on the list, in outline form, with one to three others offset under each one, presumably allies of the main suspects. At the bottom was a list of four different individuals, separated from the others by a horizontal line. Every single name on the entire list belonged to an immortal Daughter.

"And these names at the bottom?" Rebecca asked.

"They seem to be working independently for their own purposes. None has betrayed the People that I can tell, but each one is in some way involved with the companies Alexiou controls. It could be nothing."

Or it could be something. Daughters were an independent bunch, scattered across the globe in support of the various interests of the People or in pursuit of their own agendas. Usually, those agendas centered upon education, training, or finding a mate, but not always. Sometimes, the Daughters' curiosity put their noses in business that was better left alone. At other times, it led them into situations that ultimately benefited the People. A person on the scene was usually a much better judge of a situation than a distant administrator. Rebecca had always had a firm policy of never ignoring a Daughter's innate instincts in pursuit of bureaucratic regulations. Any of the individuals on Jerusha's list could be in similar situations, simply waiting for matters to come to a head before reporting in, but how to tell?

Rebecca folded the paper in half. "Thank you, Jerusha."

Jerusha nodded. "Do you want me to pursue this?"

"No, dear. I think it best for you to return to your duties in London."

"Ok, but if you need me..."

"I'll call."

Jerusha rose, kissed her mother's cheek, and left the library.

The door snicked shut. Rebecca closed her eyes and dropped her head against the back of the sofa. All this time, the People could've been combatting the rise of the next generation of the Shadow Enemy, and instead, someone had hidden the needed information, stolen it from under her very nose. Chances were good that the one who'd done so was someone Rebecca trusted. The betrayal cut deeply, sapping her energy. What a fool she'd been. How could she not have known? Had she become so complacent in her duties that these manipulations had slipped by her?

More importantly, what was she going to do about it?

Rebecca rose and secured the list in her personal safe. She needed time to think through everything Jerusha had told her, but she didn't need the list for that. The names had already burned themselves into her memory.

THE WEEKS PASSED SLOWLY as summer hit its apex and waned toward fall. After that first date, Maya stopped resisting James and saw him as often as they both had time, usually with Dierdre in tow.

The teen's near continual presence made it impossible for them to explore a physical relationship. Maya was in no hurry, but that first kiss had kindled a longing for something deeper. As they spent more and more time together, squeezing in moments between work, family, and life, they were becoming closer, maybe even developing a solid friendship, an odd situation for her. She'd never been friends with a man she wanted the way she wanted him.

Meanwhile, James seemed determined to act the gentleman. She was equally determined that he not. Their first stolen kiss, shared in his lab with the door conspicuously locked, he backed her against the wall and kissed her so sweetly, she melted under his touch. His hands skimmed over her waist and back and shoulders, and though he nibbled gently on her neck, he made no move to go any farther.

That would never do.

Since he wouldn't, Maya took the initiative a little at a time, starting with their third kiss, in her office hidden behind the cabinet holding her supplies. She snuck her hands under his shirt and stroked his stomach, dug her nails lightly into his back, and blossomed for him, leaving herself completely open to his touch.

A few days later, he cornered her in his office and pushed her against his bookcase, exploring her mouth in a greedy kiss. She dipped a finger into the edge of his waistband, and he moaned and rocked into her, pressing his growing erection against her. He unbuttoned the top buttons of her shirt and feathered kisses along her collarbone, and his hands grew bold, grasping her bottom, fitting her against his need as he murmured encouragement, urging her into boldness. A knock on his door startled them apart. Maya glared at the door, her heart pounding, her skin deliciously tight and achy. Five more minutes and they would've been on the floor, making love. How much more could she take?

One memorable Saturday afternoon, they got a little too carried away. Dierdre ran over to a friend's house on an errand, leaving Maya and James alone. They put a movie in and settled on the sofa, both fully aware that Dierdre could be back at any moment. What started as an innocent kiss ended with him pushing her onto the couch, aligning his body on top of her, his mouth greedily devouring hers. He pushed her t-shirt up and was unhooking her bra when Dierdre came in, her mind and hands thankfully preoccupied with texting. Maya shoved her shirt down and bit back a panicked giggle, and a pink tinge crept into James' cheek beneath his hot gaze.

"Later," he whispered, and she agreed wholeheartedly. Later would be great. It was the when that was the problem.

They were more careful after that, sneaking kisses when they were alone, holding hands when they weren't, whispering promises to one another at the end of each day. It was simply a matter of time before they consummated their relationship. Only the lack of opportunity kept them from doing so.

The Friday of Labor Day weekend, James left early to pick Amelia up from Hartsfield International Airport for her week-long visit. Maya corralled Dierdre into a thorough house cleaning. Having both girls around would lessen the chance for sex. Frustrating, yes, but unavoidable. James would be with Amelia while Dierdre was on her camping trip. Maya didn't begrudge his time with his daughter, far from it, but time alone with him would be splendid, just him and her and a comfortable bed. How could she have forgotten how hard it was to have sex with children around and how deliciously frustrating the long wait was?

Maya scrubbed her bathtub, expending some of her pent up sexual energy making it shine. Other than the lack of sex, there was only one thing keeping her growing relationship with James from being perfect. She had yet to tell him the truth about herself.

After their first mutual meeting with Director Upton, James had only twice brought up the documents the IECS held that might have bearing on the artifacts recovered at Sandby borg. The first time had been directly after the meeting, when he'd confronted her and she'd asked for patience.

The last time had been a mere week ago. As the translations progressed, it was becoming clear that they formed some sort of story. James had mentioned early on that the artifacts seemed to have a pattern, and this story might be it, so he thought. The documents carried by the slain Daughter began with what Maya believed was a scene from the Legend of Beginnings, the oasis that had, according to the few historical accounts they'd found, served as a sanctuary of some sort for the Seven Sisters after they were cursed with immortality for committing a mortal sin. The narrative jumped over large periods of time as it was told from document to document. When laid out side by side from the oldest story to the newest, it was clear that there *was* a narrative of sorts, in spite of the massive gaps.

As soon as they'd begun to suspect the documents' narrative theme, James had wanted a crack at the documents he knew Maya was holding back, and he'd not been happy at all when she continued refusing access.

Maya scrubbed harder as doubt ate at her. James would inevitably learn the true nature of the People. He'd have to be brought in or he'd have to leave the project. There were no other choices. Either path would end their burgeoning relationship. With another man, it might not matter, but this man was a different story. She was beginning to care about him. No, she had to be honest. She wasn't just beginning to care about him. She was beginning to fall for him. If he learned the truth about who and what she was and rejected it, rejected her, could she handle that? A queasy uneasiness rippled through her. No, his rejection would hurt her deeply and possibly even break her heart.

James had to be told, sooner rather than later, but not just yet. Please, not yet.

ANOTHER MISERABLY HUMID DAY in the South, James thought as he waited for Amelia to disembark. The air conditioning in Hartsfield International didn't quite override the sun or the heat exuded by the large number of bodies jostling from terminal to terminal.

At last, he spotted her bopping toward him to music only she could hear, and his heart melted. His little girl. Had she grown an inch over the summer or was that just his imagination?

Amelia saw him and waved, a huge smile on her elven face. They pushed their way through the crowds toward each other. James enfolded her in a fierce hug, then took her carry-on, and they braved the crowds searching for her other luggage to the accompaniment of her excited chatter.

During the two-odd hour drive from Atlanta to the IECS, they made plans. Or rather, Amelia told him all the things she wanted to do that week and he nodded and rearranged his week in his mind. Six Flags and the Mall of Georgia were musts, as were hikes in the forests surrounding the IECS.

Because he'd promised, she reminded him.

Her phone beeped. Amelia stopped talking in mid-sentence and flipped through her phone.

"Who's that?" James asked.

Her fingers moved rapidly over the keypad, absorbing her attention. "Dee."

"Don't think I know her."

"Dee as in Dierdre, as in your girlfriend's daughter."

"Er." James' mind went blank. He couldn't say Maya wasn't his girlfriend. As seen from the outside, that's probably what their relationship looked like. He just didn't think of her that way, hardly at all unless he counted pretty much every minute he spent daydreaming about her. "How do you know Dierdre?"

"She messyed me the week after you came down here. On Facebook? And then, she introduced me to a bunch of her friends. It's, like, really cool at her school."

As Amelia chatted on about all the things she and Dierdre had talked about, concern wiggled its way through James. It's not like Dierdre had gone behind his back, though she had, or that he had a problem with the girls getting to know one another, which he didn't. That was great. But shouldn't one of them have said something to him or Maya?

On the other hand, Dierdre was a pretty independent young woman. It might not have occurred to her that she needed to ask permission or at least discuss contacting Amelia with an adult before doing so. From what he could tell, she'd been raised to be a problem solver. See the problem, find the solution, fix it. Obviously, that's what she'd done with Amelia. What bothered him were her motivations. Had Dierdre reached out to his daughter as part of her overall plan to throw him and Maya together or because she wanted to get to know Amelia, or both?

Maybe she was just being considerate. He was liable to be at the IECS for months. Hopefully, Amelia would visit him a lot during that time. She'd enjoy having friends there, enjoy having younger company than his when she was around.

He pushed the concern aside and spent the rest of the evening enjoying his daughter's company, and tried not to worry about how Amelia would react to his deepening relationship with Maya.

AMELIA'S REACTION to Maya turned out not to be a problem, thanks to Dierdre paving the way. After a while, it became apparent that she'd convinced Amelia that James and Maya would be perfect for one another. The two teens were now in cahoots, their heads bowed together more often than not, giggling about one thing or another.

They visited Six Flags and the Mall of Georgia, thankfully not on the same day. Amelia insisted they go with Maya and Dierdre, whose schedule had loosened up when the summer term ended. He and Maya rearranged their schedules, and he refused to feel guilty. They'd made a lot of progress on the artifacts, more than he could've hoped to achieve in such a short time.

He was certain progress would've been even speedier if Maya weren't holding something important back from him.

It was one of the few points of contention between them, but it was a doozy. Why did Maya continue to insist that he didn't need to see documents pertinent to their work? He suspected the Sandby borg artifacts were of life-altering importance to her. Yet, she didn't trust him enough to open up about it with him and it stung.

The week leading up to the Labor Day weekend was a happy one, in spite of his worries. In that time, James got a glimpse of what life would be like if Maya and Dierdre were part of his and Amelia's family. The two girls were joined at the hip. Amelia had not only accepted Maya, she hung on the older woman's every word, much the way Dani and Indigo had when he'd first met them. For her part, Maya treated Amelia essentially the same way she treated Dierdre. Maybe someday, Amelia would accept a more permanent relationship between him and Maya.

The longer he knew Maya, the more frequently the idea crossed his mind.

The four of them had dinner together at Maya's house the evening before Dierdre was scheduled to leave for her two-day camping trip. Amelia hadn't asked to go, and he wasn't sure how he felt about that. He wanted to spend time with his daughter, but he was so close to losing control where Maya was concerned. One more passionate kiss and he might forget where they were and make love to her on the spot, location be damned. Considering that they had two teenagers underfoot, that might not be such a good idea. Cold showers and long hours at the gym weren't going to cut it for much longer, though.

Over dessert, Dierdre caught Amelia's gaze and waggled her eyebrows. She turned to James, eyes wide, and said, "So, we were thinking what with this camping trip and all, maybe Amelia should come along. I mean, otherwise she'd just be stuck here with you two 'cause all our friends are going camping."

A whiff of excitement shot through James. "Do you want to go, Amelia?"

"Well, sure, Dad." Amelia focused her gaze on the piece of fruit on her fork. "It'd be great, but I don't want you to be lonely or anything."

"You don't sound like you really want to go."

"Oh, yeah, I really do. It's just, you know, we're supposed to spend time together, me and you. The camping trip would be fun and all. They're going to hike and go swimming in this lake over the mountain and tell ghost stories and stuff, and Dierdre said I could share her tent, and there's lots of neat people going." She sighed and fixed a pitiful look on her face. "But I can stay here if you want me to."

Across the table, Maya covered her mouth with her napkin, her almond shaped eyes glittering. Dierdre wore the same hang-dog look as Amelia.

Oh, yeah, those two were in cahoots, all right.

He cleared his throat and laid his napkin on the table. "Yes, you're right, the camping trip would be fun."

Dierdre and Amelia glanced at each other wearing identical smiles.

"But I think you should stay here with me."

Amelia swung around, her mouth open. "Dad. Really?"

Dierdre's hands dropped into her lap. "Yeah, really, Dr. T.?"

Maya snickered, and James grinned. "Kidding. You can go, if you really want to."

Dierdre pumped her fist. "All right."

"Thanks, Dad." Amelia jumped out of her chair and hugged him tight. "You won't regret it."

The two teens raced out of the room, their excited chatter overlapping. Maya stood and stacked empty plates into a pile. "You know what this means, don't you?"

Immediately, his mind shot straight to the weekend ahead, alone with Maya, no teenagers to take into consideration. His skin tightened and his blood burned and desire pooled in his groin. "Oh, yeah."

Her mouth curled into a small smile. "It means we have to do the dishes."

"Oh, yeah. That."

He stood and helped her clear the table, but the dishes waiting to be cleaned didn't keep him from anticipating the coming weekend.

TWELVE

The girls packed and unpacked and repacked while Maya made the necessary calls securing a place for Amelia on the camping trip. As soon as the arrangements were made, Maya went to the attic searching for extra gear.

James followed her up the narrow stairway, close on her heels. "Amelia already knew about this camping trip."

Maya paused and peered over her shoulder. "Oh?"

"Dierdre tracked her down on Facebook not long after I got here."

"Did she really?"

"Yeah." One corner of James' mouth lifted. "She's something else."

"She's something all right." Maya pursed her lips. "Did you tell her she could?"

He shrugged. "No, but no harm, no foul, right? Besides, she was right. Amelia needs friends down here."

"Maybe," she said. And maybe Dierdre should learn to respect other people's privacy, especially where their kids were concerned. "I'll talk to her."

Maya and James dug through the attic, rounding up an extra sleeping bag and other gear Amelia might need. They dumped it in the foyer next to the front door, then Maya tracked down her errant daughter. She found Dierdre in her room lying across her bed, chatting to Amelia.

Dierdre's gaze fell on Maya. She sat straight up. "Uh-oh."

"Amelia, could you give us a few moments, please?" Maya asked.

Amelia slid off the bed. "Sure thing. I gotta talk to my dad anyhow."

Maya shut the door behind the perky teenager and speared her daughter with a stern look. "James just told me you contacted Amelia without his permission."

"Oh."

"Yes, oh. What were you thinking, Dierdre?"

Dierdre clasped her hands together in her lap. "Well, she was coming down anyhow."

"That didn't give you the right to..." Maya blew out a breath and sat on the edge of the bed. "You should've asked first."

"If I'd asked, you could've said no."

"And we could've said yes. You're a woman among the People now, Dierdre.

That means acting like one, not tearing off on a wild hair whenever you feel like it."

Dierdre's eyebrows furrowed and her gaze turned hot. "That was hardly a wild hair, Mom. All I did was find Amelia and see if she wanted to be friends, and we are. She's really funny and sweet, and..."

Maya placed a hand over her daughter's. "And what, Squiggles?"

"Forget it. You wouldn't understand."

"Try me."

Dierdre shook her head, sending her braids flying around her shoulders. "You gonna ground me now?"

"That would hardly be fair to Amelia, would it? She probably wouldn't feel comfortable going on the camping trip without you."

"Probably not. She's kind of a girly girl, you know?" The mutinous set of Dierdre's mouth softened into a smile. "Thanks."

"Don't think you're getting out of it that lightly. We'll talk about this later, once Amelia's gone back home." Maya stood and made her way to the door. "Almost packed?"

"Yes'm." Dierdre scrambled off the bed and bounded across the room, then threw her arms around Maya's neck. "You're the best, Mom."

"You, too, Squiggles."

They went in search of James and Amelia. Maya turned the incident over in her mind as she helped the teens finish packing, certain Dierdre's motivations for contacting James' daughter weren't nearly as pure as she'd let on.

THE NEXT MORNING dawned clear and bright. James and Amelia came by for an early breakfast. After, the four of them piled into his car with the camping gear stowed in the trunk. Dierdre and Amelia huddled together in the backseat, giggling over who knew what. Maya sat quietly in the passenger's seat listening to their chatter, mulling over the coming weekend.

From the moment James had given permission for Amelia to go on the camping trip, Maya's thoughts had lingered on what would happen when she was finally alone with him. Was she ready to be with him that way? Surely after all these weeks she must be, but instead of the calm excitement she'd expected to feel, butterflies danced in her stomach and molten heat slid through her blood, consuming her.

Half an hour after leaving her house, they arrived at the campers' meeting point, the head of a local, well-known trail. Maya helped Dierdre and Amelia with a final check of their camping gear while James filled out Amelia's paperwork. After hugs and goodbyes, the group set out, Johnny Linton between Dierdre and Amelia, one long arm slung around each of their shoulders.

James leaned against the hood of his car, his eyes narrowed on the departing group. Maya lingered with some of the other parents, watching the camping party until they disappeared around the first curve of the trail. She inhaled slowly and stuffed her fingers into the pockets of her shorts. Making sure the girls got off to a good start wasn't procrastinating, was it? And besides, she didn't want to seem overeager.

The last stragglers rounded the curve and the other parents drifted to their cars and left. Maya slipped into the passenger's seat of James' car and buckled in as he started the car and eased out into the string of departing vehicles.

The drive back to her house was made in near silence. Maya clasped her hands together in her lap and watched the passing scenery. Her heart skipped and the butterflies in her stomach tangled into a knot, and her mind twisted over the possibilities. Would he want to stay? Leave? Go out? None of the above?

James pulled into her drive and turned off the car. He twisted his hands around the steering wheel. "Dinner tonight?"

"Sure."

"Six ok?"

"Anytime's fine." She drew in a slow breath and blurted, "Do you want to come in?"

The corners of his mouth tilted up in a soft smile. He faced her, and his eyes were hot, greedy, and so beautiful, her heart skittered to a stop. "Yeah. I'd like that."

They got out of the car and walked into the house together, shoulder to shoulder. James waited patiently as she unlocked the door, then slipped inside behind her. She shut it and rested her forehead on the cool, wooden door.

"You ok?" he asked.

She turned, putting her back to the door. He was standing at the foot of the stairs with his hands stuffed into the pockets of his shorts and his shoulders hunched. The butterflies dissipated, leaving only the heat, and she held her hand out. "Can you do something for me?"

He stepped closer and slipped his hand into hers. "Anything."

"Kiss me," she breathed. "I want to feel you, all of you."

James tugged her into his arms and lowered his mouth to hers, claiming her in a soft kiss. She opened for him and wound her arms around his back, clinging to him as he deepened the kiss, tasting her in slow sweeps of his tongue and gentle nips of his teeth.

It wasn't enough.

She eased her hands under his t-shirt and caressed his bare skin. It was smooth and warm, his muscles firm under her touch, and she wanted so much more, the fierce burn of passion, the eager touch of his hands roaming over her bare skin, him inside her, stroking them both past pleasure into ecstasy. She wanted all of that, craved it, and she wouldn't settle for anything less.

She broke the kiss and panted, "James, please."

"Yeah," he said. "Me, too."

His hands fumbled with the hem of her shirt, yanking it up and over her head. He pulled his shirt off and dropped it on top of hers, then pressed her back against the door, holding her there with the weight of his body. His skin skidded across hers, creating a sweet, sweet friction. "Better?"

"Much."

He slid an open-mouthed kiss down the side of her neck, trailing beautiful heat. It rebounded inside her, pinging through her blood, and settled between her thighs, intense, liquid fire. She moaned and dug her fingers into his back, reveling in his bare skin melding with hers, the moist heat of his mouth, the delicious feel of his erection pushing against her core through their clothing.

His mouth met hers again. She fumbled with the fastening on his shorts, aching to feel him. Her fingers were too clumsy, her need impatient. She delved a hand into the waistband, following the silky line of hair trailing from his navel downward.

His hand gripped hers, holding it in place inches from where she wanted to be, and he tore his mouth away from hers. "Bed," he said, his voice gruff.

"Here."

"Bed, now." He gritted the word out and ground his erection into her. "Please, Maya. Don't make me wait any more."

She caught his earlobe between her lips, sucking gently. He shuddered and moaned, and she rubbed her face against his neck, hiding her satisfied smile. "Upstairs."

He glanced over his shoulder at the stairs, then dropped his forehead to the door. "Jesus."

She laughed, low and husky, and pushed him gently away from her. Urgency drove them up the stairs as fast as they could manage, trailing shoes and clothes as they went. They tumbled onto her bed, rolling together, landing with him stretched out on top of her, their hands joined, her arms pinned above her head. She rolled her hips upward, urging him to take her.

"Wait." His hand skimmed down her side and rested on her hip, pushing it into the mattress. "Let me..."

She laughed and shifted beneath him, and his erection prodded at her core.

"Oh, God," he moaned, and slid into her, filling her completely. He flexed his hips, seating himself within her, and a wave of something close to ecstasy tore through her. She gasped and lifted her knees, pulling him in deeper.

He buried his face in her neck and murmured, "That's it."

He moved against her, slowly finding a steady rhythm, deepening his thrusts, the pleasure building with each sharp push of his hips. She raised her hips in counterpoint to his and tightened her hold on his hands, and the heat building within her peaked sharply and erupted into a million shattering pieces. He thrust into her a final time and came, spilling into her on a low, shuddering moan.

They lay like that for a long while, their breaths slowing from gasps to sighs, their bodies cooling in slow increments. James slipped out of her, rolled onto his back, and tucked her tightly against his side. Maya snuggled into him, draping herself over him, and laughed. They were lying catty-corner on the bed, the duvet wrinkled and bunched beneath them, but what a beautiful, delicious rush it had been.

He kissed the top of her head and relaxed under her.

"Don't go to sleep," she said.

"I'm not," he promised, his voice soft and sleepy.

She huffed out a sigh. "Under the covers with you."

"In a minute."

The air conditioning kicked on, blowing a stream of cold air into the room. James sucked in a breath and shifted onto his side, facing her. "That's really cold."

"I tried to get you under the covers."

"Next time I'll listen." He smoothed a hand up and down her back. "You ok?"

"Mmm." Ok was probably not the word. More like smug, satisfied, womanly. Content.

"Not too rough?"

The concern in his voice tickled her. He hadn't been rough at all. She ran a leg over his, enjoying the crisp hairs scratching against her skin. "Just right."

"We, ah, got a little carried away." His cheeks flushed and his eyes closed, crinkling the laugh lines at their corners. "Actually, we got a lot carried away."

"It's ok."

"I'm clean, promise. I haven't had sex, er..." He cleared his throat. "It's been a long time."

"Me, too."

His mouth opened, closed. He blinked and cleared his throat again, and she bit her lip, containing a laugh. She kissed his nose and rubbed her fingertips through the spattering of hair on his chest. "There's nothing to worry about, really. It's a no harm, no foul situation."

Emotions flickered across his lean face, hope, relief, and something indefinable. "Really?"

"Cross my heart."

It was the closest she could come to saying, *Hey, James, I can't get pregnant right now because I'm immortal and only ovulate about once a year, twice if I'm lucky*. She wasn't ready for that conversation and neither was he. Maybe they never would be.

She pushed the gloomy thought away and kissed him lightly. "Shower?"

"Together?"

"Sure."

A slow grin stretched across his mouth. "Well, if you insist."

And she did.

THAT NIGHT, after a quick supper in her kitchen, Maya put in a movie and cuddled with James on the couch. Without Dierdre around, they could hold hands and share intimate caresses and long kisses as the movie played, a quiet background to their passion.

Maya felt no guilt whatsoever in taking advantage of her daughter's absence.

And since Dierdre was gone, Maya didn't hesitate to squeeze in as much time as she could with James, making up for the time they'd miss when Dierdre and Amelia came back from the camping trip. "Stay with me tonight."

His hand paused in mid-caress on her thigh. "Are you sure?"

"I am." She settled against him, rubbing her temple across his shoulder. "You don't have to."

"I want to. You have no idea how much. I just want you to be sure."

"I'm sure."

She cupped his cheek and kissed him, and they forgot about the rest of the world for a while.

After the movie, James made a quick trip to his on-campus apartment for clothes and toiletries. Maya slipped into the shower. As the water sluiced over her, her mind lingered on their shower together earlier, after the first time they'd made love. He'd taken the soap and run it over her, exploring her as he hadn't done before, and she'd done the same, touching him, kissing him, molding herself to him. The water was cold by the time they got out and continued their explorations in her bed under the warmth of the duvet.

Now, she hurried through her ablutions. He'd be back soon and she wanted to be ready for him. She chose her outfit carefully, a black lace bra and panty set covered by a short kimono-style robe, and did a quick mirror check of her hair, smoothing the frizz out with her fingers. Satisfied, she dimmed the lights in her room and turned down the duvet.

Downstairs, the front door creaked open. Maya's heart leapt into her throat. He was back. Her eyelids fluttered closed and the heat, sated during their earlier interlude, rocketed through her, coalescing into a greedy, eager yearning. How could she want him again so soon?

She shook the thought off and forced herself into a measured step out of her bedroom and down the stairs toward the foyer.

James glanced up and fumbled the bag he was carrying, dropping it. "Um. Wow."

She rested her fingers along the stair railing and smiled. "Ready?"

"Oh, yeah," he breathed. He bounded up the stairs behind her, his bag forgotten, and followed her into the bedroom. His hands slid around her, spreading warmth under the slow, steady touch. "That is a spectacular outfit."

She snagged his hands and pushed them away, holding them against his thighs. "My turn."

He grinned. "If you insist."

She tugged his t-shirt off and dropped it on the floor. His bare chest gleamed in the dim light. She raked her nails lightly across his stomach, and he sucked in a breath, tightening the muscles under her fingertips. She flattened her palms against him and explored him slowly, learning the feel of smooth, warm skin stretched over hard muscle, memorizing every curve and bump and dip of his lean body.

He'd apparently vented his sexual frustration at the gym, and she couldn't complain a bit.

His hands grasped her hips, digging into the skin there. "Maya, come on. Let me touch you."

She dragged hot, open-mouthed kisses down his neck and over his chest as her fingers unfastened his shorts. "Bed," she said, deliberately echoing his earlier plea.

"Ok." He sat down on its edge and pulled off his socks and shoes as he watched her, a small smile curving his mouth.

Maya shrugged her robe off. It slithered to a heap on the floor. James' eyes followed it down, then slid upward along the long length of her legs. She stepped out of the robe and strolled toward him, slow and easy, and a hot glow sparked in his gray eyes.

She pushed him back onto the bed and straddled his hips, lowered her head and kissed him gently, and he kissed her back, teasing, nipping kisses, beautiful and light, setting off a cascade of molten need within her. She rubbed herself over his rigid length. His hips jerked upward, meeting hers in a bold thrust, and she smiled. This was what it meant to be a woman, to revel in the way a man reacted to her, to savor his hitching breaths and shuddering sighs and the desperate need twining between them.

She broke the kiss and trailed hot kisses down his lean form, nuzzling her nose into the silky hair covering his chest, dipping her tongue into his navel, grazing her teeth along his skin above the waistband of his shorts. She shoved them down, taking his boxers with them.

James lifted his hips and wiggled out of his clothes. "I should've let you do this the first time."

"I liked our first time exactly the way it was."

His expression softened. "Yeah, me, too. It was perfect."

She unfastened her bra and slid it off her shoulders, baring herself to him. "Maybe we can reach perfection again."

He propped himself up on his elbows, his warm, gray eyes running over her nearly nude body. "I think we already have. Why don't you come over here and let me test that hypothesis?"

"Only if I can touch you, all night, everywhere." She shimmied out of her panties and dropped them on top of her robe. "Over and over again, any way I want."

"Yeah, I think I can handle that. Come here."

She crawled onto the bed, skimming her stomach over the tip of his erection, sliding her skin across his, aligning their bodies. "You rang?"

He moaned and dropped back against the bed. "I take it back. Much more of that and I'm going to come before we ever get started."

"That would be a shame." She rubbed herself along his length in long, easy strokes. "There's so much more waiting for you."

"Tease," he said gently, and she tilted her hips back, taking him into her in one smooth rush.

She undulated her hips in slow circles, her eyes on his, her palms flat against his chest. "You feel so good, James, so right."

"God, Maya."

He pushed his head into the bed and arched into her, and his hands roamed over her body, cupping her breasts, brushing her nipples, gripping her hips, urging her to move faster, harder, and she did, working her body against his, their gasps overlapping in a wanton symphony. He thrust into her and came, and his release throbbed through her, pushing her over the edge into her own release.

"James," she cried, and he slid a thumb over her clit, sending her high again.

Maya leaned over him, panting as her heart slowed. His eyes were closed, his chest sheened with sweat. A pulse beat furiously at the base of his neck. She dipped her head and sucked lightly, tasting the salt of his skin. Would they ever get around to having leisurely sex or would their need would always be so demanding, so consuming, so blissfully unrepentant?

"Mmm," he moaned. "You're insatiable."

"Complaining?"

"What?" His eyes popped open. He flipped her onto her back and braced himself on his elbows above her. "No. Are you kidding? No."

She laughed and trailed her fingers through the moisture on his skin. "Positive?"

"Absolutely no complaints here." He brushed his lips against hers. "In fact, if you give me about five minutes, I think we can go again."

He made good on his word, loving her with the patience of a man with all the time in the world. Afterward, they showered and fell back into bed, holding one another as sleep pulled them into its insistent grasp.

THIRTEEN

Dani sat in the living room of Dave's apartment, her gaze glued to Godzilla stomping around Tokyo on Dave's TV, eating a bowl of popcorn she'd popped in Dave's microwave while she waited for the man himself to make an appearance.

It had been a month and a half since she'd blackmailed him into this little bargain. He'd held up his end of the deal, to an extent, but now, just when his information was getting good, he'd gone walk-about on her. It was time for a little come to Jesus talk with him, just to remind him of the way things stood.

After all, her patience only went so far.

A scratching noise sounded at the door, followed by a click, and it slid quietly open. A moment later, Dave's shadow fell across her. Ten to one, he had his gun drawn. Big guy was a bit paranoid.

"What are you doing here?" he asked, enunciating each word carefully.

She took her time selecting a piece of popcorn, picking through the popped kernels in search of just the right one. "The mountain didn't come to Mohammed, so Mohammed picked the lock on the mountain's door and helped herself to some popcorn. You should get a better lock."

He grunted, set his gun on the coffee table, and dropped onto the couch beside her. He closed his eyes and dropped his head back against the sofa's plush leather.

"You look tired, Davy boy." She shook the bowl in his general direction. "Have some popcorn."

He opened one eye and peered at her, then dipped a hand into the bowl.

They munched in silence, riveted to the movie. Beside her, Dave relaxed, his body gradually sinking into the cushions. He was sitting close enough for the heat radiating off his body to warm her, a not unpleasant feeling. He was at least two hubbas, more if he'd smile every once in a while, but not Mr. G-Man. He took himself way too seriously.

She, of course, had no such problem. Why be serious when there was so much fun out there, waiting to be had?

The movie came to its inevitable end and the credits rolled. Dani set the bowl of popcorn on the coffee table and stretched her legs out, mimicking Dave's sprawling posture. "So, Davy boy. Any news on the artifact front?"

He sat up and rubbed a tired hand over his close-cropped hair. "You are one persistent lady."

"Hey, you're lucky I let you watch the rest of the movie."

He shook his head, a half smile flirting at one corner of his mouth. "Very generous."

She arched one eyebrow. "Was that an actual joke? I didn't know you had it in you."

He grunted again, closed his eyes, and slumped into the sofa. "I know where all the artifacts are."

"Well, why didn't you say so?" Dani sat up, bouncing around on the sofa, facing him. "Tell Dani all."

"Mmm." He yawned, snuggled deeper into the cushions, and crossed his arms over his broad chest. "Maybe tomorrow."

Dani gaped. Tomorrow? What did he mean, tomorrow? This wasn't friggin' *Annie*. She narrowed her eyes and ran through her options. What could she do to get Stoic Dave to talk tonight?

"Don't." His voice was flat, uncompromising, and sounded an awful lot like a warning.

"Don't what?"

"Don't do whatever you were about to do." He yawned again and sat up, rubbing his eyes with the fingers of one hand as he stood. "I'm beat."

"So you're, what, going to bed?"

"For a blonde, you're pretty bright." He pointed to the door set into the wall behind and to the left of the TV. "Spare bedroom. It's yours, if you want it."

"I know what's in there. You were gone a long time and I got bored." Dani sat back on the sofa and eyed him. "Aren't you worried I'll get mad and, I don't know, tell somebody you're double dipping?"

He shrugged out of his t-shirt, scratching his chest in a half-hearted stretch, his well-formed muscles stretching and flexing. "If you were gonna do that, you'd've done it by now."

Dani's heart flipped in her chest and her mouth went dry. Her eyes dropped to the smooth muscle and the line of blonde hair leading from his navel downward. It disappeared into the low-slung waistband of his jeans, and she bit the inside of her cheek, holding back a sigh. Dave out of his clothes was a sight to behold, shooting him to at least a two point five on the Hubba Meter. That was all this was. She couldn't be attracted to him, not to straight-laced, by-the-book Dave Winstead. No way.

"I could still do it," she said, and hid a wince. Where had that quaver in her voice come from?

"Good night, Dani."

He strolled into his bedroom and shut the door.

Dani sat back on the couch, flummoxed. She'd totally intended to rat Dave out if he didn't get her the information she'd requested, right up until the moment he took off his t-shirt and her heart went thumpity-thump.

A soft snore drifted to her from behind the closed door and Dani shook her head. She cut the TV off, slipped into the spare bedroom, and readied herself for bed, amused in spite of herself. A well-muscled chest had thwarted her blackmail scheme. She must be getting soft in her old age, that or going barmy. She smiled, slipped into the guest bed, and snuggled under the covers. Well, at least she could enjoy the view on the way to Crazyville.

THE WEEKEND'S IDYLL couldn't last no matter how much James wanted it to. He spent nearly every minute with Maya, talking about everything, laughing at the silliest things, making love with her over and over again. He watched her practice with her short staff, joined her at the gym to lift weights, and went with her to the grocery store.

The sly, knowing glances following them when they were out in public didn't bother him as much as they would've before his arrival in Tellowee. Now, he played along, holding Maya's hand, standing a little too close to her, stealing soft kisses in the produce aisle.

She dug her elbow lightly into his ribs. "Cut it out."

"Hey, we gotta feed the rumor mill." He draped an arm around her shoulders and brushed a kiss across her temple. "If they're talking about us, they're giving somebody else a break, right?"

She shot him a disgruntled stare, but she didn't shrug his arm off or shy away from his touch.

Part of him hoped that by firmly entwining his name with Maya's in the public sphere, it would help cement their private bonds. She was still holding something back, something that might be important. She didn't trust him, either, but he took the long view more and more often. Someday, she might feel free to open up to him. He could wait, if that's what it took, though he hoped he wouldn't have to for much longer.

Work took a back seat to their time together. That bothered him less the more time he spent with her. He'd been in the middle of translating a frustratingly difficult passage before Amelia's visit. Maybe the break would give him a fresh perspective.

That night was his last night with Maya. Tomorrow morning, they'd leave her home and pick up the girls, and their idyll would come to an end. Even after Amelia went back to Connecticut the day after the Labor Day festivities, Dierdre would be there. With her around, there'd be no more hot kisses whenever the mood struck, no more long, intimate caresses, no more sex.

He was beginning to think he couldn't do without Maya's touch for long. At the rate they were going, he was pretty sure *long* was less than a day.

Maybe they could sneak off campus for nooners.

Naw. Nothing got by this crowd, and eventually it would get back to Dierdre. Much as he liked the teenager and wanted her to accept him, she had no business poking her nose into her mother's sex life. Dierdre being who she was, though, he was pretty sure she'd try. That was a line they'd have to draw. God willing, they'd have to draw it soon.

He and Maya went out for supper that night in Clayton, winding their way along the sidewalks through tourists up for the long weekend, enjoying the local bands playing on the square. Afterward, when they made it back to her home, he pulled her up the stairs, undressed her slowly, and made love to her to the rhythm of a thunderstorm breaking over the neighborhood. They fell asleep wrapped around each other with rain pinging against the tin roof overhead.

JAMES WOKE UP curled around Maya, his stomach to her back, an arm thrown across her waist. It was still dark outside, the sun not yet above the mountains. He snuggled closer to her, marveling over the perfect fit of her body against his.

He dozed, his mind drifting from Maya to the camping trip to the translations. A scene flashed before him in a dreamy sequence, of seven women, a grove of trees, a horse-like animal, the scene from the cylinder seal, one he'd never really understood. There wasn't enough context, and not nearly a large enough sample for a solid interpretation. He'd talked himself hoarse trying to convince Maya to open up and share what she knew, and her continual refusals were frustrating as hell. Whatever she hid from him could hold the answers they needed. Why didn't she see that?

He murmured and shifted, still half asleep. The scene blurred, shifting into an oasis he'd visited before Amelia's birth. The strong equatorial sun glimmered off the water trapped in a pond. Trees shaded the banks, offering respite from the heat to the sparse vegetation below. Travelers through that area visited the sanctuary often, refilling water bottles, sharing a light meal at the midpoint of their journey.

A section of the translation he was working on popped into his mind, rousing him from sleep. He tried to push it away. God, it was too early for that, way too early for work and sanctuaries and...

His eyes popped open and he sat straight up in bed, wide awake. Why hadn't he made the connection before? He scrambled out of bed, jostling Maya in the process.

She rolled over and peered blearily at him. "What are you doing at," she squinted at the clock and grimaced, "five forty-eight in the morning on our day off?"

"Gotta go." He yanked on clothes and stuffed his bare feet into running shoes. "Be back soon."

He kissed her soundly, ignoring her sleepy protest, and raced out of the bedroom. He'd found the key. Holy cow, he'd really done it. If he was right, and it felt so, so right, he'd just found a way to unlock the document he was working on, and maybe something that would help them understand the entire collection taken from the anomalous grave at Sandby borg.

FOURTEEN

When Maya woke again, James was still gone. She snuggled into his pillow, breathing in the clean, woodsy scent of his shampoo. Something tender shifted and slid through her, filling her with an aching need.

Her stomach clenched into a knot. She hadn't been able to tell him about the Daughters or herself, about the long, lonely years she'd waited to find someone, and now it might be too late. Her heart was on the precipice, ready to make the fall into love. Would he despise her when he found out the truth or would he forgive her for holding back so long?

No more fear.

She inhaled his scent one more time, making it part of herself, then got out of bed and readied for the long day ahead.

He came in an hour later while she was on the phone with Director Upton, several hours after he'd left their warm bed. His grin was triumphant and a tad smug. She eyed that grin as the director issued instructions. What had he been up to?

He wrapped his arms around her waist and drew her tightly against him, her back to his stomach. Her eyes widened and she clutched the phone to her ear.

Paper rattled on the other end of the line. "Will tomorrow morning be too soon?" Rebecca asked.

"Ah, mmm-hmm," Maya murmured.

James pushed aside her hair and scraped his teeth along the side of her neck, and she gasped.

"Maya," Rebecca said. "Are you still there?"

Maya cleared her throat. "Ah, yes, Director. Sorry. I'm a little...distracted."

James tugged her more firmly against him, rubbing his erection against her bottom through the thin layers of their clothing. "Hurry up," he whispered. "I need you."

"Tomorrow's fine, then," Rebecca said.

James yanked Maya's shirt up and cupped her stomach, skimming his fingers along her skin, teasing her with his light strokes. Her eyes slid shut. "Of course, Director. We'll be there."

109

"I'll see you then." Rebecca's voice took on a sly edge of humor. "Oh, and Maya? Tell James I said hello, would you?"

"I'll do that." Maya hung up the phone and clucked her tongue. "That was naughty."

His breath feathered over the side of her neck. "You liked it."

"Well, yes, but that's not the point."

He tugged her around and captured her mouth with his, and every coherent thought drained out of her head, everything but him. He seduced her slowly, pushing her a little higher with his mouth and his hands, and made love to her there in the kitchen, in the bright light shining through the windows into the heart of her home.

Later, after her breaths calmed and her heart found a sane rhythm, she said, "The director called."

They were still leaning against the wall, his body holding hers upright, his hands circling in lazy strokes along her sides. He buried his face in her throat and nipped at her pulse. "I gathered."

"She wants to see us tomorrow as soon as you get back from taking Amelia to the airport."

"Any idea why?"

"Something important came up and she wants to brief us on it. She didn't say what."

"Tomorrow's fine." He eased away and smoothed her hair back. "How much longer do we have?"

She glanced at her watch. "Maybe an hour. Why?"

"Shower," he said, and the low flame burning within her jumped and writhed and ached.

An little before lunch, they dressed and drove out to the trailhead. A few minutes after they arrived, the group straggled into the parking area, Dierdre and Amelia near the rear. The girls pushed their way through the crowd, Johnny Linton close on their heels, and stowed their gear in the trunk of James' car, chattering in excited bursts about the weekend's events.

Johnny kissed them both on the cheek before heading off, and James frowned. "That boy just kissed my daughter."

Maya pursed her lips, hiding a smile. "He's been known to do that."

"You don't say." James narrowed his gaze on the departing teenager. "I think it might be time for the *you're not old enough to have a boyfriend* talk."

Maya snorted. "Good luck with that."

"Hey, Amelia listens to me." The frown softened and a small smile tugged at his mouth. "Sometimes, when she wants something."

The four of them stopped by Maya's house so Dierdre and Amelia could clean up. After, they wandered through Tellowee, eating lunch at the café, walking the streets with the other residents, enjoying the mid-day parade. Johnny Linton tracked them down and draped a casual arm around Dierdre and Amelia's shoulders.

James stuffed his hands in his shorts and scowled. "Does he have to do that?"

Maya tucked her arm through his elbow. "Do you really want an answer or are you just grumping because your daughter has male friends?"

"He's not looking at her like he wants to be friends, exactly."

"Relax, James." Maya rested her head on his shoulder and skimmed her hand up and down his arm. "He won't do anything she doesn't want him to."

"That's what I'm afraid of," he muttered, and Maya laughed, tickled by the gruff honesty.

At suppertime, James cornered Johnny at the grill while Amelia and Dierdre helped Maya prepare side dishes. She listened with one ear while the girls gossiped and giggled. They'd become such fast friends and seemed so close, no doubt thanks to Dierdre's meddling. Maya couldn't complain. It had eased Amelia's path toward accepting her father's relationship with a woman other than the teen's mother, hadn't it? And maybe everything would work out there, if Maya could find the courage to tell him the truth about herself.

If he could accept that truth without coming to hate her for it.

They watched the annual Labor Day fireworks from Maya's backyard, Johnny sitting on a blanket between Dierdre and Amelia, Maya and James behind them in folding lawn chairs. She threaded her fingers through his, enjoying his warmth, giving him her own in return.

The fireworks ended in a dazzling display of light and sound. Johnny said his goodbyes and, much to James' disgust, kissed both of the girls goodbye before shaking James' hand and dropping a kiss to Maya's cheek.

"Affectionate booger, isn't he?" James asked.

"It's our way," Maya said gently.

Dierdre skidded to a stop in front of them, Amelia not far behind. "So, like, me and Meely had an idea."

Maya huffed out a laugh. "Oh, you did, did you?"

Amelia nodded, her gray-green eyes wide in her pretty face. "We don't have to leave until in the morning, you know?"

"I did know," Maya said, matching the teen's solemn tone. "And?"

"Well, see." Dierdre pursed her lips and rocked back on her heels. "We kinda wanted to stay together tonight."

James shook his head. "We really need to get back to the apartment so Amelia can pack and rest for the trip."

"Come on, Dad," Amelia said, her expression melting into a plea. "It'll be months before I can come back. I bet Maya will let us both stay the night. Please?"

"You can use the spare bedroom, James," Maya offered. "The girls can bunk together in Dierdre's room. There's plenty of room for both of you here."

Dierdre clasped her hands together under her chin, her expression a twin to Amelia's. "You wouldn't want to deprive your only daughter of friendship, would you, Dr. T.?"

He laughed. "All right, all right. I guess it won't hurt, as long as it's ok with Maya."

His gaze slid to hers, and the hot gleam burning there sparked an answering call within her. They wouldn't spend the night together, not with Dierdre and Amelia in the house, but there was nothing keeping him from sneaking into her bed after the girls were safely asleep, and back into his own after making love to her one last time.

And that's exactly what he did. As he moved over her, rocking them both into sweet oblivion, Maya clung to him, desire tangling with a bone deep fear that it would be the last time she'd ever hold him that way.

JAMES AND AMELIA left for the airport early the next morning, not long after the sun peeked over the hills.

Maya rose and showered, dressed in casual work clothes, then stripped and remade her bed. It would be a long, long time before he made an appearance there again, if ever, once he learned what she was. Better to make a clean break of it rather than wallowing in what might've been.

Dierdre loped downstairs just as Maya took her first sip of coffee. The teenager rubbed her flat stomach under the sweatshirt she'd pulled on over ragged shorts, stretching and yawning her way to the refrigerator. "Mornin', Mom."

"Morning, Squiggles. Did you and Amelia have fun last night?"

"Yeah. She's coming back for Thanksgiving. We're kinda making plans to hang out together then." Dierdre sat down at the kitchen table and bit into a strawberry, chewing it slowly. Her gaze dropped to the plate of fruit and cheese she'd scrounged. "Johnny's got a crush on her."

Maya set her mug on the table. "I thought he had a crush on you."

"He did, but that was ages ago. He wasn't for me 'cause, you know." Dierdre hunched her shoulders and her lips trembled once, then firmed. "I just knew."

Maya reached across the table and squeezed Dierdre's hand with her own, inwardly cursing the fate awaiting any immortal Daughter. To search forever hoping to find love, only for it to crumble under the weight of the passing years and the fickle nature of the human heart. "I'm sorry."

"No biggie. We were too young anyhow, but now that Amelia's gonna be coming down, it'd be cool if they hooked up."

"I wouldn't count on her coming down again, honey."

Dierdre glanced sharply up. "You didn't tell him."

Maya sighed and skimmed a finger around the top of her mug. "I couldn't, not yet. I just wanted some time with him as a normal couple before all that got in the way."

They sat in silence, Dierdre picking at the food on her plate, Maya running her fingers over the ceramic mug.

Dierdre screwed her face into a frown and pushed her plate away. "D'you think he's the one?"

"I don't know. He might be."

"You love him?"

Maya sipped her coffee, grimacing as the lukewarm liquid hit her tongue. "Yes, I think so."

"But you don't trust him."

"We've not been together very long, but maybe, in time."

"You didn't trust my Dad."

"Oh, honey."

A helpless fury rose in Maya. Dierdre's father had been so special, so warm and loving, and Maya had hoped he'd be the one. She'd clung to that hope for years, right up until a Marine chaplain had shown up on her doorstep the week before Dierdre's fourth birthday with the news that Eddie had been killed by friendly fire. He'd died a long time before Dierdre should've formed an attachment to him, but she'd always missed him, and it tore at Maya every single day.

"I loved your father very much, Squiggles, but he just wasn't the one. I'd change that if I could."

Dierdre nodded, her expression glum, so different from her normal demeanor. "Sometimes I hate being a Daughter."

"I know."

"It sucks having this stupid curse hanging over you." Dierdre's eyes filled with tears. She blinked up at the ceiling and swiped the cuff of her sweatshirt across her face. "I liked Johnny, too."

"Me, too. I'm sorry he's not the one."

"Yeah. But if I can't have him, I guess Amelia going out with him's the next best thing." Dierdre's eyes dropped, meeting Maya's, and her lips twitched. "That sounded horrible."

Maya bit her lip, trying to contain her humor. "Maybe just a little."

"No, a lot. I can't believe I said that."

Dierdre she snorted out a laugh. Maya's own laughter escaped, and they burst into giggles, laughing hard in the early morning sunlight, accompanied by the occasional car whizzing along the street outside.

Dierdre sighed out her last laugh and swiped her face again. "Sorry, Mom. I guess the whole thing bothered me more than I thought."

"It's ok, Squiggles. Love is hard no matter how old you are."

"Yeah, I guess. I'm glad Johnny's still my friend, though, and if he had to fall for another girl, at least Amelia's, you know, sweet and everything."

"That she is," Maya agreed, and she breathed a silent prayer to the Lady Ki, thanking Her for giving her daughter a resilient spirit.

AMELIA BUBBLED ENTHUSIASTICALLY about her time in Tellowee all the way from Maya's house to the airport, right up until she kissed James goodbye and boarded her plane. Any other time, he would've loved listening to her, but after two nights of little sleep and an early morning drive through rush hour traffic, his mind was muddled and his nerves were frayed.

The lack of sleep was his fault, and time well spent. Maybe there'd even be a repeat in the near future. Surely Dierdre had sleepovers.

Or did teenagers still do that?

Traffic was heavy on the drive back up. Was it ever not in the Atlanta area?

He tuned his radio to a local blues station and let his mind drift, to Amelia and her new-found friendship with Dierdre, to Maya and his deepening feelings (Did she feel the same?), to work and the translation he'd finished early the day before after an epiphany brought on by the intimate company of a good woman.

Hmm. Maybe he'd have to try that again the next time he was stuck. Him and Maya in bed for a weekend, skin on skin, breaths mingling, bodies joined so intimately, he couldn't tell where he ended and she began. He grinned and tapped his fingers against the steering wheel in time to Steve Ray Vaughn. Well, it was worth a try, anyway.

When he was ten minutes out, he called Maya with a heads up on his arrival time. Not long after, he eased into his parking spot outside his apartment, then ambled to her office, whistling tunelessly. Her door was open, so he went in, closing it softly behind himself.

She was seated at her desk, seemingly immersed in a report. Her hair was twisted into some sort of knot at her nape. Stray curls had escaped, framing her face, softening the strong lines of her cheekbones. She hardly ever wore make-up, not that he cared. With or without it, she was one of the most beautiful women he'd ever met.

Maybe that didn't have anything to do with make-up or clothing or the radiant glow of good health she exuded, but with the woman he'd come to know over the past few months. Under her reserve, he'd discovered a warm, wickedly humorous woman with a deep love of family. Her work wasn't just a job. It really mattered to her, and he admired that about her. No, he admired all of her, every single aspect, the lover he'd come to know, her steady relationship with her daughter, the woman who'd brought down a skilled fighter calmly and with a deliberation few could match. If he wasn't careful, that admiration would morph into something deeper, something stronger, maybe something lasting and true.

He stepped around her desk and kissed her cheek. "Hey, gorgeous."

She put the report down, stood, and edged away from him.

He closed the distance between them, slid his hands around her waist. "What's wrong? Morning after jitters?"

"Hardly." She placed a chaste kiss on his cheek. "How was the trip?"

"Driving through Atlanta is like racing the Indy 500 on a bicycle with flat tires."

She smiled, relaxed, fiddled with his collar. "It's not that bad."

"Mm-hmm. Keep telling yourself that."

He bent to kiss her, and she turned her head slightly away. A shaft of worry speared into him. "Are you sure everything's ok? No second thoughts?"

"Everything's fine." Her gaze drifted over his left shoulder and pinned itself there. "Really."

He eased back and studied her. This didn't feel right, but other than pushing her, and he was pretty sure that would piss her off, what could he do? "Ready to meet the director?"

"Sure."

They walked together to Director Upton's office, a foot of space between them. Over the weekend, they'd gone hand in hand everywhere. Now, she seemed reluctant to touch him.

He shoved his free hand into the pocket of his slacks, tightened his grip on his briefcase, and forced himself to follow her lead. Maybe if she weren't so cold, the distance wouldn't bother him. They were at work, and if there was any place for circumspection, it was there, but this... This wasn't like Maya at all, and hadn't been the entire time he'd known her. Even that first day, she'd been warm, open, receptive. The woman beside him had hardened herself, shutting him out as surely as if she'd shut a door in his face. What was going on?

He opened the door for her and followed her through. After the meeting, he'd get to the bottom of her sudden about-face. He had other things he wanted to talk over with her, but they'd start with the distance she'd deliberately put between them.

Director Upton was ready to see them when they arrived. She met them at the door to her office and directed them to the sitting area on one side, waving them onto the settee. "I have good news. Dani called. She's located all of the missing artifacts and is putting together teams to retrieve them."

"Er," James interrupted. "By retrieve you mean...?"

Rebecca's gaze remained steady. "Some things you may not wish to know, Dr. Terhune."

"Ah. The police won't be involved?"

Maya crossed her legs and folded her hands together in her lap. "Law enforcement agencies tend to be inefficient when dealing with stolen artifacts."

He'd had first-hand experience with that, but shouldn't they at least be consulted?

"In this case, there's a real danger that the artifacts might be sold or removed to a place where we can't track them," Rebecca added. "Specifically, they may have fallen into the hands of our, ah, rival."

James' eyebrows shot up. "The IECS has a rival?"

Maya's lovely mouth turned down at one corner. "So to speak. This rival hasn't been active in a while. Has something changed?"

Rebecca hesitated. She and Maya shared a look James couldn't interpret, but worry grew in the pit of his stomach. He'd only known Maya a short time, true, but he'd never known her to show fear, not until that moment. If anybody had asked, he'd've said she wasn't capable of fear.

A cold chill shivered down his spine. What kind of rival generated fear in the fearless?

"Possibly," Rebecca hedged. "That's not something we need to worry about for the moment. Right now, we should all concentrate on translating and interpreting as many of the artifacts from the Daughter's grave as we can, and quickly. If you need my help or the help of anyone else, please use it. These artifacts are our top priority."

James stared at her. "Er, Daughter?"

Maya ignored him. "Of course, Director."

"I'll let you know when Dani has retrieved the artifacts."

Not if, but when. Wasn't the director placing too much confidence in the effervescent Dani? She seemed capable, but she was young, maybe too young for the job she'd been given.

Which he wasn't going to think about. The whole thing was illegal from start to finish. He didn't have a problem with that. The artifacts had been stolen and should be returned, but was it really necessary to steal them back?

Rebecca's reclined in her chair. "Oh, and Maya? Please bring James up to date, today if possible."

It wasn't a request. He glanced between the two women, noting the cool command of one and the weary resignation of the other. What the hell was going on?

Maya nodded. "That was the next item on our agenda, Director."

"Good. Please keep me updated on your progress."

They chatted for a few minutes more, then left. James pulled Maya aside in the hallway as soon as they were out of earshot. "What was that about?"

"I have a few things to show you. It won't take long."

She led him to the IECS museum, housed in the same building as his office. He'd only visited it once, and that briefly. Between the translations, his burgeoning relationship with Maya, and his personal project, his time for explorations of the campus at large had been limited. Now, he admired the displays of ancient amphorae, weapons, armor, and ephemera, including some documents carefully enclosed in hermetically sealed cases.

Maya jerked her chin toward the back. "This way."

They threaded through a maze of artifacts, some dating back millennia according to the description plates James studied as they went past. She stopped in front of a door with biometric security and pressed her thumb to the pad, then entered a code, waiting for the lock to click before entering.

A small room spread out before them, maybe ten feet long on each side. In the middle stood a glass case containing several fragments of ancient documents in a variety of media, much like the collection they'd found in the Sandby borg grave. A plaque was mounted to a stand next to the case.

Maya lifted a hand toward the case and plaque. "Go ahead."

James placed himself squarely between the two objects and bent down, peering intently at the fragments through the protective glass. "What are these?"

"Pieces of an origin myth. We call it the Legend of Beginnings. It describes seven sisters who were cursed with immortality for slaying the men of their tribe."

"Fascinating." He shifted his stance and skimmed over the plaque's text. "Who were the sisters?"

"You'd know them as forerunners of the Amazons."

"No kidding." He straightened abruptly. "Wait. Why have I never heard this before?"

Maya gazed steadily at him, her face a stony mask. "Because we've done everything we could to erase it from history."

James gaped at her. "Why? If you have proof the Amazons were real, it would turn history on its collective ear."

"Yes, it could, but it would also open the path to knowledge, a knowledge of the Daughters who sprang from the Sisters, who shared the curse of the Sisters, and who live today with that curse."

"What are you saying?"

"The Seven Sisters were real, James, and so is the curse."

James ran a hand over his hair, ruffling it. "So the Sisters, what? Became immortal and had children who were immortal, too, and these people survived to modern times?"

"Not the Sisters, no. They all died millennia ago, but yes, their children still live and many of them are immortal."

The blood drained from his head and he swayed. Either Maya was crazy or she was...crazy. What other explanation could there be?

He'd been sleeping with a crazy woman who believed immortal Amazons roamed the streets of America. A short, harsh laugh burst from him. Jesus. "Come on, Maya. You don't expect me to believe that."

Her shoulders tensed, hunching slightly. "Believe what you want, but it's true."

"What proof do you have?"

"Do you need proof?"

"Yeah, maybe I do."

"The proof is here. It's been here all along. Haven't you noticed the unusual number of young, athletic women at the IECS?"

Yeah, he had. Tom had brought up that very thing the first night they'd met. His heart dropped like a stone in his chest. Then the exhibition, the gymnastics, the graduated displays of combat. The unusually focused nature of the students, their physical discipline, and, sweet God above, survival and weapons training.

And the weapons in Director Upton's office. Rebecca the Blade, her husband had called her.

Was it true? Were these women really immortal descendants of the Amazons?

He paced away and back again, facing Maya and the improbable tale she'd spun head on. "Are you one, an immortal?"

"I am."

"And Dierdre?"

"The sins of the mother, James," she said softly, and the sadness in her voice echoed through the room and straight into his heart.

"Dani and Indigo and..."

"All of them, yes, though a handful of the Daughters you've met are mortal."

"My God."

"No, James. It is to a goddess that we owe our salvation. For every curse, there is a path to redemption. The Lady Goddess offered the Sisters such a path and their descendants have the same choice."

He waited, his muscles tense, hoping she'd tell him, and praying equally hard that she wouldn't.

"All we have to do is trust a man, submit our will to him." She laughed, the short sound bitter and entirely humorless. "Sounds easy, doesn't it?"

Not so much. Their time together was beginning to make an awful lot of sense to him, and not just the lack of trust. "You've never trusted me."

"I've never trusted any man, James," she said, her voice barely louder than a whisper. "But I've come the closest with you."

"And if you did trust me? What then?"

"I'd become mortal and live my life as a normal human."

"What about Dierdre?"

"Each individual must break her own curse."

"So you used me to try to break the curse."

Her face paled beneath its natural brown. "It wasn't like that."

He barked out a laugh. "Right."

"I swear, James, it was never like that. I knew there was a chance, but I also wanted to get to know you, just because," she shrugged and glanced away. "I was attracted to you from the start."

"And you enticed me here to, what? Test my mettle? See if I measured up?"

"You were invited here solely to work on the artifacts and assist with translations of other collections. The attraction between us was an unexpected bonus, for my part, anyway, but it played no role in your being here."

He shook his head and rubbed the nape of his neck. How could he ever believe that after she'd hidden so much from him?

"If you believe I'm immortal, that the Sisters existed and their Daughters still live, why is it so hard to believe I wasn't using you?"

"I'm not so sure I believe any of this." Everything she'd told him, everything that had ever happened between them, spun around and around in his head, and it was just too much. He needed to be alone, needed to be away from her and the secrets she'd kept. "I need to think."

"James, please."

She reached toward him, and he drew back, stepping out of her reach, her flinch no more than a tickle along his numb heart. One touch and he might just say to hell with it, to hell with everything, and fall back into bed with her. That wouldn't solve anything. She'd still cling to her tale, and he'd still have to deal with it.

She threaded her fingers together in front of her. "You'll have the time you need, but please don't take too long."

"Sure," he agreed, though how could he possibly know how long it would take to deal with the load she'd just slung at him? Hell, he didn't even know if half of what she'd said was true, and he hadn't even begun to sort out his feelings for her. A sharp pain set up residence in his left temple. Any way he went, he was sc-sc-screwed.

Maya's grip tightened and the skin over her knuckles whitened. "Until you've come to terms with this, please don't leave the campus."

He opened his mouth, closed it again. Where would he go? Who would he tell? He finally croaked out a shaky, "Why?"

"You're a security risk. We can't have you wandering around unaccompanied until we know you can be trusted."

"Jesus, Maya. Isn't that taking the trust issue a little far?"

"Unfortunately, we've learned this the hard way."

"And if I can't be trusted?"

"That's not a situation you need to worry about."

"Yeah, I think it is, since it concerns me," he shot back. "What would you do?"

She hesitated, then admitted, "You'd be taken care of."

"Taken care of. As in eliminated? Killed? Wiped from the face of the planet?"

"Don't be melodramatic," she said, her voice sharp and impatient.

"Then don't jerk me around."

She gazed at him for long moments. "I care about you, James."

He searched her face, looking for signs of duplicity, and saw only sincerity in the tense paleness of her skin, in the worry clouding her warm, golden-brown eyes. It was hard to believe this woman, sweet Maya with her gentle laughter and beautiful touch, could be a cold, deadly killer. On the other hand, he'd witnessed her fight with India. Maya had controlled the outcome, a sign of her skill and resolve, and a warning to anybody foolish enough to cross her.

"That wouldn't stop you from *taking care* of me, would it," he said slowly.

"Please don't put me in that position."

"Ok." He inhaled deeply, exhaled on a huff. God, he needed to think, needed some space, needed time to sort through everything. "I'm going now."

"Take care of yourself, James," she said softly.

118

"Yeah, sure."

He stumbled to the room's entrance, too overwhelmed to care how he must appear to her. What did it matter? She was old, immortal, implacable, and he was just a man. He opened the door, slipped through it, and glanced back. Maya skimmed her fingers along the edge of the glass case. A lone tear streaked down her face and her lips trembled, and God help him, he wanted to go back in there, pull her into his arms, and tell her everything was going to be ok. He closed the door and walked away, leaving her to her secrets and him to the task of mending the dent she'd made in his heart.

FIFTEEN

A BLESSED NUMBNESS settled over James during the walk to his apartment. He slipped inside, grabbed a beer out of the fridge, and slumped into the sofa, one hand on his stomach, the other holding the beer.

The sun dropped behind the hills and the security lights came on. The beer grew warm in his hand. Moisture leaked down the sides, pooling unnoticed on his skin. His conversation with Maya played over and over again in his head, a never-ending loop of revelation and disbelief.

Questions battered him into exhaustion, about Maya's veracity, her sanity, the implications of a millennia-old culture existing in modern times, virtually hidden from the rest of the world, and about the implications to himself and Amelia, to his personal work, and to the work he was doing for the IECS.

Which had probably been founded as a shelter for these women, a sort of sanctuary, not unlike the one he'd found referenced in the Sandby borg artifacts. He scowled at the darkened TV across the coffee table. He'd forgotten to tell Maya about it. He'd forgotten to tell her a lot of things.

He lifted the beer to his mouth and sipped, then grimaced. Damn it. It was too warm to drink. He peeked at his watch and sighed. It was after midnight by a long shot and he still hadn't sorted out all the questions rattling around in his head. He needed to get it out, maybe talk to somebody else, but who?

Phil and George were out of the question. They were just too young and they probably had no clue they were living among immortal Amazon-type women. Phil would probably love that. He loved being at the center of the local singles scene, and that scene suddenly made an awful sort of sense. The guys had been right. It was kind of like a meat market.

Tom might be a good sounding board, but he probably didn't know about the Daughters, either, and without him, James was stuck with too many questions and no way to resolve them.

A light bulb went off in his brain. Robert Upton. Of course. James glanced at his watch again and cursed under his breath. Still a long way 'til a decent hour. First thing after the workday started, he'd go to Dr. Upton's office and quiz the older man. Maybe *he* had the answers James needed.

He spent a restless night staring at the ceiling in his bedroom, out the window, at the closet door, and finally fell asleep in the predawn hours of morning. He awoke groggy and irritable, shivered through a quick, cold shower, and dressed, then set out in search of Dr. Upton.

The campus came to life as he walked along the paths winding between the buildings. Dew clung to the grass, carrying the chill of late summer. Fall would be there soon. He could already smell it in the air, a comforting scent that triggered a wave of nostalgia for his own days as a student.

Dr. Upton's office was located in the same building as his. James had discovered that not long after Maya's fight with India when he'd consulted with Dr. Upton on some hard to read documents. He hadn't been back since, but the building was well laid out, not that large in the scheme of things, and virtually impossible to get lost in.

He jogged the last few feet to Dr. Upton's office and groaned. The other man's office hours didn't start until later that morning. He leaned against the wall and scrambled for a way to fill his time, anything to keep his mind busy while he waited.

The museum. Right. He could go there and do what he should've insisted on doing the day before, attempt to authenticate the fragments of the origin myth.

The museum was open, the air hushed, as if no one were in. He wandered through the exhibits, rereading the posted descriptions. Several of the artifacts were ancient, others equally as rare, and still others were displayed for no apparent reason. There was no overt theme to the items on display. Maybe they'd all been owned by Daughters or pertained to them in some way, or maybe some of them even dated back to the time of the Seven Sisters Maya had told him about.

He found the door to the room housing the origin myth, scowled at the security system, and backtracked to the museum's entrance.

A guard was strolling through the first row of exhibits, her sable hair coiled into a bun at the nape of her neck, her all black uniform sharply pressed. She smiled. "Dr. T, hello. Maetyrm Maya said you might stop by."

He shuffled to a halt. One of these days, maybe he'd get used to everybody in Tellowee knowing who he was, even when he hadn't met them. "Er, she did?"

"Of course. Director Upton, too. They said you might want to study the Legend of Beginnings up close." The guard swept her hand toward the back. "If you'll come with me, I'll show you how to access it and key in a password for you."

"Ah, thank you," he said, and followed her toward the rear of the museum, listening attentively as she walked him through the procedures for entering the room. She opened the door for him, nodded once, then closed it, leaving him alone.

He inhaled slowly and moved to the display case. The plaque he'd paid scarce attention to the day before contained a summary of the myth. Seven Sisters lived with their parents in peaceful coexistence with the People, a band of Neolithic, nomadic hunter-gatherers that included the sisters and their parents. The men of the People murdered the girls' parents and enslaved the women of the People. The sisters fled and wandered the land for many days, finally coming to rest in an oasis known as Sanctuary where they lived and trained for seven years.

The eldest daughter, Kiya, dreamed of a way to free the women of the People. The sisters set out, hoping to right the wrongs done by their fellow tribesmen. They located their former tribesmen and slaughtered the men, then freed the women and children. Upon seeing the blood of the men, the god An cursed the sisters to immortality, never to bear sons, never to know peace. The goddess Ki saw that An had been unjust and used all of her strength and power to modify the curse, giving the sisters a way out.

Redemption, Maya had said.

The myth ended with a warning to remember the past. A small offset section contained a note about rumors of a lost prophecy detailing how the curse might be broken for good.

James rubbed his eyes wearily. If Maya had shown him this from the start, it would've helped him tremendously. He'd suspected as much, but now with the proof laid in front of him, a slow burn roiled in his stomach. By holding this information back, she'd deliberately jeopardized their work. His gaze fell on one of the smaller fragments, on the symbol it had taken him so long to understand, vivid proof of the harm she'd inflicted on their work. *Sanctuary.* Now he knew exactly what kind of sanctuary the translation referred to.

But why? This work was vitally important to her, so why not tell him from the start?

James thanked the guard and left the museum, trudging toward Dr. Upton's office, his mood no better than it had been before he'd studied the legend. He knocked on the door, tried the doorknob, and stuck his head inside.

Robert took one look at James and sighed. "So, now you know, do you?"

James dropped into one of the chairs in front of Dr. Upton's desk. "Oh, yeah."

"You're wondering if it's all true or if there are a bunch of crazy women running around pretending to be Amazons."

James stared, then scrubbed his hands across his face. Right. The other man had probably had a very similar reaction to his own. He'd forgotten for a minute who Robert was married to. "Is it true?"

"Oh, yes. Took me a while to get my mind around it, too, but eventually I realized that Rebecca is one of the sanest, most stable women I've ever met. And then, of course, there's the fact that I've known her immortal daughters for decades, and they've never aged a single day in all that time."

"Jesus," James breathed. "Really?"

"I wouldn't lie." Robert threaded his fingers together over his chest and leaned back in his chair. "Look, I know you have questions, but the best place for you to find those is with Maya. It'll be better coming from her because she's lived it. I just married into it."

"No, I mean, yes." James slouched in his chair, regarding the older man carefully. The questions humming through his mind were coalescing into a simple handful, and with that narrowing came an uneasy acceptance. Maybe Maya was telling the truth after all. Maybe she wasn't as crazy as he'd thought she was, and maybe he'd been wrong to jump on her the way he had. "I guess I just needed to hear somebody else say it."

"That helps," Robert said, grinning. "It also helps to get drunk. Nothing like seeing the bottom of a cup to help a man make sense of things."

James scowled. He'd tried drinking and ended up pouring it down the sink. "Couldn't go off campus last night."

"Maya put you on lockdown, did she? Well, you should've called me. I'd've taken you out myself and we could've gotten drunk with style."

James hunched his shoulders. "I didn't think of you until the middle of the night."

Robert's chuckle boomed through the small office. "Better late than never."

James attempted a smile. His mouth made it halfway, wobbled, and collapsed into a frown. "Did Director Upton threaten to kill you when she first told you?"

Robert's bushy eyebrows shot toward his thinning hairline. "What? Surely Maya didn't say that. That's not how the Daughters deal with men, I assure you."

"Er, actually, she said she'd have me *taken care of.*"

Robert's expression cleared and he threw back his head, laughing in earnest. "She's really got you by the short hairs, doesn't she? Normally, if a man doesn't fall in line, the Daughters simply remind him of the consequences. A good thrashing usually does the trick. Humiliating, yes. Life threatening, no. It's been centuries since they've actually killed a man for not falling in love with them."

Heat spread up James' cheeks and his shoulders hitched an inch higher. How was he supposed to know that? "So, she won't actually kill me, then."

"Son, if you're stupid enough to let a woman like Maya Bellegarde slip through your fingers, dying is the least of your problems."

They chatted for a few minutes more before James left. Dr. Upton had set James' mind at ease in a way only a man could. Ok, so it had been embarrassing, but he was a little more grounded now. His mind was settling, and he was beginning to believe that Maya had told him the truth, about the Seven Sisters, about herself.

The question that stuck out to him the most, the one that really worried him now that he'd stepped onto the long road to belief, was what this meant to him and Maya. How could he continue a relationship with her, knowing that at least part of her was in it for some sort of mystical cure? Or had she been truthful when she'd insisted she was with him out of an honest attraction? Could he ever be sure? Did certainty really matter?

He stuffed his hands in his pockets and shambled along the path outside his office building, head down, feet aimless. He'd done most of the pursuing. She'd been the reluctant one and had only warmed up to the idea of being with him after spending a lot of time around him. Maybe she really had been telling the truth, about that part anyway.

All of that aside, he wasn't ready to forgive her and he couldn't quite face her yet. His stomach rumbled, reminding him of the time, and James veered off toward the cafeteria. Food first, then translations, then lots and lots of sleep. Tomorrow was soon enough to deal with Maya.

THE HOURS TICKED BY. Maya took her work home to avoid even a sight of James and vowed not to cry. It was her own fault for not telling him sooner, before they'd started dating. At the very least, she should've told him before they'd made love the first time.

Dierdre had the week off from school, so they had movie night, Dierdre's choice. Naturally, she picked the sappiest love story in their DVD collection. Maya's vow not to cry lasted right up until the part where it looked like the leading couple would never get together. Tears trickled down her cheeks and she sniffed, trying to hold them back. Dierdre laid her head on Maya's shoulder, and they finished watching the movie together, each silently considering a bleak, loveless future.

Sleep eluded Maya. She rested in bed, her eyes following the light the moon cast into her room as it moved through the shadows. James had every right to be angry and no reason to believe her. She'd left instructions for him to have access to the Legend and to any documents in the Archives he needed. He was a man of science and he'd want something other than her word as proof. It shouldn't bother her, but it did. All his talk of her trusting him, and then he scoffed when she finally told him the truth. Trust was a two-way street. Why couldn't he see that?

She avoided dwelling on their relationship as much as possible and threw herself into work and training, driving herself to physical exhaustion. Still, the hours bled slowly by, sleep eluded her, and the dull ache in her heart refused to soften.

Two days after Maya showed James the Legend of Beginnings, Director Upton called. Her voice was terse and to the point. "We have a serious problem, Maya. Do you know where Dr. Terhune is?"

"He should be on the compound. Why?"

"We can't find him. The guards don't remember him leaving, and he's not in his office, his lab, or his apartment."

Uneasiness pinched at Maya. Surely James wouldn't have left the IECS, not after her warning. "Have you tried the gym? Or maybe the running paths. He likes to run."

"I'll send someone out to check. It's of vital importance that I speak with him as soon as possible."

Dread joined the uneasiness, mixing queasily in Maya's stomach. She placed a hand there and inhaled a shaky breath. "What's wrong?"

"It's Dr. Terhune's daughter. She's been kidnapped."

"Blessed Ki," Maya breathed. "I'll be right there."

She hung up and yelled for Dierdre, racing through the house searching for her daughter.

Dierdre poked her head over the rail at the top of the stairs. "What's wrong, Mom?"

Maya took the stairs two at a time and bustled her daughter into her bedroom. "Amelia's been kidnapped."

"Oh, no." The color leached from Dierdre's face. She staggered to her bed and dropped onto its edge. "When? Who? *Why?*"

"I don't know, Squiggles. I don't know anything yet." Maya brushed her hair back, tugging on the strands. "I want you to pack, enough for a week at least. I may have to leave and I want you safe while I'm gone."

"Ok. I..." Dierdre's expression crumpled. "You'll get her back, won't you? I mean, she's just a mortal and she's a girly girl and she doesn't know how to protect herself."

Maya sat down beside Dierdre and draped an arm around the teen's shoulders. "Don't worry. We'll get her back."

And Maya would, no matter what it took.

She helped Dierdre pack and half an hour later, dropped her daughter off at her dorm. As soon as her daughter disappeared up the stairwell to her room, she jogged to

Director Upton's office. The director's receptionist waved her through. Maya shoved open the door and came to a full stop. Rebecca was alone in her office.

Maya shut the door and strode to the director's desk. "Have you found James?"

"He's being brought up now."

The door opened and James was pushed inside, an irritated scowl fixed on his face. He wore running shorts and a ragged t-shirt with the arms and neck cut out, both soaked with sweat. His gaze zeroed in on Maya. "What the hell? Can't a man enjoy a damn run without being man-handled? I was still on campus."

"That was my doing, Dr. Terhune," Rebecca said, "and I apologize for the rough treatment. A matter of some urgency requires your presence, and I'm afraid security got a little carried away bringing you here."

"Next time, just ask," he grouched.

"Of course. Would you like to sit?"

"I'd rather get back to running, if you don't mind. It helps me think, and suddenly, I find myself with a lot on my mind."

Maya glanced away and crossed her arms over the ding in her heart.

Rebecca sighed and sank gracefully into the chair behind her desk. "All right, then, to the point. Dani called in a couple of hours ago. Your ex-wife was found dead in her home. I'm sorry to have to break the news to you like this. "

"Oh, my God. What happened?"

"The police are still investigating, but she may have been murdered."

James' skin paled. "Where's Amelia? She wasn't home, was she? Is she all right?"

"We don't know exactly where she is, but we're certain she's alive. We've received a ransom demand."

"A ransom..." He staggered to a chair and sank down, his elbows on his knees, his head hanging. "For what? I don't have the kind of money a kidnapper would demand."

"Not money," Maya said. "Artifacts. Specifically, the artifacts from the Sandby borg grave."

"You're kidding."

"We believe the person behind this is the same one who had the other artifacts stolen in the first place," Rebecca said. "It seems he'd like the complete set."

James swiped a hand through his hair and sat back in the chair. "Why Amelia? I have no authority over the artifacts."

"She was vulnerable," Maya said flatly. "That's why we have this compound, James, because we're hunted. It helps us protect ourselves and our families."

James turned furious eyes on her. "You let her leave knowing she might be in danger."

Maya returned his glare. "If I thought she was in danger, I would never have allowed her to leave. How can you think otherwise?"

Rebecca raised her hands. "Getting angry won't help."

Maya sucked in a breath, forcing her frustration aside. "Sorry, Director."

"Our enemy has been silent for decades, James," Rebecca said. "We had no reason to believe Amelia was in any danger. This is simply not something we could've predicted."

He cleared his throat and fixed his gaze on his knees. "What can we do to get her back?"

"We're going to hand over the artifacts. More specifically, you and Maya will hand them over." Rebecca placed her hands flat on her desk, her expression as calm and even as her voice. "Once you have Amelia and return to the IECS, you may continue working on the translations using the images we've made, just until we can get the artifacts back. In the meantime, you and your daughter will be protected. On this, you have my word."

James ran a hand over the wet strands of his hair, ruffling them into a tangle of dark spikes. "Fine."

Maya breathed a small sigh of relief. Having his cooperation would smooth their way considerably, though it wasn't as necessary as he probably believed. "When do we leave?"

"As soon as you can pack. Dani is trying to track Amelia's location as we speak. We've been given a time and place to meet, but it would be nice to have another option."

"I'll call the airfield and have the plane fueled."

"No need. I did that as soon as I tracked the two of you down. I also took the liberty of having the artifacts in our possession packed for transport. You'll be escorted to the airfield. We're putting security on alert here and sending word out to as many of the People as we can reach. The Shadow Enemy is back. Best be wary."

Maya bowed. "Of course, Director."

She grasped James elbow, tugging gently, and he stood, following her without question. Outside, his steps gradually slowed, then stopped. "Does anything good ever come from meeting with her?"

"Sometimes."

"Hunh." He ran a hand over his hair, shaking some of the moisture out of it. "What time do you want to leave?"

"Will forty-five minutes give you enough time?"

"Yeah, sure."

He stood there, staring out into space, his shoulders slumped, dark circles marring the skin under his eyes. "Will you get her back?"

Maya curled her fingers into fists. She wanted to touch him, to hold him, to comfort him in any way she could. He wasn't ready for that. Maybe he'd never want that from her again. "I will."

"Ok." His gaze met hers, and the desperate fear burning out of his gray eyes tore at her. "Is Dierdre safe?"

"She's on campus now and won't leave until we return with Amelia."

"That's good, then."

He made no move to leave. As gently as she could, she said, "We need to go soon."

"Yeah. Sorry."

"I'll meet you at your apartment."

"Sure."

Still, it took a moment for him to leave. Maya watched him long enough to make sure he was headed toward his apartment, then jogged to Dierdre's dorm and outlined the plan to her daughter.

Dierdre's eyes were red and puffy. She wrapped herself in Maya's embrace and cried into her mother's throat. "You have to get her back, Mom. You just have to."

Maya smoothed Dierdre's hair back and rocked her gently. "We will, Squiggles. I promise."

She stayed as long as she dared, then said her goodbyes, promising to call with news as often as she could. On her way out, she tracked down the dorm mother and filled her in. Dierdre would need people around her, friends and people who cared about her, and until Maya returned, that would have to do.

She ran back to her house, redressed in comfortable travel clothes, and grabbed her bug-out bags, one holding enough clothing and toiletries for three days, the other containing a small weapons cache. After a call to check on the plane's status, Maya locked her home tight and strode back onto campus, determination marking every stride she took.

JAMES STEPPED INTO HIS APARTMENT. The door snicked shut behind him, jerking him out of the daze he'd slid into. Too much had happened over the past week, too many shocks, too many surprises. He stood there a minute, sorting through everything, and settled on the one thing he could do something about. He had to save his daughter, and then, somehow, he had to find a way to tell her about Linda.

Dear God. How on earth could he possibly tell Amelia her mother had died, that the woman who'd given birth to her, sheltered her, loved her in her own absent-minded, full-hearted way, would no longer be a part of her life?

He flinched away from it. Maybe by the time they'd found Amelia, he'd have the words she'd need from him, and if not, at least she'd know she still had him.

He stripped and stepped into the shower, allowing the water to wash everything away. Amelia kidnapped, forcibly taken for a purpose beyond his control or doing, her mother dead, him embroiled in a generations-old struggle between immortal Amazons and a deadly enemy. He shuddered and stepped out, dried off quickly, and threw on the first set of clothes his hands fell on.

He dragged out his suitcase and randomly tossed items inside. Clothes, toiletries, the book on his nightstand. A knock at the front door interrupted him. He hustled through the apartment and jerked it open. Dierdre stood on the other side, her tear-stained face pale. James opened his arms and she stepped into them, clinging to him.

"Shh, now," he murmured. "We'll get her back."

"I know, Dr. T." Dierdre sniffled into his chest. "Mom's the best at this kind of thing. You'll see."

James wasn't so sure. Maya was all he had, though, so he'd just have to trust her, wouldn't he? "Come on back. We can talk while I finish packing."

Dierdre followed him to the bedroom, took one look at his suitcase, and managed a shaky laugh. "Good thing I'm here, Dr. T. You'll never survive New York like that."

She repacked his suitcase, taking out the shorts he'd thrown in, pretty much all he'd packed, and adding in sturdy jeans, t-shirts, and a couple of sweatshirts. "Ok, undies and toiletries now. You're gonna need more than toothpaste and a razor, Dr.

T."

James huffed out a laugh. "Bossy."

"Somebody's gotta keep you in line." She waited while he gathered toiletries and stuffed them into his suitcase, then closed and zipped it. "I heard Mom told you about the People."

"Yeah?"

She shrugged. "We don't keep many secrets."

"Right. Well, that was a pretty damn big secret."

"You don't understand, Dr. T." The skin around her eyes tightened and her mouth pursed, and she looked so much like Maya, James' heart thumped hard against his sternum. "It's our way of life, our *whole* way of life. That's what's on the line every time an outsider learns about the People. They got Amelia and she's just a mortal, not even blood kin. All they're doing is holding her for ransom. What do you think they'd do to us?"

Clearly something bad, judging by the tone of her voice. He apparently had a lot of history to learn and no time to absorb it all.

"They took Mom once, when she was little." Her voice dropped to a harsh whisper and her hands curled into fists against her thighs. "The Shadow Enemy killed her parents while she watched. If the servants hadn't helped her escape, Mom would've died, too. We're blood enemies, Dr. T., and they won't stop until we're all dead, all of us."

The blood drained out of his face. "Jesus."

Dierdre's hand wrapped around his forearm. Her fingers dug into his skin, bruising him, and her hard eyes searched his face. "You have to protect her, Dr. T. My Mom. You have to bring her *and* Amelia back. Promise me."

He pulled Dierdre into a hug, rocking her in a futile stab at comforting her. If Maya was in a danger so great she couldn't protect herself, what could he possibly do to keep the promise Dierdre wanted him to make? He couldn't fight or wield a staff or shoot a gun, thanks to his parents' pacifist objections and his own complacency. By God, if he made it out of this situation in one piece, he was going to learn how to protect himself and Amelia and the two Daughters he had somehow grown to love. Never again would he be in this situation, no matter what he had to do, even if it killed him in the doing.

SIXTEEN

Dani fit binoculars to her eyes and studied the scene below. After tracking down the artifacts, with a lot of help from her favorite undercover Feebi, she'd assembled teams to retrieve them, then been foiled when Dr. Terhune's daughter was kidnapped and a ransom demand issued. Amelia had been brought here, to a warehouse not far from the docks. It was too much to hope that the missing artifacts had been moved here as well, but a girl could wish, couldn't she?

Once she'd checked in, Dani had been given strict instructions to *observe only* while Maya and James made their way north to the Big Apple. The same teams that had been intended for artifact retrieval would now be used to provide backup for Maya.

It was a shame, too. Kicking butt and taking names was a lot more fun than waiting in the wings surveilling.

Of course, if things turned bad here, she'd go in, orders be damned. A kid had been taken and was being held by some very bad people. No way would Dani leave her in there alone, not for long.

A footfall scuffed on the roof behind her. Dani glanced over her shoulder. Two men were behind her, one lanky and lean, the other a couple of inches taller than her and stocky, hired thugs from Dave's crew. The Blessed Mother knew she'd observed them often enough. They ambled slowly toward her, spreading out in a futile attempt to flank her, and satisfaction burst through her. Wasn't it just her luck that they were spoiling for a fight, just when she felt like fighting?

She stood and bestowed her best come-hither smile on them. "Howdy, boys. What brings two nice men like you to a dump like this?"

They glanced at one another. Lanky's eyebrows shot toward his crew cut.

Stocky shrugged. "Boss said not to pay no mind to the broad's yapping."

Dave, that rat bastard.

"Hey," Dani snapped. "The only yapping anybody's doing is on your end, you lily-livered, speckle-sided son of a goat farmer."

Stocky grinned and waggled his fingers at her. "Put your money where your mouth is, sweetheart."

Dani grinned back. Fight it was.

Lanky leapt toward her, arms open. She slapped her palms over his ears, and down he went, screaming. She nudged him with one booted foot, satisfied he'd be down for a while. Nobody ever saw that one coming.

Stocky grabbed her from behind, locking his arms around her chest, pinning her arms in place. Dani admired the firm steel of his arms and the flat, muscled planes of his chest (A girl had to take her pleasure where she found it, didn't she?), then threw her head back sharply into his face. He dropped her and staggered backward, blood streaming from a cut on his lip.

Well, damn. She'd missed his nose.

Lanky was on his hands and knees, struggling to his feet. She kicked upwards, catching him in the stomach, and he collapsed onto the rooftop with a muttered, "Oomph."

Dani hitched her hands on her hips. "Come on, guys. Y'all are making this way too easy."

A small pinch in her arm startled her. She looked down. A tranquilizer dart protruded from her clothing. She whirled around, staggering, and glared at Dave. He lowered a small tranquilizer gun and tucked it into the back of his jeans as he walked toward her, one corner of his mouth quirked up in that almost smile of his.

Her vision blurred, taking the world with it. He'd shot her with a tranquilizer. He'd really shot her. "Son of a...," she said, and sank into oblivion.

She woke slowly, groggy from whatever Dave had shot into her. She lifted one eyelid, had her eye burned by a shaft of too-bright light for her trouble, and shut it again. Son of a bitch. Where had he taken her?

She calmed her breathing and listened. Shoes scuffed against concrete. Water dripped, pinging metallically in an irregular rhythm. Something clicked nearby, maybe a light switch. Somebody's breath hitched, a near sob, as if he or she had been crying.

Dani shifted as subtly as possible, testing her arms and legs. They were nearly immobile, her arms bound behind her at her wrists, her ankles wrapped tightly together. She clenched one hand into a fist and wiggled her arm back and forth, trying to get a feel for the material holding her. It felt a little sticky. Duct tape maybe?

She opened her eyes a slit, allowing them to slowly become accustomed to the light. The room spun once, then snapped into focus. A rectangular folding table had been erected about fifteen feet in front of her and to the side. A lamp sat on its surface, along with water, packaged food, and what looked like a first aid kit. Dave stood in front of the table watching her, his blunt features a hard mask.

Another man was beside him, dressed in a fashionable black suit with a red tie. He appeared to be in his late thirties, and was trim and clean-cut with black hair and vivid blue eyes. He might've been handsome if not for the cold amusement etched into his features.

This one she didn't know, in spite of the weeks of recon she'd done. Ol' Dave had been hiding things from her. She narrowed her eyes in his direction. That's ok, 'cause she knew where he lived. He had to sleep sometime, didn't he?

Other people were spread around what looked like the interior of the warehouse she'd been casing before that rat bastard tranqed her. She counted two, four, blinked as her vision blurred, and estimated instead. At least twenty just in her line of sight and probably more she couldn't see, both inside and out. Great.

The hitched breathing came again to her right. Dani shifted her head slowly, avoiding sudden movements. The tranq would filter out of her system soon. Until then, she'd take it nice and slow.

She finally turned her head far enough to the right to locate the source of the breathing. A pretty, young girl with deep reddish-brown hair was tied to a chair some eight feet away. Her face was tear-stained and too pale, and her lips were pressed tightly together. Dr. Terhune's daughter, had to be. Dani examined the girl from head to toe, searching for any signs of injury, but could find none other than some redness around the girl's wrists where she'd likely been straining against the ropes.

The kid got ropes and she got duct tape. Go figure.

"She's unharmed," the man in the suit said. His voice was low and smooth. The toney accent held an undertone of the Mediterranean.

"And I should believe you, why?" Dani asked.

He bowed slightly, almost mockingly, in her direction. "Forgive me. We haven't been introduced. My name is Lukas Alexiou. You would know me better as the leader of the Shadow Enemy."

A chill raced along Dani's skin. *This* was the famed Shadow, the leader of the People's mortal enemy? He looked like he should be watching an opera, not cutting down innocents left and right.

"My word is my bond, Miss Nehring," he continued. "In fact, I believe now that we've met, we have a little business to attend to." To Dave, he said, "Please bring me the man who killed this child's mother."

Two men pulled a twenty-something man forward. His clothes were torn and blood-stained, and his face was so bruised and battered, he would've been hard to identify even for kin and friends.

Lukas studied the man coldly. "I gave very specific orders for this mission. What were those orders, John?"

The beaten man mumbled something too low for Dani to hear. Amelia sobbed once, cutting it off with a sharp inhale.

"Correct," Lukas said. "The woman was not to be harmed. Retrieve the girl, do no harm. A very simple request, John, yet you disobeyed me and killed a woman, leaving a mess that must now be cleaned up. What do you have to say for yourself?"

John shook his head slowly and whispered, "She came at me with a cast iron skillet."

"I don't care if she came at you with a shotgun," Lukas screamed, startling everybody except Dave. "She was not to be harmed!"

The man broke into helpless sobs. Dani's lip curled into a sneer. Why did men always resort to blubbering when faced with retribution?

Lukas cleared his throat and smoothed a hand over his hair. "My apologies, ladies. Incompetence brings out the worst in me. Mr. Winstead, if you please."

Dave stepped forward and, with a blank expression, backhanded John, knocking the bound man to the ground. John's blubbering came to an abrupt halt.

Lukas sighed and straightened his cufflinks. "Much better. Now, on to business. Miss Terhune, I realize you are not a Daughter, but given your father's situation with Maya the Protector, I think it fair to say that you will soon be adopted by the People as one of their own."

Dani sucked in a quick breath. How could the leader of the People's enemy possibly know something as intimate as Maya's relationship with James Terhune?

"Because of this," Lukas continued, "I am willing to follow the People's tradition and allow you the right to kill this man for what he did to your mother."

"No." Amelia closed her eyes and turned her face away. "I don't want to."

"Oh, but I insist. It is the People's way, is it not, Miss Nehring, vengeance in the face of injustice?"

Lukas' tone was light, playful even, and he smiled, a vacantly pleasant expression. Dani shivered. The man was about as sane as an escapee from the loony bin. She had to find a way to deal with him, though, and fast. She glanced at Amelia, young, mortal Amelia. "She's not old enough. Fourteen is the age of decision."

"But in these circumstances, with her mother murdered before her very eyes, surely we can waive a few months and allow her to avenge that death."

"No," Dani insisted. "In that case, her nearest relative would step in for her. Since she doesn't have a relative here, exacting vengeance falls to me."

Lukas threw his head back and laughed, the sound grating across Dani's nerves. "I was told you were a canny warrior, Miss Nehring, and now I can see how very true that is. Of course, I cannot let you kill my man here. Why, we would have to untie you for that, and then you would try to kill us all. What a shame that would be."

Dani gritted her teeth. Crazy he might be, but Lukas Alexiou wasn't dumb, more's the pity.

"No, we shall wait for Miss Terhune's father. He and Dr. Bellegarde should be here bright and early tomorrow morning. I regret that we shall have to leave you tied to that chair. I've been told you could create quite a bit of mischief for us if we allowed you to roam freely."

Dani shot a killing glance at Dave. He returned her gaze with a stony one of his own.

Lukas glanced between the two of them and folded his hands together at his waist. "Why, is this a love match in the making? Will yet another Daughter succumb to frail mortality through her love of a mere man?"

Dani rolled her eyes skyward. "Oh, yeah, that's exactly what it is."

"Mr. Winstead does seem rather fond of you. Perhaps I shall give you to him once this unpleasant situation is resolved. On the contingency that he not harm you, of course. Can't have one of the Daughters bruised, can we?"

Dave grunted.

Dani smiled sweetly. "Sure, give me to him. I'll make sure he suffers for it."

Lukas clucked his tongue. "Now, Miss Nehring, that is not the way one treats a lover."

"We're not lovers, ergo..."

"I know what it's like to love a Daughter," Lukas murmured. He walked over and bent down, putting himself on eye level with her, and brushed a loose curl away from her face.

Dani swore he did it with tenderness, but still, his fingers brushing against her bare skin repulsed her. She quashed a flinch as his hand withdrew. "Who did you love?"

He eased upright, his gaze fixed on a scene only he could see. "I have loved her for an eternity, and always will. She betrayed me, yet love her I do. Can you believe that?"

She scrambled through the tales she'd heard of doomed alliances between Daughters and members of the Shadow Enemy. None matched with this man. "If she betrayed you, why do you still love her?"

"I have no idea," he said, and it struck Dani as the most honest thing he'd said.

"No matter." He shook his head and returned to Dave's side. "She and I shall be together again soon. It has been foretold."

"Care to share that foretelling with me?"

Lukas laughed again, this one softer, almost genuine. "What do you think this little scenario is about but the Prophecy? Surely Dr. Terhune has gotten that far along with his translations."

Dani's lips thinned. She was just a soldier in the war between their peoples. Her knowledge of those kinds of things was limited to what she needed to know for the missions she undertook, and only that.

"I have only come across it once before, you know. That's why I had to have these artifacts. My father destroyed the first mention of it when he learned..." Lukas' voice trailed off and his eyes glittered, cold, ruthless, determined. "Well, that's a story for another time. He paid for what he did, and I have searched since then for another version in the hopes of finding *her*, the woman I am meant to love. She and I will be together, Miss Nehring."

"Ok, well, if you'll tell me who she is, I'll be sure to warn her."

He smiled. "Oh, my sweet, you are a breath of fresh air and I have thoroughly enjoyed our conversation."

That made one of them. For her part, the whole incident had confused the hell out of her. The only thing she was sure of was that Lukas Alexiou was as mad as the Hatter.

"But, we must be going. I have instructed my colleagues not to harm you. Unless you want me to kill one of them for doing so, please do not antagonize them." He walked over and, bizarrely, pressed a kiss to the top of Dani's head. "They will be forced to retaliate and the whole thing will spiral downward from there. Be a good girl, will you?"

"Sure," she said, though she had no intention of doing any such thing. Staying where kidnappers put her wasn't in her nature, and it wasn't a lot of fun either. She glanced around, tallying the number of men around her with a clearer eye. There was a lot of fun to be had inside that warehouse and she didn't want to miss a minute of it.

Lukas patted her head, smoothing her hair back. "There, now. That wasn't so hard was it?"

He pivoted and left. Dave speared Dani with a long, intense glare, a warning unless she was sadly mistaken, then followed the Shadow Enemy's leader out of the warehouse.

Dani turned and met Amelia's fearful gaze evenly. The sight of the girl tied to a chair pissed Dani off good. She inhaled through her nose and pushed it aside. Anger didn't make for a clear head, and she needed every wit she could scrape together if she was going to get them out of this mess. "You ok, kid?"

Amelia jerked her head up once, then down. "Yeah. You?"

"Never better. Give me a few minutes to get out of this duct tape and we'll be on our way."

A man wandered over, Stocky from the rooftop. His lip had been cleaned, though it was still cracked. Maybe he'd have a nice scar as a reminder not to mess with Daughters. He pointed to two other men and gave them instructions to drag John out of the way, then turned a murderous stare on Dani.

She cocked an eyebrow and smiled coyly, suppressing a weary sigh. It was gonna be a long night.

AN ESCORT MET MAYA at James' apartment nearly an hour after they'd parted ways outside Director Upton's office. Maya stowed her gear in the trunk of one of the luxury SUVs the IECS maintained for just such occasions. The sturdy vehicle was equipped with bulletproof glass, armor plating, and other security upgrades. The gas mileage was horrible, but it was one of the safest vehicles available to them.

James yanked the door open as Maya was raising her hand to knock. He held a small carry-on bag and a slightly larger suitcase. She grabbed the suitcase and waited while he locked his apartment door, studying him from under lowered eyelashes. The skin under his eyes was still too dark and there were lines on his face she'd never noticed before. He moved slowly, deliberately, nothing like the steady, energetic man she'd come to know. Everything that had happened since Labor Day flashed through her mind, the last time they'd made love, telling him about the People, Amelia's kidnapping and the death of his ex-wife. She bit her lip and followed him down the stairs and outside. He probably hadn't slept well since then, and at least part of it was her fault.

The air in the back of the SUV was uncomfortably tense during the ride to the airfield in Gainesville and the airplane the IECS kept there for dignitaries and to provide emergency travel. Maya and James were driven straight to the hangar, and from there escorted out to the waiting plane.

Four other people were already on board, all immortal Daughters renowned for their skills as warriors. Alafair originally hailed from the Anglo-Saxon kingdom of Wessex. Brigid was also from what had become the British Isles. She smiled politely at Maya and James as they approached. Hawthorne's fiery temper had led to more than one unfaithful man losing his head, and probably good riddance. The fourth Daughter, Greta, had immigrated to the Midwest with her immigrant grandchildren some hundred years before and had settled in the South after their deaths. Maya greeted each of them with a nod. Thank the Blessed Mother the director had been able to gather such a good group on what amounted to a moment's notice.

James settled into a seat next to a window, to the rear of the four women seated together near the front of the passenger area.

The plane was too small for privacy, as much as Maya would've liked it. She sat down across from him, relaxing into the seat. "You should get some rest. We're not liable to get much once we arrive in New York."

He scraped a hand across his face and yawned. "Don't think I could."

"At least close your eyes for a while."

He did, drifting into sleep a few minutes later, likely lulled by the steady thrum of the plane's engines. Maya found a light blanket and draped it over him, then took a pillow from the overhead storage and tucked it gently under his head.

He was too pale. Poor man. To have his ex-wife murdered and his daughter kidnapped on top of everything else. Even with her strength, there were things Maya couldn't protect him from. She slumped into her seat, arms crossed over her stomach, her legs stretched out in front of her. The darkest side of the curse she lived under wasn't the continual fighting, the ever-present prickle of knowing someone was coming after you. It was being unable to protect those that meant the most from the life she and the other immortal Daughters were doomed to live.

Maya deliberately emptied her mind and closed her eyes, dozing off and on during the short jump to New York. A few minutes before they landed, she woke James, giving him time to pull his thoughts together while the pilots went through their landing routine.

Not long after, Maya, James, and the four Daughters loaded themselves and their gear into two vehicles and headed for the home of a mortal Daughter who'd agreed to house them overnight. Night had fallen while they were in the air. Maya fixed her gaze on the streetlights whizzing by as they made their way along the crowded causeways. James sat beside her, staring out the opposite window.

So much distance separated them, physical, emotional. It might as well have been a mile as the length of the backseat. Sharp regret roiled through her. Damn it, she should've told him sooner, should've given him a chance to come to terms with it before they made love. Maybe they could've avoided the distance that had sprung up between them. Maybe if she'd told him before, he wouldn't have reacted the way he had and they could face this threat together.

When their vehicles rolled to a stop along the sidewalk outside Ella Deyton's home, the lights in every room of the house seemed to be on. Ella had only been mortal for three years. She and her now husband had met while Ella was in New York on vacation, taking a break between one duty and the next. They'd fallen in love and married, and though Ella was a Southerner by birth, she'd opted to live with her husband near his family.

Ella's husband, Greg, opened the door and invited them in, leading them through the house into the kitchen. Ella was sitting at a small table, nursing her infant son. Upon seeing the child, Hawthorne, Greta, Alafair, and Brigid instantly melted from battle hardened warriors into cooing admirers, all crowding around the infant as if he were the next Messiah.

Maya lowered her head, hiding a smile. In a way, he was. The birth of a Son was always heralded, not least because it was preceded by the breaking of a curse.

Ella and Greg had prepared a meal for them, so they sat and ate and talked, sharing and gathering news. James sat quietly, eating his fill, his attention apparently on the discussion bandied back and forth around him. Maya leaned close and whispered, "You ok?"

He nodded and jerked his gaze away from hers.

Ella put Maya and James in a bedroom together, apologizing for the lack of space as she paired the four Daughters off and led the immortal women to other rooms. Maya followed her through the house, noting where the other Daughters would bed down and making sure they had what they needed.

A short while later, she returned to the bedroom she and James had been assigned. He was staring blankly at the double bed, his hands stuffed into the pockets of his jeans, his shoulders slouched.

Maya closed the door and cleared her throat. "Ella doesn't know we're, ah, not together. I can sleep somewhere else, if you'd rather."

"We're both adults," he said flatly. "I think we can handle sleeping in the same bed for one night."

They took turns getting ready for bed in the room's bathroom, then turned the lights out and settled down on opposite sides of the mattress, not touching, not speaking.

An odd pressure filled Maya's chest and climbed into her throat. She turned on her side away from James and buried her face in the pillow, determined not to regret the past. She couldn't undo it no matter how often she second-guessed herself, and it was futile to try.

The mattress shifted. A warm arm slid around her waist as James curled around her. "Don't cry."

She placed a hand over his, holding him to her. "I'm not."

"You're sniffling."

She sighed. Busted. "Not on purpose. Go to sleep. You need the rest."

His arm tightened around her. After a long moment, he said, "I haven't forgiven you."

"I know."

"I probably will, though."

The pressure in her chest eased slightly. "Really? You're not still mad?"

He huffed out a short laugh. "I'm pissed about the whole thing, you hiding things from me, my daughter getting mixed up in this blood feud, and Linda being killed. She was a good woman, Maya. She didn't deserve to die."

There was nothing she could say to that, nothing at all. She stroked her fingers over his hand, comforting him as much as she could.

His breath feathered across her shoulder. "Will you tell me about your life?"

She turned over, facing him, tangling her legs with his. "Someday."

"Dierdre told me a little."

"Oh?"

"She came by while I was packing and we talked."

"Hmm. Dierdre breaking the rules to talk to you about my past. Now, there's a surprise."

He laughed softly. "She loves you."

"I know."

"Don't ever hold anything back from me again."

"Only if I have to," she promised.

He blew out a breath, then kissed the tip of her nose. "I guess I can live with that."

Maya snuggled into him, breathing in his woodsy scent, so grateful for his touch, she ignored the uneasiness continuing to ping through her gut.

SEVENTEEN

THE HOUSEHOLD WOKE EARLY. Daughters streamed up and down the stairs and in and out of rooms, comparing weapons, discussing possible scenarios, rehashing plans. Once dressed, Maya riffled through her weapons bag while James brushed his teeth and shaved. She sorted them into two piles, those she could possibly conceal and the ones she'd carry in specifically so they'd be taken.

James came out of the bathroom and let out a low whistle. "Are those really necessary?"

"Yes." She perused him from head to toe. "How comfortable are you wearing an ankle holster?"

He shoved his hands in his pockets and fixed his gaze on the mini-arsenal she'd assembled. "No idea. Never worn one before."

"Please tell me you've at least shot a gun."

"Er, well, no."

Maya pressed the heels of her hands to her eyes. "When we get back to the IECS, you're learning how to shoot."

"Ok."

She opened her eyes wide. "Ok?"

"Yeah." He hunched his shoulders, let them fall. "We need to learn how to handle ourselves better, me and Amelia, especially if we're going to be..."

"Going to be what?"

He rubbed a finger over the tip of his nose and his lips twitched. "You know. You and me."

She definitely wanted a you and me with him, later, when they'd sorted out Amelia and the artifacts and went home to Tellowee.

"Right." She selected her Keltec .380 from one of the piles. "Ready for a crash course in guns?"

He accepted the gun gingerly. "Ready as I'll ever be."

She ran him through the basics of holding and shooting the gun, and exchanging clips. He was a fast learner, but still fumbled with its unfamiliar feel.

The third time he bobbled it, she said, "Just relax."

"It's really light." He brought the gun up again, attempted a two-handed hold, and dropped his hands. "This isn't as easy it looks on TV."

"No, it's not. Try not to put both hands up when you're shooting." She pulled his arm up and adjusted his one-handed grip. "The pistol is too small for that. If you're not careful, you could take a finger off."

He paled. "Er, gotcha."

"Point the gun as if it were your finger, ok? And remember. Aim small, miss small. The range for this gun is short, so wait until your target is within about ten feet and aim at the torso. Otherwise, you'll probably miss and piss somebody off."

"That would be bad," he said mildly.

The ankle holster gave him a little trouble. Maya made him walk around the room with the holster on, both with and without the gun inserted. Eventually, he walked naturally, casually. She helped him put a clip holder on the inside of the opposite ankle and had him walk some more. When she was certain he was as comfortable as he could be, she chambered a round in the Keltec, ejected the clip, loaded another bullet, then slipped the magazine back into place, inserting the gun and the extra clip firmly into their respective hiding spots.

"Ok, you're set," she said. "All you have to do now is draw, point, and shoot."

James peered down at his ankles. "Ah, what about the safety?"

She nodded. At least he knew that much about guns. "This gun has no safety. The first time you fire it, you'll have to pull back firmly on the trigger, about an inch. After that, shooting will be a lot easier."

"If it's that easy, how do I keep from blowing a hole in my foot?"

"It won't go off until you pull the trigger," she assured him. "Just make sure that if the police come, you take the gun off and kick it away from yourself before you can be seen holding it. Carrying a gun in New York without a permit is a felony. Better to get rid of the gun before you're caught with it, ok?"

Maya sorted through the remaining weapons and handed him a wickedly sharp folding knife. "Carry this in your coat."

He slipped it into the inside pocket of his jacket and eyed her as she tucked weapons of all shapes and sizes in every location they'd go, ending by strapping her short staff to her back.

"Won't they search us?" James asked.

"I'm counting on it." She smiled as she adjusted the fit and angle of the staff. "I'll be heavily searched. That's why I'm carrying all these weapons. Chances are good they'll miss one."

"Right."

"You, on the other hand, will probably get off lightly, since you're a man."

"Is that some kind of reverse discrimination?" He cocked his head, a small smile lifting the corners of his mouth. "I think I'm offended."

"Discrimination is discrimination, no matter whom it's perpetuated on," she said lightly. "These people are far more scared of Daughters than they are of a mortal language expert."

"Ah. Ok. I won't take offense then."

"Good." She stood on tiptoe and kissed him. "I'd hate for you to be offended because I'm a better fighter."

"What can I say? I'm really secure in my manhood."

She patted his cheek. "You should be."

THEY LEFT ELLA'S HOUSE a short time later, James, Maya, and the four Daughters they'd traveled north with all crowded into one vehicle, an SUV outfitted exactly the way the one in Tellowee had been. Maya sat on James' lap, creating just enough room in the backseat for Hawthorne and Brigid. The closer they came to the meeting point, the more his body tensed and the harder his fingers dug into her hips.

Three blocks away from the meet, Alafair stopped the SUV and everybody piled out. She and Greta jogged off in one direction, Hawthorne and Brigid in another, each pair heading toward the teams already in place. As long as Maya, James, and Amelia were in no danger, those teams would hold back. If the situation turned deadly or if an opportunity arose to regain the artifacts, they'd move in with the fury and ferocity of their warrior ancestors.

Maya slipped into the driver's seat, James into the seat beside her. His hands were unsteady on the seatbelt. It slipped out of his fingers and he grimaced. "Sorry."

"Don't be. Everyone's nervous their first time out."

He cut a side-eyed glance at her. "It's that obvious, huh."

She smiled and tucked her hand into his. "Only to someone who's been through it before. Ready?"

He jammed the seatbelt in place and stared out the windshield. "As I'll ever be."

She started the SUV and eased onto the road, driving carefully, her eyes scanning the road ahead and the area around them. They reached the meet a few minutes later. The abandoned warehouse was situated in a block of outdated industrial buildings. Some of the upper windows of the warehouse were broken and the tin roof had a huge dent in it. Weeds grew through cracks in the pavement and along the sides of the buildings, catching trash as the wind blew through the alleys and along the roads. Half a dozen burly men gathered at the main entrance, guns holstered at their sides.

Maya parked fifty feet away and cut the engine. "Remember, I'm your security. Don't go in if I can't go with you. That's not part of the deal, ok?"

James scrubbed his hands down his thighs. "Sure."

"Follow my lead and try to stay behind me if things go south. Only use your gun if we're separated."

He hunched his shoulders around his ears. "I'd already forgotten about it."

"That's ok," she said, her voice calm and even. "You'll move more naturally if you forget it's there and that'll deflect suspicion away from you. As long as you remember it's there if you need it, you'll be fine."

James inhaled slowly, releasing the breath on a huff. "I'll remember."

"Ideally, you'll never have to use it. That's what I'm here for."

Two men separated from the group and walked toward them, one waving his hand at Maya and James. She opened her door and yelled, "Stand back. We're getting out now."

The men stopped and waited as Maya and James exited the vehicle and retrieved the three cases of securely packed artifacts from the SUV's cargo area. As Maya suspected, she was thoroughly searched with a surprising professionalism. Sometimes, the Shadow Enemy hired mercenaries and thugs to do their dirty work, and they weren't always concerned about how well they did the job.

Nearly all of her weapons were located and confiscated. The only two she had left were a small knife she'd tucked into the front waistband of her jeans and the staff. One man pointed at it. "Boss says we should take everything."

Another man snorted and waved the first man off. "It's just a stick. She can't do nothing with a stick."

Maya smiled sweetly. Oh, the naïveté.

The men were much less thorough with James, catching the knife, but not the gun. Maya trained her eyes on the men, well away from James' ankle and the weapon hidden there. Hopefully, he wouldn't have to use it, and neither would she.

The artifacts were inspected last. Maya refused to hand them over, instead opening each one herself, displaying the artifacts for the man apparently in charge. At last, he nodded and waved toward the door. Two men escorted Maya and James inside, walking to the side and slightly behind them.

The brightness of early morning dimmed inside the warehouse. The poor condition of the exterior belied its sturdiness. Boxes stacked on pallets were located at regular intervals throughout the front half and the concrete floor was clear of dust and debris.

The back half of the warehouse was full of people. Maya counted eighteen men scattered across the room, plus two men standing near two people secured to chairs. The older man was dressed in a fashionably tailored suit, solid black. The younger wore jeans and a t-shirt under a light jacket. Like the other men, the casually dressed one had a handgun holstered at his hip, while the man wearing a suit appeared to be weaponless

The occupants of the chairs captured Maya's attention. As expected, Amelia was one, but what was Dani doing there? Director Upton had issued strict instructions for the younger Daughter to hold back, orders Dani wouldn't have broken without good reason. Had something unexpected happened?

Maya snagged James' elbow and halted twenty-five feet away from Amelia and Dani.

The sharply dressed gentleman stepped forward and held his hands out, palms up. "Welcome, friends. You're right on time."

"We have the artifacts," Maya said. "Release the girl and we'll turn them over."

"What? No time for a little chat?" His mouth twisted into a mocking smile. "Let's at least exchange introductions. I shall go first because, well, it's my party. Lukas Alexiou, and this is my right-hand man, David Winstead."

Maya assumed a bored expression and bit her tongue.

"And you are Maya the Protector, I presume, accompanied by the talented James Terhune. It is a pleasure to meet you both. Mr. Winstead, would you please cut Miss Terhune loose? Careful now."

Winstead pulled a pocket knife out of his jeans and cut the ropes securing Amelia to the chair. She rubbed her wrists and allowed the man to pull her up by the elbow without protest.

Lukas cleared his throat and adjusted the knot in his tie. "Before we begin, I must take a moment to express my deepest condolences to you, Dr. Terhune, on the death of your ex-wife. It was never my intention that she be harmed. The gentleman responsible will be dealt with appropriately, I assure you."

James sucked in a breath, and Maya cringed inwardly.

"Thank you," he said, and Maya sighed. At least he'd stuck to a tactful response.

"I see my men left you your staff, Dr. Bellegarde. I tried to impress upon them the importance of removing all your weapons, but they simply could not believe a woman wielding a stick could be dangerous. Would you care to give a small demonstration for their benefit?"

"Perhaps another time," Maya said.

"Of course. I trust you'll not feel the need to use your staff while under my protection." Lukas' gaze dropped to the cases James held. "And now, for business. Mr. Winstead, would you be so kind?"

Winstead murmured to Amelia and she stepped forward hesitantly, walking slowly across the concrete floor until she stood in front of her father. The teenager partially blocked Maya's view of Alexiou and Winstead. Maya shifted subtly to the side, positioning herself with a clearer path to them.

"Dad," Amelia said, her voice trembling. "Mr. Winstead told me to take two of the cases back to him."

James tensed. "Can't you stay here and let me take them back?"

"No," she whispered. "He told me to do it."

"Give them to her," Maya said softly.

James' lips thinned. "You better know what you're doing, Maya."

He gave Amelia the two cases he held. She gripped the handles tightly, walked slowly toward Dani, and handed the cases to Winstead. He set them on a table set off to the side, then nudged Amelia and murmured to her. She nodded and retraced her steps, taking Maya's case, returning with it to Winstead's side, and giving it to him without a fuss. He caught her arm and held her in place beside the table.

Lukas opened the cases, inspecting the contents carefully, his eyes wide. "Lovely," he murmured. "Thank you for bringing these. They'll make a beautiful addition to my collection." He glanced at Winstead and shut the cases, one by one. "Alas, we seem to have a small problem. This is not the complete set."

Maya stiffened. "That's everything the IECS holds except the skeleton."

"Please do not lie to me, Dr. Bellegarde," Lukas said, a chill underlying the pleasant tone of his voice. "Where is the armband?"

"Sweden," she said promptly. "If you want it, you'll have to negotiate with Dr. Lindberg and his team."

Lukas drew the handgun smoothly from Winstead's holster and pointed it at Amelia's head. James gasped and stepped forward, and Maya grabbed his arm, stopping him cold.

"No more games," Lukas said. "Give me the armband now."

Maya's jaws snapped shut. "I don't have the armband. If I did, I'd give it to you."

"Would you?" Lukas asked softly. "Would you really? Perhaps with a little more incentive."

He shifted and pointed the gun at James and his finger tightened on the trigger. Winstead jerked Amelia away from Lukas. Maya shoved James with her left hand, hard, and with her right, she unsheathed her staff and threw it in one fluid motion.

The staff sailed through the air, tumbling end over end.

The gun went off, its loud bark echoing in the warehouse.

The bullet hit below her left clavicle, pinching Maya's skin, the force of the impact pivoting her around.

Time slowed. Her gaze fell on James sprawled across the cold concrete floor. He scrambled to his knees, shouting at her. Winstead covered Amelia's head with a large hand and shoved her face into his chest. Dani screamed, her face contorting as she struggled against her bonds.

And Lukas Alexiou, the man of the hour, gaped at Maya, his expression so full of sorrow and shock, it wrenched her heart.

She staggered to the side and blackness crowded around the edge of her vision.

Daughters poured into the warehouse from every entrance, avenging angels hell bent on loosing their fury on the unsuspecting Shadow, and Maya sagged to the floor, energy draining from her in a dizzying rush.

JAMES SCRAMBLED UPRIGHT, stumbling to Maya's side as she staggered sideways. He caught her, eased her onto her hands and knees, and knelt beside her.

"Amelia," she said, her voice strained.

James swiveled around, scanning the room in frantic bursts. Amelia was huddled beneath the table not fifteen feet away, hands over her head. Winstead was hustling Lukas Alexiou toward a rear exit. He stopped and scooped up a screaming Dani, threw her over one broad shoulder, and grabbed Alexiou's elbow, nearly dragging the older man in his wake. Dani kicked and twisted, her screams unintelligible over the sounds of Daughters flooding into the building, engaging the men Winstead and Alexiou left behind. Winstead smacked her bottom hard, and Dani squawked. A moment later, the three slipped outside and were gone.

James shifted his attention to his daughter. "Amelia!"

She glanced up and began crawling toward him, dragging Maya's staff in one hand and a small box in the other. By the time she reached them, Maya was lying flat on her back, her skin unnaturally pale, her breathing shallow. James pressed his hands against the bullet wound. Blood seeped through his fingers, coating everything in its path in a sticky, red mess.

Amelia reached him and opened the box, a first aid kit. She sifted through it, tossing aside items willy-nilly. She ripped open the packaging on a large piece of gauze, nudged his hand aside, and slapped it over Maya's wound.

Maya moaned. Her eyes fluttered open and she swiped weakly at Amelia's hands. "Need to get up."

James placed a restraining hand on her unwounded shoulder, holding her in place. "We're taking care of you, Maya. Just hold still, ok?"

"Protect you," she wheezed out. Amelia removed one piece of gauze and exchanged it for another, pushing firmly against the wound. Maya grimaced and gritted her teeth. "Let me up."

"You're bleeding too much," he said flatly. "There's a hole in your shoulder, and I don't care what you say, I'm not letting you get up."

"Right arm...still good."

Amelia sat back abruptly, her young face nearly as colorless as Maya's. "We're out of gauze and she's still bleeding."

"Here." James yanked his jacket off, then his t-shirt, the cool dampness of the warehouse chill against his bare skin. He folded the t-shirt in a rough square and handed it to Amelia. "Use this. If that doesn't work, I'll look for something else."

Amelia glanced over his shoulder and squealed, and James whirled around. One of Alexiou's goons was heading their way, eyebrows lowered, his mouth a thin line. James' heart dropped like a lead weight into his stomach. They were defenseless with Maya wounded and flat on her back.

The gun. He mentally smacked himself in the forehead and fumbled with the ankle holster, trying to remember Maya's instructions as he pulled the tiny gun out from under his pants leg.

"Aim small, miss small," James muttered. He aimed and pulled the trigger, and pulled. The goon was almost on top of them and closing fast. James squeezed harder, praying the gun would go off in time. After a small eternity, it fired, recoiling against his hand with a loud bang. The goon staggered sideways and blood spread across his torso in a dark patch. James squeezed the trigger again. Almost immediately, it went off, the sharp report carrying across the warehouse.

The goon dropped to the floor with a thud. Behind him, another goon was running toward them. James fired the tiny gun and missed. Damn. The gun had a really short range. He'd forgotten all about that.

"Small gun, small range," he mumbled, then laughed shakily. His life was becoming a litany of catch phrases for handling weapons.

Maya coughed, drawing his attention away from the second goon. "Get out."

"I'm not leaving you here, Maya."

"Go," she insisted.

"I'm staying here until we can move you. You have to trust me."

"Do," she said, and passed out.

Pain exploded through James' jaw and he dropped the gun. The momentum of a punch carried him backwards across Maya's body, jostling Amelia in the process.

For the love of God. They were in the middle of a mini-war zone. How could he have forgotten that other goon?

Amelia scrambled for the staff with bloody hands while the goon hoisted James up by two beefy fists clasped in a punishing grip around his upper arms. She swung the staff like a baseball bat, connecting with the goon's back. The goon loosened his hold on James. She arched back for another swing, and James wiggled, struggling to get free. She swung again, solidly connecting with the goon's back. He dropped James and rounded on Amelia. She shuffled slowly backward, staff cocked on her shoulder, her mouth set in a hard line.

James scrambled along the ground for the gun, both eyes fixed on Amelia. Where was it, where was it? His hand connected with metal and the gun skidded sideways. Damn it. He glanced down, swiped it up, and launched himself across Maya's prone form, jabbing the gun into the other man's back. The goon froze in mid-reach. Amelia swung, hitting the hefty man in the jaw. His head popped around and he swayed. James shoved his shoulder into the goon's side, and the man fell, thumping into the concrete floor.

James braced his hands on his knees. "Good swing, honey. Maybe you should try out for softball next year."

Amelia wheezed out a breath and her eyes went wide. "Dad, geez."

"It's just a suggestion." He held out his hand. "Give me the staff. I'll hold off the goon squad while you take care of Maya."

He laid the gun on the floor beside Amelia as she leaned over Maya, then stood guard over the two of them with the staff cocked back over his shoulder in a two-handed grip.

Bodies littered the floor, more than James remembered seeing as they walked in. Most were men, though a few Daughters had fallen. At least a dozen conflicts were still raging through the warehouse. Very few of the men had their guns out. James studied them as he turned in slow circles. Empty holsters, guns well out of reach. Right. They'd been disarmed.

A cold chill slithered down his spine. He swung around and glimpsed a woman he'd never seen before standing beside the table. She was small and delicate. Her hair hung past her shoulders in a straight, black waterfall. She wore a knee-length emerald lamé jacket over an incredibly short black sheath paired with black, thigh-high boots. Her hands gently stroked the artifacts in the still-open cases. She closed one of the cases and picked it up, then pivoted toward the back entrance.

"Hey!" he said.

She stopped and peered over her shoulder, a small smile on her beautiful mouth. She blew him a kiss, and in two blinks, she was gone.

James dropped his guard and stared at the spot where she'd been. She couldn't have just disappeared. Maybe he was hallucinating. He rubbed his eyes with the heel of one palm and glanced around. Maya on the floor, Amelia hovering over her, Daughters gleefully hacking at men with staffs and assorted weaponry. Nope, not hallucinating, yet only two cases lay on the table.

Another goon broke free from a Daughter and loped toward them. James swung the staff in a circle, testing its weight. Time to make good on his promise to Maya.

EIGHTEEN

People buzzed in and out of the waiting room, doctors and nurses, police officers, those waiting on loved ones. James, Amelia, and several Daughters huddled together out of the way, waiting for Maya to come out of surgery. They'd brought her to the Emergency Room on the pretext that she'd been mugged. Two officers had come by not long after and taken statements. James had given them some totally made up malarkey. Nobody would've believed the truth anyway.

And now they waited as a surgeon attempted to remove the bullet where it had lodged against Maya's shoulder blade.

Daughters trickled in and out of the waiting room, some sporting bruises and cuts, others bandages or stitches. James had long ago lost track of their names. One brought James coffee and Amelia juice, another brought sandwiches, still another brought clean clothes. They'd both been grateful, especially Amelia. Maya's blood had soaked through her pants and part of her t-shirt, and had nearly dried by the time they made it to the ER.

A number of Daughters also brought updates. Lukas Alexiou and his man, Winstead, had escaped with Dani to parts unknown. A team had been sent after them, primarily to recover Dani. Director Upton had been updated and was apparently already on her way to New York. Two cases of artifacts had been recovered at the warehouse and securely stored in an unknown location.

James didn't mention the woman in the green coat. He still wasn't sure he hadn't imagined her, but if he hadn't, the director was probably the first person who needed to know about her.

They'd been waiting two hours when a Daughter walked in and sat down beside James. She was athletically slender with auburn hair and hazel-green eyes, and was dressed as many of the other Daughters were in comfortable casual clothing. "Hello."

God. Another Daughter to remember. "Hi."

"I'm Annette. You must be James."

James nodded, hitching his thumb at his daughter. "Amelia."

"Nice to meet you.'

"Likewise."

Slow humor spread across her oval face. "You don't know who I am."

"Ah, no. So many people have come in and out."

She snickered. "She must not've told you. I'm Maya's eldest daughter."

"Her eldest..." James heart sank into his stomach. Maya had *promised* not to hold anything else back from him. "Just how many of you are there?"

"Just me and Dee."

"Are you sure? Because Maya's surprises keep popping out of the damn closet with surprising regularity."

Annette patted his arm. "She probably hasn't had time to explain everything yet."

James inhaled sharply and rubbed his forehead. "Yeah, probably. A lot's happened over the last few days."

They passed the hours chatting, waiting for an update on Maya's progress through surgery, post-op, and then in recovery, no visitors allowed. James called his family, letting them know Amelia was safe. Annette took a quick break to update Dierdre on Maya's condition. Amelia fell asleep, curled into a chair beside James with her head propped on his shoulder. A familiar looking Daughter (Greta maybe?) pulled out a deck of cards and started a game of no-stakes poker with several others.

Talking with Annette and watching the impromptu card game absorbed James' attention, pushing out the day's events. Amelia's tear-stained face as she took the cases of artifacts from him. Dani tied to a chair, helpless. Maya shoving him out of the way and taking a bullet for him, then lying in a pool of her own blood.

So much blood.

His stomach twisted into a sick knot. She'd come so close to dying. He was sure, or as sure as he was of anything, that the only thing separating Maya from death was the curse.

The surgeon pushed his way through the waiting crowd and discussed Maya's prognosis with them. Annette, as her official next of kin, took the lead, though she included James and Amelia in the conversation. The surgeon emphasized Maya's needed for recovery time. A hysterical laugh bubbled up from James' gut. Maya was immortal. She had all the time she needed.

That night, she slipped into a coma. The days passed slowly and her wound began to heal, but she didn't wake up. James and Amelia stayed at the hospital during the day, leaving only to eat, sleep, clean up, and pass regular updates along to Dierdre. They took turns reading to Maya or talked softly in the waiting room when the hospital staff chased them out of her room. Annette slipped in and out frequently, as often as duty allowed. Getting to know her had made their wait slightly more bearable.

A rotating team of Daughters stayed with James and Amelia, acting as security while another team protected Maya. Director Upton had expressed her deep concern that James and Amelia were vulnerable, and he'd put up no resistance to the security detail. He didn't think he could stand having Amelia taken again.

A week after Maya had been shot, James and Amelia sat at her bedside, Amelia reading, James watching her. She'd closed herself off since the kidnapping. That couldn't be good. Didn't she need to talk about it, maybe start coming to terms with what had happened with her mom and everything else?

He crossed his arms over his chest and cleared his throat. "Can we talk?"

Amelia glanced up, smiling. "Sure. What's up?"

"I thought maybe we could talk about your mom."

Her smile faded. She marked her place in the book and tucked it into her lap. "Can't we talk about something else?"

"I know it's hard, sweetheart." He reached across Maya's body, holding his hand out to her. "I know you miss her. It's not good to bottle it all up inside."

"I just don't wanna talk about it. I just don't..." She sniffed and turned away. "I can't."

He sighed and withdrew his hand. "Ok. I'm here if you need me, if you want to talk. I'll listen."

She nodded and closed her eyes. "Can I finish my book now?"

"Sure, sweetheart."

He slumped into his chair and scrubbed a hand over his nape. Maybe she just needed more time. Maybe when they had Linda's funeral, Amelia would gain some kind of closure or something, or maybe being back in Tellowee with Dierdre and her new friends would help. At least she knew he was there for her, and that's the only way he could figure out to help her.

One day slipped into the next with no real change in Maya's condition. The hope James held that she'd wake up began to fade. Sitting at her bedside gave him too much time to think, about the things she'd told him, about that day at the warehouse. Was there anything he could've done differently? If he'd known how to fight, would Maya have pushed him out of the way and taken a bullet for him or would he be the one lying there? If he'd accepted everything she'd told him, the People, the curse, her own immortality, would that have changed the outcome?

Two weeks after Maya's injury, Director Upton had Maya transferred to a hospital near the IECS under the care of a doctor with a broad experience in the People's peculiar physiology. James, Amelia, and Annette accompanied Maya back, along with a small staff of nurses and the cadre of Daughters acting as security.

As soon as the IECS' private plane touched down in Gainesville's airfield, James relaxed. They were almost home. Here, he and Amelia could rebuild their lives in a safe environment where nobody could get to them, and here, Maya would find the help she needed. At least, he hoped she would.

REBECCA SAT BEHIND HER DESK, waiting for the arrival of Dani's FBI agent. The past few weeks had been an uproar of activity and uncomfortable revelations. Important artifacts had been found and then stolen. The Shadow Enemy had resurfaced, headed by a man about whom the People knew very little. And a traitor lay in their midst.

The latter had occupied Rebecca's thoughts through an uncounted number of sleepless nights, draining her energy and sapping her strength. Still, she had to find a way to deal with those events and the ones yet to come. Through it all, the People must survive. That had always been her driving concern.

Her secretary buzzed with the message that David Winstead had arrived. Rebecca studied him as he entered, the broad shoulders and tall frame, the no-nonsense haircut, the stony expression. He looked like a thug, moved like a dancer, and, from what she could tell, had the strategic skills of a chess grandmaster.

A smile touched her mouth. Yes, he would do nicely.

"Mr. Winstead." Rebecca stood and held out her hand, measuring his grip as he shook it. "Welcome to the IECS. I trust you had a pleasant trip."

"Pleasant enough," he said, his voice low and rough.

"Please, won't you sit?" She perched on the edge of her chair. "I appreciate your coming on such short notice and breaking your former engagements to assist us."

He dropped into a chair in front of her desk. "Not like I had a choice."

"Hopefully, our business won't take much of your time. I presume you're still undercover with Alexiou?" He nodded once, and she continued. "I'm curious. What excuse did you give him for coming here?"

"Told him I was coming after the girl." He shrugged and one corner of his mouth tilted up in a half smile. "Alexiou has a soft spot for women. Took a shine to Dani in particular."

Rebecca tamped down her concern. Having the leader of the Shadow Enemy *take a shine* to a Daughter could never be good.

A ruckus sounded outside her door, and Rebecca sighed. Voices raised in anger, something banged against the wall, and the doors to her office flew open, revealing a furious Dani. Her gaze zeroed in on Dave and she froze. "You low-down steaming pile of goat feces."

"Dani!" Rebecca said. "Mr. Winstead is a guest here."

Dani inhaled a long, slow breath and her hands unclenched. Her green eyes were bright, though, and bored holes into the hapless agent's broad shoulders.

"Please have a seat, Dani. We have much work to do."

Dani stalked to a chair and flopped into it, her glare steady. Rebecca bit back a sigh. At least her youngest hadn't killed the poor man. What a public relations nightmare that would be, and it would forever ruin the relationship Rebecca had carefully cultivated with the director of the FBI.

She flattened her palms on the surface of her desk. "I have several reports from Daughters who were at the warehouse last week during the exchange. Only two cases of artifacts were recovered. Mr. Winstead, by any chance is the third case in Alexiou's possession?"

"No, ma'am," he said flatly. "I left all three cases on the table when I took Dani and Lukas out of harm's way."

"I would've been better off if you'd left me there, you Neanderthal," Dani hissed.

Rebecca sighed. "Dani, please."

"He threw me over his shoulder and spanked me!"

Rebecca pursed her lips, hiding a smile.

"And then he let me 'escape' through a sewer. It ruined my favorite pair of boots." She rounded on Dave. "You'll be paying for those, Ape Man."

Dave's stony expression remained unchanged.

Dani slouched into her chair, her pretty face set in a scowl. "My hair still smells like sewage."

And that was the sticking point. Dani could be called many things, but vain she was not, except when it came to her hair. Rebecca eyed the lustrous, golden curls. If it were her, she'd be upset about the smell, too. That didn't help the situation they were in now, though.

"Let bygones be bygones, daughter. We need to focus on tracking down the missing artifacts." Again. Would they never be able to hold all of them in one place? "Now, several Daughters reported seeing a woman at the warehouse during the fight. One Daughter thought this woman took the case."

"No one recognized her?" Dani asked, her voice almost calm.

"Unfortunately, no. I was hoping Alexiou had electronic surveillance installed in the warehouse."

Dave nodded. "He does. Shouldn't be hard to gain access."

"Thank you. All I ask is that you not mention our involvement in your investigation."

"If I can. Alexiou wants the artifacts as much as you do. Pretty sure he'll do what he has to to get them back."

"Of course," Rebecca said. "Any idea why?"

He lifted one shoulder in a quick shrug. "Something about the Prophecy of Light."

Rebecca sucked in a breath. "What did he say about it?"

"He was never really coherent when he talked about the prophecy," Dave admitted. "Kept mentioning a woman, though, and I got the feeling she was somehow tied to it."

"Someone he loved who betrayed him." Dani shot a glare in Dave's direction. "Alexiou talked about that after Mr. Caveman here drugged me and tied me to a chair. Sadly, I now know how it feels to be betrayed."

"It was duct tape," Dave said evenly, "and I was protecting you."

"Do I look like I need your protection?" Dani snapped.

"As a matter of fact..."

Rebecca tapped one palm against the top of her desk. "Children, could we please stay on task?"

"Sorry, Maetyrm," Dani muttered. "Alexiou got a little weird about this woman. I couldn't figure out who he was talking about, except that he believed she was a Daughter."

"Did he ever mention a name?" Rebecca asked.

Dave leaned forward and braced his forearms on his thighs. "No, never, but he dreamed about her a lot. Sometimes, he'd wake up screaming in the middle of the night, but he never called out a name, that I know."

Rebecca sighed. "A name would be incredibly helpful."

"To be honest, I'm not sure he ever met this woman in real life. Until the artifacts were found in Sweden, I thought she was all in his head."

"I'd appreciate it if you'd pass any additional information you learn on this woman, her relationship to Alexiou, and the Prophecy of Light back to me."

"If I can," he said.

"Good. Now, I would very much like it if the two of you could put aside your differences long enough to track down the missing case of artifacts. Start with the woman in the warehouse. The resources of the IECS and the People are at your disposal."

Rebecca stood, signaling the end of the meeting. Dani and Dave rose as well.

"Got a few things to clear up before we start," he said.

"If you could stay here a day or so before you clear those things up, I'd consider it a personal favor," Rebecca said. "We have a great deal of background material available that may assist with your efforts to recover the artifacts. Dani will fill you in. And, of course, my husband and I would enjoy having you over for dinner tonight, if you have the time."

"Appreciate the offer," he said. "If you'll excuse me, I need to make a phone call."

"Of course."

He nodded to Dani and left. As soon as the door swung shut behind him, Rebecca came around the desk and gathered Dani in a tight hug. "I was so worried about you, daughter."

"I was ok. The big lug really was trying to protect me, more's the pity."

"Don't be so hard on him, then."

"Oh, don't worry. He can take it."

They chatted for a few moments more, as much so that Rebecca could take the time to assess Dani's condition as anything. Dani wasn't her child by birth, but the younger Daughter was still hers in all the ways that mattered. A mother's worries never ended, not when a child was placed in her care, and not when that child was a woman fully grown.

Rebecca cupped Dani's shoulders. "Don't forget dinner tonight, darling. The boys will be so excited to see you."

"We'll be there."

"Try to be polite to Mr. Winstead in front of Robert. Otherwise, he'll get ideas and you'll never hear the end of it."

Dani rolled her eyes skyward. "Don't I know it."

"Would you rather take Mr. Winstead to the Archives or the museum to fill him in?"

"The museum. He'll like all the weapons. They're about his speed."

"Dani," Rebecca chided gently. "He's our best lead on the artifacts. Try to be nice to him."

"All right," Dani said, her mouth twisted into something between a smile and a grimace.

"Oh, and darling, if he betrays the People, don't hesitate to do what must be done."

Dani's expression hardened. "Of course, Maetyrm."

Rebecca shooed her daughter out, then put her hand on her abdomen over a growing knot of unease. Something unpleasant was about to happen, something holding the potential to cause a great deal of harm. She was certain the days ahead would be brutally unkind to her daughter, and equally certain there was nothing anyone could do to stop it.

MAYA'S TRANSFER BETWEEN HOSPITALS went off like clockwork. The new hospital, located half an hour outside of Tellowee, was staffed with medical personnel who understood the slightly different physiologies of immortal Daughters. Unfortunately, they were of little help.

Ethan Phillips, a well-built doctor in his early thirties with auburn hair and light green eyes, took over Maya's care. He introduced himself to James as a member of the People, a son of a Daughter whose curse had been broken when she'd fallen in love with Ethan's father. The young doctor relayed the information as casually as most stated their name, unknowingly corroborating Maya's story. James tucked the knowledge and Ethan's ease with it away for future reference.

On the third day after Maya's arrival, Ethan tracked James down and asked him to step outside Maya's room for a brief update. "There's really nothing physiological keeping Maya in a coma. The bullet caused relatively little damage and the wound is healing rapidly."

James sighed and scrubbed a weary hand over his face. "So, what's keeping her in a coma if not her injuries?"

"There are a few possibilities. Do you mind if I ask you a personal question?"

"Sure."

"How deep is your relationship with Maya?"

Heat rushed into James' cheeks. "Er, pretty deep."

"Hmm." Ethan cleared his throat and tapped Maya's chart against his thigh. "It's possible your relationship with her somehow triggered her change from immortal to mortal."

"She's broken the curse?"

"Maybe," Ethan hedged. "The curse and everything associated with it is mystical in nature, not physiological, including an individual's removal from the curse's influence. If the curse is a factor here, there's nothing medical we can do for Maya except keep her comfortable and hope for the best."

The sit-and-wait policy did not a thing to ease James' concern for Maya, but his conversation with Dr. Phillips did give him a lot to think over. If Maya had somehow broken the curse, did that mean she trusted him or maybe even that she loved him?

He tried not to get his hopes up, but the thought eased some of his doubts about their relationship.

Amelia settled in at the on-campus school better than James could've hoped, thanks in large part to Dierdre's influence. He took the two of them shopping to replace the clothes Amelia had left behind in Connecticut, thrilling them no end in spite of the gloom of Linda's death and the lingering concern over Maya. As soon as the police cleared Linda's house from investigation as a crime scene, James planned to have a moving company go through it and store everything until he and Amelia found a more permanent home. He'd never allow her to go through that house again, not after she'd watched her mother die there.

The police were still investigating Linda's murder and pressing James for any information he could give. Director Upton had advised him not to reveal his knowledge of the killer's identity and whereabouts. Doing so would focus attention unnecessarily on James. The police would want to know how he knew who Linda's killer was, potentially opening up a can of worms he just didn't have the energy to deal with, not then, maybe not ever, so he held his tongue. When Linda's body was released, he and Amelia would go back to Connecticut for the funeral, but that might not be for a long while.

After Maya's first week at the new hospital, Annette returned to work, promising to come back as soon as Maya woke up, and as often before then as she could manage. She kissed James on the cheek and told him how glad she was her mother had someone so good in her life. He hadn't known what to say to that.

With Annette gone, he, Amelia, and Dierdre fell into a routine. While the girls were in school, James worked at Maya's bedside, occasionally taking breaks to talk to her about his progress. The girls came to the hospital once school was out, accompanied by a protective escort. After a good visit, he drove them to his on-campus apartment, fed them supper, and helped with homework.

As often as not, Dierdre spent the night, sharing Amelia's bed. The two of them talked until they fell asleep, and when James checked, they were usually facing one another in the double bed, holding hands as if they needed the comfort even in sleep. James spoke with Director Upton and Dierdre's dorm mother about Dierdre's continual presence. Both women assured him that she was far better off in his and Amelia's company than alone while Maya was in the hospital.

Everybody seemed so accepting of his role in Maya's life, as if when she woke up, everything would magically be ok between them. Even he was beginning to believe it.

The girls settled in, his work on the artifacts progressed to the point of near-completion, and Maya remained in a coma. Summer turned to fall. The nights grew chilly enough for coats and tourists came out in droves on the weekends to see the turning leaves.

One night three weeks after their return to Georgia, while James was making supper and listening with half his attention to Amelia and Dierdre gossip about boys, Dr. Phillips called. Maya had come of the coma and was asking for them.

NINETEEN

MAYA SHIFTED on the hospital bed. She was groggy and stiff, and her shoulder twinged every time she moved. It had nearly healed while she was unconscious, so Doc Phillips said, but she was still oddly aware of it.

As soon as she'd regained consciousness and buzzed a nurse, he'd slipped into her room and examined her from head to toe. She'd been lucky the bullet had hit as high as it had, he'd said. A little lower and closer to the center of her body and it would've punctured a lung. A hit in the other direction would've shattered her arm socket. She could've lost the use of her arm or, worse, the arm itself.

"So I'm lucky to be in one piece," she'd murmured, earning a sharp glance and a sharper retort.

"You're lucky somebody was there to stop the flow of blood and watch over you," he'd said. "A few more minutes and you would've died."

Maya's eyes slid shut. The curse didn't really grant immortality. It just made Daughters really hard to kill. That hardiness aside, when somebody tried to kill you and kept trying, sooner or later, it would catch. She'd trusted James to watch over her when she was too weak to do it herself, trusted him to do what he had to in order to protect him and her and Amelia. For the first time in her life, it had felt right trusting a man. Her faith had apparently been well placed.

The door to her room burst open and Dierdre tumbled inside, followed closely by Amelia and James. Maya grinned. Here they were. She held out her arms and caught Dierdre as she leapt onto the bed, accepted a prim hug from Amelia, and finally, James' kiss on her forehead.

He settled into a worn chair at the side of the bed. "It's about time you joined us."

Dierdre slid off Maya and sat on the side of her bed. "Yeah, Mom. You need to come home real quick. Dr. T. is a terrible cook. He's about starved us to death."

Amelia hid a giggle behind her hand and James sputtered out an aggrieved, "I am not."

They filled her in on the events of the past few weeks. Amelia had enrolled in Tellowee's high school one grade behind Dierdre and was taking her first ever martial arts class.

Maya cut a side-eyed glance at James. How could she tell him that Amelia learning how to defend herself wouldn't have kept her from being kidnapped? He might change his mind, and Amelia really *did* need to learn defensive skills, at the very least. So did he, something she'd take care of as soon as she was able-bodied.

Dierdre shared the news that she wasn't playing volleyball. "Mom, it's, like, ninth grade. I've got three more years to play. Besides," she said, her eyes wide, "you needed me more."

Maya squeezed her hand. "My sweet Squiggles."

James propped an elbow on the chair's arm and rubbed a finger over his smile. He was quiet while the girls rambled about everything from shopping to school to boys, heavy on the boys. They'd have to talk soon. She had so much to tell him, but not here. Not in front of the girls.

The doctor kept her overnight for observation, then released her into James' care with the warning to take it easy and report back if she had any problems.

James bypassed her house and took her straight to his apartment, settling her onto the couch with the solicitude of someone looking after the terminally ill. After the third time he asked if she needed anything, she finally snapped. "I'm fine, James, really. Please quit hovering."

He slumped onto the sofa beside her and took her hand in his, chafing warmth into her skin. "You were in a coma for more than a month. I think I can be forgiven for hovering."

Maya rested her head on his shoulder. "You can stop now. I'll be fine."

"Promise?"

"Yes."

Maya closed her eyes, content to rest on the sofa beside him. The injury had sapped her strength more than she'd expected it to.

James brushed his cheek across the top of her hair. "Dr. Phillips said you might be mortal now. Any chance you might've broken the curse?"

Maya sighed and buried her face in his throat. "When I was lying there, after Alexiou shot me, I tried so hard to get up and protect you and Amelia."

"I know, sweetheart. Shh. Don't think about that now."

"No, it's... You leaned over me and asked me to trust you, and I realized right then that I did. I trusted you, so I stopped fighting and I believed in you, and it was like this huge weight lifted off of me." She clutched his hand, holding him to her, allowing his strength to bolster her own. "I've never felt that free before."

"And you think that was the curse breaking?"

"Maybe," she said softly. "Maybe I'm scared of hoping too hard."

"Maybe you shouldn't be so afraid of what hope can do." He cupped her jaw and tilted her face toward his, his eyes soft and warm. "I love you, so much. I want to try to work things out with you."

"Ok."

"Just ok?"

She smiled and draped her legs over his lap and curled her fingers into the smooth cotton of his shirt. His arm around her back was hard and strong and comforting. Three hundred years she'd waited to find him, or nearly so, and now, here he was at last. "Yup, just ok."

"Not, 'Of course, James, I'm madly in love with you and want to be with you forever'?"

"Sure."

"Sure, what?"

Her smile widened into a grin. "Sure, I'm madly in love with you."

"Really?"

"Really."

"What about the forever part?"

"If you insist," she teased.

He kissed her then, slowly and gently and with much more patience than she probably deserved, and she kissed him back, showing him in the best way she could how much he meant to her. After, she told him about Annette and about Dierdre's father, and about her parents.

He hugged her close, surrounding her with his gentleness. "Dierdre said you watched them die."

"I was very young, maybe four or five. It's hard to remember that far back."

"It's ok." He cleared his throat, and when he spoke again, his voice was softer, hesitant. "Ah, I just realized I don't even know how old you are."

"Two hundred and ninety seven on my last birthday. I was born in 1716 in New Orleans."

"Wow. You're a real cradle robber."

She laughed. Her shoulder twinged and she winced. Being mortal wasn't all it was cracked up to be.

James smoothed his hand up and down her arm. "What happened to your parents?"

"My mother was a young Daughter out on her first real mission alone. She was sent to investigate my father, a Frenchman in New Orleans on business. He was suspected of aiding our enemy."

"The Shadow Enemy?"

"Right. Mámá entered his household as a slave. She was a mulatress, so it wasn't hard for her to blend in, but she was educated and beautiful and charming. From what I've pieced together of that part of her life, it was relatively easy for her to gain Pápá's trust. He took her as his mistress and she became pregnant."

"With you."

Maya nodded. "They fell in love. The Shadow Enemy discovered their liaison and came after them in the middle of the night."

"Dierdre said the servants protected you?"

"They did. Some of them died trying to smuggle me out, but not before I watched my parents being killed. I can still remember my mother drawing a sword and challenging her attackers even as they cut her down."

"That's an awful thing for a young girl to have to live with."

It was, but it wasn't the most horrible story she'd ever heard. Other Daughters had pasts so tragic, none dared speak on them. And at least Maya had survived to pass down what little she knew of her mother to her own children, preserving the memory for generations to come. "It's the price we pay for our heritage."

"I'm sorry."

His words surprised her. "Why?"

"Because you've had to live with this for so long."

She pressed a kiss to his cheek, lingering with her lips against his skin, repaying a measure of his kindness. "There's nothing anybody could've done to change that."

"I know." He threaded his fingers through hers and stroked his thumb across her skin. "But there might be a way to stop this war between the People and the Shadow Enemy."

"What?" She jerked upright and stared at him. "How?"

"Labor Day morning, when I raced out of here so early. Do you remember?"

Maya narrowed her eyes. "I was enjoying that early morning cuddle before you woke me up."

He kissed her forehead. "That morning, I had an epiphany of sorts that's helped me translate the remainder of the Sandby borg texts."

She opened her mouth, and he touched his finger to her lips, silencing her.

"Even the Linear A tablet," he continued. "Sanctuary. That was the symbol I needed. It brought everything else into context, and from there, it was just a matter of time until I figured all of it out."

Her breath whooshed out of her. "Sanctuary as in where the Seven Sisters sought refuge?"

He pressed his lips together. "I think so."

"Does Director Upton know?"

"I've told her some, but not all," he admitted. "I wanted to share this with you first."

"James," she chided. "She needs to know this."

"She knows enough to get started," he assured her. "But there's more."

"I love it when you say that."

He grinned and brushed the tip of his nose across hers. "The rest of the tablet contained a prophecy. I've been studying the fragments in the museum, about the origin myth? And I think the Linear A tablet might contain the Lost Prophecy."

She jumped into his lap, ignoring the pain in her shoulder. "You are a language god."

She kissed him soundly and coaxed him into taking her to bed, and showered him with enough affection to last him a lifetime.

SUPPER THAT NIGHT was a madhouse. Amelia and Dierdre insisted on cooking. The menu was a little creative and they talked over each other as they turned the efficiency kitchen into a disaster area.

James supervised from the relative safety of the table. It was good to see Amelia regaining some of her natural effervescence, though she refused to talk about her ordeal. It had been a month since her mother's death and her own kidnapping. How long did it take for somebody to heal from that kind of trauma? He slouched into the hard backed chair and scowled. Surely healing meant talking about it, at least a little.

A few minutes after the four of them sat down to eat, Maya said, "I called Director Upton earlier and made an appointment for us to see her in the morning so we can discuss the rest of your work."

James passed a plate of lopsided pancakes to Amelia. "What time?"

"As soon as the girls get off to school. I hope that's not too early."

"Not a bit. Besides, it's nice to start the day with positive news for a change."

Dierdre bit her lower lip and gazed at him with wide, hope-filled eyes. "What kind of news, Dr. T.?"

Maya winked at him. "James is nearly finished working with some documents, the ones he came here to translate and study. He thinks he's found a reference to the Lost Prophecy."

Dierdre gaped. "No way!"

Amelia's fork clattered to her plate and her already-pale skin whitened. "The Prophecy of Light?"

James and Maya exchanged a glance. "How did you know about that, honey?" James asked.

"Mr. Alexiou talked about it when he kidnapped me. Well, he didn't kidnap me personally but, you know, after."

Maya laid a comforting hand on Amelia's arm. "At the warehouse?"

"Yeah, then," Amelia said. "He was kinda crazy, but he wasn't mean to me or anything, except for, you know, tying me up and stuff. And even then, he got mad about Mom..." Tears welled up in her eyes. She sniffed them back and glanced down at her plate. "He wanted me to hurt the man who killed Mom."

A slow heat burned through James' veins. Goddamn Alexiou. He'd managed to pack a lot of harm into a few days. James inhaled a sharp breath and managed a calmly spoken, "What did you do?"

A tear slipped down Amelia's cheek. "I told him no, then Dani said she'd do it, and Mr. Alexiou laughed and told her he couldn't untie her."

"What did he say about the Prophecy, Amelia?" Maya asked gently. "Do you remember?"

"I don't remember all of it. I was really scared, you know?" Amelia shifted toward him, her brows furrowed, and grasped James' hand. Her fingers dug into his skin, biting through flesh into bone. "But he went on and on about it. Something about loving somebody for a long time and how she betrayed him, but he still loved her, and how they'd be together again."

James cupped her hand. "Did he say who?"

"No. He just said he'd been looking for the Prophecy and something about his dad. I think something bad happened. You know, to make Mr. Alexiou crazy."

"Why didn't you tell me this before?"

"I didn't want you to be mad at me." Amelia's face crumpled and a sob escaped her throat. "Mom was trying to protect me when that guy killed her. It was my fault she died."

"No, honey." James rose and pulled her into a hug. "It's not your fault. You had nothing to do with that, ok?"

Maya and Dierdre slipped out of the room, tears trickling down Dierdre's furious face. She and Amelia had grown so close, and from Dierdre's expression, it appeared she'd taken Amelia under her protective wing, much the way her mother had done with him.

He held Amelia through a storm of tears and quiet sobs, murmuring softly to her, reassuring her that everything would be ok, even if it never was again. How could it be when her mother was gone? Linda might not have been the best parent when it came to remembering the little things, but she'd loved Amelia so much. She'd been a good mother, and he hated that Amelia had lost her, that Linda's life had been wasted on the whim of a madman.

Amelia's tears wound down. James dried her tears and, when he was sure she was ok, encouraged her to get ready for bed. As soon as she'd scooted off toward the safety of Dierdre's friendship, he began cleaning dishes off the table. Maya joined him a few minutes later.

"Dierdre ok?" he asked.

"Yes. Amelia?"

"She will be." Somehow, some way, his daughter would be fine, no matter what he had to do to help her get to that point.

Maya helped him load the dishwasher, and after, he sent her off to rest on the couch while he finished. Somehow, the girls had managed to strew flour from one end of the little kitchenette to the other, and had dirtied what looked like every pot, pan, and cooking utensil while they were at it.

James scowled at a gooey egg beater and dunked it under running water. He'd been lumping Dierdre with Amelia as if she weren't just his daughter's friend and the child of his lover, but part of his family. He and Maya hadn't quite settled things that afternoon, but they would, and soon. He loved Maya and he knew she loved him, too, but they couldn't keep playing at being together. If they were going to act like a family, they should *be* a family.

He was just old-fashioned enough to want to be married to the woman sleeping in his bed while his daughter was under the same roof. If he had his way, that's exactly where Maya would be later on that night, and exactly where he wanted her to be for the rest of their lives.

He stuffed the last dirty dish into the dishwasher, turned it on, and padded into the living area. Maya was curled up on the couch fast asleep, her face half buried in the pillow. She'd overdone it. Hadn't he told her to take it easy for a while?

He scrubbed a hand over his hair, ruffling it into an untidy mess. Ok, there were only two beds in the apartment. The girls were in one, and it might be manly, but he wasn't sleeping on the couch, not on Maya's first night home. He strode into his bedroom and turned down the covers on his bed, then crept into the living room and carried her through the apartment. After everything they'd been through, he couldn't stand not having her near. Tomorrow they'd settle the issue of family, and soon, maybe they'd be one.

THE NEXT MORNING, Maya and James dropped Dierdre and Amelia off at school. Maya stared through the passenger's side window of James' car, following their progress through the school grounds as they mingled with their friends and disappeared into the school's entrance.

James had insisted on driving, though the entire IECS campus was scarcely a mile across. Hardly a difficult walk on a bad day, let alone a bright, fall morning like that one. Maya hadn't argued nearly as hard as she should've. She was still a little weak and her shoulder wasn't healing nearly as quickly as she was used to her body healing. She sighed and rested her forehead on the window. Maybe it would never heal properly, but it was a small price to pay, all things considered.

"She'll be ok, won't she?" James asked.

"She will be, once she's had time to adjust." Maya shifted in the seat, facing him. "Kids are more resilient than we give them credit for being."

"Yeah, I guess." He glanced away and ruffled his fingers through the hair at his nape. "Are we in a hurry?"

"We don't have a set time we need to see the director, if that's what you mean. Why?"

His mouth thinned. "This isn't how I wanted to do this."

"Do what?"

"Ask you to marry me. We never really got around to that yesterday."

"Hmm."

"I mean, I thought I might ask you to dinner and give you a ring or something." He huffed out a short laugh and shook his head. "Lame, I know, but it's traditional, right? But here we are in a car watching our daughters walk to school together and..."

Maya laid a hand gently on his forearm. "Here's fine, especially if you'll just go ahead and ask."

"Yeah?" A slow grin curled the corners of his mouth and crinkled the corners of his eyes into a smile. "I love you. Marry me."

Her own lips twitched into a grin. "Ok. When?"

"Today would be great, maybe tomorrow. A week, tops."

She laughed and kissed him, savoring the slow press of his mouth against hers, the warmth of his skin, the quiet love they'd found. Her heart turned over and something beautiful and light bubbled through her, spilling over into their kiss.

"Mmm." She pulled back, breaking their embrace before they got carried away. "Director Upton's waiting."

He groaned. "You had to remind me."

He started the car and eased into the road, and a few minutes later, parked outside the building housing the director's office. Rebecca was waiting for them and sat quietly through James' update on his recent findings, her hand palm down on the report he'd given her, covering his translation of the Prophecy of Light.

"Thank you, Dr. Terhune," she said. "I hope you'll consider continuing your work with the IECS."

He leaned back in his chair and glanced at Maya. "Actually, my work with the Sandy borg artifacts is nearly finished. I've even managed to piece together a loose narrative based on them."

Rebecca arched an elegant blonde eyebrow. "So you'll be leaving us then?"

Maya smiled. "I've almost convinced him to stay on permanently, Director. James has asked me to marry him."

"And you said yes. Congratulations to the both of you. Will you be holding a traditional ceremony?"

"A traditional ceremony?" James asked.

Maya groaned. "She means a traditional wedding of the People."

"And that's different from a regular ceremony, how?"

"You don't want to know," she said firmly. To Rebecca, she said, "We haven't gotten that far yet."

Rebecca tilted her seat back. "You will, of course, take him to see the Oracle."

Maya nodded. There were some traditions worth keeping, and that was one. "Of course, Director."

"Good then. Dr. Terhune, please let me know what I can do to assist with any additional work you do regarding the Sandby borg artifacts."

"There is one thing. I understand Tom Fairfax has been updating the Archives' cataloging system and adding better inventory lists." James leaned forward and met Rebecca's gaze evenly. "I thought we might want to search the Archives for documents related to Sanctuary, anything that might help us understand the records from the Sandby borg site better. Would it be possible for him to do that while I work my way through the rest of the Sandby borg items? He probably has the best grasp on how to find things at the moment, and we could really use some help."

"Yes, of course," Director Upton agreed. "I also have another recommendation, someone who assisted heavily when we first began building the Archives here. I can't guarantee she'll come, but I'll try to persuade her of the importance of the work being done here."

James rose and shook Rebecca's hand. "I appreciate that."

"Anything to assist with your work, particularly if it helps us locate Sanctuary," Rebecca said.

Maya and James left not long after. As soon as they were in the car, he said, "Ok, I know you guys have a long history together, but sometimes I feel like you're speaking a different language. What is the Oracle?"

"If you'll drive to the Archives, I'll show you."

"The Oracle is in the Archives."

"Yes and no. I promise I'll explain, but it's better if you see this with your own eyes." She gripped his hand, a silent plea for understanding. "Much like the origin myth."

"Ah. Ok."

He drove them to the Archives' parking area and helped her out of the car, his hands gentle. She let him, not necessarily out of a need for assistance. She enjoyed his touch, enjoyed having him near, and she was beginning to rely on his strength as much as her own.

Maya signed out a golf cart and showed James around the Archives. He'd never been beyond the reading room before. As they traveled deeper and deeper into the mountain housing some of the People's most valuable items, she outlined its history.

"Members of the People who originally settled here came because it was a frontier, a place where they were free to live as they chose. They befriended the local tribes, including the Cherokees, and eventually founded the town of Tellowee."

"So Tellowee is a Cherokee name?" James asked. "I wondered."

"It means 'white oak grove,' and yes, it's Cherokee. The People discovered a system of caves here and eventually expanded and modified them into the Archives, as technology improved and necessity demanded. The mountain is solid granite, but the caves could be humid."

"Hence the need for technology."

"Right. More importantly, the People could fall back here in an emergency, and they often did."

He gazed around them, his eyes roaming over the concrete-lined halls and the doors spaced at irregular intervals. "I can imagine. This place is huge on the inside."

Maya turned into one of the older, narrower tunnels and slowed their speed. "We've added to it over time. The area we're in now is part of the original cave system, whereas the Archives is housed in the newer sections. Technology," she reminded him. "And because we have the room and the security, many of the other settlements of the People have opted to send some of their holdings here."

He jerked around, facing her. "Wait. Tellowee isn't the only one?"

She shook her head, sending a mass of kinky curls flying around the sides of her face. "There are a handful of places like Tellowee around the world, places where the People can live in relative peace."

"How many of you are there? Surely not that many."

"There are nearly three thousand immortal Daughters at the moment, more or less, and more mortal Daughters and Sons. We stop counting the number of mortals after the second generation from immortality."

Maya eased the golf cart to a stop outside the entrance to the Oracle's chamber and nodded to the two Handmaidens flanking a large, heavy door. "Here we are."

One handmaiden entered information into a keypad affixed to one side of the door, then waited while Maya pressed her thumb to the scanner plate and entered a second code. The door's lock released, and the Handmaidens pulled the door open, allowing James and Maya to enter.

Here, the tunnel was even narrower, wide enough for just two people to walk side by side. The light fixtures were recessed into the walls and gave off a scant glow. The dim lighting combined with the close quarters and a damp chill turned the tunnel slightly spooky. In spite of the creep factor, younger Daughters somewhat irreverently called it the Tunnel of Love.

After twenty feet, the tunnel widened into a roughly round room with concrete walls, floor, and ceiling. Seven alcoves were evenly spaced around the room, each containing an artifact lit by a small spotlight, each one believed to have been a possession of one of the Seven Sisters. Two Handmaidens guarded the tunnel's terminus. Two others stood at attention in the center of the room at the foot of a rolling gurney draped with cloth. A fifth Handmaiden sat in a chair next to the bed, book in hand. She glanced up when Maya and James entered and smiled sweetly at them.

On the platform, a woman lay prone. She was dressed warmly and covered from head to toe by a transparent veil. A quiet reverence filled Maya. This woman had come to play a central role in the People's rituals, binding them together as surely as any legend or prophecy or shared history.

James stood stock still at the entrance, his avid gaze cataloging every detail of the room, from the alcoves to the Handmaidens to the woman at its center. "The Oracle?" he asked quietly.

"Yes." The reading Handmaiden marked her place in the book and moved out the way. Maya twined her fingers with James' and led him to the Oracle's side. "This is her."

"Did she give the People the Prophecy?"

"Nobody knows where the Prophecy came from." Maya shrugged and considered the sleeping woman. "It's possible she did, but it would've had to have been a very long time ago, before our written records begin."

James tilted his head to the side. "She doesn't issue prophecies, but you call her the Oracle?"

Maya pursed her lips, stifling a laugh. His confusion was natural, and so very endearing. "She was found in a cave, a grotto, really. I think it was somebody's idea of a joke. You know, mysterious woman in a cave, the mystical elements of the curse and the People's origins?"

"Gotcha. So who is she?"

"We don't really know. She's been this way for as long as anyone can remember, and we have some very old Daughters."

James dipped toward the Oracle and exhaled sharply. "She's not breathing."

Maya snagged his arm and tugged him backward. "Relax. She doesn't breathe. In fact, she doesn't move at all, not that anyone can see. We think she's in some sort of mystical stasis."

"So you just put her here and what?"

"Protect her. Watch over her." Maya lifted the veil away from the Oracle's face and torso and folded it carefully below her waist. "Hope she wakes up so we know who she is."

James cleared his throat. "Er, should you be doing that?"

"It's ok. This is part of the tradition. When a Daughter breaks her curse, she comes here with the one she trusts to pay homage to the Oracle."

"So you trust me, then? Your curse is broken?"

She smiled up at him, this man who meant so much to her. He'd earned her trust and ensnared her heart, and managed to save her in the process. "Yes and yes."

He slid an arm around her shoulders, and she leaned into him, thankful for his presence, grateful he'd taken a chance on her and had the patience to wait for her trust to grow. After a while, she took one of the Oracle's hands in her own and explained quietly how she'd met James and what he meant to her. When she'd emptied her heart and run out of words, she pressed a kiss to the Oracle's hand, surprised as she always was that the sleeping woman's skin was warm and soft, kept so by some force beyond Maya's reckoning.

"Can I touch her?" James asked.

Maya arched a single eyebrow. "You really do like older women, don't you."

James shot her an exasperated look. "One at a time is more than enough for me, sweetheart. I wanted to thank her, like you did. Can I do that?"

"I don't see why not."

James lifted the Oracle's hand and bent down to whisper softly, as if she really were asleep and he didn't want to wake her. Then he kissed her hand as Maya had done and stepped back.

Maya reached forward to draw the veil back across the Oracle's body.

The Oracle gasped and arched upwards. Her eyes shot open. "Gulnar?" she rasped. "Gulnar nadji?" She collapsed against the gurney and her body jerked, her limbs flailing against its metal sides. Maya snagged James' elbow and pulled him out of the way as five Handmaidens raced to the Oracle and braced themselves on either side of her, containing her on the gurney.

Maya's hand tightened on James' arm. "What did you do?"

"I talked to her, just like you did," James said, his voice shaking.

"What did you tell her?"

"I told her what you did, how we met and how I love you, and then I told her we'd found the Prophecy of Light and that we hoped to use it to break the curse."

The Oracle sagged and stilled. One of the Handmaidens radioed out. Another ripped the cloth away from the gurney's edge. Two others unlocked the wheels and rolled the Oracle carefully out of the cave. In a few moments they were gone. The remaining Handmaiden escorted them out past the two Handmaidens standing guard and left them at the golf cart.

Maya and James navigated their way to the Archives' entrance in silence. When Maya turned in the golf cart, the guard on duty relayed the information that the Oracle was on her way to the hospital near Tellowee.

James walked beside Maya to the car, head down, his expression pinched. "I'm so sorry, Maya. If I would've known she'd react to me..." He shuffled to a stop and stared at the sky above them, clear blue and cloudless. "Has no man ever spoken to her before?"

She threaded her arm through his and rested her head on his shoulder. "She has a lot of visitors, James, Sons and men like you who've become part of the People. It almost certainly wasn't your presence that triggered her seizures."

"Still, maybe I shouldn't have told her about the Prophecy. Maybe it would've been better if I hadn't said anything at all."

"I think you did exactly the right thing."

The Oracle had awakened, if only for a moment. James couldn't know what that might mean. He had no idea of her importance or of the significance of what he'd said. Maya turned the possibilities over, studying them carefully. Could the Oracle be connected to the Prophecy somehow? Is that why she'd woken now or had it simply been her time to wake up? And what was it she'd said? *Gulnar nadji.* Nothing Maya recognized, but maybe someone else would know the phrase.

All of that would be resolved in time. The Oracle would be cared for and maybe she'd even wake up for good. The curse would be broken, their enemy defeated, and the People saved. The hope that these things would come to pass was greater now than it ever had been before. Maya tucked the worry and hope away. For now, she had more pressing matters to think about, a family to build, a life to live, and a love to bind it all together.

She took James' hand and kissed him softly, absorbing his heat into her own, and with it some of his worry. He relaxed against her and she knew he'd be ok, that he'd go on to fulfill his promise to the Oracle. He'd help the People break the curse, and he'd love Maya forever. That was what she'd waited for her whole life, a man she could love without reservation, someone who loved her just as fiercely.

She intended to enjoy every moment with him.

The Prophecy of Light

*In the days of Shadow
The Light will awaken
Daughters and Sons will gather
Where the bones of the Sisters shall lie
The storm will rise, but
The bow of the Enemy will unbend
And the Light of the People
Shall see into the darkest Shadow
Two paths lie before the People
Strength brings victory
Weakness is death
Only the Light can decide
Which one to follow*

Book 2
Light's Bane

ONE

DANIELLA NEHRING stood behind a string of yellow police tape and stared at the remains of the man left in a dark alley in one of the Big Apple's worst slums. He'd been beaten before being killed, or possibly he'd died while being beaten. Either way, it had been an ugly death, and probably no more than the man had deserved. He'd killed the ex-wife of an ally of the People a few weeks ago. Now, her death had been avenged.

A cool, early morning breeze blew over Dani, wafting the scent of filth and decay through the alley and into the street. A small crowd gathered behind the police tape. The crime scene had briefly stirred interest in the neighborhood's residents, mostly among passers by. A few mothers pulled their children away, but for the most part, the locals were unconcerned. Death was a regular visitor here. Already, the crowd was thinning as people drifted back to their normal routines.

Dave Winstead stood beside Dani, as still and resolute as Lady Liberty, his strong features stoically set under a battered Chicago Cubs baseball cap. Though he knew the man whose body had been found in the alley, Dave made no move to identify him, surprising Dani not at all. Doing so would lead the police directly from Dave to Lukas Alexiou, an antiquities dealer that had been the victim's former employer, and probably the one that had ordered the man's death.

Nobody crossed the leader of the Shadow Enemy without feeling the lash of repercussions.

Dave turned and walked away, and Dani followed silently behind. She put the crime scene firmly out of her mind, instead admiring the broad expanse of Dave's shoulders tapering to narrow hips, the loose-limbed stride that covered ground quickly without being hurried. At six three, Dave topped Dani by less than a hand, though he out-bulked her by a mile. She'd had a lot of chances to observe him building that muscle, and one memorable close encounter with his naked chest.

Not close enough to touch, true, but close enough for the play of light on muscles to imprint itself into her mind in a way she wouldn't forget anytime soon. She'd pulled that memory out a few times, running it through her head to keep from smacking Dave down when he did something stupidly male.

Shame to ruin a fine chest that way.

They walked until the streets grew cleaner and the buildings less shabby, with open businesses instead of broken and boarded up windows. The dull hopelessness of the people they passed was gradually replaced by industry and neighborliness. Dani's stomach growled every time they walked by a restaurant and she caught a whiff of frying food, an unpleasant reminder that she hadn't eaten breakfast before Dave had dragged her to the murder scene.

They caught the subway after walking for blocks and eventually wound up at the building where Dave lived.

Dani had been to Dave's apartment only two times, first when she'd broken into it to gain his help in the search for some stolen artifacts, and then earlier that morning when she'd arrived in the city after a long flight from Atlanta. He'd offered her his spare bedroom, and Dani had accepted. They'd be working closely together for a while, though expedience played only a part in her decision. Deep down, she hoped to gain another glimpse of his bare chest.

In spite of the grim events greeting her arrival in New York, Dani smiled. A girl had to take her fun where she could get it, and the sculpted muscles of Dave's bare chest promised a lot of that in the not so distant future.

He was one of the most stoic men she'd ever met, she reflected as they climbed the stairs to his apartment, and also one of the most thoughtfully cautious. As an undercover FBI agent tracking black market antiquities, he had to be in order to protect his identity and, therefore, his job. His caution had annoyed her a few weeks back, when he'd drugged her and duct taped her to a chair, ostensibly to protect her. Then, he'd had no idea she was a decades-old, kickass warrior. He'd only thought to keep her out of harm's way and under a watchful eye as the People exchanged artifacts for kidnap victim.

So he said, anyway. That incident, along with his *allowing* her to escape through New York's sewer system, still pricked her temper.

Think of his chest, Dani.

When they were in his apartment, Dave locked the door behind them. Dani waited while he did the usual check for bugs. Paranoid? No. She'd found a couple herself in her initial sweep of the apartment. Her favorite Feebi was being watched, by more than one party. Why, he wouldn't say, but she just knew he knew.

Dave Winstead was frustratingly silent on a lot of matters. No amount of prodding could pry information loose if he didn't want to talk. The only thing she hadn't tried yet was sex, not because she wasn't attracted to him, but because she knew it wouldn't work. And, she hated stooping to such underhanded tactics if a more savory one would do the trick.

So far, she hadn't found the secret to manipulating him. As far as she could tell, he was simply unmanipulable. She'd already tried blackmailing him by threatening to tell the wrong people that he was working undercover. That had seemed to work for a while, until he'd called her bluff the weekend before Labor Day. She had no idea why he'd continued to help her then, and only an inkling of why he helped her now.

Fact was, she needed his help. When the Sandby borg artifacts had been stolen from under her nose a few months back, she'd tracked them from Sweden to London to New York. Part of those artifacts had been recovered, but one crucial tablet had been stolen again by an unknown woman. Dave had originally played a critical role in helping Dani pinpoint the artifacts' location in New York. Now he was going to help her track that woman, in part by giving Dani access to Lukas Alexiou's property.

Dave shrugged out of his jacket and hung it on a coatrack nailed to the wall behind his front door, then took off his battered baseball cap and hung it on another peg. Dani hung her jacket up beside his and followed him into the kitchenette.

He opened the refrigerator and rummaged inside. "Hungry?"

She leaned a hip against the edge of a counter. "Starving. Whatcha got?"

"Omelet ok?"

"Sure."

Dave pulled eggs, vegetables, cheese, and a small package of ham out of the fridge and laid everything on the counter. When he began rinsing the veggies, Dani said, "Need help?"

He looked at her directly for the first time since she'd arrived at his apartment earlier that morning. "You cook?"

Hmm. How could she test him without lying? "I can press buttons on a microwave as well as the next woman."

He grunted and turned back to the cutting board.

She bit back a smile. What a caveman.

He moved efficiently around the kitchen, chopping and stirring and whisking. Since he seemed to be working through something, she left him in silence. It was more fun watching him anyway as he shifted from counter to stove and back again, his well-toned muscles playing subtly beneath his clothing.

They ate at the tiny table he'd shoved into one corner of the kitchen. It was just big enough to seat two people, as long as nobody minded knocking knees occasionally.

At her first bite of the omelet, Dani moaned and barely stopped herself from shoving another bite in immediately after the first. "Good stuff."

"Thanks."

"Where'd you learn to cook?"

"Mom." He relaxed against the back of his chair and pinned her with one of his patented expressionless stares. His slate gray eyes glinted in the sunlight pouring through the window's blinds. "She said if I wanted to eat, I had to learn to cook."

"Wise move."

Dani took another bite of her omelet, savoring the burst of flavors across her tongue. Dave watched her eat for a minute, then turned back to his meal. When they'd both finished, she carried their plates to the kitchen and turned on the faucets in the sink.

"You cooked, I'll clean," she said.

He grunted what might have been an agreement and began clearing the counters, putting away unused vegetables and raking organic material into a small bowl.

"What's that for?" Dani asked.

"Compost. 201C has a garden on the roof."

"Does 201C have a name?"

"Sure."

Dani waited, her hands immersed in sudsy water. "And the name is...?"

He flicked a finger down her nose. "Mind this."

The casual gesture caught her by surprise. "Knowing your neighbors' names isn't nosey."

He settled back against the counter beside the sink, arms crossed over his chest, feet spread apart for balance. "It is if they're not your neighbors."

"They'll be my neighbors for the next few days. What if I need help?"

"You won't."

"But what if you're gone and, I don't know, the sink backs up."

He shook his head slowly. "Where I go, you go."

Dani rinsed the last dish and put it in the drainer, then shook her hands over the sink, slinging off excess water. He leaned around her and snagged a dish towel from the drawer beside the sink, and his body rubbed against hers, male and muscled and warm.

Pinpricks of heat slid over her skin. She cleared her throat and focused on the dishes. "Thanks."

His mouth quirked to one side in a small lopsided grin. "Welcome."

He settled back into his pose beside her and watched her expectantly.

"What?" she asked.

"I can hear questions burning through your mind. Spit 'em out."

Dani leaned her hip against the counter beside him, taking care to keep a decent distance between them. "I know you have a plan."

"Yeah."

"Care to share it with me?"

"Got some things to do first."

"And I'm supposed to, what? Sit around and twiddle my thumbs like a good girl while you go out and do my work for me?"

He considered her for a minute. "Would you?"

She bit her tongue and fought for patience. Neanderthal Man had only an inkling of who and what she was. Smacking him down every time he acted like a caveman wouldn't help them get this job done. "Not the little woman type," she said flatly.

"I know." His mouth quirked into another grin. "Just wondered if you'd follow my lead."

"Only as long as you're useful."

"Fair enough."

He pushed away from the counter. Dani followed him out of the kitchenette and as far as the doorway of his bedroom. She propped against the doorframe while he rummaged through his spare possessions.

She'd explored this room thoroughly the first time she'd come to Dave's apartment. The only furniture in the room was the Queen-sized bed draped with a black comforter, a nightstand holding a lamp, and a matching chest of drawers. Two small, hand-thrown pots rested on the top of the latter, one filled with change and the other with knickknacks. The nightstand held some well-worn, paperback Westerns. Other than a backup service weapon and his clothing, stacked neatly in the chest of drawers and hung just as precisely in the closet, the room contained nothing else, not photos or letters from home or an old annual or even pictures on the wall. Just the things he needed to get by from day to day.

Dave tapped a small pile of ephemera gathered on top of his chest of drawers. "Spare key and my cell number." He walked toward the doorway and Dani moved out of his way, standing aside while he put his cap and jacket back on.

"Where are you going?" she asked.

"Out. Back soon." He zipped his jacket and locked a no-nonsense stare on her. "Don't bother the neighbors."

He walked out and shut the door behind himself, and Dani stared after him. He'd left, just like that, giving her no idea of where he was going or what he was doing. She'd come to New York to do a job, a job he was integral to, and he'd just...left.

"What happened to *where I go, you go?*" she muttered.

She pivoted on her heel, marched to her bedroom where she'd stashed her gear earlier, and slapped the doorframe as she passed. Dave Winstead was the most infuriatingly frustrating man she'd ever met, and she'd encountered a lot of men in her time.

She yanked clothes out of her suitcase and put them away in the closet of the spare bedroom, then set her toiletries out in the apartment's only bathroom. Her irritation with Dave had evaporated by the time she finished, so she took out her laptop, a notebook, and a pen and concentrated on work.

She called Rebecca with an update on the crime scene she and Dave had visited that morning. Her mother would pass the information along to James Terhune, whose ex-wife, Linda, and daughter, Amelia, had been victims of the dead man.

Her mother had another interest in that information. The world at large knew Rebecca Upton as the director of the prestigious Institute for Early Cultural Studies. In reality, heading the IECS was only part of her job. Rebecca served as the primary strategist in the People's ongoing war with the Shadow Enemy, directing efforts to keep the People safe and undermine the Shadow's operations. Knowledge of those operations was critical to Rebecca's efforts, and so a file on the crime scene would take a permanent place among the IECS'S holdings.

Near the end of the call, Dani asked after Maya Bellegarde. The Daughter had been badly wounded in the attempt to regain Amelia. Maya, a respected member of the People, had once been Dani's teacher. When Rebecca told her Maya was still in a coma, Dani gritted her teeth. A wave of helpless fury rolled over her and she slapped her laptop closed and slid it onto the couch. If Dave hadn't duct taped her to a chair, she might've been able to affect the outcome of that exchange and keep Maya out of harm's way. Instead, she'd been forced to watch as Lukas Alexiou aimed a gun at her friend and pulled the trigger. Who cared what the man's intentions had been? Maya had been hurt, and Dani hadn't been able to stop it.

She popped off the couch and paced in short, quick strides across Dave's living room while she finished talking to Rebecca. When the conversation ended, she hung up and rubbed a tired hand across her neck, already regretting the excess emotion. Hadn't she learned yet how futile it was to fret over the past? There was no going back. Lingering on what couldn't be changed was a waste of energy.

Dani dropped her phone next to her laptop and stalked into her bedroom. She changed into yoga tights and a matching tank top and found a suitably large empty spot in Dave's living area to use as a workout space.

Her muscles were tense, taut. She rolled her shoulders and deliberately emptied her mind, then stretched into a series of Yoga postures. She blocked out the feel of Dave's body brushing against hers, the bruises and wounds littering the body of the dead man, blood dripping down Maya's chest. She moved until she felt clean and whole, then put herself through a series of katas to erase the last of the useless emotions weighing on her. Anger and frustration and helplessness, gone, pushed away through positive action.

When she felt more balanced, Dani threw a ragged sweatshirt on over her workout clothes and settled down in Dave's living room with a bottle of water and a stack of notes to review. The sofa's leather upholstery molded itself to her body, and she relaxed into it, enjoying its cushy comfort. Dave's apartment might be Spartan, but he had good taste in furniture.

She focused on work for the rest of the morning, using it to keep her mind active and away from thoughts of the frustrating man whose apartment she temporarily shared.

DAVE SLIPPED through the mid-day pedestrian traffic, his pace steady and unrushed. He entered a local business, stepped out its back door, and circled around in a randomly circuitous path, hopefully confounding the tail he'd picked up as soon as he'd stepped outside.

He'd discovered he was being followed weeks before his first meeting with Dani, when she'd tried to blackmail him into trading information for her silence. He'd played along, in part because he'd hoped it would lead him to the people tailing him. Instead, he'd been drawn into a millennia old struggle between the immortal Daughters and what Dani's people called the Shadow Enemy.

He'd been sent undercover by the FBI into the heart of that enemy, unaware of their secret function. His official assignment was to infiltrate Lukas Alexiou's businesses and gain the man's trust in order to stop the black market trade of ancient artifacts coming through the city of New York. After his assignment had shifted to include helping the People, specifically Dani, track a distinct group of artifacts, Dave had wondered if his initial job hadn't had a deeper purpose, aligned much more closely with his new job than he'd been told.

He couldn't shake the feeling that there was more to the whole situation.

His mind drifted to the first time he'd met Dani, when she'd stepped out of the shadows into his path. He'd pinned her to a tree, thinking her no more than a young woman impulsively digging into his past. Over time, he'd discovered there was more to her than that. Just last week, he'd learned that she was a seventy-four year old warrior, yet she looked no older than twenty-five, and that on a bad day. And still, he burned with the memory of that first encounter, the mindless attraction, the press of her lithe body into his, her sweet breath panting across his mouth.

He'd known she was trouble from the get-go, that even thinking about starting a relationship with her would end badly, but since learning who and what she was, he couldn't get the idea out of his head. She was dangerous to him, a distraction he couldn't afford, but he couldn't find the strength to push her away.

It didn't help that she was the reason he was there.

Half an hour after leaving his apartment, Dave stopped at a telephone booth and called his handler, Stuart Hampstead, to check in. Stu was a bit of a weasel. An annoying prankster, he never failed to be in the wrong place at the right time. He was also a brownnoser, something Dave personally despised, but not a bad man. Dave had tried hard to like him and found the simple emotion beyond him where the other man was concerned.

"Hey, man," he said.

"Dude, where are you?" Stu said in an urgent whisper. "I been looking all over for you."

Dave paused, caution tightening his spine. He'd been assigned to the People a week ago by the Director of the FBI personally, a move that should've filtered into the right ears by now.

"Listen, things are getting hinky around here," Stu rushed on. "For God's sake, somebody came in and raided my computer today looking for info on you. Then it got back to me that you're being watched, but nobody knows why. You are in deep shit, my friend."

"I'm exactly where I was told to be," Dave said flatly.

"If you say so," Stu muttered. "Just be careful, man. Be real careful. And don't leave the city again without telling me."

Dave disconnected the call and scowled. He'd left word for Stu in a roundabout way letting his handler know what he was up to. Somewhere, a connection had failed. More importantly, Stu had apparently not been kept in the loop.

He considered the implications, then dialed another number and left a brief, coded message before dropping the phone in its cradle. That one would take a while to ferment, leaving him plenty of time to work on Dani's problem. He headed back toward his apartment, not bothering to hide his route, and grunted when he picked up a tail. A block from home, he pulled out his phone and called Alexiou, arranged for a visit the next day, then called an old friend and lined up tickets for that night's game.

It would cost him, but he had a feeling he'd need a bribe to coax Dani into following his lead.

He swung by a souvenir shop and picked up a present for her, hoping to sweeten the pot. Fifteen minutes later, he unlocked the door to his apartment, half expecting her to be gone. He faltered in his tracks when he saw her sitting on the sofa wearing calf-length tights under an old sweatshirt with the collar, hem, and cuffs cut out. Her blonde curls were piled into a loose bun on top of her head, random strands haphazardly framing her pale, oval face. She'd propped her bare feet on his coffee table and was knitting something, her delicate hands moving rapidly through the stitches, emerald cat's eyes hidden as she focused on the work.

His heart turned over with a solid thump. Most women were too intimidated by his silent bulk to stick around long enough for him to come home to them. Sure as hell, none of them felt comfortable enough around him to dress down.

This woman wasn't afraid of him and it turned him on, softening him to her when he needed to be hard, focused.

He shut the door softly, turned the locks automatically, and hung his jacket and cap up. Time to face the music. He was almost looking forward to it.

TWO

D AVE HADN'T RETURNED by the time Dani finished reviewing her notes, so she pulled out her knitting, a handicraft she'd picked up as a child. The repetitive nature of the stitches and the gentle clack of the needles were peaceful, soothing, a welcome contrast to her normally hectic schedule.

She loved having handmade clothes. It reminded her of growing up in Rebecca's household, the safest, happiest time of her life. Her adoptive mother's daughters had rotated in and out on an irregular basis and treated Dani like a doll, dressing her in homemade clothes. Spoiling her. Loving her unconditionally. Her life there had almost made up for not knowing her natural parents.

Dave come in, and she ignored him, still a little angry at him for walking out on her like that. He locked the door behind himself and meticulously hung up his jacket and cap, then dropped down on the couch beside her. His massive shoulder rubbed against hers, and a small frisson of awareness sparked in her.

His gaze locked onto her hands.

"What?" she asked.

"Thought you weren't the little woman type."

"I'm not." She waited for him to reply, then snorted. Dave, saying more than one sentence at a time? Not likely.

Dani set the knitting project aside and shifted to face him, deliberately putting a few inches between them as she drew her legs up onto the couch, folding them in front of her to add another barrier. She rested one hand on her feet and rubbed lightly.

"Cold?" he asked.

"I'll put socks on in a little while. Where were you?"

He ignored her and pulled the small folded blanket off of the back of the sofa. He spread it over her lap, reached under it, and grabbed one of her feet.

She jerked at her foot, firmly trapped in his hands. "Your hands are colder than my feet."

"Nope."

She jerked again, then realized how silly the two of them must look, playing tug of war over her feet. It was a small thing, so she gave in and draped her legs over his lap, leaning her shoulder against the back of the sofa to maintain balance.

He wrapped his hands around her feet under the blanket, chafing them gently, warming them, exploring each one from the tip of her toes around the arches and heels and up her ankles and calves, right up to the bottom edge of her Yoga tights and back again. His work-roughened hands left tingles on her bare skins. Her earlier tension melted away, lulling her.

"Marry me," she said.

His slate gray eyes widened. "What?"

"You cook, you clean up behind yourself, and you give good foot rubs. What more could a girl ask for?"

One corner of his mouth turned up in that lopsided grin of his.

"So, where'd you go?" she asked.

His hands slowed under the blanket until one rested on her ankles and the other on her knees, tucking her legs firmly against his body. "Made some calls."

"And?"

"We have a meeting with Alexiou tomorrow, his place."

"Great." Dani blew out a worried breath and rested her head against the back of the sofa. "Couldn't you have found a more neutral location?"

"He's expecting me to check in, spend some time with him." His eyes swept over her, setting off tingles of another sort low in her abdomen. "You bring a dress?"

"Ah, no. Why?"

"He'll expect you to dress for supper."

She sat straight up. "No. Absolutely not. We were supposed to get information from him, not fraternize."

"Dani," he said, his rough voice even. "Fraternizing with Alexiou is my job. He's already asked us to eat with him, and after, he'll expect us to use my room there."

"What do you mean *us*?"

"Stay the night." His gaze was steady, firm. "Together."

Dani wiggled her legs and yanked them back. "No."

His grip tightened and his eyebrows lowered over his slate colored eyes. "Yes."

Dani gave up and left her legs on his lap. "Look, Neanderthal Man, other women might fall for your little ploys, but I see right through them."

"Alexiou thinks I'm infatuated with you. Unless you want me to turn you over to him, you will help him believe that."

"You've got to be kidding me." Dani flopped back onto the sofa and slapped her hands over her eyes. "Couldn't you find a way around that?"

When he said nothing, Dani peeked out from behind her hands. His expression might as well have been granite, it was so hard, and he seemed completely unmoved by her exasperation.

"Mr. *My way or the highway* Winstead," she murmured. She'd have to give in to him, *again*, either that or go home a failure. "Ok, ok. Just don't think I'm this easy all the time."

"If you were easy, you'd already be in my bed."

His voice was so matter of fact, Dani gaped at him. What a piece of work. Like she'd sleep with such a domineering, over-sized hunk of a caveman.

Even if he was nearly a three hubba guy.

Hey, even she had some standards, and the line stopped at sub-human species.

"We could take a test run," he said.

She sucked in a breath, ready to scorch him with a scathing comment. His mouth quirked into one of his almost-smiles, and all the anger rushed out of her. "You made a joke. Wow."

He smiled then, a full blown stretch of his mouth that lit up his face, shaving years off his appearance. Smiling, he was boyish and charming, a far cry from his normally stoic demeanor. "Had to try," he said with a rumbling laugh.

She stifled her humor and the urge to goose him into more laughter. Dave happy? Yeah, more than three hubbas. "What's next, then?"

His fingers shifted and curved around her leg, rubbing gently along the back of her thigh. "Game tonight."

Heat spread up Dani's body and her toes curled. Man, she was easy. "We're going to a game."

"Football."

He pulled a hand out from under the blanket and grabbed something laying on his other side that Dani hadn't noticed him carrying, then plopped a cap on her head. She tugged it off and gave it a good look-see.

"You got me a New York Giants hat. What a sweetie," she said, deliberately keeping her voice flat, hiding her surprise over the gift. It touched off a schmoopy romantic chord within her. Other women liked jewelry and fine dining. Apparently, sports paraphernalia and a football game were her things.

He shook his head at her in a silent chide.

"Why are we going to a game?" she asked.

"Information."

She bit her lip, oddly disappointed that the gift was work related. Which should've been obvious. All Dave thought about was work.

"And fun." He brushed a fingertip across the tip of her nose. "Haven't been to a game in a while. Thought you might like to go."

"Sure."

"Better get going then."

Dave tugged the blanket off her legs, and Dani scooted away from him. He stood and held out his hands to her, and she took them, allowing him to pull her up. Her body bumped against his as she rose and his hands fell to her waist, steadying her, pulling her closer than was probably necessary. Maybe.

He gazed down at her, a curious look on his face, like he didn't know quite what to do with her.

That made two of them. She didn't know what to do with him either.

REBECCA UPTON stood at one end of the conference table waiting for the members of the Council of Seven to file into the room. Each was accompanied by at least one assistant, who attended the meeting to take notes and perform other small tasks for the councilmembers.

As was customary, Lydia took the head of the table directly opposite Rebecca's position. Lydia descended from Kiya, the eldest of the Seven Sisters, the progenitors of the modern People. She was a small woman and beautiful, with silky black hair and large brown eyes set in a pale, oval face. Though still immortal, because of her great age she appeared to be a few years older than the younger immortals at the table, all of whom appeared to be in their early to mid-twenties.

It was the hardest aspect of their lives to explain, even beyond the curse granting Daughters immortality. While immortal Daughters appeared ageless to mortals, the natural aging process had only slowed, not stopped.

The other councilmembers assumed their places between Lydia and Rebecca, with representatives of the elder sisters sitting closest to Lydia. Anya, the sister of Rebecca's mother, represented the line of Abragni, the youngest of the Sisters, and so sat on Rebecca's left.

Rebecca furtively studied her aunt as the councilmembers and their retinue situated themselves around the IECS'S largest conference room. Anya had become mortal in 1948 when she'd fallen in love with her now-deceased husband, Goddess keep him, and had submitted her will to his, a necessary condition preceding the lifting of the immortal curse placed upon the Sisters and their female descendants. Her hair had faded to white over the years, but was still worn in two long braids, an unbroken habit left over from Anya's childhood. Her pale blue eyes twinkled mischievously, a trait that had sent Rebecca into giggles during her own childhood nearly a thousand years past.

They had always been close. Anya had been her biggest supporter in Rebecca's bid to direct the IECS, yet it was Anya's name heading the list of possible traitors Rebecca's own daughter had compiled and turned in a few weeks prior.

That knowledge had thrown Rebecca. Betrayal by one she loved dearly, by a woman that had, truth be told, been as much a mother to Rebecca as her own mother had been? It was unthinkable.

When everyone was settled, Rebecca sat down and called the meeting to order, greeting each councilmember in turn for the record being kept by her own assistant.

Had the Seven Sisters ever dreamed the People would grow large enough to need such bureaucratic necessities as meeting minutes?

Rebecca flipped the report in front of her open. "We have several items on the agenda today, beginning with old business. For your convenience, page three of your reports summarizes the discovery of a Daughter's remains in an anomalous grave at the Sandby borg site."

She paused for a moment, allowing everyone adequate time to review a summary of the information the IECS had accumulated on the archaeological dig at the fifth century Swedish land fort. That burial had prompted her to send Maya Bellegarde to investigate further, to the benefit of the People. Not only had the grave contained an armband adorned with the Eye of Marnan, it had also held a cache of documents pertaining to the People's history. The last meeting of the Council had taken place not long after the Daughter's grave was uncovered and artifacts from it, including a portion of the texts, were stolen by person or persons unknown, and had eventually fallen into the hands of their ancient enemy.

"The big question is, of course, who was that Daughter?" Rebecca met the gaze of each councilmember in turn. "Hopefully, everyone has had an opportunity to review memories and any personal records for information on the identity of this Daughter. She was wearing the Eye of Marnan. Could she have been of that line?"

Miriam, a small, dark-haired immortal Daughter of the line of Marnan, slowly shook her head. "We're still looking into it. That time period was a particularly violent one for the immortal Daughters of our line. Many were killed or went missing, never to be heard from again. But we are looking, and not just in the records of our line. Every descendant of Marnan whom we can reach is searching, even the ones long mortal." She smiled, a sweet expression at odds with her normally serious countenance. "We are eager to claim her."

"Of course." Rebecca returned the councilmember's smile. Whenever possible, the People kept meticulous records of the lineages of all immortal Daughters and mortal children to the second generation from immortality, but many gaps remained, particularly in the eras when the People were hunted relentlessly.

"I'd like to remind everyone to make certain their families are submitting DNA tests to our labs. Our head geneticist assures me that she'll be able to take a DNA sample from the Sandby borg Daughter's bones. Having adequate genetic samples from the living population will facilitate a match between her and us."

"We shall ensure it," Miriam said.

"Our geneticist would deeply appreciate that. Does anyone else have anything to add?" When no one spoke, Rebecca continued. "Then please turn to page five."

Rebecca took the Council through the events that had occurred just after the last meeting: bringing in James Terhune to translate and interpret the documents found in the Sandby borg grave; the kidnapping of James's daughter, Amelia, by the Shadow Enemy, who had demanded the Sandby borg artifacts as ransom; and the botched exchange during which Maya Bellegarde had been wounded.

"Two cases of the artifacts were recovered," Rebecca explained, "but one case was taken from the warehouse by an unknown woman."

"You are tracking this woman, I presume," asked Miriam.

"Daniella Nehring is working on discovering the woman's identity as we speak," Rebecca assured her. "We should have a photograph of her from warehouse security within the next few days. If necessary, a copy will be circulated among the People to facilitate identification."

"And the Shadow Enemy?" asked Phœbe, a mortal Daughter of the line of Eleni. "Shall we pursue them as well?"

"That is one topic we must discuss today, and it is a subject that pains me." Rebecca folded her hands together on top of the table. "We have been led astray, my sisters. The Shadow Enemy has not lain dormant these past few decades, as I and many of you have been told, but has instead increased in strength and numbers. This information has been deliberately hidden from the People, possibly by one of our own."

Gasps rose around the table and from the host of assistants scattered around the room. Rebecca was careful not to scrutinize any one individual too closely, but took note of each one's reaction. Anya frowned, but otherwise remained impassive, and Rebecca's heart sank. Surely her aunt wasn't complicit in the betrayal of the People.

"Please, be calm." Rebecca pitched her voice over the gathering whispers as people shifted and spoke to their neighbors. "We're investigating and, with the cooperation of each of you and the People at large, I have faith that we'll get to the bottom of this matter in a timely fashion."

"Are you certain there is a traitor among us?" Gwendolyn, a mortal Daughter of the line of Lilleni, asked softly.

"It's unthinkable," said Isolde, a mortal Daughter representing the line of Bagda. "The People are stronger than that and united in our cause. Why would anyone betray us?"

"Nonsense, Isolde." Anya gazed one by one at each of the women gathered around the table. "Most of us are united in our need to break the curse, but there are those among us who enjoy their immortality and subtly undermine the efforts of the larger group. Surely you've not forgotten the rise and destruction of the Eternal Order?"

A tense silence descended upon the group.

"They are gone now, with no survivors," said Eleanor, an immortal Daughter representing the line of Ganenda.

"I have heard rumors," Gwendolyn began.

Isolde hissed out a breath. "Half-truths and fairy tales. They were never much more than a myth."

"Hardly." Anya's voice held a hint of censure. "Though they were certainly before your time."

"Surely this is a moot point, as the Eternal Order is defunct," Miriam said. "We are much more rational now, much more tempered in our manners as a people. Could any of us ever openly betray the common cause simply because some among us wish to have longer lives?"

The discussion continued among the council members. Rebecca let the conversation wash over her, mentally noting each individual's reaction. It was hard to believe that any one of these women, who'd devoted large portions of their lives to the People, could ever betray them.

When the debate had gone on for several minutes and was in danger of collapsing into tedium, Lydia spoke. "Enough." She waited until she held everyone's attention before continuing. "Rebecca will continue her investigation. Until she discovers the exact nature of the betrayal and knows who has been doing what, our discussion is pointless." To Rebecca, she said, "You will have our full cooperation."

Rebecca nodded politely. "Thank you. Now, if there are no other questions on that matter, we have a few other items to discuss."

The meeting continued as they usually did, in depth and at length. Rebecca had refreshments brought in and listened to the concerned whispers among the councilmembers' retinues. Several hours after it had begun, Rebecca adjourned the meeting, weary after the ordeal of measuring every single person in the room. A persistent ache built behind her eyes and she longed for a glass of chilled wine, a steamy bath, and her husband's kind embrace, not necessarily in that order.

As the councilmembers filed out, Anya pulled Rebecca aside. "You look tired, kaetyrm. These past few weeks have been difficult, yes?"

"It's been busy."

"Why have you not told me of your concerns?"

Rebecca rested her hands on the table, watching the final stragglers as they huddled near the room's exit. When she was certain she couldn't be overheard, she said, "I don't know whom to trust."

"Bah! You were always so cautious," Anya scolded. "Now, you don't trust your own family?"

"I have reason not to."

"What do you mean?" Anya lowered her voice. "Say it plainly."

"I have a list of people whom I suspect may have been hiding information about the Shadow Enemy and who may be in league with them. Your name is at the top."

Anya gasped and stepped back, and the color leached out of her wrinkled face. "I would never betray the People. Never!"

"And me?" Rebecca rubbed her forehead, suddenly weary of the entire matter. "Would you betray your sister's daughter?"

"You and I have much to discuss, child, but not here. Here is not safe. Too many blasted ears." Anya cupped her hands over Rebecca's shoulders and squeezed gently. "You must trust me until then."

Rebecca couldn't bring herself to assert that, yes, she trusted her aunt, but she unbent enough to kiss Anya's wrinkled cheek goodbye. Family had always been so important to her, as it was among most of the People. It was what banded them together against the world. Surely she could give her mother's sister time to explain herself before branding her a traitor.

As Anya walked out of the room, followed closely by her staff, Rebecca was torn between loyalty and duty. She would have to choose one eventually, but not until she had more information. She gave instructions to her assistant to close down the conference room, then went home to try to regain her perspective.

THE GIANTS were losing, again. Dave slouched in his seat and watched the disaster unfold on the field below them, one ear tuned to Dani's grousing.

"Next time, I get to be the winning team." She slapped the Giants cap he'd given her against her thigh. "Look at that. My sisters can run faster."

After meeting her mother and seeing Dani in action a time or two, he could believe it. The People were a fiercely athletic bunch. "Chiefs is my home team."

"Convenient." The Chiefs scored a touchdown, and Dani's shoulders slumped. "I thought you said we were going to have fun."

"We are."

She turned a withering glare on him, sniffed, then focused on the game.

He left her alone, content to watch the game and her reaction to it. She'd told him flat out she wasn't a Giants fan, but had decided to root for them just this once. "To match the hat," she'd said. He'd been surprised to learn that she knew the Giants' dismal record before going into the game, that she was competitive enough to mourn their poor performance, and loyal enough to shoot a dirty look at him every time the Chiefs made a good play.

Or maybe she was still pissed that he'd left her alone most of the day and wouldn't tell her where he'd been.

In the third quarter, he spotted the reason he'd brought her to the game. "Hot dog?"

She nodded, her attention fixed on the play in progress.

He held up two fingers to an elderly man whose ebony face and white curls glowed under the stadium's lights as he walked up the stairs carrying a tray of food. Dave pulled out his wallet and extracted several bills folded precisely, passing them to the person next to him, who passed them down the line to the concessioner, who took the money and passed two steaming, wrapped hot dogs back to Dave in the same manner.

Dave handed one to Dani. She muttered a thanks, unwrapped the dog, and took a hearty bite.

He ate his own in silence, amusement curling through him as Dani hastily swallowed a bite and yelled at the refs for making a bad call, her voice joining the roar of the crowd. He bided his time, waiting until the end of the quarter before judging enough time had passed.

"Need a refill?" he asked.

"Sure." She scrounged around under her seat one-handed, her attention on the game, and handed him an empty cup to throw away. "Get me a coke, wouldja?"

"Pepsi ok?"

"Coke, Pepsi. Whatever." The Giants fumbled the ball, and she yelled, "Butterfingers!"

He kissed the top of her head, dodged her hands slapping him out of the way, and pushed through the filled seats, wending his way to a mostly empty section of the tunnels surrounding the stadium. The concessioner was already there, hovering in the shadows of a side tunnel, his thin body stooped over his tray.

"Hey, man," the old man said, his wrinkled face creasing into a smile. "Where you been?"

"Busy."

Dave grinned and held out his hand. Jimmy had been his first contact in New York and had guided him through some tough moments on his rookie undercover assignment.

Jimmy grasped Dave's hand, his smile widening into a chuckle. "You work too much, man. Got to take some time, get some relaxation." His twinkling eyes narrowed. "That why you bring company to the game? Never seen you with a woman before."

"Sorry, Jimmy. She's work."

"Son, all women is work. What you need?"

"Information. Can you have Junior meet me three days from today?"

Jimmy stroked arthritic fingers over his chin. "Well, now, I suppose so. Where at?"

"You know where. About ten in the morning?"

"Sure, man," Jimmy agreed. "We got to get the network going?"

"Yeah."

"Must be important to bring you out of hiding. Is it that woman you got?"

"In a way."

Jimmy shook his head. "She too pretty to be that kinda trouble."

Dave grinned at the old man. "Jimmy, all women are trouble."

Jimmy cackled, picked up his equipment, and shuffled off.

Dave located a concession stand and bought two drinks. He made it back to Dani in time to see the Chiefs score. She burst out of her seat, jeering with the home crowd. A tendril of warmth crept through him. She was beautiful to watch, no matter what she was doing.

She plopped into her seat and leaned casually against him. "What'd the old man have to say?"

Dave draped an arm around her shoulder, drawing her closer. "Later," he whispered against her ear, and she shivered.

Somehow, he wasn't surprised that she'd figured out what he was up to. It just meant he'd have to be more careful in the future. *Protect her*, he thought, and turned his attention back to the game.

THREE

HE MORNING after the game, Dave hurried Dani through a string of posh boutiques searching for appropriate dinner wear. So sue her because she hadn't brought a dress. She'd never expected he'd drag her to eat with the *leader of the People's enemy*. When she made that point to him, he stared at her stonily and said, "Guest or hostage. Your choice."

She gave in, again, and ticked a mark on her imaginary score card: Caveman 3, Dani 0.

How was it that she was more than twice his age and he still got the better of her?

In the third shop they visited, he pulled out a tight, emerald Lycra sheath for her to try on, and she immediately put her foot down. No way was she going to dinner dressed like a tart.

That evening, as they pulled into the drive of Alexiou's country home, Dani congratulated herself for gaining the upper hand. The elegant black halter dress she'd chosen suited her and the occasion perfectly, especially paired with the delicate evening jacket the sales girl had recommended. The strappy heels she'd found to go with the dress put her just below eye level with Dave. It made her feel as if they were on a more equal footing. Whether they were or not was another matter entirely.

The Alexiou estate was as luxurious as Dani had expected it to be. Dave had broken his laconic stoicism and shared details of the main house's construction during the pre-Black Friday boom at the height of the Industrial Revolution. It sat on a hundred acres of prime rural real estate in upstate New York, far enough away to be an escape from Alexiou's holdings in New York City, not so far as to be a hard commute.

The main house was three stories of Gothic Revival architecture, grim and imposing, with impeccably manicured lawns and a long, circling drive paved with cobblestones. Alexiou's driver stopped the car at the front entrance, and Dani waited like a well-mannered lady for him to open the door and hand her out.

Though doing so was pointless. At her age, if she didn't know how to get out of a car on her own, there was no hope she ever would. Still, she was determined to be polite, even without Dave's glowering reminder. She needed access to the warehouse's security footage in order to complete her job. Without it, she might as well be searching for a needle in a haystack. So, polite she'd be, even if it killed her.

The driver was an elderly man, stooped and gray, with the sweetest smile and a twinkle in his faded periwinkle eyes. "If you will, sir. I'll have your baggage sent to your room and the dear lady's as well, yes?"

Dani patted his hand gently, charming the old man into a blush. "You're very kind."

Dave leveled a strange look on her as they walked up the stairs leading to the main entrance, barred by two heavy, wooden doors.

"What?" she said. "I can be nice."

He grunted and swung the door effortlessly open on a brightly lit, ornate foyer. A uniformed man stood at the base of the stairs opposite the front door. He took their coats and informed Dave that "Master Alexiou" was waiting for them in the parlor.

Dave slid his arm around Dani's waist and guided her to the parlor tucked away behind the foyer. The room's door opened onto an opulently furnished sitting area. A fire crackled in the fireplace set into one wall, throwing a welcome warmth into the chill of New England's early fall. A baby grand piano sat on the opposite side of the room, its finish gleaming in the room's dim lighting.

Lukas Alexiou rose as they approached, as did the room's two other occupants, a man several years Lukas's junior and a young boy of maybe seven with sun streaked hair and tanned skin.

"Ah, Mr. Winstead. At last." Lukas shook Dave's hand, then gripped Dani's in firm fingers and lifted it to his lips. "Ms. Nehring. How delightful it is to see you again, and under much more favorable circumstances. Please, allow me to introduce my brother, Marco, and my nephew, Steven."

Dani nodded to each in turn, receiving a cold glare from Marco and a curious stare from his son. Marco looked a lot like his older brother, with dark hair, blue eyes, and sharply chiseled features. His son was quite different, his lighter features and rounder face inherited, Dani guessed, from his absent mother.

"Mama says if I'm not a good boy, the Daughters will eat me in my sleep," Steven said solemnly, his serious gray eyes guileless. "Are you a Daughter?"

Marco uttered an appalled, "Steven!"

Dani ignored him and knelt in front of the boy. "I am, but I only eat boys who are at least this high, Master Steven." She held her hand well over his head. "As long as you're a good boy and mind your mother, I promise not to eat you."

"Okey dokey." He burst into a smile, showing a gap in his front teeth. "I'm this many. How many are you?" He held up one hand with fingers spread wide and Dani revised her estimate of his age downward.

She ruffled the silky curls of his hair and grinned. "More than that."

Dave helped her solicitously back to her feet. The warmth of his hard grip on her elbow simmered through her.

Marco held his hand out for Steven. "Time to wash up."

Steven obediently took his father's hand. As he bounced out of the room, he said, "Did you hear, Daddy? She said she wouldn't eat me."

"Cute kid," Dani said.

Something close to fondness softened Lukas's features. "He is a very special child. I appreciate your kindness."

Dani shrugged. "Children should be loved and protected."

Lukas inclined his head toward her. "A point on which we both agree."

She bit her tongue, holding back a harsh reminder that not long ago, he'd used a child as a pawn in the war between their peoples.

A uniformed man glided into the room and announced dinner. Lukas insisted on escorting her into the dining room, chatting affably with her, and Dani gritted her teeth. Polite. She had to be polite if she wanted to track down the artifacts.

Compared to the parlor, the dining room was simply furnished, almost sparse in its starkness. The walls were painted a deep purple above darkly stained wainscoting. Framed landscapes dotted the purple at even intervals. Windows on one end of the room went from nearly floor to ceiling and were covered with layers of draperies, the top one sage green in color. A long buffet occupied the opposite wall, to the left of the room's entrance. A massive wooden table ran down the center of the room.

Five place settings were set at one end of the table. Lukas led Dani to the opposite side and seated her two places down from its head. Dave sat down to her right, while Lukas took his place at the head. Marco and Steven came in behind them and settled on Lukas's right-hand side, with Steven in a booster seat across from Dani.

She caught Steven's eye and winked. He grinned at her and blinked both eyes hard at her.

As soon as they were settled, servants entered the room bearing trays of plated food. Dani groaned under her breath when she realized the meal would be served as courses.

Which is what she got for flirting with Steven instead of paying attention to the table setting.

"I hope you enjoy the cuisine, Ms. Nehring," Lukas said as the servants stepped away from the table. "We have a new chef, trained here in New York. I haven't the patience for haute cuisine. Thankfully, Chef Ephraim has a lovely way with our local dishes."

"I'm sure it will be wonderful," she murmured. She'd had her share of fine dining in her youth, and had enjoyed it then, as well as the attention lavished on her as she rose to a loose sort of fame. Now, she preferred simple and wholesome, more in keeping with the People's traditional diet, and was relieved that the chef apparently did, too.

As one course followed another, Dani allowed the men's conversation to flow around her, contributing only when directly addressed. She sampled each course instead of eating heartily, not from fear of poison or drugs. Dave would never allow that, she was sure.

She narrowed her eyes into slits. On the other hand, he'd shot her with a tranquilizer dart, so maybe he'd only allow other people to drug her.

As accustomed as she was to taking care of herself, to seeing to her own safety, it amazed her how secure she felt around him. That security unsettled her, and she tried to shake it off. Dave was not a man she could trust. He'd already betrayed her in a misguided attempt to protect her. She couldn't afford to forget that he might do so again.

After the meal, they retired to the parlor, a society ritual she could've done without. She waved away Lukas's offer of an after-dinner drink and sat beside Dave, who passed as well. He draped his arm behind her along the top of the settee. The material of his suit jacket brushed against her upper back and the heat of his fingers, curved around her shoulders, seared her skin through her own jacket.

The evening dragged on. The men continued their small talk. Dani tuned it out. She didn't want to know what they were discussing. Steven fidgeted beside his father, yawned, and his shoulders slumped. Poor kid must be bored to tears. She knew exactly how he felt.

She hated the polite tedium of society gatherings, and had since she'd left the pretense of that life behind. There were some things she hadn't forgotten, like the music that had lured her from Rebecca's home into the limelight. The piano on the other end of the parlor called to her, a sharp reminder of her forgotten love.

"Would you like to play, Ms. Nehring?" Lukas asked.

Dave's hand tightened against her shoulder, and Dani hesitated. She hadn't played in years, but at Lukas's casual invitation, her fingers itched to stroke the piano's keys. "If you don't mind."

Lukas's eyes glinted and a small smile played around his refined mouth. "Please, help yourself."

Dani rose and strode calmly to the piano, raising its lid. She settled herself on the stool, adjusted her length to the pedals, and rested her hands on the keys. Rachmaninoff, she thought, and began playing the opening measures to Prelude Opus 3 No. 2 in C# minor, allowing the music to pull her into its seductive beauty as it moved from a sedate adagio to wildly passionate and back again, carrying her emotions with it.

She played the entire piece, pleased at her near flawless performance, if not by the inner turmoil of passion it stirred. The final notes of the piece faded slowly. She closed the lid on the music's beauty and returned to her place on the settee amid the men's polite applause.

"Marvelous, Ms. Nehring," Lukas said. "It's such a shame you left the stage."

"Everybody grows up, Mr. Alexiou."

"True," he agreed. "Still, I heard you were quite talented in your youth. I believe our grandparents even attended one of your performances."

Dave's stare bored into her, unnerving Dani. They didn't discuss the past or their personal lives, but if her turn at the piano surprised him, it didn't show. She shifted her gaze around the room, searching for a change of subject to ease the discomfort his stare caused, and noticed Steven curled up beside his father, fast asleep. "Poor kid. I guess my playing did that."

"It's past his bedtime," Marco said, his voice glacial. "If you'll excuse me, I'll take him to his room."

Marco picked his son up and walked swiftly out the door without another word. When he was gone, Lukas sighed and set his empty glass on a side table. "My apologies, Ms. Nehring. Marco is not as...enlightened as I am when it comes to the People."

"I'm not enlightened at all when it comes to the Shadow Enemy," she retorted.

Beside her Dave tensed and his arm tightened painfully around her shoulders.

Lukas laughed lightly. "And why should you be? We are blood enemies, are we not? Still, you were kind to my nephew. Perhaps there is hope for a reconciliation in the future."

"Not likely."

"Dani," Dave warned, his gravelly voice a soft rumble.

"It's quite all right, Mr. Winstead," Lukas said, his gaze steady. "The enmity between our peoples has a long and bloody history. Progress cannot be made overnight, but that is why we are here tonight."

"How do you figure?" Dani asked.

"Unlike my brother, I believe there should be peace between our peoples. I would like to see the hostilities ceased, if not today, then certainly in my lifetime."

Dani sucked in a breath, trying and failing to temper her anger. "Is that why you're building an army and stealing artifacts and kidnapping innocent children?"

"We did not steal the artifacts, Ms. Nehring. I merely took advantage when they became available for sale."

"What are you saying?"

"I'm saying," he said, his voice calm and precise, "that the Shadow Enemy was not responsible for the theft of the Sandby borg artifacts."

Dani considered that for a minute, uncertainty tugging at her. Why would he lie? On the other hand, why would he tell the truth? "If not you, then who?"

Lukas shrugged. "Perhaps you will discover that during your investigation of the mysterious woman."

She eyed his casual unconcern, certain he was hiding something. He had to've gotten the artifacts from somebody, possibly even the person that had stolen them. "An investigation you'll voluntarily assist."

"Of course. I have as much to gain from uncovering this woman's identity as do the People."

"Sure," Dani scoffed.

"Believe me or not, Ms. Nehring, but this, at least, is truth."

Dave stood and held out a hand to her. "Bedtime."

The single word held a hard, flat anger. Dani slid her hand in his and rose, ignoring the heat rippling through her blood. He could be mad if he wanted to. It wouldn't stop her from needling the truth out of his boss.

"Good night, then." Lukas stood and nodded to Dave. "I shall see you bright and early in the morning, Mr. Winstead. Ms. Nehring, please make yourself at home here."

"Thank you," she murmured, aiming for gracious, probably missing by a mile. It was hard to be anything good or kind in the presence of a man responsible for so much destruction.

Dave led her upstairs, his strides slow and even, but Dani knew he was still miffed with her. Well, too bad. He'd dragged her into this situation. Surely he couldn't blame her for taking advantage of it to learn what she could, and tweaking Lukas's nose while she was at it.

She risked a sideways glance at him and sighed. His face looked like it had been carved out of granite, it was so hard. Looked like she was going to get chewed out good this time.

DAVE LED DANI into the bedroom he used at Lukas's estate and shut the door tightly behind them. "Get into your nightclothes. We're going to bed."

Dani snorted. "Forget it, Ape Man."

Dave gritted his teeth. In two strides, he was at her side, his hands latched around her upper arms. He yanked her body into his, firmly quelling her struggles, and brushed his mouth against her ear. "We're being watched."

She stopped struggling. "You're just saying that so you'll have an excuse to paw me."

"I'm saying that because it's true. Installed the cameras in here myself. They're everywhere except the bathrooms."

"Great, only, I didn't bring pajamas."

Weariness seeped through him and he sighed. "You knew we'd be sleeping here."

"Yeah, but I didn't think you'd really make me sleep in the same bed as you."

He bit back an oath and released her, then stalked to the chest of drawers and pulled out one of his t-shirts. He tossed it to her and jerked his chin toward the bathroom. "Help yourself."

She tossed her head and flounced out of the room. God, she drove him crazy. He'd told her they'd be sharing a room, told her it was the best way, but had she listened? Oh, no, not pigheaded Dani. Why did everything have to be so difficult with her?

He loosened his tie and yanked it over his head, tossed it onto the chest of drawers along with his belt. He hung his suit up, then stripped out of the button-down shirt, t-shirt, and socks he'd worn under it. He lobbed those into the dirty clothes basket and dropped onto the edge of the bed.

A whole night alone with Dani, his t-shirt and their underwear the only things between them.

He switched the bedside lamp on, grabbed the Western he was reading, and stretched out on top of the covers. Frustration clashed with desire, tearing at him. She was so beautiful, so real, and he wanted her so much, need burned through him every time she was close, roiling, aching, consuming need. The night ahead loomed large, distracting him from his book. Her half naked under the covers next to him, her lithe body relaxed in sleep. He sucked in a breath and forced his attention onto the words in front of him.

Dani sashayed out of the bathroom carrying her dress, evening jacket, and heels, her long, supple legs bare beneath the hem of his t-shirt. She jerked to a stop, her emerald eyes wide as they roved down the length of his body and back up again.

He watched her out of the corner of his eye as she shook her head and continued walking to the stack of luggage resting on one side of the room. The lamplight glimmered over the toned muscles of her legs. She leaned over and his t-shirt rode up, flashing lacy underwear.

Heat roared through him and his body hardened.

Deliberately, he turned his attention back to the Western, ignoring her. She grabbed her bag of toiletries and went back into the bathroom, and walked out a few minutes later smelling like toothpaste and soap. He marked his place in the Western and took his turn in the small room, brushing his teeth, washing his face, anything to give his erection time to soften.

The weather was supposed to be nice that weekend. Maybe they'd go out to another game. He needed to call his mom, check on the family. Hey, how about those Yankees?

When he reentered the bedroom, she was lying on her back under the covers, staring at the ceiling. His penis stirred back to life and he cursed under his breath. One look at her and he was a goner. Hell with it. She'd just have to deal. He cut off the lamp and slid under the covers next to her, ignoring her stiffness.

He propped up on one elbow beside her. Moonlight streamed through the windows, throwing silver glints across her pale features and the loose curls of her hair flowing across her pillow. Her eyes were wide, solemn. In anybody else, he would've said she was apprehensive, but not her. Not his Dani. She was strong and tough and beautiful.

She blinked up at him, and his heart skipped and jumped and softened. He brushed her hair away from her face and slid a silky strand through his fingers, just to see how it felt curling around his skin. Cool, smooth, beautiful, exactly like her. He scooted closer to her and bent toward her, intending only to kiss the tip of her pert nose.

She flinched back, out of his reach. "I'm not having sex with you."

He rolled on top of her, settling himself into the juncture of her thighs. Her body was warm against his, giving, and he stifled a groan. It felt so good to nestle against her, for her sex to cup his erection.

"What are you doing?" she hissed.

"Not having sex."

He rubbed his mouth over hers, easy and gentle, and she melted under him, hitched in a sharp breath, curled her fingers over his ribs. He darted his tongue out, tasting her lips, and she opened to him. Honey. That's what she was, pure, womanly honey. She stroked her tongue against his, and desire burst through him, strong and swift, fever bright. Her wet heat teased him through their underwear, the only barrier between them, and he tangled his hands in her hair. Had to control it, had to protect her. He couldn't rip the fabric away and slide into her tight, slick beauty.

He groaned. God, yes, he wanted that, wanted to push into her, please her, wanted to feel her come around him, her nails digging into his skin, her breath panting across his skin.

He broke the kiss while he still could and feathered kisses over her jaw, flicked the tip of his tongue against her earlobe. "Keep it down. Somebody's probably listening."

"Fine." She shoved against his chest. "Do we have to do this?"

He skimmed his face over hers and nipped her other ear, breathing into it as he spoke. "Alexiou thinks we're lovers."

She bit his shoulder, and he winced. "Who told him that?"

"Nobody." He grazed his lips over hers in a swift, teasing taste. "You'll be safer if he believes it."

"I'm not having sex with you," she gritted out.

"Don't have to. You don't have to do anything you don't want. Chrissake, Dani, help me out here."

"This is just an excuse for you to get your hands on me."

He breathed out a laugh. "Of course, it is, but there are better ways to do it."

"Like what?"

"Like coming to your room when we're alone in my apartment." He touched his lips to hers again, licked the tip of his tongue into the corners of her mouth. Her breath shallowed and thinned, and his hips jerked against hers, reflexively seeking her heat. "We could've done this a long time ago and you know it."

"Mmm. Maybe after I saw your chest."

His lips curled into a satisfied smile and he filed her admission away under, *How to get Dani to have sex.*

She skimmed her hands up and down his ribs, petting him. "So you want to put on an act for Alexiou's benefit."

"To protect you." He rocked against her, rubbing the length of his erection against the core of her body, taunting himself with the promise of her warmth. What he wouldn't give to make it real, to sink into her, to know all of her. "How well can you fake it?"

"Oh, Davy," she said loudly. "Give it to me, you stud."

He bit back a laugh, and his anger over the way she'd acted earlier evaporated. "Cut it out, Dani."

She batted her eyelashes. "You asked."

He buried his face in her neck, and her hair tickled his nose. He breathed in her scent, absorbed it, held it deep in his lungs. It would have to tide him over for a while, maybe a long while.

She moaned softly and turned her head to the side, giving him better access, and her hands tightened against his ribs. "Keep that up and it won't be an act."

"Mmm. Really?" Another item for the file. Dani liked his face rubbing into her throat. Good to know.

He kissed her again and braced himself on one forearm above her. He stroked down over her body, cupped her breast through her t-shirt. It filled his hand, fit perfectly in his palm. Would she let him taste her there, let him suck her nipple into his mouth? Would she arch under him and beg him to never stop?

Her breath hitched and shuddered across his chest. "You're trying to seduce me."

"Not me."

Though, maybe he should try, just once. He shifted and bit her nipple gently through the t-shirt, and laved the flat of his tongue over it. It hardened under his caress. Yeah, that was good.

She gasped and cupped his head, pressing him against her. "Yes, you. If it meant doing your job, you'd sell your own mother out."

"Not quite." But close enough to the mark to sting a little.

He skated his hand across her ribs, curled his fingers around them, and rubbed his thumb over the underside of her breast. The thin material of her t-shirt dragged against her skin, the friction tantalizingly light. She arched her back, pushing her breasts into him, silently begging for more.

He gave in. Why shouldn't he? She was here, she wanted him, and he needed so much to please her. He scraped the pad of his thumb around her nipple through the shirt, over and over again, and ached to know more. Would she let him touch her like this skin on skin or would he never know what she felt like, no barriers, no holds barred, just her?

"This feels like sex," she said.

"Honey, if this were sex, I'd already have you naked with my face between your thighs." He cupped her breast, strumming the nipple. "My mouth on your sex, licking and teasing. Just for starters." Unable to resist the temptation, he sucked her nipple into his mouth through her t-shirt, nibbled the hard little pebble, released it on a groan. "If we were at home, I'd put my mouth there now, taste you, figure out how to make you come using my tongue and my fingers buried inside you."

"Oh." She drew the word out into a needy moan and her eyelids fluttered closed. "Wow. I think I just came a little."

He laughed, low and rough, and she shivered. It was exactly the reaction he'd craved. "I want to be there, Dani. Tell me you want it, too."

She breathed his name, a soft, whispering sigh, and his control wavered. Couldn't take her, not here, but he could please her. He slid his hand between them, yanked his underwear out of the way, and slid the tip of his erection over her pussy through her underwear. Her fingers bruised his skin and she writhed beneath him, and he *burned*. He slipped a finger under the edge of her panties into the slick folds of her core, hot, wet honey. What would it feel like to slide his erection into her, to have that wet heat surround him? Just once, he wanted to know. He dipped his finger into her, probing her tight core, and she moaned. Greedy satisfaction thrummed through him. Yeah, that was it. That was what she needed.

He eased his finger in and out, and grimaced. She was tight and small, too small for him. He'd never fit, even if they could have sex, and he wanted that, wanted it so badly it messed with his focus. He pulled his finger out and circled it around the nub of her sex, shifting his fingers experimentally over it, discovering exactly what pleased her, and she rewarded him with soft cries and twisting hips.

Her breath panted out of her as he caressed her. She raked her fingernails down his back, scoring the skin lightly, gripping him to her, silently urging him on. When he was sure she was close to an orgasm, he covered her and yanked the blankets up, preserving at least some of her modesty, and rocked against her, hard and fast, his erection caught between them. She slid her legs down his and rolled her hips up, meeting every thrust with one of her own.

He grazed his cheek over hers and whispered, "Can you come like this?"

"Probably," she gasped.

He licked her ear and braced himself on one forearm, gripped her bottom and fitted her to his thrusting hips. She writhed and arched and her hips undulated, and his control slipped dangerously close to breaking.

Had to pull back, had to, but God, it was so good. The silky fabric of her underwear skidded along the underside of his dick, scalding him, shoving him closer to the edge. He wrenched himself back and focused on her. She was close, so close. He could help her the rest of the way. "Want to?"

A strangled laugh choked out of her throat. "What a question."

He took that to mean *yes* and captured her mouth with his, absorbing the soft sounds of her passion as he rubbed against her, bringing her closer to orgasm. He sucked gently on her lips, tangled his tongue with hers, and she shuddered and cried out her release, and his body tightened. He reined himself in, but just barely. She was so beautiful, so hot. It was all he could do to groan like he'd come and rock against her in a fake aftermath. After a minute, he rolled off her and threw an arm over his eyes, and breathed through the high of almost being inside her.

Dani rolled over with him, slid an arm across his sweat-slicked chest, and rubbed a knee over his legs. A hum of satisfaction purred out of her, raking over his skin, and his breath whooshed out. Good thing she hadn't purred like that when he was on top of her or nothing would've stopped him from being inside her.

Her knee grazed his erection and she stilled. "You didn't come," she whispered. She brushed a hand lightly along his body and rested it over his hard length. "Why didn't you come?"

"Have to get up early in the morning." Her fingers folded over his dick, stroking him, and he arched into her. So close, so close. He put his hand over hers and squeezed. "Once I start, I won't stop until you have nothing left to give."

"Sounds like it might take a while," she said, her voice sultry sweet. She tightened her grip in spite of his restraining hand and licked his shoulder.

He shuddered. Her tongue on his skin, her hand nearly encircling his erection. Was she trying to kill him? "All night long."

"Davy, the things you say to a woman." She breathed out an amused sigh. "At least let me finish you."

He squeezed her hand a little harder. "You can owe me."

She huffed and sat back, and jerked her hand out from under his, resting it on his lower abs. "Are you placating me?"

Her fingers toyed with the line of hair leading from his navel to his erection, and his stomach muscles clenched as she eased her touch lower. "Mmm. Someday, you can do anything you want to me."

Her hands on him and her mouth on his skin and, God, sinking deep into her core? He shuddered and his hand slid away from his erection. He'd meant what he said, every word, and it shamed him to know he was close to doing just about anything if it meant falling into her. "Just not tonight, ok?"

Her eyes narrowed into hard, green slits in the dim lighting. "You've had your way for far too long, Farm Boy."

Her hand swept down and skidded across the tip of his erection, and a ripple of pleasure spasmed through him. He grappled with her, desperately trying to control her hands, and somehow, she won and engulfed him, stroking him hard.

"They'll see," he gritted out.

She flashed a wicked smile. "Let them see me pleasure you."

She captured his lips and her tongue danced with his, and her hand. He hissed in a breath and gripped the sheet underneath him in tight fists. Her hand was soft and firm, all at the same time, stroking him from balls to tip and back again in a delicious imitation of what he wanted to do to her. She broke their kiss and feathered small caresses along his neck, and her teeth nipped his skin sharply.

His control shattered and his hips found their own rhythm, matching the delicious strum of her touch. "God, Dani. Don't stop."

Her hand moved faster, harder, and the pleasure built in him, sharp and heavy.

Make it real, make it last, his body clamored, and he thrust the need away. He could give her this, give her this small thing, come for her the way she'd unraveled for him.

"Gonna come," he said, and the orgasm roared through him, devouring his strength and will. His seed spilled across her hand and onto his abdomen in hot streams, and heady bliss throbbed through him in slowly diminishing waves.

Her hand stilled and slid to his hip, and she sighed. "Better?"

He wheezed out a laugh. "You're kidding, right?"

She rose over him, her woman's power shining from her like a beacon. "Be right back."

"Mmm." He sank into the mattress, so loose he couldn't muster the energy to move. He closed his eyes, reveling in the pleasure she'd given him, letting it wash everything else away. Water ran briefly in the bathroom. Dani's light footsteps padded across the floor. Something cold hit his stomach, and he opened his eyes. She was standing over him, washcloth in hand, cleaning ejaculate off of his abdomen.

"Sorry," she murmured, and toweled him dry.

He watched her walk back into the bathroom, hips swaying under his t-shirt, and something shifted in him, filling him with an unfamiliar tenderness. Every time he pushed it down, it bobbed back up. Finally, he quit resisting and tucked it away to mull over when his head was clear and his heart wasn't tangled up in the passion they'd shared.

She reentered the bedroom and slid into bed, nestling her back against his side. "Nice moves," she said softly. "Where'd you learn 'em?"

He sighed, glad for the distraction. "Kansas."

"Har."

"Seriously. Nothing to do there except play ball, drive a tractor, and make out."

"Is that why you, ah, left?"

He rolled over and tucked her against his chest, ignoring the rightness of holding her. "Yeah."

"The women in Kansas must've raised statues in your honor."

He laughed and nuzzled her neck. "Go to sleep, Dani."

She sighed and, to his surprise, did just that. He relaxed against her, his body still humming from her touch, and lost himself to dreams.

FOUR

THEY DROVE BACK into the city the next morning in one of Alexiou's cars. The scenery flashed by, shifting slowly from countryside to suburbia to urban. Dani risked a furtive sideways glance at Dave. His eyes were glued to the road. One massive hand rested on top of the steering wheel, the other loosely cupped the gear shift.

He'd barely spoken to her, and then only in the terse, monosyllabic grunts she'd come to expect from him. The considerate lover of the night before might as well have never been.

She sighed and leaned her head against the window, closing her eyes against the light. What had she expected? When she'd woken up that morning, the space where he'd slept had been empty and cold. The night's interlude had revved her into a quick shower. She'd bounced down the stairs looking for him, going first to the dining room, where a sleepy-headed Steven was eating a light breakfast in the presence of his nanny. The woman had looked at Dani as if she were a monster and her arms had tightened protectively around the little boy. Dani hadn't been able to resist hissing at her, making Steven laugh. It had the unfortunate side effect of frightening the woman into grabbing him and rushing out of the room.

He'd smiled at Dani over the nanny's shoulder, blown her a kiss, and blinked a two-eyed wink at her. The little flirt.

She'd roamed the house until she'd discovered Dave holed up with Lukas. Her hopes of finding Lover Boy had been dashed when he'd reverted to Caveman, ordered her to pack while he finished conferring with Lukas, and then dragged her off the estate with the speed of a greedy relative carting a rich aunt to the loony bin.

Damn it all. For a minute or two, something like fondness had overridden her irritation over his domineering manhandling. Good thing he'd reminded her what he was really like. Otherwise, she'd be falling at his feet begging for a repeat of last night, except harder, longer, and with a lot more nudity.

Her mind drifted back to the moment when he'd defined sex. *If this were sex, I'd already have you naked with my face between your thighs.* His hand stroking there, his mouth on her neck.

As the images of the night before played through her mind, warmth pooled at the juncture of her thighs and she squirmed in her seat. He'd stoked her passion so easily and barely slaked it, the bastard. She should've left him hanging. Would've served him right.

Maybe she just needed to get laid. When was the last time she'd bothered to take a lover, to sate desire with sex instead of violence? She prodded her memory and scowled. Long enough to forget her last lover's face, and for a Daughter with a sharp, endless memory, that was saying something.

Right. As soon as she got rid of Dave, she'd find a new lover. Easy peasy, no more problemo.

Her stomach clenched into a knot and she sighed. What was it with her and the big lug? Yeah, sure, he was growing on her, but was he growing on her so much even the thought of taking another lover bugged her?

He seemed completely unaffected by the previous night. His tight control was so firmly entrenched, it might as well have never been breached. Did she mean that little to him? Maybe his protectiveness toward her was all in her head. Maybe she really was just a job to him.

Maybe while she was considering asking for more, he just wanted to get rid of her.

The doubts circled in her head, eating at her. No man had ever turned away from her before.

The car came to a stop, interrupting her spiraling thoughts.

While she'd been lost in her head, they'd driven all the way through the city and arrived at the entrance to Alexiou's corporate headquarters. Dani got out when Dave did, following him silently as he gave instructions to the valet and checked them in with security on the main level. They took the elevator to the tenth floor and checked in with the receptionist. The woman flirted outrageously, flashing cleavage and dropping enough innuendos that Neanderthal Dave blushed.

Dani assumed an expression of bored amusement throughout the spectacle, earning her a disgruntled glare from Dave. Hey, if he wanted her to help him get out of tricky situations with women, A, he shouldn't be so damn desirable, and B, he should be nicer to her.

They wended their way to the room holding Alexiou's video surveillance of his city properties. As Dave had explained when they'd first made plans for her visit north, all security video was looped into one constantly monitored system. Digital copies were saved on external hard drives for at least a week before being erased. After the botched exchange where Alexiou's forces had been overrun by Daughters, Dave had had security save that day's video so they could use it as training footage. Now, it would serve as a lead on the woman who'd waltzed in during the middle of that fight and stolen a case of artifacts out from under their collective noses.

The man on duty bumbled upright when she and Dave entered the monitoring room. He was a few inches shorter than her, with the thin, mousy build of a life-long computer geek.

Dave shook the man's hand. "Good morning, Henry."

"Morning, Mr. Winstead, Miss." Henry fumbled, then burst into a nervous smile. "Right, the security footage. Got it right here."

Henry dug out the appropriate hard drive and hooked it up so that it showed on a free monitor, fawning over Dave with enough deference that Dani rolled her eyes.

"Cut it out," Dave muttered.

"When they stop kowtowing," she hissed.

Henry flopped into his chair. His fingers flew across the keyboard. "So, I took the liberty of searching through the footage to find the best angle. Here. This is where she comes in."

His fingers rapped against keys and the video moved forward. The woman entered the warehouse through the same door Dave had carried Dani out of, moving quickly enough that Dani had no doubt the woman was a Daughter. The woman went straight to the table holding the cases of artifacts, sorted through them, closed one of the cases, and picked it up. She halted abruptly and glanced back over her shoulder, then wiggled her fingers at somebody off camera. A few seconds later, she was gone.

Dani frowned. "Is there another angle with a better view of her face?"

Henry blushed a deep red, at being addressed directly by a woman, Dani guessed, but diligently tapped at the keyboard. The video jumped and flickered. "Thought you might ask. Here's another camera. Watch this."

The video rolled again, this time from a different angle, one closer to the entrance the woman had used. She picked up the case of artifacts and turned, and Henry tapped the keyboard, slowing the video. Nearly every person in it halted except the woman. She appeared to be moving languidly through frozen vignettes. At the exit, she glanced up and smiled at the camera. Henry stopped the video and swiveled toward Dani and Dave, a huge grin on his thin face.

"Can you print that?" Dave asked.

"You bet." A few more taps and a whirring sounded. Henry rolled the chair around and pulled a sheet of paper out of the printer. "Voila."

Dani peered around Dave's arm. "It's a good picture. Can you make a few more copies of this and maybe put that footage on a thumb drive for me?"

Henry beamed at her. "Sure. Won't take long."

While Henry flipped through the warehouse's security feeds, Dani studied the woman framed in the picture. Bless him, Henry had enlarged the footage. The woman's face now covered most of the letter-sized paper. The color was poor, though better than the black and white videotape Dani had expected. The woman wore her black hair straight and long. Her violet eyes stared directly into the camera and her pale, oval face was stretched into what might've been a pleasant smile except for the coldly calculating pleasure in the woman's expression.

Goosebumps broke out along Dani's skin. No way was this a woman she wanted to meet in person.

But the face nagged at her. Dani tried to pinpoint it in her memory, sorting through the many faces she'd witnessed over time. Henry swiveled toward her brandishing two thumb drives, and Dani tucked her efforts away. If she'd ever met this woman, she'd ferret it out of her mind. Eventually.

She and Dave left shortly afterward, taking with them a stack of paper duplicates and the digital footage Henry had so kindly captured for them.

They walked back to the building's entrance in silence. Dave had the valet bring Alexiou's car around and drove her to his apartment. They trudged up the stairs together, carrying their luggage, nodding at the curious greetings of the few people they met going up.

As soon as they were safely inside and Dave had done his routine sweep for bugs, Dani said, "What's the plan?"

"Get that footage to Director Upton. Tomorrow, we'll meet with somebody who can help us canvas the city for the mystery lady."

Dani nodded. She'd already planned to carve time out to speak to Rebecca, though the meeting came as a surprise. "And tonight?"

His mouth curved into a mischievous smile. "Tonight, we have fun."

DANI REVIEWED the footage Henry had given them, then dumped it into cloud storage and e-mailed a link to Rebecca. Alexiou's security tech had been kind enough to include a still shot of the unknown woman's face, which Dani attached to the e-mail. While she was waiting for the e-mail to send, she called her mother.

"Hello, sweetheart," Rebecca said. "How's New York?"

The creak of a chair drifted through the static and Dani smiled. She'd caught her mother at work. Some things were reliable as clockwork, and that was one of them. "Dirty, but illuminating. I have a present for you, coming by e-mail."

"A present?" Warmth entered Rebecca's voice, and a hint of playfulness. "You were always my favorite, you know."

Dani laughed. "You say that to anybody who brings you gifts."

"And it's always true, darling. Hold on. Your e-mail just popped up. The attachment's opening." Rebecca gasped. "Oh, no."

Dani tensed. "What?"

"This is Lilith Cæstus."

Dani's breath caught in her throat and cold fear slithered down her spine. She'd never had a run in with the ancient Daughter, but rumor had it she was mad as a Hatter and viciously ruthless. Anybody who crossed her ended up dead, or worse, depending on Lilith's mood. She liked to feed on her victims, draining their blood or eating their flesh, sometimes both if she was really pissed, and usually while they were still alive.

Foreboding skittered through Dani's blood. No Daughter had taken on Lilith and lived to tell the tale. Even the Shadow Enemy steered clear of her.

"Be careful, Dani," Rebecca said, her voice shaky. "Lilith is not a Daughter to be trifled with."

Nausea roiled in Dani's gut. It was never good when a Daughter as old and powerful as the Blade trembled in the face of an enemy. "I know, Mom. I'll be careful."

"Once you locate the artifacts, let me know and I'll send a team in to help you." Rebecca inhaled a slow breath. "Do not under any circumstances confront her on your own. Is that clear?"

That would be easy. Only a fool went against such a Daughter alone, or maybe somebody with a death wish. "Yes, Maetyrm."

"Good." A chair creaked in the background. Rebecca cleared her throat. "Good. Well, now that we know who we're up against, I can have someone pull what we have on Lilith and send you information on recent contacts and hideaways."

"That would be great." Dave entered the living area and set a steaming plate of clam linguini on the coffee table in front of her, then sat down beside her, his own plate in hand. Dani nodded her thanks and returned her attention to the phone call. "How long do you think it'll take?"

"I'll put a rush on it. The sooner you can track Lilith down, the sooner we can deal with her and move past this."

"We'll work on tracking her down from this end, too. Dave has some ideas on that."

"All right. Keep in touch, darling, as often as you can."

"I will, Mom." Dani closed her eyes and clutched the phone tightly to her face. "I love you."

"Love you, too. Be careful."

Dani hung up and placed her phone on the coffee table. Uneasiness clung to her, and with it, the raw fear that something bad was about to happen, something really bad. It pinged through her gut, leaving behind an unfamiliar dread.

She shoved it aside and picked up the plate of pasta Dave had brought her. "We have a name. Lilith Cæstus. Ring any bells?"

Dave shook his head. "Who is she?"

"A Daughter. Big surprise, huh?"

His mouth turned down at one corner. "Explains the speed."

"Yeah. Could be trouble. She's old, like, really old, and not somebody you want to meet in a dark alley." She twirled her fork through the steaming pasta, pushing noodles around as her mind worked. "Or any alley, to be honest. Rebecca's going to see if the IECS has any recent info on her. She should have something back in a day or two."

They ate in silence, the only sounds in the apartment the scrape of utensils against dishes and the muted roar of traffic on the streets far below.

It was nice to share such a peaceful meal, and it calmed her after the horrible instinct prodding her to *run, run, run*. One good thing about Dave. He wasn't a chatterbox. Of course, that was kind of annoying when a woman needed information, which, sadly, she often did.

He was so closed off, so tightly controlled, and not at all trusting.

She could understand that. Being a Daughter meant being careful not to trust the wrong person.

"Why do you call her Rebecca?" he asked, startling her out of her reverie.

"'Cause that's her name."

"Thought she was your mom."

"She is." Dani set her plate back on the coffee table and curled up facing Dave. "But she's not my birth mother. Rebecca took me in when I was a baby and raised me as her own."

He placed his plate beside hers and stretched out, arms crossed over his chest, his long legs sprawled in front of him. "Who's your birth mom?"

"Dunno. Rebecca never told me. I only know that she was a Daughter."

"And your dad?"

"He died a long time ago."

Something unidentifiable shifted across his features. "Sorry."

"Don't be. I never knew him."

An old, familiar ache throbbed through her heart and she stood. Hadn't she resigned herself to never knowing her parents a long time ago? Hadn't she made a deal that she'd never regret what she couldn't change?

She grabbed their plates and headed into the kitchen, Dave following silently behind her. She plunked the dishes in the sink and ran water, added dishwashing liquid. Dave leaned his very fine rear against the counter next to her and stared.

"What?" she asked.

"You're sad."

"What, are you Dr. Phil now?"

His features tightened into his customarily stony gaze. "Don't."

Shame filled her. She blew out a breath and closed her eyes, trying to find her balance. "Sorry. Really."

He shifted closer, and she opened her eyes. He brushed his lips across her forehead. Some of her sanity returned, and she mustered a smile for him.

"I've got this," she said, and to prove it, she turned the faucet off and plunged her hands into the sudsy water.

He picked up a dish towel and settled on her other side. "Sure."

She didn't make a fuss at his breaking the *You cook, I clean* rule. His presence was comforting. With him there, the unpleasant foreboding eased a little. With him, the loneliness plaguing her since childhood didn't seem so big. So what if she'd never known her parents? So what if half of her was missing because she *didn't even know her mother's name*? No biggie.

Or not. Rebecca had never understood that not knowing left a gaping hole in Dani's sense of self, in the way she thought about herself, and in the way others thought about her. Being a Daughter and not knowing one's lineage, not even knowing which Sister was your ancestor? It was nearly unheard of. Because of it, Dani had skirted the edge of acceptance, like the proverbial red-headed step-child, and never really fit in anywhere, no matter how hard she tried.

She shoved the self-pity out of her heart and focused on enjoying Dave's muscled arm rubbing against hers as they made quick work of the kitchen clean-up. Fun. That was her middle name. Dave had said tonight would be fun. Somehow, she doubted that, but it was better than dwelling on things she had no control over and couldn't change anyway.

Her gut pinged again. She sighed and rolled her shoulders, easing some of the tension. Something was coming, something big. Hopefully, she'd be ready when it got there.

THE STENCH of stale sweat permeated the gym. Dave spotted Dani on her bench presses, quietly impressed by the nonchalant way she'd handled coming there. He would've bet money on her being used to weight training on machines, if at all, but she was more than familiar with lifting free weights. In spite of the girly yoga outfit she wore, there was no missish fussiness at the grime, no coy attempts to under-lift, no pretense of ignorance, and absolutely no flirting with the guys. Just a straightforward, down to business workout.

It impressed the hell out of him.

When he'd taken her clubbing the night before in a useless attempt to ferret out information about the Daughter Lilith, he'd expected Dani to balk, especially since he'd promised her fun. But she'd gone along, as if she'd expected exactly what he'd delivered. Kinda took the fun out of teasing her when she did that, but what the hell. At least she hadn't complained.

They hadn't learned anything, but he'd expected that. New York City was a big place. One night canvassing bars wouldn't put much of a dent in the work ahead of them.

As Dani slowly dropped the weights to her chest and pushed them up again, Dave reflected on the information Director Upton had promised to send. Knowing the names of Lilith's contacts and her last-seen-ats would make a huge difference to his and Dani's work, allowing them to tailor their efforts. What they were doing now was just a shot in the dark, but it was at least working toward the end goal. Plus, it kept Dani busy. She had more energy than any three people he knew. Finding a good outlet for that energy was another matter.

His mind immediately drifted to that night at Alexiou's, when he'd found a very appropriate outlet for her, and he cursed inwardly.

It was all he could do to focus on his work with that memory playing in his head. Worse was the need to build another memory just like it, only fully nude and with a lot more contact.

Dani finished her reps and they switched places, adding weight to the bar to meet his workout needs. He laid back on the bench, adjusted himself in relation to the weights, and lifted, copying Dani's slow bunch and press movements.

Truth time. He was attracted to Dani and had been since the minute he'd laid eyes on her.

Hunh. Maybe that was a bit of an understatement.

The more time he spent with her, the more he got to know her, and the more he got to know her, the more he wanted her. He liked her, from the tomboyish bounce in her step to her innate sense of fun.

And then there were the tight workout clothes she wore. When she'd first shimmied out of her sweat suit, revealing the skin-tight Lycra tights she wore underneath, he'd about bitten his tongue off. So yeah, the attraction between them was growing, like a wildfire consuming a forest. On his part, anyway.

On the flip side, starting a relationship with her was a surefire path to heartbreak. The job had to come first, not just the job they were on now, but the one he'd been given on that bright day more than a decade ago. That was the important one. Fear clenched his gut every time he thought about failing. Failing meant losing Dani, maybe permanently. That couldn't happen. He wouldn't let it. If it meant breaking her heart or hurting her to keep her safe, then so be it.

They finished their workout in silence, then stowed the weights they'd used in their proper places for the next person. Dani sipped sparingly from a bottle of water, her one concession. When he'd pointed out that there was a water fountain at the gym, she'd said flatly, "Forget it. I'm not drinking after a bunch of dirty men."

Junior walked in while they were finishing and nodded.

Dave set the last weight onto the rack. "Be right back."

She arched an eyebrow and put her water up, then wandered to the boxing ring in the center of the gym.

Junior made a beeline for Dave. He was a small man, wiry and lean, his ebony skin smooth, and a street hustler, honest and sharp as a tack. He was also part of a network of people just like him, people hiding in plain sight and, because of that, could gather a lot of information without anybody noticing. "Gramps says hello."

"Where's he at?"

Junior shook his head. "Arthritis. Eats his bones up sometimes."

"Sorry to hear that."

"Yeah, man. He was sorry he couldn't come. Nothing makes him better like reliving his glory days."

Dave grunted. "Not much to these glory days. Just need help finding a woman."

Junior eyebrows shot up. "Way I hear it, you got a woman. What you need another one for?"

"Jimmy tell you that?"

"Naw, man, my eyes did." Junior grinned, flashing a row of straight, white teeth, and jabbed a finger toward the center of the gym. "She something, too. Though, if she was my woman, I wouldn't let her near Raoul."

Dave pivoted toward the room's midsection and stifled a sigh. Dani was climbing into the ring, bare-headed, her slender hands encased in sparring gloves, along with a stout Hispanic man known locally as Hammer Head. Raoul was a street fighter. Fists like hammers, a nasty tendency toward head blows, and he wasn't known for playing by the rules. Out of all the men Dani could've picked to fight, she had to choose the most dangerous one there.

"Mm, mm, mm." Junior scuffed a foot over the concrete floor. "You better get her outta there, man. Raoul, he ain't so fond of the ladies, you know what I mean? And that's on a good day."

Dave considered it for a minute. He could try to pull Dani out of the ring and probably get a blistering earful for his troubles or he could trust her to take care of herself. He eyed Junior. "Twenty says she takes him."

Junior dark eyes widened. "Man, what you know that I don't?"

Dave smiled and held out his hand.

Junior glanced back a the ring. "You sure you don't wanna get her outta there?"

Dave wiggled the fingers of his outstretched hand.

Junior sighed and slapped Dave's hand. "All right, man. Your loss."

The gym's owner stepped into the ring to serve as the ref, and Dave relaxed. Leon was a former boxer and had a strict sense of fairness. He huddled with Dani and Raoul, likely setting the rules for their bout, then jogged out of the way, one hand raised in the air. When Leon's hand fell, Dani and Raoul began circling each other.

Raoul moved first, two quick, right-handed jabs aimed at Dani's delicate jaw. She ducked back, eluding the jabs, and Raoul swung a hard, left-handed punch toward her ribs. Dani caught his hand, shoved him aside, and elbowed his kidneys as he passed.

Junior groaned and rolled his eyes at Dave. "Now I see why you bet me."

"Sucker," Dave said mildly, and Junior grinned.

Raoul popped back up, bouncing lightly, a nasty grin on his face. Dani grinned back. The two went into a flurry of punch and counterpunch, using whatever parts of their bodies were handy to try to make contact. Raoul never did. Somehow, Dani evaded his punches, weaving and blocking like she knew what he was going to do before he did. The blows she landed were bruising and well-placed, designed to do enough damage to slow her opponent, but not enough to permanently injure him. Eventually, Raoul made a mistake and dropped his defense during a roundhouse kick aimed at her thigh. Dani scrambled back, avoiding the kick, then back-handed Raoul, her moves so quick, she blurred. He spun around once and thudded onto the mat, and she bounced out of the way, a satisfied grin on her face.

Groans and scattered applause sounded across the gym, and Dave guessed more than one bet had been placed on the outcome. Junior dug out his wallet and passed a twenty dollar bill to Dave.

Leon stepped across the mat and knelt beside the prone figure. Dani stood patiently nearby, hands on hips, murmuring something to Leon as he checked Raoul over. When Raoul stirred, Dani wisely left the ring and bounced her way to Dave, pulling the sparring gloves off as she did.

Junior whistled at her. "That was some fight. Say, you wouldn't be interested in—"

"No," Dave said, "she wouldn't."

Dani rounded on him. "Hey! Maybe I—"

"No," Dave repeated. "Junior, it was good to see you again. Tell Jimmy I said hello and let me know if I can do anything."

Junior shook his head, a grin playing over his thin face. "Sure, man. Later."

Dave grasped Junior's hand, leaned in for a shoulder tapping man hug. "Later."

Dani hooked her hands on her hips. As soon as Junior was gone, she said, "You know, it's been a long time since I let anybody dictate what I could and couldn't do."

"Get used to it."

A dangerous glint glimmered into her green eyes, and perverse pleasure sparked through him. Good. Now maybe she'd realize he was serious about protecting her. Mad she'd get over. Hurt was a lot harder to heal from.

She pivoted on her heel and marched to the workout bag he'd brought, dug her sweat suit out, and yanked it on, pointedly ignoring him.

He tugged on his own sweats and a light jacket. What he wouldn't give for a shower. Lunch first. After that workout, Dani would need food, and she deserved a reward for knocking Hammer Head to the mat.

She sashayed out of the gym, bumping fists with a couple of the regulars as she went. He followed at a slower pace, enjoying the day and the smooth roll of her hips. A block away from the gym, a sunny smile replaced her irritated grimace and the spring popped back into her step.

She never held a bad mood for long.

When he was sure she wouldn't bite his head off, he said, "Lunch?"

"Yeah. I'm starving."

"Thai?"

"Sure." She slowed and matched his stride. "So, that man you passed the thumb drive to. Will he help us?"

He didn't bother asking how she knew he'd slipped something to Junior. She seemed to catch everything that went on around her. He should be used to it by now.

"Yeah."

"Good." She threaded her arm through his and sighed. "You know, you should've let me take him up on his offer."

"No."

She laughed. "Dave, sweetie, I used to eat men like Raoul for breakfast."

"Why?"

She shrugged and tugged him back into a walk. "Why not? Besides, it's good money."

"Thought you worked for the IECS."

"Sometimes," she acknowledged. "Not always."

He steered her to a little hole in the wall located a few blocks from the gym. Not much to look at, but the food was terrific. They sat at a secluded booth in the back corner and ate hunched over Tom Yum Gung. He teased her into laughter, and enjoyed it, enjoyed her. She was easy that way, casual and relaxed. Soothing when she wasn't bouncing off the walls, and even then, he liked being near her.

They finished eating, and Dave relaxed against the back of the booth, content to listen to her rambling chatter. A shift in light toward the front of the restaurant caught his eye. Stuart shoved his way through tables to the waiter, his expression angry, and Dave tensed. He'd made damned sure they weren't followed when they left his apartment that morning, so how the hell had Stu found them?

Dani lowered her gaze and folded her hands on the table in front of her. "What is it?"

Dave shook his head and sank lower in his seat, one eye on Stu harassing a college-aged waiter. A minute later, Stu huffed out of the restaurant. Dave raised a hand and called the waiter over.

"That man," he said softly. "What did he want?"

The waiter grimaced. "He was looking for somebody. I told him to get lost. We don't want trouble."

"Did he say who?"

"Yeah. Some chick with black hair." The waiter snorted. "Like, this is a Thai restaurant. Do you know how many people with black hair come in here?"

Dave dug out his wallet and passed the man a twenty. "If he comes in again, keep putting him off, ok?"

"Sure, man." The waiter slipped the money into his apron. "My parents would freak if they knew somebody was in here asking questions."

"Don't tell them," Dave advised, and the waiter shrugged and headed toward another table.

Dave led Dani out of the restaurant, checking the street as subtly as he could. She'd have questions, but those could to wait until they were somewhere safe. He turned the incident with Stuart over in his mind, adding it to the mix of other oddities he'd been collecting. The pieces were beginning to take shape, but he couldn't quite make out the picture they formed yet. He needed more information, always more. He'd give it a little time, and then he'd see if he could shake the pieces up a little.

FIVE

THEIR TIME settled into a routine of morning workouts and evening searches, interspersed with meeting the day-to-day needs of food, laundry, and other chores. They were becoming friends of a sort, Dani thought, in spite of their mutual distrust. She was beginning to recognize Dave's moods and differentiate between one stony expression and the next, enough that she now knew when he was teasing just by the way he looked at her.

Problem was, he didn't look at her the way she really wanted him to, and it was beginning to frustrate her.

A few days after she received Lilith's name from Rebecca, Dani sat with Dave on his overstuffed leather sofa, watching a movie with him after a long day of chasing down false leads and trying to generate new ones. She'd found a yarn store a few blocks away that carried some nice wool and had snuck away from him and purchased enough yarn to clothe a small army, or one really large FBI agent.

Dani smiled to herself as she worked through a basic Gansey sweater pattern in a slate gray wool, the same color as Dave's eyes. As soon as she'd spotted the yarn, she'd grabbed enough to make him a sweater. He'd been so patient when she'd measured him, standing perfectly still as she wrapped the tape measure around his clothed body, following her every move with that intense look she'd come to know and, truth be told, enjoy.

More fool her, but she was growing fond of the big lug.

She'd already finished a fisherman's cap for him and tucked it away where he wouldn't find it. She had a strong feeling he'd need it soon, and she'd learned never to ignore her gut instinct, especially when it came to men.

The sweater would take weeks to complete, but even so, she expected it to be ready well before winter ended. Whether they'd still be working on tracking down Lilith or not, she'd make sure he got it.

An uncountable mix of emotions swelled through her and her hands paused in mid-stitch. Chances were good they'd find the artifact soon, and when they did, she and Dave would go their separate ways. She was beginning to dread that time. They weren't exactly friends, but they were getting there. And there was no doubt whatsoever that the attraction she felt for him grew stronger every day.

Unfortunately, he didn't seem to feel the same way. Other than the occasional casual or polite touch, Dave appeared to have a strictly hands-off policy where she was concerned. She'd caught him looking a time or two, but that was it. It was almost like he'd completely closed off that part of himself, or near enough. Being unable to break through that wall of control was frustrating, but damned if she'd beg, no matter how much her body and, she admitted reluctantly, her heart wanted her to.

The movie they were watching was an old favorite, where a woman became a princess but lost her true love in the process. When the scene between the princess and the pirate came on, after he defeated the man who'd kidnapped her, Dani dropped her knitting into her lap and stretched her hands and fingers out, rotating her wrists to ease the strain of holding the needles. She risked a glance at Dave. He sat beside her in his usual imitation of a statue, moving only to sip slowly from a bottle of Straub Lager. Every once in a while, he grunt or shook his head. On rare occasion, his mouth quirked into a reluctant half-grin. She thought he might be enjoying the movie, and it pleased her more than it should have.

A chill shivered through her. Living in the South had apparently thinned her blood. Earlier, when a freezing rain had brought a halt to their search for Lilith, they'd returned to Dave's apartment for a late supper and a movie. She'd changed into her spare workout tights, and Dave had promptly pushed her back into her bedroom for warmer clothes. Even after changing into old sweats and a pair of hand-knit wool socks, she shivered.

She, who'd spent more than one night out in worse weather dressed only in leathers and wool accessories.

Maybe she was getting old.

Dani grimaced. A mortal human of her age would have one foot in the grave already. Immortal Daughters, on the other hand, expected to be in peak physical condition until they were killed or became mortal. Neither was an easy accomplishment.

When another chill hit her, she set her knitting aside, exasperated, and scooted forward on the couch. Something warmer to wear it was, though having to dress so warmly was getting really old.

Dave set his lager down and reached for the lap blanket draped over the sofa's back. He tugged her against his side, spread the blanket over her lap, and casually threw an arm across her shoulder, his gaze never leaving the movie.

Oh, wow, he was warm. She curled her knees up under the blanket and snuggled into his welcome heat. This was no time to be Daughterly, after all. A woman could freeze to death clinging to her pride.

"Better?" he asked softly.

"Yeah." She tucked the blanket under her chin. "Thanks."

He grunted in typical caveman fashion, and she smiled. He really was a sweet man, in spite of his strong resemblance to a Neanderthal.

As her body warmed, she yawned and a wave of fatigue hit her. The past week had been hectic and she hadn't gotten enough sleep. Her eyelids fluttered closed and she yawned again. She could listen to the movie, just for a minute...

What felt like half a shake later, she opened her eyes. The movie's credits rolled over the TV screen, and her body was sprawled on top of Dave's on the sofa. His heart thumped steadily under her cheek. One of her hands had worked its way under his shirt and rested against warm, bare skin. She jerked it out, appalled to have betrayed herself in sleep, and struggled to sit up.

The arm he'd draped across her back tightened, holding her firmly in place. "Sleepy head," Dave rumbled, a hint of laughter in his voice.

"Sorry," she muttered, and tried to sit up again.

Her knee grazed Dave's groin, and he grunted. "Steady now."

A mortified wave of heat washed over her and she buried her flaming cheeks in his chest. "Sorry."

"'S ok." He shifted onto his side, taking her with him, and she eased away. He scrubbed a hand over his head and stood, ambled to the TV and turned it off.

Dani sat up, taking the blanket with her. Somehow, he'd managed to keep her covered while she slept, and warm. As soon as she pulled the blanket off, the chill returned, and she heaved a weary sigh. She'd be warmer in bed. Maybe if she wore her sweats as pajamas it would help.

Dave pulled his long body into a stretch. His shirt rode up an inch over the waistband of his jeans, exposing a small strip of his abdomen.

Her gaze zeroed in on his bare flesh. What would he taste like there, smooth and warm, rough and manly? She shoved the need away. Really, she'd had enough of her body for one night.

She picked up her knitting and tucked it carefully into its bag, then shuffled toward her bedroom.

"I can turn up the heat," Dave said, startling her into a full stop.

He was looking at her with an expression she couldn't quite pin down.

She shook her head. "You already have it on seventy."

His steady gaze shot through her, and she shifted her weight, then winced. She'd given in to her nerves. What kind of Daughter did that? She huffed out a sigh and continued to her room.

He crossed his arms over his wide chest and leaned a shoulder against the doorframe.

Amusement. That's the expression he was aiming her way.

"You can sleep with me," he said.

She narrowed her eyes at him. "That's what you said the last time and look how that turned out."

"No sex this time."

"Uh huh. That's what you said the last time."

"Nobody's watching now."

She snorted. "Like that would stop you."

"True."

"Then no." She made the words as flat as she could, and ignored the tiny little happy dance her body had done when he'd agreed with her.

"Flannel sheets."

She stared at him, aghast. "You have flannel sheets? Why don't I have flannel sheets?"

"Haven't gotten yours out yet."

She shot a withering glare at him, set her knitting in its proper place, and rummaged through her clothes, searching for something warmer to wear. It would serve him right if she made him take her shopping tomorrow.

Her cellphone beeped. Dani grabbed it and opened a text from Rebecca. She read it swiftly and grunted, then groaned. How come she'd picked up Caveman Winstead's bad habits? Why couldn't he pick up some of hers instead? She answered the text quickly, then placed her phone on top of the nightstand next to her bed.

"Mom's sending a courier with info on Lilith," she said. "Should be here tomorrow."

He grunted, and she rolled her eyes.

"What are you doing?" he asked.

"Looking for warmer clothes." She stepped away from the chest of drawers and hooked her hands on her hips. As warmly as she'd packed for this trip, she hadn't packed warmly enough. Next time she came to New York in the fall, she'd bring her thermals.

"Stubborn." Dave walked to her and cupped his hands over her shoulders. "Come sleep with me so you'll be warm."

She closed her eyes and bowed her head. On the one hand, Dave had already dinged her pride enough. Sometimes he was a tad too domineering, and she gave in to him way too often. On the other hand, she was friggin' cold. With desire thrown into the mix, it really wasn't much of a contest, but she had to at least put up the pretext of being firm on the rules.

"No sex. Promise?"

He brush his lips across her forehead. "Sure."

She frowned. "Kissing is sex."

"Give it a rest, Dani."

"Fine." She opened a drawer, grabbed a t-shirt, and thumped the drawer closed. "Dibs on the bathroom."

She stretched her nightly routine out in a futile attempt to calm the happy dance down and lectured her body sternly on appropriate behavior. Cuddling was fine. Groping was not. No kissing, no hands below the waist or legs above mid-thigh, and absolutely no peeking.

When she exited the bathroom into Dave's bedroom, Dave was sprawled out on top of the covers, dressed only in his underwear, reading a paperback novel. An eerie sense of déjà vu hit her. She shook it away and ignored all that smooth skin, the play of light over muscle. The bump in his underwear where his sex lay hidden.

Heat shuddered through her. Ignoring Dave? Yeah, right. Maybe when hell froze over.

"Your turn," she said.

He stuffed a bookmark into the book and set it aside, probably exactly where he'd gotten it. He scooted off the bed and padded into the bathroom, and she admired his long, muscled form.

You sure about the groping? her fun side asked.

Absolutely, positively certain, her downer side said.

When he closed the door, she shook herself into action, climbed into his bed, and curled into a ball under the blankets as she sank into black flannel. If the promise of flannel sheets was all it took to get her into bed with a man, maybe she was too easy. Then again, at least she was warm.

The light clicked off and the mattress shifted. Dave curled around her and hooked an arm over her waist. His legs brushed her feet, and he hissed in a breath. "Icy feet," he murmured.

She shifted them away from him, and he snuggled closer, draping one leg across her feet. His body heat seared into her from head to toe. "You're like a furnace, Dave."

A low laugh rumbled from his chest. "Complaining?"

"No." She sighed and relaxed into him, grateful for the warmth. She was pretty sure she would've never warmed up completely on her own, flannel sheets or not.

"Getting sick?" he asked.

She yawned. "Daughters don't get sick. Hardly ever."

He kissed her neck and brushed his cheek over her hair. "G'night."

"Night." She yawned again and faded into sleep, oddly secure surrounded by his warmth.

DANI WOKE the next morning to sunlight streaming through the blinds, warm and content and well-rested. She'd had the sexiest dream. Dave with his hand between her legs, whispering encouragement to her while he coaxed her body into waves of beautiful pleasure. A satisfied smile slid over her face and she rolled over to rag Dave about the dream.

His side of the bed was empty.

Dani huffed and flopped onto her back. That man. What did he think, that he could just...

She paused in mid-thought. What exactly had Dave done that was so bad? Ok, so, the first time they'd shared a bed, he'd broken the no sex rule, but that was nothing compared to the method he'd used to break it. Her body tingled at the thought of what he'd done to her, and what she'd done to him that night, and clamored *more, more, more* every blasted time she was around him, like a starving Oliver Twist holding out a perpetually empty bowl.

The second time, he'd shared his body heat and warmed her through and through, and hadn't laid a hand on her otherwise, except in her dreams.

Drat the man.

Did he have to be so considerate and then leave her hanging like that? Couldn't he just once wake up with her instead of leaving her wondering, dreading his inevitable return to stoicism?

That was what bothered her the most. She'd break through just enough to see what kind of man he could be, only to have him default to laconic Neanderthal.

Maybe it really was one-sided. Dani squinted at the light rippling across the ceiling. Maybe he was just humoring her or...

No. She'd played the maybe game before where Dave was concerned. Damned if she'd do it again.

Resolved, she flung the covers off, relieved that the room seemed mostly warm. She straightened the bed without actually remaking it, which she refused to do, Dave's neat tendencies or not. That's why she'd hired a cleaning lady for her own place, somebody possessed of far more patience with such things.

Dani grabbed her clothes, decided on a shower, and since she was still dressed in a t-shirt and undies, took the connecting bathroom as a shortcut, hoping to avoid Dave's flat gaze.

The thought of how unattractive he must find her was just too depressing to face right then, especially after the intensely sensual dream she'd had.

She opened the bathroom door and paused in midstride. The shower was running. Her heart flipped over in her chest and tingling heat gathered between her legs. Dave was in the shower. She closed her eyes, hand still on the doorknob. Sweet Lady Ki. All six foot three of Dave, water running down his nude body, his hands scrubbing soap over bare skin.

"In or out," he said gruffly.

Ok. She was an adult. They'd already been intimate, sort of, so what was the big deal? She'd just walk through and not look at Dave *naked under the running water* and everything would be fine.

That plan lasted long enough for her to close the door and walk halfway across the tiny floor, and then she gave in to curiosity. Just one peek. She could handle that, right? One teeny, tiny peek at him...

It was her undoing.

The shower curtain was clear and showed every single inch of bare skin down the right-hand side of his body. His forehead rested against his forearms, braced against the shower wall, with his back to the spray. Water sluiced over his muscled back and down his firm bottom before sliding across his spread legs.

His skin pebbled in goose bumps and she realized abruptly that he was taking a cold shower. Her gaze automatically slid to his groin and she swallowed. He was half-hard, even under the bracing water. While she watched, his erection grew and lengthened, jutting away from his body in a primal display of his sexuality.

Her mouth went dry and memory surfaced, of her hand on that length, circling it and sliding against the velvet skin, of Dave coming, his body arching off the bed as he rode the crest of an orgasm.

He faced her and his arms fell to his sides, framing his body, every muscle shown in spellbinding relief. Need clawed its way over reason. *Poseidon*, she thought weakly, and subconsciously raised his hubba factor a notch.

Her gaze flew up, clashing with his, and she swallowed. Predatory desire etched itself into his expression. He reached up and slid the shower curtain back. The rings screeched against the curtain rod, jolting her into action. With a small squeak, she turned and fled, slammed the door to her bedroom shut, and leaned against it, heart beating a quick double-time in her chest.

Immediately, she tapped her fists against her forehead. Idiot. Daughters didn't flee. They *pursued*. What on Earth had possessed her to run?

The flinty need Dave had aimed at her popped into her mind. That look, like a lion stalking an antelope. By the Goddess, if she'd ever doubted that Dave wanted her, that episode should put her mind at ease once and for all.

She laughed weakly, both ashamed of her reaction and thankful for her near escape. Clearly, she wasn't ready for anything more with Dave, so maybe it was good that he had the strength to hold back. Maybe if she'd anticipated his desire, she'd have been ready for it and accepted his invitation, but maybe it was better this way. A little time to think over this thing between her and him, take into account the way he'd looked at her...

Her breath caught in her throat and need trembled through her muscles. A little time, yeah, but not too much. She wanted him, craved his warmth and his strength. A sigh pushed its way out of her lungs. Yeah, that was it. Think it over, accustom herself to the idea, then act.

The water turned off in the bathroom. Dani shoved away from the door and gathered clothes, dawdling to give Dave plenty of time to dry off and perform whatever strange ritual men endured at the start of their day.

When she was sure Dave was finished, she slipped back into the bathroom and rushed through her toiletries, half afraid he'd walk in on her, half afraid he wouldn't.

And was disappointed when he didn't.

She walked out of her bedroom fully dressed, her hair pulled into a ponytail, and was surprised to find him in the kitchen, apron on, cooking thick slabs of ham. She hesitated at the kitchen door then, determined to be casual about the whole thing, walked up to him and leaned lightly against his back, her hands on his waist, intending to thank him for sharing his warmth the night before.

He stiffened, and she jerked away from him. Ok, well. Obviously he wanted her but didn't *want* to want her. Her chest tightened and she swiveled on her heel. Whatever. This assignment would be over soon, and the back and forth thing he kept doing would end with it.

A carton of eggs sat on the counter next to a bowl and, needing something to keep her hands busy, she broke half a dozen into the bowl, setting the shells aside for 201C's compost bin. One hand curled into a fist on the counter. 201C, the neighbor whose name Dani had never learned, because Dave didn't trust her or didn't want her around or whatever the hell was going on in that ape-like mind of his.

A warm body nestled against her back and Dave's hands wrapped around hers. She closed her eyes. She'd have to give up that familiar heat, have to give up his gentle touch. Why did she always have to let go of people, just when she'd gotten used to them? For once, why couldn't she have somebody stable in her life, somebody who was all hers and only hers?

Dave tugged the bowl out of her hands and set it farther back on the counter, then turned her gently around. Her eyes popped open. While she'd had her back turned, he'd cut the eye off under the ham and removed the apron covering his plain black t-shirt.

He cupped her face, stroked his hands over her skin and hair. "Dani."

She shuddered and leaned into him. "What?"

"Sorry." He brushed his lips across her forehead and pulled her into a hug. "You've never touched me before. It startled me."

She frowned into his chest, breathing in the mingled scents of soap and fried ham. "Sure I have."

"Not first."

She thought back over the months she'd known him, all the times they'd been intimate or just close, and sucked in a breath. He was right. She'd accused him, in her mind at least, of being too controlled, of being standoffish, but hadn't she been the same by refusing to touch him? She had no problem getting physical with people she liked, her family and friends, even casual acquaintances. Why had she held back with him?

The answer slapped at her immediately. She'd known from the start that something about Dave was special. *Something* had whispered to her the first time she'd seen him. *Something* had urged her to follow him and learn about him and find a way to fit him into her life. Up until that moment, she'd thought it was because of the job she was doing. It wasn't unusual for her instincts to lead her like that, and she trusted them nearly implicitly.

What if this time, though, they'd lead her to *the* man, the one she could love above all others, the one that could help her break the curse? What if, deep down, she'd known that and had subconsciously tried to avoid it, while craving him so deeply, she'd driven herself into a frenzy of conflicted emotions? Like running out of the bathroom when faced with his stunningly beautiful arousal.

She rubbed her face against his hard chest and wrapped her arms around his waist, reveling in this small intimacy. She was being stupid, melodramatic, like a teenager in the throes of her first crush. Which she was far from being, but still. She'd never come this close to loving a man before, not this way.

And she was scary close to falling for him.

Her stomach knotted into a tight fist, and she tensed. Falling for Dave? She barely knew him, and what if he hurt her? What if...

She huffed out a tiny laugh and relaxed. She was *still* being an idiot. She could enjoy whatever was happening between her and Dave or she could dread it. As long as he was playing nice, why not enjoy it?

She tilted her head back and met his gaze. His face had softened into boyish charm. He brushed his lips teasingly over hers, then claimed her mouth in a gentle kiss.

Heat stole through her and she *mmmd* into his mouth. A simple kiss, soft and sweet. Why weren't they doing that more often?

She pressed her chest into his, and he slanted his mouth across hers, deepening the kiss. His tongue traced the seam of her mouth, and she opened for him, and moaned when his tongue pressed inside. Her fingernails dug into his skin through his shirt. So good. It was so good to be with him, so good to feel. She met him touch for touch and gave herself over to the need roiling within her, a need he'd roused and only he could answer.

He slid his hands down her back, gripped her bottom, and lifted her onto the counter, pushing himself between her legs, aligning their bodies core to core. Even through their clothing, his erection pulsed against her. He tore his mouth away from hers and trailed open-mouthed kisses down her neck. She tilted her head, granting him access, and shivers whispered through her as he mouthed her sensitive skin.

His hand slid under her shirt, smoothing upward against her bare skin, and he cupped her breast, kneading her through her bra while he sucked gently at the base of her neck. Her breasts tightened and her nipples pebbled, and she *wanted*. She wanted his mouth on her bare skin, she wanted the pressure of his tongue along her breast. His hands drifted to the waistband of her workout tights and pushed it down, and his fingers slid inside and stroked over her slick core.

"Come for me, Dani," he murmured.

The words echoed her dream, and she slammed abruptly into awareness. "What?"

He stilled, his muscles taut, his fingers pressed intimately against her.

She tugged at his shoulders, trying to get him to look at her, and he eased back, his expression stone hard. Deliberately, he flicked his fingers across the nub of her sex.

Pleasure rippled through her and her focus wavered. "Dave, we need to talk."

He flexed one finger into her pussy and nipped her lips. "Later."

He nibbled his way across her jaw and down her throat, trailing moist heat, and rational thought melted away. Dani closed her eyes, savoring the sharp build of pleasure in her blood. His finger slid slowly in and out of her and his thumb rubbed her clit, and he sucked the skin over her pulse into his mouth and licked, and she gasped and clutched his shoulders and bit her lip around a plea for more.

"Come for me, Dani," he murmured, and she moaned and breathed his name, and reality fractured in a magnificent wave of bliss, carrying her along in its wake.

He cradled her and peppered small kisses over her face, and a thread of an unknown emotion spiraled through her. Satisfaction? Tenderness? She sighed and stroked his chest through his t-shirt. What did it matter? She'd figure it out eventually. In the meantime, they had a whole afternoon to kill.

He eased his hands out of her tights and picked her up.

"Where are we going?" she asked.

"Bed," he said, satisfaction thrumming in his voice.

Her heart skipped a beat and she sucked in a breath. Great minds apparently thought alike, and this time, he was going to be in her, moving over her, stroking his rigid erection into her pussy. Her stomach muscles tightened and heat pulsed between her thighs. Sweet Goddess help her, but she wanted that.

Halfway across the living room, the doorbell rang. Dave halted and glared at the door.

Dani pressed her lips together, containing her humor. "Probably the courier. Put me down."

His arms tightened around her and he turned the glare on her.

"Won't take but a minute," she promised, and he let her go, his expression caught between reluctance and annoyance.

She knew exactly how he felt.

She checked the peephole, then flung open the door and beamed at her brother. He was nearly as tall as Dave, though leaner, with his father's dark hair and height.

"Bobby!" she said and enfolded him in a bear hug. "What are you doing here?"

He smacked a kiss to her cheek. "Business."

She eased back, grabbed his hand, and tugged him inside. "People or personal?"

"Both." He tugged a small, flat package out of the back of his jeans and handed it to her. "Mom sent this for you."

Dani ripped the seal open and pulled out a wad of paper. "She didn't tell me you were coming."

"I asked her not to. Wanted to surprise my baby sister."

She snorted. "In your dreams, kiddo. I was the one changing your diapers, not the other way around."

He laughed and draped an arm over her shoulder, then stiffened against her.

Dani glanced up. Dave was glowering at them, his arms crossed over his chest, his feet set in a wide-legged stance. His expression flummoxed her. What was wrong with him? "Ah, Dave, you remember my brother, Bobby, don't you?"

Dave nodded. "Upton."

"Winstead," Bobby gritted out.

Dani rolled her eyes. Men and their pissing contests. Why didn't they just whip out their penises, compare sizes, and get it over with?

Dave's phone beeped, drawing everyone's eyes to his pocket. He dug it out, checked the message, and stuffed it back into his pocket. "Gotta go."

"Where?" Dani asked, and was surprised not at all when he shook his head and walked into his bedroom, shutting the door behind himself.

Bobby's arm slid off her shoulders. "A man of few words, I take it."

"You have no idea."

Dave came back out of his bedroom wearing a turtleneck in place of the t-shirt he'd had on when he walked in. He stalked toward Dani and, ignoring Bobby, pulled her against him. His expression softened as he gazed down at her. "Feed the boy."

Bobby sputtered out a protest, and Dani snickered. Dave hardly had a right to call Bobby *boy*. The two men were too close in age. Dave's mouth quirked into one of his lopsided grins, and she shook her head. Why did he have to needle Bobby like that?

"Come back soon?" she asked softly.

"Mmm."

He leaned down and kissed her, exploring her mouth slowly, and her body hummed as need reignited within her.

So he was making a point to her brother with the kiss. That didn't keep her from enjoying it and wanting more.

"Don't burn the eggs." With one final peck, Dave let her go. He spared a hard glance for Bobby, grabbed his jacket and cap, and shut the door quietly behind himself.

She locked up behind him and turned back to Bobby.

"What was that about?" he asked.

"Which part?" she responded lightly. She headed toward the kitchen, leaving him to follow or not.

"Well, we can start with that kiss and work our way out from there. Winstead seemed awfully proprietary." He stopped in the kitchen's doorway and crossed his arms over his chest, assuming a posture eerily like Dave's. "You're having sex with him, aren't you?"

"No, I'm not." Which was absolutely true. Mostly. "But we were about to when you rang the doorbell."

Bobby's expression twisted into mock disgust. "TMI, Dani."

"You asked."

"What about the eggs?"

Dani grinned. "He thinks I can't cook."

213

"No." His own face split into a grin. "Really?"

She laughed. "Yeah."

"You're so bad."

She winked at him. "Brother, you have no idea."

SIX

URING THE WALK to the trattoria, Dave struggled to regain control of the desire roaring through him. As much as he tried to keep a tight grip on his mind, focusing it with all his will on the task ahead of him, it kept drifting back to the near miss with Dani. Every time it did, heat shot into his groin and his dick hardened. They'd been building toward sex for months now, months of teasing and hinting and playing. If Dani's brother hadn't knocked on the door, Dave would be inside her, pleasing her, satisfying her, finding his own release.

Watching her lose herself in passion, her lean body writhing, eyes closed as she savored his touch, and touched him in return. Her slim hands sliding over his skin, stroking him, her mouth trailing hot, wet kisses across his body.

He wanted that, craved it. More, he wanted *her* to want it.

He wandered through the streets, automatically taking steps to lose the tail he'd picked up when he'd left his apartment. His mind lingered on Dani, on the memory of her walking in on him in the shower, her dazed expression clinging to his body. That one incident told him everything he needed to know about how much she wanted him. And after, she'd touched him and let him touch her. She must be softening toward him.

He rubbed a hand over the ache in his heart. If she was softening, he was already a goner, had been since pretty much the night he'd walked into his apartment and caught her watching a Godzilla marathon. She was beautiful and funny and smart, she could kick anybody's ass, and she liked monster movies. How could he *not* fall for her?

That should concern him, but he pushed it away, ignoring it. They'd locate Lilith soon, and when they did, he'd bind Dani to him as much as any man could hold a Daughter. Never for long unless the curse could be broken. A lot of men had tried with Dani. None had succeeded. She'd never even had a child that he could find, something most Daughters had already done by her age.

He should know. He'd studied enough of the files Alexiou kept on the People, probably for the same reason Dani's people and every other organization known to man kept them, including the FBI. To keep track of enemies and allies.

215

Though, that he knew of, the FBI didn't have files on immortals.

He stopped at a pay phone and called Stu, left a message on his handler's voice mail, then dialed Jimmy and checked in on Junior's progress, which was squat. Even with the stuff Bobby had brought from the IECS, Dave felt better having his own info coming in, so he asked Jimmy to have Junior keep digging.

Dave exited the phone booth, tested for a tail, and walked randomly for a while, just in case. He slowed his pace a block from the Italian café, subtly checked for stationery watchers, and spotted the woman he'd called the day Dani had arrived in New York.

Meredith Cartwright sat at a shaded table, sunglasses blocking the morning sunlight, that day's *Times* opened to the business section. Her slim figure was dressed in a sharply tailored navy suit and her shapely bare legs were crossed beneath her fashionably styled skirt. She was meticulously groomed, brown hair hanging loose over her shoulders, make-up just so.

He'd seen that hair disheveled beneath dim lighting, her naked body swaying over his. He'd known from the get-go that she wasn't for him, and had let her persuade him anyway. It'd been a mistake, but they'd both been adult enough not to let it interfere with their jobs. In a way, they were even friends, if an FBI agent could be on friendly terms with a spook.

He sat down in a metal chair across the table from her.

She folded the paper precisely and set it aside. "Well, well, well, the mighty Dave Winstead, as I live and breathe. Long time, no see."

Dave folded his arms across his chest. Every single damn time they met, she had to play her games. That crap got old after a while.

"Still a talker, I see." A waiter pivoted toward their table, and Meredith waved him away. "Tell me, Davy, what have you been up to that's worthy of having two agencies keeping tabs on you?"

His eyes narrowed. "Know the FBI's watching and Alexiou's brother."

Meredith tsked and folded her hands in her lap. "Getting a bit rusty in your old age."

"Who else then?"

"Well, I could tell you, but I'm not certain it's worth my job."

"You're kidding."

"Afraid not." Concern flickered across her expression and was just as quickly gone. "The only way I could meet you is because people know we were intimate."

Dave grunted. "And you let people think we were starting up again."

"Naturally. We could, if you'd like."

Her sly smile irked him into a scowl. Dani's face popped into his head. As beautiful as Meredith was, he wasn't even tempted. "Water under the bridge, Mer."

"Your loss." Her eyes flicked away and back. She leaned forward and her voice dropped to a low whisper. "Whatever you're doing, Dave, get out now, while you still can."

He braced his forearms against the tabletop. "Tell me what you know."

"I can't, or not enough anyway." She swallowed and her gaze darted to something over his shoulder. "What I can say is that it's not you they're after, but some kind of tablet. An ancient artifact of some sort, and I'm certain the search is being pushed by someone *outside* the agency."

The artifact Lilith had stolen. Had to be. "Who?"

"No idea. Really." She reached across the table and cupped his hands between hers. "Be careful, Dave. Everything I've run across tells me that whoever is after this thing will do anything to get it, and they don't care who gets hurt in the process. Do you understand?"

"Yeah." He flipped his hands and held hers, squeezing them gently. Lovers they might never be again, but he still cared about her.

She leaned across the tiny table and pressed her lips to his in a gentle farewell. "I can smell her on you, you know. The willowy blonde you're seeing."

Dave narrowed his eyes and tightened his grip on her hands. "Leave her out of it, Mer."

"She's already involved." Meredith pulled her hands out of his, stood, and tucked the newspaper under her arm. "Try not to get yourself killed. Shame to let a body like yours go to waste."

She turned and walked away, heels tapping against the concrete sidewalk. He watched her go, mind in a turmoil over their conversation. The FBI and the CIA were both watching him, and the latter at least was looking for the artifact. Likely, they were using him to get to it. What was on that tablet that was so important? And who could be pressuring two powerful organizations into putting manpower on that kind of a search?

A shadow passed over him. Bobby Upton dropped into the chair Meredith had just emptied, and Dave sighed.

"Nice little woman you've got there, Winstead." Bobby slouched into the chair and crossed his arms over his chest, pinning a harsh glare on Dave. "And right after you left my sister, too."

"Butt out, Upton," Dave said flatly.

Bobby leaned forward, a dangerous glint in his hazel eyes. "You screw with my sister, you screw with me. You got no business toying with her like that."

"Cool it, kid. The only toying going on between me and Dani is in the bedroom." Which was mostly true.

Bobby vaulted out of the chair, anger vibrating from his stiff body. "You son of a bitch. She's half in love with you and you're fucking cheating on her. Stand up so I can beat the shit out of you."

Dave unfolded to his full height and glared down at Dani's brother. By God, the man had balls. "I'm not cheating on her, Upton. That was business."

"Business doesn't usually involve kissing a leggy brunette."

"She was yanking my chain. That's it."

A sharp pain shot through the base of Dave's skull. First Meredith, and now Bobby. All he needed was for Stu to show up and his day would be complete.

Why had he let Dani open the door that morning?

He yanked out his wallet, sorted through his cash, and threw a decent tip on the table. "Walk with me," he told Bobby, and turned on his heel, not caring if the other man followed or not.

Bobby fell into step beside him.

Dave rolled his shoulders. Well, damn. Now he had to talk. "Meredith works for the CIA. Analyst, and a former lover."

"How former?"

"Very." Dave ducked into a cut-through alley. "What man would be fool enough to cheat on a woman like Dani? She's more woman than most men can handle."

"Plus, she'd skin you if she found out."

"There is that," Dave agreed mildly.

They weaved in and out of the lunch-time pedestrian traffic as the city's noise rose up around them. People talking, bicycles whirring past, drivers beeping their horns to try to speed up log-jammed streets. So different from his life in Kansas, so alive in an artificial way that contrasted sharply with the natural rhythms of his father's farm. Chaos versus peace, machine versus nature.

A sudden longing to be home tugged at him. He could take Dani, introduce her to his folks, show her what life was like on a farm. They'd love her, probably treat her like another daughter. His sisters would fall into an easy friendship with her, the way women did, and maybe it would ease some of the loneliness that sometimes slipped through Dani's mask of cheerful unconcern.

They picked up a tail two blocks away from his apartment, and Dave slowed.

"I see them," Bobby said, his voice low. "How long have you had those?"

"Few months. Since before Dani."

"Any idea why?"

"Was hoping Meredith would know."

Bobby stopped on the street corner, waiting for the pedestrian signal. "Did she?"

"Sort of."

Bobby didn't ask for an explanation, and Dave didn't offer one. It would all come out anyway when Dani filed a report with Director Upton, but for now, he was still mulling it all over and didn't feel like sharing.

When they reached his building, Dave asked, "Coming up?"

"I've already said my goodbyes. Got a job here." Bobby shrugged, his eyes focused on the building. "Should last a couple of weeks, so if you need my help..."

"We'll call."

Bobby's hard eyes fixed on Dave. "Just so you know, if you hurt her, I'll kill you."

Dave grunted. "If I hurt her, you won't have to."

Bobby nodded and slid into the crowd.

Dave walked into the building. The tension of work slipped away from him and his heart lightened. Dani was upstairs waiting for him, hopefully as eager as he was to pick up where they'd left off.

THE THREE MEN sitting across from Rebecca were as different from one another as men could be. Tom Fairfax, an archival expert, was a tall, slim man with black hair just beginning to gray. At forty, he was the eldest of the group by almost a decade. Phil Walters had the square jaw and clean cut looks of an All-American athlete, and hid his intelligence behind that veneer. He was working on his doctoral dissertation, a project he hoped to complete before his next birthday, the milestone age of thirty. George Howe was a geneticist and the youngest of the three. He was a few inches shorter than the other men and slightly pudgy, with the keen, sharp mind of a genius.

The People would need their expertise in the days to come.

Rebecca had called them into her office together because they were friends, having banded together in some instinctual ritual of manhood when faced with the largely female population housed in and around the IECS campus. They would need each other's support to understand the secrets hidden here. She just hoped their curiosity overcame their skepticism.

"Gentlemen," she said. "Thank you for coming on such short notice. I appreciate that you've each had to shift your schedules around in order to talk to me."

Tom's lean face creased into a friendly smile. "Whatever you need."

"Thank you. What I'm about to tell you may seem strange, but please believe that it's true, and that your discretion in this matter is of the utmost importance."

She didn't miss the curious glances the men exchanged or the raised eyebrows, but simply pressed ahead, explaining the true purpose of the IECS and the people living in Tellowee, and ending with the nature of the curse shrouding the People's past, present, and future.

"I know it's hard to believe," she added, "that a curse of immortality could be laid down upon seven women and then passed to their daughters. I imagine you have questions or would like proof aside from my word."

The men's expressions held no surprise, nor shock, disbelief, or any of the other emotions she'd observed in the expressions of the people she'd briefed in the past. If anything, the men seemed a little smug.

"We've already worked a lot of that out." Phil grinned, unabashed. "Kinda hard not to, as long as Tom's been here."

Tom crossed his arms over his chest and slouched in his seat. "You should really think about rotating your experts out more frequently."

"Yes, I suppose so," she said. "You never said anything."

"And risk losing access to the work here, or worse?" Tom shook his head. "That would be stupid."

"And you're anything but."

Phil waggled a thumb at George. "'Sides, peewee here's got a girlfriend. He wouldn't leave her without a fight."

George hid a blush behind one hand. "Geez, Phil. Tell everybody, why don'tcha?"

Rebecca arched an eyebrow. She was well aware of how male guests were treated by the many Daughters living in the area, but hadn't known of a liaison involving the shy prodigy.

"Andrea," Tom said, his voice low. "He's still torn up because she's stronger and tougher."

"She's an immortal Daughter, trained since birth to defend herself and her People," Rebecca pointed out.

Tom shrugged. "Well, then there was the shotgun."

Rebecca glanced between the men. What in the world was Tom talking about?

"Late night date," Phil said cheerfully. "Stepfather didn't like where George here put his hands."

George groaned and sank lower in his chair.

"Ah." She remembered the uncertainty of first love, though hers had occurred centuries ago. Her thoughts drifted to her husband, her heart's best love, come to her so late in her long, long life. "Your intelligence is likely just as intimidating to her, Mr. Howe. Though, if I were you, I'd take pains to avoid kissing Andrea in front of her stepfather. He's a good man, but his temper runs high where his family's concerned."

George muttered something under his breath that sounded like, "Now you tell me."

Rebecca stifled a laugh. Poor child. But he would learn. "Have you any questions, then, that the three of you haven't yet worked out?"

The men traded shrugs, then Tom said, "I think we have it."

"Well, I suppose I should let you all get back to your work, then. Need I explain the consequences of breaking my trust?"

Phil snorted. "That goes without saying."

Rebecca inclined her head. There was a reason she still participated in the regular competitions the People held. Each of these men had witnessed her and other members of the People fight, Sons and Daughters alike. Poor Mr. Howe had apparently learned the skill of a Daughter firsthand. They were reasonable men and intelligent enough to understand the need for discretion.

And if they weren't, she would deal with them, as the People always had.

As the men shuffled out of the room, Rebecca said "Mr. Fairfax, could I have a moment more of your time, please?"

"Of course, Director. Just a minute." To Phil and George, he said, "See y'all tonight?"

"We'll be there with bells on," Phil said as he led George out of her office.

The door shut behind them, and Tom perched on the edge of a chair in front of her desk. "Guys' night out. You needed something?"

"When Dr. Terhune informed me that one of the documents from the Sandby borg grave mentioned a possible location for Sanctuary, he also asked for your help in sifting through the IECS archives. Is this a task you feel comfortable assuming?"

"Yeah, sure. We're still trying to update the inventories and catalogue, but I can pass those off to somebody else, if it's ok."

"Please do. Finding Sanctuary is important enough that we need our top minds on it."

"Sounds like. And this is the place where the Seven Sisters went after their parents were killed, right?"

"Yes. We've been searching for millennia. Rumor has it even the Sisters couldn't find it again, once they'd left." She paused, uncertain how much she should share. Of course, he would be, and had been, working with their entire collection. Sooner or later, he'd figure it out. "Some believe Sanctuary is an allegory, others that it was real but mystically hidden from the Sisters, similar to the Garden of Eden in the Christian Bible."

"Right. God threw Adam and Eve out because they'd eaten from the Tree of Knowledge and knew sin."

"Exactly, except in this case, the Sisters' sins occurred well after they left. We believe they wanted to return to Sanctuary, but the path was hidden from them by An, the god that cursed them."

"So it might be a real place or it might not, and if it is, it could be hidden?"

She smiled. "You see why we've had so much trouble finding it."

"Yeah." Tom grinned and rubbed his hands together, and his hazel eyes glimmered. "Nothing like a challenge to keep a man busy."

"I hoped you'd say that." Rebecca folded her hands together on top of her desk. "I've called someone in to help you."

"Really? Who?"

"The original archivist. She's a bit...difficult. Absolutely brilliant, but not an easy person to work with."

"And who is this paragon?"

"My daughter, Moira." Rebecca sighed and rubbed the sharp pang in her temple. Amazing how merely speaking the name of her temperamental middle child caused a headache. "She's Irish and a bit high-strung. I wouldn't put her off on you except she has a better understanding of the Archives than anyone, with the possible exception of yourself."

Tom shrugged. "We'll find a way to get along."

Oh, if only dealing with Moira were that easy. Rebecca cast a glance skyward and sighed. "Let's hope."

Somehow, though, she couldn't see her daughter taking the time to get along with anyone, particularly if it spited her mother. It had taken all of Rebecca's knowledge and skill to persuade Moira to leave Ireland.

"When will she be here?" Tom asked.

"She's Irish. She'll be here when she gets here, and that's the best we can expect from her."

And she prayed to the Lady Goddess that Moira would have mercy on them all when she arrived.

DANI WAS SITTING in the living room when Dave entered his apartment, feet tucked under her on the leather sofa, making notes and riffling through the papers summarizing the IECS'S information on Lilith. He hung his jacket and cap up and ruffled a hand over his hair, studying her as she worked. She'd pulled a blanket over her lap. He bumped the thermometer up a notch. She wouldn't ask him to do it, and Daughter or not, she seemed to be catching a cold.

He walked over and dropped down beside her on the sofa, shoulder to shoulder with her. She shifted subtly away from him, and he sighed. That was Dani. One step forward, half a mile back.

"There's a good chance Lilith's not in New York," she said. "Nearly all of the IECS'S recent information on her indicates she's in Atlanta."

She handed Dave two sheets of paper, stapled together at one corner. He scanned the nearly two dozen dates and places where Lilith had been spotted over the past five years. There were two incidences in New York City, aside from the one at the warehouse, and a spattering in other parts of the country or overseas. The vast majority were in the Southeast, and there, Atlanta was a clear hub. Several of the entries were marked with an asterisk, a few with double asterisks.

She cleared her throat. "I thought we could check out the two here tonight and head to Atlanta on the IECS'S plane tomorrow morning."

Dave grunted and handed the papers back to her. She stuck them back in her pile of notes, fished around, and handed him another stack of stapled pages, this one with entries going back twenty years, many also marked with asterisks. He studied them, searching for patterns, then flipped a fingertip against the top page. "What do these asterisks stand for?"

"Daughters killed or mortally wounded, sometimes Sons."

"And the double star?"

"Lilith's involvement uncertain but probable."

He dropped the paper on the table with the others. Dani had yet to look at him and an uneasy tension vibrated off of her. What had happened while he'd been out? "What's wrong?"

Her hand flew swiftly across the paper her eyes seemed glued to. "Nothing."

"Liar," he said, deliberately keeping his tone light.

She looked at him then, her face cold and hard, so unlike her normally open, animated expressions. "You've been with another woman."

Upton. That fink. "No."

Dani threw her pen down and met his gaze. A dangerous fire glinted in her eyes. "Now who's lying?"

She pushed herself off the couch and stalked into her bedroom, shutting the door quietly behind herself.

Dave stifled a curse and scrubbed his hands over his head. So help him, the next time he saw Bobby Upton, he'd give the man the beating he deserved for ratting out that kiss to Dani.

He stood up and went to his bedroom, pausing in front of her door on the way. It was suspiciously quiet on the other side, no tears, no ranting, no breakables banging off the wall. He blew out a harsh breath. Maybe they both needed time to cool off, and he could give her that. He changed into running shorts and a long-sleeved athletic top, then veered into the bathroom to relieve himself. While washing his hands, he glanced in the mirror and groaned. A smudge of rose red lipstick smudged one corner of his mouth.

Christ. No wonder Dani was pissed.

He scrubbed it off with a wet washcloth and vowed never to even look at another woman unless Dani was there to witness it. By God, he'd nearly exhausted his control where she was concerned. One more thing, just one more, and he was going to toss her over his shoulder, haul her to the nearest bed, and fulfill every sexual promise he'd ever made to her, spoken or not.

He tossed the washcloth down on the bathroom counter, jotted a quick note for her letting her know he'd gone out for a run, and tucked his phone and a spare key into the tiny waist pocket of his shorts. Blowing off steam pounding his feet against pavement seemed like a better idea than hunting Upton down and pounding fist into face.

He came back an hour later, his body tingling inside and out, his mind clear and calm. Dani's bedroom door was still closed, and he sighed. Was she gonna live in there or what?

He trudged into the kitchen and fixed a protein shake, drank it standing up, and focused on the night ahead. The chances of finding another trace of Lilith in New York were slim to none, but they had to check those addresses out, just in case. Maybe they'd get lucky. Probably not.

It was their last night here. Maybe they could go out, do something fun. Check out a movie, see the sights, anything to coax her out of her snit and back to her normal, cheerful self.

Dani padded into the kitchen dressed in a green wool sweater and black leather pants, her footsteps quiet on the carpeted floor. Her skin was pale, her hair mussed, and a faint, red crease mark marred her cheek.

"Nice nap?" he asked.

She grunted.

He swallowed the last of his drink and rinsed the glass out, placing it in the sink to wash later. He wanted to pull her close and finish what they'd started that morning, or just hold her until she forgave him for being an idiot.

Though he damn well had *not* kissed another woman. What kind of fool did she take him for? He wasn't the kind of guy to snuggle up to one woman and make out with another, never had been.

Anyway, a man could be kissed without kissing back, couldn't he? And, hell, what was a little kiss between friends?

She shuffled across the kitchen floor to the refrigerator, stifling a yawn. Somehow, he didn't think he'd persuade her of that, particularly if she found out he and Mer had had sex.

Only once, six years ago, but still.

Dani pulled out a carton of orange juice, and he found a glass for her. She mumbled a thanks and poured herself some juice, then put the carton away. He followed her into the living room and sat down on the edge of the sofa beside her, resting his forearms on his thighs.

He studied her, trying to gauge her mood. Was she ready to talk to him again or was he going to have to grovel some? "I know this place. Good home cooking. We could go there tonight."

She cut a side eyed glance at him. "If you're trying to apologize, forget it."

"We have to eat, and they make a helluva good cheesecake."

"Bribery won't work."

"Chocolate truffle with hazelnuts."

She sipped the orange juice. A small smile tugged at her mouth. "Ok, look, I could forgive you for the flannel sheets, but withholding chocolate truffle cheesecake is just cruel."

"And the lipstick?"

The smile dropped from her face and her expression hardened into stone. "Some things are unforgiveable."

She closed her eyes and leaned her head against the back of the sofa, probably to shut him out, not that it would work. He tugged the glass carefully out of her grip, set it on the coffee table out of the way, and pulled her into a one-armed hug. Her body went stiff as a board, but at least she didn't struggle.

He brushed a tender kiss over the top of her head. "Let me explain."

"You're going to anyway, aren't you."

He chafed a hand gently along her arm. "I'm being followed."

"Knew that already."

"Meredith put out feelers for me, trying to figure out who and why."

"Alexiou, the FBI."

A small swell of pride welled up within him. Smart, clever Dani. "The CIA, too." She relaxed into him. "Tell Dani all."

So he did, beginning with the first time he'd noticed the tail, going through his suspicions about his assignments and his handler, and ending with his meeting with Meredith.

"Why didn't you tell me this before?" Dani asked.

He shrugged. "Used to working alone."

"Dave, come on. We've been working together for months, off and on. You should've told me about this a long time ago."

"Yeah, maybe." He sighed. "Are we ok?"

"No," she said flatly. "We're not ok. I don't care who that woman was. If you want to be with me, you can't run around kissing every woman you know."

"Christ, Dani, it wasn't like that. She kissed me."

She stood and stared coldly down at him. "You had a choice, Dave. Accept it or back away. Which one did you choose?"

He stifled a grimace and pushed himself off the couch. "I chose not to do anything. That's not the same thing as acceptance."

"You're splitting hairs, Caveman." Temper flashed in her eyes and her cheeks flushed pink. "If you can't keep your lips off other women, don't even think about putting them on me again."

He bit back a curse and walked away before he did something stupid, like drag her into the bedroom and show her exactly how he'd put his lips on her, other women be damned. "Shower," he said, and went into his bedroom, shutting the door on her glare.

SEVEN

THEY LEFT NEW YORK early the next morning by the private plane Bobby had arrived in, after a night spent checking the two addresses on their list. Dani had caved and let Dave take her to the restaurant he'd suggested, persuaded as much by the promise of cheesecake as anything.

After all, it was the little things that made life worth living. Freshly made chocolate truffle cheesecake with a dusting of hazelnuts certainly fit that bill.

As she'd suspected, the remaining New York addresses the IECS had for Lilith were useless. One was a seedy dive, filthy to the point of health code violations. Unsurprisingly, nobody remembered seeing the Daughter, even after a generous bribe.

The second was a restaurant in Manhattan, and ditto. Of course, it had been weeks since Lilith had been spotted at either location, and then probably from a distance. The Daughter's reputation preceded her and left a rash of conveniently blank memories in its wake.

The list of Lilith's known relatives among the People had ended the same way, with call after call unanswered, including one to Lydia, Lilith's niece and a member of the Council of Seven.

It was like chasing a ghost with only rumor to go on and hoping to catch it in a butterfly net.

They'd come back to Dave's apartment late. Dani had finished packing, ignored Dave and his tempting flannel sheets, and fell into a restless sleep. She'd woken up in the middle of the night with him standing by her bedside, pulling another blanket over her. He'd softly kissed the tip of her nose and left, his nearly bare body glimmering in the dim light shining through the room's window.

If the rat bastard weren't so sweetly considerate, she might have an easier time hating him.

She'd seen the lipstick, An curse him, and the pain of betrayal had hit her hard. She'd only just kept the hurt from showing. In spite of Bobby's texted warning, she'd believed in the big lug. Dave wouldn't kiss another woman while dangling Dani on the hook. Drug and kidnap her, keep her in the dark, and waltz her in front of the People's most dangerous enemy, sure, but not cheat. Until she'd spotted that lipstick, she hadn't thought he had it in him.

How wrong could one woman be?

Dani stared out the window of the plane watching the clouds float by, her mind in turmoil, her heart an aching mess. She still had a hard time believing it. Dave had seemed so sincere in his denial. Bobby had backed that up, even as he warned her to be careful, but she'd seen the lipstick with her own eyes.

They landed in the regional airport near Gainesville and gathered their bags and gear, the transition through security made easier by the size of the field. Rebecca had sent a car to pick them up. Dani directed the driver, one of the IECS'S security complement, to her apartment in Buford.

Dave hadn't spoken since they'd left New York. In anybody else, the silence would worry her, but he seemed to prefer it, always had. Dani let him take the front seat, just so she could avoid his protective presence and the thoughtful gaze he trained on her. His possessiveness should irritate her. Instead, it simply drained her.

The driver dropped them off outside her apartment. She thanked him and led Dave inside and into the elevator.

It was a small place in a good neighborhood, located close enough to Tellowee and her family's base to be convenient, but far enough away to feel independent. The neighbors were friendly, mostly young married couples, a few with children, and the elderly building super was an Audrey Hepburn fan.

It helped to have things in common with your neighbors.

Most everybody was at work when she brought Dave in. She unlocked the door and pushed it open, hung her keys on their hook by the door. The apartment smelled like lemons and pine cleaner, thanks to her cleaning woman. The wooden floors gleamed in the midday light shining through the windows on the opposite side of the room. The right wall contained pictures of her family, rows and rows of memories captured in individual moments. The left, though, held her pride and joy, a collection of weapons she'd assembled over her lifetime, some ancient, others modern, including the weapons she used on a regular basis.

Contentment filled her and the tension tightening her muscles eased. It was good to be home.

Dave dropped his luggage on the floor inside the entrance and locked up behind himself. He pulled out his electronic sweeper and ran it around the table sitting just inside the apartment, the coat rack, the door frame, and Dani bit her lip, hiding a smile. How could she still find him so adorable after what he'd done to her?

Remember the lipstick, she reminded herself, *and not his chest, that gloriously magnificent muscled chest, naked with water running over it.*

Dave pulled a small chip from behind a framed poster of one of her singing engagements way back in the day, and her amusement died. She dropped her bags beside his and did a manual sweep of her bedroom and bathroom while Dave finished the living area and kitchen. Somebody had violated her home. If she ever found out who, things would not end well.

They found three bugs in all, plus a miniscule camera positioned strategically under an end table and aimed at the front door.

Nothing else was out of place, but nothing would be, damn it all. The cleaning lady would've wiped away any traces of an intruder, thinking Dani herself had made the mess.

Dave held the bugs and camera up, and she nodded. He destroyed and threw the camera in the kitchen trash, then ran the bugs under water, frying their circuits.

Dani mulled the situation over. Was there a way to avoid having the camera, at least, put back in place or were they doomed to have the friggin' thing replaced every time they stepped out of the apartment? The last thing they needed was somebody monitoring their movements, no matter who was doing it.

And who *had* done it? Surely not the same people that had been following Dave. How could anybody possibly have known they were coming to Georgia and beaten them here to set surveillance up? Or had it simply been put in place as a precaution, when Dave started working with her?

Dave reentered the living area, and Dani shrugged her questions away. They had other work to do. With any luck, solving one problem would lead to a solution for the other.

"Only one bed." She jerked her chin toward the living area in the great room. "The couch folds out or you can go to a hotel."

Dave folded his arms across his chest and slowly shook his head. "Not leaving you."

"Have it your way."

Of course, if he hadn't *kissed another woman* he could be having his way with her right at that moment, in the luxury of her Queen-sized bed. "I'll make some space for your stuff in my closet."

"Thanks. Lunch?"

"Sounds good."

He walked toward the kitchen, separated from the living area by an island, and skirted the four-person wood dining table shoved against the wall. He opened the refrigerator and looked inside. Immediately, he jerked away from it and turned wide, slate gray eyes on her. "It's empty."

"Yes," she agreed mildly. "I've been gone a long time."

He shut the fridge door. "You don't even have mayo. Who doesn't have mayo?"

"We'll stock up later." She pulled out her phone and waggled it at him. "Chinese?"

"Sure."

He yanked open the closest kitchen cabinets, probably checking to see what she had in stock. If the fridge had shocked him, the lack of supplies in the cabinets would give him apoplexy.

She called her favorite take out place and ordered for the both of them.

When she finished, he said, "You have phone numbers for take out on your phone?"

"Who doesn't?" She grabbed one of his bags and gestured toward her bedroom. "I'll show you where you can put your things."

The delivery boy arrived while they were stowing Dave's clothes. Dani set her laptop up on the dining table, brainstorming with Dave as they plowed through Kung Pao Shrimp and General Tso's Chicken.

Halfway through, Dani retrieved the lists of addresses Rebecca had sent them and pointed out a handful clustered in and around the northeastern section of the

Greater Atlanta area. She typed one of the addresses into Google Earth and circled her fingertip around a section of the map highlighted on her laptop's screen. "I'm pretty familiar with this area. We can start there tonight with this group of bars and work our way outward."

"Good a place as any."

She typed in another address, refocusing the map. "Meantime, what about hitting this cluster? It's not far from here."

He slouched into his chair. "Lot to cover in one day."

She stood and picked up her plate and utensils. "Yeah. And?"

"How about we stock up today and do the second cluster tomorrow? That'll give us time to find the owners and maybe track Lilith that way."

She shrugged and took her dirty dishes into the kitchen area. "Sure. We should add the addresses of Lilith's nearby relatives to the list and visit them while we're out."

"Dani, wait." The chair scraped as he stood and his footsteps echoed as he crossed the wooden floor.

"What?"

The corner of his mouth turned up in that lopsided grin of his. "You cooked, I'll clean."

She smiled, unable to resist his humor. "I ordered. That's not the same thing."

"Close enough."

She shuffled out of his way, scrounged paper and a pen, and began a list of staples. Mayonnaise. Beer. Fruit. Cheese. She eyed the list. Hunh. Maybe Dave should do this part.

He dumped their dishes into the sink and ran water over them. "Wanna try something else."

"Like what?"

"Paper trail. Everybody leaves one."

She tapped the pen against the counter. Good ol' Dave and his government-molded mind. "And you have a lot of ways to track paper, don't you?"

The look he shot at her over his shoulder carried all the smug authority of the FBI. She turned back to the list without another word. Cute, adorable Dave. Too bad he was such a Neanderthal.

When he finished the dishes, he settled his hands on her waist and leaned into her, his cheek next to her temple. His warmth seeped into her skin, melting away the *back off* she'd mentally prepared. Would she ever really learn to resist him?

He drew her into a companionable argument over the list and the menu. Dave insisted he wasn't willing to risk her cooking. Dani shot back that it was *her place, her rules*. It was the most she'd ever heard him talk at one time and, funnily enough, it warmed her to him even more.

Remember the lipstick, she thought, and not a whiff of betrayal or hurt reared its protective head. Damn the man. In less than twenty-four hours, he'd managed to erode all her carefully erected barriers, and she'd let him. Was she really ready to have her heart broken by a man who couldn't even keep his lips to himself? She gritted her teeth and hardened herself to him, dragging a shield around her tender heart inch by reluctant inch.

DAVE SAT on the sofa, watching Dani's TV, waiting for her to get out of the shower. After their staples run and a quick supper of sandwiches, he'd called his folks just to say hello, and listened to his mother ramble about grandbabies and church socials, and his dad grump about the weather and crop futures.

Some things never changed, except that every year it seemed his sisters popped out another baby. If not them, then a cousin or a neighbor or a friend of the family. His mother had dropped hints that it was time for him to settle down and give her a grandchild. He hadn't told her he might've found somebody to do that with. First he had to convince Dani that he hadn't kissed another woman.

Stubborn as she was, that might take a while.

The muffled sounds of her getting ready sounded through her bedroom door. A few minutes later, she walked out. He twisted on the sofa, intending to ask her if he could take a turn in the shower, and his brain fritzed out, erasing every thought in his head.

She wore a white long-sleeved shirt tied under her breasts. The front gaped open, exposing the edges of a black, lace bra. Her midriff was bare to the waist of a pleated plaid skirt that was just long enough to cover the essentials. Sheer black, thigh-high stockings encased her slender legs, held up by a garter belt. Its straps showed against the stretch of bare skin visible between the bottom of her skirt and the top of the stockings. Her shoes looked like platform Mary Janes. She'd pulled her hair into pigtails and put on just enough make-up to pass for a Goth vampire hooker doing a school girl imitation.

He zeroed in on her navel, where a silver ring glittered against her smooth, tanned skin. That hadn't been there yesterday. If it had, he'd have already had his mouth there, tonguing it.

He stood slowly, barely managing not to stumble over his own feet.

"Jesus, Joseph, and Mary." His voice was strangled and tight, and his dick poked at the fly of his jeans. "You're not wearing that out."

"Yes, I am." She sashayed past him. Her hips swayed with each step and the skirt swished against her finely crafted ass. She bent over the dining room table and gathered the pages of Lilith's sightings and contacts together, and her skirt rode up, baring the smooth, creamy skin high on her thighs. His control teetered on the edge of shattering.

"Are you wearing underwear?" he blurted out, and winced. Holy cow. Where had his good sense evaporated to? What kind of question was that to ask a woman who was barely speaking to him?

"Shower's open if you want." She peered over her shoulder, still bent over. "I laid some clothes out for you."

She turned back to the table and reached for her laptop, and the skirt rode higher, revealing a narrow strip of black satin between the completely nude cheeks of her ass. A vision popped into his head, of her bent all the way over on the table, her ass bared to his gaze, of pulling that strip aside and burying himself in her, of sliding in and out of that tight, wet heat until she begged for release.

"We don't have all night, Dave."

Her voice broke through the vision, scattering it, and he fumbled desperately for his focus. Lilith. Bars. Shower.

Right.

He headed toward her bedroom, walking slowly enough to accommodate an incredibly inconvenient hard on, and stripped off his clothes as he went, not caring if she saw the effect she'd had on him. By God, if she couldn't handle it, maybe she should wear more clothes, like a muumuu or a parka or something.

His gaze fell on the outfit she'd placed on the bed for him, and he groaned out a laugh. Black t-shirt, tight jeans, and the motorcycle boots she'd insisted he bring from New York. A fisherman's cap rested on top of the stack of clothes and he recognized it immediately. She'd knit that for him while they were in New York. An odd wave of tenderness wove through the gripping need, ratcheting his desire higher until it burned through him.

Please God, let her forgive him soon.

IT WAS a long night. The first two bars were washes. Both were too upscale for Dave's tastes, with modern fixtures, trendy music, and enough artifice to last him a lifetime. They were places where people went to be seen, not to grab a cold one and hang out with friends.

The bouncers at both greeted Dani with smiles and fist bumps, and let her and Dave cut through the lines of people waiting to get inside. When he asked, she told him she taught classes on self-defense and crowd-management, and had gotten to know a lot of security personnel and local law enforcement agents as a result.

She blended in with the highbrow set better than he would've thought, in spite of her outfit. Thank God she'd covered it with a knee-length leather jacket before they'd left her apartment, but only between bars. Once inside, she stripped it off and headed for the dance floor, her body twisting sensually to the beat of the music blasting through the air, studying the crowd beneath lowered lashes while he wandered casually around the perimeter searching for Lilith or hangers-on. He'd just as casually slipped a small picture of the Daughter to the bartenders, along with a tip, with little luck. None had seen Lilith recently. One bartender recognized her as an infrequent guest, but knew nothing about her. Dave left his card at each bar with the request that the bartenders call if she came in.

The third bar on their list, Bones, was grubbier, darker, and not anywhere close to trendy. It was housed in a series of brick buildings, with the adjoining walls knocked down and columns put in to support the roofs. Skeletons, whole or in pieces, were scattered along the walls next to voodoo dolls, shrunken heads, African shaman masks, and other tools of dark magic. Euro techno throbbed in the background. Nearly everybody was dressed in black and sported enough piercings and tats to float all of Atlanta.

Once inside, Dani peeled off her jacket and gave it to the coat check girl, then threaded through the crowd to the dance area and joined two girls dancing with each other.

Dave squeezed into a spot at the bar, ordered a pop, and watched her move to the music, his body thrumming with the need he hadn't been able to freeze out with an icy shower. The bartender set a cup of fizzing soda in front of him, and Dave swiveled away from the floor and pushed a picture of Lilith across the bar. "Seen this woman?"

The bartender stepped back, pale hands resting against the bar, dark eyes suspicious. Like most of the bar's inhabitants, he was covered with piercings. A tattoo of a dragon peeked out from the rolled up cuff of his black, long-sleeved shirt. "Who wants to know?"

Dave leveled a hard stare on the man. "A friend."

The bartender pushed the picture back. "She comes in sometimes."

"Anybody with her?"

"Yeah. She's got a whole gang." The bartender snorted and his wide mouth twisted into a sneer. "They think she's a vampire or some shit."

"You don't?"

"Naw, man, but she sure ain't right." The bartender twirled his finger around one temple and whistled. "You know what I mean?"

"Yeah, I got it." Dave pulled a business card out of his wallet and passed it across the bar with a twenty. "Call me if you see her."

"Sure, man. You want change or a tab?"

"Keep it."

Dave put his back to the bar and propped against it, drink in hand, automatically homing in on Dani's position. She'd danced her way deeper into the bodies writhing on the dance floor, far enough that it took him a minute to figure out what he was seeing and another minute for it to seep into his disbelieving mind. Dani was cozied up to some skank, tatted kid, her back to his chest, his hips grinding against her ass. She twisted around and smiled down at the kid, who flushed and stuttered and dug his fingers into her hips.

Hell with that.

Dave slapped his cup onto the bar and stalked through the crowd, shouldering people out of the way. A deep vein of jealous anger throbbed through him. What the hell was she thinking, messing with a kid like that? They were supposed to be working. They were supposed to be *together*.

When he reached Dani, he grabbed her arm and growled a warning to the kid. "Mine."

The kid scrambled back, hands in the air, and disappeared into the seething crowd.

Dave yanked her against him. "What the hell?"

She wound her arms around his neck, molding her body to his, and smiled at him through gritted teeth. "He knows Lilith, you Neanderthal. Now dance or I'm gonna make you go home."

He grunted and settled her more firmly against him, his anger pounding to the music's steady beat. With her Mary Janes on, she was nearly as tall as him. Their bodies aligned perfectly, hips against hips, her breasts pressed into his chest, their mouths so close, their breaths mingled.

Her gaze dropped to his lips. "Dave."

She whirled in his arms, and he sprawled one hand along her bare midriff over the cold chill of her navel ring. Glorious heat pooled into his groin. He was gonna put his mouth there later. She'd like that, wouldn't she, having a man worship her? And oh, yeah, would he worship her.

He gripped her hip with his other hand and lead her in a grind, her firm ass against his erection. Her hands covered his, pressing them against her skin, and he pulled her back into his chest. "Tease."

She turned her head and smiled wickedly, her lips inches away from his own. He should kiss her, give her a little of the heat rocketing through him, maybe get some back. He leaned in to do just that, and a tingle went up his spine, halting him a hair's breadth from claiming her mouth.

"Dance," Dani said.

"She's here."

"I know." Dani pivoted and wound her arms around him, kissed him softly, so good, so sweet. "Do you need a minute?"

He was never going to calm down while she was plastered against him, and damned if he wanted to let her go. "We go as soon as she's settled."

"Tell me when."

Dave dug his fingers into Dani's hips and brushed his cheek against hers, his gaze pinned to Lilith winding gracefully through the bar. "When we get home, I swear, I'm bending you over the dining room table."

"Try it and die, Farm Boy."

"Maybe you'll like what I do to you." Lilith disappeared into a knot of people, and Dave reluctantly released his hold on Dani. "Ready?"

Dani took his hand and led him through the crowd toward the far side of the building. Lilith sat at a small table, basking in the attention of the group fawning over her. Up close, she was coldly beautiful, her eyes nearly vacant behind what had to be violet-colored contacts, her black hair flowing straight to her shoulders. Her dress was a skin-hugging black. It bared her arms and enough cleavage to entice most men into sin.

Her gaze zeroed in on Dani and Dave as they approached.

"Mmm, darlings," she said, her voice a low, accented purr. "Look what the People dragged in."

"Lilith," Dani said flatly, her body relaxed.

Dave shifted to stand beside her and crossed his arms over his chest, his expression blank.

"How charming," Lilith said. "You know my name."

The group around Lilith tittered behind pale hands.

"You have something belonging to the People," Dani said.

Lilith leaned back against her chair and slid her hands down her torso. "Why, I'm certain I haven't a thing with me but what I'm wearing."

Dani ground her teeth together. "Don't play games. We know you have the Prophecy tablet."

Lilith rose abruptly. The people surrounding her fell silent and edged subtly away from her. She walked slowly around the table, her hips swaying, and stopped in front of Dani, one hand extended. Dave snatched her wrist, and Lilith turned an unimpressed stare on him.

"Your pet is protective, Daniella."

Dani cut a side-eyed glance at him, and he let go. "How do you know my name?" she asked.

Lilith's hand fell away. "I make it my business to know."

"Where's the tablet?"

"I'm certain I have no idea." Lilith pivoted toward her sycophants. "Have you seen a Prophecy tablet?" She turned in a slow circle, arms spread wide, her wide-eyed gaze raking over the silent crowd gathering around them. "Has anyone seen this tablet?"

She dropped her arms. Her gaze flicked to Dave, then settled on Dani. "He's quite handsome. Perhaps you would consider a trade. Him for information."

Dani snorted out a laugh. "All I want is the tablet. Him, you can have, if you can take him."

Lilith shifted her stance and ran a hand down Dave's chest and across his stomach, then cupped his penis, caressing him through his jeans. Her vacant gaze bored into him and dark chills shivered across his skin. He held his body loose, controlling his first instinct to grab Dani and run, as far and as fast as he could.

"Daniella, darling, didn't Rebecca teach you to be more careful with your toys? I might break him and then you wouldn't have anything to play with."

Dave nodded at Dani. "That belongs to her."

"Did Rebecca not tell you?" Lilith squeezed him, her touch just shy of painful. "She belongs to me, to do with as I will. To kill, or not." She released him and stepped back. "That is her destiny."

"I don't believe in fate," Dave said.

"But she does. Isn't that right, little Dani?" Lilith smoothed a hand over one of Dani's pigtails. "You look so like your father."

Dani stiffened, and Dave placed a restraining hand on her back.

"What do you know about my father?" she asked.

"I know all, see all." Lilith's smile held no humor, only a flickering sadness, gone as soon as it touched her face. "As does Rebecca. Have you not asked her?"

"Do you have the tablet or not?"

"I think...not. But perhaps I do. Who's to say?" Lilith stepped back and her icy expression turned to stone. "It's past your bedtime and my patience grows thin."

"We'll be back."

Lilith's hollow laugh echoed in the dead space around her. "Until then, darling girl."

Dani pushed through the crowd surrounding them, and Dave followed. The muscles around his spine tightened and the hair on the back of his neck bristled. They were being watched. Not a damn thing he could do about it. Dani picked up her coat, and they left Bones and went back to her apartment without a single word passing between them.

EIGHT

A S SOON AS they entered Dani's apartment, Dave rounded on her. "What did you think you were doing?"

Dani shrugged her coat off and hung it on the coat rack. "What are you talking about?"

He gritted his teeth. "Lilith. Why did you push her like that?"

"I had it under control."

"You had it under..." His voice trailed off. Yeah, she'd had it under control, all right. That's why Lilith had felt free to touch his friggin' penis in the middle of a crowd of onlookers. Thank God his erection had softened under her touch. "Ok, fine, you had Lilith under control. What about the boy?"

She arched her eyebrows, her expression curious, nothing more. "Which one?"

"The one you were having sex with out on the dance floor."

"I have no idea what you're talking about."

She whirled away, and he grabbed her arm, halting her in mid-step.

"Is this some kind of childish revenge for Meredith?"

She shook her arm and her cheeks flushed bright pink. "I was doing my job."

"Like hell."

"Back off, Farm Boy."

"When you can be reasonable about this."

She laughed, a furious bark of sound, and yanked her arm out of his grip. "You left me hot and bothered and went straight to her. Sorry if I can't be reasonable about it."

"She kissed me," he said, enunciating each word carefully, "to say goodbye."

Dani snorted. "Yeah, right."

"Chrissake, Dani, I don't want another woman." He scrubbed a rough hand over his head, ruffling the short strands. "I want you."

Her look shouted *liar* and had enough hurt behind it to crack his heart. "It's not enough to want, Dave."

He cupped her shoulders and squeezed gently. "I've wanted you since the first time I saw you."

Her mouth opened and closed, and her shoulders relaxed under his hands. "Really?"

"The very first, when you stepped out of the shadows wearing that Goth vampire porn outfit."

A coy smile tilted the corners of her mouth up. "So, it's the clothes you like."

"Like what's under the clothes." He skimmed his fingertips down the bare skin between her breasts, and her heart skittered under his touch. "In here."

"Yeah?"

"I swear it."

She bit her lip. "You're trying to talk me around."

"Maybe a little." He touched his forehead to hers, searching for the words that would make her understand. "Seems like a lifetime you've been in my dreams, in my heart."

"Why should I believe you?"

"Because it's true. Feels like I've spent my whole life looking for you." He slid his arms around her waist. She leaned into him, and he bit back a sigh. That was what he needed, her against him. "Why would I risk losing you?"

"I guess I just don't know if I can trust you, after everything that's happened between us."

"I never put you in harm's way, Dani, never. Don't turn me away again."

He kissed her then, hard, demanding, greedy. She opened for him, and primal need surged through his blood. He flicked his tongue into her mouth, tasting her, and she moaned and dug her fingers into his muscles through his t-shirt. This is what he'd been waiting for, her satiny skin under his hands, her body arched into his, everything she was open to him.

Her phone rang. She broke the kiss and rocked back on her heels, her gaze hooded and dreamy, her beautiful mouth slick and red, her breaths panting out of her lungs.

He tightened his grip on her waist. "Not this time, Dani. Please."

"Ok." Her hands drifted down his chest and tugged his t-shirt out of his jeans. "Off."

He yanked the shirt off, let it fall to the floor, and pressed his mouth against hers, walking her backward. The backs of her thighs hit the dining table, and his earlier vision clogged his head, of her bent over the table, of lifting her skirt and pulling aside the strap of her thong, of sinking into her tight, wet heat. Later. He could do that later. First, he wanted to taste her. He lifted her onto the table and settled between her thighs.

She stroked his chest, learning him from collarbone to bellybutton. "I've wanted to touch you since the first time you pulled your shirt off in front of me."

"Should I cut a Godzilla movie on, bring back the feeling?"

Her eyes cut to his beneath the dense curve of her lashes. "You're getting bold with your humor."

Because I feel safe with you. He bit the thought off before it could meander to the funny feeling in his chest where his heart beat a rapid *rat-a-tat-tat.*

She tugged him down, her hand firm on the back of his neck, and molded her mouth to his. Her other hand drifted across the muscles of his chest and trailed heat wherever she touched, all the way down to the erection he'd sported since she'd walked out of the bedroom earlier, dressed like a naughty school girl. He pulled his mouth away from hers and pressed open mouthed kisses down her neck, nipping the skin with his teeth.

She inhaled a sharp breath. "I love it when you do that."

"Mmm." He licked the flat of his tongue all the way up the slender column of her neck, and she shuddered and moaned and clung to him. His file of *things Dani likes* was growing by the minute. "Tell me what else you love."

She exhaled a laugh. "Every single damn thing you do."

He laughed against her neck, tugged her shirt aside, and traced his tongue along the line of her collarbone, tasting her skin. Pure silk, warm honey, beautiful woman. "So if I—"

"Yes."

She tilted her head, silently encouraging his explorations, and fumbled with the ties of her shirt.

He brushed her hands aside and soaked in the view of her firm breasts barely covered by the black lace of her bra. He skimmed his hands over them, memorizing the rough feel of the lace contrasted with the smooth silk of her skin. "What if I—"

"Goddess, yes."

She undid the front clasp of her bra, then propped her hands behind her, her cat's eyes molten.

He spread her shirt and bra wide, framing her upper torso with fabric, and flicked his thumbs across her nipples. "Remember that night at Alexiou's?"

Her lips tilted into a sensuous smile, the secret, knowing look of a seductress. "Mmm. Good times."

His hands drifted to her flat stomach and the silver ring glinting against her skin. "Remember what I told you I'd do if we ever had sex?"

She bit her lower lip and flicked her eyes down his body, and her sweet gaze burned into his skin. "I remember."

"Gonna do that now."

He wrapped one arm around her back, cupped her breast, and sucked her nipple into his mouth. Dani threw her head back and her gasp shot through him, stoking his desire. He licked his way to her other breast and suckled her. She was so good, so ripe. Her nipple hardened under his tongue and her legs wound around his waist, and her panted breaths morphed into kittenish mewls in the back of her throat.

It was beautiful, the way she shivered under his mouth. The arch of her back pushed her breasts up, like she couldn't get enough, didn't ever want him to stop. Now that he'd tasted her, now that he knew what it could be like with nothing between them, he wasn't sure he could.

He skimmed the backs of his fingers down her stomach, teasing her skin, then delved under her skirt, searching for her core hidden beneath her skimpy thong. She was hot and wet, and he ached to taste her. He eased back and flipped her skirt up, baring her upper thighs, and bunched the material around her waist. Above it, the navel ring glinted against her flat stomach, and below it was her pussy, covered by a thin, satiny strip.

He yanked the thong away, breaking the fragile material. She was so slick there.

He pressed his hands tight against the tops of her thighs, pushing them wider, and slid his thumbs along the sensitive creases on the outside of her sex, then farther in, along the plump lips. Her hips shifted on the table, and he glanced up.

She was watching him, an odd light glowing in her beautiful face. "I want you so much."

Her soft, breathy voice cut him to the core. She wanted him. God, yes. "Gonna taste you now," he said, and barely recognized his own voice through the thick need.

He knelt between her legs, lifted them onto his shoulders, and flattened one palm against her stomach, holding her in place. His first taste was a long lick along the seam of her body. The honeyed liquid at her core melted into the back of his throat, and he groaned. She was pure, womanly sweetness. His erection pushed against the tight material of his jeans, aching, and he fed it, fed the molten need building in him with another long lick, with his tongue delving into her core, and the nub of her sex sucked into his mouth in a slow, nibbling tease.

She dropped back against the table. "Holy Mother, don't stop."

He laughed, low and husky. He wasn't going to stop, not until she came so hard, she forgot everything but him.

He slid one finger into her slick heat, pushing in and out in an imitation of what his body demanded. Her hand cupped the back of his head and her hips rotated up in rhythm to the sucks and licks and nibbles of his mouth. She felt so good there, tasted so good, and he never wanted it to end.

Her grip tightened around the back of his head. "Dave. I'm... I'm close."

He pushed a second finger into her, and her pussy pulsed around him as her hips writhed against his touch. God, yes, she was hot, ready. Her hand slipped away, and he quickened his pace, stroking his fingers in and out of her while his tongue flicked across her clit, pushing harder and faster, hitting the special spot inside her core over and over again, and she came on a long moan, her body arching off the table as she ground her sex against his mouth. He pulled his fingers out and licked her core again and again, savoring the taste of her release.

Her breaths slowed and her hips stilled, and she lay limply against the table. "Are you sure the women in Kansas didn't raise at least one statue in your honor?"

He laughed. "Not a one."

"Crying shame."

He kissed his way up her stomach, flicked his tongue around the navel ring. The cool metal was so at odds with her warm, tanned skin, and he savored the difference, pushing his tongue into her navel, lifting the ring, tugging at it with his teeth.

Her hands skimmed up his arms in butterfly touches. "Having fun?"

He *mmmd* against her skin. "I like this."

"So piercings turn you on?"

"Just yours."

He pushed himself upright and drank her in, the golden skin, firm and smooth, the satisfied smile teasing her mouth, the wet folds of her core. She'd opened to him, accepted him, let him move her, and he wanted to give her so much more, needed to touch her, to love her.

He fumbled with his jeans, unfastened them, and shoved them and his underwear down, releasing his throbbing erection. Pre-cum glistened along the tip. She rubbed one finger along the sensitive slit, spreading moisture around the head of his dick.

"I want to put my mouth here," she said, and his hips jerked forward, begging her to. Her mouth on his dick, sucking him in, teasing him, her tongue stroking over his skin. His balls tightened and his tongue tangled up in his mouth and his breath pushed out of his lungs, and he was dizzy with her and everything she could do to him.

Not yet, though, not until he satisfied her again.

He gripped his erection and rubbed the tip of it against her pussy, sliding it up and down along the soaking wet folds, then pressed into her. Her body devoured him inch by inch and the broad head of his erection disappeared into the slick folds of her sex. So tight, a wet-hot glove that clung to his skin as he rocked in and out, trying to seat himself fully, and raked the need higher.

Sweat broke out on his skin and he grasped her hips. She sucked in a breath, and he glanced up, meeting her gaze. Satisfaction and womanly power hummed out of her. A small smile played across her mouth, like she knew exactly what it was doing to him to go slow, to give her body time to adjust. The muscles of her core squeezed around him, and his hips shot forward. He flexed his hips, gaining a scant inch, and his muscles strained and shook.

"Don't wanna hurt you," he gritted out.

Her smile gentled. "You're not."

He slid in and out of her slowly. Her pussy yielded a little more with each stroke, and at last, he was buried in her to the hilt. He stayed like that as long as he could, waiting for her to be ok. Her body gripped him so tightly, so good, so good.

His teeth ground together. He couldn't hurt her, not now. Had to go slow. Had to take it easy.

"Dave." She slid her hands over his and squeezed gently. "Please."

"Ok," he said. "Ok."

He moved then, settling his hips into a hard, steady rhythm, his erection sliding in and out of her in agonizing pleasure as skin met skin. He bent over her, kissing her, and his tongue emulated his thrusts into her pussy. She wrapped her legs around his waist and her arms around his back. She took him, all of him, and her sharp passion exploded around him. Her body jerked and her pussy pulsed, and her pleasure shot him over the edge, shattering him as he pumped into her, spilling his release into her willing body in an orgasm that went on and on, sapping his strength with its intensity.

When he came back to himself, they were both panting, their bodies glistening with sweat. Dani was limp under him and her arms splayed across the table. He kissed her lips gently. He wanted to stay there forever, just like this, her sated and warm beneath him, him buried deep inside her.

He eased away from her and brushed a hand over her hair, and she smiled at him, her eyes closed, contentment purring through her. His heart thumped in his chest, echoing his satisfaction and something more. Tenderness, completeness, and an emotion he refused to define.

He stood and shucked his clothes down his body, then chuckled. He still had his boots on. He yanked his briefs and jeans back into place, and zipped his jeans up. "Up and at 'em."

She opened one eye, then closed it and sighed. "I'm fine here, thanks."

He snagged her hands, pulled her up, and scooped her off the table.

Her eyes popped open. She gasped out a laugh and wrapped her arms around his neck. "Mmm. I likey."

He grinned at her and strode into her bedroom, then dropped her onto the bed.

She bounced and shrieked out a laugh. "I can't believe you just did that."

"Believe it."

He sat down next to her and took his boots off.

She settled behind him, resting her head against his shoulder, her hands stroking his skin. "Davy."

He set his boots on the other side of her nightstand. "Not gonna make me talk, are you?"

"No." She sighed and pressed a kiss against his back. "It was good."

"Yeah."

"Again, Farm Boy?"

He twisted around and tackled her, and pressed her into the soft duvet covering her bed. "As you wish."

She smiled and tugged him down, and he let loose the fierce need scorching him, feeding her fire as long as she wanted him to.

THEY EVENTUALLY wound up in the shower. Water streamed out of showerheads set into either side of the massive stall. Dani won the soap battle and talked Dave into letting her wash him. He braced his forearms against the tiled wall between the two showerheads, his back to her, feet braced apart, and let her touch him at her leisure.

She started at his neck and scrubbed her soapy hands over his beautiful form, massaging gently as she washed, learning his body, the ridges and dips of muscle bunching at his shoulders, running down his spine, the tufts of hair under his arms. He was ticklish there, touchy, and she teased her fingertips over the sensitive skin, reveling in the sharp inhales of his breath and his low moans.

Dani reached around him and soaped his pecs, thumbed his nipples, then dipped her hands lower and bathed his washboard stomach. Her breasts pressed into his back, rubbing across the skin, and her nipples pebbled as desire licked at her.

She wanted him so much, even after he'd pleasured her three times that evening, and found release twice himself. His body hardened under her slow caresses, the muscles rigid. If she skimmed lower, she'd encounter his arousal, firm and beautiful.

Instead, she soaped her hands again and ran them over his hips and around his bottom, then knelt beneath the spray and gave his legs her due attention. She shifted on the tub's floor to wash his left one and noticed a small mark on his left hip, maybe half an inch square, so small it would go unnoticed unless he was nude and somebody was right next to him, as she was.

She scraped the pad of her thumb across the mark and frowned. "I thought Feebies couldn't have tattoos."

Dave glanced down at her through his arms, one corner of his mouth quirked up. "Can't."

She clucked her tongue. "Dave, you naughty boy. When did you get it?"

His grin faded. He closed his eyes and rested his forehead against his braced forearms. "When I was sixteen."

She shifted closer and gasped. His tattoo was a triangle set on point with a half circle dropping from the top line. Sweet blessed Mother. To know this symbol, he had to've been in danger. It was the only way he could've seen it. "You have to tell me about this."

"Can't," he said flatly. "Promised I'd never talk about it."

She pulled herself upright and tugged his arm down. He turned slowly, reluctantly, and met her eyes, his own expressionless. "Do you know what that symbol is, who it represents?"

His dispassionate stare bored into her.

She tightened her grip around his arm. "An assassin, a dangerous one."

"Right."

"You have to believe me." A tremor shuddered through her and her heart stuttered in her chest. Sixteen. If things had worked out differently, he would've died, and she never would've known him. "Did you see her? Did she tell you her name?"

"She didn't threaten me, Dani. Can't say more than that. I promised."

"Why do you wear her symbol?"

"To remember."

"To remember what?"

He shook his head slowly, frustrating her with his silence. She'd get no more out of him that night, but that didn't mean she had to let it drop forever. "Promise me you'll be careful."

He stoic expression softened into a smile. "Always am."

He cupped her face and tilted it up, and kissed her, soft and sweet. She let the fear slide away as he stoked her passion, building it swiftly, overwhelming her. He lifted her high, pressed her back against the shower wall, and slid into her, sheathing himself in her heat. She wrapped her legs around him and held on as he made love to her under the water cascading over them, punctuating their gasps and sighs and sharp releases.

Reality swirled around her, breaking the spell of his touch. He was watching her with such tenderness, her heart flipped over and she slid the rest of the way into love.

She closed her eyes against it. He'd break her heart someday. She just couldn't find the energy to care while fresh from his touch. She'd have to deal with heartbreak, knew that with a startling, bone deep certainty, and still, she loved him.

Goddess, she was stupid.

Dave shifted and slid out of her body, leaving her achingly empty. He washed her quickly, running the soap over her while she stood docile as a statue, love and heartache and dismay warring within her.

He switched the water off and lifted her out of the shower, toweled them both dry, and bundled her under the covers of her bed next to him. She snuggled into his embrace, her mind drifting through the many secrets Dave had yet to share with her.

A COLD BREEZE woke her. Dani opened bleary eyes to the pre-dawn light glowing dimly through her bedroom windows. The curtains of one window billowed, stirred by a light breeze. It was October, too cool at night to keep her windows open. She distinctly remembered checking them the day before to make sure they were locked. Had Dave gotten too hot and opened one?

The covers slid down as she sat up, exposing her to the cool night air. Goose pimples popped up on her skin and she chafed her hands over her bare arms.

A figure stepped into the light, and Dani froze.

It was a woman dressed in a hooded leather knee-length coat and calf-high boots over jeans and a tank top. She stepped farther into the room, revealing the full face mask she wore over her features. The Woman with No Face, whose symbol was tattooed on Dave's left hip.

An eerie calm settled over Dani. Her weapons were too far away. She wouldn't reach them before the Woman got to her, but she could stall long enough to give Dave a chance to get away.

She reached back and jostled him gently, trying to wake him, her eyes fixed on the woman steadily drawing closer.

"He will not wake."

The flat voice floated from behind the mask, and fear sparked through Dani. She shifted onto her knees, loose and ready for whatever the Woman threw at her. "What have you done to him?"

The Woman halted a foot away from the edge of the bed. "Nothing, child. He has his role to play, as do you."

"What's his role?"

The Woman remained silent, her dark stare a grim weight.

"What's my role?" Dani asked.

"You know this."

"To retrieve the tablet containing the Prophecy of Light."

"No, child."

"Then what?"

"Your task is to destroy the Daughter calling herself Lilith. Can you not see this?"

Dani's breath shallowed. "She said my destiny was to die at her hand."

The Woman nodded slowly. "That is one path."

"What if I do?"

"He will mourn you for as long as he lives."

Dani placed a protective hand on Dave's arm. "And if I live?"

"Then he will give you the seven you desire."

The seven, the number of children each Daughter strove to bear, in honor of the Seven who had borne them. An unspeakable longing filled Dani. Her body heavy with Dave's child, his eyes shining up at her out of the face of her son. Could that ever be?

"This is your choice," the Woman said.

Was it really? Did Dani, at her young age, truly have it in herself to defeat a Daughter of Lilith's age and strength? "What if I can't? What if I'm not strong enough?"

"You will find the strength." The Woman slowly smoothed her hand over Dani's hair, almost tenderly. "Blood will out."

Dani held herself still under the caress. The Woman would as soon kill her as anything, if reputation held true. The knowledge did nothing to deter Dani's innate curiosity. "What is my blood?"

"You know this."

"No, I don't."

"You have the gift of sight, the gift of prophecy, if you would but use them. Open yourself, child, and find your path."

The Woman touched a single finger to Dani's forehead and something loosened within her mind. The mask lifted. In the low light, a face took shape. The pale, oval features loomed closer and closer, close enough for Dani to recognize her own face staring back at her under the mask's foreboding surface.

She gasped and sat straight up in bed, her heart pounding, air wheezing in and out of her lungs. She groped around searching for Dave and sagged on top of him. A dream. It was just a dream.

The morning's chill blew across her skin. Dani whirled around. The curtains covering her windows billowed out and a small piece of paper fluttered next to her pillow. She picked it up by its edge using her thumb and forefinger. A single symbol was etched onto the paper, the symbol of the Woman with No Face, and Dani's heart sank. It hadn't been a dream, none of it had. One of the most sinister figures in the People's history had visited and gifted Dani with a reminder.

She flipped the bedside lamp on and got out of bed, shut and locked the bedroom windows, then secured her apartment's other entrances. When she was finished, she cut the light off and surrounded herself with Dave's warmth, her mind tangled into knots over everything she'd learned.

NINE

THE OMEGA did a steady business nearly every night of the week, thanks in large part to its distinction as the only bar in Tellowee, Georgia. Tom Fairfax sat at his usual table, surrounded by the three men he'd formed an easy friendship with during his time in the area. All three of the other men had eyes on women, though for entirely different reasons.

James Terhune kept a close eye on his girlfriend and, if rumor had it, soon to be wife, Maya Bellegarde. Maya was seated at the bar, talking with friends, looking hale and hearty for a woman who'd come out of a weeks-long coma just a few days before. But that was a Daughter for you. Nothing kept one down for long, short of a beheading.

Across the table, George Howe mooned over his own love interest, a security guard at the IECS named Andrea. She was playing darts with her stepfather, who wasn't overly fond of the shy geneticist. Poor kid.

Phil Walters, the last of their group, looked at all the women. As far as Tom knew, Phil had no interest in any particular one, which seemed to suit him and the women just fine, judging by the number of dance partners and dates lining up for the younger man's attention.

Tom had an eye on a woman, too, a beautiful Irish Daughter who drank like a fish and cussed like a sailor. She was standing at the bar watching a soccer game and painting the air blue with her comments. He winced at a particularly foul combination of words and hid behind his bottle of beer. Honestly. How many times could one person say the eff-word in one sentence?

She cursed again, and Tom counted. Apparently the magic number was eight.

When Rebecca Upton had first told him she was bringing her daughter in to help him, Tom had been ecstatic. He loved working with the IECS'S current head archivist, Naomi Spillfeite, who readily admitted she'd taken the position not out of any particular expertise, but to fulfill her duty to the People. Naomi was a dream to work with, sweet in spite of her age and eager to learn. But he'd longed for a colleague who really spoke his language, somebody with a deep understanding of archival issues and a real knack for the work, somebody like, he imagined, the IECS'S first Archivist.

In his mind, he'd built Rebecca's daughter into a paragon of beauty, intelligence, and reason, all near-universal traits of the People. He'd imagined her as an equal, truly sharing the workload, and chatting with her over coffee, communing on an intellectual level, and maybe someday a visceral one.

His imaginings hadn't come anywhere close to reality.

Moira the Reluctant was, indeed, one of the most beautiful women he'd ever seen. Her strawberry blonde hair capped delicate features and she had a perfectly toned body, usually clothed in casual corduroys and a wool sweater. She was also coarse, rough, and brutally tactless. Mother and daughter bore a startling physical resemblance to each other, but their manners were shockingly different.

James shifted in his seat and sipped his water. "You've been quiet tonight."

Tom shrugged. "Not much to say."

James followed the direction of Tom's gaze. "That's one of Director Upton's daughters, isn't it?"

"Yeah." Tom sighed, sat back in his chair, and tried hard to lever his attention away from Moira. "She's supposed to help out in the Archives."

"You don't sound happy about that."

"Rebecca warned me Moira was difficult, but—"

Moira plopped her mug onto the bar and snapped out a particularly vile string of invectives. A Daughter sitting at the bar whirled around and retorted something equally harsh, and their conversation quickly devolved into a shoving match. Maya and her friends glanced around, then turned back to their conversation, like it was nothing for a fight to erupt in the middle of a peaceful bar in the middle of rural Georgia.

Tom hid a wince behind a sip of beer. Where Moira went, trouble soon followed.

James's eyes crinkled at the corners. "I see."

Tom snorted, lifted his beer, set it back down without taking a sip. Moira swung and connected a solid right-hand pop to the Daughter's jaw. Will, the bartender, pulled out a wooden bat and rapped it against the edge of the bar. The two women swung around and pinned murderous glares on him. He glared steadily back, unintimidated. Took a lot of courage, as far as Tom was concerned. Either one of those women could probably wipe the floor with Will in a fight, no matter what kind of specialized training he'd had as a Son. Still, it worked. Moira and the Daughter went back to the game, and Tom went back to brooding in his beer.

"She's beautiful," James said.

"Yeah, she is."

"In that special kind of way?"

Tom sighed and scrubbed a hand over his jaw. "Let's just say, the first time I saw her, I dropped a box of files and nearly swallowed my own tongue."

"Hit you that hard, did it?"

"You could say that."

Tom's gaze drifted to her. She was alternating between cheering and jeering the game playing on the television hanging in one corner of the bar. Somebody scored and she wiggled her bottom. His body reacted and, to his absolute disgust, his jeans tightened uncomfortably over his unruly dick. "She's just not what I expected."

"They never are," James said.

Yes, but couldn't she at least be civilized? "How am I going to get through the next few months with her?" The question slipped out, and Tom slumped into his seat. First his dick and now his mouth. Which part of his body was he going to lose control over next?

"The way any of us do," James said. "One day at a time."

"Not a lot of help there, pal."

The game ended. Somebody dropped change into the jukebox and the inevitable slow song drifted out of the speakers. If there was one thing Daughters loved to do besides fight, it was dance. Couples paired off and drifted onto the dance floor, and Tom scowled. Fat lot of good a slow song was doing him. He couldn't even stand up without giving away his attraction for Moira.

James set his beer on the table and stood, his gaze zeroing in on Maya. "I'll give you some better advice, then."

"Yeah?"

"Dance with her. Worked for me."

That was true, and not just for James and Maya. Andrea always sought George out for a dance, no matter how hard her stepfather glared at the couple. Phil never lacked for a partner, even if it wasn't the same one twice.

Tom narrowed his gaze on Moira. She had her back against the bar, elbows propped on its surface, and was sneering at the people filtering onto the dance floor. He was torn between the desire jangling through his body and distaste over her crudity. No matter what, he had to find a way to deal with her. They were going to be working together for months, possibly even years. With that in mind, he inhaled a deep, fortifying breath and pushed his way through the crowd toward Rebecca Upton's fiery, Irish daughter.

THREE LONG DAYS passed after the Woman's visit, three days of checking addresses and following leads and uncovering squat. There was no sign of Lilith at any of the places they'd checked, not one. Nobody knew her, nobody had seen her, nobody was talking, particularly not her relatives. Every single one refused to answer their phones or their doors. If Dani hadn't seen Lilith with her own eyes, she'd be hard pressed to prove the other Daughter actually existed.

Dani checked the cobbler she'd put in the oven half an hour earlier. Not quite done, she judged, and shut the oven door. It had been an uphill battle convincing Dave to trust her cooking. He'd come around, though, once he'd had a taste of her blueberry muffins. They'd shared cooking and cleaning duties since then or ate out if their search for Lilith kept them on the road through mealtimes.

Warmth shuddered through her. They'd been sharing a lot of things since the first time they'd made love. Her bed, their bodies, any handy piece of furniture available. Outside of her apartment, Dave was calm and carefully controlled. Once they were alone and safe behind a closed door, he was so much more open, with his humor and charm, with his passion. Since their first night together, she never woke up without him wrapped around her.

Rebecca had invited them to Tellowee to celebrate Moira's homecoming over a large family meal. Dani had accepted for them both, then talked Dave into it. It would be interesting to see the reactions Dave's appearance generated among her family and the other guests likely to be at her mother's home, given his role in recent events. Nothing like dropping the Shadow Enemy's right-hand man into a group of Daughters to stir things up a bit.

Her gaze crept toward where he sat, sifting through their dwindling list of leads. Her heart skipped a beat and she sucked in a deep breath. They would find Lilith soon. The inevitable discovery was gaining momentum, rushing toward them with devastating, unstoppable fury. When they found Lilith, Dave would leave, taking Dani's heart with him. She could feel it, deep down, and she dreaded it more and more every day.

Since the Woman's visit, Dani's intuition had built in strength and certainty. She'd always relied on her instinct to guide her, but now it was telling her things she simply didn't want to know. Lilith coming, Dave going, the end of the world as Dani knew it and other unsettling portents. If this is what it meant to have the *gift of sight*, as the Woman had put it, then thank you, but Dani would rather do without.

Dave stood, startling her out of her reverie. He stretched his long body toward the ceiling, and she melted. She loved him so much, needed him in a way she could never explain, and she wanted him, more than she'd ever desired another man.

He met her gaze and stalked toward her, and Dani scrambled away from him, laughing. He caught her in two long strides and buried his face in her hair.

She curled her fingers around his hips and tilted her head to the side. "Dave, quit."

He shoved her hair aside and scraped his teeth over her skin, then licked gently, and she struggled to focus around the heat building in her.

"We have to leave soon or we'll be late," she said.

He cupped her bottom and yanked her against him, aligning her hips with his. His erection pushed against her through their jeans, rubbing exactly where she needed it to. "Won't take long."

"I am not going to my family's home straight from having sex with you."

He sighed and rested his forehead against hers. "It might be our last time together."

Alarm skittered through her. "What? Why?"

"Me, in the middle of your family, obviously your lover." He nibbled her lips, licked the sting away. "I might last five minutes."

She laughed and swatted his arm, and wiggled out of his embrace. "You're more likely to catch flak because of working with the Shadow Enemy. Far as I know, Rebecca's the only one who knows you're an FBI agent."

"Bobby knows, but good point." He scrubbed a large palm over his close-cropped hair. "Who else is supposed to be there?"

"Half the town, most likely." She waited a beat, then added, "Including Maya Bellegarde and James and Amelia Terhune."

Dave winced. "Shoot me now."

She slid her hands around his waist and sank into his hard warmth. "I'll protect you."

"You'll be the first in line to take a punch."

"True. Don't worry. They think you've defected to the light side."

"Right."

She laughed and kissed him, then shooed him out of the kitchen while she checked on the cobbler.

They drove her Starmist Blue '57 Thunderbird. Dani pulled the protective cover off, and Dave bent over it reverently, touching it like a man touched his lover.

Like he touched her.

He walked around it, checking the finish and the sleek lines. "Where'd you get her?"

"Bought it when I left home, right off the showroom floor, after I'd earned enough money to pay for it outright." She patted the hood fondly. The Thunderbird held a host of good memories and represented a lot of lessons learned. "I've tried to keep it in good condition."

"She's a beaut."

She cocked her head and considered him, and because her heart was so full of love, she did something she'd never done before. She tossed the keys to him and enjoyed his grin.

It was a small thing to make somebody so happy, but oh, it felt so good.

Not one cloud marred the clear, October blue. It was warm, so they put the top down and turned the radio up, and hummed through the Sunday morning traffic clogging the roads.

They arrived at Rebecca's house not long before noon to an already crowded driveway. Dani helped Dave put the top back up on the Thunderbird, then snagged the cobbler and led him inside. The living room was empty. They followed voices to the kitchen and found Rebecca and Maya standing side by side near the sink, prepping side dishes. Both women swiveled around, and Maya's gaze narrowed coldly on Dave.

Rebecca dried her hands on a dish towel and pulled Dani into a careful hug around the warm cobbler, then squeezed Dave's arm. "You made it. We're almost ready to eat."

Dani wedged the cobbler into an empty spot on one counter. "I brought dessert."

Rebecca lifted a corner of the tinfoil covering the glass baking dish. "Peach cobbler? Your father will love it."

"I made it just for him." Dani scooted around her mother and hugged Maya. "Don't be too hard on him," she whispered. "He's not what he seems."

"He'd better not be."

Dani straightened and stepped back. "Maya, you remember Dave Winstead."

Maya nodded once, her expression carefully blank.

Dani glanced back at Dave and rolled her eyes. He'd crossed his arms over his chest and settled into a wide-legged stance, and his expression was as stoic as Maya's.

The door opened behind him and Maya's daughter, Dierdre, bounced in two steps ahead of James Terhune's daughter, Amelia, their chattering voices overlapping one another.

Dave's shoulders tensed and he turned slowly toward them.

Amelia skidded to a halt. Her eyes widened and the color leached out of her face under evenly trimmed mahogany bangs. She latched onto Dierdre's arm and whispered, "Mr. Winstead. You can't make me go back."

Dierdre stiffened and shot a venomous glare at Dave, and Dani panicked. Before she could act, Dierdre shook Amelia's hand off and backhanded Dave. His head snapped around, and Amelia shrieked.

Dani leapt into the space separating Dierdre and Dave. "Dierdre, no. Just wait a minute and let me explain."

Dave shoved Dani behind him and held her there with one arm.

Dani glanced helplessly at her mother. Rebecca was smiling behind her hand. Maya leaned casually against the counter and shook her head, and Dani sagged into Dave's back. Great. No help from the two adults in the room.

Dierdre swung again, and Dave caught her arm and yanked her against his chest, her back to him, her arms trapped against her torso, her feet bicycling into his shins. He bent down and whispered softly to her.

"Liar," Dierdre spat out. She kicked back, and Dave deftly avoided the blow.

"Just listen, kid," he said, and he kept whispering until Dierdre relaxed and stopped struggling. He let her go in increments and stepped away from her, his hands up, palms out.

Dierdre blew a strand of hair away from her face and glared at Dave. "Is he really with the FBI?"

Dani caught Dave's subtle nod out of the corner of her eye. "Whatever he told you, it's the truth."

"Yeah?" Dierdre snorted. "He still deserves a good ass kicking."

"Dierdre," Maya said.

Tears welled up in Dierdre's dark eyes and her hands bunched into fists at her sides. "He hurt Meely."

Amelia threaded her arm through Dierdre's. "Mr. Winstead didn't hurt me, I promise. He kept Mr. Alexiou from shooting me."

"You swear?" Dierdre asked.

"I do. C'mon, Dee. Let's go back outside."

Dierdre's hands relaxed, and Dani's relief whooshed out of her. Thank Ki for Dave's endless well of patience. If not for that, they could've had a real mess on their hands. What had she been thinking, bringing him into the heart of her family?

Dierdre speared Dave with a final glare. "Grampy Robert said the burgers are nearly ready and y'all should, like, bring out the other stuff so we can eat."

"We'll be out soon, sweetie," Rebecca said. She shooed the girls out, and they rushed out as quickly as they'd entered, their feet clattering on the outside steps. Rebecca resumed her stance against the counter. "That went well."

"Fat lot of help you were," Dani said. She tugged Dave's head down and winced. A bruise already bloomed along his jaw. Pride welled up over her concern. Dierdre had a wonderful fighting form, graceful and strong. Someday, she'd be a fine warrior, just like her mother, and a protector of the weaker ones among her kin and friends.

Too bad she'd had to demonstrate her growing skill on Dave. Dani prodded his jaw and her heart sank into her gut. What if her family and friends never accepted Dave, even when they learned that his place in the Shadow Enemy was a front? She'd hoped for a smoother transition and a little more understanding, but what if the people she loved could never forgive him for doing his job?

Dave hooked his hands on her waist. "I'm fine, Dani."

A hand holding a bag of ice appeared in Dani's peripheral vision, and she turned toward a grinning Maya.

"My daughter packs a punch, Mr. Winstead. Best put something on that bruise now."

He snagged the ice and held it to his jaw. "She's pretty tough."

"But fair. She'll come around."

Maya picked up two platters of side dishes, bumped her hip into the screen door, and went outside.

Dani jerked her chin at the hallway's entrance. "Bathroom's the second door on the left. I'll be there in a minute."

He nodded and left, gingerly pressing the ice to his jaw. A minute later, the bathroom door shut behind him.

"You're in love with him," Rebecca said. "Oh, sweetie, what were you thinking?"

Dani heaved out an exasperated breath. "What any woman would think, Mom."

"And how does he feel about you?"

Dani glanced down at the floor, hiding the fear roiling through her. "I think he cares about me."

"But you're not sure." Rebecca crossed the kitchen and pulled Dani into a hug. "Do you think he could love you?"

Dani nestled in her mother's embrace, drawing comfort from it. "I think so, but there's so much more."

Rebecca smoothed her hands over Dani's hair, then cupped her shoulders. "What is it?"

"We had a visitor a couple of nights ago. The Woman with No Face."

"Sweet Goddess. What did she want?"

"I think she wanted to warn me or something."

Dani took a deep breath and related everything to her mother, Dave's tattoo, their conversation about it, the Woman's visit.

"The Woman sought him out," Rebecca said slowly.

"He wouldn't say, but because he wears her symbol..." Dani shrugged. "How else could he know about it?"

"And the Woman specifically said you were to fight Lilith?"

"Not in so many words, but yeah. She didn't seem to know the outcome, though."

"Always two paths," Rebecca murmured. She squeezed Dani's shoulders, then eased back and crossed her arms over her chest. "There are so many things you don't know, my sweet girl."

"Like what?"

Rebecca hesitated. "Lilith has killed nearly everyone who's confronted her."

"I know. You sent me the list."

"No, Dani, you don't understand. She killed six of her own daughters when they tried to put her down as a group."

The breath wheezed out of Dani's lungs. "All six at one time? And they couldn't defeat her?"

"No one has."

"Then how can I?" A sudden hopelessness overwhelmed Dani. The two paths the Woman had told her about, killing Lilith or dying by her hand. How much hope did Dani have of overcoming the older Daughter and taking the path that led to a life with Dave?

"You'll find a way," Rebecca said, and her voice held a certainty Dani wished she could embrace. "I have faith."

A footfall scuffed on the linoleum. Dani whirled around. Dave was framed in the doorway, his expression a fiercely determined mask. He'd heard. Maybe not all, but enough. He'd heard and he intended to do something, follow her into battle, throw himself between her and Lilith.

Her eyelids fluttered shut. Whatever happened, she had to protect him, had to keep him safe no matter what risk she faced so he could live on.

Even if she didn't.

TEN

THE NOISE MADE by the crowd gathered at Rebecca Upton's house was nothing new to Dave. He'd grown up with three sisters and a large, extended family, and didn't blink an eye at the mix of generations, from a brand new baby to an elderly aunt, or the way they interacted, talking over each other, laughing and cutting up, and generally doing what families did. The difference between one and the other was that with this crowd, the age of the individual couldn't necessarily be deduced from how old they looked, with the exception of the very young.

At lunch, he managed to squeeze in next to Dani at a table full of other women, mostly Dani's adoptive sisters. Moira, the guest of honor, sat across from him, her hair a muted fire under the early autumn sun. Earlier, Dani had let it slip that Moira had been born in the sixteenth century and never left her homeland, if she could help it.

Rebecca's next youngest daughter, Charlotte, sat at the end of the table to his right, bouncing a toddler on her knee, with another of her children sitting between her and Dave.

Margaret, a cold-eyed woman Dani had introduced as one of Rebecca's eldest children, sat to Dani's left next to Anya, Rebecca's aunt, who appeared to be about eighty, maybe ninety, but was probably a lot older.

All of Rebecca's daughters bore a strong resemblance to their mother, with small differences taken from their fathers. Charlotte's hair was a mousy brown, Margaret's ash blonde, but the shapes of their faces and the way they held themselves reminded him strongly of Rebecca.

Dave let their conversation flow by without participating, and they ignored him, discussing childbirth, men, and other womanly matters as if he weren't there. He didn't mind. It was fascinating to hear the women talk and to see how Dani interacted with her family. She was at ease here, relaxed and loose in a way he'd never seen her before. As the conversation slipped around him, he watched her, touched her in small ways, and enjoyed the almost absent-minded way she leaned into him.

"So, Dani, how many hubbas does this one rate?" Charlotte asked, grinning slyly.

The question sharpened his focus on the discussion.

Dani held up four fingers and wiggled them, and the other women arched their eyebrows in his direction. Even Margaret shot him an appraising look.

"What?" he asked Dani, and she shook her head, mischief lighting her emerald eyes.

"Is that with or without clothes on?" asked Charlotte.

"Without." Dani slid a sideways glance at Dave. "In the shower."

Heat stole up his cheeks and he gritted his teeth. Of all the things she could've shared, why did it have to be of him naked?

Moira groaned. "Poseidon. The bastard always was her favorite."

Dani inspected her fingernails, then casually buffed them against her shirt. "Personified."

"Were you in the shower with him?" Margaret asked, her voice as cold as her eyes.

"Not that time."

"Well, now, if I had a man to look at me like that, I don't know as I'd ever let him leave the blessed shower," Moira said in her lilting voice.

Charlotte sighed. "Too bad I've already found my heart."

"I haven't," Margaret said, and her steely gaze told Dave exactly what she wanted out of him.

Moira laughed. "Oy there. Margaret Mary wants a taste."

"Mine," Dani said firmly and squeezed Dave's thigh.

Anya frowned. "Now, girls. He's not a piece of meat to be haggled over."

"Oh, he's definitely a full meal," Charlotte said, and all the women laughed, even Margaret.

Dave endured their good-natured ribbing while he finished eating. The little girl sitting next to him drew him into a conversation about burgers, the sky, and brothers. Becka, he thought her name was, after her grandmother, the director.

As soon as he could, he slipped away from the chattering women, dumped his empty plate in the trash, and wandered into a quieter spot of the enormous yard. The noise and chaos of Dani's family faded away behind him and his mind drifted to the conversation he'd overheard between Dani and Rebecca. Dani hadn't told him about her late-night visitor, and it worried him. Why hadn't she woken him up when the Woman had come? He was a light sleeper, always had been. Why hadn't he woken up on his own during Dani and that woman's conversation?

More worrying was the fact that Dani thought she had to face Lilith alone. No way was he going to let her. He wouldn't have before when she was only a dream to him, and he wouldn't now when she was all too real, in his heart, in his life. She'd spoken to her mother about the seven children he'd give her if she survived, and the idea expanded and filled him. Dani growing large with his child? Yeah, he wanted that. Now all he had to do was make it a reality, and he would. As soon as they were finished tracking Lilith and retrieved the artifact she'd stolen, he'd find the words to tell Dani how he felt and convince her to marry him. There was a happy ever after in it for both of them, if he could just win her over.

He sighed and rubbed a hand over his nape. That would come, in time. No use worrying over it until then.

His gaze fell on a playground visible over the hedge guarding the edge of the yard. It held the kind of equipment he'd played on as a kid, monkey bars and slides and really tall swings. A basketball goal loomed over a paved court big enough to hold a game on. If he were more familiar with Dani's family, he'd jog over there, find a ball, maybe shoot some hoops. It'd been a while and he missed the feel of the ball in his hands, the tinny sound of it hitting the court, the camaraderie of teammates and the high of playing in front of a crowd.

A footstep scuffed in the grass behind him. James Terhune halted beside him. He was half a head shorter than Dave. The barest hint of gray shot through his dark hair and laugh lines radiated away from the corners of his eyes. He was lean and athletic, fit in a way that came solely from regular exercise.

Dave sighed and wiggled his sore jaw, resigned to confrontation. Hey, if things worked out just right, maybe James could smack Dave's other jaw and he could have a bruise on each side.

"I didn't get to thank you," James said.

"For what?"

"For pulling Amelia away from Alexiou when he drew that gun."

The day James and Maya were supposed to ransom some of the Sandby borg artifacts for Amelia. The exchange hadn't gone the way any of them had hoped it would. "Couldn't leave her there."

"It was a good thing."

Dave bit back a response. He'd just been doing his job, but even without the job, he would've tried to protect her. "She ok?"

"She will be. Now that we know what happened." James stuffed his fingers into the front pockets of his jeans. "She wouldn't talk about it for a long time. Being around Dierdre helps, though."

Dave grunted. His jaw didn't really appreciate the time he'd spent around the volatile Daughter.

James ducked his head, grinning. "She'll come around."

"Amelia or Dierdre?"

"Both." James pointed at the basketball court. "You play?"

"College." A lifetime ago, when he'd still believed finding and protecting Dani would be easy.

"Really? Me, too."

"Where at?"

"UConn. You?"

Dave grinned. "Notre Dame."

"The Fighting Irish. Horse or one on one?"

"You find the ball, you can have your pick."

James laughed. "Horse, definitely. You've got me on reach."

Dave turned back to the view, lighter somehow, and settled in to wait for James's return. A door slammed open, laughing voices spilled out of the house, and Dave glanced over his shoulder. James jogged toward him, ball in hand, a sheepish expression on his face. He was leading a small crowd of people, mostly women.

"Sorry, man," James said. "They caught me looking for a ball."

Dave shrugged it off, content to play even with a crowd.

"Shirts versus skins!" a woman called, and a collective groan went up from the few men present.

It ended up being women versus men. The women insisted all the men take their shirts off so nobody would get confused. Dave shot James a skeptical look at the transparent ploy, but the other man just shrugged and said, "What can we do?"

Bobby Upton, Bobby's cousin Will, and a teenager named Johnny Linton joined James and Dave's side. The other men opted to sit out, including Charlotte's husband, Howard, and Rebecca's husband, Robert, who'd rolled down to the court in a wheelchair.

Dave hadn't spoken to Bobby since they'd seen each other in New York. He'd made a conscious effort to stay out of the other man's way that day, hoping to keep the peace, but he hadn't forgiven Bobby for telling Dani about Meredith and deliberately leading her to the wrong conclusion. He didn't want to spoil Dani's day by fighting with her only brother, so he reeled it in. One afternoon playing nice with Bobby wouldn't kill him.

The men who were playing took off their shirts while the women huddled together and chose a team. Bobby stripped his off, revealing a tattoo on his upper left arm, of a sword, point down, outlined in black, the blade in red. An elaborate shield was inked into Johnny's arm in the same place. Will had one, too, a stylized circle bisected vertically by a simple line.

Dave elbowed James. "What's up with the tats?"

"It marks their lineage, in honor of their mothers. All Sons get one when they turn sixteen. It's sort of a right of passage."

Sixteen, the same age Dave had been when he'd gotten the small tattoo on his left hip. The strong urge he'd had to sear that mark into his flesh had never really left him, though he'd had a very different reason for marking himself than the other men had.

Bobby picked up the ball and lobbed it to Johnny, and the two warmed up near the goal. Bobby turned his back, and Dave spotted another tattoo, an intricate black line drawing of a bird in flight holding two rings in its claws.

"What about that one?" Dave asked James.

James's eyebrows veed. "It's in the right place to be a wife's mark. Maya's trying to talk me into getting one."

"Didn't know Upton was married."

"He's not." James stripped his shirt off and tossed it onto the grass. "Let's warm up before the ladies get out here."

The women broke apart, and Dave groaned. Dierdre led Dani, Moira, Margaret, and Charlotte onto the court. The challenging glint in the young Daughter's dark eyes boded ill for Dave. Oh, well. At least he had four other men to deflect some of her blows, and if that didn't work, he'd toss her in the sandpit.

Robert and Rebecca declared themselves referees and the game began.

It was a roughly competitive match. After a while, Dave relaxed and enjoyed the tussle, in spite of the elbows hitting his ribs, sometimes deliberately.

The men were taller, but what the women lacked in height, they made up for in speed and sheer grit. And elegance, he thought after Dani made a particularly beautiful fade away to score. She moved like a dancer, graceful and strong, and handled the ball like it was an extension of her body, the way a true athlete would.

Dave took full advantage of guarding her, brushing closer than regulation permitted. She shoved him out of the way with whatever part of her body was handy. During one play when Dani had the ball, she made the mistake of turning her back to him. Dave wrapped an arm around her waist, yanked her into full contact with his chest, and popped the ball out of her hand from behind, sending it speeding toward Johnny.

Dani squawked and yelled, "Call the foul, Dad!"

Robert winked at Dave. "What foul?"

Dani narrowed her eyes and mouthed *peach cobbler*, and Robert gave her a hangdog look.

The women scored their fifteenth point, ending the game to the cheers of the onlookers on the sidelines and the groans of the men.

"We let 'em win," Bobby said, "or else they gripe and nag until they get a rematch."

His sisters protested loudly, and the group fell into good-natured bickering, with appeals to Rebecca, who refused to be drawn into the argument.

As soon as Dave tugged his shirt back on, Dani looped her arm through his. "Thanks for playing."

Dave grunted and trailed with her behind the rest of the crowd heading toward the Upton residence.

She rested her head against his shoulder. "I hope they weren't too hard on you."

"A few bruises. Nothing permanent."

"Poor baby. A little TLC when we get home will make it all better."

He kissed her upturned mouth, and one of her sisters let out a long, piercing whistle. He scowled at Dani. "When can we be alone?"

"Soon," she whispered, and pulled him into another kiss.

He intended to hold her to that.

REBECCA SHUT the dishwasher and turned it on. After the impromptu basketball game in the park behind the house, she'd sent most of her guests to the matinee to gain some peace and quiet. Robert had stayed behind, opting for a long nap before the lot trooped back in. Bobby had headed for the airfield in Gainesville on his way to New York. Anya had insisted on helping with the cleanup. Her aunt had other reasons for staying, but Rebecca had avoided conversation as long as she could.

She really didn't want to know if Anya had betrayed the People.

It was cowardly, yes, but avoidance was preferable to the action Rebecca would be forced into if her aunt was a traitor. Her mother had died centuries past, but Rebecca still carried the sting of loss in her heart Who would want to lose another family member, long before death made it a necessity?

Anya padded into the kitchen carrying yet another load of plates and cups. She dropped them into the trash can, then stretched backward, her silver braids swinging. She was dressed in comfortable jeans and a peasant style blouse and wore turquoise and silver jewelry around her neck, wrists, and fingers. Anya often joked that she'd just been hanging around until the 1960s came along so she could find her true spirit.

"Dani's young man is a handsome one," Anya said.

"Four hubbas, I heard."

"He seems to care for her." Anya pulled the trash bag out of the can and fastened it shut. "Though it concerns me that he has such close ties to the Shadow Enemy."

Rebecca leaned a hip against the counter. "It may not be that much of an issue. Dani told me he wears the mark of the Woman with No Face."

"But how? Why?"

"He won't tell her. From what Dani can gather, he's had the mark since he was sixteen." Rebecca tapped her fingers against her leg. "The Woman has been known to prophesy."

"But what could she have said to him, and at such a young age?"

"Who knows? Perhaps something to do with Dani."

"As tightly as he clings to her, it's a distinct possibility."

"What do you mean?"

Anya set the trash bag aside. "Bobby told me that young Winstead is incredibly protective of Dani. Quite proprietary."

"Bordering on possessive. I've noticed."

"It's concerning, particularly if he refuses to break his ties with our enemy."

Rebecca inhaled a cleansing breath, exhaling slowly as she chose her words. "I believe he will, in the end."

Anya's cornflower blue eyes sharpened. "You know something."

"I do, something I'm not at liberty to discuss without Mr. Winstead's permission."

"As long as it works out in the end." Anya settled against the counter next to Rebecca. "Now, while we're on the subject of the Woman, I think it's time I shared my own secrets."

"Should we sit for this conversation?"

Anya huffed out a short laugh. "No. I think this one is best gotten over with quickly. The Woman visited me many years ago, right about the time you assumed the directorship at the IECS."

"Just after Bobby was born," Rebecca murmured.

"Yes, just so."

"What did she want?"

"To kill me, I thought, but she had bigger things to discuss than the death of one mortal Daughter. She said your fate was intertwined with the end of the curse."

Why hadn't the Woman told Rebecca that? "Really."

"She also said that I must allow the Shadow Enemy to grow in whatever way I could."

Rebecca gaped. "But why?"

Anya shrugged. "Who knows?"

"She must have told you something."

"Only that there was one within their ranks who must be protected if the curse was ever to be broken."

Rebecca mulled over Anya's remarks, struggling to fit the knowledge into the puzzle the Woman presented. "What does it mean?"

"Who knows? Sometimes, I feel as if the Woman has been directing us all along, guiding us toward the path she wants us to take."

"In some cases, it would appear so, with Dani and Dave, and now you." Rebecca rubbed her fingertips over her closed eyelids. "Who else has she been directing?"

"Anyone or no one. She has her own mind, it seems."

"If only we knew her identity."

"That way be dragons," Anya cautioned.

"I know." Rebecca pushed herself away from the counter. "Let's hope the truth will out and that she is truly on our side."

Anya pulled Rebecca into a hug. "Aye, child, else we're all doomed to suffer forever, and our children with us."

ELEVEN

RIGHT AND EARLY the next morning, Dani stepped into the shower, her mind fixed on their few remaining leads. They would've canvassed every address on their list at least once within two more days, canvassed, interviewed, broken into a couple on the sly, and noted all the ones that were for sale for later investigation. It was frustrating to have to fall back on the less focused methods they'd used in New York to track Lilith, particularly when Dani's gut screamed that the other Daughter was nearby, somewhere.

Dani scrubbed her skin, her brow furrowed. She had an idea, a long shot. Ok, a *really* long shot, but with Dave's help, it might generate a credible lead. At least, they could add to the People's knowledge of the Shadow Enemy, if Dave would go for it.

He might not, considering how damnably loyal he was. In this case, surely he'd see that his loyalty was misplaced. Surely.

Her gut twisted into a sick knot. His job might still be more important to him than she was.

The shower door opened and cool air brushed over her wet skin. The second showerhead came on, blasting cold water along one side of her warm body, and she squealed. She aimed a scowl over her shoulder as Dave shut the shower door behind himself.

He smirked and wrapped himself around her, strong and warm, melding skin to skin. "Missed you."

"I haven't been up that long."

"You should've waited for me."

"Says the man who keeps leaving me in bed alone."

He nuzzled her throat and a thread of humor wound its way into his gravelly voice. "You weren't ready to wake up next to me then."

"Oh, really? How do you figure?"

He thrust his erection gently into her lower back. Her body softened, anticipating what always happened when one of them was aroused, and she blew out an exasperated breath. She was so easy. Worse, he knew it.

Distraction, that's what she needed, if only to get her mind off how putty-like she was whenever Dave was around. "I have an idea."

His arms tightened around her. "Oh?"

"Not that, you perv. Honestly. I want to check the properties Alexiou and his family own around here."

"Why?"

"Just a hunch." She wiggled her way around, facing him. "I thought you might be able to help me figure out which properties to hit first, since you're more familiar with the Alexiou family."

"Sure."

Tension slid out of her muscles and she relaxed against him, enjoying the skid of her wet skin along his and the desire thrumming through her blood. "I want to stop by the yarn store today while we're out."

He skimmed his hands down her back and cupped her ass. "You have a closetful."

"There's no such thing as too much yarn. Besides, it's on the way to Lydia's house. I want to pay her a personal visit."

He lifted her by her ass and pressed her into the wall between the two showerheads.

She wrapped her legs around his waist and clutched his shoulders. "We're wasting water."

The tip of his erection prodded her pussy, and she sighed as he eased into her, filling her completely. He braced a hand on the shower wall beside her head and his hips flexed against hers. "Nope. Checked already."

"Checked what?"

"Shower water's recycled."

"Oh." She closed her eyes, smiling in spite of herself. "Of course it is."

He thrust harder, and she clung to him through the passion building so easily between them.

THEY DRESSED, eventually, and followed up on the last of the leads Rebecca had given them. Dave insisted on driving. She should never have given him the keys in the first place. Even though she'd covered her Thunderbird and they were driving the Jeep again, it had set a bad precedent.

Give Dave a millimeter and he took a mile.

The first address on their list, an abandoned shopping center, was a no go. Dani checked the date and snorted. Three years had passed since that sighting, just long enough for the economy to take a toll on the neighborhood and drive out what few businesses were left.

Dave parked and they checked the building's perimeter and peeked into dirt-smudged windows. Dani jotted down the information printed on a sign taped to one of the glass doors and placed it with contact information for other properties for sale on their list. Once they'd gone through all their leads, they'd pose as buyers and have a real estate agent open those particular buildings for them. They ran the risk of tipping Lilith off to their investigation that way, but it beat breaking and entering when it wasn't absolutely necessary.

After they finished at the first property on their list, Dani directed Dave to the yarn store she wanted to visit. It was on their way and she didn't drop by often because she lived so close to another yarn store, so it wouldn't hurt to stop, would it?

He didn't buy her rationalization, and she was fine with that, as long as she got her yarn fix.

The bell dinged when Dani pushed the store's door open. Ginny, the shop's owner, called out a greeting and appraised the two of them over the top of her cheaters. A couple of other women were knitting at the table centered in the middle of the store. They looked up, spotted Dave, and their conversation ground to a halt.

It wasn't that he was a man. Plenty of other men came into the store, if not as knitters then with their craft-loving significant others. And it probably wasn't because of his looks, either. Dave wasn't ugly, but he wasn't quite handsome either. His light brown hair was cropped too short and his features seemed permanently set in a stoic mask. On the other hand, his size and physique would cause a stir anywhere, even when covered by his trademark plain black t-shirt and jeans and the jacket she'd insisted he wear because it was *cold,* for crying out loud.

If she was a little smug because those women would never see Dave in all his glory, then so be it. That was nothing to be ashamed of, and holding that secret knowledge inside herself warmed her through and through.

They wandered along the wall of yarn. Dave seemed fascinated by the colors and textures, and she relaxed. His enjoyment left her free to concentrate on the new sock yarn Ginny had stocked. Dani sorted through it, picking out enough to make Dave, Robert, and Bobby a pair each in a beautiful blue, brown, and buttercream self-striping yarn. From the solids, she selected one skein each in deep purple and lime green to make leggings for her niece, Becka. Wouldn't she look lovely attending ballet lessons in colors so suited to her bright, outgoing personality?

Ginny drifted over after helping another customer. She was a small woman in her late fifties with her hair dyed a bold copper. She wore a hand-knit Aran crafted in natural wool over jeans, and slip-on Crocs over hand-knit, pink and green polka dot socks.

"You've never brought a man in before," Ginny said, her scratchy voice low. "He's a big one. Tell me you're buying for him today."

"Sorry, Ginny. I picked up yarn for him in New York."

"There goes today's profit. Where'd you find him?"

"New York."

Ginny's penciled-in eyebrows shot high. "They make Yankees that big now, do they?"

"He's from Kansas." Dani peeked to see what he was doing. He had a skein of yarn in his hand and was running it between his fingers, an odd look on his face. "Farm boy, born and bred."

Ginny shifted and glanced at Dave. "Looks like he's found something."

"Let's hope not. I'm still working on the Gansey I started for him in New York."

"Speak for yourself. I can see business picking up with him around."

"I'd better see what he's got before you get ahold of him."

Ginny held out her hands. "I can hold your yarn at the counter for you. Want me to go ahead and wind these for you?"

"Please." Dani handed off the yarn she'd picked out and threaded her way through displays to Dave. "Whatcha got?"

He held out the moss green merino wool he'd been fondling. "Can you make a sweater out of this?"

"Sure. Who for?"

He hunched his shoulders and a blush tinged his cheeks. "Ah, me?"

She cocked her head, studying him. "I'm making you a sweater now. Don't you like it?"

"Yeah. It's..." His gaze dropped to the yarn in his hand. "This is the same color as your eyes."

"My eyes are lighter than that."

"Not when we're, ah, together." The color deepened on his cheeks and he lowered his voice. "It'd be like having you surround me all the time."

"Oh." She drew the word out as pleasure rushed through her. Farm Boy wasn't shy. He wanted her. She bit her tongue around the need to blurt out how she felt and pressed a soft kiss to his mouth. "That's the sweetest thing a man's ever said to me."

A pattern popped into her mind, a saddle shoulder turtleneck in stockinette stitch with a slight negative ease. It would be perfect for his build. She took the skein of yarn from him and checked the yardage and gauge, mentally calculating how much she'd need, then pulled down skeins and compared dye lots.

He sucked in a breath. "Jesus, Joseph, and Mary. How many do you need?"

"A lot. You're a big guy. Here, hold these."

She stacked yarn into his arms and led him to the register where Ginny sat knitting a shawl in a lace weight yarn the same color as her hair. Had she actually hand-dyed the yarn to match it or chosen it because of the similarity in color?

"We're ready," Dani said.

Ginny peered at them over her cheaters. "I see he talked you into another sweater."

Dani slanted a look at Dave. No woman in her right mind would turn down his sweet plea, especially after that blush. "How could I resist?"

"How indeed," Ginny said, smiling. "Want me to wind these, too?"

"That would be great, thanks." Dani patted her pockets and sighed. She'd left her wallet in the car, something she wouldn't have done if she'd been driving. "Keys, Farm Boy."

He crossed his arms over his chest and gave her *the look*. "Why?"

"So I can get my wallet."

"I'm paying."

"No, you're not. My yarn, my money, now give me the keys."

"My sweater, my money."

Dani tried to ignore Ginny avidly watching their byplay. "Give me the keys," she gritted out, "or I'll take them."

He arched an eyebrow, as if daring her to try, and Dani lost her patience.

"You are such a domineering *man* sometimes," she accused in a harsh whisper. "Why does everything have to be your way?"

"Knitting is a lot of work." His tone was even, reasonable, and it irritated her all the more. "It's only fair that I buy the yarn."

"Why do you have to be so damn rational?"

"Because I'm right."

Of course he was. He *always* was. "Fine. You can buy the yarn for your sweater, but I still need to get my wallet so I can pay for the other yarn."

He shook his head slowly, his expression unmoved, and she sighed. He wasn't going to budge. She'd have to unless she wanted to cause a scene, and she really liked coming to this particular yarn store. So, a scene was out. She'd have to give in to him *again*. It was a bad habit she wished she could find a way to break.

She rubbed her forehead against the ache sprouting there. "Ok, but..."

Just this once, she meant to say, but a sharp pang in her chest caught her breath and the words faltered on her tongue. Her heart pounded and sweat broke out along her skin, and her muscles stiffened. Another sharp pang hit her, and her body rebounded as if she'd been carrying a heavy weight and it was suddenly gone. She staggered into Dave. Her vision blurred, her mind spun, and she slumped as dizziness overwhelmed her.

He lifted her high, then set her down. The dizziness passed slowly and eventually her mind sharpened. Something cold was pressed to her forehead. She lifted a heavy hand and prodded it. A washcloth. She blinked her eyes open. Ginny was hovering over her and Dave knelt beside her and she was... She glanced carefully around. On the settee used by the friends and family members knitters brought with them when they shopped.

Dave had one hand on the pulse at her wrist and gently stroked her hair with the other. "You ok?"

She inhaled a shaky breath, judged that the worst was over, and pushed herself upright on the settee. "Yeah."

"What happened?"

She searched her mind, stumbled across a possible cause. Her stomach clenched into a knot and sank like a stone in her gut. No, that couldn't be it. Surely not.

Ginny patted Dani's arm. "I'll just finish winding your yarn."

Dani mustered a wavering smile. "Thanks, Ginny."

As soon as Ginny was out of earshot, Dave said, "Are you pregnant?"

"*What?*"

Ginny looked up from the yarn winder, her penciled in eyebrows high.

Dani lowered her voice. "No."

A strange look crossed his face. She thought it might be...disappointment, but that couldn't be right.

"You sure?" he asked.

"Dave, I'm not pregnant." She glanced back at Ginny. The shop owner was pointedly ignoring them. Dani lowered her voice to a whisper anyway, just in case. "Daughters always know when they ovulate. There's absolutely no chance I'm pregnant."

One corner of his mouth turned down. "Then what?"

She shook her head. Her mind spun around in a dizzying circle and she winced. "Later, ok?"

She scooted forward on the settee, and he pushed her gently back down. "Stay here."

"I'm not a puppy," she gritted out.

He stood and dug his wallet out of the back pocket of his jeans. "Humor me."

Worry lingered in his voice, a bare thread underlying his flat, gravelly tone, and she relented. Which is what had gotten her into this mess in the first place. She dropped her head into her hands. Too late to change that. She'd already let the damn horse out of the barn by giving in to him over and over again.

Lilith. Dani still had to deal with the other Daughter, and if she was right, her biggest weapon was gone. She should be afraid, shouldn't she? But it wasn't fear slumping her shoulders and draining her emotions. It was resignation. She looked at Dave, just looked at him as Ginny slowly drew him out while he paid for the yarn. The big lug really had grown on her, until she loved him, until she submitted to him. Not enough to make her feel less of a Daughter, but enough to break An's curse.

What chance did she have now to defeat Lilith and have a life with Dave, without the toughness that went hand in hand with immortality? None.

Dani sucked everything in, the hopeless dread, the worry, the regret, and stiffened her resolve. She had until they found Lilith to figure out how to defeat the other Daughter as a mortal. To do anything else would mean giving up Dave, and now that she'd found him, she wasn't giving him up, not for Lilith, not to death, not for anything.

TWELVE

D AVE TRIED to talk Dani into resting for a day or two after her dizzy spell at the yarn store, with no luck. She was adamant about not being pregnant, but other than that, she wouldn't tell him what was wrong.

It worried him on several levels, some he didn't want to examine too closely. He wanted to make her a permanent part of his life, no question, but he hadn't planned on having kids right away. After she'd nearly passed out, three things had hit him simultaneously. He was no longer on the verge of falling in love with her, but had already taken the plunge. He wanted her to be the mother of his children. And he wanted that as soon as possible. All he had to do now was talk Dani into it.

Right after he figured out how to solve all the other problems they faced.

She'd insisted on continuing their investigation. After leaving the yarn store and again earlier that afternoon, they'd hit the other addresses on their list, exhausting the leads Director Upton had given them. Even the family members were a no-go. Lydia, a councilwoman on the People's ruling body, had been home, but her assistant had turned him and Dani away. Tomorrow, they were going to make appointments with a real estate broker to gain access to properties on their list that were for sale. After that, they'd begin tracking down any of the Alexiou family's property in the area.

It wasn't beyond possibility that Lukas or some member of his family owned property in Atlanta. The People had a significant settlement nearby, which demanded at least an outpost, but the Alexious were, by nature, businessmen. Whether any of their property actually led to Lilith was another matter, but Dave was sure they'd find at least one substantial property owned by the Alexious in the Greater Atlanta area.

That night, they sat in Dani's Jeep outside Bones, the nightclub where they'd first met Lilith. It was the only lead on their list that had panned out and the only one with the real potential of a repeat visit, as far as he could tell. All of the other sightings had been at businesses. Lilith had to sleep sometime, didn't she? Yet nobody had managed to track her back to a residence. Worse, she'd left no paper trail that he could find through all the resources at his disposal. How could anybody in the twenty-first century not have at least a driver's permit?

While they waited, Dani alternated between making notes on possible avenues to explore and knitting a sweater for him. He studied her out of the corner of his eye.

Her hands were close to a blur as she worked the needles and the sweater was quickly taking shape. How could she possibly see the tiny stitches in the dim light?

There were so many things he didn't know about her, things that could never be put into a file, no matter how extensive it was. Things like why she was obsessed with yarn and when she'd started knitting. Why she'd left home at such a young age to pursue a life on the stage.

What it was like growing up not knowing her parents.

He scrubbed a hand over his hair. They didn't talk about things like that. He relied on her chattiness to carry their conversations, and a lot of times, she avoided talking about herself. Maybe he should push her to open up more, share some of her life with him.

Problem was, he didn't know how to open up and draw her in. Sex would only get him so far, no matter how great it was. How long would it take for his silence to push her away and out of his life?

The line leading into Bones shifted, drawing Dave's attention. He spotted movement in the shadows around the side of the building and bit back a curse. Stu. What the hell was he doing in the Atlanta area?

Dani shoved her knitting into its bag. "What's wrong?"

He jerked his chin toward Bones. "My handler. Stay here."

"Damn it, I'm not a puppy."

He got out of the Jeep, ignoring her, and headed after Stu. A car door slammed shut behind him and he pinched the bridge of his nose. "Just once, could you please do what I ask?"

Dani leveled a frosty glare on him. Hell with it. If they didn't move now, they'd lose Stu. She'd be safe enough this time, but the next, she was by God staying in the car even if he had to tie her to the seat.

Dave scanned the street as he crossed at a casual stroll, Dani close behind him. The bouncer recognized her and waved them inside. Dave led her through the sparse crowd, his gaze roving around the interior.

Stu the Weasel slipped through a Staff Only door on the far side of the room.

Dave cut across the dance floor and followed Stu through the door into a brightly lit hallway. Three doors lined one side, spaced at regular intervals. Dave jiggled handles as he and Dani passed. Locked, every last one, unsurprising given the area's high crime rate.

The hallway veered off at a sharp right angle. Dave stuck his head around the wall. The adjacent corridor was empty and led straight to an outside exit. He jogged to it, Dani hot on his heels, and opened the door into a service street running behind the nightclub. Except for a dumpster, some litter, and what were probably employee vehicles, it was deserted.

A wall ran the length of the other side of the street, separating it from an empty lot. Dani grabbed his arm and pointed to the left, and Dave just made out a figure hurrying into the darkness down another empty street set perpendicular to the service alley.

They followed at a full blown run, keeping pace with each other, their feet pounding on the pavement. Ahead of them, the figure startled and turned, then took off at a dead run away from them across the street into another alley.

They stopped at the place where the figure had disappeared. It was a dead-end leading straight into another building. Doors were embedded into the walls on either side and at the far end. Dave checked the doors on the right, Dani the ones on the left. All were locked or chained shut, including the door at the end.

Dave looked up, searching for another exit out of the alley. There were none that he could see. Stu, or whoever had run from them, had accessed one of these doors, but which one?

He caught Dani's eye and jerked his head toward the entrance of the alley. They walked out together, and Dave memorized the address.

Dani elbowed him. "Perimeter?"

He nodded and they walked around the corner of the block, casually studying the businesses at street level and the entrances to what might be residences on the upper floors. When they turned the next corner, they slid into a streaming crowd of night owls. Dani twined her fingers with his and leaned into him, and Dave slowed his pace, falling into the role she'd assigned him. Just two lovers, out for an evening stroll after supper.

They turned another corner, and the pedestrian traffic dwindled and dropped off completely. They searched the dead-end alley again, then headed for Dani's Jeep.

They'd found no trace of Stu, but Dave didn't doubt his own eyesight. His handler had been here, at a location linked to a woman who'd stolen an artifact out from under the noses of both Alexiou and the People. The likelihood of Stu not being involved seemed slim, especially coupled with the agent's suspicious behavior over the past few weeks.

Finding out what Stu was up to had just hit the top of Dave's list of priorities. Dave settled into the Jeep next to Dani and resumed his surveillance. Nobody wanted to be on his radar, especially not somebody associated with a target.

THEY ARRIVED home hours later, bone weary and gritty. Dani unlocked the door and stopped dead in her tracks. A dark-headed woman sat on the couch, bathed in the soft glow of light emanating from the TV as Godzilla wreaked havoc on Tokyo.

Dave leaned into Dani and pushed the door open, and his big body tensed against hers. She inhaled a deep breath and walked all the way in, then rolled her eyes. Dave had palmed his gun. Sweet, paranoid Dave. She shook her head and waited until he put it away before approaching the couch.

The woman flipped the TV off using the remote and rose gracefully. Her dark, emotionless gaze flicked to Dave, then settled on Dani. "Rumors have reached me of a young warrior who seeks my aunt, Lilith Cæstus."

Dani bowed. Crap. A member of the Council of Seven breaking into her apartment? Not good. "Maetyrm Lydia. If I may, this is David Winstead. He's helping me search for Lilith."

Lydia nodded. "The FBI agent who masquerades as Lukas Alexiou's right-hand man."

Dave hissed in a breath and muttered, "Does nobody know how to keep a damn secret anymore?"

Dani stifled a wince. Had he completely forgotten that most members of the

People had better than average hearing, and immortal Daughters the best?

"I learned not from others, young Winstead, but from my own resources. One does not survive millennia without learning how to ferret out information."

Dave nodded stiffly. "And you've gathered a lot of information in your life."

Dani elbowed him in the ribs. He shot her a hot glare.

Lydia observed them placidly, her head cocked slightly. "I have indeed, including the information you now seek."

Dani pinched the back of Dave's arm. "Any help would be appreciated, Maetyrm."

"A residence, a paper trail." Lydia lifted her hands in an elegant shrug. "These things are easily hidden by one such as Lilith."

A cold chill raced up Dani's spine and she shivered. She hadn't shared the specifics of their search with anybody except her mother.

"And easily found by one who knows her well," Lydia continued.

"Why would you help us track down your own kin?" Dave asked flatly.

Dani groaned and shifted into a loose protective stance in front of him. He might as well have asked why they should trust the councilwoman. That kind of affront usually ended poorly for the doubter.

A small smile tilted the corners of Lydia's mouth upward. "It is time."

"For what?" Dani asked.

"All things happen for a reason, when they are meant to be. The players step forward, the pieces fall into place, and Light's Bane soon meets the hand of the People's Scourge." Lydia's gaze settled on Dani, eerily sharp. "The time of the Prophecy is nigh, my child, and we all have our roles to play."

Dani choked on an inhaled breath. Lydia's words echoed the Woman's, uttered less than a week ago.

Lydia's expression softened and she cupped her hands over Dani's shoulders. "Have patience, child. You shall have that which you most desire and your kin will claim you, as they would have if they had but known you. This I vow."

Dani pressed her lips together over the million questions humming through her mind. Lydia knew more about her family? She knew where Dani belonged? Why had she never said anything? Why had she let Dani grow up among another family?

Propriety be damned. A woman deserved to know her kin, deserved to know her lineage.

Didn't she?

"I have written down what you need in order to find Lilith." Lydia's hands slid away and she stepped back. She touched her fingertips to Dave's sternum. Her gaze slid to Dani's. "He will do."

Dave barked out a hard laugh, and Dani sighed. Not many men met the approval of a Daughter as old and powerful as Lydia. That Dave was one proved his worth.

"Thank you, Maetyrm," she said.

Lydia inclined her head once. "We shall meet again very soon, my child, though not under favorable circumstances, I fear."

Dani saw Lydia to the door, then locked it tight. When she turned, Dave had settled into his favorite pose, arms crossed over his chest, feet planted wide on the floor. He was glaring at her, his slate gray eyes hot.

"What?" she asked as slipped past him and picked up the slip of paper Lydia had left there. It had a single address on it, along with the next day's date and a specific time.

"Do all Daughters break into other people's apartments and watch Godzilla?"

Dani laughed. "You're just mad 'cause I only did it once."

"Once was enough."

"Once is never enough, Farm Boy." She studied the sheet of paper. "I know this address."

"Yeah?"

"If I'm right, it's an old cotton mill, converted into a factory decades ago. I think it was abandoned in the '80s."

Dave grunted. Poor guy looked as tired as she felt. Sleep first, then. There was no hurry to research, no pressure to follow leads, not now that Lydia had stepped up and helped them.

Why the other Daughter had decided to do so was anybody's guess, the councilwoman's words to the contrary.

Dani stuck the address with her notes and headed toward the bathroom, stripping down as she walked. They were both grubby. All she wanted right then was a long, hot shower, a good cuddle, and eight hours of solid sleep.

Dave slid into the bathroom behind her and tugged off his shirt. "What did she mean?"

She stepped into the shower and turned the water on wide open. "Which part?"

He finished shucking his clothes and lobbed them into the hamper. "Light's Bane. The People's Scourge."

"I don't know what Light's Bane is, though it must have something to do with the Prophecy of Light. But when I was younger, on the streets earning my living with my fists, my nickname was the Scourge."

"Right." Dave smirked and stepped into the shower behind her. "You're not an enemy of the People."

"You're thinking too broadly."

Dave soaped his hands and ran them along her skin, sparking the heat of desire that never quite winked out.

Dani closed her eyes and leaned into him. "Think more specific, like a weapon used to inflict pain or the person wielding it."

"Mmm." His hands skimmed down her back and cupped her ass, kneading it gently. "So you're the People's weapon."

"You could say that."

His hands fell away, and she opened her eyes. He'd started washing himself. She held her hand out for the soap and took over. This was her favorite part, running her hands over his body, memorizing the curves and plains of his muscles. Passion had little to do with it. She enjoyed him, enjoyed pleasing him, and, Ki help her, she really was fond of the big lug, over and above the love strangling her heart.

"The rest was just confusing," she said, "which actually makes a weird kind of sense. Lydia's really old and from the line of Kiya."

Dave grunted. She glanced up. Shadows darkened the skin beneath his closed eyes. He didn't need long explanations about the intricate workings of the People keeping him out of bed. She finished washing him quickly and sluiced the soap off of him, then turned the water off.

They were in the middle of drying off when he said, "I don't follow. What does Lydia being descended from Kiya have to do with anything?"

Dani hung up her towel and squirted body lotion into her palm. "Sometimes when descendants of the Sister Kiya get very old, they develop the ability to commune with the Lady Goddess."

"Commune as in speak to the dead?"

"More like an oracle."

She finished rubbing lotion into her skin, tugged on a t-shirt and clean undies, and crawled into bed. Dave cut the lights out and joined her, fully nude, and she snuggled into his embrace.

"Some Daughters like Lydia, can glimpse the future," she said. "Usually it's just a heightened sense of awareness. Like instinct, but more."

How could she explain it to somebody who wasn't of the People and didn't have a lifetime of dealing with Daughters touched by the Great Lady's wisdom?

Dave's breath puffed out on a soft snore, and Dani smiled. He must've drifted off as soon as he'd wrapped himself around her. Figured. At least she wouldn't have to struggle to explain Lydia's gift of sight now.

A light went off in Dani's head and her eyes popped open. *She* had that extra awareness. It had always been there, a muted ping in her gut directing her actions more often than not. Since the Woman's visit, it had grown, developing into something more. Why hadn't it occurred to Dani that she might be of the line of Kiya, whose descendants carried that exact instinct to a much stronger degree than other members of the People?

Dani closed her eyes. It was a long time before her epiphany faded and she fell into sleep.

THIRTEEN

DANI MANNED the computer, tracking down information on the address Lydia had given them while Dave fixed a quick Southwestern scramble for their lunch. They'd slept in that morning trying to make up for the late night. He'd woken up wrapped around her and figured he must've fallen asleep in the middle of their conversation when they'd gone to bed.

He peeked at her, sitting so primly at the dining table, her hair pulled into an untidy knot on top of her head. An hour ago, those golden curls had spilled wildly around her shoulders as she rode him to release. Desire pooled into his groin and his dick hardened. He'd pleased her for a long time, and been rewarded with her soft moans and beautiful releases.

With another woman, he probably would've already gotten tired of the sex, the effort of getting to know her, the rituals of courtship and romance. Not with Dani, and he suspected he never would.

He finished cooking the scramble, divided it between two plates, and added some of the fruit Dani ate by the handfuls. He set her plate on the table beside the computer, and she glanced up and smiled.

He kissed the top of her head, caught a whiff of her lemony shampoo, then settled down with his own plate. "Eat."

Dani picked up her fork and stuffed a bite into her mouth. She sat back and *mmmd*. "Wow, this is good. Do you know a Pinico Alexiou?"

"Lukas's uncle. Why?"

"He owns the factory located at the address Lydia gave us last night."

Dave dug into his own meal. Dani's hunch had played out. The Alexious were involved much more deeply than he'd known, apparently, and were possibly connected to Lilith. He pulled his phone out of his jeans pocket and texted Lukas. *What's in the Gainesville GA factory owned by Uncle P?*

A reply popped up almost immediately. *Unknown.*

Dave stuffed his phone back into his pocket.

"What?" Dani asked.

"Don't think Lukas knows about that factory."

Dani snorted, and Dave shrugged. During more than two years working undercover in Lukas's operation, he'd learned that the family kept as many secrets from each other as they did from the outside world.

Dani focused on the laptop, her expression carefully neutral. "If we find out what's going on, will you tell him?"

"Yeah."

She pressed her lips together, the only change in her expression

Weariness slammed into him and he slumped in his chair. There were still so many things he hadn't told her, so many things she wouldn't understand. Why he'd stayed on with Alexiou. Why he kept the other man in the loop. How in the end he was helping her as much as he was helping either the FBI or Alexiou.

After eating, they traded places so Dani could wash dishes while Dave researched. He reviewed the information she'd found on Alexiou holdings in the South and jotted down what he knew about several. They'd have to investigate the others, but they could do that as a team.

Dani joined him after finishing in the kitchenette, and he turned the computer over to her. He had his own laptop with him, went everywhere with it, if he could, but hadn't taken it out much since coming to Georgia. Dani's laptop was state of the art, an indulgence, she'd told him, but a practical one. And she knew how to use it, teasing data out in ways even he, with all of his training, couldn't do.

He sat back and watched her work, absorbing the energy radiating out of her. God, she was sexy from the tip of her pert nose all the way down those long, shapely legs of hers.

She glanced up. "What?"

He leaned forward and captured her sweet mouth with his, exploring her slowly, savoring the catch in her breath and the curl of her fingers into his. How had he lived so long without her, without her touch and her taste, without her easy warmth, without her heart?

He eased away and squeezed her hand. "Beautiful."

She flushed and turned her attention studiously to his notes on the Alexious.

He laughed, earning a disgruntled stare from her, and headed into the bedroom to put together a weapons bag for their trip to Gainesville.

Her closet overflowed with clothes, shoes, accessories, and enough yarn to last even an immortal Daughter for decades. An image of Dani's hands flying through the stitches as she knit sprang into his mind and he mentally revised his estimate. It was more than any woman except her could get through in at least twenty years.

He'd tucked his own bag of weapons away underneath sacks of the stuff. When he pulled it out, one of the bags of yarn teetered. He dropped his bag and grabbed the yarn bag, panicking in a way he never did on the job. Not two days ago, Dani had dropped her knitting bag on the stairs as they were going out. He'd watched in horror as balls of yarn scattered everywhere, unraveling into a holy mess as they bounced down the stairs. He'd helped her untangle and clean every single one, and his fingers had fumbled with the tiny strands.

He shuddered. Never again. Dani could knit anything she wanted, and he was happy to support her interest, but he sure as hell didn't want to tangle with her yarn even one more time.

271

He retrieved his weapons bag without a major unraveling and escaped the closet, well aware of his close call. Dani entered the bedroom while he was sorting his weapons onto the bed, deciding what they might or might not need during their trip to Pinico's factory.

She leaned her head against his shoulder and hooked a finger through the belt loop in the center of his back. "Whatcha doing?"

"Had a hunch."

Her shoulders slumped and she shivered.

He put the gun he was checking down and draped an arm around her slender shoulders. "What's wrong?"

"You're not the only one with a hunch."

He frowned. Dani's hunches were usually spot on, but not always good. And he wasn't throwing her into danger when he didn't have to. "You can stay here."

She scowled and smacked his chest. "I thought we settled the little woman thing."

"I'm bigger. You're female."

"Har."

She eased away and riffled through his weapons, settling on a knife with a single-edged, two-inch wide blade as long as her hand. She flipped it, testing its weight, and eyed the blade critically.

"You can use it," he said.

She threw the knife onto the bed and dropped down next to him. "Got my own."

"What are you taking?"

"A sword, a dagger, and a Bersa .380."

"Hmm."

"Honey, I'm a weapon unto myself. A scourge, remember?"

"Don't get cocky."

Fire shot into her emerald eyes. "Confidence isn't the same as cocky."

"I know," he said, his voice softening. He'd seen her fight and knew what she could do. That wasn't his worry. What nagged at him was that as good as Dani was, he suspected Lilith was much, much better.

He shrugged a two-seater shoulder holster on over his t-shirt, chambered a round in his Glock, and engaged the safety, then slid it into the holster under his left arm. He stuck extra magazines on the other side for balance. Dani stood and helped him adjust the fit, picked up the knife she'd tossed down, and clipped it to his belt.

Why had she given him a knife, that one in particular?

She frowned at the weapons on the bed and yanked his bag closer. "Handcuffs?"

He unzipped an inner compartment. She pulled out one of the two pairs he'd tucked away and grinned, waggling her eyebrows as she dangled them between two fingers. "Wanna try 'em out, Farm Boy?"

"In your dreams." He caught the handcuffs when she tossed them at him, put them in his back pocket, and followed her out of the room. "Why handcuffs?"

She paused beside the sofa. "I think you'll need them today, or maybe the next time. I can't tell."

"You, what?" He fumbled for a minute, searching for a good way to ask. "Saw it?"

"Nope. Just a hunch."

A hunch involving handcuffs? Yeah, that didn't sound good. Dave rolled his shoulders, trying to shrug off his unease, but no matter what he did, it lingered as Dani retrieved a sword mounted on her wall and they finished prepping for their visit to the factory.

THE DRIVE to Gainesville through the beginnings of rush hour on Highway 365 seemed to take forever. Dani drove. She knew exactly where the factory was. No need for directions. The location was right in her head, preserved by her ever-vigilant memory. They took the Jeep and sat in silence, the radio off, each uneasy at going in essentially blind, not knowing what they were heading into.

Probably not much. Even if Lilith was there, negotiation and reason would be the first lines of defense. And if that failed, well, that's why Dani had brought her sword.

The factory was on the outskirts of the northeast Georgia city, not far from the airport where they'd arrived by plane from New York. As they neared, traffic thickened and the roads jammed up with more and more people leaving work for home.

Dani exited the Interstate onto Brown's Bridge Road, pausing at traffic lights, adjusting for traffic, and finally pulled into the factory's parking lot. She parked the Jeep and switched off the engine, then pointed to the left. "This is it. There used to be dozens of millhouses out through there, built back around the turn of the last century when cotton was still king and labor was cheap."

"You were there?"

"Har. That was a little before my time."

"What about the layout of the factory?"

Dani shrugged. "I found a plat on the tax assessor's website, but couldn't dig up a plan for the building. My guess is the main area is open. Likely all the equipment is gone, so it should be fairly empty unless gangs or homeless people have set up residence."

"Offices?"

"Sure." She opened her door and slid out, stretching as Dave got out and slammed his door shut. "Probably off to one side. Maybe upstairs. Shouldn't be difficult to figure out once we're in."

He crossed his arms over his chest, settling into his default stance, and studied the factory in the early evening light. "Security?"

Dani judged the overgrown parking area, the knocked out windowpanes, the faded *for sale* sign that had been tacked to the side of the building at least a decade ago. "Unlikely."

"Stay in the car."

"You're kidding, right?" He shook his head, and she choked down her anger. "Don't go there, Dave."

He scrubbed a hand over his nape. "Dani—"

"Forget it," she said flatly. "Perimeter sweep?"

He nodded and pivoted toward the entrance, and she followed. Unease reverberated in her gut. Hadn't she grown out of fits of nerves about, oh, fifty years ago? Strangely, she wasn't worried about facing Lilith, not today, only of what *else* they might encounter in this odd location.

Surely Lydia hadn't led them into a trap.

They examined the building together, testing doors, peering into low set windows. It was too dark to see much, but Dani got a sense of space and figured she'd been right about the layout.

After a few minutes, they found a set of doors, chained shut. A rusted key lock dangled off of equally decrepit chains. Dave tugged hard on the lock.

"I've got bolt cutters in the Jeep," Dani said.

He shook his head and tugged again. The lock gave and she huffed out a laugh.

"Rusted, not locked," he said.

He pulled the chains through the door handles. The scrape of metal against metal drowned out the roar of traffic on the nearby road, and Dani winced. Not the quiet entrance she'd hoped for. Dave wrapped massive hands around the door handles and yanked, and the right one opened smoothly.

"That's odd," she whispered.

Dave grunted and entered, and Dani stepped into the interior behind him onto the factory floor, a largely empty space extending all the way to the building's roof. It was surprisingly clean and eerily reminiscent of the Alexiou's warehouse in New York where Lukas Alexiou had nearly killed Maya Bellegarde. The air of abandonment on the outside juxtaposed starkly against the well-maintained interior.

Rows of doors occupied both the left and right sides, running the full length of the shorter ends. A metal staircase on the right-hand side led to more doors on a second floor. A hallway bisected the doors on the left. Dani could just make it out in the dim lighting filtering through the filthy windows and the open door behind them.

She fished a small flashlight out of her back pocket at the same time Dave flipped his on. The focused beams did little to brighten the area directly in front of them. On the far side, close to the building's opposite outside wall, crates of all shapes and sizes were stacked in neat rows. She elbowed Dave and pointed, and they walked toward them, their footsteps echoing in the cavernous space.

They were still yards away when she realized what she was looking at. Some of the crates were wooden and labeled "ammunition" in large, stamped letters. Other crates were actually plastic storage boxes. Dani knotted her empty hand into a fist. Probably weapons.

"So close to Tellowee," she murmured.

"An hour?"

"If that."

They opened several of the boxes at the forefront and discovered enough weapons, munitions, and explosives to take down a small city, or a well-fortified complex.

The Alexious were planning for war.

Dani's breath hitched and stuttered. Her friends and family, cut down by an army of Shadow Enemy foot soldiers. She rounded on Dave. "Did you know about this?"

"No."

The word was flat, uncompromising, and unaccountably, she believed him. Her relief whooshed out, carried by her first easy breath since they'd entered the factory.

"What about Lukas Alexiou?"

"Doubt he knows." He stepped away from the cache of weapons and rubbed the back of one finger across his chin. "He wants peace, badly. Don't think he'd do this."

"Then who?"

"The factory's in Pinico's name, so probably all of the uncles." He glanced at her, his slate gray eyes hidden in the creeping darkness. "Maybe Marco, too."

Steven Alexiou's bright face popped into her mind and her eyelids fluttered shut. Blessed Ki. He'd be dragged into the conflict between the People and the Shadow Enemy no matter what else happened. The sins of the father, right? And of the mother.

Footfalls scuffed against metal to their right. Dani whirled around and peered into the darkness, and discerned the figure of a man stepping carelessly down the staircase from the upper rooms.

Dave took one look and cursed. "Handler," he muttered, and was gone in a loping run.

The man raced back up the stairs.

Dani took off behind Dave. Maybe this time they'd catch Dave's handler and figure out what the man was up to. If they did, she hoped Dave would turn the man over to the FBI. His handler was a distraction they didn't need, not now.

She was halfway across the factory floor when instinct prickled. She stopped and turned slowly around, searching for whatever had pricked her internal alarms, and caught movement near the entrance to the hallway to the left of the door she and Dave had entered through. Lilith emerged from the shadows followed by two Daughters, and raw fury hit slashed through Dani. She didn't know one of the Daughters, but the other was India, a vicious warrior few liked well because of her harsh and bitter outlook.

Indigo would be heartbroken if she ever found out her twin sister had fallen into league with Lilith. Dani gritted her teeth. Indigo was an old friend and a good person. She didn't deserve to be haunted by her sister's failures.

Lilith halted, and India and the other Daughter settled into place on either side of her.

"Daniella, sweet," Lilith said. "What an unexpected pleasure. I see you've found the hiding spot for my little toys."

Dani clicked the flashlight off and shoved it into her back pocket. "I see you're in league with the Shadow Enemy."

"They serve their purpose."

"Which is?"

"To stop the Prophecy. To keep the Light from rising." Lilith's voice was calm, conversational, as if she were reciting a list of errands. "To remain immortal, to feed the rush of power and gain the adoration of mere mortals, so easily manipulated."

Light's Bane, Lydia had said. Could this be what she'd meant?

"The Prophecy has to be fulfilled or our People will never have rest," Dani said.

Lydia clucked her tongue. "Why, you've quite fallen for that nonsense. I thought better of you, darling."

"Sorry to disappoint." Dani drew her sword, felt more than heard the metal part from its leather sheathe. "But really, all I came for was the artifact."

"Not today, dear child. I'm quite late for an appointment, but I shall leave a playmate for you." Lilith beckoned India forward with an impatient flick of her hand. "India, sweet, you know the rules. No mortal wounds."

India drew the sword strapped to her back, a dark pleasure lighting her even features. "Yes, Maetyrm."

"Until we meet again, Daniella," Lilith said, and left the way she'd come, taking the unknown Daughter back through the darkened hallway.

Dani stepped forward to follow, and India shifted into her path.

For Indigo, Dani tamped her irritation down. "Leave now and I'll give you a day to flee before I tell Rebecca you've betrayed the People."

India's scornful laugh grated across Dani's nerves. "I haven't betrayed my people. I've embraced them."

"You're not of Lilith's line."

"My father descended from her, many generations removed. My An-cursed mother never knew, but Lilith did."

Dani swung her sword in a circle, testing its weight, and eyed India. Winning against another Daughter, especially one of greater age and skill, could be tricky. How could she manipulate India and diffuse the situation without harming her or coming to harm herself? Dani eased subtly to the left.

India readjusted her stance with a loose-limbed swing of her sword, blocking the hallway's entrance. "Lilith sought me out. She'd heard I disapproved of the path the People took and offered me a place at her side. How could I refuse such a generous offer?"

To betray closer kin and follow a woman bent on the destruction of the People? "How indeed?" Dani murmured.

India twisted her wrist, and her sword arced in a vicious swing toward Dani's head. Dani swung her sword up, deflecting India's blow to the side, and punched its heel into India's gut.

India sucked her stomach in, avoiding the blow, and whirled into another attack. Dani blocked again and threw her full weight into India, shoving her away.

India skipped backward, a malicious grin blossoming on her face. "That bitch Rebecca's trained you well."

Dani reined in her temper. India was trying to get a rise out of her. Unless she wanted to die, and Dani absolutely didn't, she wouldn't allow India to needle her. "Be careful what you say about my mother."

India smirked. "Your mother?"

Dani remained silent. It was a sore point, that Rebecca was her adoptive mother, but mother she was still. Nobody was allowed to scorn the relationship.

India cocked her head and her grin faded. "You haven't figured it out yet. Incredible."

Dani stared the other woman down, ignoring the tendril of dread creeping through her.

"That bitch never told you." India spat onto the concrete floor. "You follow her so blindly."

"Be respectful. I won't tell you again."

"You're no match for me." India inhaled deeply and grimaced. "Not now. The stench of mortality clings to you, little girl."

Dani patted her hand over a fake yawn. "Is this where you start the monologue about how you're really saving me from myself by trying to kill me?"

"This is where I tell you who you really are, Daniella, the Scourge of street trash and the daughter of Lilith, the Bane of the People."

Dani's heart squeezed to a halt in her chest, then thumped back to life in a hard gallop. Her arm fell and the sword's tip scratched into the cold, concrete floor. "You're *lying.*"

Even as she said it, a certainty grew in her, a recognition of the *rightness* of India's words. A voice drifted through Dani's mind, the voice of the Woman with No Face on the night she'd visited Dani. *Blood will out.* At the time, Dani had thought she descended from a good and noble Daughter, but this. This was untenable. Lilith was a cold-blooded murderer. Her every action over the past two millennia had been to thwart the People's destiny, and *that* was the blood coursing through Dani's veins, warming her heart, feeding her mind? There was no nobility there, and no hope for redemption.

India's expression softened into rare compassion. "It's not a lie, Dani. You're the last of her children, the last of her line. And it's your fate to die by her hand, as so many have done before you."

Dani struggled with the emotions flooding through her, the dismay and anger, the sheer betrayal. Rebecca hadn't told her, hadn't warned her. Why had her mother... No, not her mother. Why hadn't the woman who'd taken Dani in told her the truth?

India lifted her sword, and Dani automatically settled into a defensive stance so deeply ingrained, her body would respond even if she were half dead and blind. It was only after India began cautiously stepping backward that Dani registered the rapid footfalls echoing from behind her.

Dave. Her heart crumbled into dust. Blessed Ki. She'd have to tell him. He'd have to know, and when he did, she'd lose him. She'd never hoped to keep him, but she'd wanted a little more time.

She pushed the emotions down, hardening herself against the pain, and prepared to protect him.

A shot rang out, startling her.

"Your pet has come to your aid, little mortal." India re-sheathed her sword, her backward stride lengthening. "If the sex is as bad as his aim, you might want to find a new one."

The footsteps slowed as Dave drew level with Dani, his gun aimed at India's chest. "That was a warning. Next time, you're dead."

"Two against one," India said. "At least you've outgrown that ridiculous notion of fairness Rebecca tries to instill in everyone. Come to Bones on Sunday, little aunt. At dawn. Don't be late."

She backed away, disappearing into the growing shadows.

When she was gone, Dani sheathed her own sword, her hands shaking. Adrenaline, maybe shock. The knowledge of who she was, of what she'd become in the space of a heartbeat, rushed into her, rearranging everything she'd once been, and she swayed under the impact of its blow.

Dave grabbed her, steadying her. "Are you hurt?"

Dani shook him off and clamped down on the tears threatening to overflow. India's words rang through her mind, and betrayal spiked again, morphing into white hot anger. "I need to talk to Rebecca."

"Now?"

"As soon as we can get there."

She turned her back on him and walked away. She needed answers, needed *something*, and the only person who could give them to her was the very one that had hidden the truth from Dani since taking her in as an infant.

FOURTEEN

HE UPTON HOME was quiet when they arrived. Through a haze of emotion, Dani remembered that Bobby was still in New York and all of Rebecca's immortal daughters were likely out on jobs, as Dani was.

Except, she wasn't Rebecca's daughter, was she? The bitter thought hit her harder at that moment than it ever had before.

Dave had stayed quiet on the drive out as he drove them northeast from Gainesville. She'd let him drive. Her focus was shattered and she couldn't risk hurting him with her inattention to the road. Her only rational thoughts were to protect Dave and to gain an answer from Rebecca. Strange how bad news narrowed a woman's purpose.

Dani walked into the house, followed closely by Dave. Rebecca and Robert were sitting in the kitchen around a table full of steaming food.

Rebecca glanced up and paled, and her fork clattered against her plate. "You know."

The beautiful voice Dani had always associated with comfort and love held a world of sorrow.

Rebecca held a trembling hand out to Dani. "I wanted to tell you."

"But you didn't." Furious tears welled up and Dani blinked them away. "Why?"

"How could a mother break her daughter's heart?"

"You're not my mother," Dani retorted.

Rebecca flinched, and satisfaction hummed through Dani, mingling with her bitter fury. So it hurt Rebecca to hear those words? Good. Great, even. Maybe now she'd understand how Dani had felt for years, *decades*, not knowing who she was, believing her family to be good and noble, as Rebecca's was. What a lie. What a complete and utter farce her entire life had been.

Robert threw down his napkin. "Dani!"

"No, Robert." Rebecca laid her hand on her husband's arm and managed a tremulous smile. "She has a right to be upset."

Robert leaned back in his chair, frowning.

Rebecca scooted her chair back and stood. "I would like to speak with you privately, Dani. Mr. Winstead, please help yourself to supper."

Dani followed Rebecca to the library, down the long hall with framed pictures filling every inch of wall space. Rebecca loved having those pictures, reminders of her children and grandchildren, of the kin that had lived long enough to be captured in paintings or photographs. Dani's gaze fell on a picture of her and Jerusha taken after Dani had become an adult and come home, never to return to the stage. 1964. Dani smiled faintly and some of her anger faded. Rebecca had taken the picture with her brand new Polaroid. When the pictures developed, they'd all laughed at the crazy things they'd done, hamming it up for the camera.

Rebecca had settled onto the leather sofa in the library by the time Dani entered, her roiling emotions muted for having remembered the love, the community that Rebecca had provided for her. Dani sat on the other end and curled up facing Rebecca. Since marrying Robert and buying this house, Rebecca always chose to have serious discussions with her children on this couch.

The tears threatened again and Dani pushed them down. She'd get through this one conversation as rationally as she could. Mourning could come later, when she in bed, surrounded by the comfort of her lover.

"In the summer of 1939," Rebecca said, "I was roaming around the States between jobs. The Great Depression was at its height here and Europe was no better. Germany in particular was not doing well. Hitler had risen to power, bringing the Nazis with him, and Jews and other non-desirables were being tormented even then."

She took a deep breath and knotted her fingers together in her lap. "The People were more prepared than others to ride through that time. We had set aside our own farm land, cared for largely by our mortal kin, and had savings in gold and other tangibles rather than relying on government-issued money.

"We were in a rare lull in fighting the Shadow Enemy, so I was at loose ends. I was in Chicago. I don't remember why I was there or what I'd been doing that day, but I'd just come back to my hotel room for the night. The Drake. Maybe I'd gone out to supper or the theater. At any rate, when I opened the door, a woman stepped out of the shadows, the Woman with No Face. I was terrified. There I was without my primary weapon being confronted by, well, you know. All I could think was how stupid I was to not have a weapon stronger than a dagger on me."

Dani wrapped her arms around her knees.

"She stepped forward out of the shadows, rather dramatically, and pointed to a bundle on the bed," Rebecca said. " 'She is yours now,' she said. 'You must care for her as if she were your own. Do not fail in this.' Then she was gone. It wasn't until much, much later that I learned the truth, that the Woman had stolen you from Lilith not long after your birth and brought you to me to raise."

Questions filled Dani's mind, so many questions. "Why did the Woman take me?"

"Who knows why she does anything? All I can tell you is what I learned, some of which you already know. Your father was a Nazi soldier, very low in rank."

"You told me," Dani murmured. Rebecca had given her a picture of him on her fourteenth birthday. At the time, she hadn't questioned the gift, but now she wondered. What had Rebecca done to obtain that picture? What sacrifice had she made on behalf of her adopted daughter?

"Lilith killed him before you were born." Rebecca reached over, closing the distance between them, and grasped Dani's hand, squeezing it briefly. "I don't know why. She was always unstable, never quite right in her mind. She killed her other daughters at about the same time you were born. I think they learned about you and were coming to protect you. When they failed, the Woman took you instead."

"Why, though? Why would I need protection from my own mother?"

"I don't know. I'm sorry." Rebecca unfolded her legs and pushed herself off the couch. She unlocked the safe hidden behind her desk and pulled out a single envelope. "Not long after the Woman brought you to me, I received this."

Rebecca handed Dani the envelope and sat down. It was flat, about the size of Dani's hand, and tied with a faded red string. Dani carefully untied the string and set it aside. The outside paper wasn't an envelope. It was a plain piece of parchment, folded over into an envelope, protecting another piece of parchment folded into thirds. Dani smoothed out the inner parchment, a handwritten lineage. At the bottom was the word "Daughter" below her parents' names. Lilith's lineage was denoted generation by generation from her to Kiya, eldest of the Seven Sisters.

Dani glanced up from the paper. "You named me for my father. I mean, I knew that, but it just now hit me. I guess I should be grateful you didn't name me after her."

"How could I, knowing what she was?"

How, indeed? "Why didn't you tell me before?"

"How could I? I knew it would break your heart. It was selfish of me, I know, but I couldn't stand to see you hurt like that. Besides, I always got the feeling I should wait to tell you, until you were ready." She held her hands up, palms out. "It never seemed like the right time."

Of course not. The right time, the best time, was probably now. Dani refolded the papers, tied them back together, and laid them on the empty cushion between her and Rebecca. "I face Lilith this Sunday."

Rebecca pursed her lips, her skin haggard under the soft lights of the library. "I'd like to go with you."

"It isn't your place."

Rebecca didn't quite control her flinch. Shame flooded Dani. She could've been kinder, hadn't meant to be otherwise.

"At least take someone with you," Rebecca said.

Dani hesitated. "Is Margaret in town?" At Rebecca's nod, Dani let out a breath she hadn't known she'd been holding. "Her and Moira, then. They're handy in a fight, and there'll be other Daughters there."

"Lilith has managed to sway People to her side?"

"India Furia and another Daughter I didn't recognize." Dani described the unknown Daughter briefly and outlined the scene at the warehouse, including the large number of boxes and crates held in the factory. "Lukas Alexiou's uncle Pinico owns the factory. Lilith admitted she was working with them."

"It's time to prepare, then."

"Yes." Dani stood and stared down at the woman she'd always called mother. A bitter anger ate at her, twined oddly with the love she held for Rebecca, the head of the only family she'd ever known. Forgiveness was beyond her right then. As long as Lilith lived, as long as that was unresolved, Dani had no intention of seeking it. Maybe it was wrong of her, maybe not, but she refused to soften.

Rebecca's gaze fell to her knees. "Your father had another child, a son."

The news had no effect on Dani. She was nearly beyond feeling anything outside of the emotions aroused by learning of her heritage and Rebecca's betrayal.

"He was a year older than you and lived just long enough to have a child of his own."

"A son." His image popped into her mind, unbidden, so real she could almost feel his presence. "My nephew."

"He lives in Raleigh now with his family. I thought you should know."

Dani whirled away from Rebecca, away from the face that had suddenly aged, the hands clenched tightly together in her lap. The tears brimming in eyes that never shed them.

Dani stalked out of the library into the kitchen. Dave was talking quietly to Robert. The two men looked up when she entered, and Dave rose abruptly.

"I'll go to her," Robert said. He pushed himself up from the table and leaned against it while Dave handed him his crutches. When he drew abreast of Dani, Robert stopped and looked her firmly in the eye. "She loves you, more than you can know."

Dani's mouth trembled and she firmed her lips. She stepped out of Robert's way. His crutches thumped against the wooden floor as he walked slowly out of the room.

Dave pulled her into a hug, cradling her against his solid strength.

"Dave." Her voice cracked and wobbled, and she sniffed into his chest. "Take me home, please."

He tucked her under his arm and led her outside, and drove her home.

Dani focused on the passing scenery, a flimsy defense against the image of Rebecca sitting on the leather couch, her shoulders slumped, tears welling up in her pale, blue eyes.

DAVE DROVE quickly through the evening traffic from Tellowee through Gainesville to Dani's home. She sat quietly looking out the window, watching the lights pass, lost in her own thoughts.

He'd learned a lot that night about Dani, from India and Robert. Not from Dani herself. That stung, more than he'd ever admit. They didn't talk, true, not like a couple should, but she should've shared some of the things she'd bottled up inside herself.

She followed him up to her apartment, waited while he unlocked the door, her every action jerky, stiff, like she was moving on autopilot. He shut the door behind them, then did his usual, probably-paranoid check for bugs and other electronic devices. They hadn't found any after his first evening here, but he checked anyway. Never hurt to be cautious, and tonight of all nights, he didn't want to be overheard.

Dani wandered into the middle of the room, staring out the windows at the nighttime sky. He kept an eye out for her while he worked his way around the room, searching for bugs. After a few minutes, she settled in front of a buffet sitting against one wall where rows of framed pictures stood. Her fingertips grazed gently along the tops of the frames, touching each one in turn. Halfway down the row, she stopped and picked one up.

Dave finished his sweep and wrapped himself around her, his chest to her back. The photograph she held was old, black and white, and of a man in a uniform.

"My father." She ran a finger along the face, over the eyes tilted exactly like hers, across the curve of a cheek that was achingly familiar. "Rebecca gave this to me when I turned fourteen. The age of decision."

She set the photograph down and leaned against him. "I don't know how much you know about that time in a Daughter's life. It's almost like adulthood for mortals. We have the authority to make most of our own decisions, step out onto our own paths, if we like. Seek revenge, as Amelia could've done when her own mother was killed, if she'd been a little older."

Dani shivered, and he tugged her around and rubbed his hands up and down her back, slowly warming her.

"I had the chance then to pursue my family's identity and I didn't. Don't know why." She barked out a short laugh and laid her head against his chest. "I'd always wanted to go to New York, to sing and dance and be in front of people. I chose that path instead of looking for my family."

"No shame in that, Dani."

"No, I guess not. Maybe I didn't want to know. Maybe I already sensed it was more than I could handle."

"Tell me."

"What do you want to know?"

"What that Daughter said that upset you."

She hitched in a breath, and he tightened his hold, rubbed his cheek against her hair, anything to comfort her.

"Lilith is my mother," she said.

Lilith, who was little better than a cold-blooded killer, the mother of Dani and all the goodness seeped into every inch of her, from her laughter to her heart and back again.

Dave cupped her head in his hand and pressed her into his chest. "You're not her."

"To the Daughters, it doesn't matter. Blood is everything. Don't you see?"

He didn't, no, because he wasn't of the People. But he wanted to see. He wanted to understand. "Tell me."

Her shoulders hunched and her breath feathered through his shirt, warming him. "Blood will out. That's what she told me. The Woman with No Face. The one whose mark you wear? She came to me and told me that *blood will out*, and now I find out I'm the child of a monster. Two, if you count my father. It never bothered me before, what he was, what he did. I never thought of it because I never knew him, because he died before the Nazis committed the worst atrocities."

The sorrow in her words echoed into his heart. "You're not them."

"Am I not?" Her soft laugh held no humor, only the bitterness of the disillusioned. "What does it matter? I have to stop her, keep her from killing anybody else, and I don't know how."

"You'll find a way."

"Such simple faith."

"Yes, but truth, too."

She wrinkled his shirt between her fingers and buried her face in his throat. "I'm mortal now."

His mind shot back to what he'd overheard in the factory. She'd passed out at the yarn store, then India had derided Dani's mortality, and he'd wondered. They just hadn't had a chance to talk it out around everything else that had happened. "How?"

Her hands tightened against his back. "I think I gave in to you too many times."

"And that was it?"

"No."

"Tell me."

She heaved an exasperated sigh, and some of his worry drained away. She was coming back to him, getting back to normal, finding her balance.

"That's it right there, Caveman," she said sharply. "You're so domineering, so *male*, and I keep giving in on the small things because it's easier than arguing all the time."

"And that's enough to break the curse?" he asked, incredulous. If that was all it took, all of the Daughters would be mortal by now.

"Hardly. For the curse to be broken, two things have to happen. Submission, big or small, and a certain, ah, depth of emotion."

Did she have to dance around everything so cautiously? "Depth of emotion?"

"Love, you idjit," she said drily.

"Really?"

"I wouldn't knit a Gansey for just anybody, you know."

Her voice held a hint of teasing affection, and his heart soared, expanding inside his chest, filling him to the brim. "You love me."

"I never said that—"

He picked her up, cradling her in his arms, and kissed her into silence. She loved him. God, she really loved him, and he loved her, and now, they could be together.

He carried her into the bedroom and dropped her on the bed. She shrieked and scowled, and scrambled away from him. He crawled in behind her and pinned her to the bed. "Say it."

Her generous mouth tilted into a small smile. "What?"

He yanked her shirt up and blew a raspberry on her belly, and she giggled and shoved at his shoulders.

"Tell me you love me," he said.

"Forget it, Caveman."

She wiggled against him, trying to escape, and her shin grazed his groin. Her eyes went wide. "Oops."

He scooted up and captured her mouth with his, exploring her the way he had the first time he'd kissed her, the night she'd stayed in his bed at Alexiou's.

She moaned and cupped his face between her hands. The color of her eyes had deepened to the exact color of the yarn he'd picked out, and she was looking at him like he was the only man she'd ever known. "Dave. Make love to me."

He undressed her slowly, worshipping every inch of her body with his mouth, his hands, filling her when she was ready, showing her in every way he could how much he adored her, and she shuddered into a sweet, sweet release and carried him away with her love.

After, he dozed, curled around her, enjoying the feel of her wrapped in his arms. He woke when she slipped quietly out of the bed, and watched her dress and throw together an overnight bag.

"What are you doing?" he asked.

She paused in the middle of zipping up the bag. "I have a few things to take care of before Sunday."

He sat up, ignoring the blankets as they slid off him, and waited her out.

"A nephew I didn't know about until tonight. He lives in Raleigh." She dropped the bag, sat down beside him on the bed, and wrapped her hand around his forearm. "I know you're worried, but I'll be fine."

"Who said anything about worry?"

She leaned in and kissed him gently. "You're nearly vibrating with tension."

"Let me go with you." It wasn't a request, but the demand rising up inside him that he voiced, the fear of leaving her in a vulnerable position, of her risking her life when she didn't have to.

"Not this time." She brushed a hand over his hair and kissed him again, then stood. "I'll be back on Friday, Saturday at the latest."

God, was there anything he could say or do that wouldn't piss her off or drive her away, anything to make her stay or let him go with her?

"I'm taking the car, so use the Jeep if you need it, ok?"

She picked up her bag and walked toward the door.

"Be careful," he said.

She nodded. "You, too."

Her footsteps scuffed softly against the carpets she'd scattered everywhere. The outer door opened and closed, and the emptiness of her apartment echoed back at him.

She loved him, and because of that, she was mortal.

Jesus, Joseph, and Mary. She had to fight Lilith as a mortal.

He cursed his own stupidity and tossed the covers back. In his arrogance, he'd pushed her into losing the best weapon she had, her immortality, because he'd been impatient, because he'd wanted her for so long, since before he'd even known her.

He couldn't give her back her immortality, and wouldn't if he could, but he could do everything in his power to help her come out the other side of her fight with Lilith intact.

Starting with figuring out what that weasel Stu was doing in Atlanta. He'd escaped Dave's grasp twice already, both times through wiliness. By God, it wouldn't happen again.

Dave threw on the first clothes his hands landed on and carefully selected a series of weapons. Time to go hunt down a rodent.

FIFTEEN

DARKNESS FLASHED by the car, broken in irregular intervals by the lights of late-night restaurants, gas stations, and other cars. The trip from Buford to Raleigh was pure interstate. Miles of good road whizzed by so quickly, Dani lost track of how long she'd been driving.

Her heart was numb, but her mind buzzed with questions, with the wonder of having blood family so nearby. Now that she was mortal, she could reach out to them, forge friendships, maybe get to know them.

If she survived Lilith.

There was no question in her mind, no hesitation, that she would meet her birth mother in battle in three days. The outcome was less certain, but it would be what fate deemed. As Lilith and the Woman with No Face had said, destiny ruled the lives of the People.

Dani's hands tightened on the steering wheel. If she survived Lilith, she'd reach out to her mother's family, to Lydia and Lydia's children, and to the children of her sisters, if there were any. She honestly didn't know. Strange that she knew so little about her mother's family, in spite of the fact that Lilith was one of the more notorious Daughters.

Dani hit the outskirts of Raleigh as the sun peeked over the horizon, blinding her with its brilliance in the pale pink sky. She found a hotel, parked, and registered, and crashed in her room with the Do Not Disturb sign turned outward.

She woke to an empty stomach, showered quickly, and ordered a pizza. While she was waiting, she turned the TV on to a local news station and pulled out the phone book, searching for her nephew. There was no entry, so she opened her laptop and searched the Internet.

It didn't take her long to find his family. Nehring wasn't a common name, and the father had named the son after himself, as he had been named after his own, and Dani's, father.

The waiting was the hardest part. Daniel Nehring, her nephew and the third of that name, was an engineer in his late forties. She called his home and left a message detailing a made-up story about searching for her roots, then settled down at her computer to do enough research to lend plausibility to her cover story. When she was finished, she called her attorney and added Dave and Daniel's children to her will, then turned the TV to a movie and pulled out Dave's sweater, soothing herself with the rhythmic click of needles creating fabric.

At 6:05 p.m., Daniel returned her call, and they chatted amicably about family and roots. Dani took a page from Maya's book and manipulated the conversation to her favor. By the end of the call, Daniel suggested they meet for lunch the next day, and hung up likely thinking it had been entirely his idea.

She went out, roaming the streets of Raleigh, stumbled on a Goodberry's and ordered a cup of maple almond frozen custard, and ate it as she walked, her mind deliberately emptied of anything but taking the next step.

Dave texted her, and she answered, letting him know she was ok, then texted Margaret and Moira to confirm that they could meet her on Sunday.

She was warmed by Margaret's response (*Anytime, little sis*) and amused at Moira's (*Bludy fckin hell, cldnt u pick a fckin decnt hr*).

The warmth of the day had seeped out of the air, replaced by the chill of night, by the time Dani settled in for the evening in her hotel room with her knitting and a sappy romantic comedy. She resisted the urge to text Dave, ignored Rebecca's call and then Bobby's, and turned in early.

She found a yarn store the next day after checking out of her hotel and bought enough yarn to make Dave roll his eyes, if he could see her. She should've brought him along, needed the raw comfort of his presence, his warm strength. As much as she wanted him, some things a Daughter had to do on her own. Turned out, meeting her long lost family was one of them.

The chain restaurant where she'd agreed to meet Daniel was located about halfway between her hotel and his office. She left her car in the hotel's parking lot and walked, enjoying the crisp air of fall, and spotted him entering the restaurant. He turned as she neared, and they stared at one another.

The physical resemblance between them was odd, with their golden hair and tilted emerald eyes, high cheekbones and an intangible something that eluded Dani. His jaw was stronger and he was slightly taller and more muscular, his hair was fading to gray, but there was no mistaking the family connection.

She stopped next to him. "Daniel."

He shook her hand. His slender hands were callused, like a laborer not a paper pusher. "Shall we?" he asked in a voice tinged by a strong, Germanic accent.

Dani nodded, and they walked into the restaurant together.

After the hostess seated them and they'd placed their orders with a waitress, they sat in awkward silence, staring at each other surrounded by the noise of the mid-day crowd. Dani broke the silence. "I have a picture of your grandfather, if you'd like to see it."

His shoulders relaxed as he exhaled. "Yes. We have so little information about his life, it would be wonderful to see a photograph."

Dani dug the framed picture out of her messenger bag and passed it across the table to him. "I can make a copy for you when I get home."

Or leave instructions for Dave to send it back, if she didn't survive Sunday's face-off with Lilith.

Daniel held the framed picture gingerly. "The family resemblance is remarkable."

"Strong genes."

He chuckled, a low rolling sound that awakened her own humor. After taking another good look at the picture, he handed it back to Dani, retrieved his briefcase, and opened it. He pulled out a file folder and spread it out on the table.

"I thought you might like to have copies of some of the things we do have on the Nehring family. Newspaper clippings, a photocopy of pages from the family Bible, things such as that." He rifled through the folder's contents and pulled out three pages that were clipped together. "This is the prize, though."

Dani scanned the pages, mentally translating the German script into English as she did. It was an account of her father's brutal murder, or what the local police had been able to piece together of it. She noted the date and read it again through the sorrow crushing her heart. He'd been so young, then. Not an innocent, no, but too young to die the way he had.

"My father didn't live long enough to pass along any stories of his father, my grandfather," Daniel said, "and my mother had no stories, either, so I was very happy to discover these clippings in the family Bible last year after my mother passed."

"I'm sorry to hear of her death," Dani murmured.

"It was an accident. Very unexpected. She always said *Grossvater* Daniel was murdered because he was cheating on his wife and the affair caught up with him."

Dani glanced quickly down at the papers in her hand, struggling to keep her expression blank.

He sat back in his chair. "You know something."

"Only rumor."

"Then there is no harm in telling me, is there?"

Surely a little information would do no lasting damage. "Yes, he was having an affair."

"How do you know?"

"From stories passed through my own family." She placed the photocopied newspaper clippings carefully back into the file. "I haven't been able to verify it, but all the facts fit."

"Yet your kinship is not close."

"Close enough for this." Closer than he would ever know. She slid the folder across the table to him. "Everybody loves a juicy piece of gossip, even if it's decades old."

"True." Daniel's face creased into a smile and the laugh lines around his eyes hinted at his age. He opened the folder to the last page. "These are yours to keep, but I wanted to show you this one in particular."

He pulled out the paper, a picture of a young couple on their wedding day. "My parents."

"Such a handsome couple." Dani ran her fingers over the smiling faces. Her brother and his wife. She'd never know them now, never hold his face in her hands, never hear his laughter, never know if he could've been the family she'd always longed to have. "I wish I could've met your mother."

"She would have loved you. Family was everything to her. It broke her heart to leave our homeland, but after my father died, there was nothing holding her there."

The waitress brought their lunches, and Dani tucked the folder away. They talked until their meal was finished and she soaked in all the stories he told, of his life and his father's, of his two children, both in college, of all the things she would've kept track of if she'd known about them.

Over dessert, he said, "You must come by and meet my family."

"I wish I could." Dani sipped the coffee she'd ordered with the slab of pecan pie the waitress had talked her into trying. "I have a meeting tonight with my attorney back in Atlanta."

Daniel's eyebrows furrowed. "Nothing troubling, I hope."

"Just some minor changes to my will." She tapped her bag over the folder he'd given her, so full of precious memories. "Thank you for sharing. I'll get a copy of that photograph to you as soon as I can."

"No rush. You'll come back soon to visit, won't you?"

"As soon as I can," she promised, and left not long after. He hugged her and the simple gesture, given so sweetly by her nephew, drove her to the brink of tears. To learn of her family when it might be too late. Facing the possibility of never really knowing them was as heartbreaking as the thought of losing Dave, but it steeled her resolve. With so much to live for, how could she possibly not fight all the harder?

DARKNESS FELL hours before Dani unlocked the door to her apartment, bone weary after her long drive from Raleigh and the meeting with her attorney. He hadn't been happy about staying late at work on a Friday night. Too bad. Some things couldn't wait for normal business hours.

The Jeep hadn't been in the parking lot of the apartment complex when she'd pulled in. A spurt of panic shot through Dani that Dave had gone for good, before her gaze fell on his Cubs baseball cap hanging from the coatrack. He never went far without it, which probably meant he'd gone out to a place where he was afraid of losing it.

She unpacked, scrubbed off the grime of travel in a long, leisurely shower, and had a snack while she waited. An hour later, his key snicked in the lock and an eerie sense of déjà vu hit her. Her watching Godzilla on the couch waiting for him to come home. Dave was right. Daughters on the hunt needed to find a better MO.

He dropped down beside her, pulled off the cap she'd made him, and tossed it onto the coffee table. "Didn't expect you back 'til tomorrow."

She threaded her fingers through his and leaned against his shoulder, content for the first time in days. "It went pretty quickly."

"Learn anything?"

"My nephew looks a lot like me."

"Handsome, then. I think I'm jealous."

She hid a smile against his shoulder. "He's my nephew, not a prospective lover."

"But you'll love him, just because he's family."

His astuteness surprised her. Of course, she would love her nephew. Family meant so much and hers was too precious to take for granted. "Are you worried you'll lose my affections?"

He untangled his hand and tugged her into his lap. "Nope."

"Pretty confident, huh?"

His slate-colored eyes lightened and a soft smile curved his hard mouth. "Yup."

And he was right. No worries there, not for him.

His chest was warm under her cheek. She yawned and snuggled against him, closing her eyes. "Let's stay in tomorrow, do homey, couple things. You can cook for me."

"Anything you want."

She drifted then, and when he carried her to bed, she scooted under the covers, half asleep, and reveled in his warmth.

They woke late and, true to his word, Dave cooked for her. They watched TV, played a heated game of Monopoly, and made love to the rhythm of the October rain pounding down on the roof above them.

It was a bittersweet heaven, to have this time with him, and she wanted to enjoy every minute while she could.

That night, she listened to him breathe as the rain pattered against the windows. She'd snuck a copy of her will into his bag while he was in the kitchen cooking supper and thought she was cleaning her gear, along with clear instructions on what to do with the few pieces of memorabilia she hadn't specifically named in it. He would do the right thing. It was what she loved best about him.

Rebecca would look after him, if Lilith won. On this, Dani also had no doubt. The People took care of their own.

Two hours before sunrise, she slid out of bed and dressed, careful not to wake Dave. She chose her leathers for their durability and strength, and checked her sword carefully, in case she'd missed anything the night before. The other weapons, she left. Against anybody but Lilith or one of the older Daughters, Dani's body was her best tool, and her sword would take care of anybody, or anything, else.

When she was ready to leave, she retrieved Dave's spare set of handcuffs and placed the key on the nightstand next to his side of the bed, far enough away that he couldn't easily get to it. As gently as she could, she attached one cuff to the metal railing of the bed's head and the other to Dave's right wrist. The snick of the second cuff snapping into place woke him. Bless him, but he'd learned to sleep more deeply since coming to Atlanta.

He blinked sleepily at her and scrubbed a hand over his head. "You're up early."

She kissed him on the forehead and stepped away from the bed. "Yeah.

"When'd you get up?" He reached for her and metal skidded against metal as the handcuffs slid along the headboard's spoke. He twisted his head toward his arm, then swiveled back to her. "Unlock the handcuffs, baby."

She shook her head and backed up another step. "I can't."

"I have to come with you. I have to protect you." He tugged carefully on his arm, and when he spoke, a thread of panic wound through his rough voice. "Can't do that if I'm chained to the bed."

"This is something I have to do on my own."

He yanked at the handcuffs with both hands. His muscles strained in the glow of the streetlights shining dimly through the windows, refracted by the rain. "Don't do this, Dani, not alone."

"Stop, Dave, please. You'll hurt yourself." She swallowed back the tears clogging her throat. She was only making things worse by lingering, only hurting him more, and she couldn't bear to watch him suffer, not because of her. "I'll text somebody to come get you when I get to Bones."

She turned her back on him and left, and the tears that had threatened slid down her cheeks. He was wrong, so wrong. He was never supposed to protect her. That was her job, her duty as a Daughter, to protect the man she loved. Chaining him to the bed was the only way to keep him safe. Lilith couldn't reach him here and that was the important thing, wasn't it? He had to live, no matter what happened.

"Dani. Goddamn you, don't walk away from me." The covers rustled and his fist thudded into the wall. "Let me go. I need to be with you. Dani!"

She shut the door and kept walking as his hoarse pleas slowly faded behind her

It took a long time for her hands to stop shaking long enough to start the Jeep, and nearly as long for resolve to overcome heartache and get her out of the parking lot. She swiped her tears away and fought for calm as she drove to Bones. Dave was safely out of harm's way, and she couldn't afford to worry about him if she wanted to return to him.

And, oh, how she wanted that, to tell him every day what she held in her heart, to hear him say those words back to her, to marry him and have children and extend her family as far as she could. All she had to do to gain those dreams was kill her mother.

Sorrow spun through her, knocking her into another tailspin, and her tears morphed into harsh sobs. She pulled over on the side of the interstate and hid her face in her hands. Is this what she was reduced to, crying like a child over the hand fate had dealt her? Rebecca would be so ashamed of her. The People didn't whine over what had to be done. They faced it head on, spine straight, shoulders back, weapon high. Wasn't that the way Dani had always tried to live? Wasn't that the example Rebecca had set for her daughters?

Dani sniffed back her tears and eased onto the highway. The Scourge had never backed down from a fight before, and she wasn't about to now.

The sun hovered below the horizon when Dani arrived at Bones, emotions firmly under control. The remnants of last night's rain glistened along the streets under the fading streetlights. She parked at the curb behind a cherry red Miata. Moira and Margaret were propped against its trunk, sipping steaming liquid out of fast food cups. Both were dressed snugly in black leathers and carried swords strapped to their backs.

Dani heaved a sigh. They'd actually come. Thank the Lady Goddess, her adoptive sisters hadn't abandoned her. She texted Rebecca and asked her to check on Dave, then pulled off her jacket and strapped metal braces around her forearms, the only armor she allowed herself. The guards wouldn't protect against a bone-breaking direct hit, but they could deflect blows away from her body.

She unbuttoned the sleeves on her jacket, then got out. The early morning chill shivered through her. She shrugged her jacket back on and ignored the pointed glances Margaret and Moira exchanged.

Moira's eyes glimmered over the cup she held to her mouth. "Oy, there. Ye're late."

"Where's the pet?" Margaret asked, eyebrows arched.

"Dave," Dani said, "got a little tied up and couldn't make it."

"Ooo, sex games." Moira winked saucily, her pretty face mischievous under the black toboggan she wore. "And Margaret Mary missed all the fun."

Dani ignored her and focused on Bones. She described what she knew of its layout to her sisters while they waited for the sun to rise. Just as the star's leading edge crested the horizon, a car's engine purred nearby. Dani's heart leapt in her chest. Now what?

A beat up Bronco pulled up to the curb behind her Jeep.

Margaret jerked her chin at the new arrival. "Who's that?"

Dani shrugged and wrapped her hand around her sword's hilt, just in case. "No idea."

Half a dozen Daughters spilled out of the Bronco, laughing and talking. Lydia got out of the front passenger's seat, her mouth curled into a small smile, and Dani's hand fell away from her sword. She stepped into the street and nodded toward the councilwoman as the other woman approached.

Lydia bussed Dani's cheek. "You look well, cousin."

"I'm sorry." Embarrassment overrode confusion and Dani blushed. "I mean, thank you, but what are you doing here?"

"Come to help," called one Daughter. At the same time, another said, "Heard there was a rumble."

"We have come to stand beside our kin," Lydia explained in a low voice, "as I told you we would."

"Oh." A dam broke inside Dani and a well of emotion shoved its way out of her heart. Hope, love, longing. Her family had come for her, not just her adoptive sisters, but her blood kin. It was more than she'd dared to dream, given what she was about to attempt. "Thank you."

"We could not let you face her alone, even when this task falls solely to you."

Dani firmed her lips against a fresh spate of tears as Lydia introduced the Daughters who'd accompanied her, risking Lilith's displeasure to stand against their bloodthirsty elder.

Bones' front door screeched open. A mortal human stepped out, her skin pale against her flowing, black dress. She beckoned them closer, and Dani recognized her as one of Lilith's followers. The twenty-something sycophant probably had no clue exactly how far in over her head she'd fallen.

Dani followed the mortal inside, her steps careful, her senses alert. Margaret, Moira, and Lydia fell in behind her, and the other Daughters behind them. Generic pine cleaner lingered in the air. Its harsh sting failed to mask the underlying stench of alcohol and stale sweat. The only clear spaces were the dance floor and the narrow walkways between tables. If they had to fight through this mess, it could get ugly.

Behind her, Lydia hissed. Dani turned around and followed Lydia's pointing finger to a skeleton pinned to the far wall.

"The bones of a Sister," Lydia said.

Dani didn't ask how her cousin knew. She and Lydia were of the line of Kiya, who channeled the will of the Lady Goddess. Sometimes, as Dani was learning, they gained a few spidey senses in return for their devotion. If she ever got out of this mess, she'd be sure to pay homage to the Great Lady, for her life, for the extra awareness Ki granted, and for the gift of having Dave in her heart.

A door opened on the far side of the club and Dani swung around. Lilith glided out followed by India, the Daughter whose name Dani had never learned, a handful of other Daughters, and more than two dozen mortal humans, at least one of whom was, if Dani's gut could be believed, a Son.

"Daughter." Lilith's cold voice rang across the nearly empty room. "Where's your pet?"

"He had a little run in with standard issue handcuffs," Dani said.

"Pity."

"You'll never have him, Lilith."

Lilith laughed, cold and humorless, and the hairs on the back of Dani's neck bristled.

"What was lost can always be found again," Lilith said.

"You'll never get past me."

"Oh, darling." Lilith's hand rose. In it, she held a gleaming, double-edged sword. "Such arrogance will be your downfall."

"Did you bring the artifact?"

Lilith covered a patently fake yawn with her free hand. "Your repetition is tedious."

"Like mother, like daughter." Dani walked slowly onto the dance floor, stopping close to its center, and raised her voice. She wrapped her hand around the hilt of her sword and felt the soft *shink* of metal against leather as she drew it. "Kill the Daughters. Capture the mortals. Lilith is mine."

She stabbed her sword into the air above her head and yelled a war cry. One by one, the Daughters behind her unsheathed their swords and joined her, their voices rebounding through the room into a deafening song, and the mortals flinched away from the fierce challenge.

Dani cut the war cry off and cocked her sword, readying herself. Lilith raced onto the dance floor, her body a blur, and swung her sword in a vicious swipe at Dani's neck.

SIXTEEN

DAVE ALTERNATED his efforts between the handcuffs and the headboard, tugging at each one until the skin on his wrist cracked and bled. The spindle on Dani's wrought iron headboard refused to give. The paint scratched off to bare metal. Except for that, it was undamaged. So were the agency-issued handcuffs chaining him in place.

The sky gradually lightened as the sun rose. Dave slumped against the headboard and closed his eyes. He was too late. Dani's fight with Lilith had probably already started, and there was no way he could get there in time to take the blows for her, to protect her as he'd promised to do so long ago.

At sixteen, he'd been a hell-raiser, unfocused, undisciplined, and cocky, thanks to an innate talent with a basketball, and had been well on his way to becoming a farmer, like his dad and granddad before him. He hadn't minded. Working with the land, tilling it, coaxing it to grow crops while the sun beat down overhead. There were worse ways to make a living. He'd had no ambitions beyond nebulous plans to marry Sue Ann Jenkins, raise a passel of kids, and take over the farm after his dad retired.

One fine spring day while he was in town running errands for his mother, steeped in the freedom of a newly-licensed driver, *she* had stepped into his path. He'd never forget her face, hauntingly beautiful, as cold and deadly as a glacier in the North Atlantic, or her words. *Protect her,* the woman had said, and when he'd asked who, her icy gaze had pierced him so intently, fear had trembled through him.

The woman hadn't spoken again, though her voice had whispered through his mind. *She will find you.* The vision that followed had imprinted itself indelibly into his memory, of a woman whose face he couldn't see, of an epic battle between good and evil of which the unseen woman was just a small part, and of his place at her side, protecting her from *everything.*

That encounter had changed his life. After that, he'd had a purpose beyond the land and his family, and had known exactly what he had to do in order to achieve the promise he'd made himself that day: to prepare himself for the woman who was going to be his so he could protect her the way he had in his vision. He'd snuck out a week later and sealed that purpose with the tattoo on his hip, taken from a symbol etched into a slip of paper he'd found after the woman had left. He'd buckled down in school, studying harder than he ever had before, and started developing his athletic skills instead of coasting on native talent. It had led him exactly where he wanted to go, to a good college on a basketball scholarship, and eventually to the FBI.

Since then, he'd waited and watched and learned, and never stopped preparing himself.

He'd recognized Dani as the woman he was supposed to protect not long after she'd found him. Once he did, it had been a short step from protecting the girl of his dreams to loving her.

And in loving her, he'd failed her.

A chill shivered over him. Dave's eyes popped open and he glanced around, searching for the cause. A woman drifted out of the room's shadows. She was dressed in a hooded coat and wore what looked like a wooden mask over her face. He scrambled upright in the bed. Jesus, Joseph, and Mary, he hadn't even heard her come in.

She paused at the side of the bed and peered down at him through the mask's eye slits. She pushed the hood back, then took off the mask, and Dave's breath whooshed out of him. It was the woman that had given him his mission fourteen years ago. Incredibly, her coldly beautiful face hadn't aged a day.

He sank into the mattress. She had to be a Daughter. Who else could remain ageless after a decade and a half? "Who are you?"

"I have many names, child."

"The Woman with No Face?"

"That and others." She cocked her head to the side. "You must go to her now."

"Can't go like this." Dave lifted his arm and tugged, ignoring the pain in his wrist as the handcuffs jingled against the headboard. Bitterness seeped into his voice. "Thought I was supposed to protect her, and she left me here."

"Sweet child." The woman ran a gloved hand lightly over his hair. "Daniella does not need the strength of your arm. She is a capable warrior in her own right."

"Then why am I here?"

"Why do you ask what you already know?"

The Woman picked the handcuff key up off the nightstand and handed it to him, holding only the very edge. He took it and thanked her gruffly, and twisted awkwardly around. Why the fuck had Dani cuffed his right wrist, his dominant hand, instead of his left? He managed to insert the key into the lock and release himself, then flexed his fist, checking the damage he'd done to skin and muscle while fighting the cuffs.

"Tend that before you go," the Woman said.

He stood, taking the sheet with him. "I will."

The woman edged out of his way, her face pale and absolutely emotionless.

"Will we meet again?" he asked.

"Look to your heart."

She stepped slowly back into the diminishing shadows and slipped out an open window into the early morning air.

He headed into the bathroom, half his mind on her, the other half on what he had to do to get to Dani. Why had the Woman come, exactly when he'd needed help? How had she known, about Dani, about the fight, about everything? He shrugged it off. The hows and whys weren't important, only the outcome. Dani needed him. It was his job to love her, to watch over her, to make sure she never felt alone again. That was what mattered, not how they'd gotten to this place in their lives.

He rummaged for a bandage, slapped it on his wrist, and dressed. Holster on, guns checked, extra ammo. He tucked the handcuffs into his back pocket and locked up behind himself.

And broke every traffic law he could to get to Dani before it was too late.

He eased Dani's car to a stop behind a beat up Bronco and raced to the door, cursing when he tugged and found it locked. Angry shouts came from around the back of Bones. He followed them at a full-out run through the narrow alleyway separating the nightclub from an adjacent building. He burst into the street behind the club and stumbled to a halt. Two Daughters, swords strapped to their backs, were dragging bruised and bleeding people out the back door and forcing them against the wall running between the street and the park. Another Daughter tackled two men before they could make the far edge of the park and brought them down in a flurry of punches.

He caught the attention of one of the Daughters as she opened the back entrance. "Dani?"

She eyed him coldly from head to toe, and her gaze lingered in a few places he'd rather they hadn't. "I see what all the fuss is about. Come on."

She led him through the hallway into Bones' public area. The club's main floor was in shambles. Tables and chairs were scattered in pieces, the mirror behind the bar was broken, and people were everywhere, fighting or moaning on the floor. A couple looked like they might be dead.

He sorted through the crowd, searching for Dani, and spotted Moira dragging a screaming woman off the dance floor by her hair. Moira tossed the struggling woman into a pile of subdued people to his left and winked at Dave, grinning in spite of the bruise blossoming on her cheek.

Margaret and Lydia were engaged in fights on opposite sides of the club, their swords flashing nearly too fast for him to follow.

And in the dead center of the dance floor, Dani exchanged lithe blows with Lilith, her expression calm, her breathing even. Oh, thank God. She was safe. She was fine. He just had to get to her, was all, and keep her that way.

A tight grip latched onto his arm. He glanced down at the Daughter that had led him inside.

She tugged his arm. "You'll distract her."

Dave sucked in a breath. She was right. Dani couldn't afford to divide her attention. As long as she was holding her own, he wouldn't interfere. The minute she lost it, though, all bets were off.

The Daughter released his arm, waded into the pile of people huddled together, and dragged two out and down the hallway. Dave assessed the situation on the floor more closely. Everything was under control. He wasn't needed just yet, so he settled against a wall and enjoyed the spectacle.

Three women cornered Margaret against a table, trying to pin her, ducking around the Daughter's sledgehammer-like blows. Moira waded in, sword sheathed, and wound her hands into two women's hair. She snapped her fists toward each other, and the women's skulls cracked together.

Dave winced and scrubbed a hand over his own close-cropped hair. Good thing he kept it short. Otherwise, no telling what Dani's sisters would do to him.

Lydia had her back to another Daughter, their swords swinging steadily as they attacked and counterattacked. He examined their opponents closely. The man they were fighting had a tattoo on his upper left arm and their female opponent fought with the same ferocity as Dani and her sisters. Dave grunted. Members of the People, had to be.

A woman he didn't know was fending off a scrawny man near the bar. Dave squinted at the fighting couple. Something seemed familiar about the man. Mousy hair, thin shoulders, underhanded attacks. Dave swore and shoved away from the wall. Stu, that friggin' weasel. It was about time Dave pinned his handler down. The other man had evaded him the whole time Dani was gone, and now Dave had a mountain of frustration waiting to be meted out.

He pushed his way through ruined furniture, deftly avoiding the skirmishes still raging, and stopped beside Stu and the Daughter. She swung the pool cue, and Stu ducked. Her blow glanced off his shoulder. Stu stumbled and lost his balance, and Dave struck. He grabbed the other man's nape and pinched hard, then yanked Stu into a half Nelson.

The Daughter rested the pool cue on one shoulder.

"Friend of mine," Dave said.

Stu squirmed in Dave's hold. "Aw, shit, man."

"Doesn't look too friendly to me," the Daughter said, "but you're welcome to him."

She wandered off, drawing her sword as she went.

"Dave, man," Stu said.

Dave jostled the other man. "What are you doing in Atlanta, Stu?"

"Business," Stu gasped out. "Ease up, man. You're choking me."

"Kinda the point." Dave flexed his arm and straightened, lifting Stu off the ground. "I hate liars."

Stu snapped his elbow into Dave's ribs, and Dave grunted. In one smooth motion, he released his grip, palmed the back of Stu's head, and slammed it into the bar. Stu groaned and staggered, and Dave dug out his handcuffs.

One good thing about Dani leaving him the way she had. He'd remembered to bring the friggin' handcuffs.

He cuffed Stu's hands behind his back, then jerked him up by the collar of his jacket and frog marched him to Bones' far corner.

Moira stood guard over the people still waiting to be dragged outside and bound. She nodded toward Stu. "See ye've caught a fish, there."

"Couldn't let you have all the fun," Dave said.

"Was me, I'da thrown him back."

He barked out a laugh and shoved Stu into the pile face first, then fished out his cellphone and hit one of the few numbers he had on speed dial. He waited while his call was relayed, ground his teeth together when he reached voice mail, and left a terse message.

Moira grabbed Stu's shirt and twisted him around. "Feckin' mortals," she muttered. She ripped the shirt, exposing Stu's tattooed upper arm.

"Isn't that a mark of lineage?" Dave asked.

"That it is." She straightened and rested her hands low on her hips. "This one's a little scrawny to be a Son."

Stu wiggled around onto his back and spat at her. Moira backhanded him, knocking Dave's handler out cold.

"Diluted blood." She wiped her hand across her eyes, smearing blood seeping from a cut at her temple across her pale skin. "Can't be closer than three generations to immortality for a tap like that to knacker him."

"Could he have other traits?"

"Why?"

"This isn't the first time I've tried to catch him."

"Slipped away on ye, did he? Well, that's to be expected, what with ye being a slow-witted farm boy and all."

He ignored the jibe and turned to check on Dani. The other fights had petered out one by one while he'd been dealing with Stu. Lydia and the Daughter whose back she'd had were searching the pockets of the Son they'd been fighting as he sprawled on the floor, groaning softly.

Margaret joined Moira, her fingers gingerly probing a cut behind her right ear. He studied the bodies strewn across the floor. There was something wrong there, something missing.

Or someone.

"India," he said.

Margaret and Moira exchanged glances.

"Do you know her?" he asked.

"Yes." Margaret's shuttered gaze swept the floor, her blue eyes glacial. "She was here when we came in."

Moira muttered a long string of inventive curses, and Margaret slapped a hand against her thigh.

Good to know he wasn't the only one worried. With India gone, the chances of permanently stopping the threat posed by Lilith and her tagalongs lowered significantly. Damn it, they'd needed to round everybody up, not let a Daughter slip away unnoticed.

A sharp cry from the dance floor snagged Dave's attention. He whirled around, automatically searching for Dani. She staggered sideways, and he leapt forward. Margaret and Moira snagged his arms, holding him in place. He struggled against their grips, dragging them behind him as he marched toward his heart, his mind narrowed to one goal.

Protect her.

In the center of the room, Dani tumbled to the floor, and Lilith swung her sword downward in a killing blow.

AT LILITH'S first, testing blow, Dani's focus snapped into place, allowing her to sense the events around her without distracting her from the fight at hand. While she and

Lilith battled, Dani perceived when her allies won a fight or were injured, when the mortals tried to escape, and even when India slipped away from the fight. All of these things, Dani sensed from a distance, as if they occurred on the other side of a closed window, distorted by the glass, leaving her untouched. Able to react if she needed to. Able to focus as long as she and Lilith's fight went undisturbed.

Nobody came anywhere close. As Dani and Lilith traded blow after blow, their swords dancing quickly in thrusts and parries, not a soul bothered them. Dani spared no thought to that unusual occurrence, not even gratitude that because others let them be, she could concentrate her will on Lilith.

Dave's entrance registered as a bare ripple through Dani's awareness. His anger smacked against her, and she shrugged it off, dismissing it. Nothing she could do about that now, or would. She'd done what she had to. Maybe someday, he'd understand.

The other fights dwindled as the Daughters supporting her subdued the mortal humans, and then the immortal ones.

Her breath was coming in short bursts, her muscles warmed from trading blows, when Lilith slipped under her guard in a lightning quick thrust, stabbing Dani in her side. She stumbled and tripped backward over the remnants of a chair. A furious male roar sounded from the back of the room. She caught a flash out of the corner of her eye and rolled away just in time to avoid a heavy downward blow from Lilith's sword.

Dani rolled onto one knee and fingered the cut in her side. No real damage had been done aside from the rip in her new leather top. She scowled at Lilith. "That was just mean."

Lilith smoothed a hand over a seam that had suffered under one of Dani's earlier thrusts. "Payback's a bitch, darling."

Dani pushed to her feet and swung her sword loosely around, readying it. She spared one brief glance for Dave. Margaret and Moira had each wrapped themselves around one of his arms and another Daughter was behind him, her arms around his waist. All three pulled backward while Dave strained forward, his muscles bulging as he dragged the three women with him toward the dance floor. Lydia stood in front of him, a placating hand flat on his broad chest, and Dani relaxed and tuned the scene out. Lydia had it under control. Nothing would get past the councilwoman.

Malicious greed glinted in Lilith's violet eyes. "The boy will be mine."

Dani smirked. Lilith must be worried if she resorted to a transparent attempt at psychological warfare. "He'll never yield to you."

"Are you so certain?"

"He prefers women who are sane and, well, sane, so yup."

Lilith's delicately arched eyebrows snapped together and the tip of her sword wavered. "I take what I want."

"Good luck with that."

Dani whirled and backhanded her sword toward Lilith's neck.

Lilith scuttled out of range and her scowl deepened. "Men are weak, yet you seem so certain of him."

"Yup."

"And that is all the answer you will give?"

"It's all you deserve."

Lilith sucked in a breath. "I am your *mother.* You will *answer me.*"

"My mother is Rebecca the Blade." Dani's voice rang through the nightclub and the noise inside it abruptly stilled. "You're just the whore who gave birth to me."

Lilith screamed her fury into the silence around them. She lifted her sword and attacked in fierce, lightning fast blows. Dani's stomach shriveled into a hard knot. She'd made a huge tactical error. Lilith crazed would be a more dangerous opponent than Lilith sane, and would therefore be much harder to defeat.

Lilith's anger raged against Dani in unceasing waves. Over and over, the older Daughter struck, her sword flashing again and again as she lashed out. Her relentless attack pressed Dani in slow, backward circles around the dance floor as she countered and deflected.

With every step, Dani's strength dribbled out, one minute drop at a time. The muscles in her arms and shoulders began a slow burn and a smidgen of panic wound its way through her gut. She forced herself to keep moving by sheer dint of will, swinging her sword up, dancing back or around, avoiding direct hits wherever she could, and desperately searching for a gap in Lilith's defenses.

A second flash of silver shot out and pain stabbed through Dani's right thigh. Awareness hit too late. Lilith had drawn a second blade, a knife just long enough to sneak in under Dani's guard. Fear washed through her. Not good, not good, not good. Lilith stabbed her again, just above the first wound, and Dani cursed under her breath.

She staggered and dropped to one knee. Her grip loosened as she scrambled to right herself, and the sword fell out of her hand, clanging onto the parquet floor. She deflected Lilith's next blow with her forearm against Lilith's wrist, twisted her arm until she held Lilith's hand over the hilt of her sword, and pressed downward, forcing the sword's tip into the floor. Lilith jabbed the knife around in the same motion, and Dani caught that hand, too, then yanked her mother down and butted her in the forehead. She shoved, and Lilith staggered back, off balance.

Dani catapulted forward, ignoring the throbbing pain in her leg, and tackled Lilith, crashing them both into the floor. Lilith's head cracked sharply against the wood and she moaned. Dani straddled her mother, pinned Lilith's sword hand under her knee, and scrambled for Lilith's sword. Something sharp pierced her side and she hissed in a breath. Had to hurry, had to hurry. There! Her hand curled around the hilt of the sword. She yanked it to her, lifted it high, and slammed the tip down into Lilith's chest.

Lilith coughed and blood gurgled out of the wound in her chest. "Daughter. The Light. Stop." Her eyes rolled back and she stilled, and was dead.

Dani sagged against the sword, her strength nearly gone, her breath ragged and harsh. Sweet, blessed Ki. She'd really done it. She'd killed her own mother, killed the woman she should've loved, would've adored if things had been different. If Lilith had been sane, if she hadn't slaughtered her own daughters and Dani's father.

A tear rolled down Dani's cheek and she sniffed. Sound rushed inward, overwhelming her with the sheer weight of its volume. Lydia crouched beside her, murmuring soft, unintelligible words.

Dave skidded to a stop and dropped to his knees beside her. "I've got you, Dani. You're safe now."

And he surrounded her, holding her tightly to his chest, right where she belonged.

Her vision blurred and dimmed. From far, far away, Margaret said, "Watch the knife!" Moira cursed a blue streak. Somebody else asked something about a head, and Lydia said, "She's done enough."

Strong arms lifted her and warm lips pressed against her own, and her gut said, *This one*, and she fell down, down, down and heard no more.

SEVENTEEN

HOSPITALS UNNERVED Dave more than he'd ever admit. It was irrational and unfounded. He'd had no loved ones die or suffer in a hospital, no lingering illnesses or surgery to account for the unease, just a simple dislike he refused to examine.

A man was entitled to one phobia in a lifetime.

Dani was still as death on the hospital bed, her gentle breathing accompanied by the beep and whir of machines. Lilith's last strike had glanced off one of Dani's ribs, ripping a gaping, messy wound in her side. She'd lost a lot of blood there and from the wounds in her thigh, and would wear the scars for the rest of her life, physical reminders of her mother's death by her own hand.

If he could carry that pain for her, he would.

The trip from Bones to the hospital outside Tellowee had been one long, panic-filled blur. Moira had driven the Jeep while Dave sat in the back with Dani, desperately pressing bandages to her wounds as her blood welled up between his fingers. Lydia had ridden with them, leaving the other Daughters behind to clean up Bones, interrogate Lilith's followers in an attempt to find the artifact, and contact the families of the dead so they could bury their kin.

Lydia had had the foresight to call ahead to the hospital. A Dr. Phillips had met them there and taken Dani directly from the Emergency Room into surgery. The wound in her side had been stitched, as had the ones on her thigh. A small cut to her abdomen had also been bandaged.

Except for those injuries and assorted bumps and bruises, she was fine. After asking several pointed questions about Dave's relationship with Dani, Dr. Phillips had said that she'd likely passed out from fatigue, shock, and a loss of blood. She was sedated now, resting. Dave perched on the edge of an uncomfortable chair and held her fingers, trying not to jostle her. He should let go, he really should. He just couldn't bring himself to.

A commotion sounded outside Dani's room, then the door swung open. Rebecca stepped inside, her strides sharp and frantic. She came to an abrupt halt at Dani's side.

"Is she ok? What happened? No, sorry." Rebecca pressed a hand to her chest and breathed out a shaky laugh. "Moira told me on the phone on the way here. I was waiting for the call, waiting for..."

"I know," Dave said. He rose and went around the bed, then helped her gently into a chair.

"Mortality. It's not for the faint of heart."

He sat down and draped a hand over Dani's uninjured leg, comforting himself with her warmth, with her presence.

Rebecca stared at Dani, her expression tautened by grief and something else he couldn't name. "When you know you're going to live a long time, you act differently, *feel* differently, about yourself and the world around you. Emotion is..." She seemed to struggle for a minute. "Strong, but more easily controlled when you're immortal. You're in it for the long haul and can't give in to anything that might sap the energy you need to survive the eternally long centuries."

She wrapped her hand around one of Dani's feet, gripping her tightly through the sheet. "Your children are strong and you train them to protect themselves and the People, and while you hope they find a way to break the curse, you pray they don't because being mortal means being weak. Being mortal means relying on others to help you protect yourself. It's why we value strength and intelligence and reason, because those are the traits our children need to survive. It's what *we* need to survive."

He didn't know what to say, didn't think she needed a response even if he'd had the words.

"You will leave her," she said, her voice thick and strained. "You will leave and it will break her."

"I have to leave," he acknowledged. "I'll be back."

"Will you?"

The question was as sharply pointed as the ones Dr. Phillips had aimed at Dave. What was it about him and Dani that gave everybody the right to stick their noses in? "Yes."

"How can I trust you?" Rebecca nodded toward Dani. "How can she?"

If he hadn't been able to tell Dani how he felt, how could he tell somebody else? Yes, he had to leave. His handler had to be dealt with. So did Lukas Alexiou. Dave had a lot of thinking to do about the direction his life was going to take from there on out. One truth cut through everything, though. He couldn't live without Dani. Wherever she was, there he'd be, too, but he had business he had to take care of first.

The silence stretched between him and Rebecca. People came in and out of the room, quietly checking on Dani. Lydia poked her head in the doorway, and Rebecca left to confer with her. Margaret and Moira dropped back to back onto the room's other hospital bed and fell asleep waiting for news. Rebecca came back in and more chairs were scrounged to accommodate Lydia and some of her kin.

The women talked, their voices low. Somebody brought in sandwiches from a local deli, but Dave wasn't hungry enough to bother with food. Nurses came in periodically to check on Dani, as did Dr. Phillips, and all the while, Dave's thoughts circled chaotically in his head.

Bobby arrived hours later, looking bone weary, Robert not far behind him on crutches. Dave gave up his seat for the older man and leaned a hip against the side of

Dani's bed.

"Winstead," Bobby said gruffly. "You look like hell."

Dave grunted. "Haven't looked in a mirror, have you?"

"I see Dani didn't kick you in the nuts over that CIA chick."

"No thanks to you."

"Hey, man, anything to help."

Rebecca leaned forward and tapped her fingers on the bottom of the hospital bed. "Boys, why don't the two of you go to the house and get cleaned up?"

"I just got here," Bobby said.

"And you can just go home and take a shower. You stink of travel." Rebecca folded her hands in her lap and stared the two of them down. "Dr. Phillips is keeping Dani sedated until tomorrow morning at least. She won't wake for a while, so you might as well go do something useful instead of standing around sniping at one another."

Robert coughed into his hand, and Dave narrowed his gaze on the smile the older man couldn't quite hide.

Bobby's shoulders slumped. "Come on, Winstead."

Dave glanced at Dani. She was surrounded by family and didn't need him right then, but how could he leave her? On the other hand, Rebecca was right. Dani wasn't going to wake up anytime soon. "Need to run by Dani's and grab some clothes."

Bobby snorted. "What, are you living with her now?"

"Butt out," Dave said flatly.

"When you get your hands off my sister."

The two of them squared off, heads down, hands bunched into fists at their sides.

Rebecca stood abruptly. "This is neither the time nor the place for such foolishness. Honestly. If the two of you don't start acting like adults, I shall be forced to take you both in hand."

Bobby stepped back with a muttered, "She can do it, too."

Dave glanced at Dani's brother. "At the same time?"

"Child's play."

Dave turned an assessing glare on her. "Hmm."

She returned it with a cool stare. "Play nice," she said, enunciating the words, "or I'll show you exactly what I'm capable of."

Dave bit back the urge to say, "He started it." He brushed a kiss across Dani's forehead and walked out of the room, away from the curious stares of her family.

A HEAVY WEIGHT rested on Dani's eyes. She struggled to open them and failed. Nearby, something beeped after every beat of her heart. Her body was stiff under cool sheets, except her left leg. Oddly enough, it was burning up. She tried to shift and discovered that it was pinned, and searched her mind for a reason she might not be able to move it. She'd handcuffed Dave to her bed and driven to Bones. Margaret and Moira and Lydia and her other kin had been there. The fight with Lilith came easily to mind, and with it a kind of muted heartache over what she'd had to do. Then blackness, a blessed, drifting peace.

She tried to open her eyes again and succeeded in achieving a blurry vision. It was still dark, but she could just make out the far wall, institutionally neutral behind a really bad landscape. Dave sat in a chair beside her bed, his head and one hand covering her left thigh. A curtain hung out of the way behind him, and beyond it, a woman rested on another bed.

Dani strained her eyes, blinked, and her vision swam into focus. A hospital. She was in a hospital. She lifted her head and blinked again, trying to focus on the other bed. Energy drained out of her and she flopped back into the bed. She'd figure out who it was later. Maybe.

Dave stirred and raised his head, and his hand squeezed her thigh. "You're awake."

"Where am I?" she asked.

"Hospital near Tellowee."

He stretched into a stand, and even half-drugged and disoriented, a small curl of desire fluttered in her abdomen.

Good to know at least something was working right inside her.

He helped her sit up and held a lidded cup with a straw to her mouth, and she drank, relishing the cool relief of water sliding down her parched throat.

"Time is it?" she asked.

He set the cup aside and stroked his fingertips over the back of her hand. "Four a.m."

"How long have I been out?"

"A day."

She dropped her head back against the bed and closed her eyes, weary inside and out. A whole day, she'd been out, recovering from her fight, from the aftermath, from... Her eyes flew open. "My car?"

One side of his mouth quirked up. "You're lying in a hospital bed, worried about your car?"

"I love that car." She smiled, tried to. "It's a classic."

He scooted a chair closer to her bed and sat down. "It's fine, baby. Get some rest."

Dani nodded and drifted off. When she woke again, the sun was fully up and shone brightly through the lone window. Dave was still in the chair by her bed, fingers tapping away at his laptop.

He glanced up, closed it, and set it on the nightstand by her bed. "How do you feel?"

"Like I got run over by a truck." Dani wedged a hand between her hip and the edge of the bed and shoved herself upright. Her head swam and dark shadows danced at the edges of her vision, and she groaned. "What did they put in my I.V.?"

"Drugs." He raised the bed for her, then gave her a sip of water. "Hungry?"

"Starved. Tell me you're gonna take me home and feed me."

"Sorry. Dr. Phillips wants to keep you another day."

"Figures." She shot a sour grimace at the closed door. "Maya got to go home the day after waking up from a coma, but I have to stay here another day. How is that fair?"

"Did Maya lose a couple pints of blood from a four-inch long, inch deep knife wound?"

"Well, no," Dani admitted, and didn't add that Maya had been shot. By the time the other Daughter had come out of the coma, the bullet wound had nearly healed.

Rebecca entered, looking fresh and lovely. Dani's heart squeezed painfully in her chest. Not now, please. She just couldn't deal with her adoptive mother now, not on top of everything else.

"Good, you're awake." Rebecca shut the door behind herself and popped the tray up on the bed. "I knew you'd wake up hungry, so I snuck some breakfast past the nurses. Honestly, as close as this place is to Tellowee and as often as we send business their way, you'd think the cafeteria would provide decent meals for us."

A decent meal turned out to be scrambled eggs, bacon, fruit, and a cup of yogurt. Dani ate, using a full mouth as an excuse to not join Dave and Rebecca's conversation.

"You'll be pleased to know that Margaret dropped your handler off at the FBI field office in Atlanta," Rebecca said. "They were very happy to recover him."

Dave rubbed his hand across Dani's knee, warming her. "Hunh."

"I'm sure you'll want to speak with him yourself."

The remark was so pointed, Dani's nerves tingled and popped.

"When I'm finished here," Dave said mildly.

Dani's heart sank into her stomach. He was leaving. Of course, he was. He still had a job to do and he wouldn't abandon it for a mere woman, Daughter or not. Her appetite faded and she scooted the eggs around on her plate.

Dave nudged her. "Eat."

Dutifully, she took another bite, chewing and swallowing without tasting a single bit of it.

"What about the artifact?" he asked.

"Lydia's daughters were very...persuasive." Rebecca sat back in her chair, her smile smug. "I've sent a team in to recover it and should hear something back by tomorrow at the latest."

They talked on, discussing the removal of the Sister's remains from Bones back to the IECS, where their geneticist would attempt to extract DNA and possibly identify which Sister they belonged to. After the fight, Rebecca had sent in a team to thoroughly clean the nightclub before it opened again. Of course, somebody was bound to be suspicious when they realized a lot of furniture was missing. Dani vaguely recalled the mirror behind the bar breaking, but maybe she'd just imagined that.

Bobby and Robert drifted in about the same time that Dani finished her breakfast, and they might as well have opened the floodgates. Margaret and Moira stopped by. Lydia and several of the Daughters Dani had met the day before dropped by, too. Friends who lived nearby came in, and pretty soon, the sheer number of well-wishers overwhelmed Dani, sapping what little energy she'd gathered.

She dozed off and woke no telling when to a whispered argument between Dave and Bobby that pulled her between amusement and exasperation. What was Bobby's problem with Dave, anyway? They had so much in common, their age, their work in similar fields, and their love of all things athletic. At one time, she'd hoped they'd eventually be friends. Instead, Bobby seemed determined to dislike Dave. That wasn't like Bobby at all. He liked everybody and usually went out of his way to charm and schmooze.

After Bobby stalked out, Dave flopped into the chair beside her bed and smoothed a hand over his close-cropped hair.

"You're leaving," she said.

He gazed at her steadily, his expression neutral. "Eventually."

"When?"

He hesitated, blinked. "Two days."

She closed her eyes. So soon? Wasn't he even going to wait until she got out of the hospital?

"I'll be back," he said.

"Will you?" The question sounded tired, as tired as Dani felt. She couldn't hold him here, couldn't keep him, and he hadn't asked her to go with him. Wasn't that a good kick in the gut.

His hand gripped hers, strong and warm and gentle. "Brought your knitting," he said gruffly.

She opened her eyes, amused in spite of the small crack in her heart. "Did you?"

"Knew you'd be bored."

A faint hint of pink tinged his cheeks, why she had no clue, but she let it drop. Let him keep his secrets, along with his thoughtfulness. "Where is everybody?"

"Sent them home so you could rest."

"That must've been quite a feat."

"Rebecca helped."

Rebecca was one problem Dani wasn't ready to face, not yet, maybe not ever. "Can I take a shower?"

"Sponge bath." One corner of his mouth quirked up into that adorable half smile of his. "Doctor's orders."

"Oh, and I guess you want to be the one to give it to me, huh?"

His slate gray eyes heated and the smile dropped from his mouth. "If you insist."

An answering heat pooled between her thighs and she scowled. Traitorous body didn't know when not to give in to the enemy, even if he was sexy as sin and twice as charming.

The hours passed more quickly than Dani would've thought. She tried knitting and gave up when it irritated the skin around the I.V. needle the nurses refused to remove. Somebody had left a deck of cards, so she and Dave played poker around visits from half the town of Tellowee. Dani's families, adoptive and blood kin, were a near constant presence, and a surprising comfort.

Dr. Phillips released her the next day. Dave drove her back to her apartment and fussed over her in such a quiet way, Dani didn't have the heart to tell him she could take care of herself. They watched movies together, and Dani nearly cried when Dave put in her favorite about the love between a farm boy and a woman who became a princess.

Later that night, he helped her bathe, tucked her in bed, and walked away.

Dani pushed herself upright. "Where are you going?"

He kept his back to her. "The couch."

"You're sleeping on the couch? Why?"

"You need rest."

"Would you look at me? Just, look at me, please?"

His shoulders hunched. "I'll be in here."

"You're leaving me."

He faced her and frowned. "Just sleeping in here so you can rest."

"No, I mean, you're leaving tomorrow." Her breath hitched in. "Stay with me tonight."

"You're in no shape for sex."

Heat flooded her cheeks and her heart cracked in two. "Is that what you think of me, that all I want is sex?"

"No." He hesitated, glanced away. "Can't control myself when I sleep, I want you so much."

"Oh." That dream she'd had in New York the night she'd gotten so cold and he'd seduced her into his bed with the promise of flannel sheets, of him with his hand between her thighs, the mind-blowing orgasm, and Dave, naked in the shower the morning after. "That's why you're sleeping on the couch?"

He shrugged, and she melted.

"Dave, come to bed. It's ok, really. Humor me, ok? I really don't want to spend our last night together alone."

"I'm coming back," he insisted, but she ignored him, folded down the covers, and patted the bed beside her.

He looked at her for a long moment, so long, she thought he'd leave anyway. Finally, he turned off the lights, undressed, and climbed into bed beside her. He lay on his back, tense and unmoving.

That wouldn't do, not on their last night together. She draped her injured leg over his thighs and rested her head on his chest.

"This isn't a good idea," he said.

She skimmed her hand over his flat stomach, and smiled when his muscles tightened under her palm. "Shush. Nobody asked you."

He laughed then, a quiet, comforting rumble. He embraced her, holding her gently, and she relaxed, happy to have him for a while longer.

She slept deeply and woke on a gasp. He was sitting on the side of the bed, fully dressed, and something dark twisted insider her.

He stroked her hair, pushing it back from her face. "Sleepy head."

She caught his hand and brought it to her cheek, rubbing her face against the calloused warmth. "You're leaving."

"You keep accusing me of that."

"Because it's true. When is your flight?"

"Have to go by the field office in Atlanta first."

"And you won't be back here before your flight for New York."

"No."

She sat up carefully and pushed the covers off. "See? You're leaving."

His hand tightened on her cheek. "I *will* be back."

"When?"

"I don't know. As soon as I can."

"And then what? You're just going to come down here and leave..." She trailed off, unable to voice her hope that he might stay with her, leave the job he'd worked so hard to secure. A futile wish. He'd never leave his job. It meant too much for him to give it up.

"We'll work it out." He kissed her, and his mouth lingered on hers. "Promise."

But a few hours later, after they'd had lunch and he'd packed and the taxi was waiting for him; when he said goodbye with a gentle kiss that left her breathless and longing and heartsore at the same time; after he left her, she couldn't bring herself to put much faith in his promise. She sat on her couch, the sweater she was making for him clutched in her lap, and stared out the window, willing her tears not to fall.

EIGHTEEN

O F ALL THE THINGS Rebecca had ever had to do, sitting at work, calmly going about her day while her child was a scant hour away pining over a broken heart, was probably the hardest. Dave had left yesterday on his way to Atlanta and, eventually, New York, and Dani was alone.

Rebecca's gaze was drawn across the room to her sword, Silverthorn, won in battle nearly a thousand years ago when she'd been just a girl struggling to prove herself in a world that cared little for children and less for females.

Life was hard. She'd learned that long ago, but by Ki, why did the pain have to be rediscovered and endured by every new generation?

The door to her office opened and her youngest entered. The blessed son had been just a glimmer of hope on that fateful battlefield a millennium past. Bobby skirted the desk and kissed her on the cheek, then dropped into a chair in front of her desk.

"I have a job for you and your company, if you have room for it in your schedule," she began.

Bobby sprawled out in the chair, his hazel eyes serious in his lean face. "What kind of job?"

"One perfectly suited for the Enforcer."

He appraised her silently. "I haven't been called that in a while."

"True."

"I thought you hated that part of me." His fingers drummed an uneven rhythm on the arm of the chair. "Why would you want me to bring it back now?"

"India Furia."

He tensed, exactly as she'd expected, and speared her with a hard stare culled from her own repertoire. "I heard she escaped during Dani's fight with Lilith, that she was aligned with that Daughter and her cause. Anybody could find her and bring her in."

She sat back in her own chair, and they stared at one another, two warriors prodding the other's defenses. "True."

"Why me?"

"Because you have a stake in the outcome."

"No—"

She cut him off. "You can lie to everyone else, but not to your mother. I know where your heart lies."

"And where do you think that is?"

"Bobby, darling, don't play games with me." She leaned across her desk and folded her hands together on its top. "You've loved her since you were fourteen years old."

He glanced sharply away, hiding the heartache still evident in the stiff set of his shoulders, in the stubborn lift of his chin. "She rejected me."

"You were a child."

His low, bitter laugh grated painfully across her heart. "No Son is ever a child for long, Mom."

She couldn't deny the truth of that. No child of the People ever lived without looking over his or her shoulder, but that didn't keep their parents from trying to provide a place where Sons and Daughters could feel safe for the short time they were children. Had she not devoted decades of her life providing just such a place in Tellowee?

He sat back, his confidence apparently intact. "Besides, Indigo will never work with me to catch her own sister."

"I think she might surprise you." She handed him the folder of information she'd prepared. "You may not have to deal with her directly, if you don't wish. There are other threats I'd like your company to chase down, though India is our top priority at the moment."

Bobby took the folder and flipped through the pages it held, skimmed the summary sheet, and closed the folder. "How long have you known about this?"

"Since July," Rebecca admitted.

He rubbed a finger across his mouth. "It's not like you to sit on intel."

"I've had others doing deeper backgrounds on the subjects."

"And now you're ready to strike." Bobby tapped the folder's edge against his leg. "I have people I can assign to this now. In a couple of weeks, I can put nearly the whole company on it."

Tension drained out of Rebecca's muscles. "I appreciate that. Have your assistant draw up the contracts and we'll work out a retainer and payment schedule."

"I'll bring it by tonight after work."

She held a hand out to him. "One other thing, if you have a moment."

"Sure."

"It's about Dani's relationship with David Winstead."

Bobby scowled.

"Nothing to say for yourself?" she asked.

He huffed out a harsh laugh. "Me? What have I done?"

"Every time you're around the man, you antagonize him. That cannot continue should he and Dani deepen their relationship."

"Yeah, there's the problem right there. Son of a bitch has already left her high and dry."

"Bobby," she said sharply, and he winced. Good. Perhaps her tone would filter through this nonsense if her words didn't. "Dave has business he must attend to. Surely you, of all people, can understand that."

"Right. Business."

Rebecca studied her son carefully. "Is it Dave you're worried about or something else?"

He glanced away and jiggled his leg, bouncing his knee. "There's a reason I was called the Enforcer."

"I'm aware," she said drily.

"You don't know the half of it." He met her gaze evenly, and in his eyes was a mountain of regret. "I've done things, Mom, been things that would give most people nightmares, just like he has. Is that the kind of man you want Dani to have?"

"What you're really asking is whether that's the kind of man Indigo would want, isn't it?" She stood and walked around the desk, then sank into the empty chair next to him, one comforting hand on his forearm. "Oh, sweetie. Is this why you've been antagonizing Dave?"

"He's not good enough for her."

She cupped her hands around his handsome face and turned it toward hers. "You must resolve this, darling, or it will eat the very heart out of you."

He rested his forehead against hers and gripped her wrists. "She never wanted me, not when I was mostly innocent, not when my heart was pure. She'll hate me now, hate what I've done, hate me."

"Bobby, my precious son. Don't give up until you know for certain how she feels."

"But—"

"No, darling, no buts. You will approach her and work with her, and perhaps the two of you can at least find some middle ground in friendship." Rebecca kissed his forehead and eased away. "I love you."

"Love you, too, Mom."

He stood and left, and she turned in the chair, watching him walk away, a strong warrior with his mother's skill and his father's heart. Would he never make peace with his past and find his heart again? If he didn't, she'd have to step in. He'd suffered long enough. For his own good, she would approach Indigo and set things right.

Truly, a mother's job was never done.

THE EARLY OCTOBER MORNING chilled Dani to the bone for the second time in less than a week. This time, she didn't have the luxury of a leather jacket to ward off the cold. She got to keep her pants on, a minor blessing, even if she was barefoot. The grass on the IECS'S athletic field was crisp and dewy, wetting her feet as she trudged through it, but at least the first frost hadn't hit yet.

She gripped her shield in her left hand and her spear in her right, and joined the ring of six other women standing around the bier Lilith's corpse rested on, each holding a shield and spear. Lydia, as the eldest of the deceased Daughter's kin, stood at the head as the honorary mother figure, with Dani to her right as the closest living kin. Dani didn't recognize the other Daughters. Lilith's granddaughters, probably, or volunteers roped into helping out of tradition.

The lack of curiosity about her own kin didn't even register. She was still stiff and sore from the wounds Lilith had delivered four days before, and her heart had fled along with the big lug she'd fallen in love with. Nothing else really mattered.

He'd texted when he'd arrived in Atlanta, but hadn't called. She hadn't expected him to, even if she'd wanted to hear his voice, needed to hear him tell her he'd be back.

And now, here she stood at the funeral of the mother she'd only learned about two weeks before, alone among the crowd of people who'd shown up more to make sure Lilith was really dead than anything.

The crowd shifted silently around the ritual circle. Lydia lifted her shield and spear and raised her voice in a mighty cry. One by one, the other women joined in and then the people around them until the noise was strong enough to reach Ki, a plea for mercy and grace upon the deceased.

Lydia cut her voice off abruptly. She hit the butt of her spear against the ground twice, then tapped the head of the spear against her shield. Thud, thud, hit, thud, thud, hit. Dani and the other women picked up the beat and swayed in a slow, funereal waltz as Lydia sang the first stanza of a traditional requiem, honoring the deceased's role as a daughter. The circle shifted to the left, and Dani stopped at her mother's head and picked up the song, singing, "Mother, mother, giver of life, Mother, Mother, justice is thine."

The words were meant to be ironic, to tweak the nose of the god that had cursed them to immortality. The People believed that when a Daughter died, she joined Ki on an eternal plane where the curse could never reach her again. It was the justice An had denied them with his unjust thirst to repay the blood the Sisters had spilled millennia past.

The words had never been as ironic as they were now. Surely Lilith had met justice at the tip of her own sword and her soul, if she'd ever possessed one, was languishing in a torturous state with the very god that had bequeathed the immortality she'd clung to so fiercely.

The circle shifted again. The Daughter beside Dani sang her part, and on around until Lydia stood at the head again. The song ceased and quiet settled over the field. All eyes turned toward Dani, but she couldn't bring herself to voice words of praise for the Daughter who'd harmed so many. Instead, she skipped to the next step in the ritual and slammed spear against shield, jumping and landing with each blow. The other Daughters in the circle joined in as if they'd anticipated her. The still raw wounds in Dani's thigh protested the movement. She ignored them and sang out an ululating cry, ending the circle's portion of the funeral.

When enough time had elapsed to be respectful, Dani cut off the cry and stepped back with the other Daughters. Seven Sons stepped forward, dressed similarly to the women, in leather vests and pants, their feet bare. Bobby had stepped in as a substitute for Dani's closest male kin. Even gratitude for that small kindness eluded her.

The men lifted the body off of the bier using the handles on the stretcher placed underneath it, three to a side and one at the front. The Daughters fell in beside the Sons as an escort, and behind them, the people that had attended the first portion of the ritual formed a loose line.

The funeral party led the crowd away from the field through the IECS campus to the small cemetery situated behind the main building, where a pit had been dug. The Sons carefully lowered the stretcher into the pit and stepped back, and the Daughters comprising the circle took their place and shoveled dirt into the grave over Lilith's corpse.

Originally, the ritual had ended with the body interred in a cave, as the Oracle had been. Over time, the funerary rite had morphed from that to immolation and then to burial, though some descendants still chose immolation.

Dani hadn't wanted Lilith's body to decay so rapidly. Justice demanded a slow, putrid rot that would, if Ki had any mercy, take years to eat away at Lilith's once beautiful shell. It was spiteful and vindictive, but Dani didn't care. Anything to ease the pain Lilith had inflicted on the world, and on Dani's six sisters, who hadn't survived their mother's wrath.

The wound in Dani's side burned and ached by the time the body was covered and the dirt tamped down. Sweat and grime caked her skin, and she wanted nothing more than to go home, take a hot shower, and hide in bed for a long, long time.

But the day wasn't over. The modern addition to their rituals of the after-funeral home visit had to be observed. In history class, and then on her own, Dani had studied the People's history and admired her ancestors' ability to adapt to the customs and social mores of the eras they'd occupied in order to survive and, hopefully, thrive. Right then, she couldn't dredge up that admiration. It clashed deeply with her desire to be alone, to mourn in peace the mother she'd barely known, and to adjust to her new role as the daughter of one of the most reviled women in the People's history.

So she went to Rebecca's house, took a quick shower, and changed into warmer clothes. She endured the condolences and the sly, speculative looks from people who knew her only in passing, and the more genuine concern of her friends.

She picked at a plate of food Jerusha put together for her, and nearly cried when Lydia introduced her to the other members of the circle. Her nieces, the children of the sisters she'd never known, and only a handful at that. She, who'd longed all her life to know her birth family, had finally found them, but at a much greater cost than she'd ever anticipated having to pay.

Dani drifted through Rebecca's crowded house, through the family that had adopted her as their own and the family that now claimed her by right of blood. Through it all, she wished Dave was there to hold her and comfort her, to ease some of the burden resting squarely on her shoulders.

More, she wished she'd told him how very much she loved him before he left, and prayed to the Lady Goddess that he loved her enough to return to her.

NINETEEN

S TUART HAMPSTEAD'S skin was sallow and flabby under the harsh lights of the interrogation room. His clothes were rumpled from his brawl with Dave and torn where Moira had man-handled him. Stu had managed to pull his shirt up over the tattoo on his left arm, but everybody knew it was there now. Everybody knew he'd gone rogue. Only Dave had an inkling of what the tattoo meant, and he wasn't about to share, either.

He sipped lukewarm coffee out of a waxy cardboard cup and observed Stu's questioning from the wrong side of a two-way mirror. Nicodemus Hutley stood beside Dave, hands on hips, his eyes narrowed as Stu evaded and avoided every question put to him.

Hutley was an imposing man, nearly as tall and broad as Dave, and hefty around his waist. He was sharp and intelligent and canny, and at fifty-three, was in the prime of his career with the FBI as the Special Agent in Charge of its field office in Atlanta. He didn't waste time on small talk and had no patience for rodents, two things he and Dave had in common.

"Let me have a go," Dave said.

"No can do, New York," Hutley said in the slow drawl of a rural south Georgian. "You're only here to observe and assist."

"Kansas," Dave murmured. "I'm from Kansas."

"Is 'at so? Hmm." Hutley fingered his stubbled chin and appraised Dave from head to toe. "You kinda do look like a farm boy."

Dave grunted and rubbed an absent-minded hand over the sharp longing piercing his heart. *Farm boy.* Damn it, he missed Dani. The longer Stu held out, the longer it would be until Dave could see her again. "I can get him to talk."

"Son, if we can't get him to talk, what makes you think you can?"

"He was my handler. I know him."

"Hunh." Hutley turned his attention back to the interrogation room. "Give us another day."

Dave snorted. The only way the FBI had been able to hold Stu this long was because they'd charged him under the Patriot Act as a terrorist. Dave had been only too happy to help things along by describing the amount and kinds of weapons housed at Pinico Alexiou's factory in Gainesville. Hutley had gotten a warrant on Dave's testimony, raided the factory, and found exactly what Dave had told him they'd find. Word was Washington hadn't taken the implications well.

For three long days Dave had spilled his guts to Hutley, then to Hutley's men, and then to Hutley again. For three days, he'd watched Stu sit with smug confidence in that interrogation room, not saying a damned thing. For three long, long nights he'd been alone in a hotel less than an hour from where Dani slept, and now on the fourth day, when Dave was the best resource to break Stu, Hutley wanted to wait.

Dave ground his teeth together and snagged his fleeting patience, holding it right where it was. He needed to do something, anything, to move things along. Since Hutley wouldn't let him work on Stu and Dave had told them everything he could, except for the whole *immortal Daughters* thing, he excused himself and went back to the hotel. He changed into workout clothes and spent hours in the hotel's gym, pounding the frustration and anger out of his system.

His phone rang at six a.m. the next day. He checked the number, then answered. "Yeah?"

"He's ready for you," Hutley said.

Dave's mind snapped to attention and a bone deep satisfaction spurted through him. "Be there in thirty."

Stu was in the same clothes and the same chair in the same interrogation room as the day before. Dave walked in, thick folder in hand, and straddled a chair on the opposite side of the table. He opened the folder carefully, more for show than anything. "Hello, Stu."

Stu rat mouth curled into a sneer. "If it isn't the little pet. How's that Daughter you're screwing? I heard Lilith sliced her up good."

Dave stared at the other man, face expressionless. Damned if he'd let Stu get a rise out of him. "Why did you leave New York?"

"Because you left New York. I had to keep an eye on you, didn't I?"

"That's not how it works."

Stu shifted in his chair, a small smile playing over his thin lips. "Now you tell me."

"What were you doing at the Alexiou's factory in Gainesville?"

"Minding my own business. What about you?"

"You know why I was there."

"Really? Hunh." Stu rolled his eyes to the ceiling. "What was that now? Oh, yeah. You were chasing me and losing."

Dave ignored the jibe. "Who put the weapons and ammunition in that factory?"

Stu jolted forward across the table and hissed, "You know who did that. Why are you asking such ridiculous questions when there are so many other answers out there?"

Dave closed the folder and pushed it aside. "Ok, then. Give me some answers."

Stu's high-pitched laugh bordered on hysteria. "Lilith was my great-great-great-grandmother."

Dave nodded. He'd already worked that much out. Not the exact relationship, no, but that Stu was somehow descended from Lilith.

"She came to me, sought me out when she learned I was with the FBI. A little favor for the family. I'd heard the stories, that my great-great-grandmother was a Daughter, a woman who betrayed her own mother, but not before she'd born a Son. My great-grandfather. It was all very hush-hush, because how do you tell mere mortals about such things?" Stu slouched into his chair. "She wanted me to arrange a meeting, to act as a go-between. The Alexious and herself."

"What did she want with the Alexious?"

"The enemy of my enemy. She wanted to align with them against the People, to stop the Prophecy from being fulfilled."

"Is that why you had people following me?"

"You and that Daughter, what's her name? You were getting too close, you and all the rest. Lilith wanted to know what you were up to, so I kept tabs, had people follow you."

"And the CIA?"

Stu snorted. "No idea, really. She didn't tell me everything."

Dave considered the other man, the hollows under his eyes and the sincerity shining from him. "Why are you telling me this?"

"Because it's not over, man." Stu glanced at the two-way window behind Dave and lowered his voice. "You think you got the head, but this ain't no snake. It's a hydra. Cut off one head, two more grow back. We're gonna win. We're gonna stop the Prophecy, and there ain't nothin' you can do about it."

"Why do you care so much?"

"'Cause they're gonna make me immortal, too, let me reclaim my birthright."

"Is that what Lilith told you?"

"She didn't say it outright," Stu admitted. "But they got rituals, they got ceremonies. I know it can be done."

The anger and betrayal drained out of Dave, leaving only pity. He pushed himself off the chair and gathered Stu's file. "There's no way to become immortal, Stu. I've checked. You know I have access to all of the Shadow Enemy's records. The People's, too."

"No way, man. Lilith wouldn't leave me hanging like that."

"Lilith's dead," Dave said flatly, "by the hand of her last daughter. She was using you."

The color leached out of Stu's skin and his hands trembled as he folded them together on the table. "You're lying."

"Believe what you want."

Dave walked out of the interrogation room, leaving Stu to the tender mercies of Nicodemus Hutley.

IF EVER a woman deserved to mope, Dani figured it was her, so she did. She stayed at home, only leaving to shop for groceries. More often, she ordered in. She spent her days knitting, watching sappy movies, and doing long, slow stretches to keep her muscles from atrophying until she'd healed enough to work out again.

Running, lifting, sparring. Any of those would've been better than sitting at home, pining for Dave and mourning a mother she'd never known, but until Dr. Phillips gave her the go ahead, she was taking it easy.

Rebecca called, and Dani ignored her, then ignored Margaret, Moira, Charlotte, and Bobby when they showed up and Jerusha's persistent overseas phone calls. That was the thing about big families. There was always somebody else to nag you.

Dani finished Dave's sweater, washed and blocked it, then laid it folded on her unused dining table. He'd been gone for nearly two weeks. At first, he'd texted a few times each day, then once a day, and then every couple of days. She'd already resigned herself to his absence, but her heart continued to cling. *Time to move on*, her mind insisted. *Give him some time*, her heart countered.

Unable to stand it anymore, she boxed the slate-gray Gansey up and had her cleaning lady ship it when she came by. Then tortured herself by beginning a saddle shoulder turtleneck for him using the moss green yarn he'd picked out the day she'd become mortal.

What a masochist.

The Monday before All Hallows' Eve, a firm knock rapped on Dani's door. She paused the movie she was watching, set her knitting aside, and checked the peephole. Great, just what she needed. More nagging. She heaved a sigh and opened the door.

Rebecca stood at the threshold, dressed in one of her svelte suits with a wool coat thrown over it, warding off fall's chill. "May I come in?"

Dani opened the door wider and stepped aside. Rebecca pulled off her coat and hung it up next to Dave's baseball cap. Dani endured Rebecca's hug and kiss, then led Rebecca to the sofa where they sat down at opposite ends, facing each other.

"We're having a party for Halloween," Rebecca said. "Everyone in Tellowee's throwing their doors open this year, making a big fuss. We'd love to have you come celebrate with us."

Dani bit her lip. She didn't exactly feel like celebrating, what with killing her mother and all. Rebecca deserved better than hearing that, though. "We'll see."

"It's just a few days away. Robert would love to see you."

"How is he?"

"Better. He's trying a new regimen and it's doing wonders for the MS." Rebecca leaned forward and slid cool fingers along Dani's forearm. "He misses you. We all do."

Dani glanced away, ashamed. She couldn't dredge up the energy to care, hadn't found a damn thing to care about since Dave had left, not even her family, such as it was.

Rebecca's hand fell away and she sat back. "This has to stop, Dani. You can't spend your time mourning for Lilith and pining for Dave. It's not healthy."

"It's only been a few weeks. I think I'm entitled to that much time to mourn the mother I barely knew."

Rebecca flinched, and Dani's shame morphed into guilt. She hadn't meant to sound so harsh, hadn't meant to take her bitterness out on her adoptive mother.

"I suppose so." Rebecca's gaze dropped to her knees. She smoothed her skirt idly, seemingly lost in thought. "You're never going to forgive me for not telling you about Lilith, are you?"

Dani lifted one shoulder in a half-hearted shrug. "You did what you thought was right."

"Yes." Rebecca pinned a hard stare on Dani. "Yes, I did. It was the only thing I could do. Surely you can see that."

Over the past few weeks, Dani *had* thought about that. She'd considered how much she'd wanted to know who her parents were and how much Rebecca had sacrificed to raise her, knowing whose daughter she was. Rebecca had kept the past a secret to protect Dani, just to give her time to grow up and love and live before the truth caught up with them all.

Before Lilith found her and killed her.

"You should've told me," Dani said, "but I can't blame you for hiding it from me."

Rebecca nodded, and Dani clung to the hope that maybe, someday, this woman would understand that there was nothing to forgive.

"Have you heard from your young man?" Rebecca asked.

"He's texted."

"No calls?"

"He's not much of a talker."

"I gathered."

"So, any word on India?"

Rebecca's lips pressed into a thin slash across her face. "Bobby's working on that."

"Does Indigo know?"

"If she didn't before, she does now. Bobby sent someone to read her in or went himself."

"Hmm."

Bobby had always had the hots for Indigo, since he was a kid, really. Something had happened between them when he was a teenager. Nobody knew exactly what, or if they did, they weren't telling, but Dani *did* know that neither had walked away unscathed. Indigo had buried herself in work as far away from Tellowee as she could get, and Bobby, well. Bobby had spent a long time running from his demons.

"I told him the same thing I'm telling you," Rebecca said. "You can't let the past eat away at your heart, darling. You're too good for that, too much the angel."

Dani laughed, and was surprised at the rancor bubbling out of her. "Hard to be an angel when you're mother was a murderous bitch."

"Dani." Rebecca scooted closer on the couch. "Her blood running through your veins has no bearing on what kind of person you are."

"Sure it does." Dani gazed up at the ceiling, struggling to hold her tears in check. Seemed like she was crying more often than not, and really, what kind of Daughter wallowed the way she had? "The sins of the Mother. Isn't that the code we live by?"

"No, darling, it isn't." Rebecca smoothed a hand over Dani's hair, brushing back the wisps that had fallen out of her haphazard bun. "The first time I saw you, I knew you'd grow into a great warrior."

Dani sniffed and laid her head on Rebecca's shoulder. "Really?"

"Of course, darling. After the Woman with No Face brought you to me, I looked down at you, lying in a blanket. Do you remember that blanket? You carried it around until you were, oh, five or six, I think."

"I don't remember," Dani said softly.

"Well, you did. It was rather cute." Rebecca tugged Dani into her arms, holding her close, soothing her. "But the first time I saw you, it was still new, handmade, and you were lying there looking up at me. Your eyes were still blue. It was a long time before they lightened to green, but they were piercing, intelligent. You couldn't have been more than two months old, but you were already so aware.

"I took one look at you and I fell in love. I knew then, right at that moment, that you would be my daughter, not because the Woman had given you to me to raise, but because I loved you."

"Oh, Mom." A tear streaked down Dani's face and she swiped it away. "I'm so sorry."

"No, my sweet child. There's no need for that."

"I've been awful."

"You've been human. These past few months have been tough on you, but you've handled it so well. Others would've run from the task you were given, but you stood your ground, and you won. You have to make peace with the past in your own way, but please know that I am so very, very proud of you for finding the courage to do what you had to do."

Rebecca stayed through supper and watched the rest of the movie with Dani. On her way out, she reminded Dani of the Halloween party, and Dani promised to be there. She picked up Dave's turtleneck and worked on it a while before doing a set of slow stretches and getting ready for bed.

Rebecca was right. Dani had never been tested before, not really, and she'd found her courage in the days leading up to the fight with Lilith. More, she'd found her faith. She'd believed in herself or, at least, believed in the justness of her cause. And now, she needed to draw on that faith and believe in Dave, believe that he'd come back to her and love her and let her love him.

But as the days passed and October's blue skies faded to November's gray with little contact from Dave, Dani found it harder and harder to cling to the faith that had given her the strength to face Lilith.

TWENTY

LUKAS ALEXIOU'S estate blustered against the rural New York landscape exactly the way it had the last time Dave had been there. Rain threatened in the steely clouds overhead and cold seeped straight through muscle to bone. The trees had shed their leaves weeks ago, leaving the forests barren and gray. It was a perfect backdrop for an autumn day in New England.

After helping pull as much information out of Stu as he could, Dave had finally left Atlanta for New York, where he'd spent another two weeks wrapping up his business there. He had only a few things left to do, including saying goodbye to Lukas Alexiou.

He should tell Dani that, tell her he'd be back soon. He fished his phone out of his pants pocket and opened it, trying to find something new to say. *I love you.* No, he wanted to tell her that in person. *I miss you.* Surely she already knew that.

Do you love me?

He turned his phone off and stuffed it into his pocket. Next time, she was coming with him, business or not, and then he'd show her how he felt, as often as she wanted him to, more if she'd let him.

When Dave entered Lukas's study, he and Marco were engaged in a silent test of wills, staring daggers at each other behind the massive, antique table Lukas had converted into a desk. It was an old, familiar scene. Lukas ran his empire with an iron fist while Marco resented not having control of his own life and, more importantly, the Alexiou money.

Marco glanced at Dave and sneered. "And here he is now, the traitorous FBI plant, come to check on his little assignment. How was Atlanta, Dave? Did you have fun aiding the People in their war against us?"

Dave crossed his arms over his chest and settled into a wide-legged stance. Little shit could peck at him all day. Didn't mean Dave had to react.

A muscle in Lukas's firm jaw flexed. "As I said, Marco, I've known all along about Mr. Winstead's work with the FBI. He told me so himself, the moment he entered my employment."

Marco gaped. "Isn't it against the Bureau's policy to disclose that kind of thing?"

"I asked for a little leeway," Dave said.

"Why would you allow a government spy into our heart?" Marco asked.

"Because I wanted to know who was running black market antiquities through my stores, brother, and this was the best way to learn."

Marco's eyebrows snapped together and his hands clenched into fists. "You trusted an outsider over your own family, over your own brother."

"Yes, I did, precisely because I suspect that someone in my family chose to betray my trust by dealing in black market goods."

Marco blanched. "You think I betrayed you."

"I merely voiced my suspicions." Lukas sighed and sank into his chair. "We must keep our interests legitimate and above-board. I've explained that to you and the uncles over and over again, yet none of you will listen to reason."

"Because your *reason* has more to do with making peace with the People than protecting our own interests."

Lukas's voice whipped out like a lash. "That's enough, Marco."

"No, it isn't. You let him bring that abomination here, under the same roof as my son."

"Be careful what you say about Dani," Dave warned.

Marco sneered and dismissed Dave with a slash of his hand. "You sidled up to this man instead of trusting your own family. Pinico was right. You're weak and addlepated."

Lukas stood slowly and pinned an ugly stare on his brother. "Remember who you're talking to, Marco. It's not just the purse strings I hold here. If you push me, I shall push back."

"We'll see, brother."

Marco marched out of the room, rage nearly vibrating out of his slender body.

Lukas pressed his palms into the top of the desk and his cold gaze followed his brother's progress. As soon as the door slapped shut, he sighed and turned toward the window. "You have siblings, do you not, Mr. Winstead?"

Dave plopped into a chair in front of Lukas's desk. "Three sisters."

"I always wanted a sister. Instead, I have a brother who resents his place in the family hierarchy and my position at its head. Of course, he has no idea what I did to get there." Lukas rubbed his long fingers in slow circles against his temples. "Since the age of thirteen, I have devoted my time to building my family's holdings and finding a way to make peace with the People. The two are not as mutually exclusive as Ms. Nehring believes."

Dave didn't see how the two could possibly be anything other than contradictory, but who was he to say?

"You doubt me, Mr. Winstead." The corners of Lukas's mouth turned up slightly. "Have faith. All will turn out as it should, though I doubt anything will be as painless as we would like."

Nothing ever was. Hadn't he learned that the hard way with Dani? Watching her fight Lilith alone, watching her fall, having to leave her while she was healing. He sucked in a breath around the agony throbbing through his chest. He hadn't even told her he loved her, hadn't been able to find the words.

Lukas's hands fell to his sides. "War is imminent, Mr. Winstead. Can you not feel it? And now you've come to tell me you're leaving, knowing how much I shall need you at my side in the long days ahead."

"Dani needs me more."

"True. She's quite lovely, such a charming companion. If my heart weren't already taken, I might try for her myself."

Charming wasn't the way Dave would put it. Feisty, stubborn, and maybe a little arrogant. He wouldn't take her any other way. "She'd drive you batty in a week."

Lukas laughed and his shoulders relaxed. "She might at that. Still, I couldn't let you leave without wishing you good fortune. I also have a gift for Ms. Nehring, a small token of my esteem for the both of you."

He walked to his desk and picked up a parcel wrapped in kraft paper and tied with twine. Dave took it and hefted the light package in his hands. "What is it?"

"A small something from our collection of artifacts related to the People. I knew to whom these belonged the moment you told me who had taken the Prophecy artifact." When Dave hesitated, Lukas added, "Please. Open it."

Dave untied the twine and opened the heavy paper. Inside rested an ancient pair of something similar to sparring gloves. They were worn and nearly falling apart, and had smears of what looked like dried blood along the edges.

"Cæstus," Lukas explained. "Used to protect one's hands during a bout of Pankration, an ancient Greek sport."

Dave examined the cæstus, turning each one gently in his hands.

"We had reports of a Daughter who fought," Lukas said, "but no one recorded her name."

"Lilith Cæstus," Dave murmured. He hadn't ever considered that her name might mean something.

"Perhaps Ms. Nehring will be pleased to have this memento of her mother."

Dave gently rewrapped the gloves. "She will. Thanks."

"You're quite welcome, although as a wedding present, it's hardly adequate."

"Don't know if she'll have me," Dave admitted.

Lukas smiled. "My dear Mr. Winstead. How could she possibly resist?"

They talked for a while, discussing plans for filling Dave's spot. In his time in Lukas's organization, Dave had come to play a vital role. He'd be difficult to replace, mostly because Lukas trusted only rarely, the primary reason Dave had asked for permission to break the Bureau's sacred rule when he'd gone undercover. Full honesty had been the only way he could earn Lukas's trust and effectively play the role the FBI had assigned to him. It had been risky, but it had worked, and Dave had provided valuable information to the FBI and Lukas during his time there.

Before he left, Lukas asked Dave to stay in touch, a promise Dave easily made. In spite of occasional crazy spells, Lukas was a good man, or as good as a man could be in his position. And, it might help to have the ear of the Shadow Enemy's leader.

Dave arranged for the clothes he kept at the Alexiou estate to be shipped, then drove back into the city. Somewhere between Atlanta and New York, he'd made the decision to leave the FBI and move to Georgia to be with Dani. He didn't know what he'd do there yet or if she'd even have him, but he couldn't stay with the FBI and have her in his life, too. The job was too hard and consumed too much of his attention.

Before she'd found him, it had been a way to stay sharp while he waited for the mysterious woman he was supposed to protect. Now, it was just a job, and damned if he'd let it come between him and the woman he loved.

He was going to tell her that, soon as he could.

Just a few more days. Surely he could wrap up his life in New York soon and get back to her by then.

A WEEK AND A HALF before Thanksgiving, Dani stood at the side of her bed pondering the shipping box resting on the duvet. It was half full of Dave's things. It had been so long since she'd heard from him, so long since he'd even texted, she'd finally given up on him coming back. Sitting around moping wasn't doing a damn thing for her state of mind, so she'd found a box and started packing away his things. For the past week, the open box had sat on her bed. At night, she dumped it onto the floor so she could sleep, but during the day, back it went so she could stare at it some more. And now, here she was again with bedtime upon her, and she had to make yet another decision, pack his things for shipment or move the box to the floor for another day.

She hadn't been able to bring herself to add his beloved Cubs hat to the pile, not yet, but she had to do something, didn't she? She couldn't keep hoping for something that would never happen, no matter how much she wanted it to. It wasn't healthy or right, and she was tired of hurting.

Familiar, aching sadness buffeted around her heart and unshed tears clogged her throat. She sniffed them back and glared at the box. Why couldn't she just finish the job and send the damn thing off?

The front door's knob rattled. Dani padded out of the bedroom and picked up the gun she now kept close to hand along the way. Her wounds had healed well. Dr. Phillips had cleared her for almost every activity, but her scars still pulled uncomfortably when she moved, distracting her during training. A gun needed simpler movements to use than her staff and had the added effect of being more intimidating.

She was halfway across the living room when the door opened and Dave walked in. His face was haggard. Shadows marred the skin under his slate colored eyes and his clothes were rumpled.

Dani stumbled to a halt and shock rooted her to the middle of the floor. "What are you doing here?" she blurted out.

The corners of his mouth turned down and his eyebrows furrowed. "Isn't that kinda obvious?"

Dani set the gun down on an end table. "I thought you were gone for good."

The line between his eyebrows deepened into a scowl. "I told you I'd be back."

"Yeah, but that was before I didn't hear from you for weeks on end." She crossed her arms over her chest and tapped a foot against the hardwood floor. "You've got a lot of nerve using that key after all this time."

Dave dropped his bag near the entrance and stalked toward her, all animal grace and male attitude. "Chrissake, Dani."

She held up a hand, palm out. "Stay right there. I'm not so beat up I can't take you down."

"Really." He smiled, the cold-blooded snark of a predator stalking its prey. "Let's test that."

She scuffled backward, bumped against the couch. Dave lunged forward, snagged her around the waist, and tossed her over his shoulder, and she swore a blue streak. Damn it, how did he keep getting the better of her?

She wiggled and squirmed, trying to break free, and pounded a fist into his back. "Let me go, you Neanderthal."

"Forget it, Dani. It was a long flight from New York and I'm tired. Last thing I want now is a fight."

He marched into the bedroom, shoved the box containing his things off her bed with a sarcastic, "Nice," and tossed her onto the bed. She rolled over and scrambled away from him, and he yanked her back and covered her body with his.

She twisted underneath him. "Get off me, you big lug."

"Forget it. I told you I don't wanna fight."

She punched his upper arm, and he grabbed her hands and yanked her arms over her head, pinning them against the bed. She slid a knee between his legs, grazing the sensitive skin of his upper thighs.

He dropped his full weight onto her. "Cut it out, Dani."

"Let me go."

"No."

His breath panted against her neck, and she shivered as heat raced down her traitorous body. Dave was *persona non grata*. Apparently her body hadn't gotten the memo yet.

She bucked her hips into his, twisting them in a weak attempt to unseat him, and encountered a full-blown hard on. Her eyelids fluttered shut and she stilled.

Oh, that was good. Was she so easy that having him on top of her and obviously ready for sex quelled her will to fight? What was wrong with her? He'd abandoned her right when she needed him most, and then waltzed back into her life like what he'd done was no biggie. His hips pressed into hers and his breath huffed out, and she stifled a moan. Why did he still feel so good?

As soon as she stopped struggling, Dave eased some of his weight off her and touched his forehead to hers. His mouth was so close. She could kiss him, savor the delicious slide of his mouth on hers, and...

She jerked her face away. What the hell? Two minutes back, and she was already giving in to him again.

He sighed and rubbed the tip of his nose across hers. "I love you."

Sharp anger burst into a raging flame within her. "You've got a funny way of showing it."

"I couldn't call."

"Why? Did the FBI take away your phone? Oh, no, I know what it was. You just forgot my number, right?"

"God, Dani."

She eased her head to the side and studied him. His mouth was a thin slash across his face and his shoulders were hunched. If she didn't know better, she'd say he was uncomfortable, but not Dave. Oh, no. He fit in everywhere, blended, molded himself to the circumstances. Uncomfortable wasn't in his vocabulary.

"What's wrong?" she asked.

"I didn't call because if I heard your voice, I was afraid I'd lose it."

"What's that supposed to mean?"

He released her hands slowly and braced himself above her on his forearms. She lowered her arms and pressed her hands against his chest. The beat of his heart thumped hard against her palms through layers of muscle and bone, and she stroked him, just because she could.

"I had to wrap things up," he said.

A muscle ticked in his jaw. Without thinking, she smoothed her fingers over his cheek, soothing him. He nuzzled his face into her palm and kissed it, and his eyelids slid shut. "If I heard your voice, I was afraid I'd never be able to stay away long enough to finish what I had to do."

"You could've told me that."

"I tried to. Didn't you get my texts?"

"I did, all three dozen or so, and I'm pretty sure not a one said, *I can't call because hearing your voice would push me over the edge.*" She swatted his shoulder, and did it again because, damn, it felt good. "You could've told me you were thinking about me."

"I did. I mean, I was." He kissed the tip of her nose. "Thinking about you. Every minute, I wanted to be here."

"And you didn't tell me this, why?"

"Wanted to tell you in person."

"Then you should've called." She heaved an exasperated breath. "I've been dying here, worried about you, thinking you'd left for good."

He nuzzled the side of her face, pressed a butterfly kiss to her cheek. "You knew I'd be back."

"No, Dave, I didn't."

She pushed hard against his chest, and he rolled away and propped up beside her on one elbow. She sat up cross-legged and stared down at him, and her heart flipped over in her chest. He looked so vulnerable, almost afraid. She'd never seen him look that way, not in the middle of sex, not the day her curse had broken, not even on the day he'd left her, promising to come back to her.

She slowly shook her head. "All I had was your word backed up by, what? A lot of steamy sex?"

His eyes went molten and he reached for her. She pushed him away, and he flopped onto his back and slung a forearm across his eyes. "It wasn't just sex, not for me."

"How was I supposed to know that?"

"I showed you how I felt, every day."

She bit her lip. "I don't understand."

"It was never about the sex, Dani." He sat up and faced her, and in his gaze, she saw the love she'd so badly wanted him to feel for her. "Come here."

He opened his arms, and she frowned. "You're not getting off that lightly this time."

He reached out and pulled her in, tucking her body against his in spite of her struggles. He brushed his face against her hair and said, "Stubborn," and she sighed because he was so big and warm and comfortable.

"Better?" he asked.

She gave up on the anger and decided to bring it back later, when he least expected it. Sneak attacks were always more fun than a frontal assault. "Yeah."

He chafed her arms through her sweater, warming her. "You were cold."

She laughed and relaxed into him. "These days, I'm always cold." And he always knew. A light popped on in her head and she stiffened. "This is what you've been doing?"

"Mmm."

"This whole time, you've been drawing me in, with your flannel sheets and your home-cooking and your manliness?"

"Manliness?"

She ignored the humor in his voice and smacked his arm. "You seduced me with flannel sheets."

"Only a little."

"And that's all you're going to say?" She dropped her voice, imitating his low rumble. "'Dani, I love you. I show you with flannel sheets.'"

He laughed softly and his arms tightened around her. "Sounds about right."

"So, let me get this straight. When you rubbed my feet and let me sleep in your bed when I was cold and cooked for me and helped me find my mother and let my family beat you up at basketball, what you were really saying was that you loved me."

"Yeah."

"Unbelievable."

"Not so much."

He told her about the day he'd met the Woman with No Face, how at the age of sixteen, he'd seen a vision of Dani fighting Lilith and known that it was his job to care for her, how he hadn't known what that meant until Dani chained him to the bed and faced Lilith alone.

"When did you figure out I was the person the Woman meant for you to protect?" Dani asked.

"Not long after you found me, before you came to my apartment the first time."

The night he'd taken off his shirt and she'd drooled over the wide expanse of his naked chest. Suddenly, that night made a lot more sense. Everything did.

What an idiot she'd been. Of course, Dave wouldn't say the words. He never said any more than he had to. She knew that, had known it all along, and still, she'd expected him to, what, text and call and be schmoopy boy, when he'd been schmoopy boy all along. Nearly everything he'd done had been not so much to protect his job as she'd believed, though he'd done that, too, but to care for her. In that moment, her whole view of him realigned.

She should've believed in him, should've known he'd be back, even if he hadn't called. It was so clear to her now, what she meant to him, how much he loved her. She'd been so stupid to hold back on him.

No more of that, not ever again.

She nuzzled her cheek into his chest. "What did you bring me?"

"How do you know I brought you something?"

"Because you love me. Now give."

"Greedy."

He eased away from her, walked into the living room, and reentered the bedroom carrying an oblong package wrapped in brown paper. Dani's heart skipped a beat. She reached out hesitantly, wrapped her hands around the package. Something *off* emanated from it, bad vibes or something. Not anything that could hurt her. Dave would never do anything like that.

Except drug her. And force her to escape through the sewer. And make her spend the night at the Alexiou estate.

She narrowed her eyes at him. Her boots had never recovered from her little adventure in the sewer, and she still hadn't forgiven him for the drugs. On the other hand, that night at Alexiou's had been absolutely beautiful, so maybe it all evened out.

Dave cleared his throat and nodded toward the package. Dani unwrapped it slowly and stared at the ancient sparring gloves the brown paper had protected. "Where did you get these?"

"Alexiou. He said they belonged to Lilith. Cæstus, when she participated in Pankration way back in the day."

"But why did he give them to you?"

He shrugged. "He likes you."

"You're kidding."

"'Fraid not." He crossed his arms over his chest. The corners of his mouth tilted in that almost smile she adored. "He told me if he weren't already taken, he'd try for you himself."

She focused on the gloves and shoved aside the image of the Shadow Enemy's leader making a play for her heart. Thank the Great Lady he hadn't, but he'd given her such a thoughtful gift, the only memento she had of her mother. Maybe someday, in the distant future, she'd resolve her feelings for her mother and everything that had happened. Maybe then she could cherish the gloves for what they were.

"Please tell him I said thank you," she said.

"You can tell him yourself when we visit him early next year."

"You're kidding!"

Dave threw his head back and laughed, hard. She twisted her mouth into a frown. Honestly, it wasn't that funny.

His laughter faded to a huge smile. "I'm kidding."

She harrumphed and folded the paper carefully around the cæstus. "I want to take these to the IECS, have those smears tested. Maybe have them restored. After that, would you help me find a way to display them?"

"Sure." He sat down on the edge of the bed and held his left hand out. "Got something else for you."

A small box rested in his palm, exactly the size and shape to hold a ring. Her heart flipped and trembled, and she swallowed. "Is that really for me?"

"If you want it."

He placed the box carefully in her hands, and she stared down at it. What if it wasn't a ring? What if it was something else, a necklace or a bracelet or a pebble? This was Neanderthal Dave, after all. No telling what he'd put in there.

His hand squeezed hers. "You gonna open it?"

She inhaled a deep breath. Ok, so, she was a Daughter and Daughters were courageous. Brave. They never backed down, never ran from trouble, so whatever it was, she could handle it, right? Quickly, she flipped open the box, and the breath she'd inhaled rushed out on a wave of hope and disbelief. Inside was a ring with a square emerald set in silver, surrounded by tiny diamonds. Dave plucked it out and slid it on the ring finger of her left hand.

"What... What's this?" she asked.

He tossed the box over his shoulder and pressed her onto the bed, then covered her body with his. "You know."

"Say it, just this once."

He kissed her instead, long and slow and easy, and everything in her heart welled up inside her, the love, the longing, the need to hold onto him and never let go. Did he really feel the same way about her?

He eased away from her, breaking the kiss. "Marry me."

"Why should I?"

He nibbled her lower lip and skimmed a hand under her sweater, warming her skin with his. "You know why."

"Say it," she insisted.

"I love you."

She inhaled sharply. "Dave."

"Will you?"

"I'm thinking," she teased, and his gentle laughter rumbled through his chest into hers.

He rolled along the bed, taking her with him, landing on his back with her sprawled across him. "Come to Kansas with me. Want you to meet my folks."

"I don't know," she hedged. "We've been living in sin for a while. They might not like me, seeing as how I've debauched their only son."

"They'll love you."

"Marry me first."

"Why should I?" he countered, and she grinned and said, "Because I love you, Farm Boy."

"Guess I'll have to, then."

They made sweet love, sealing the promises of their hearts. After, when they were curled around each other and the heat of passion ebbed slowly from their bodies, he held her carefully, tenderly, and his embrace held its own message.

Turned out, some things were better shown than said, and Dave was a master at showing his heart.

EPILOGUE

THE WOMAN stood on the balcony looking into the apartment at the couple lying on the bed, wrapped in each other's embrace. Once, she would have envied their happiness and the fragile mortality the girl had found. Daniella had a far better life in store for her, now that her mother was gone, but there were still trials for the young couple to face, more difficult than the troubles most couples endured.

The vision of the time to come had been quite clear, the outcome less certain.

Weariness settled over the Woman and she fingered the scar around her neck, a permanent reminder of who and what she was. The People thought her an object of horror, of death. Few knew her true objectives, and even fewer saw her actions as the mercies they were.

The threads of fate tangled into a knot so thick, even she couldn't always sort them out, but she had no need to. The Lady Goddess guided her, always and forever. It was Her will the Woman followed now, and had for so long she'd forgotten how to live another way. She had excised the People of the evil embedded within them and nurtured the goodness until it took root and flourished.

She glanced at the couple, lying so peacefully together. Sometimes, even she needed help rooting out the bad.

The light in the bedroom extinguished, and the Woman turned away, satisfied that the Goddess's will had been fulfilled in this instance.

She jumped lightly onto the rail of the balcony and balanced there as she studied the suburban landscape. The world had changed so much in the passing millennia of her life, and yet, some things remained unchanged. The People endured in spite of their enemies and the Lady Goddess watched over them all with a benevolent eye.

Blessed be Ki.

The Woman stepped off the rail into the night.

And let the darkness consume her.

Book 3
The Enemy Within

ONE

INDIGO DUPREE surveyed the packing boxes strewn throughout her new apartment with a light heart. *Home*. For fourteen years, she'd lived out of a suitcase, roaming from job to job, never staying still for long. It was time, past time really, to put roots down again, to settle somewhere. Time to stop running.

It was purely a coincidence that growing roots landed her in Tellowee among the past she'd left behind. Her mother lived here now with her new husband and a baby on the way, hopefully the long-desired son. A new baby to spoil and love and cherish.

The yearning to push life from her body, to become a mother and hold a babe of her own, whispered through Indigo. She had few regrets in her life. Not having a child was one of them.

Another regret, a stronger one, tightened its grip on her, of a boy on the brink of manhood and a kiss she could never forget.

She shoved the memory away and picked up a box.

Being a Daughter wasn't all it was cracked up to be. Near-eternal youth had advantages, true, but it came with a memory that never faded, never blurred. The mistakes of a long past piled up on one another like poorly stacked blocks, resting on the sanity of the moment, waiting for one false move to send the whole stack toppling.

What would it be like to be mortal, worried only about things like finding a place to walk her dog, if she had one, or saving up for a new pair of outrageously impractical heels?

Indigo paused in the middle of slitting open the tape of the box she'd chosen, turning the notion over in her mind. Mortal women didn't look over their shoulders, trying to stay one step ahead of an ancient enemy. They didn't worry about breaking a curse or finding a lasting love. Ok, sure, they worried about love, but not the way an immortal Daughter did. An immortal Daughter who couldn't find a love strong enough to take her heart and will was doomed to a restless life, always on the run, never to find solace.

The doorbell rang, startling Indigo into dropping the box she held. She frowned at the door. In town less than a day, and already visitors came a-calling. Gossip spread quickly in the sleepy Southern town. A handful of people knew she'd moved back to

Tellowee and she'd just left the house where most of them lived, all except Dani Nehring.

Her frown lifted at the thought of her friend, who lived only an hour away. When Indigo had called the week before, Dani had sounded near rock bottom. Indigo had finally teased enough information out of the suddenly tight-lipped Daughter to learn that Dani had had a rough go of it since their time in Sweden, between falling in love, becoming mortal, and finding, then killing, her long lost mother. Indigo had invited her to come out, maybe have pizza and catch a movie, but she hadn't really expected Dani to take her up on the offer, not yet. Still, Indigo hurried to the door, anxious to see her friend.

When she pulled open the door, her heart skittered in her chest, then sank like a stone. Bobby Upton stood at the threshold, a solid six feet of lean muscle, unruly chestnut hair, and hazel eyes. His face was thinner than she remembered, his eyes harder, but he looked strong and fit in a black, form-fitting turtleneck tucked into low-slung jeans.

Her gaze drifted unconsciously down his body and her breath caught in her lungs. He'd filled out handsomely since the last time she'd seen him. He'd always been tough, with the lean, quick build of his father. His shoulders seemed broader now, the muscles more defined under his clothing. The cockiness he'd worn like a badge as a teenager had mellowed to cool confidence, apparent in his loose stance and calm gaze. He held himself like a man ready to handle anything thrown his way, not a boy eager to take what he wanted.

The man before her wouldn't *need* to take anything. He'd simply have to ask and it would be willingly given.

She sucked in a breath, appalled at the direction her mind had taken, and jerked her gaze to his face. His wide mouth was tilted into a smug smirk. A bloom of heat and color worked its way into her cheeks and her mouth snapped into a thin line.

Ogling Bobby Upton. Atta way to keep the upper hand.

"Indigo."

His voice was low and smooth. Awareness shivered up her spine and she closed her eyes against it. Why had he, of all people, shown up at her door?

"May I come in?" he said.

Her eyes popped open as her skin went hot, then cold. She swung the door shut, anything to keep him on the other side, *please, Goddess.*

His hand shot out, catching the door in mid-swing. "We need to talk."

"I don't have anything to say to you," she said, and bit the inside of her cheek at the breathless note in her voice.

His jaw tightened. "This is business."

She threw all her weight behind her hold on the door, and glared at him when his one palm, flat on the door's surface, was enough to counter her strength. His smirk was a little too smug, a little too knowing. Drat him. Fourteen years and he still got the best of her.

She clenched her jaws together and gritted out, "Still not interested."

He shoved the door hard, popping it out of her restraining hand, and stepped inside, a dangerous glint in his eyes. Her heart raced as she scrambled back. The last time she'd seen that look, bad things had happened, *really* bad things.

Or really good ones, depending on the point of view. His hand skimming under her shirt, teasing her skin with the soft, sure grazes of his fingertips. His mouth claiming hers, demanding her surrender as he pressed her against an unforgiving concrete wall. Her body melting under the onslaught of his heat, then voices spilling out into the hallway and her jerking away, keeping them both from making a terrible mistake.

She turned from him, away from the stain of memory and regret. "What do you want?"

"I'm here about India."

Indigo stifled an irritated sigh. Why did people always come to the good twin when the bad one erred? "What has she done now?"

"Fallen in with some very bad people."

"India *is* very bad people, Bobby."

"Ever hear of Lilith Cæstus?"

She sucked in a breath. Dani's mother, the ancient Daughter who had wreaked havoc on the People and anyone else she could lay hands on over the past couple of millennia, now dead by her only surviving daughter's hand. "Please don't tell me India was with Lilith when Dani stood against her."

"Ok, I won't."

Indigo wilted under the mildly voiced sarcasm. Hearing that would break her mother's heart. India had always been difficult, zagging when Elizabeth told her to zig, lashing out at everything that came her way, good or bad. The reckless anger had only grown worse as she aged.

"She's just the tip, Indigo," he murmured.

His voice washed over her like a caress, a distracting shiver of possibilities. She pushed her reaction away. Duty was a hard mistress, duty to family the hardest, this one in particular. Bobby Upton in her home. The things a woman did for family. "Ok, fine. Come in and close the door. You can help me unpack while you fill me in."

He shut the door and locked it, and walked toward her in a loose limbed gait, like a man ready to claim what was his. *Blessed Goddess.* Her breath caught in her throat and her heart raced and his heat surrounded her as he neared, and she caught his masculine scent and went dizzy with need. She steeled herself against it and brought herself ruthlessly under control.

Bobby dug a knife out of his pocket, picked a box, and carefully slit the tape holding it closed. "It's been a madhouse around here lately."

"I heard." Indigo breathed out a silent sigh of relief when her voice sounded relatively normal. "Have all the Sandby borg artifacts been recovered yet?"

"No." He unpacked china, set it on the counter, and dropped packing material onto the pile she'd started. "The one Lilith stole from the warehouse in New York a couple months back? That one we have, but as far as we know, the Shadow Enemy has the others."

Her hand went to the spot on the back of her head where she'd been hit earlier that year, during the theft of a cache of documents from the Swedish dig. "No word on the original thief, then?"

At his silence, she glanced up and caught him watching her with a peculiar expression on his face, his eyes intense, his mouth set in a thin, hard line. Her hands trembled when he stepped closer, and then his fingers sifted through her hair, probing the back of her head with a light, firm pressure.

She pulled back to escape his touch, to still the tremors in her body and the needy ache pooling low in her gut. He clasped her shoulder with his other hand, holding her in place while he examined the spot where she'd been hit.

"I was worried about you," he murmured. His breath warmed the skin of her face, and she steeled herself against his nearness. He was so close, his heat and strength there if she wanted it. She'd given in to him once for a few brief moments fourteen years before. It had ended with both of them running as far and as fast as they could. How could his mere presence chase that regret and memory away so easily?

"It was nothing." She tried to step back again and he let her go. "Long healed."

His expression closed as he turned away from her and opened another box. "Mom believes someone's actively working against the People, hiding the Shadow Enemy's movements, maybe undermining other common goals, like breaking the curse."

She plucked at the box she'd crumpled beneath nerveless fingers. "There are always a few who go against the grain."

"This feels like a concerted effort. Organized." He caught her gaze, holding it with the intensity of his own. "It's possible India picked up where Lilith left off. If she did, she probably has at least a rudimentary control of Lilith's followers. If not her, then someone else, but our priority is finding India. I wouldn't ask for your help if I didn't need it."

"She and I were never close."

"But you understand her in a way few other people do." His gaze went hard and flat. "I could always ask your mother for help."

She gaped at him. How could he even suggest that? "She's pregnant."

"Hard to miss."

"And you would ask her to go after India? Are you insane?"

"I have a job to do, Indigo."

"And you don't care who you hurt to do it, is that it?"

"I always care who I hurt," he snapped. "That doesn't mean I can neglect my duty."

"Duty," she scoffed. "You're Rebecca the Blade's son, all right."

"You have no room to lecture me about duty."

She flinched away from the harsh grate in his voice. "Bobby..."

He cut her off with a dismissive slash of his hand. "I'll find India with or without you." He pulled a business card out of his pocket and tossed it onto the top of the box she held. "I'm briefing a team tomorrow morning at ten thirty. Be there if you want to help."

He stalked out of her apartment, shutting the door firmly behind himself. She exhaled a shaky sigh and slumped against a stack of boxes. Her first day in town and she'd totally blown it. Bobby's face popped into her head, the hot rake of his eyes, the gentle pressure of his fingers sifting through her hair. She shivered as the heat he'd stirred reignited. Why had she answered the door?

Right. She'd expected anyone, anyone at all, other than Bobby Upton, the very reason she'd left Tellowee in the first place. If he'd come about anything but India, she'd ignore him. She was good at that, but duty called, that wretched beast, and her duty, if what he said about India was even halfway true, was to chase down and contain her errant twin, whether she wanted to or not.

Her gut roiled and the muscles around her spine tightened. Why did he have to be the one going after India?

Indigo scrubbed her hands over her face and pushed him out of her mind, determined to keep him there as long as she possibly could.

THE NEXT MORNING, the office hummed with activity as duties were assigned and discussed alongside a hefty dose of weekend gossip. Bobby sat in his office with the door open, listening to the hustle and grind with the satisfaction of a man invested in it. When he and two of his closest friends, Hiro Okada and Drew Martin, had started BDH Security & Protection Services two years before, they'd hoped for success and never dreamed of achieving it so quickly. It was one of life's unexpected pleasures, kind of like seeing the woman of his dreams again after nearly a decade and a half.

The night before, he'd left Indigo's more than a little frustrated and spent hours afterward sweating her out of his system. A punishing run on the treadmill and an hour in the pool swimming lap after lap as if the Shadow Enemy were on his heels hadn't been enough to purge her memory. He'd fallen into bed exhausted and dreamed of her soft, lithe body all night long, of kissing her, of sinking into her, of the little mews of pleasure she made when he touched her.

He rubbed a hand along his chest, over the ache he'd lived with for fourteen years. There was no other woman for him. It had been a hard lesson, one learned when he was barely a man. Now if he could just come to grips with it and her rejection, maybe they could both have some peace.

The intercom buzzed, interrupting his mood's downward spiral.

"Mr. Upton?"

Laura Ellenburg's voice drifted through the line, as clipped and efficient as the rest of her. She'd been the first person he, Hiro, and Drew had hired when they'd started BDH. They'd snagged her right out of business college, impressed by her composure and organizational skills, though she'd barely been twenty at the time. In the two years since, they'd never had a reason to regret it. She was always on time, kept the office running like a top, and, with her waif-like figure and doe eyes, was easy on the eyes to boot. Laura was like the little sister none of them had ever had, and they treated her that way whenever she let them.

Bobby scooted his chair closer to his desk and punched a finger at the phone. "Yes, Laura?"

"There's a woman here to see you." Her voice held a prim, disapproving edge under the stiff formality she seldom dropped. "A Ms. Indigo Dupree. Should I have her make an appointment?"

A sudden heat filled his veins, enough to have his blood humming under his skin. He stifled it ruthlessly. She was probably there about India, damn them both. "Send her back, please."

He walked around his desk and watched her through the open door of his office as she strode past the reception desk, her heart-shaped face set in the lines of someone undertaking an unpleasant task. Her long black ponytail swished with every step and her eyes glittered like sapphires against the pale ivory of her skin. She wore drab olive cargo pants and a loose white cotton shirt, and carried herself with the innate confidence of a woman who knew how to handle herself.

His traitorous heart skipped a beat, taking his breath with it, and he cursed low and long. When would he learn?

She stepped into his office, shut the door, and caught his gaze with her own. "I'll help you find India, but I have conditions."

He leaned back against the edge of his desk and crossed his arms over his chest. That was a Daughter for you. Always laying down the law and expecting the man in her life to toe the line. If he hadn't gotten tired of it at the age of ten, it'd be funny. "Such as?"

"I work alone."

"No," he said flatly. "No one here works alone."

"Then I work with anyone but you," she shot back.

The pleasure of her presence evaporated abruptly. "Sorry, Indi. Everyone else is taken."

"How can you possibly know that?"

"Because I do."

"Fine," she gritted out. "Then promise to keep your hands to yourself."

"No can do."

She turned on her heel, heading for the door. Hell with that. He was damn tired of her walking out on him, pushing him away, letting his heart rot in the dank heap of loneliness he'd endured nearly half his life.

He caught her arm and jerked her around. "Why don't we just get it over with?"

Her eyes widened with what he would've sworn was panic. "I don't know what you're talking about."

"Another kiss," he explained patiently. "We're both thinking about it. Let's just do it so we can move on."

"In your dreams."

A muscle twitched in his jaw at the snap in her voice. She had no room to talk about dreams, no leave to remind him of everything he'd lost when she'd pushed him away. He yanked until she fell into him, hissed in a breath when she struggled against him, trying to break free. Goddess, it was so good to have her there, to feel her once again the way a man always wants to feel the woman he desires. He hardened his grip, tightened it until their bodies were melded together, and called himself ten kinds of fool for enjoying her weight pressed into him.

She stilled as something very Daughter-like flashed through her expression.

"Don't do anything you'll regret later," he warned.

"I doubt I would regret it."

Her hands gripped his waist hard enough for her fingernails to dig into his skin through his shirt. She raised her head to look at him, and his gaze zeroed in on her lush, red mouth, so close to his own their breaths mingled. The world went still and faded around them, and he lowered his mouth to hers, slowly enough to give her time to pull away, and not nearly fast enough for the desire raging through him.

When his lips were a hair's breadth from hers, she murmured, "The blinds are open."

He tore himself away from the temptation of her sweet lips and the promise of another taste, and glanced up. Margaret Mary stared at them through the windows separating his office from the main hallway, her eyebrows raised. Of all the people in the office who could've caught him fondling the woman of his dreams, it had to be his sister. By the Lady Ki. A Son couldn't do anything without his female relatives knowing about it.

He cursed inwardly and let Indigo go, and clamped down on the need roiling through him as she pushed herself carefully away from him.

She sat down on the love seat and crossed her legs, fixing him with what he thought of as her teacher stare, uncompromising, hard, and always right. "And that is why you need to keep your hands to yourself, Bobby."

Irritation whipped through him, mixing with the need still zinging through his gut. "Forget it."

Her gaze never faltered. "When a woman says no, it means no."

"When you say no, I'll stop touching you."

"I said no." She took a deep breath, let it out slowly. "Repeatedly."

"You've never said no, not once. In fact, I'm pretty sure the last time we did this you were begging for more."

Her brows snapped together into a fierce scowl and she stood abruptly. "This is never going to work."

A knock rapped on the door and Laura poked her head inside. She glanced from him to Indigo and something shifted in her expression, too quickly for Bobby to catch. "Meeting's in five," she said, then closed the door on them.

"That's my cue to leave," Indigo said.

"Wait." Bobby held his hands up when she backed away. "At least come to the meeting. You can always leave after if you decide you really don't want to help."

After a long moment, she nodded and allowed him to lead her to the conference room with a gentlemanly hand on the small of her back. She didn't pull away. A spurt of triumph shot through him at her acceptance of his touch. Small, intimate touches, delivered so frequently and casually she never gave them a thought, seducing her so gently she never saw it coming.

Hell, doing that would be no problem. He slid his hand up her back until the ends of her ponytail brushed along his skin, teasing him with every step. No, touching her wouldn't be a problem at all. Knowing he could never have her, that was the thorn that kept him from trying for her again.

Two

T HE REST OF THE LEADERSHIP TEAM was seated around the round conference table when he and Indigo entered the meeting room. Bobby introduced her first to his partners and former military buddies, Hiro and Drew. Hiro was the great-grandson of Japanese immigrants and the son of fierce traditionalists who'd raised him to respect the customs of their homeland. He was slender and fit, and more disciplined than any of them, except Margaret. Drew was a Yankee from Boston, a Southie with the burly Irish build of his forefathers and a brawling attitude to match. The three of them had been through hell together and seen each other out in one piece, forging a bond of friendship so strong it bordered on brotherhood.

The two men sat with their backs to the left wall. Zenalisa Jones, their tech expert, had taken her customary spot opposite them, her thin frame slumped sulkily in her chair. Not long after they'd opened, Zena had shown up on their door demanding a job. It had taken her five minutes to hack their system, and less than that for them to hire her. When they'd gently probed her background, she'd given them such a dead-eyed look that they'd backed off. Even Hiro, with his soft touch and gentle voice, hadn't been able to pry it out of her.

"You've met Laura, our office manager, and you remember my sister, Margaret."

"Of course," Indigo murmured politely.

Bobby led her to a seat on the far side of the table and sat her to his left next to Zena. "I've asked Indigo to sit in on this meeting since she'll be helping us with a job I've just contracted."

Drew groaned and sat back in his chair. "We're overbooked now, Bobby."

Bobby sat back in his own chair and drummed his fingers lightly on the arm of his chair. "We can rotate this in as people become available."

Hiro pulled his notebook forward and began making notes. "What kind of skill sets are we talking about?"

"Whatever we need to unearth spies and possible traitors," Bobby said bluntly.

Drew pulled his lower lip between two fingers before speaking. "Corporate espionage or treason?"

"That depends on how you look at it. It's for the Institute for Early Cultural Studies." Bobby caught the slight puzzlement in Margaret's otherwise blank expression.

"Wait, your Mom asked you to do this?" Drew's thuggish face twisted into a leer. "Will she be coming by?"

"That's my mother you're talking about," Bobby reminded him.

Margaret leaned forward and pinned Drew with a menacing glare. "Mine, too."

"Her, I'm afraid of," Drew said, then pointed at Bobby. "You, not so much."

Bobby narrowed his eyes. "I can still kick your ass."

"Here we go." Hiro rolled his eyes to the ceiling in a long-suffering look. "You guys remember we're trying to run a business here, right?"

Indigo leaned forward to catch Hiro's eye. "Are they always like this?"

"Usually, they're worse." Hiro gave her an assessing look that had Bobby's temper flaring. "I'm the nice one of the bunch. A good lover, too, when you get tired of Upton."

"We're not lovers," Indigo said with a small smile. At the same time, Bobby said, "Hey!" and Drew said, "Dibs on the new girl."

"Children." Margaret's voice was quiet but firm, and drew everyone's attention. "The matter at hand?"

Bobby cleared his throat and split a dirty look between Drew and Hiro. "I've got preliminary profiles on a list of suspects and info on the possible shark and its victim. Zena and Laura, I need the two of you on research. The rest of us will divide up the list of names."

"I'll need the paperwork," Laura said.

"Everything's on the secure internal server and I'd like to keep it that way." Bobby looked at each of them in turn, allowing the weight of his gaze to hammer in the absolute necessity of his request. "That means no sharing anything over the Internet, no talking about this over an unsecure phone line, and no internal memos."

"Gonna be hard to work that way," Drew said.

"We'll make it work," Bobby said. "Just so you know, Indigo's twin sister is on that list. They're identical, so make sure you're talking to the right one before spilling anything."

Zena snorted. "If they're identical, ain't no way to tell 'em apart."

Bobby clamped down on his impatience. "You'll figure it out. Our objective is to ferret out the traitor and bring him or her in for questioning. The people on this list are dangerous. All of them are trained in hand to hand and multiple weapons, so use caution. Don't be afraid to ask for help."

"What's the time frame?" Hiro said.

"However long it takes. Sooner's better, though." Bobby stood. "Tie up what you can this week. Delegate everything else. I'll speak with each of you in detail over the next few days, but plan on devoting time to this contract in earnest beginning next Monday. Margaret, I need a word."

The meeting broke up as it always did, like a flock of noisy geese heading for warmer weather. When Indigo rose from her chair, Bobby caught her arm. "Stay," he said, and waited until she resumed her seat before turning his attention to his sister.

Margaret appeared to be in her mid-twenties, though she was centuries older, one of their mother's eldest children. At five ten barefoot, she was just two inches shorter than him, though her ice blue gaze regularly cut him down a notch or two.

When she worked, which was nearly always, she dressed in comfortable shirts and cargo pants and kept her ash blonde hair pulled back in a ponytail. Today, she was dressed in black from head to toe and appeared ready to take on a small army.

He was pretty sure she could do it, probably already had a time or two in her long life.

At his request, she moved across the room with a lethal grace until she was close enough to carry on a low conversation.

"What do you know about the Eternal Order?" he said.

Her expression remained coldly assessing. "Aren't you a little old for fairy tales, brother?"

He gave her the look that comment deserved and pulled a sheet of paper out of his pocket. "I found this in the file Mom gave me."

Margaret took the paper from him, unfolded it, and read the two lines of text it contained before passing it to Indigo. "And?"

"Don't play games, Margaret. Tell me about the Eternal Order."

"It's a myth." She leaned a hip against the edge of the conference table and folded her arms across her chest. "A tale used to scare children into being good. Nothing more."

"How do you explain that paper, then?"

"I don't," she said calmly. "There's not enough there to explain."

"'The Eternal Order. Margaret knows.'" He barked out a laugh. "Sounds pretty straight-forward to me."

"Sounds like a con to me," Margaret shot back.

"I'll find out sooner or later."

"When you do, let me know." She turned on her heel and left the room.

Bobby waited until the door swung shut behind her before turning to Indigo. She was staring after Margaret with an odd expression on her face.

"What's wrong?"

She shook her head. The light danced off her ponytail as it shimmied. "It's nothing, really."

"Spill it."

She pressed her lips together. "You know what the Eternal Order is, don't you?"

"I've read the fairy tales," he said drily, and she frowned.

"They're not fairy tales." She folded the paper in her hands into a precise, even rectangle. "It's an ancient order made up mostly of immortal Daughters bent on keeping the Prophecy of Light from being fulfilled. They were wiped out centuries ago."

"Are you sure?"

She nodded, though her expression remained uncertain. "Surely the Council wouldn't hide their existence from the rest of the People. They were so powerful then, so dangerous. No one was safe."

Which was an excellent reason to keep their return a secret. "I'll see what I can find out."

"No, Bobby." Her hand shot out to grip his arm and her eyes went round in her face. "Leave it be. If the Order's been hidden this long, exposing them can only bring trouble."

He considered her for a moment, took in the fear on her face and in her warm grip. "If I didn't know better, I'd think you were concerned for my safety."

She dropped her hand from his arm. "I'd show the same amount of concern for anyone."

"Liar."

"Think what you will." She stood and handed him the paper. "I'll try to give you an answer on whether or not I'll help track down India by this weekend."

"That's fine." He rose and inched closer to her, lured by the sweet fragrance of her skin. "I'll be by later tonight with supper."

"That's not necessary."

"I insist," he said mildly. "You need to eat and we have things to talk about."

She narrowed her eyes at him. "You're just trying to weasel your way into a kiss."

He held up his hands in mock surrender and managed to edge closer. "You still need to eat."

"You're not going to twist me around your finger like you do everyone else, Bobby." She put her hands up to ward him off. He slid in under her guard and gripped her waist, reeling her in until their bodies touched from waist to knee. Exasperation flickered through her expression. "You never give up, do you?"

"Would you believe me if I said I can't help myself?" He lowered his head to breathe in her scent, let himself go dizzy with it. "That no matter how much I tell myself to back away, something keeps pulling me to you?"

She rested her hands lightly on his chest and kept her gaze locked there. "That doesn't make it right."

"Doesn't make it wrong, either," he countered. "Now, do you want Italian or Chinese?"

The hesitation on her face lingered for a long moment before her lips tilted into a smile and a ghost of a dimple appeared in her cheek. "Barbecue. Sweden has terrible barbecue."

He laughed even as he reined in the happiness zinging through him. "I know just the place."

"Six o'clock, then. Don't be late."

He let her go and watched her leave, her gait smooth and sensual as she strode away.

He sat back down to give his body time to cool off. He must be out of his ever-loving mind to pursue Indigo, even if she was the only woman to ever hold his heart.

INDIGO VISITED HER MOTHER after leaving Bobby's office, then went shopping for groceries and other essentials. She ran into several people she knew, and said hello, asked about family and work. It was nice to be back among the People again.

She flipped on the radio to keep her company as she put away groceries, sang alone with the songs she knew, and danced to the ones she didn't. Her mood lightened with every song. She slipped off her shoes, padded across the wooden floor on socked feet, threw the windows wide. An early autumn breeze blew in, bringing with it the smell of fallen leaves warmed under the sun shining brightly in the clear azure sky. Indigo leaned out the window and turned her face into its warmth, and smiled from the sheer joy of being home.

With a contented sigh, she pulled herself back inside and surveyed the work waiting for her. The number of boxes needing her attention had dwindled by half in the frenzy of unpacking she'd done after Bobby left the day before.

Her breath shallowed as she remembered his hands in her hair, his body pressed against hers, and warmth of another kind heated her blood. Her heart screamed at her to *Run, as fast as you can*, but Indigo pressed it down with a deep inhale of air. Her mother needed her, needed the comfort of kin during the last few weeks of her pregnancy, and Indigo wanted to be at the birth of her next sibling. Bobby would give up eventually. Perhaps they could forge some sort of friendship when he did, as she had with the rest of his family.

A little nagging voice in her head cried *Delusional!* and her heart twisted at the thought of not holding him again, of never knowing what it would be like to kiss Bobby without guilt clinging to her.

Not that she wanted to, of course.

A chill breeze crossed her skin. Indigo snapped to attention, then groaned at the time on the apple-shaped clock she'd hung in the kitchen. Half an hour spent mooning over a man she didn't want and couldn't have regardless. It was shameful, how easily her thoughts slipped to him. She burst into a frenzy of activity to drive him out of her head.

The afternoon passed quickly as Indigo puttered. By the time the first shadows of dusk crossed the room, she'd unpacked everything she could, polished the few items of furniture she'd kept, and updated her calendar with to-do lists for the week.

She was rummaging through the fridge for supper when the doorbell rang, startling her, and immediately a flush heated her cheeks.

Bobby.

She hurried to open the door. He stood on the other side looking as casual and confident and dangerous as he had that morning. *Run, run, run*, her heart urged as it beat double time in her chest. She ignored it and stepped back to let him in.

"Sorry," she said as she shut the door behind him. "I forgot you were coming by."

"Well, that put me in my place." He set the bags he was holding on the kitchen counter and started pulling containers out. "I thought you might be pining for company by now."

"No," she said, then winced. Butterflies danced in her stomach, so she took a deep breath, hoping against hope for them to calm. "I mean, I've been too busy to pine for anything today."

"So I see." His eyes darted around the room, and she felt a moment of pride that she'd managed to set the apartment mostly to rights before his arrival. "Looks like there's not much left to do."

"Oh, well, there's still lots of work." She busied her hands with the bags he'd brought, pulling out cartons of food and placing them on the counter. "I don't even have a couch or a bed yet. Haven't decided if I really want a TV. What kinds of channels can you get on cable here?"

She glanced up when he didn't answer. He was watching her with an intensity that jangled her nerves. "Or I could try satellite," she finished lamely.

"There are other options." His gaze held hers for another moment before he broke it and turned to the cabinets. "Where are the plates?"

"To the left of the fridge."

She pulled out silverware and serving spoons, helped him dish out food on two plates and pour tall glasses of chilled sweet tea. They sat at the rickety table she'd been carting with her from place to place for nearly a century and a half, one of the few pieces she'd kept over the years, simply because it held so many memories.

Bobby talked her through the pros and cons of cable, satellite, and Internet access while they ate, and teased her gently when she confessed to not being a huge fan of television programming. She relaxed gradually until it seemed like the most natural thing in the world to sit next to a handsome, lethally sexy man, sharing a meal and a long, winding conversation.

Their talk eventually turned to local gossip, then to their families, before hitting a personal topic.

"So, when's your mother due?" Bobby sat back and pushed his plate away, unfolding his mile long legs under the table.

"A few weeks." Indigo scooted her legs out of the way to make room for him. "We're all hoping for a boy."

"I bet." He nudged her legs gently with his own under the table. "Your mom will be happy to have you near."

"I hope so. India's made it a little hard on her."

"Mmm. She was always so bitter."

"That's one word for it." She stood, fighting the restless unease that filled her whenever she thought of her twin, and gathered their plates. "When Mom became mortal and married Glen, India flipped out. Apparently, she screamed at Mom about being weak or some nonsense and Mom kicked her out."

Bobby rose and followed her to the sink. "I bet that was something to see."

"I'm glad I missed it." Indigo took a deep, soothing breath as she boxed up the leftovers and stowed them in the fridge. "They've always been at odds with one another, fighting over every little thing. That's what it felt like when we were growing up, anyway."

He leaned against the counter and rested his hands against the edge. "And you hid in your books."

She glanced at him, astonished. "How did you know?"

"I know you."

"No," she said with a shake of her head, and eased back at the dangerous glint in his eyes.

"Yes, I do, and if you don't stop running from me, I'm gonna start chasing you."

Her heart jumped into her throat and excitement thrummed along her skin. "I'm not running."

"Indigo." He touched a finger gently to her mouth, traced the line of her lower lip before letting his hand fall back to his side. "You can lie to everybody else. Don't lie to me."

"I'm not..." She sucked her lip into her mouth, trying to quell the tingle his touch had caused, and only made it worse. "This is silly."

"Yes, it is."

His agreement held no rancor, though his body was stiff, ready, and his hazel eyes glittered and bored into her, tracking every single movement she made as if he were waiting to pounce.

This must be what a rabbit felt like when it faced off against a hound.

She ran water in the sink to wash the few dirty dishes instead of using the dishwasher, and struggled to calm her sudden nerves. "Why did you decide to come back to Tellowee?"

His expression relaxed into a knowing half-grin. "Same reason as you. Dad's MS has been a problem over the past few years and Mom needed help."

"I thought it was getting better."

He opened drawers until he found a dish towel and slung it over his shoulder. His hands were quick and competent as he rinsed the dishes she washed, and a little flutter went through her. What else would those hands do well?

"It comes and goes, but sometimes, they need an extra hand. Charlotte helps out when she can."

"But she's got the babies."

"Gorgeous, sweet babies, but they're a handful, and since our other sisters are gone more often than not..." He shrugged, a casual lift of one muscled shoulder. "I needed to be near family when I got out of the Army, so here I am, helping out where I can."

Her heart melted a little at his admission. "That's very sweet of you."

"Hardly."

She peered at him and saw a slight tint of red on his cheeks. "Are you blushing?"

"No."

His voice was just shy of sullen. She bit her lip against the amusement bubbling up. "What was that you said about not lying?"

"Har." He checked his watch and pressed his lips into a hard line. "I have to go. Early meeting."

"Oh." She'd just gotten used to having him around. "Thanks for supper."

"Any time." He dropped the dish towel over the drainer and cupped her shoulders with his strong, warm hands. "In fact, I vote we do this again tomorrow."

"Can't," she said, and tried to staunch the honest regret she felt, along with the flood of sensation his touch caused. "Girls' night out."

"Wednesday, then," he said, his voice firm.

"Furniture shopping." When his eyes narrowed, she added meekly, "In the afternoon."

"Come by the office when you're ready and I'll go with you. No buts," he said when she protested and brushed his lips across her forehead. "Lock up behind me."

She walked him out, half afraid he'd try more than a soft kiss, and sagged with disappointment against the closed door when he didn't even hug her. *No,* she told herself firmly as she straightened. *You're happy he didn't try to do anything. Happy, not disappointed.*

She finished straightening up from their meal, made ready for bed, and settled into her sleeping bag with *Jane Eyre.*

And stared blankly at the book, her imagination caught by the kiss yet to come.

THREE

BOBBY JANGLED THE KEYS in his hand, flipping them around on one finger as he mulled over the meeting he'd just left. When his mother had given him the names of suspected traitors to the People, he'd decided to take an individual approach to each one, in particular Isolde, a member of the Council of Seven, the People's ruling body.

He'd been raised to understand that dealing with a councilmember should be done carefully, no matter what the reason. Instead of handling her on his own, he'd approached Hawthorne, an elder who was Isolde's aunt, to at least lay some groundwork. Hawthorne had allowed him his say under her carefully impassive gaze, then said *no* in a voice as cold and dead as the dark side of the moon.

Given her reputation, he was lucky she hadn't separated his head from his body on sight.

The elevator dinged, the doors opened, and people spilled out on their way to lunch. Bobby stepped inside, punched at the button for the floor housing BDH, and studied the lighted numbers marking the elevator's progress.

Hawthorne would eventually come around. She'd been halfway there when he'd left, though he wasn't entirely sure if that was because he'd poured on the charm or if she was getting soft in her old age.

His lips twitched into a smirk. Not that he'd dare call her *old*, especially when she appeared to be about his age, if that. Immortal Daughters tended to be a little sensitive about their age, and he liked his head right where it was.

His humor faded abruptly, taking his mood with it. He'd learned the hard way just how touchy Daughters could be about their age, especially when faced with a potential suitor. Indigo had pushed him away quickly enough. Sixteen was young, yeah, but he'd been a man in the eyes of the People when he'd tried to claim her the first time, a claim that would've been legal and binding to his mother and hers. Among the People, those permissions were the most important. Not much else mattered when a Son united his life with a Daughter.

He shrugged his left shoulder, stretched his fingers over his collarbone, brushing the top of the tattoo hidden by his shirt. Permission was one thing. That tattoo was another. It forever marked him as the husband of a Daughter, claimed through love or, in his case, the drunken recklessness of a man who'd had his heart ground under the heels of a woman who hadn't wanted him.

It had taken him the better part of a decade to come to terms with Indigo's rejection, to work out the anger and hurt. They were still there, waiting to pounce, but over time, he'd found a way to chain them back so they didn't eat at him every single moment. He'd spent years atoning for the damage he'd done trying to exorcise that pain. His past would always haunt him, nothing he could do about that, though he and it had made an uneasy truce, sort of.

His mind drifted to the conversation he'd had with his mother the day she'd hired him to track down those who may have betrayed the People. She'd been spot on when she'd said he felt he wasn't good enough for a woman's love. *Indigo.* His heart lurched in his chest. Mom had said he had to find a way to deal with the past or it would eat the heart out of him, but he knew the truth. His heart was still there, even if it was battered and filthy from the things he'd done after Indigo rejected him. It was there, and it still belonged to her.

He'd asked her to stop by today, to let him tag along while she shopped for furniture, and he recognized his request for what it was: A pathetic attempt to be a part of her life, in whatever small way she would have him. He would settle for friends, if that's all they could be, and not wish for more. He didn't deserve more, no matter what his mother thought. Maybe before he'd let his emotions rule his life he could've had Indigo, but not now, not after the things he'd done, not unless they could both forget the past and the hand fate had dealt them.

Goddess knew he wanted her enough to try, even if all they could ever have was friendship.

The elevator doors opened. Bobby stepped out into the reception area and spotted her dressed in a shimmering, red flowy shirt over form-fitting leggings that highlighted the lush curve of her bottom and the strength in her legs. The breath whooshed out of him in a rush and every nerve in his body went on full alert.

Yeah, friends. How's that working out for you?

He shook his head to try to clear it, and noticed the tense set of Indigo's shoulders as she faced off against Laura, whose normally professional face was drawn into a thunderous scowl.

What the hell.

He ignored the sudden ache in his temples and stalked toward the two women, resigned to sorting out whatever problem had cropped up between them.

INDIGO SMOOTHED HER SHIRT DOWN over her flat stomach, then tugged at the hem to make sure the fabric hung correctly. Above her, digitally created numbers lit up in sequence as the elevator rose toward the floor housing Bobby's company. Her stomach jumped when the elevator dinged, signaling a stop. It wasn't because of nerves, couldn't be. Bobby had asked her to drop by today and offered to go shopping with her. She'd made a considered, rational decision to allow him to accompany her, for selfish reasons that had nothing to do with the attraction sparking between them.

No, not attraction. *Tension.* There was still *tension* between them, left over from that unfortunate day. She didn't want to dwell on that. It was in the past and best left alone. Better to look to the future, a bright future where she was welcome in the Upton household among people she'd known for decades prior to Bobby's birth, and could visit there without any *tension* between herself and the beloved Son because she and he had resolved it.

That the Son in question had a strong back and owned a truck big enough for hauling furniture was merely coincidental.

She walked out of the elevator toward the reception desk. Laura was sitting in for the BDH receptionist again. There was nothing sinister or untoward about the young woman, yet her presence jangled Indigo's nerves even more. Laura dressed smartly, held herself well, and apparently managed the office with a ruthless efficiency that would make Rebecca Upton proud. Indigo ignored the niggle of envy and pasted a pleasant smile on her face.

"I'm here to see Bobby," Indigo said.

"Mr. Upton is out of the office at the moment." Laura's wide brown eyes were cold behind her wire-rimmed glasses. "Would you like to make an appointment?"

Indigo tried to ignore the sinking feeling in her gut and failed spectacularly. So, it was like that. What was Bobby doing spending time with her instead of Laura? "Would it be all right if I wait?"

"That would be futile. Mr. Upton indicated he would be out of the office the entire day."

"Since he asked me to meet him here this afternoon, that's unlikely." Indigo gritted her teeth, searching for her normally endless patience. "I'm sure he'll be back soon. I'd very much like to wait for him."

Laura rose and rested her fingers on the phone in front of her. "Mr. Upton did not tell me about a meeting. Therefore, he will not be back. You should make an appointment and go before I call security."

Indigo huffed out an annoyed breath. Before she could reply, the elevator's doors opened. She glanced around. The nerves she'd managed to settle jumped back into play at the sight of Bobby stepping out, his expression caught between irritation and anger.

"What's going on?" he said.

Indigo opened her mouth to reply. Laura beat her to the punch.

"Ms. Dupree arrived without an appointment." Laura shot a heated glare at Indigo over the top of her glasses. "I informed her that you would be out today."

"I will be," Bobby agreed. "Indi and I are going shopping."

Laura pressed her lips together with what was surely disapproval. Indigo just refrained from giving the other woman a *so there* look. When had she stooped to such childish gestures? Right. That would be the day Bobby Upton had sauntered back into her life.

Bobby ran a hand casually down Indigo's back. She shivered at the touch, though it didn't distract her from the venom that flickered across Laura's face a moment before the young woman arranged her features into a professional mask.

His voice dropped as he leaned into Indigo. "I need to make some notes before we go. It won't take long, if you don't mind the wait."

"I'm a little early." Her irritation over the intractable Laura faded. "In fact, I deliberately came early to see if you wanted to have lunch with me. My treat, in return for your expert shopping help."

Laura gave a patently fake cough into her hand.

"Sure," he said. "Want to wait in the office while I catch up?"

"That would be lovely."

"Go ahead, then." He pulled out a set of keys, selected one, and handed it to Indigo. "I'll be right there."

She took the ring of keys from Bobby's hand. and headed toward his office, ignoring Bobby and Laura's quiet conversation behind her. The blinds were pulled down tightly against the row of glass windows between the main area and his office. Indigo unlocked the door and flipped the light switch on as she went in, closed the door, and dropped the keys on his desk.

She wandered around his office, exploring the books shelved neatly along the length of the wall behind his desk. Pictures and memorabilia sat at regular intervals, interspersed among the books. She examined each in turn as she skimmed book titles. There was a picture of Bobby with his family when he was about ten and another right beside it of him as an infant, held gingerly in his father's arms. Indigo sighed at the love on Robert's face as he gazed down at his son, touched at the depth of expression.

There were the obligatory sports photos and a few snapshots from Bobby's time in the military. In one, he and Drew bracketed Hiro. All three were dressed in camouflage and wore somber expressions. From the thinness of their bodies and their relative youth, she guessed the photo had been taken on graduation day for advanced training of some sort.

She'd deliberately fostered a lack of knowledge about Bobby as subtly as she could. Maybe it was time for that to change.

Two shelves down was a photo of Bobby with Dani draped over his back, both laughing with the carefree zest of youth. The memories of the day it was taken popped into her mind. Labor Day, about a month before Bobby's sixteenth birthday. The whole town had come out for the annual national holiday and made a day of it with races and contests and food and fun. It had been a wonderful day, though she likely wouldn't remember it as brightly if her life hadn't changed so completely not long after, immortal memory or not.

She stroked a finger over the picture, oddly disquieted at the joy in his young face, and the hardness that had grown into it since.

Because of her.

Indigo inhaled deeply and pushed the guilt away as Bobby opened the door to his office.

"Sorry about that," he said. "I don't know what's gotten into Laura. She's usually so good with people."

Indigo moved out of the way as Bobby came around the desk, and took a seat on the sofa beside the door while he leaned over his desk and made notes on the large calendar there.

"Really?" she said.

"Really, what?"

His expression was blank, his body relaxed and loose except for a slight tightening around his eyes. Indigo considered him and couldn't quite tamp down the smug amusement. He really had no clue why Laura had acted the way she had. Whatever feelings Laura had for him, they weren't returned, not in the same measure.

"Nothing," Indigo said.

He speared her with an intense gaze that left her needier than it should've, then shrugged. "I'll give you a key so you can come in and work."

"I haven't agreed to help you yet."

"But you will."

"You have a lot of confidence in your ability to persuade me."

"Mmm. Persuasion, charm, bribery. Whatever it takes."

He jotted down a few more notes, checked his watch, and threw his pen onto the desk. His eyes slid down her body so briefly she would've missed it if she weren't paying attention. A frisson of heated awareness shivered through her at the glint of approval in his gaze.

"So, where are we going?"

"Wherever you want." She stood and noted the way his gaze followed her movements, almost as if he couldn't help looking. His words from a few days before floated through her mind. *Would you believe me if I said I can't help myself?* It appeared he really couldn't. It pleased her, inexplicably, irrationally. "Would you mind driving?"

"I don't mind." He picked up the keys from his desk and crossed the room to stand beside her. "Probably for the best anyway, since I brought the truck."

She pressed her lips together to stifle the humor tugging at her. A strong man with a truck indeed. "I appreciate that."

He opened the door and placed a hand on the small of her back in a touch that warmed her through and through. "Figured you'd want to get that furniture in as soon as possible."

She let him escort her through the building, and noted with uncharacteristic spite that Laura had abandoned her post. "You figured correctly. I don't mind sleeping on the floor once in a while, but it gets uncomfortable night after night."

They entered the elevator and he punched the main floor's button with a roguish grin that made her blush. Why had she brought up *sleeping* around him, of all people?

She blew a silent breath out when he let it go and forced herself to carry on a natural conversation with him that did *not* include anything related to sleeping or beds or the attraction sparking so brightly between them.

BOBBY TOOK HER to a chichi deli a block away from his office and insisted on paying for their lunch. After they placed orders for a turkey sub each, they found a table off to one side, away from the windows and the lunch crowd streaming in.

Indigo sat down across from Bobby. "You know, I was supposed to treat you as a thank you for helping me today."

He shrugged. "Yeah, but I'm the man."

She looked up from the sandwich she was arranging in meticulous portions across the butcher's paper that held it. "What does that have to do with anything?"

"This isn't Tellowee where Daughters run amuck and bully and coddle their men into submission." He grinned at her. "This is America and I'm the man. Here, when we take beautiful women out, we pay."

She paused with one quarter of her sandwich halfway to her mouth. He thought she was beautiful. After all this time and all the things that had passed between them, the heartache and disappointment and anger, he still thought she was beautiful. A gooey warmth nudged at her heart, right where her resolve was supposed to be. How was she supposed to fight him off when he said things like that?

He raised his eyebrows and pierced her with a look that seemed to see right through her. "No rebuttal?"

"I'm not letting you pay every time we go out."

"You say that like this is an official date."

She gave him a quelling look. "Besides, this lunch was my idea."

"Still the man." When she started to speak, he nudged the plastic basket holding her lunch with a finger. "Are we gonna argue or eat?"

"I wasn't arguing," she said primly. "I was clarifying."

"Uh-huh." He took a bite, chewed thoughtfully as his eyes lingered on her. "How did you like working on the Sandby borg site?"

"It was fun, right up until the robbery. Dr. Lindberg, the man in charge of the dig," she said when he raised a questioning eyebrow, "he was a lot of fun to be around. A bit of a rascal, too, but only around his wife. I think they've been married fifty-five or six years now, and are still very much in love."

He glanced down at his sandwich, hesitated, then took a bite of it almost mechanically. She nibbled at her own sandwich as the silence dragged on between them. Why had she mentioned the l-word around him? No matter what had passed between them, he deserved better than to have her prod an old wound. She sipped from her bottle of water, searching for a safer topic. "How did you meet Hiro and Drew?"

His shoulders relaxed as his gaze lifted and a smile tugged at his mouth. "In the Army. We went through, ah, training together."

"Training." She took another bite, waited for him to elaborate. "What kind of training?"

"Can't say." His grin grew a fraction. "Classified."

"Honestly, Bobby."

"You're so fun to tease." He held up his hands at her impatient look. "Ok, ok. We went through OTC together."

She inhaled sharply and said in a harsh whisper, "Delta Force?"

"Mmm. Pretty much everything after that really is classified."

"But the Delta Force, Bobby? That's so dangerous."

His expression hardened. "I enlisted for the danger, Indi."

No, he'd enlisted to escape what had happened between them and the Army had taken him in like the lost soul he'd been. A wave of guilt flooded through her, dimming her pleasure of the day. He could've been killed or, worse, captured and tortured, all because she'd been too cowardly to handle his heart properly. "I can't believe your mother allowed that."

"I was sixteen. Didn't give her a say in the matter."

"You weren't sixteen when you were selected for OTC."

"No, I was a little older." His grin returned, though his eyes held a dangerous glint. "And thanks to your training, Maetyrm, I had an interesting enough skill set to attract the right kind of attention."

"So you slew them with your mad grammar skills, huh."

"That wasn't the only thing you taught, and you weren't the only teacher I had."

Her appetite fled abruptly and she pushed her basket away. Every Daughter and Son went through rigorous training from an early age. Martial arts, gymnastics, outdoor survival, weapons training, and a host of academic skills that placed them well above their mortal human peers in myriad ways. Many wound up in the armed forces or worked as mercenaries precisely because of the intensive training they'd received as children. "How did you make it into the Army at such a young age?"

"How do you think?" he retorted. "Every teenager in Tellowee knows who to go to if they need an ID."

She'd used such services herself over the years, each time she needed to alter her identification to reflect her apparent age, which hadn't changed in nearly a century and a half. "So you paid someone to fake a birth certificate and school records," she guessed.

"Something like that." He nudged her basket again, inching it closer to her. "You need to eat. We've got a long day ahead of us."

"I'm not hungry."

"Eat anyway."

"Bobby." She rubbed her suddenly damp palms over her thighs. Everything he'd been through since the moment she'd fled from him had been her fault. Every day under the Army's thumb, every day in a backwater hell, surrounded by people who would as soon kill him as spit on him. All of that because of her. "I'm sorry."

"Why?"

"You know why." She took a deep breath, tried to exhale the guilt and worry tangled up with her nerves. "You joined the Army because of me, because I pushed you away."

"I joined the Army because I wanted to be there." He speared her with a flinty gaze. "Don't ever try to own that again. Being there was my choice. If I hadn't liked it, I wouldn't have kept re-upping."

She sat back in her chair, nonplussed.

"Seriously. You're not to blame for what I did." He switched chairs, taking the one beside her. "Here, guess I'm gonna have to feed you, since you won't feed yourself."

"You'll do no such thing," she said, though she smiled and ate her lunch, as he'd no doubt intended her to.

Their conversation drifted to other things, to Indigo's relief. How Hiro, Drew, and Bobby had schemed and plotted and finally opened their business together two years before, after they'd gotten out of the Army. About her travels during the last decade, mostly from one archaeological dig to another, with a short stint as a teacher at another of the People's centers in Europe. And about trivialities. Books read recently, the best grocery stores outside of Tellowee, who was dating whom in the insular community.

Gradually, the awkwardness faded between them. Sometimes, she thought

Bobby might be holding back, especially when he talked about Hiro and Drew. He was very open about what he did share, though, and she tried to be as well. They were working toward some sort of friendship, after all. If he touched her hair as they talked or held her hand when they wandered through crowds, she put it down to his solicitous nature. He was a toucher. She'd seen him do the exact same things with his sisters, during that *before time* she refused to dwell on. If her hand tingled from the warmth of his touch and sparked off a chain reaction of dizzy heat that rocketed through every cell in her body, well, that was her problem. She could deal with it.

After lunch, he drove her to a huge furniture store in Buford. Once inside, she paused in awe of the sheer size of the selection.

"Bobby, really." She looked around at row after row of furniture grouped into functional settings for every room in the house. "I only need a serviceable sofa and a bed. We'll never sort through all of this in one day."

"Sure we will." He placed a hand on the small of her back. "C'mon."

Indigo allowed him to guide her through a series of artfully arranged living areas. He stopped at a grouping consisting of a large couch, a loveseat, and a recliner, along with a coffee table, matching end tables, and more accessories than she would ever need.

She bit her lip and searched for a polite way to tell him no. "I don't need this much."

"You don't have to take the whole thing." He grinned, took her hand, and led her toward the couch. "Let's try it out."

He sat in the middle of the couch, pulled her down beside him, and draped a friendly arm around her shoulders. A tang of his soap tickled her nose, sharp and masculine, like Bobby. She shivered when his hand grazed her upper arm through the thin sleeve of her blouse.

The couch was soft and cushy, easy to snuggle into. Maybe a little too easy, especially with an attractive man sitting next to you with his arm draped over your shoulders. "This is comfortable."

"Sturdy, too." He patted the cushion with his free hand. "Easy to clean. This model has a fold-out bed."

"A useful addition." She turned to look at him and her breath caught in her throat. His mouth was inches from her own, sensual and tempting. "You've done this before, I take it."

"Mmm." He rubbed a finger over her lower lip, slowly, carefully, as if he were memorizing the shape and texture. "The extra bed comes in handy when you've got a large family."

"I suppose it does," she murmured. His gaze dropped to her mouth and his arm tightened around her shoulders, drawing her closer, and she put a hand on his chest, to stop him or encourage him, she didn't know.

He blinked and drew back a moment before she heard footsteps approaching. Indigo stood, as much to pull herself together as anything, and managed a smile for the salesman walking toward them. The not-quite-kiss she shoved out of her mind. She couldn't do a thing about the heat that lingered from Bobby's touch.

In the end, she chose to take the sofa and a recliner in a deep chocolate brown, not because they were sturdy and easy to care for, but because Bobby looked so comfortable there. Since he looked comfortable, she reasoned others would as well.

Buying the sofa had absolutely nothing to do with her sudden need to encourage him to drop by her home. Nothing at all.

Bobby talked her out of looking for bedroom furniture at that store, saying only that he had something else in mind. She let it go and set her attention to haggling the price down on both pieces, then arranged for them to be delivered to her apartment. When they left the store, Indigo said, "Just out of curiosity, why aren't we taking the sofa back with us?"

"Because we need the room for your bedroom furniture."

He helped her into his truck before walking around and getting in himself. Once they were underway, she shifted in the seat, studying his profile. He drove with his eyes fixed on the road and his left hand at the top of the steering wheel. His right hand rested on the bench seat between them, edging closer to her in tiny increments.

"What was wrong with the furniture at that store?"

"It's not what you're looking for." He merged onto the highway and accelerated to match the flow of traffic. "I saw the way you eyed the coffee table in there."

Her lips curled into an unladylike sneer. "It looked fake."

"It's cheaper wood with a veneer. Still wood, but not the kind you're used to."

"Oh? What kind of wood am I used to, then?"

He glanced at her long enough for his mischievous grin to reignite the desire he'd stirred in her earlier, a heat her body hadn't quite forgotten. "The real kind. Trust me. You'll love what I have in mind."

"How do you know?"

"You liked the sofa, didn't you?"

She settled back into her seat. Following his lead wasn't so hard, but trusting him to pick out furniture for her? What woman in her right mind would allow a man to have a free hand there?

They ended up at a climate controlled storage unit not far from Tellowee. Bobby helped her out of the truck before he unlocked one of the units and rolled the door up. His unit was packed from wall to wall with items draped in protective sheets and cardboard boxes of all shapes and sizes.

She followed him into the cool interior, peering with him under each sheet he lifted. "What is this?"

"Furniture. Mostly wood." He moved a box and pulled the sheet off of a low rectangular object, revealing a Mission-style coffee table. "Some other stuff I'm saving for..." He shrugged casually as his voice trailed off.

"What?"

"Stuff. This table would look great with your new couch."

He appeared so uncomfortable, she let the moment pass and turned her attention to the coffee table. "Is that wormy chestnut?"

"Yup, with a hand-rubbed oil finish. You'll need coasters and can't put anything warm down on it, but it should suit you."

She knelt to run a hand over the smooth finish, down a perfectly aligned joint. It must have taken hours for someone to craft this one piece alone. "I can't take this."

"Sure you can."

He stepped deeper into the unit, lifting sheets as he went.

"It wouldn't be right." She stood reluctantly. "You're obviously saving it for a very special purpose."

"Yes," he agreed mildly. "Here's the bed for you."

He flipped back one of the sheets, revealing an intricately carved headboard. Indigo stepped closer, her body brushing against his in the tight space as she did, and ran a hand over the design.

"It's beautiful." Questions popped into her mind one after another, so many she had a hard time choosing between them. Finally, she settled on, "Where did you get it?"

"I made it. Most of the design elements are from the Book of Kells." He stroked a hand down her hair, then rested it on the small of her back. "The wood's walnut, from a tree that used to stand near the house. Do you remember?"

"The one lightening struck not long after you were born," she murmured, and found herself leaning into his warm comfort.

"Dad did a lot of woodworking back then, before he knew about the MS. He salvaged what he could, had it sawed for furniture." He moved to stand behind her, dropped his hands to her hips, and drew her back until their bodies were pressed firmly together. "I found it when I got out of the Army."

When he spoke, his breath puffed gently against her ear, sending a shiver along her skin. She eased forward fractionally, away from the delicious press of his body against hers, away from the heat and temptation. His fingers dug into her hips, holding her in place.

Distraction. She need to distract him, or maybe herself, before one of them gave in and did something they might both regret or, worse, enjoy. "It must've taken hours to make this."

"Mmm." His hands eased around to her stomach as he nuzzled his face into the juncture of her neck and shoulder. "You smell like wildflowers in the spring."

"Focus, Bobby," she said, and winced when her voice hitched.

"I am." He licked her neck above the collar of her shirt, and she shuddered at the feel of his tongue on her skin. "I'm trying to talk you into taking the headboard."

She breathed out a laugh. "Is that what you're doing?"

"Say you'll take it."

He pressed a kiss to her neck, just above where he'd licked, and blew gently along the moisture left behind. Heat raced through her, pooling between her legs in a rush of warmth and wetness. She melted into him and tilted her head to the side, silently begging him to continue. Goddess above, what he did to her.

He nipped at her earlobe with sharp teeth, eliciting a needy gasp from her. "Say it slowly, though, will you? I kinda like the persuasion part."

She rested her hands on his, to keep them in place, to learn the feel of him, which one, she didn't know or care. "Tell me why you're lending it to me."

His sigh feathered along her skin as he drew away, stealing the warmth of his touch from her. "You don't want to know."

"Yes, I do." She twisted and caught his heated gaze with her own. "What's so bad that you can't tell me?"

"It's not that big a deal." The warmth drained from his expression, leaving his beautiful hazel eyes cautious and cool. He dropped a perfunctory kiss to her cheek and stepped away from her. "This is the stuff I made for my own house. Since I'm living with Mom and Dad and it's just sitting here, I thought you might like to use it."

She held no illusions that he was being completely honest with her. Whatever he was holding back was his secret to keep. She should absolutely respect his privacy, and she would, right after she found a way to weasel it out of him. "I'll take it, but only if you promise to tell me when you need it back."

"I won't, not for a while." He pulled the sheet free and handed it to her before hefting the headboard.

"I can help."

"Not without ruining your outfit, which I like." He stopped and raked a gaze over her body from head to toe, intensifying the memory of him behind her, warm and firm and strong. "A lot."

Her limbs went limp and weak at that expression, edgy, needy, and so very, very appreciative. "Oh. Um."

Her eyes fluttered closed. Could she be any more of a lovesick girl around him? *Friends*, she recited desperately. *We're going to be friends.*

She clung to that mantra as they loaded and unloaded furniture. By the time they made it to a mattress store, she had herself well in hand, right up to the moment when Bobby helped her pick out a mattress by sprawling out on a few of the displays. An image of him naked in the bed he'd made flashed through her mind, and her muscles clenched with a desperate, fierce need to have him there. *Friends* might not be exactly where they were headed. All the ignoring in the world couldn't make that thought go away.

FOUR

B Y THE END OF THE WEEK, Bobby managed to squeeze in time to speak with Zena and Laura about their upcoming assignments. Zena's sneer at the extra work had been expected. It was her normal way of dealing with change.

Laura, though, had been downright frigid to him since he'd spoken to her about Indigo, which seemed out of proportion to what he'd told her. *Don't hassle her. She's family.* Somehow, it had been enough to send Laura into a tizzy.

He took a sip of coffee and grimaced at the harsh, bitter taste. She'd stopped making the coffee, too, leaving it to early-riser Drew, who burned water trying to boil it.

A knock sounded on the door. *Speak of the devil,* Bobby thought, and waved Drew and Hiro into his office.

He'd deliberately left briefing his closest friends until last so he could ponder how best to approach them. They'd shared so much over the years, but he'd always managed to hold the story of the People back. He'd never known how to tell them he was descended from a group of immortal Amazons living under a curse, and he still wasn't sure he wanted them to know now. Telling them would help them understand the real threat the People faced. Leaving them in the dark might make them unnecessarily vulnerable.

They'd probably think he was nuts. No, not probably. Definitely. Who wouldn't?

Hiro and Drew sat down in the two chairs placed opposite his desk, and he was struck once again by how different they really were. Each had joined the Army for the same reason he had, to escape. Drew often spoke of his childhood in Boston as a dead-end choice between running drugs or working in the factories. Either one meant a hard life and an early grave. Hiro's choices had been less harsh. His parents had wanted him to go to college, become a corporate schmuck, and marry a "good Japanese girl," who they'd already picked out for him. He'd said no by enlisting the day after his eighteenth birthday.

Bobby had been running from the woman who'd unwittingly captured his heart.

And now here they were, operating a security business catering to corporate schmucks, all still single, and none of them headed for an early grave, an outright miracle given some of the assignments they'd pulled. All in all, it wasn't a bad life, especially now that they were out from under Uncle Sam's thumb.

Hiro crossed an ankle over a knee and rested his elbows on the arms of his chair. "I know we have other business to discuss, but I wanted to get this out of the way. India visited me a couple of nights ago."

Drew straightened in his chair and muttered a curse. "Me, too. Snuck into my house in the dead of night like she owned the place."

Bobby rubbed a hand over tired eyes. He'd have to disclose the whole bit, immortality, curse, and all. "What did she do?"

"Why aren't you surprised?" Drew said. "Goddamn woman broke into my house and you take it like it's nothing."

"Oh, it's not nothing, but it could've been a lot worse." Bobby sipped his coffee and grimaced. "Stop making coffee. I'd rather do without."

Drew's eyebrows snapped into a mulish scowl.

Hiro's expression was calm, his voice even. "What do you mean, worse?"

"First, tell me what she did," Bobby said.

"Other than break into my goddamn house? Tried to bribe me to turn on you, that's what, and then threatened to kick my ass when I said no." Drew crossed thick, muscled arms over his chest. "And if you don't like my coffee, maybe you shoulda been nicer to Laura."

"I haven't done anything to Laura," Bobby said.

"India," Hiro said with some emphasis, "tried to bribe me as well. Do you think she's approached anyone else?"

"If you didn't do anything, then why is she sulking?" Drew said with a pointed glare.

"All I said was, leave Indigo alone. That's it. And I was nice." Bobby heaved a sigh. "India would know better than to approach Margaret, but the others, yeah, she probably has."

"Why not Margaret?" Hiro asked.

"If you were so nice, then why's Laura in a huff?" Drew asked.

Bobby ignored him. "Margaret would've torn her to pieces on sight."

Hiro nodded. "Margaret the Frigidaire..."

Bobby winced. "Don't let her catch you calling her that."

"I'm not stupid," Hiro said.

Drew snorted. "Says who?"

"Margaret might be cold, but she's stronger, faster, and a better fighter than India." Bobby sat back, gauged his timing, and said, "Plus, she's a few centuries older."

"Back to Laura," Drew began, then snapped his jaws together with an audible click. "What was that?"

"I believe he said Margaret's a few centuries older than India." Hiro's voice held a hint of dry amusement. "Exactly how old is Margaret?"

"She'd kill me if I told you." Bobby rubbed a finger across his mouth, hiding the smile threatening to rise. "Just keep pretending she's twenty-nine-ish and your head is safe."

"And how is it that Margaret's managed to live that long?" Drew said. "Takes more than a wish for that to happen."

"She's immortal, or close enough."

"And you are, too, then." Drew's expression lightened as he leaned toward Hiro. "I knew we shoulda had his head checked after that last mission. All the fungi. Went straight to his brains."

"It's a wonder he has any left," Hiro agreed.

"Seriously, guys." Bobby rolled his eyes skyward. "Did you never wonder why we rotate women out of here so frequently?"

"Because we like to keep 'em hot?" Drew said, and yelped when Hiro casually backhanded him on the arm.

"Because people tend to notice when someone doesn't age," Bobby said. "Because these women are busy chasing an ancient blood enemy and protecting their kin."

Drew sat forward in the chair. "You're serious about all this?"

"As serious as death." Bobby took a sip of his coffee without thinking. "Dammit, Drew, stay away from the coffee machine."

"I told you..."

"I think you'd better start at the beginning," Hiro said.

"Right." Bobby pushed his coffee mug away to keep from picking it up out of habit. "About ten millennia ago, Seven Sisters avenged the deaths of their parents and were cursed to immortality by an angry god, and at the same time, were cursed to never bear sons, only daughters."

He took them through a brief history of the People as they knew it, and explained how the Lady Goddess had tempered the curse, providing an out for each immortal Daughter, and how the People had searched relentlessly for a way to break the curse for good, so that no Daughter would be born with the same, crushing burden. He told them of the Shadow Enemy and their thirst for the blood of the People, and the many battles waged over time as the Daughters struggled to find peace. Finally, he filled them in on the recent finds at Sandby borg, of the discovery of the Prophecy of Light and its translation by a team at the IECS, and the hope they all had that the Light would choose the path that would end the curse, if only they could figure out what the Light was.

When he finished, the room fell into a long silence. Hiro stroked his mouth thoughtfully and Drew tapped a nervous beat on his thigh.

When they remained silent, Bobby said, "C'mon guys. Would I lie to you?"

"You bet your ass," Drew said. At the same time, Hiro said, "Absolutely."

Bobby sucked in a breath, straining for patience. "I mean about something important."

"Hunh." Drew stabbed two fingers at Bobby. "There was that time in Reno, with that hooker you tried to pass off as your sister."

"Because she *was* my sister, you moron." Bobby jerked a thumb at the wall behind him. "There's the picture of us together when I was a kid."

"Uh-huh," Drew said, skepticism heavy in his voice. "I guess those drug lords in Afghanistan were your sisters, too."

"No, those were really drug lords," Bobby said. "And that was a little lie for the greater cause, so it doesn't count."

"What about Madrid, when he snuck two hoochie girls into the CO's hotel room and blamed you," Hiro said to Drew. "Islamabad."

Hiro and Drew shared grins and said in unison, "The camel derby."

Bobby dropped his head into his hands. When had he lost control of the conversation?

"Do you remember the name of that jockey?" Hiro said.

"Who cares about him. It was the sister I wanted." Drew sighed out a smile. "Good times."

"I didn't actually lie about the camel or the jockey," Bobby pointed out. "Or the jockey's sister, who, by the way, was a man and not related to the jockey *at all.*"

"Are you sure?" Drew said. "Because I had my hands..."

Bobby interrupted. Some things, a man didn't need to know about his friends. "Positive, and it's still not a lie."

Hiro spread his hands in a mild shrug. "You didn't tell us about it beforehand, so close enough."

"Ok, all right. I fudged a couple of times." Bobby sat back in his chair and rubbed a hand across his hair, ruffling it. "But I never lied about anything important and you know it."

"True," Hiro said.

Drew shrugged one shoulder. "I always wondered why that hooker looked just like your sister did twenty years ago."

Bobby shot him an exasperated look and ground his teeth together. "Jerusha's not a hooker, and if you call her that one more time, I'm gonna..."

"Boys," Hiro said, and waited until Drew and Bobby exchanged pointed glares before continuing. "Let's say this story is true. Why didn't you tell us before?"

Bobby barked out a laugh. "Do you think you would've believed me before?"

"If you'd needed us to." Hiro's gaze was steady. "Are you immortal?"

"No. Children born to Daughters who've broken the curse are always mortal."

"Are you sure you didn't sniff a fungus or something?" Drew said.

Bobby fixed a withering glare on him.

"Who exactly is your mother sending us after?" Hiro folded his hands across his waist, his dark eyes patient, steady. "Members of the Shadow Enemy?"

Bobby shook his head. "When I said traitors, I really meant traitors. Mom thinks some of the Daughters have, for whatever reason, been manipulating information somehow, either hiding it from the People or giving false data to us. The problem is, these Daughters may be working alone or they may be working together, or some combination, but they aren't necessarily working with the Shadow Enemy."

"What about India? What's her role in all this?" Drew steepled his fingers together under his chin. "And how do you know Indigo's not in on it with her?"

"For one, Indigo and India have never gotten along," Bobby said through gritted teeth. "And for another, we know for a fact that India runs with a bad crowd. I can't share the details, but Dani wasn't in the hospital a couple of weeks ago with appendicitis."

"India did something to her?" Drew's eyebrows veed over the storm clouds brewing in his eyes, and Bobby winced. Drew had a bit of a crush on Dani. Bobby dreaded having to tell his partner about his adoptive sister's new love interest.

"No, not India, but she was part of it." Bobby sucked in a breath and blew it out slowly. "Look, guys, I'm only telling you this much because India came after you.

She's dangerous. So are these other women. Some of them make Margaret look like a school girl out for a walk in the park."

"We can handle ourselves," Hiro said mildly.

"Maybe. Either way, you need to be on alert. The People we're going after are highly-skilled warriors, all of them, and they won't hesitate to kill you and everyone around you if they think you're a threat."

"Eh, why are we doing this job again?" Drew said. "Wouldn't it be better if your people handled it from their side?"

"Mom specifically asked for the Enforcer," Bobby said flatly.

"Well, damn." Drew tugged at his ear. "Hell's come to Georgia and we're all gonna die."

Hiro sliced an impatient glare at Drew. "Bobby wouldn't take any job with a high risk of failure."

"True. I like my hide where it is." Bobby sat back in his chair, amused. "That's why we're going high-tech. As skilled as these women are, most of them cling to the old ways."

"A good sword arm," Hiro guessed.

"And spear and bow, but you get the idea." Bobby shrugged. "Plus, they don't know your faces."

"If the secret weapon is Drew's mug, we're in deep shit."

Drew shoved Hiro, sending the other man's chair bobbling.

Hiro shot Drew a dirty look and righted his chair. "Are you sure Indigo can be trusted?"

"As sure as I can be," Bobby said.

"Is that your dick talking or your brain?" Drew said bluntly. "'Cause she's a smokin' hot piece of meat, bro, but she ain't worth my life."

Hiro rolled his eyes skyward.

Bobby stood and leaned across the desk, pinning Drew with a deadly stare. "Watch what you say about Indigo."

"If that's how you told Laura to leave her alone, it's no wonder she won't make coffee," Drew shot back.

"Laura didn't call her a tramp."

Drew stood up abruptly enough to knock his chair back. "I didn't call her no tramp."

Hiro rose and moved to stand between them. "Indigo's off limits, Drew. She's *the one*."

Drew's brows drew together with a confused frown. "The who?"

Hiro raised his eyebrows. "*The one*."

"Oh." Drew's expression cleared. "Ooooh. The lady in the cups."

Bobby glanced back and forth between them. "What?"

"The woman you talk about when you get drunk," Hiro said drily.

Bobby drew back and said flatly, "I never get that drunk."

"Oh, yes you do," Drew said with a laugh. "You used to damn near wax poetic about that woman, with her big blue eyes and her long black hair and her sweet voice. Damn me, why didn't I put it together first?"

"Because you don't pay attention," Hiro said.

Bobby dropped into his chair, appalled. "I can't believe I got drunk enough to talk about her."

Drew slouched down into his chair. "It's no biggie, man."

"You know our secrets, too," Hiro said in a reasonable tone that grated the nerves down Bobby's spine.

"Not like that one." Bobby rubbed his forehead and tried to tamp down on the embarrassment. "Any more questions about this job?"

They let the evasion pass and discussed strategies and tactics for another hour before breaking up. After they left, Bobby spent the rest of the afternoon making phone calls and catching up on paperwork, clearing his schedule. He wanted to have the weekend free for Indigo. They had no set plans, but he hoped to rope her into spending time with him, just because. They were settling into an almost easy friendship, comfortable in spite of the lightning sparking between them at the slightest touch.

He bit back a hard laugh.

Friendship, hell. What he felt for her went way beyond that. Memory teased him until he trembled with it, trembled for her. The way she'd felt in his arms a few days before, small but strong, warm and soft. The way she'd melted against him and tilted her head, exposing the graceful column of her throat to his mouth as she breathed out helpless little gasps. He'd ached and burned with the need to take her, to ease his hands into the waistband of her tights, roll them down, and bend her over the nearest piece of furniture so he could bury himself in her warm heat and forget.

Goddess knew, he had a lot to forget.

He shifted in his chair, adjusted the hard length trying to ram itself through the fly of his slacks. Damn him, he wasn't good enough for her, never would be again. Knowing that didn't kill the fierce urge possessing him, pushing him to claim her anyway.

INDIGO HUMMED as she walked up the stairs to her apartment, juggling grocery bags and keys. It had been a good week, thanks to Bobby. Furniture shopped for and arranged, a budding friendship growing between them. Maybe he would come over so she could repay his help with a hot meal.

And perhaps talk him into helping her pick out a TV.

He was handy that way.

Her breath caught in her throat when a figure stepped into the hallway in front of her. She tensed for a fight until recognition hit.

"Sister." India bowed slightly, traditionally a gesture of respect. On India, the move held enough contempt for three people.

She'd cut her hair in the past few months, chopped it off short and gelled it until the inky locks stood in disordered, finger-combed spikes along her head. The look suited her, especially when combined with the skin-tight leathers India preferred. Indigo touched her own long ponytail, smoothed down the oversized sweater she wore. Why did she always go for comfort over chic and sexy?

"India." Indigo dropped the groceries at the threshold of her door and stuck the key in the lock, leaving the keychain dangling. "What are you doing here?"

"Isn't it obvious?" India's voice took on a playful lilt. "I've come a-calling."

Indigo sighed, suddenly weary. "What do you want?"

"What, no pleasantries for your dear sister?" India tsked almost playfully. "That's no way to treat a guest."

"Just spit it out."

India's face hardened. "If that's the way you want to play it."

"It isn't a game, India. You know as well as I do that the Blade is out for your blood."

"I'm not afraid of Rebecca Upton."

"Then perhaps you should be afraid of her son, the Enforcer," Indigo snapped. "She's set the hounds on you, sister dear."

India tapped a hand against one leather clad thigh and regarded Indigo thoughtfully. "Is that concern for me or him?"

"Both. We may not always see eye to eye, but you're still my sister. If you harm another one of the Blade's children, you're dead."

"I had no hand in Dani's injuries, nor do I intend to harm the Son of the Blade." India pursed her lips. "Unless he gets in my way."

"He'll come after you. You know how persistent he is."

"Not first hand, no." India's mouth curled with mocking humor. "But you know well enough for the both of us, don't you?"

"Please, India. Whatever it is you're doing, please just stop it."

"I can't. Don't you see?" India stepped closer and held out a hand in what Indigo thought might be a genuine plea for understanding. "The Prophecy must be stopped. That's all I'm trying to do."

"That's what this is about?" Indigo breathed out a laugh. "You're trying to stop the Prophecy? By the Goddess, India, how do you ever intend to do that?"

"By snuffing out the Light." India's smile turned cruel in the pale beauty of her face. "Stop the Light, end the Prophecy, and we all live eternally."

"That's insane. No one knows what the Light is or even where to find it."

"Oh, there are people who know."

"People like Lilith Cæstus, who murdered her way across five continents." Indigo swallowed against the bitterness of contempt and fear coating her tongue. "Is that what you've fallen to, India? Murder and madness?"

"Lilith was never afraid to seize what she wanted."

"Nor was she afraid to kill anyone who stood in her way. Don't do that, India. You're better than her."

India's laugh was hollow and harsh. "You're right about one thing. I *am* better than Lilith. At least I'm not stupid enough to fall to the blade of a weakling mortal."

"Dani is no weakling, mortal or not." Indigo drew her patience around her like a mantel. "It's not too late to change your course. Bobby's asked me to help bring you in."

"Yes, I know." India's voice sounded oddly gentle. "I came to ask you not to."

"Why?" Indigo said, baffled. "I would never allow him to hurt you. You know that."

"You were always so tender-hearted," India murmured. "Even when I hurt you, you would never raise a hand to me."

A ding of metal dropping sounded from the stairwell. Indigo swiveled to check the stairs, then immediately turned back, her gaze firm on India. "You're my sister."

"Such a simple thing, the trust that implies."

India edged closer and held her arms out, waiting patiently, maybe for the trust that had never really developed between them. Indigo couldn't let it go, couldn't bypass a chance to make amends with her twin, the woman who should've been her other half. She twined her arms around India and sniffed back the tears sparking in her eyes. They'd never been close. At their age, wasn't it time for them to be?

Booted footsteps thudded on the stairs. Indigo tensed and tried to draw back, and was restrained by the hard band of her sister's embrace.

"I'll always love you, my sister. Truly, I will," India whispered. "But I can't allow you or the Son to stand in my way."

India shifted her grip and yanked Indigo around until she was secured across the shoulders, her back to India's chest. Indigo struggled briefly against the confinement, and lost her breath when Bobby appeared at the top of the stairs.

Fear stabbed at her, not for herself, but for him, for what India might do to him. "Bobby, no!"

Bobby's gaze zeroed in on India as he fell into a defensive stance, his lean form beautiful and deadly.

"My, my, my, if it isn't the Enforcer." India stepped back, dragging Indigo with her. "We were just talking about you."

"Let her go, India," he said, his voice low, his expression like granite. "She's the innocent here."

"There are no innocents among the People. Remember that, Bobby Upton."

India released Indigo and shoved her toward Bobby, then took off at a dead run down the hallway toward the staircase at the other end.

Indigo caught Bobby as he made to follow her sister, and threw all her strength into holding him back. "No, Bobby, please. She's my sister."

Bobby halted in mid-stride and pinned her with an incredulous stare. "She betrayed the People and tried to hurt you."

"She was only trying to distract you."

"You're too kind, Indigo." Bobby glanced down the hallway and sighed. "I can't believe you let her go like that, knowing what she's doing."

She eased her hold on him one stiff finger at a time. "She's my sister."

Bobby cupped her shoulders with warm, work-roughened hands and rubbed gently. "That doesn't excuse anything. You know what she's capable of, honey. You have to let me shut her down."

"I know." She sighed and looked up into his lean face, that hard, compelling face that filled her heart and dreams, and her thoughts whirled into chaos. First India and now Bobby. What was it about the two of them that sent her into turmoil every single time they were near? "I can't think about it now."

Bobby squeezed her hard. "You have to. She's dangerous."

"I know, I know." She brushed a hand over her forehead, willing her scattered brain cells into some form of coherence. "Look, come inside and we'll talk. I was going to make you supper anyway."

"Now who's trying to distract me?"

"Is it working?"

"For now, but only for now." He dropped a kiss on her forehead and let her go. "Sooner or later, you have to face this, Indi. You can't run from it forever."

Indigo sucked in a breath as his words struck home. She'd come back to Tellowee not to face her past, but to at least stop running from it. Maybe it was better that he never knew how hard she would run from something she couldn't face.

Then again, that was a lesson he'd already learned.

FIVE

INDIGO WOKE EARLY Saturday morning with a pounding heart and dread lodged heavily in her gut. She sat up in bed and searched through the groggy fog in her head for some meaning, some rhyme or reason behind the disquiet. When it failed to appear, she threw back the covers with a huff and took a long hot shower to clear her head.

Half an hour later, the fog hadn't lifted, but at least she was clean. She made her bed and took a moment to admire its fine craftsmanship. Bobby had done a good job with it and the matching chest of drawers he'd brought her the evening before. Pride swelled through her as she ran a hand along the smooth, dark finish of the headboard, bringing with it amusement.

Where Bobby was concerned, she hadn't the right to any pride. That she felt it at all showed how completely contrary she was.

A cup of tea, she decided, something to distract herself from the ever present thoughts of Bobby. No better way to start the day.

While it steeped, she threw open the curtains and reveled in the bright day blooming outside her window. A light frost coated the railing of her empty balcony. She assessed the space with a critical eye. It would be lovely filled with a display of pumpkins and corn stalks. A trip to the local produce stand should do the trick.

A firm knock sounded on her door, startling her into a gasp. She placed a hand to her racing heart and laughed at her own jumpiness. "Come in," she called.

Bobby opened the door and stepped inside, a scowl on his face. "Did you leave your door unlocked last night?"

"Of course not."

"Don't leave it unlocked while you're here." He fixed her with a disapproving glare. "And never allow anyone in without checking who it is first."

She huffed out an exasperated breath. "I'm perfectly capable of taking care of myself."

"Uh-huh. You took care of yourself real well with India yesterday."

She turned on her heel, heading toward the kitchen to check her tea. Why had she bothered to let him in? If all he could do was criticize, maybe she wouldn't anymore, no matter how attractive she found him. "I know how to break holds."

He caught up with her and snagged her in a firm grip, locking her arms in place with hard, muscled arms wrapped firmly around her torso. "Prove it."

She rolled her eyes and relaxed into him. A pleasant warmth stole through her when his body lined up with hers, her back to his broad chest and her bottom snug against his manhood. She clamped down on the sudden urge she had to wiggle and squirm, needling him into reaction, just to see what he would feel like all hard and needy behind her. "Is this necessary?"

"Absolutely."

His breath brushed against the side of her face, tickling her.

"I don't want to hurt you," she murmured.

His low laugh vibrated through her where his chest touched her back. "Sweetheart, you're not gonna hurt me."

Anger flashed through her at the smug condescension layered through his voice. So he thought she, a Daughter with decades of training and experience, couldn't take him, a piddling mortal? Weak little Indigo with her soft skin and gracious nature couldn't defeat a Son?

She lifted her legs off the floor, throwing him off balance, then slithered out of his arms when he lost his grip, evading his grabs with deflecting blows. She came around in a crouch and launched herself at him, catching him around the middle, tackling him. Their bodies hit the floor with a solid thud. They rolled, each grappling for dominance, sliding across the slick hardwood floor until they hit the side of the couch, Bobby on top. He grabbed her hands and yanked them above her head, pinning her to the hard surface. She bucked against him, a burning fury fueling her struggle, and scissored her legs, searching for an opening. If she could gain traction, she could flip him, and then she'd show him who was weak.

He dropped his full weight onto her, pushing the breath out of her lungs. Her eyes widened. His breath hit her temples in harsh puffs as his hard length pressed against her core, intimate and sweet and so very, very welcome. For a moment, she lay still beneath him, savoring his touch, savoring him, pressed against her like a lover.

No, *Goddess*, what was she thinking? He couldn't be there, couldn't love her the way he wanted to, the way she secretly yearned to have him. It would spoil everything, their budding friendship, the tender kisses and glancing touches, the warmth and need and desire, all gone because of her lack of control. *Not again, please not another decade without him.*

In a panic, she redoubled her efforts, shoving at him, and gasped out, "Get off."

"When you calm down."

He dropped a heavy thigh over hers, countering her attempt to flip him. Her leg slipped up the inside of his thigh, grazing his groin, and she stilled at his muttered curse. The anger drained out of her abruptly and their eyes met, his narrowed, hers amused.

"Oops."

"You nearly take my manhood and all you can say is oops?" His mouth twisted into a wry smile. "Have a heart, Indi, or at least think of my children."

"You don't have any children."

"Exactly why you should think of them." He levered himself off of her, grabbed the hands she held up to him, and pulled her into a stand. "Another slip like that and I won't have a love life either."

She walked into the kitchen to check her tea. "We wouldn't want that, now, would we."

Bobby followed her and visibly stifled a laugh at the disgruntled glare she aimed at him. "Tea cold?"

"Thanks to you." She dumped it into the sink and rinsed out her cup. "You owe me breakfast now, and an apology."

"Breakfast I'll give you, but why the apology?"

"Because you didn't believe me when I said I could take care of myself."

"No, I believed you, but I'm no fool." He grinned and rubbed the side of his jaw where a red spot roughly the size of her fist lingered. "It was as good an excuse as any to hold you."

She shook her head, torn between disgust and laughter, and held herself erect when he stepped forward and cupped her shoulders, rubbing them gently through her sweater.

"Have you been working out?" he said.

The concern in his voice touched her. "There's a gym here."

"Yeah, but are you using it?"

He cupped the back of her neck with one hand and trailed the other down her arm, entwining his fingers through hers. She stifled a shudder at the warm shock of desire coursing through her from such a simple touch, wiping her mind clean of their conversation. What had he asked her? Right, the gym. "Um. Not yet. No time."

"Monday morning, then, we'll start working out together. No buts," he said when she made a half-hearted protest. "We have a great training center at the office, one floor up. You'll love it."

"Oh, well." His fingers tangled in her hair, pulling gently, and her breath caught in her throat. "I suppose."

His satisfied look should've made her angry, but when he dropped a kiss to her nose, she closed her eyes and bit her lip to keep from begging him to *just kiss me already*, and forgot all about the way he'd manipulated her into agreeing with him.

They drove his truck to eat breakfast at a diner in Rabbit Town. By the time they arrived, Indigo was so hungry, she ate twice as much as she normally would, and groaned when Bobby tried to get her to eat more.

"We've got a long day ahead of us," he said as he pushed his toast toward her.

She placed her hand on top of his to stop him. "I'm stuffed, really," she said, and he let it go with a skeptical look.

He helped her pick out a TV and lamps, and when she tried to buy bookcases to hold the collection of books she hadn't yet pulled out of storage, he told her *no* in a voice that brooked no argument.

"Should've brought some from the storage unit," he said gruffly.

"You have book cases in storage. That you made?"

"Sure. Back in the back, behind your bedroom suite."

"You can't keep giving me your furniture, Bobby."

He shrugged. "It's mine to give."

"Yes, but you're going to want it back when you get married and..." The truth shuddered through her, a wildfire of knowledge and knowing. "Bobby."

"What?" He caught the sweet sadness in her look and hunched his shoulders. "It's not like that."

"Are you sure?" she said gently. "Because that's what it looks like to me."

He glanced away, but not before she saw the loss and sorrow fill his expression. "You turned me down."

"You were sixteen, Bobby. Still a child in so many ways, and my student on top of that." She wrapped her hands around his firm triceps, holding the man he'd become. The echo of that day pounded through her, the horror and embarrassment that had chased her through fourteen years of running. They bounced through her until they diminished, leaving only regret behind. "What else was I supposed to do?"

"Nothing." His face hardened into an impassive mask, sending uneasy chills down her spine. "We should head back now."

Her heart sank. She followed him through the checkout line, then out to his truck, and waited patiently while he started it, searching for the man she'd come to know behind the shell he'd erected around himself. When they hit the highway, he flipped the radio on, filling the silence that stretched between them, taut and cold and frighteningly empty.

THE COOL NIGHT AIR chilled India Furia's skin as she climbed up the side of Hiro Okada's apartment building, boosting herself from balcony to balcony in a zigzagging line upward using ropes, grappling hooks, and the strength of her own body.

It would've been easier to climb down from the roof, if he lived in a building without roving security guards and keycard locks on all the entrances, including the one in the lobby. Those effectively sealed off access to the roof. Using the balconies, which had no such protection, seemed more prudent than trying to trick his building's security. The only risks she took were being caught by night owls peering out their windows and bypassing the locks on the balcony's French door once she reached Hiro's floor.

With any luck, he'd left it open to catch a good breeze while he slept, but she doubted it. During their one brief meeting, he hadn't struck her as being either careless or a fool.

She pulled herself silently over the railing onto his balcony and stripped off her gear, piling it in one corner of the empty landing while she caught her breath.

She'd approached Hiro as she'd approached the others working with Bobby Upton, only after much research and thought. She'd initially hoped to stall the investigation or stop it all together, but they were a loyal bunch, for the most part. Of all the people she'd approached, Bobby's two Army buddies seemed the least likely to betray him. Yet here she was, on Hiro Okada's balcony, about to try again to gain his help in some way.

His face drifted into her mind as she wound the ropes she'd used into neat coils, and with it came a sensation she had difficulty pinning down. Sharp as anger, but without its rancor, and holding something close to tenderness, which was just ridiculous. Her heart held no tender emotions. They'd all been burned out of her a long time ago.

The door behind her slid open. She turned to find Hiro standing in the open doorway, braced against the frame, bare chested and wearing loose pajama bottoms. Security lights from the parking lot below played along his body, throwing his muscled torso into relief above the low-slung bottoms. She risked a glance downward, traced the sparse hair below his navel as it disappeared beneath the waistband, and caught sight of his bare feet as her gaze went lower. They were long and narrow and graceful, much like the rest of him, and her breath caught in her throat as she imagined his long, slim body nude.

She bit back a groan. What a fool she was, to risk blowing her mission because she was attracted to a man. She turned her back on him and stooped to gather her gear so she could leave, then popped upright when he spoke.

"Bit chilly tonight," he said, with no inflection in his voice, as if they'd met on the street instead of on his balcony in the middle of the night.

"A bit." She winced at the insipid reply, grateful he couldn't see her face.

"A little late for a visit, though."

She flushed at the mild reprimand, then scowled at her reaction. "You didn't have to open the door," she snapped.

His chuckle skimmed over her skin like a touch from his elegant hands, leaving her deliciously warm in places that should've been untouched. "If I hadn't, you would've broken in, and I like my locks the way they are."

She whirled around as anger rose, drowning out the softer feelings he drew from her. "I'm not so clumsy that I would've broken them."

"That temper's going to get you in trouble one day." He stepped away from the door into the shadows filling his bedroom. "Since you're here, you might as well come in."

She waffled for a moment, then stepped inside, closed the balcony door, and listened to the sound of his footsteps as he padded across the carpeted floor in the dark. The squeak of the mattress came to her. Her eyes adjusted to the darkness, picking up the dim light as it filtered through the door's glass. She zeroed in on the bed, where Hiro sat with his back against the headboard cushioned by pillows, his legs spread out in front of him.

"If you're here to try to proposition me again, you're wasting your time." He patted the mattress beside him. "I was about to watch a Godzilla rerun. As I recall, that's what you were watching the last time you broke into my apartment."

She gave a half laugh at the reminder. "So you think you've got my number now, is that it?"

"I'm just trying to be a good host." His chest rose and fall on a deep breath. "Let's not play games tonight, India. It's late, there's a good movie on. We might as well enjoy it before you try to bring me over to the dark side."

It was tempting, more than she'd ever admit. To lie beside a man, to absorb the warmth of another body through her skin with even the most innocent of touches. It had been so long since she'd had that. The loneliness of her life, usually so easy to ignore, pinged through her with a suddenness that took her breath, leaving her uncomfortably vulnerable. Was it him she wanted or would any attractive man have pulled at her emotions?

He turned the TV on with a remote, flooding the room with the flickering light of Godzilla rampaging through Tokyo. The sounds of hordes of fleeing Japanese faded when he turned the volume down. He placed the remote on the nightstand beside the bed and crossed his arms over his chest, stifling a yawn.

He looked tired. She bit her lip as another unfamiliar emotion hit her. It took her a moment to recognize guilt, and when she did, she turned to leave, then felt all the more foolish because she hadn't hardened herself against it and pressed her advantage.

"Shoes off."

She paused with her hand on the door.

"Weapons, too."

Indecision tore at her, and she huffed out an irritated breath. She never waffled. Waffling was for children and mortals, not immortal Daughters with a high-stakes mission. So he looked tired. So what? She needed information. More, she needed an in with Upton's people. Hanging around with him might bring one or the other into her grasp.

That she would be sitting on a bed in a darkened room with a man whose feet turned her on didn't enter into the equation.

"I'm bringing my gear in so it'll stay dry."

"Condensation's hell on gear," he said.

She ignored the laughter in his voice and retrieved her equipment, stowing it in a tidy pile inside the door, out of the way but close enough to grab if she needed to leave quickly. She balanced herself against the wall next to the door to take off her boots and placed them by her equipment before shucking her weapons.

Awareness crept down her spine. She glanced up and found Hiro watching her, his face an unreadable mask. "What?"

"I can't believe you took off all your weapons."

She hid genuine amusement behind a snarky smile. "I don't need weapons to defend myself against you."

She padded across the room and crawled into his massive bed, settling against the headboard a good foot away from him.

"I've got a spare set of pajamas, if you want them."

"I'm fine," she said, and ignored the small shifts he made to close the distance between them.

He ran a finger down the outside of her thigh and her muscles jumped in response. "Those leathers can't be comfortable."

His voice held just enough reasonable patience to spark her temper. Of course, the leathers weren't comfortable. She'd worn them to protect her skin against a fall, not because she'd expected to crawl into bed with him. She opened her mouth to scald him.

"Temper," he said, interrupting her.

She snapped her jaws together and started to scoot off the bed. "This isn't going to work."

His hand shot out, closing on her forearm. "It will if you'll unbend a little. You know how to relax, don't you?"

She furrowed her brows, not wanting to admit that, no, she didn't know how to relax. It was damned near impossible for a woman in her position to do so.

"Put the pajamas on, stay a while." He loosened his grip and rubbed his hand up and down her arm, sending tingles of heat across her skin. "I won't tell a soul."

She peered at him over her shoulder, taking in the sleepy plea, the soothing tone of his voice, the hand stretched toward her on the bed. He was watching her again, his impassive gaze piercing through her as if he saw everything, the aching loneliness, the years of servitude to a cause that separated her from her kin, always apart, always alert. He saw and accepted her anyway, and because of that, she yearned for him, *him*, the man who drew her like a moth to a flame, mission be damned.

So she helped herself to his pajamas and stripped down with her back to him.

A tiny thrill of satisfaction ran through her when his breath hitched.

Mmm. She stepped into the pajama bottoms as satisfaction purred through her. *He noticed the lack of underwear.*

Indigo would've gone to the bathroom, for modesty's sake. Then again, Indigo would never have placed herself in this situation to begin with.

Being the bad sister had distinct advantages.

India tugged on the pajama top before crawling back into the bed next to Hiro. He draped an arm over her shoulders, as casually as if they'd done this a thousand times before, and she accepted his touch, snuggling into him as the rest of the world faded away.

SIX

ONDAY MORNING dawned bright and early, a perfect October day with the promise of clear blue skies, once the sun rose fully.

Bobby could not have cared less. After dropping Indigo off at her apartment Saturday evening and helping her unload her purchases, he'd gone home and spent the rest of the weekend brooding. The scene in the store played over and over again in his mind, and then, just for fun, his memory had thrown in the day he'd made a play for Indigo, the day he'd become a man in the eyes of the People and decided to take the woman he wanted.

He closed his eyes, lost in the taste of her lips, the press of her hips against his, the smooth silkiness of her skin when he'd eased a hand under her shirt. Then her startled gasp and the look of pure horror on her face when she'd shoved him away, raking his young heart over the hot coals of rejection.

What was it about women that made men feel like perfect fools?

He rubbed his hands over his face, trying to wipe away the fatigue and the memories, all of them. The sooner he faced reality where Indigo was concerned, the better off he'd be. While she accepted his touch, welcomed it, even, she didn't seem to want more than friendship.

As much as he logically knew that he should stick with *just friends*, he couldn't deny that in his heart he would always want more, no matter how wrong he was for her. Friendship was just the beginning, and he hadn't even figured that out until she'd poked him in the gut with the past.

Now, how did he convince her to go beyond friendship, or should he even try? As much as he wanted her, that very past hung between them, a stain that blossomed and oozed when he least expected it. Nothing he did could ever erase it.

A tap on the door snagged his attention. Indigo poked her head in, a hesitant smile on her face.

"Hey." He forced himself to stay seated, when his body begged him to run to her. "I didn't think you'd show."

The dimple in her cheek flashed as she slid all the way inside his office. She wore skin tight black yoga tights paired with a loose sweatshirt that hung off of one shoulder, revealing the strap of a matching top. His heart nosedived somewhere south

374

of his knees. He'd never get through a workout with her in those clothes, not without his body giving him away.

"You said you'd work out with me." She held up a workout bag and waggled it. "I hope you don't mind, but I brought clothes to change into afterward. Is there a shower?"

A vivid image shot into his mind. Indigo in the shower, water running down her back and over her firm ass. He bit back a groan and tried to rein in his imagination even as his body hardened.

"Or I could go work out in the gym at my apartment complex." She sighed deeply and sat on the edge of one of the chairs in front of his desk. "Look, Bobby, I know we parted a little awkwardly over the weekend."

"I hadn't noticed," he said drily.

She pressed her lips into a straight line and gave him a prim look. "But we're still friends, aren't we? I mean, we're working toward friendship, don't you think?"

The plea in her voice was so earnest, he hated to shoot her down. "Yeah, but it's not the only thing."

Her gaze slid from his to a point somewhere over his left shoulder. She was about to lie, sure as he was a Son. *Dammit.* When would she shoot straight with him? He stood abruptly, irritation pushing him to action, and rounded the desk. She sat back in the chair, panic written all over her face, and a spurt of satisfaction pinged through him.

She should be wary of him.

He rested on the edge of the desk and pulled her up from the chair into the cradle of his widespread legs. She smelled like spearmint and soap and warm woman, and it was all he could do to keep his hands on her hips and his mouth to himself when she landed against him. His erection pressed into the juncture at her thighs, and he shuddered when she shifted and her body rubbed against his.

"Feel what you do to me, Indigo," he murmured.

She looked away, and his irritation shot straight into anger. He tangled a hand in her hair and tugged gently until she met his gaze. "Don't lie to me, ever," he warned.

"I wasn't going to lie." Her fingers curled into the thin material of his t-shirt where her hands rested against his chest. "I was just..."

"Going to lie." He slid his free hand around, cupping her lush bottom, and inched her forward, molding her to him, their cores separated by material so thin it revealed every inch of his erection, and hid nothing of her heat from him. "Feel what you do to me."

A flush spread across her cheeks. "That's a biological reaction. Any man holding a woman this way would do the same thing."

He ignored the scold in her voice. "I've held plenty of beautiful women, Indigo."

Her eyes narrowed. "Really."

"Lots of beautiful, attractive women. Dozens, even." What he thought might be jealousy flickered through her expression. "And I've never felt this way about any of them."

"You've had sex before."

The mild accusation in her voice was hard to ignore. He tamped down the guilt. So he'd sought refuge in the arms of other women after she'd rejected his young heart.

What had she expected? That he'd pine away for her, forever a virgin? God knows he'd given her his dues, starting with that drunken night nine years before when he'd bound himself to her forever and forsaken his chance at happiness along with it.

Dammit, he wouldn't feel guilty about the past either, not one second of it.

"I'm a man." He managed a casual shrug. "And I know how it feels to want a woman. There's no one like you."

"Oh." Her brows furrowed and her gaze came to rest on his mouth.

"That's it, just *oh*?"

"Well." She pursed her lips into a little moue he ached to nibble and tease. "I suppose now would be a good time to talk about where this all might lead."

"You're kidding," he said flatly.

"Or you could just kiss me." She slid a hand to the nape of his neck and scraped her nails along his skin. "If you promise to stick with a kiss."

His hand tightened in her hair and she gasped. "I don't know if I can."

"Just try," she murmured.

He let go of her hair, slid his hand down, cradling her shoulders. Her eyes fluttered closed and her breath hitched. Sweet Goddess, she was ready for him, her lips parted and slick, her face flushed with the same need gripping him. His heart raced and fluttered as he lowered his mouth to hers, and fourteen years worth of longing and memory pounded through him.

He groaned at the first touch of her soft lips on his, tried to temper the need rising in him to grind against her, to take what she so freely offered, to claim her in a primal rush. He slanted his mouth across hers and their breath mingled, hers sweet and hot on his tongue. She arched into him with a moan and slid her fingers into his hair, and his muscles tightened with a burning desire. When it threatened to spiral out of control, he pulled back to nibble at her lips, to lick at the sweet lushness and savor it, to savor *her*.

He'd waited so long for this, too long between her first sweet kiss, taken by a boy on the verge of manhood, and this one, given freely by a woman eager to have him.

She opened for him, deepening the kiss until it raged through them both. Her tongue darted out in a teasing taste along his lips, then licked against his, and his control teetered and smashed. His fingers dug into her shoulder and the firm flesh of her bottom, and he shuddered when she curled her nails into his back through his t-shirt.

A heavy fist rapped on the door.

He jerked away from her, gasping for breath through the roar in his ears and the ache in his groin. Indigo opened her eyes and he fell into the passion shining from the sparkling depths. Her lips were red and full from the kiss, her cheeks flushed, and her breaths came in short pants. Savage need rippled through him. She wanted him. Sweet Mother, she wanted him. "Indigo," he breathed, and lowered his mouth to hers.

The door opened and Drew stepped inside. "Whoops," he said, and stepped out again, closing the door behind himself.

Bobby cursed under his breath, dropped his forehead to Indigo's, and struggled to bring the desire rampaging through his body under control, to stifle the impulse to back her up against the door, push her pants down, and surge into her over and over again until she cried out with release. Need shuddered through him. *Soon, please, let her need him with the same fierce urgency.*

When the need to claim her dimmed enough for him to think around it, he said, "Why didn't you lock the door when you came in?"

"Mmm. Because we were going to work out, remember?"

He rubbed his nose against hers and loosened his grip so she could pull back enough to catch her breath. "All I remember is you telling me to kiss you."

"Selective memory," she accused gently, and nipped at his lower lip, sending a pulse of heat down his body. "Do you need to go after Drew?"

"I'll talk to him later. Kiss me again." He smacked her bottom lightly when she tried to pull away, and grinned when she yelped. "I want to make sure we're doing it right."

She pushed at his shoulders and he let her go, and braced his hands against the edge of the desk, willing himself not to reach for her again.

"This is neither the time nor the place for that, Bobby Upton."

He cocked his head and considered her. It wasn't a no, exactly. "You say that like you're afraid it might go beyond a kiss."

"It might," she said mildly. "I'd rather not take that chance."

"Does that mean there's a chance we might do this again?"

The look she gave him was both prim and haughty, and made him snicker in spite of the aching need.

"A man can hope."

"A man should get ready for the gym." Her eyes drifted down his body and widened when she spotted his erection, clearly visible through the nylon of his running shorts. She patted her chest absent-mindedly, as if trying to contain her heart, and nibbled at her bottom lip before her cheeks flushed and she jerked her gaze back to his. "Do you, ah, need a moment?"

"Probably a few."

"Right." Her gaze dropped again and her lips curved into a secretive, womanly smile. "I'll just..." She pointed at the door.

"I'll catch up."

She snagged her bag, turned part way toward the door, then stopped abruptly. "I almost forgot. Do you have time later to talk about India?"

The desire slid from him in a rush. "I can make time. Why?"

"Something she said to me on Friday." She shook her head and jerked at the bag in her hand, obviously troubled. "About stopping the Prophecy by snuffing out the Light. Her exact words."

A cold stillness filled him, chilling the heat left by her passion. "The Eternal Order?"

"Maybe." Her eyes rounded in a face gone suddenly pale. "I should've mentioned it earlier."

"We got a little caught up."

"That's an understatement," she muttered.

He laughed and pushed himself away from the desk to walk across the room and drop a kiss to her lips, and fought the urge to deepen the brief taste, to finish what they'd started earlier. "Let me get my things and I'll go with you."

"All right. I'm sorry I didn't agree to help you right away." She shifted her stance from one foot to the other. "You know. To track down India. I shouldn't have hesitated like that."

"Don't worry about it." He drew his workout bag from under his desk and hefted it. "She's your sister. I know you love her, in spite of everything."

"I do."

Her voice was gentle. A light shone from her eyes that he'd never seen before. When he reached her side, she stood on tiptoe and pressed a kiss to his mouth, a light, friendly gesture that startled him.

"What was that for?"

"For understanding." She smoothed down the material of his shirt, her hands lingering on his chest. "I appreciate it."

He cupped her shoulder and squeezed. "Hey, what are friends for?"

Her dimple flashed as she smiled, and he followed her to the elevator with his body still tingling from her touch.

INDIGO HUMMED happily as she made tea in the fully equipped break room at Bobby's office. The kiss they'd shared before their workout, and his reaction to it, lingered in her mind. The glorious touch of his lips to hers. The hard press of his erection at the juncture of her thighs.

He'd needed her, really needed her judging by the husky moans rumbling from his throat when she'd pulled him down and opened to him. Her breasts had grown heavy and wet heat had pooled in her nethers, and she'd reveled in the feel of his fingers biting into her skin. Every brush of his body against hers had sent a wonderful rush of feeling through her. Heat, desire. Need.

And not a whit of guilt or shame.

She licked her lower lip and closed her eyes to savor the taste of him clinging to her mouth, and relished the thought of touching him again without the horror of that long ago day tainting their passion.

When her tea finished steeping, she pulled the tea leaf strainer out and stirred in a touch of honey before sipping delicately at the steaming liquid.

Would he want to kiss her again?

She huffed out a laugh. *Silly Indi.* Of course, he would. He could barely keep his hands off her when they walked through a public area fully clothed. And when they were alone...

A rush of heat shivered through her. When they were alone with that heavy need between them, what would he do?

So far, he'd been a gentleman, or as much of a gentleman as a man like Bobby was capable of being. So maybe his hands strayed where they shouldn't a time or two. Maybe his mouth touched her where it oughtn't more often than not, but that kiss. *Mmm, that kiss.*

What if she enticed him?

No. They were friends, and friends didn't try to seduce one another.

Did they?

She knit her brow, mulling over the ethics of seducing a friend.

Of course not. That would be...wrong. And deceitful.

The memory of his hand on her bottom, pressing her against him, popped into her mind. She wanted to feel that again, feel his need, let it consume her.

Dare she seduce him?

No, she thought again, and allowed her lips to curl into a secretive smile. But she could think about it, couldn't she?

The break room's door opened. Indigo glanced over her shoulder and barely stifled a groan at the considering stare on Margaret's face.

Margaret Mary, Bobby's oldest and most deadly sister, who had nearly caught them kissing the week before.

"Margaret," Indigo said.

"Indigo." Margaret stalked forward and grabbed a mug from the cabinet above the sink, helped herself to the coffee. "How's your mother?"

"Very well, thank you."

"I'd like to drop by when the baby's born, pay my respects."

Indigo sipped her tea and watched Margaret carefully, waiting for the other shoe to drop. One could never tell what was going on behind Margaret's cold eyes. "I'm sure she'll love to see you."

Margaret leaned her bottom against the counter and regarded Indigo with equal caution. "Do they know the sex yet?"

"They wanted it to be a surprise."

"Mmm. Are you fucking my brother?"

"No." Indigo sighed and gripped her mug tightly. "Not that it's any of your business."

"Maybe I think he can do better."

"Maybe you should let him decide," Indigo shot back.

"If you hurt him again..."

"Is that what this is about? Protecting your brother?" Indigo compressed her lips into a thin line. "Or are you using him as an excuse to keep me from helping him?"

"Maybe a little of both," Margaret admitted. Her gaze was fixed on Indigo as she sipped from her mug.

Indigo weighed her options, considered the other woman, and took a calculated risk. "Are you a member of the Eternal Order?"

Margaret sputtered out a laugh. "What makes you think that?"

"Oh, get real, Margaret. Like I could draw any other conclusion after you brushed Bobby off last week."

"I'm not a member of the Order," Margaret said evenly.

"What about the High Guard?"

Margaret's expression remained blank and cold. "I couldn't tell you even if I wanted to."

Indigo tapped a finger against her cup. "Will you hinder Bobby's efforts to track down the People's enemies?"

"Why would I do that?"

"Because he might get in your way."

"No." Margaret's lips twitched into what might have been a smile. "In this instance, his agenda is my own."

"I see."

"Do you?"

The two of them locked gazes and shared a moment of understanding Indigo would've been hard pressed to explain to anyone else.

When the silence stretched thin, she said, "I care about Bobby."

"See that you do."

Laura walked in and flushed when she spotted Indigo.

Margaret freshened her coffee and lifted the mug in a salute to Indigo on her way out. "Have fun."

"Thanks," Indigo said drily, and girded herself for the next battle.

SEVEN

BOBBY SQUEEZED TIME from his schedule to drive to Tellowee and see his mother without making an appointment. It would likely piss her off, but that was ok. He wanted answers. Now that Indigo had confessed her fears about India's ties to the Eternal Order, he would damn well get them.

He caught Rebecca as she entered her office.

"Bobby." She raised on tiptoes to kiss his cheek before continuing into her *sanctum sanctorum*. "What a pleasant surprise."

He followed her in and closed the door behind them. "Do you have a minute?"

She turned a puzzled look on him, an elegant one, and his heart softened. He'd heard the stories of her youth, about the young girl who had wielded a sword with such dazzling cunning that it had been given to her. She'd used it to cut a swathe through generations of armies in Europe, Africa, and Asia, first as a soldier and eventually as a leader. That sword rested in a case in the corner of her office, protected by glass, unlike the woman who stood before him. Her heart had fallen to his father, the charming history professor with a bent for genealogy, and now it was Bobby's as well.

He waited for her to take a seat behind her desk before dropping into one of the chairs in front of it. "How's Dad?"

"Better. The new medicine is working very well." She leaned forward in her chair and pierced him with a questioning stare. "We missed you this weekend."

"I stayed at the office. We officially started work on the IECS job today and I wanted to be ready."

She dropped her eyes to the desk and shifted a paper.

Uh-oh.

"I thought you might have spent the weekend with Indigo."

"Why would you think that?"

"You're working with her, aren't you?"

"That doesn't mean I'm seeing her." Which he wasn't. Exactly.

"True. Are you at least on speaking terms?"

His mind drifted to the kiss they'd shared that morning, the weight of her body against his, the way she'd curled her fingers into his hair and pulled him down for more. "Sort of."

"Are you trying to get along with her or are you being stubborn like your father?"

Bobby breathed out a laugh. "Mom, really. We're getting along fine."

"Well." She narrowed her gaze on him and he struggled not to shrink beneath it like a child caught with his hand in the cookie jar. That steely gaze had likely brought down a hundred armies all on its own. "As long as you're trying."

"I am." And he was. If he were trying any harder, they'd be married with babies on the way.

A little girl with Indigo's sapphire eyes, holding her hands up and calling him Daddy.

Indigo round with child, glowing softly the way expectant mothers did when they were happy and healthy.

Indigo under him, her ebony hair spread out across his sheets, her body caught in rapture as he stroked into her until she came, over and over again.

"Bobby?"

He looked up to find his mother watching him with raised eyebrows.

"Sorry. Work." He cleared his throat and shifted in his seat. "Lots going on."

"Of course."

A knowing smile played across Rebecca's mouth, and heat rose in his cheeks. Dammit, why couldn't he get his mind under control and off of Indigo?

"What brings you by today?" she said.

"India Furia." He leaned forward and pinned her with a sharp stare. "She's been visiting my team members, threatening them if they don't back off."

"Not an unexpected development."

"Not much of one, anyway. She stopped by Indigo's on Friday, mentioned her plans for stopping the Prophecy."

Rebecca's gaze remained steady. "Any specifics?"

"Just a threat to snuff out the Light." He kept his gaze as careful as hers. "Indigo thinks India's part of the Eternal Order."

The corner of Rebecca's eye twitched in an otherwise neutral expression, and his heart sank. "When were you going to tell me?"

"About what?"

"Don't play games with me, Mom."

They faced off against one another, cool stares clashing across the desk.

"Some things are better left unknown."

The careful note in her voice set him on edge. "I'm not risking my people on an unknown."

"Life is an unknown, Bobby." She swiveled in her chair to look out the windows running along one side of her office. "You're old enough to understand that."

His jaws clenched at the reprimand. "I've been old enough to understand that for a long time."

"True."

She sounded sad, regretful even. For the first time, he noticed the faint lines around her eyes and the gray in her ash blonde hair. His gut twisted into a hard knot. Sweet Goddess. When had she gotten old on him?

"Tell me about the Order," he said softly.

She sighed and swiveled back to face him. "I can only tell you so much."

"Then tell me what you can."

He reached across the desk and waited for her to take his hand, as she'd done when he was a little boy. She'd always been there for him, protecting him, loving him. Now, maybe it was his turn to return the favor.

"Sweet boy." Rebecca clasped his hand in hers. "You were always my favorite."

He grinned. "You say that to all of us."

"And it's always true." She squeezed his hand gently before letting go. "I suppose you're going to share everything I tell you with your team."

"Not all of them. Hiro and Drew, yeah."

"And Indigo?" she said with a coy tilt of her head.

"Let's not go there again."

"I want you to be happy."

He let his gaze go flat over the humor. "You're stalling."

"Only a little. So you'll tell Hiro, Drew, and Indigo, whom you aren't seeing."

"Mom."

"Don't approach Margaret," she warned.

"Too late. Now spill."

Rebecca pressed her lips into a thin line. "The Eternal Order is real."

He rolled his eyes skyward. "I got that part."

"Don't be smart, young man." Rebecca tapped the top of her desk with one finger. "I can still put you in your place, if needs must."

He rubbed a finger across the smile that rose. She could indeed, and would probably always be able to. "Yes, ma'am."

"And don't think I can't see that smirk. Honestly. Kids these days."

They shared a grin, and then Bobby listened while his mother told him everything she could about the Eternal Order and its struggle to stop the Prophecy from being fulfilled.

REBECCA LEANED BACK in her chair and watched her youngest child as he left her office. Trying to find a balance between giving him the information he needed and protecting the larger interests of the People had exhausted her.

Bobby had probed her knowledge relentlessly, seeking the information he needed to close in on India Furia and other possible traitors to the People. An intelligent mind focused ruthlessly on the overall objective, exactly what the People needed to defend themselves. Her mother's heart filled with pride that her son would be the one to solve this problem and bring their enemies to justice.

The intercom buzzed, announcing her next appointment. She picked up the phone's handset and instructed her receptionist to give her a moment before sending anyone in.

She took a sip of cool water, relished the feel of it trickling down her throat, and ignored the fatigue that seemed to dog every movement she took these days. A quick make-up check in the hand-held mirror she kept in her desk reassured her that she didn't look nearly as old as she felt.

Of course, if she felt her true age, she would feel old indeed.

She still had a couple of decades before she hit the millennium mark, and hoped she'd be around for it. Robert had promised her a party to end all parties as a celebration. She intended to hold him to it, but first, she had to lead the People through their current crisis.

The door opened to admit Sigrid Glyvynsdatter, their in-house genetics specialist, and George Howe, a young man whom Rebecca had invited to the IECS to assist Sigrid in gathering and analyzing DNA samples from living members of the People, as well as from the remains of the dead.

The two were opposites in nearly every way. Raised in the time of the Vikings to be a ruthless and fierce warrior, Sigrid had, like most immortal Daughters, maintained her warrior's form, lean and quick, and had the grace and confidence to match. George was slightly dumpy, and fidgeted himself into a nervous frenzy whenever his co-worker's frosty gaze rested on him. Though they were both brilliant scientists, their mindsets were often at complete odds.

Strangely enough, it brought out the best in both of them. Rebecca had personally hoped the two would find love together, but the unpretentious Mr. Howe had apparently already given his heart to another Daughter. Sigrid showed no signs of challenging the other woman's claim.

George sat down in one of the chairs situated in front of Rebecca's desk. Sigrid handed Rebecca a folder before seating herself.

"Our report," Sigrid said in a voice still thick with her native tongue.

Rebecca flipped it open and skimmed through their latest findings. "Anything of special note?"

"Nothing untoward or unexpected," Sigrid answered.

George slumped slightly in his chair.

Rebecca closed the folder and pinned him with a curious stare. "Would you like to add something, Mr. Howe?"

"No." He cleared his throat and slid a little lower. "Only, if we could just..."

Sigrid turned a glacial stare on him, and he halted in mid-word.

"Yes?" Rebecca prompted.

"Mr. Howe would like to send some of our samples to off site labs," Sigrid said.

He tugged at his collar and shifted in his seat. "It would speed up our work tremendously."

"And leave it open to infiltration by others." Sigrid dismissed his argument with a decisive blink. "I'm concerned about receiving results that have been deliberately tampered with, or possibly having samples stolen outright."

"Concerns noted," Rebecca said. "Mr. Howe, our labs will simply have to be sufficient."

"Yes, ma'am." His shoulders hunched miserably. "Can we at least bring in some more people, maybe equip another room to use as a lab?"

Rebecca raised a questioning eyebrow at Sigrid, who looked briefly skyward.

"It would ease some of the workload and hasten our work," Sigrid admitted.

"All right. I'll expect a formal request on my desk by the end of the week, along with a list of names of appropriate personnel," Rebecca said. "Have you made any headway on identifying the Sandby borg Daughter?"

George perked up. "Some. We found a small amount of DNA in her bones and are testing it now."

"Good. I want to be informed as soon as you know anything." Rebecca clasped her hands together and rested them on the desk. "How's testing of the general population going?"

"Slowly. Many of the older Daughters are resistant to being tested." Sigrid unbent enough to twist her lips into something resembling a wry grin. "But it's coming along. It would be helpful if we could dedicate one person simply to record keeping."

"Whatever you need."

George and Sigrid exchanged a look.

"What?" Rebecca asked.

George leaned forward, confidence entering his posture for the first time since he'd entered the room. "We've started testing the skeleton found at that nightclub Bones a couple of weeks ago."

"Very interesting," Sigrid murmured.

"How so?" Rebecca asked, intrigued.

"The bones are old." George's cheeks flushed with excitement. "Possibly old enough to be a Sister, if I understand the timetable correctly."

"Perhaps not that old," Sigrid cautioned. "But old, indeed. This could help us cement some of the lineages that are in question now."

Rebecca pressed her lips together, trying to quell her own excitement.

"I'd like to expand testing to later generations," George said. "Later, of course, once we've finished testing the remains held at the IECS and known members of the People."

"Of course," Rebecca said. "I bow to your good judgment."

George burst into a frenzy of technical talk that went straight over Rebecca's head, about mitochondrial DNA, which she had at least heard of, and a host of new tests and research that left her dizzy. When Sigrid jumped in with her own opinions, Rebecca sat back and listened to them argue, and allowed the promise of their research to lift her hopes. Perhaps one day, the mysteries of the People's history would be fully unraveled.

EIGHT

THE LONGER INDIGO SPENT around Bobby and his crew, the more impressed she was by their efficiency and effectiveness. By the end of the first week, Hiro and Drew had rounded up and questioned two of the Daughters on their list.

Of course, it had taken a whole team to persuade each of the Daughters to answer questions and BDH had run through its in-house supply of bandages as a result, but the job had been done. They'd questioned the Daughters, thoroughly checked their stories with the help of Zena and Laura, and let the Daughters think the scrutiny was done. It wasn't. Bobby assigned rotating teams to keep tabs on the women's movements and contacts, funneling the whole through his own hands to stay on top of their progress. Hiro and Drew were equally as bad, focusing intensely on each step of their assignments, seemingly to the exclusion of everything else.

She and Bobby worked closely together, though she focused on India and he on coordinating the entire operation. When they were at BDH, they usually holed up together in his office with her set up on the couch and him at his desk. More often, they were on the road, tracking leads and gathering information.

The days were long and hard, lasting well beyond what Indigo had expected, and effectively kept her from acting on any tentative thoughts she might have had to seduce Bobby. Not that they didn't spend time together, because they did, but it was usually at BDH or on the road.

He hadn't stopped touching her. His hands lingered on her waist, brushed through her hair, slid under her shirt when they were alone, caressing the skin of her torso. His lips found hers in odd moments, at times tender and fleeting, at others fiercely demanding, until Indigo gasped with pleasure and bit her tongue to hold in pleas for more.

More was something he never requested, never pushed for.

It bothered her more than it should have. She replayed their kisses over and over again in her mind until her body hummed with frustrated passion, and began to wish she'd never said no to him in the first place.

That day still stood between them, not because she couldn't move past it, but because Bobby couldn't. His eyes lingered on her far more than he likely realized. In them she caught a haunted longing that left her wondering exactly what was going on in his stubborn, male head.

On Halloween, she took a short break to pass out candy with her mother and step-father at their house in Tellowee. A bittersweet envy filled her as she watched Glen fuss over her mother's rounded form. They were so in love, so intent on one another. As soon as was polite, Indigo made her excuses and slipped out, ashamed of the jealousy gnawing at her over their obvious happiness.

Another week passed, the list of suspects grew, and more people were brought in for questioning. Word got out that Bobby was on the prowl and some of their sources dried up.

Hiro and Drew were only too happy to take teams out and renew those sources.

Margaret, on the other hand, seemed content to observe and take a back seat to the main action.

Indigo hadn't told Bobby about her conversation with his sister in the break room or shared her suspicions that Margaret was more heavily involved than she let on. Indigo hadn't forgotten, though, and in her spare time began to dig quietly into the other Daughter's movements over the past few centuries, searching for answers to a conundrum only she could define.

By the middle of the third week, Indigo's nerves were stretched thin. They were no closer to discovering India's whereabouts or her possible connections to the Eternal Order, and had been unable to fully eliminate any of the other names on their list. Bobby seemed as focused as ever on their end goal.

She was ready to scream with frustration.

The only things that kept her from doing so were their morning workouts and their evening work sessions. Each morning, they met at the gym on the floor above BDH and spent an hour lifting weights, swimming, or sparring. Each night, they would grab supper and eat it at Bobby's desk or in the break room, or go to her apartment to continue working.

As gently as she prodded, their conversation never lingered on the past. It ate at her, the things she'd done, the things he'd done because of her.

Nearly two weeks after Halloween, they met at her place for supper, a roast she'd put in the crock pot that morning before she'd left for work.

Bobby sidled up behind her while she stood at the counter, waiting for the microwave to heat the mashed potatoes. His arms came around her waist and she leaned back, drawing comfort from his warmth.

"Mmm." He nuzzled the side of her neck and pressed a chaste kiss there. "How can you still smell so good after the day we've had?"

"It's called soap," she said with a laugh.

His tongue raked over her skin, sending a wave of heat through her. "I think it's called Indigo."

The microwave dinged and she pulled free to check the potatoes. Bobby took plates out of the cabinet. His clothes tightened over his lean, fit body as he stretched up. She bit back a sigh. What would he say if she yanked his shirt up and licked her way down his torso? Surely he wouldn't mind if she took just a nibble or two.

That's depraved, Indigo, one part of her chided, and another answered with, *Yes, but do it anyway.*

"What are you smiling about?" Bobby asked, bringing her abruptly back to reality.

A flush crept up her cheeks and she cursed her fair skin. "Nothing," she said, which was true enough. Her inner ramblings were nothing he needed to hear.

The phone rang, saving her from the inquisition gathering behind his narrowed eyes. Without moving his gaze from her, Bobby reached out a long arm and picked up the receiver. "Hello."

She crossed her arms over her chest, struggling between laughter and outrage. If he felt free to answer her phone, maybe he was a little too comfortable in her home.

He leaned back against the counter while he listened and gave her an arch look. After a moment, he said, "We'll be there," and hung up.

He turned to rummage through her silverware drawer and she huffed out an exasperated breath.

"Who was that?" she said.

"Who was...? Oh, on the phone." He pushed the drawer shut and dropped forks and knives on the counter. "Your step-dad. He's at the hospital with your mom."

Nervous excitement flitted through her, making her bounce. "The baby?"

Bobby grinned as he picked her up and whirled her around once, right there in the kitchen. "On its way."

She clutched at his shoulders, as much to hold him as to counteract the dizziness. "We have to go."

"Supper first."

He let her slide down his body, and she hitched in a breath at the feel of his hard muscles rubbing across hers.

"No, no time," she said and caught his hand. "We need to go."

"You need food, sweetheart." He dropped a kiss onto her forehead and turned to dish up two plates. "Besides, babies are slow. You can spare five minutes to fuel your body."

"Oh, fine," she huffed, but took a plate when he offered it. He was right. It could take hours for the baby to come, and they hadn't eaten in so long her stomach dug into her backbone in protest.

They ate standing at the counter, then stored the leftovers in the fridge and washed up before leaving. Bobby drove, leaving her to fret during the short distance to the hospital. To distract herself, she pressed a hand against his thigh and held on as if he were her anchor, and not the man she found herself wanting more and more with a need that bordered on desperation.

BOBBY EDGED THE TRUCK up over the speed limit in the twenty minute drive from Indigo's apartment to the hospital outside Tellowee, not enough to get caught, but enough to shave time off the drive.

Indigo's face was pale and tense. Nerves or excitement, he figured, or maybe both. Two minutes after hitting the highway, she'd latched onto his thigh as if she were afraid he'd abandon her. Her fingers tightened hard enough to leave bruises, sending a pulse of pleasure through his muscles at the sweet pain of her touch.

Maybe if she'd placed her hand a little lower on his leg, it would've been different, but she'd unthinkingly rested it so that her pinky brushed against the fly of his jeans every time he moved his leg.

So maybe he jiggled it a little more than he should have, but by the Goddess, even that small touch sent him to heaven.

He took a curve a shade too fast and inhaled sharply when her hand slipped and her knuckles grazed his erection through his jeans. When the road straightened out, he grasped her hand and reluctantly moved it closer to his knee where it wouldn't be so distracting.

Hospital first. Touching later.

The paleness of her hand contrasted starkly with the dark blue of his jeans in the night's shadows. Would she touch him like that if they were alone in her apartment? Maybe if he coaxed her into it she would. He glanced furtively at her, ran his gaze along the drape of soft fabric over firm breasts, the toned muscles of her thighs, and shifted as the heat and need ratcheted higher. Yeah, maybe he would.

He parked in the first empty parking spot he came to and hustled Indigo out of the car and into the hospital's after-hours entrance. She held his hand as they took the elevator to the floor housing the maternity ward, her breath humming shallowly in and out of her lungs as she watched the elevator's numbers light up. When the doors opened, they stepped off it into a crowd of friends and family.

Bobby trailed behind Indigo, letting her lead the way, speaking to the people he knew, which was nearly everyone. Tellowee was a small community and his mother a well-known member. Politicking, as she called it, had been bred into him at an early age.

After Indigo found a nurse and received an update on her mother, they squeezed onto one of the waiting room's couches. He draped an arm over her shoulders and pulled her close, as much because of the tight space as anything.

She completely missed the curious stares directed their way.

Bobby met each one with a steady gaze, raising smiles on some faces and scowls on others.

As much as they all liked to believe otherwise, there weren't so many People that gossip didn't spread like the wind, and was remembered far longer. Nearly everyone who knew him and Indigo had probably at least heard that they'd had some difficulties when he was a teenager, although few would know exactly what those difficulties were. For him to show up at an important family event with her and show such casual affection was bound to raise a few eyebrows.

What would those same people say when Indigo took him as her lover?

It was bound to happen, maybe would've already if they hadn't been so busy at work. He hadn't missed the way her eyes followed him, the flush that crept up her pale cheeks when he caught her staring, shy and sweet and sexy all rolled into one. She had the cutest habit of drawing the corner of her bottom lip into her mouth when she was thinking about sex. Every time she did that, his penis saluted. Every. Single. Time. It was getting so he couldn't be around her without the damn thing standing at attention.

He'd taken to jerking off in the shower, his senses surrounded by steamy heat and the memory of her fingers tangling in his hair, the taste of her skin on his tongue, the curve of her ass under his hand and her back arched, pressing her breasts into his chest; and his fist, working his erection hard and swift, willing himself to come just so he could maintain a little control around her.

Sometimes it even worked.

He shifted on the couch, cleared his throat, leaned forward over the near painful erection pushing against the fly of his jeans. The need he had for her never eased. The urge to sink into her and feel her slick heat wrapped around him was never far away. Just the thought of being with her like that, of joining his body with hers and having her accept him, sent desire pulsing through him, low in his gut. He pushed it back, fixed his attention on the game of Rummy someone had started while he'd been lost in thought, and breathed a silent prayer.

Sweet Lady Ki, please let her be ready soon.

An hour passed so slowly Bobby shook his watch to make sure it was running, and was still surprised at the digital numbers on its face. People came and went, stopping by to offer their good wishes or staying to help pass the time.

His mom dropped by, took one look at Indigo squeezed up against him, and furrowed her brow. He wasn't sure if she was issuing him a silent order to behave or if she was concerned about the implications of his and Indigo's position. Since several people were squeezed into tighter spots in the waiting room, he thought it was probably the latter.

Indigo barely noticed. She pretended to play cards, but her eyes roamed continuously to the area where her step-father would come out when the baby was born.

Another hour passed before that happened, and when it did, a cry went up around the room at the happy smile on Glen's face. Indigo stood and pulled Bobby with her.

"It's a boy," he said, then held up his hands when a cheer rang out. "And a girl. We have two blessings tonight."

Indigo whirled and threw her arms around Bobby. He held on as she laughed and cried and pressed sloppy kisses to his cheeks.

"Oh, I have to go talk to him for a minute. Be right back." She pressed a final kiss to his mouth and darted off, pushing her way through the crowd.

He shoved his hands into the pockets of his jeans and watched her go until she disappeared with her step-father into the delivery room. Rebecca stepped up to him and threaded her arm through his.

"The day you were born," she said in a soft voice meant for the two of them alone, "your father passed out before we could even get here."

A swift, nostalgic ache rose in Bobby's chest at the familiar tale.

"Charlotte had to drive us to the hospital, and you know what her driving's like. By the time we arrived, your father was a nervous wreck, poor Charlotte was in tears, and you had nearly pushed your way out. You were always in such a hurry."

"I know," he murmured. It had gotten him into trouble more than once, and not solely on the day he'd become a man and tried to claim Indigo.

"You've slowed down a little in your old age," she teased.

He grinned at her. "Not so much as you'd think."

She placed her hand on his cheek, pressed gently until he turned his face toward hers. "There's no hurry, Bobby. There never was."

"It feels like there is, like if I don't hold her to me, she'll slip right through my fingers again."

Rebecca patted his cheek, then dropped her hand. "I think you'll find Indigo more receptive to your suit this time around."

An unwarranted hope lurched in his chest. "How so?"

"You'll see," she said simply, and he nodded, though he didn't see at all.

Indigo came out not long after, beaming, and pushed through the crowd until she reached him.

"Congratulations," Rebecca said.

Indigo's smile dimmed a notch. "Thank you, Director Upton."

"Rebecca," his mother said. "How's everyone doing?"

"Wonderful, thank you. They've brought the babies to the nursery and said we could go look."

"Then look you should." Rebecca squeezed Bobby's arm, though she directed her remarks to Indigo. "Please give your mother my best wishes. Tell her I'll stop by in a day or two to check on her."

"Thank you," Indigo said.

Bobby watched his mother make her way through the crowd with the ease of a knife through butter before letting Indigo tug him toward the nursery. His whole conversation with his mother had been off somehow, pointed in that mysterious way women had of conveying information without tipping their hand in the slightest. What could she possibly know about Indigo that would give him hope?

"Oh, Bobby, you should see them." Indigo's voice was hushed as they walked hand in hand along the corridors. The crowd fell away behind them, a distant murmur of family and friends. "They're so tiny and perfect. The nurse said I could hold them if I wanted, though I think I'd rather wait until they're out of the nursery. Don't you think?"

He let her chatter, content to wander the halls with her, enjoying the smooth silkiness of her hand gripped in his own and the light patter of her happiness. When they came to the nursery, he was surprised that her siblings were the only two residents. A nurse spotted them at the window and hurried to let them in.

"If we had other babies, you'd have to stay outside," she explained, "but since it's just these two angels and they're perfectly healthy, you'll be fine."

Indigo led him to a spot between the two hospital cradles and bounced from one to the other, cooing softly over the sleeping infants. When she wound down and found a spot halfway between, he pulled her into his arms with her back against his chest and held her. A strange feeling gripped him as they stood there, flanked by newly born babies, and he remembered the vision he'd had of a little girl with Indigo's beautiful sapphire eyes.

A sudden longing to make that child a reality hit him, hard enough to stagger him. He tightened his hold on Indigo as his heart stuttered in his chest, turned over, and thumped hard.

She sighed and leaned her head back over the yearning in his heart. "Aren't they beautiful, Bobby?"

"Mmm." He brushed his cheek against her midnight hair, breathed in the clean scent of her. "They look like little wrinkled frogs to me."

She gasped out a laugh and smacked his arm. "I can't believe you said that."

"I can't believe you took me seriously."

"Oh, you," she said, and settled back against him with a happy sigh. "Seeing them makes me want my own."

"I'm happy to oblige," he said, and felt the quiet rumble of her laughter more than heard it.

"I'm sure you would." She turned in his arms and rested her hands against his chest. "Don't you want to have children?"

Oh, if she only knew. How could he tell her that he'd dreamed of her having his children since the day she'd walked into his English class as his teacher, less than two months before his fifteenth birthday? Would it scare her off to learn how often he pictured her in his mind, round with his child, her eyes full of love and promise? "Some day. Why did you never have any?"

"Oh, well, you know. It was never the right time. Never the right man." Her gaze dropped to her hands and the happiness slipped from her face. "Growing up with India and Mámá fighting all the time was difficult."

"That was a long time ago," he said gently.

Her face lifted and her eyes filled with regret. "The past has a way of clinging to the present, no matter how hard we try to shake it."

He knew that, knew it all too painfully well. She didn't have to suffer for it, though. He kissed her then, a soft press of lips meant to comfort, to soothe, to bleed some of her sadness away so that the pleasure could fill her up again. Her fingers curled against his chest and she sighed into his mouth, and he took it, all of it and her, everything she was willing to give him.

When he could tear himself away, he said, "Let me take you home."

"Ok," she said, and her eyes lit with the promise he'd dreamed of seeing there. His heart jumped into his throat, the racing beat roaring through his ears as heat sprang between them. *Blessed Goddess.* Unless he was mistaken, she wanted more than a drive home.

NINE

I T TOOK THEM an hour to make their way out of the hospital. Her mother was being moved to a regular room when Indigo and Bobby came out of the nursery. Indigo said goodbye to her step-father and promised to visit the next day, and then there were all the well wishers and family members to deal with, and by the time they left, second thoughts pinged around Indigo's head.

Had she really agreed to have sex with Bobby or had that been her imagination?

She peered at him out of the corner of her eye as he drove, his left hand draped over the top of the steering wheel. His right one held her hand against his thigh in a casual gesture. He'd let her hang on to him on the ride over, held her hand while they were inside, stroked her back, easing her nerves.

Coming from him, such affection could mean anything. After all, this was the man who'd admitted to holding *dozens* of attractive women over the course of his young life.

Her breath faltered in her lungs and a flush crept up her face. She'd totally misread the situation. So what if he'd kissed her senseless on a dozen different occasions over the past few weeks? He'd walked away every single time in spite of the erection he nearly always sported afterward.

A shaft of pain twisted its way into her heart, bone deep and hard.

What was she doing? If he still wanted her, he would've acted by now. This was Bobby, the same person who'd tried to claim her as soon as he'd become a man in the eyes of the People. Bobby, who didn't lollygag or wait around on someone else, but stepped forward, manned up, and got the job done.

This was a man who held his sisters' hands and showered everyone he knew with affection of one sort or another. Her heart twisted again. She was no different, nothing special. Why had she allowed herself to believe she meant something to him still, just because she once had?

Indigo tugged gently at her hand, trying to slide it from beneath his. His grip firmed around it, and he lifted her hand to his mouth and kissed her fingers in a tender gesture that stung her fragile heart.

Damn him for making her believe, for making her *want*.

The minute he pulled into the parking lot of her apartment complex and parked, she jerked herself away from him and out of his truck. Her tennis shoes squeaked as she all but ran up the sidewalk and the two flights of steps to her apartment without checking to see if he followed. She fumbled with the lock, let herself in, and made it three steps inside before he caught her.

His hands gripped her waist, swinging her around until her back hit the closed door. He braced his forearms above her and leaned in until their noses touched. Her breath hitched in her lungs, caught by the heat in his hazel eyes, so deep and needy, almost desperate. She pressed her hands flat against the door, holding them there to stifle the aching need to touch him, to curl her fingers into his shirt and pull him down until their lips met. Heat pooled between her thighs and her skin tightened in anticipation and she bit her lip hard, willing herself not to give in.

"I love it when you do that," he said.

"Do what?"

He shifted and moved, traced her mouth with one finger. "When you're thinking about sex, you nibble the corner of your mouth. It makes me hard."

"Oh." Her breath came in shallow gasps. "I didn't know..." That she was doing it, that it provoked him sexually.

His laugh was low, gritty, and sent his breath feathering across her lips. "I like it."

"Oh."

His finger traced her lips again. Her lips tingled at the teasing touch and she opened her mouth and flicked her tongue out, tasting the tip of his finger. He sucked in a breath and stilled, and an embarrassed flush heated her cheeks. She turned her face away from him, away from temptation. "Sorry."

"Why? It felt great."

"Is that what this is, then? A way for you to feel great?" She pushed him away with a hurt fury that surprised them both. "Anyone will do, huh, especially poor, weak little Indigo. Is this payback for rejecting you Bobby?"

His eyes widened as he huffed out a breath, dimming the heat in his gaze not one whit. "What are you talking about, Indi?"

"I'm talking about you toying with me."

"I'm not toying with you." He gave a half laugh. "I'm trying to seduce you."

She crossed her arms over her chest and regarded him with narrowed eyes. "Really."

"Well, yeah, but that's nothing new. I've been trying to do that since I was sixteen." He ran a hand through his hair and mumbled, "Thought I was doing pretty well there, too."

She sucked in a breath. "You've been playing with me since the moment you walked through that door, with your casual hugs and kisses and those sexy little licks on my neck."

"Sexy, huh?"

"I thought we were friends." She glanced away, covering the hurt, her pride begging her to hide it from his astute gaze. "I thought you wanted me."

"I do. We are." He rubbed a finger over his forehead, shook his head. "What is this about?"

"I don't know!" She met his confused gaze with her miserable one. "I guess I just got carried away in the nursery, surrounded by babies, and you were there and made me want you, like you always do, and I'm tired of being alone when you're right there, underfoot all the damn time, tall and sexy and charming, and really, do you have to be such a good kisser?"

A gentle smile tugged at his mouth. "You said damn."

"I know." The humor of it hit her and a laugh bubbled up. "Sorry."

"No, it's ok. You should vent more often."

He held out his arms and she walked into them. The tension bled out of her in a swift rush. It felt so good, so right to hold him like this, like she was supposed to be there, surrounded by everything he was. She rested her head against his chest and breathed in the lingering hint of spicy cologne, the masculine scent that was all Bobby. "I feel silly."

"Don't." He rested his chin against the top of her head, tightened his arms around her. "Next time, though, maybe you should talk to me instead of bottling it up."

"Maybe." She drew back until she could meet his gaze. "So, was it my imagination or did you really want to have sex with me?"

"That was definitely not your imagination." He dropped a kiss on the tip of her nose. "I'll understand if you don't want to, though."

"But you're, er." She stuttered to a stop. How did one describe a man's erection in polite company?

His laugh was low and shaky. "I've been *er* since the first time I saw you."

She bit the corner of her lip, and he groaned.

"You have no idea what that does to me." He rested his forehead against hers. "It's late. I should probably go."

"What?" She clutched at his shirt. "No, wait."

"Indi, sweetheart, one more kiss that's not a goodnight and I might not be able to stop."

"Maybe I don't want you to."

He heaved a breath and looked skyward. "Maybe's not gonna cut it, not this time. If I stay, you have to be sure it's what you want."

Her heart tipped into overdrive. "I'm sure. No, I am," she added when his mouth twisted into skepticism. "I want to be with you, have for a while. I just needed time to work up to it."

"Yeah?"

She answered him with a slow, womanly smile as she took his hand in hers and backed toward her bedroom, watching the burning need in his gaze build until it encompassed them both. She left the overhead light off, flipped on the bedside lamp instead, and wavered as uncertainty flicked through her. It had been so long since she'd been intimate. None of those men had been anything like the one who stood before her, strong and confident, intent only on her. It was scary and good all at the same time.

And she *wanted* it to be.

He yanked his BDH polo over his head and dropped it to the floor, his eyes hot, demanding, and just a little dangerous. "Touch me."

She reached out and ran a finger down the center of his torso from the top of his sternum to his belly button, marveling at the taut, smooth expanse. He shivered and she pulled back, only to have him grab her hand and place it more firmly against his skin.

"It tickled," he said in a gruff voice that sent tingling chills up her spine.

She circled her fingers along his chest. His skin was smooth under her touch, the hair scattered there crisp and warm. Satisfaction purred through her when he shuddered and she did it again because she could, because he'd given her permission to touch him, freeing her to do as she pleased.

Emboldened, she moved closer and ran her hands up his ribs. On the way back down, she slowed her touch and memorized every dip, every ripple of muscle over bone. His skin was warm and firm, tougher than her own, but still smooth as satin. She ran a fingernail along the edge of his pants, teasing him. The hair under his navel was silkier, warmer, and oh so tempting. She slipped a finger into his pants there, rubbing in and out of his waistband as he sucked his stomach muscles in with a low moan that shivered through her.

"I want to put my mouth on you, here." She traced her fingers lower, skimming over the hard length hidden behind his zipper, learning the width and breadth of him through the worn fabric. "May I?"

His breath whooshed out in a rush. "Anything you want."

Oh, yes, she wanted, burned so hard with the need for him, it consumed her.

She pressed nibbling kisses along his collarbone while her hands wrestled with the fastening of his jeans, fumbling in her eagerness to touch him. He rested his hands on her waist and watched her with an intensity she could feel, his eyes taking in every touch, every breath.

When his jeans were undone, she pushed her hand into his underwear and stroked the backs of her fingers along the velvet skin of his erection. His hands dug into the skin at her waist. "That's it, baby," he murmured, and threw back his head on a gasp when she circled him with finger and thumb and stroked downward.

Desire washed over her, and power. She wanted to feel him shudder and moan while she sucked his erection into her mouth, to bring him pleasure and taste his release and know that she was the one who had given that to him.

She pulled her hand out and stood on tiptoe to take his mouth in a fierce kiss while she worked his pants down over his hips, over the firm curve of his bottom and the thick length of his manhood. He moaned when his erection broke free and rasped out her name in a voice harsh and needy, urging her on with his fierce cry. His skin glimmered in the low light. She followed the play of shadows along his muscles with her lips, darted her tongue out, tasting the saltiness of his skin, and sucked and nibbled her way down his torso until the hardwood floor dug into the bones and skin of her knees.

His erect penis jutted proudly from his body, the tip wet and ready, eager for her. She cupped his firm bottom with a steadying hand, circled his erection with the other, and licked along the slit at the end of his manhood. His hips jerked forward at the first touch of her tongue, pushing his length into her mouth.

"Sorry," he said. "Feels good."

She *hmmd*, reveled in his answering moan, and eased the head of his erection deeper, sucking gently and licking the underside until he tangled a hand into her hair, urging her to take more. She did, slipping him as far into her mouth as he would go, then let him slide slowly out as she drew away. In and out she pulled him, suckling him in the age-old kiss of a woman for the man she desired. His body arched, pressing his hips forward, and his muscles trembled under her fingers, flexing and bunching with each wet stroke.

"Indigo, please," he moaned. "I need you, so much. Let me have you."

A hint of saltiness hit her tongue and she drew back, even as his hands tightened in her hair. She glanced up and found him gazing down at her, his hazel eyes hot, his expression taut with need, and a thrill ran through her. "You want me to stop?"

He laughed, low and unsteady, and shook his head. "I don't want to come yet, either."

He pulled her to her feet and their hands tangled together, yanking at each other's clothes, dropping them onto the floor in a careless pile of his and hers, and then she pushed him onto the bed and looked her fill of him. His skin glowed golden in the low light and his eyes glittered beneath hooded lids as his own gaze drifted across her body, lingering on the lush weight of her breasts, the soft slope of her stomach, the curls at the juncture of her legs. His feet were flat on the floor, his thighs a wide frame for his erection, and the muscles of his torso bunched with the curve of his body.

He was the most beautiful man she'd ever seen, and he was *hers*.

She pressed her lips together, needing him so much. Where did a woman start with a man like Bobby, with his dangerous eyes and godlike body and a touch that sent her soaring higher than she'd ever been?

"When you do that, I want to lick your mouth until you open for me."

She huffed out a breath. "Do you catalogue every gesture my mouth makes?"

"Every. Single. One." His gaze heated her where it flicked down her body. "Come to me."

The low command shivered through her, leaving her weak and helpless.

"Don't make me wait, Indi." He held out a hand, beckoning her closer. "I need you."

She clasped her hand in his, let him tug her forward as she crawled onto the bed and straddled his waist, lifted herself above him and guided his erection with her fingers until the tip nudged at the entrance to her wet heat.

"Don't stop," he said.

"I won't. Not this time."

She shifted her hips, taking him in little by little until he was completely sheathed and her sex stretched, deliciously full. He rested one hand on her thigh, ran the other down her stomach, down, down, and delved his fingers into the folds of her sex, rubbing against the little nub hidden there.

Wild pleasure streaked through her. "Bobby," she breathed, and braced her hands against his chest. She moved over him, undulating her hips slowly, sliding over his hard length. Heat flooded through her, overwhelming her with a suddenness that took her breath. He made her *want*, made her *feel*, and it was so good, *so good*. She threw back her head and closed her eyes and met the rhythm he set with the upward thrusts of his hips and the downward push of his hand on her hip and the rub of his fingertips along her sex.

Faster and harder they flew, their breaths gasping in time to the union of their bodies. She lost herself in the need and the pleasure he gave her, in his low moans and the feel of his hands on her, until she hung on the edge of a precipice, waiting for him to join her.

He thrust up one last time and came with a groan, his release throbbing into her, and then he pinched the little nub he'd been rubbing, thrust into her again, and sent her tumbling under wave after wave of her own release.

BOBBY TUCKED A HAND under his head and stroked Indigo's back, waiting for their breaths to slow and their bodies to cool. Her weight was supported partially by her own thighs. He wished she would slide her legs down and lay fully on top of him. He wanted that, wanted to feel her skin pressed against his when she was sated and full.

She slid to his side with a sigh and rested her head on his chest, leaving him bereft at the loss of her weight.

"You're still hard." Her hand glanced along his hip and landed softly on his lower stomach, just above the base of his penis. "I thought you came."

"I did." And Goddess, it had been wonderful. The wet heat of her sex, the soft mews in her throat. Desire stirred and he reined it in. "I'll probably be like this for a while."

"Why?" Her fingers slipped closer to his sex through the thick hair protecting its base. "Was it not good?"

He laughed softly. "It was beyond good, Indigo. Better than it ever was in my pitiful dreams."

Hesitation filled her expression. He pushed her onto her back and settled on top of her. His erection slid along the wetness at the core of her body, a remnant of their shared pleasure, and he groaned with the beauty of it.

"Trust me, sweetheart." He dropped a kiss to her lips, savored her sweetness for an all too brief moment before levering himself off the bed. "We're gonna do this again soon."

Her eyes slid closed. He took advantage of her inattention to snag his shirt off the floor. In his rush to have her, he'd nearly exposed himself and the mark he carried on his back. She couldn't see it, could never know it was there.

"Is this one of those *wham bam thank you ma'ams*?"

"What? No." A choked laugh escaped his throat. "Geez, Indigo, where do you get this stuff?"

"That's what it feels like." She propped her head on an elbow and studied, her eyes cool pools of sapphire. "I'm not complaining. It was really good."

"Glad it met your approval."

She ignored his sarcasm with a quiet blink. "Great, even, but the last time I did this, I'm pretty sure there was more than two minutes of cuddling afterward."

"So you feel cheated, is that it?"

He crawled back to the bed, taking his shirt with him, and aligned their bodies. Goddess, he hated to leave her when her body was sated from their shared pleasure. He wanted her again with a greedy desperation that surprised him. Not tonight, though. Tonight, their first time, once was enough. Any more and it would hurt her.

Any more and she might see the *aenkanien*.

She shifted and rested a hand against his chest. "Yes, absolutely. Also, I'm trying to figure out why you're rushing out of here when we've barely started."

"Mom's expecting me home."

Her neck was too tempting a target to pass up. He dipped his head and licked, taking his time exploring her skin.

"Can't you, um... Do that again," she said when he nipped. "Can't you text her or something?"

"I could, but I'm not going to."

She tangled her fingers in his hair and tugged until he lifted his head. "You're really not staying the night."

"Nope," he said firmly, and hoped she didn't hear the regret or remember the erection he still sported.

She arched her hips and rubbed against him, and he sighed. She hadn't forgotten the erection.

"I can't believe this." She pushed him off and sat up, and he backed hastily away. "This is so not what I expected from you."

"Sorry," he said, and winced when she hit him, a full-blown punch in the shoulder.

"Don't you lie to me, Bobby Upton." Her voice hit him like a battering ram, beating at the guilt gnawing its way through him, degrees harder than her fist had been. "What's going on here?"

"Nothing. I just have to go."

He eased back again and she pounced, tackling him onto the bed. He fought her in a panic, deflecting her hands as gently as he could while she grappled with his limbs and tried to turn him over. Her hand slipped through his guard and grasped his penis in a firm grip. He stilled, careful not to shift suddenly. Her hand tightened, making his breath hitch.

"Indigo, be careful."

"Oh, I'm going to be careful, you weasel." She squeezed again and his breath whooshed out of his body with the pressure of her hand, somewhere between pleasure and pain. "I want to see your back."

Fear shot through him, as wild and desperate as his need for her. "No, baby. Please don't ask me to do that."

Her other hand latched onto his balls and her fingernails dug into his scrotum. "Turn over."

Her face had gone cold, expressionless, though her voice was choked with anger and hurt. He sat up slowly and, when she let go, gave her his back, exposing the tattoo he'd tried so hard to hide from her, and with it, yet another reason for her to run from him. He squeezed his eyes closed against the regret and the fear, and breathed a silent prayer to the Lady Goddess.

Please let Indigo forgive me.

The hope that She would hear his plea eluded him.

"Whose mark is it? No." Indigo's breath came in heavy, uneven pants and her hands fell away from him. "I don't want to know. Just tell me, Bobby. Tell me how you could have sex with me when you wear another woman's mark on your shoulder."

"Indi, honey, it's not like that."

"Don't call me that. Don't you dare call me that, not after we..."

Her voice quavered and broke, and with it, his heart.

"I got this the day I turned twenty-one." He shifted to face her and blanched at the tears on her cheeks. "Me and Hiro and Drew, we were home on leave and they got me drunk as a skunk. I'm not sure exactly what happened after that."

"You got married."

She said it the way other people would say, *Well, duh, you idjit,* but with a flat rancor he'd never heard from her.

"No, not exactly." He scooted closer, rubbed his forehead with shaky fingers when she cringed away. "I had this picture in my wallet, a drawing I made a long time ago when I was still young enough to believe I could have the woman of my dreams."

She curled her legs up and wrapped her arms around them, her wide sapphire gaze scrutinizing him as if he were a snake coiled to strike.

"Anyway, I guess I showed it to Hiro and Drew, probably told them where it was supposed to go. Next thing I know, I'm, er, getting sick outside a tattoo parlor with my shirt off and my back on fire."

Her tears had dried, though she held herself stiffly. "Whose mark is it?'

He breathed out a laugh. "How could you even ask?"

Her lips pressed into a thin slash across her pale face. "That tattoo is my mark, my *aenkanien?*"

He turned, putting his back to the light cast by the bedside lamp. "A dove in flight carrying an olive branch in its beak and two intertwined circles in its claws."

"It's beautiful." Her fingers touched him gently, softly tracing the intricate black line tattoo on his left shoulder blade. "Why didn't you tell me?"

"I didn't want you to feel obligated." At her sigh, he said, "It wasn't your fault that mark ended up on me. I couldn't make you take responsibility for it."

Her hand dropped away. "Who else knows about it?"

"My family." He stood and kept his back to her, ashamed to face her for the first time in his life. Of all the things he'd done to her, this was the worst. "No one knows whose mark it is, though."

Her bark of laughter held enough bitterness to have the shame curling into despair. "Your mother does."

He jerked around so quickly his head spun. "No. I never told her."

"Bobby, she knows."

"She'll never make you claim me."

"She doesn't have to." Indigo slid off the bed and stood next to him, her chill gaze steady and even and determined. "I claim you willingly."

"No." Cold anger washed over him, chased by fear. She would never love him if she were forced to take him as her mate, never, and eventually it would kill any kindness she held for him. He'd rather let her go than live with that. "Not like this."

"What else is there to be done?" She took the shirt gently from his hand. "We'll sort it out tomorrow, ok? I'll talk to your mother, pay the fines, and we'll work it out."

"So that's it, then. Bobby's made a mistake and you're gonna make it all better."

A puzzled frown crossed her face.

"What about the years I spent hacking my way through drug lords and terrorists and anyone else the Army threw in front of me, all the time I spent burning through the anger of your rejection by killing as many people as I could get my hands on?" He yanked her to him. "You gonna fix that, too?"

"Bobby, please." Indigo's eyes were round in a face that had gone pale. "I thought you'd want this."

"Oh, yeah, I want you," he ground out. "I want you so bad it hurts. It's hurt for a long, long time, Indigo."

Her hands came up, placating, seeking to gentle him as if he were a wild beast. "Bobby, please. Come to bed and we'll sort it out, I promise."

"Yes, let's do that." The fury dropped away in a rush, taking any softer emotion with it, leaving him as steely cold as the barrel of his gun. "Let's go to bed."

He rushed her, capturing her in a quick grab, and threw her onto the bed, following her as she scrambled back.

"What are you doing, Bobby?"

"Living up to my nickname."

He grabbed her foot and brought the inside of her ankle to his lips, licking the salty sweetness of her silky skin into his mouth.

"I don't understand," she said. "Can't we just talk about it?"

She tugged at her foot and he nipped at her skin, not enough to hurt, only enough to keep her still.

"Oh, but we are. Don't you want to know what you're in for?" He licked up her leg and when she squirmed, he grabbed her other ankle and held it against the mattress with a hard grip. "Don't you want to know what kind of man you're taking on?"

"I know what kind of man you are, Bobby."

He licked into the crevice of her knee. Primal satisfaction ripped through him when her breath hitched and her fingers curled into the bedspread. "Do you, Indigo?" He ran his hands up her shins and pinned her legs down just below her knees. "I was very effective at what I did."

"I know that's why you were called the Enforcer." Her muscles trembled when he sucked the tender skin of her inner thigh, scraped his teeth there. "That was a long time ago."

"What was it you said about the past clinging to the present?"

He braced his hands along the outside of her thighs, pressed butterfly kisses to her stomach, licked gently into her navel. She sucked in a breath and brought her hands up, cradling his head against her abdomen.

"You have to let go of the past sometime, Bobby."

"Not today. Today, I'm teaching you a lesson."

"What..." She moaned when he raked his tongue across her nipple. "What lesson?"

"The Enforcer is not to be trifled with." He captured her nipple in his mouth and suckled until her eyes fluttered closed and her head fell back. Her skin tasted like the sweetest nectar as it hit his tongue. He laved the velvet of her nipple over and over again, willing her to *feel*, willing her to *need*. "Tell me no, Indigo."

"Um." She cleared her throat, rolled her head against the pillow. "What am I saying no to again?"

He stifled the laugh that rose over his anger, washing him clean with its goodness. Goddess, she was cute when she was lost in passion.

"Sex. Tell me you don't want me." He rose over her and prodded the core of her body with the tip of his erection. It was all he could do to hold back, to keep from slipping into that tight, wet heat. "Tell me to stop and I will."

Her eyes popped open and she gaped. "You want me to turn you down now? Are you crazy? If you stop now, I'll kill you."

He hooked an elbow under one of her knees and pressed it against her chest as he surged up into her, burying himself in her heat in one smooth stroke. His own muscles trembled with the need to stay there, to love her until the pleasure lifted them high and her heart cried out for him. "Be certain," he gritted out.

Her hands cupped his face and her eyes softened. "Don't make me beg."

"Hook your leg around my back," he said, and when she did, he pushed into her with sharp, hard thrusts of his hips. Her eyes drifted closed and her hands gripped his shoulders so fiercely, his blood welled up under her fingertips. He welcomed the pleasure-pain and used it to focus, to hold his body in check even as she gasped and arched against him and her sweet little pussy rippled around his erection in a frenzied release.

He pulled out of her, stopping the build of his own release as her hands slid limply off his shoulders.

"Holy Mother." A secretive smile tilted her lips upward. "Remind me to make you mad again tomorrow night."

He huffed out a half-laugh. "I'm not finished yet."

She lifted her head and raked a gaze down his body. "Bobby," she said, and fell back onto the bed with a lusty sigh.

He captured her hands and pinned them above her head with one hand. Her body was slick and pink from their play, and he'd left too much of it unexplored. She shifted under him, rubbing her hardened nipples across his chest. They were round and firm and begging, and he couldn't deny them a minute longer.

He licked across her skin, tasted sweat and woman and sex. The heat in his body skyrocketed to an unbearable level at the little whimpers she made deep in her throat. He let go of her hands and flipped her over, pressed open mouthed kisses down the hollow of her spine, exploring her slowly, filling in the long years of yearning. All that time, dreaming of how she would feel under him, imagining the way she would move and sound, the way she would beg for him. Those piddling hopes had never come close to the reality of holding her, of joining with her so intimately, they became one.

He built her passion one trembling sigh at a time, savoring every inch of her until she clutched the covers in her hands and squirmed beneath his mouth. His control broke when she arched her bottom up, offering herself for him. He knelt between her legs and urged her onto her knees with her head cradled in her arms and her back sloped downward, thrusting her lush bottom into the air, and drove into the slick clasp of her core. *Sweet Mother, yes.* This is what he'd waited for, this moment when she was his, only and ever his. He'd never let her go again, not until the last breath left his body.

She moaned and pushed back against him with each thrust and he fell into her, lost as his heart thudded and his muscles tightened and she drew him in, welcoming his touch as desire built to a fevered pitch. He pounded into her until she came and called out his name, and her body clamped down on his, pulsing and fluttering, pushing him past desire into release. He gentled his thrusts as it went on and on, spilling his seed into her until he had nothing left to give.

TEN

INDIGO STRUGGLED to catch her breath, to bring her body down after the seeing to Bobby had given her. When he'd pulled out of her after that marvelous display, they'd fallen to the bed with him spooned behind her, their sweat slicked bodies sliding until they fit together, just so.

He'd lashed out, trying to scare her into backing off maybe, and given her a telling glimpse into the man hidden beneath the carefree, fun-loving veneer.

She'd reveled in the sting of his teeth on her skin, the force of his thrusts, the throb of his release. Never before had a man taken her like that, like he couldn't live another minute without being inside her.

And he'd been right. Bobby Upton was not a man with which one trifled. Lesson learned.

Giddiness swept over her and she laughed to herself until her body shook.

"Shh." Bobby spooned against her and stroked her hair. "It's ok."

She shook her head. No, it was not ok. It was wonderful, fabulous. Absolutely exhilarating.

She couldn't wait to do it again.

His arms tightened around her, pulling her flush into his sweat soaked nudity. "I'm so sorry. Do you want me to leave?"

She blinked and rolled over. His face was pale under his tan, his expression pinched and full of regret, like he'd committed the most horrible of sins.

"Why would I want that?" she said, honestly baffled.

"I hurt you." He dropped a kiss to her forehead and pulled away. "Let me get something to clean you up."

She grabbed his arm. "Wait. It's not like that. I mean, yes, you hurt me, but not..." She blew a breath out. "It's a good kind of hurt."

How could she explain the fullness in her body, the delicious tenderness between her legs, and the power of knowing that he wanted her, fierce and rough and hard and urgently, as no man had ever wanted her before? That having him bear her mark made it all the more beautiful and real?

"Hurt is hurt," he said with a skeptical look.

"Not this time." She sat up and held out her hand, waiting patiently until he took it. "I want to tell you something."

He curled around her, rubbing her nose with his in a gesture so tender it took her breath. "What?"

"I don't care what happened in the past."

He stilled in mid-rub and his eyelids slid shut. "I don't want to talk about that."

"No, listen." She grabbed his arm, holding him in place. "What you did after, well, after that day, the things you did in the Army, I don't care about that. It doesn't change what's between us."

"Indi, baby. You don't know what I did back then, all the people I hurt, all the..." He swallowed hard and nuzzled his face into the crook of her shoulder. "Don't tell me it doesn't matter."

"It doesn't," she insisted. "If you can't let it go..."

"Who says I haven't?"

She gave him the look that comment deserved. "Do you love me?"

His gentle laughter feathered across her skin, chilling her, arousing her. "You have no idea how much."

"And after all this time," she murmured. She'd always heard that once a Son gave his heart, it was no longer his. Could it possibly be true? Hope fluttered in her stomach, as jittery as nerves and twice as elusive. "Let it go, for me. Let the past not come between us anymore."

He held himself still against her for long moments, his muscles clenched, his breath a gentle brush across her throat. At last, he said, "I'll try. I swear to you, Indi, I'll try."

She exhaled the breath she hadn't known she held. It would have to be enough. "Share a shower with me?"

He drew back, studying her as desire pushed the worry out of his expression. "Are you sure I didn't hurt you?"

"Not the way you mean."

He shook his head as she led him into her bathroom, reveling in the soft smile playing around his mouth, the sheer beauty of his perfectly muscled form. As the water warmed and the tiny room filled with steam, she ran his fingers through hers, marveling at the rough callouses, so different from the tender warmth of his gaze.

"You're doing it again," he said.

"What?"

"Biting your lip." He dipped his head and licked at the corner of her mouth, catching her teeth. "Keep doing that, sweetheart, and I'll keep pleasuring you, as long as you want me to."

She laughed softly and pulled him into the shower's warm spray. Bobby posed her with her hands against the shower wall and her legs spread wide, and washed her in gentle strokes, murmuring softly to her as he ran his hands down the column of her neck and the curve of her spine; over the roundness of her bottom and into the sensitive creases beneath it; down the backs of her legs and up again, sliding over her stomach to cup her breasts and knead them; into and around every inch of her body in a slow, torturous route. Her heart thumped in her chest and her breath caught in her throat and her muscles trembled under the heat of his calloused touch.

He eased her beneath the spray, rinsed her skin off, and tilted her head back to wash her hair, rubbing her scalp with the pads of his fingertips until she tingled. By the time he finished, she was trapped somewhere between gentle need and bone deep relaxation.

"You give awesome showers," she said.

He laughed and rubbed soap across his chest. "I've always wanted to do that."

"Mmm." She leaned against the wall of the shower and trailed a finger through the soap bubbles on his chest, tracing the letters of her name, branding him in this small way as hers. "Can I do that to you?"

"Not unless you want to have sex again."

"I'd love to, but I think we probably need to talk." Still, she couldn't resist running her finger in slow spirals around his nipple. "Plus, I'm a little sore."

His eyebrows snapped together as he put the soap away. "I knew I hurt you."

"Only a little and it was good."

"You're sure?"

She gave a half laugh. "Any better and I would've melted into a puddle on the bed."

After toweling each other off, Bobby helped her dry her hair, using her blow dryer set to low and her brush to comb through the long strands, soothing her.

"Are you sure you've never done this before?" she said.

"Only in my mind." He put the dryer and brush away, and rested his hands on her bare hips, stroking the skin tenderly. "My sisters never trusted me with their hair."

"Their loss," she said, and he grinned. "Do you still need to leave?"

"Mom's expecting me." He rubbed a hand across his hair, brushing out some of the water lingering from their shower. "I can text her, let her know I'm not gonna make it home tonight."

She peered at him over her shoulder. So, his earlier excuse for leaving had really been about hiding the *aenkanien* from her. "Remember when you told me not to lie to you?"

He wrapped his arms around her, propped his chin on the top of her head. "Yeah."

"Ditto."

"That wasn't a lie, exactly."

"Close enough."

She took his hand and led him to the bedroom, and hesitated yet again, uncertain over dressing for bed or not, over where they would each sleep or how. Would she ever learn to be comfortable with this intimacy?

"Do you want to talk about it tomorrow?" He picked up the watch he'd laid on her nightstand before their shower and checked it with a slight frown. "It's getting pretty late."

She couldn't talk to him while she was stark naked. It sent her mind down too many dangerous paths. Bobby working his way up her body with nips and licks and knowing touches. Bobby filling her with his hard length and sending her over the moon again and again. She shivered as need stirred in her nethers. A nightshirt it was. She walked to the chest of drawers and rummaged for one. "I want to see your mother first thing in the morning."

"You don't have to do that." He sat on the edge of the bed and watched her pull the shirt on, his eyes following the quick stretches and jiggles she made as she shrugged it on. "I told you. There's no obligation here."

"Yes, there is." She flipped her hair out of the neckline of the shirt and sat down beside him, taking his hand into her own, his rough touch comforting in a way she could never explain. "It's not just about duty, Bobby. I'm a hundred and sixty two years old, well past the age for a Daughter to have her first child."

His breath shallowed. "You want to have my baby?"

"Yes." He looked so vulnerable, so insecure. She leaned forward and placed a gentle kiss on his mouth. "You'll be a good father."

"You don't have to claim me to have that."

"No, but since you already bear my mark, it seems like the sensible thing to do."

And she wanted it, so very much, to wake next to him each morning, to feel him move within her each day, to bring him pleasure. To feel special, needed, and to make a difference in someone else's life.

His expression shifted, as if he were waging an internal war. "Why me?"

"Because you're kind and sweet and funny." She kissed him again, let her lips cling to his for a moment. "Because you make me feel like I'm the most beautiful woman in the world."

"You are." He wrapped a hand around the nape of her neck and touched his forehead to hers. "Like a flesh and blood cross between Snow White and Wonder Woman."

A giggle bubbled over and she fell back against the bed, taking him with her. "Really? Wow." She traced a hand over his shoulder, marveling at the way his body was put together. "I can't decide if I'm flattered or not."

"Be flattered," he said firmly. He slipped his hand under her shirt and stroked the backs of his fingers along her stomach. "Are you sure about this?"

"I've never been more certain of anything."

That much was true. The number of things she was sure of at any one time wouldn't take two hands of fingers to count. The decision to take Bobby as her mate was easily the most certain thing in her life, though she refused to dwell too heavily on the whys.

"I want to live with you." His fingers moved up into longer strokes down her abdomen. "If you want me to."

"I do. We can find a house later, if you want."

"I've already got the furniture built," he said with an easy grin. "We'll need a big yard with room for a garden and a swing set."

She arched an eyebrow. "Planning ahead?"

"Since I was fifteen. I know this place near Tellowee."

So much had changed the second time Bobby walked into her life. A few weeks ago, knowing that he'd wanted her since he was little more than a child would've sent her running scared. Now, she wanted to make a life with him.

Of course, now he was a grown man.

She ran a hand over his *aenkanien* and a secret thrill shivered down her spine. He was hers now, only hers. She would find a way to make it work. "Your mother has to agree to the claiming first, and she might not. She may be offended at my treatment of her precious son."

"She knows you had nothing to do with the *aenkanien*."

"Mmm. Well, we'll see."

Bobby took a minute to text his mother, and Indigo didn't rag him. Even in these relatively safe times, the People lived in the shadow of danger. Sons and Daughters alike were still hunted and harmed on a regular basis. No need to worry Rebecca unnecessarily with those fears.

Indigo flipped off the lamp and scooted under the covers next to Bobby, and drifted into sleep as he cradled her through the long, autumn night.

INDIA SLIPPED through the balcony doors into Hiro's apartment and placed her gear in a neat pile to the side. In the light shining dimly through the glass, she could barely make out his sleeping form. It was late and she shouldn't have come. Still, it wasn't the first time she'd slid into his bed in the middle of the night, and it probably wouldn't be the last.

The hospital had been quiet when she'd snuck into the nursery to see her new siblings, the favored son and another girl. She'd stood over them as they slept, watching them as a good sister should, and her chest had tightened with unaccustomed emotion. Tenderness at the miracle of their birth. Love that they hadn't earned and wouldn't appreciate for years, if ever. And a sweet longing to have a child of her own.

Her mother must be happy.

India unlaced her boots in jerks and tugs, set them beside her gear, and yanked her leathers off as a storm of conflicting emotions raked at her. Frustration, bitterness, anger. They rolled over her, pushing out the softness, leaving her heart hard and cold.

She padded across the room on silent feet and eased into the bed next to Hiro.

He stirred, shifted, and his hand snaked under his pillow.

"It's me," she said softly, so he wouldn't pull out the knife he slept with. She wanted a fight, not a massacre.

"Mmph." He reached for her and she went willingly, letting his warmth seep into her. His hand made small circles on her back, drifting down until he cupped her bottom. "You're naked."

"I am." She rested a hand on his chest and draped a leg over his hip. "Is that a problem?"

"No. Mmm." He yawned and pulled her closer. "Let me wake up."

She kissed him instead, trying to be gentle for some reason that was beyond her when all she wanted to do was bite and punch and kick. He inhaled sharply and groaned when she nipped at his lips, maybe a little harder than she should've.

"You're in a mood." His hand squeezed her bottom. "What's wrong?"

"Mámá had her babies."

"So you snuck into my apartment and crawled naked into my bed?" he murmured sleepily.

She bit back her first smart remark and said, in the most reasonable tone she could manage, "You left the door unlocked."

He yawned again and rubbed his face against hers. "Knew you'd be back."

His comment stung, though she couldn't have said why. "I shouldn't have come."

"Wait, no. God, you're sensitive."

She reared back, not just stung but hurt. Tears popped into her eyes as her heart ached and withered. Damned if she'd let him see them.

She rolled out of his grasp and slid from the bed. The covers rustled behind her and she sensed more than heard him draw closer, following her across the room. His hand fell onto her shoulder and she shoved it away.

"What's gotten into you?" His voice was a hard, impatient rake across her raw nerves. "Jesus, India. Any other woman would be happy I left the damn door open for her."

"I'm not any other woman." She snatched her shirt from the pile on the floor. "Guess you didn't notice."

"Oh, yeah, I noticed all right." His hand snuck out, quicker than she could follow, and snatched the shirt from her hand. "If I noticed any harder, everybody else would, too."

She reached for her shirt and let out a frustrated growl when he held it out of her reach. "Give me my shirt."

"Not until you calm down." He backed up a step. "You go out there angry and you're liable to fall."

"I'm as likely to fall as you are to lose your dick." She grabbed at her shirt and stifled a scream when he held it away from her. "What is this, kindergarten? Give me my shirt and I'll get out of your hair."

"Is that what this is about?"

He dropped the shirt and lunged for her. She evaded narrowly and swung her arm out, hitting his forearms in a sweeping blow, knocking his hands to the side.

A smile flashed across his face, part satisfaction, part danger, and then he came at her, hard and fast, his hands quick and sure. She fought back, blocking and weaving, allowing him to learn her defenses while she studied his offense.

They circled around the room exchanging swift blows that flew out like lightning. The third time his strike snuck past her guard and nipped at her, barely grazing her hip, her temper flared. He was toying with her. She wanted a fight.

Her next blow caught him in the ribs, hard enough to bruise, not hard enough to break a bone. He stepped away from her, dropped his hands, and studied her, his expression flat and unemotional.

She stiffened under the discomfiting weight of his stare. "What?"

"You don't know how to play, do you?"

She'd disappointed him. Her breath shallowed in her lungs and her head went light. She shrugged, trying to throw the odd feel of it off. "Life is a struggle, not a playground. Either you win or you lose. There's nothing in between."

"India." He shook his head, snagged her shirt, and held it out for her. "Sometimes I feel sorry for you."

She sucked in a breath at the ache that sprang up in her gut. She could take a lot from him, but not his pity.

And she wanted so much more.

But there he was, watching her with an unnerving steadiness, holding her shirt out. Why didn't he just say it, just tell her to leave? Why did he have to be so gentle about it?

She dug her fingernails into the palms of her hands until the urge to apologize passed. She wouldn't beg. Men were a dime a dozen. Another one could be in her bed before the sun rose, if she wanted.

She didn't, but that wasn't the point. She could have anyone. Somehow, though, the only man she wanted was the one who stood in front of her, telling her to go without saying a word.

She reached out to snatch her shirt away and he grabbed her wrist and twisted, bringing it up and back, using it as leverage to push her face first onto the bed. He pinned her wrist to her lower back and followed her down, straddling her thighs with his own. She bucked and wiggled trying to unseat him, and he smacked her bare bottom hard, stopping her cold.

"Now that I'm awake," he said, "let's talk."

Her arm ached where he'd jerked her around and her bottom stung. She wiggled again, trying to break free, and he smacked the other cheek, a sharp blow that sent pleasant tingles radiating through her. Her muscles tightened and heat pooled between her legs. She buried her face in the bed, stifling a moan.

"Don't do that," he said in a voice as sharp as the blow he'd landed.

"What?" She kept her face buried so that her voice was muffled by the comforter. "I stopped fighting."

"Hunh. Right." His hand dropped onto her bottom over the area he'd smacked and rubbed gently. "Don't hold back your response. If you're turned on, let it out."

"I'm not."

Of course, she was. Worse, she wanted him to do it again.

"And now you're lying." His hand squeezed her bottom. "If I let your arm go, will you promise to be good?"

"Define good," she hedged.

"No more fighting."

She could stand the pain, and would have, if the fight hadn't drained out of her. "Ok."

He held her arm for long moments before releasing her. She pushed halfway up, swung her arm around gently, and prodded her shoulder, checking for damage.

"Here, let me."

He braced a hand beside her head on the bed, using the other to push her hand out of the way and rub the sore muscle. She crossed her forearms and dropped her head onto them, and sighed as his fingers dug into her skin, kneading the tension away.

"Feel good?"

"Mmm." She sighed again, a deep cleansing breath, and closed her eyes. His hand shifted to her neck with firm strokes, teasing a moan from her. "You don't have to do that."

"I want to." He shifted behind her, brushing his body against her back, and pressed his mouth where his hand had been. "If I didn't, I wouldn't keep leaving the door unlocked, which any other woman would know."

His tongue darted out, rasping across the skin of her spine, and she lost track of the conversation.

"I love your skin." His breath blew across the damp spot his tongue had left behind, and she shivered. "Soft and sweet. A little salty."

410

He licked again, lower down, then lower and lower, touching his tongue to the skin above each of her vertebrae in turn, and working his way back up with butterfly kisses. She grasped the comforter, wrinkling it in her fists, and bit her tongue to hold back the fire, to contain it and keep it from spilling out of her.

His teeth sank into the skin at the juncture of her neck and shoulder, hard enough to pull an involuntary moan from her. He pressed an open mouthed kiss to the spot and sucked lightly, and her muscles quivered with need. What was it about this man that left her weak and aching, desperate for more of anything he would give, yearning to give him something in return?

He pulled back and she shivered from the loss of his body heat. "Under the covers," he said.

She pushed up from the bed with trembling muscles and, for the first time in her life, didn't curse the weakness. He'd made her this way, made her feel something other than fury and anger and frustration, and it was good. She crawled under the covers, turned on her side, and watched him strip his underwear off, drinking in his perfectly formed beauty.

He crawled into bed beside her and draped a hand on her hip, his expression in shadows. "I want you to stop coming up from outside."

Desire drained abruptly from her. She closed her eyes and turned over, away from him, suddenly so tired it hurt.

"Could I sleep here tonight? Just for a little while." Her voice broke. She swallowed to clear it and didn't even notice the tears. "I won't come back, if I can just..." *Have a little longer,* she thought, but couldn't bring herself to say it.

"Shh. Hey." He scooted up behind her and spooned her. "I meant I want you to come up the stairs like normal people do. You can use the spare key card."

She breathed out a relieved laugh. "I knew that."

"Sure you did. That's why you're crying." He brushed his face against her hair. "I never thought I'd see that from you. Maybe a roundhouse kick or a punch to the mouth, but not tears."

"Gimme a break." She peered at him over her shoulder, catching his dark gaze in the shadows. His eyes glittered in his narrow face. Even she could see the concern etched there. "It's been a rough day."

"You want to talk about it?"

She shook her head. "That's not why I came here."

"Why did you come here?"

"You know why," she said softly.

"You could've had that any of the, what, dozen or so times you've dropped by, before, during, or after our Godzilla marathons. Preferably all three." His hand stroked her hip, soothing her. "Why now?"

Because she'd reacted instead of thinking, like she always did when her temper was high. Because she ached for him and needed him, and knew it, deep down where she never looked, in the part of her heart that craved a soft touch and a gentle voice and an end to the constant bitterness.

Not that she'd ever admit it, not to his face, especially not the part about needing him.

"When I saw the babies, it just, I don't know, made me want more. Maybe I'm tired of being alone."

"I can cure the alone part," he said. "But we should probably hold off on the babies until after the second date."

She gaped at him, saw the mischief in his eyes, and laughed, letting it roll over her until her stomach muscles hurt with the goodness of it. "Thank you," she said when her laughter died off, leaving only a pleasant warmth behind.

"For what?"

"For letting me stay."

His features tightened and her breath caught at the passion gathering there.

"I wouldn't have it any other way," he said, and kissed her like he meant it.

ELEVEN

OBBY WOKE INDIGO before he left for work, while the sun was still skimming under the mountains on its way into the sky. She mumbled and shifted in the bed, and winced when she moved her legs.

He wanted to ease the soreness with his mouth on her skin, and would when the sun finished its journey for the day. He settled for teasing kisses along her neck when she turned her face away from his, and laughed when she pulled a pillow over her head and snuggled into it.

His lover wasn't a morning person. Who knew?

He let himself out of her apartment, pulling the locked door shut behind him, and jogged down the stairs as quietly as he could. The pre-dawn air chilled his skin through his thin jacket. Time to pull out the winter one.

His truck started on the first try and he let his mind wander while it warmed up.

He could grab enough clothes to last him through the week when he went home to change before going to work.

Maybe Mom would've already left for the IECS by then.

He checked his watch and huffed out a breath that fogged in the cool air. Nope. She'd still be in the middle of her workout when he got home.

Not home anymore, though. Satisfaction filled him, followed quickly by a sharp worry. Indigo was ready to claim him, but how long would that last when she hadn't submitted to him and become mortal?

Probably not long. He'd heard the stories of immortal Daughters who settled down with lovers. It hardly ever ended well, no matter what emotions were involved. Inevitably, the man aged while the Daughter didn't, and things got ugly when one of them wanted to move on.

He couldn't imagine ever wanting to leave Indigo behind, though it wasn't much of a stretch to imagine the opposite.

She'd run from him once, devastating his young heart. A second time would kill him.

He worried over it during the short drive between Indigo's apartment and his parents' home. If he could find a way to make her love him...

No. He of all people knew love couldn't be forced. Hadn't he learned that the hard way?

But they were friends and she cared for him, and his past didn't seem to bother her nearly as much as it bothered him. Those were good places to start.

His optimism lasted until he eased his way into the back door and saw his mother sitting at the kitchen table, drinking a cup of coffee.

Well, damn.

Resigned to the inevitable, he poured himself a cup and sat down across from her, facing her without any shame, though he felt like a kid sneaking in past curfew after a night of hell raising that ended up in the morning paper.

"Good morning, Bobby."

Her voice was light and even, her gaze sharp, and he was suddenly glad he was wearing a collared shirt. He was pretty sure there was nothing to see. Indigo wasn't a kid to leave those kinds of marks and neither was he.

"Morning, Mom. Dad not up yet?"

"He's sleeping in today." She set her cup into its saucer with the barest clink. "He has a doctor's appointment later."

"I can take him," he offered.

"He informed me last night that he would drive himself." Her smile was gentle. "This new medicine has given him back a good deal of his independence."

"That's good." Bobby sipped his coffee, stifled a curse when it scalded his tongue. "Tell him to call if he needs me."

"I shall." She folded her hands on the table. "Thank you for texting me last night. I know you're a grown man and you're free to come and go as you please, but I worry."

"I know." He put his mug down, reached across the table, and grasped her folded hands, chafing gently. "I'm sorry."

"Don't be." She unfolded her hands to hold his. "I knew this day would come. I'm trying to be happy for you."

"You know how I feel about Indigo."

"I do." Her hands tightened on his and her lower lip trembled once before she pressed her lips tightly together. "I've known since you were just a boy that she would capture your heart and I would lose you to her."

"No, Mom, don't think that." He scooted forward and clasped both her hands in his. "Geez. You women with your crazy notions."

She laughed, a short sound that carried as much heartache as it did joy. "Even when you tried for her, I knew you were mine. While you were gone in the Army and out building your company. All that time, you were my little boy, right up until the moment you walked through that door and sat down across from me like the man you've become. I'm going to miss you so much."

"Mom." He huffed out a laugh. "I'm moving ten minutes away. You'll hardly know I'm gone."

"It's not the same." She sniffed and patted his hands. "I assume you want my blessing, and your father's."

"Of course, I do."

"But you'll do what you want, regardless of what I think," she said in the cool voice she reserved for adversaries, or people who'd pissed her off.

He met her steely look with his own. "As you said. I'm a man, not a child."

A flash of pride crossed her face and was quickly replaced by the hard mask of a warrior. "If she breaks your heart again, I'll have to deal with her."

"As the law allows, but only that." He picked up his mug, sipped the strong brew. "Even if she hurts me, I'm duty bound to protect her."

"And you know your duty well," she murmured.

"I'm my mother's son."

She acknowledged that with a cool nod. "Yes, you are."

"She's going to come talk to you today." He tapped his thumb against the rim of his mug. "Don't penalize her too harshly."

"You've borne her mark for years, Bobby, years when she forsook you."

"That's not fair and you know it. She only learned about the *aenkanien* last night. The decision to put it there wasn't hers."

"Still, the law is the law and I have my own duties to consider. I won't have you cast aside penniless when she's finished with you."

He hunched his shoulders, uncomfortably reminded of his earlier thoughts. "I can take care of myself."

"That's not the point. She has a financial obligation to you in the eyes of the People." She compressed her lips into a thin line. "The care of a Son who's been claimed is one of our most sacred laws."

"Just keep in mind that I'd like to have children before I'm too old to enjoy them."

Her lips curled into a smile and held such cunning, apprehension stole up his spine. "Don't worry, dear. I'll make certain you have those children."

"Mom," he warned. "Don't meddle."

Her eyes widened innocently. "I would never meddle."

"Yes, you would. Try to be good, ok? When she becomes my wife, she becomes your daughter."

"I know. She'll be a good daughter." Her smile softened and a gleam entered her eyes. "But I should be allowed a little fun, shouldn't I?"

He groaned. His mother having fun wasn't necessarily a good thing.

He checked his watch and grimaced. "I've got to get to work."

"Do you want some breakfast before you go?"

"Thanks, no. I'll catch some on the way in." He stood and dropped a kiss to her forehead, carried his coffee mug to the sink and rinsed it out. "I'm moving into Indigo's apartment tonight."

"So soon?" She rose and brought her cup to the sink. "Don't you want to wait until after a formal ceremony?"

He coughed to hide a laugh. "Ah, we've already consummated our relationship."

She blinked. "I don't like to think about you doing those things."

"You know I've had sex before," he said, and grinned when she gave a mock shudder.

"My son is as pure as the driven snow."

"If it makes you happy to think that, who am I to argue?"

He touched his forehead to hers, then raced up the stairs to shower, change, and pack enough clothes to last the rest of the week. His mother was waiting for him when he came down. She opened her arms and held him tight, and sent him off with a kiss and a look that said she had a special kind of fun in mind for Indigo.

He started his truck and rolled the worry around in his mind. Sooner or later, Indigo would have to learn to deal with his mother. She was woman enough to do it or he would never have fallen for her in the first place. Still, the worry lingered as he drove to work and spent the day trying to focus on running a business instead of on the upcoming meeting between the two women he loved best.

HOURS LATER, Indigo sat on an overstuffed love seat in the waiting area of Rebecca Upton's office at the IECS. She smoothed a hand over the bun she'd twisted her hair into, touched icy fingers to the pearls draped around her neck, and nearly jittered out of her skin in her nervousness.

Claiming Bobby wasn't the problem. That morning, she'd awakened to find him gone with only a vague, lingering memory of his goodbye kiss. In the cold light of day, she'd taken the time to consider the matter without lust clouding her mind and discovered a keen yearning to make Bobby hers in the eyes of the People.

To do so, she would have to seek his mother's approval. There was no way around it. The People's traditions blended and melded as societies changed and grew, but some things remained sacrosanct. A Son was not forsaken. There was no wiggle room there, not in their laws and not in her mind. Her duty was clear. Bobby must be claimed, regardless of the circumstances surrounding the *aenkanien* he bore.

It wasn't solely duty that drove her. She acknowledged that and then ignored it. Better to leave it alone until she could ponder the ramifications of her inner motivations.

"The director will see you now, Ms. Dupree," the receptionist said.

Indigo rose and took a deep breath before straightening the black business suit she wore. It was her least favorite outfit, but a necessity. Bobby's mother was a powerful woman. One did not face her without being well-groomed and ruthlessly prepared.

She gripped the handle of her briefcase and marched across the reception area, turned the handle of the door leading to the director's office, and entered.

It was a large room, well-appointed with a graceful Queen Anne style desk at the back and a small sitting area to the front, off to one side. Hand-woven rugs decorated the hardwood floor. Books and memorabilia rested in shelving on either side of the door. From the corner of her eye, Indigo caught a glimpse of the director's primary weapon, a sword that was thankfully still encased behind protective glass.

Negotiations such as these had gotten violent in the past. Hopefully, this one wouldn't.

Rebecca rose gracefully from behind her desk and walked around it. Her carnelian red suit hugged her figure, highlighting the power of her form and position. "Indigo. Thank you for coming by," she said, as if the meeting had been her idea instead of Indigo's.

Indigo bowed slightly. "Director."

"Rebecca. I insist."

"Of course."

Rebecca's eyes held a craftiness that sent a niggle of worry through Indigo, in spite of the accompanying smile.

"Won't you have a seat?" Rebecca held her hand out toward the sitting area. "I think we'll be more comfortable here, don't you?"

Indigo's heart stuttered in her chest. What was Bobby's mother up to? She perched carefully on the edge of a plush chair and set her briefcase on the floor beside it.

Rebecca sat down on the settee, resting comfortably against the cushions. "How's your mother?"

"She's doing well, thank you. The delivery was normal and she's recovering quickly."

"And your siblings?"

"The babies are fine." Indigo softened automatically at the thought of the babies, then pulled the emotion back, certain the director was about to strike. "They and Mámá should be able to go home tomorrow."

Rebecca folded her hands in her lap, her face a polite mask. "How is India?"

And there was the hit, a subtle reminder of Indigo's connection with a rogue element of the People. *Damn. Should've seen that one coming.* "I haven't seen her in some weeks, but I assume she's doing well."

"When you do see her, please tell her I'd like to have a word with her."

If she wanted to see India, the director would have to get in line, right behind Indigo. "As you wish."

"I understand your work at the Sandby borg site is complete. Have you decided to settle here in Tellowee permanently or will you be moving to another job soon?"

Indigo struggled to keep her expression neutral, her muscles relaxed. *Should've seen that one coming, too.* "I expect my stay in Tellowee will be long-term, considering my relationship with your son."

A flicker of amusement flashed across Rebecca's face. "Oh?"

Why had she bothered to be polite? "In fact, he's the reason I'm here."

"I'm aware." The politely amused expression never wavered. "I wonder, though, how a woman of your means and stature could possibly have the temerity to ask for my son."

Shit.

Indigo clenched her hands reflexively and nearly groaned at the mistake. *Never show weakness in front of the Blade.* It was the number one rule when dealing with a Daughter as old and powerful as Rebecca Upton.

"I assure you, Director, my means are more than adequate to care for a Son of Bobby's standing." She reached for her briefcase, pulling it onto her lap. "I have extensive documentation of my financial status, including investments and real estate holdings."

"Leave it," Rebecca said in a hard voice.

Indigo slid the briefcase onto the floor, her hope for a peaceful settlement sinking with it.

"I'm much more concerned with the matter of your abandoning him, first at sixteen when he tried for you, and then at twenty-one when he took your *aenkanien*."

"In my defense, Director, Bobby was my student when he was sixteen. It would have been unethical for me to accept his suit." Sweat pooled under Indigo's breasts and her heart fluttered against her ribs. "As for the *aenkanien*, I only learned of it last night."

"The law is the law." Rebecca pinned Indigo with an unforgiving stare. "As his mother, I have the right to seek Retribution before the Council."

Indigo's eyelids slid closed and the blood rushed from her head, leaving her dizzy. This was her greatest fear, that Rebecca would invoke the old ways of physical punishment and eschew the newer fine system. The penalties were great either way, but the fines were a relatively small matter for most Daughters, especially older ones who'd had time to accumulate wealth of one sort or another.

Physical Retribution, on the other hand, usually involved flogging the skin from the offending Daughter's back. Indigo had seen it done once, as a child, to a Daughter who had forsaken an abusive Son. It had taken weeks for the skin to grow back and years, she'd heard, for the scars to fade completely.

She'd felt the sting of the lash before. Her body jerked involuntarily at the memory. Such a punishment wouldn't kill her, but it would hurt for a long, long time and brand her as a pariah.

Bobby would be lost to her forever.

She opened her eyes. Rebecca's lips had curled into a smile that held the faintest hint of triumph.

"What Retribution will you seek?"

"Since my son is fond of your skin, I shall forego the right of Retribution through the Council and ask for a monetary penalty instead."

Indigo held in her sigh of relief. "Thank you, Director."

"Rebecca. Twenty five thousand dollars per year of your neglect, with interest retroactive from the date of the *aenkanien*, as well as five thousand dollars per year from the date of his suit to the time of the mark's application, without interest. You will put this money into a trust for the benefit of any children from your union, to revert to Bobby should your union fail or if there are no legal issue."

Indigo sat back in the chair, nonplussed. That was far less than she'd anticipated, all things given, and actually quite reasonable, given Bobby's status. "Of course."

"When will you next ovulate?"

"I fail to see..."

"Do not test my patience, child," Rebecca said. "When will you ovulate?"

Indigo clamped her teeth together. "By spring."

"Good. If you conceive a child by my son within the next two years and bear it within three, I shall waive the penalty for refusing his initial suit." Rebecca folded her hands in her lap. Indigo tensed, preparing for another strike. "If you have two children within that time, I shall match the amount of your penalty from my own coffers, to be paid into the trust."

Indigo compressed her lips together, hiding her astonishment. "That's very generous."

And the requirement of children aligned neatly with Indigo's own goals, which couldn't be a coincidence. Somehow, Rebecca was two steps ahead, while Indigo was still trying to figure out which game they were playing.

"I want my son to be happy."

"He will want for nothing."

"That's not the same thing as being happy." Rebecca leaned forward and laid a hand on Indigo's arm. "Is there any chance you could love him?"

"I care for him," Indigo said carefully. "He's a good man and treats me well. If I were to love anyone, it would be him."

Rebecca considered her, searching for something in Indigo's expression. After a moment, she squeezed Indigo's arm and sat back. "His father and I wish to pay the Son's gift."

Indigo relaxed for the first time since entering the building. "That won't be necessary."

"Oh?"

"Bobby has paid it himself, in furniture for our home."

"Ah." Rebecca smile held genuine amusement. "Still, we would like to contribute."

"Bobby is contribution enough." Indigo shifted in the chair. "If you wish to contribute beyond that, I'll leave it to him to negotiate the gift."

"I'll speak with him then. When will the ceremony take place?"

"We haven't set a date. I'd like to wait until after our current business is finished."

Rebecca nodded. "I understand you've already consummated the union."

A heated blush crept up Indigo's face. Drat her fair skin. "We have each submitted physically to the other."

"I see." Rebecca's gaze remained steady. "I shall have the contract drawn up by the end of the week. Will ninety days give you enough time to establish the trust?"

"Yes, thank you." Indigo couldn't bring herself to say Rebecca's name, no matter how often the director insisted. "I'd like to present Bobby to my mother this weekend. After that, we would love to have you and Mr. Upton for dinner."

"We'd be delighted." Rebecca rose. "I'll look forward to your call."

So much for having Bobby deal with his mother. Indigo grasped the handle of her briefcase and stood.

"Take good care of my son, Indigo." Rebecca stepped forward and clasped Indigo's shoulders in a surprisingly gentle grip. "He deserves some happiness."

Didn't they all. "I shall do my best."

Rebecca nodded and stepped back, her expression caught in a mixture of triumph and resignation.

Indigo bowed and left. When she closed the office door behind her, she took a deep breath and let it out slowly, and sent a thankful prayer to the Lady Goddess that she'd made it out of Rebecca Upton's lair in one piece.

TWELVE

INDIGO DROVE CAREFULLY from the IECS to her apartment and changed clothes before heading to the hospital to visit her mother.

No. *Our* apartment. A home that, Goddess willing, would be filled with the sounds of children by the end of the following year. A little girl with Bobby's daredevil nature and sweet smile.

Or the blessed Son.

She held that wish to herself, savored it for a long, precious moment, then let it go. It was too soon to think of becoming mortal. Her heart was still her own, even if her body wasn't, and Bobby had made it clear the night before that her body was no longer solely her own, as his was now hers as well.

Maybe he would *teach her a lesson* again that evening. A pleasant throb pulsed between her legs and she pressed a hand to her racing heart. *Mmm.* Something to look forward to.

She parked and made the short walk from the hospital's parking lot to her mother's room.

Elizabeth Andrews was a beautiful woman, tall with the black hair and blue eyes she'd given her daughters. Her heart was kind, though not always sweet, and she had no tolerance for disobedience in her children, disobedience often meaning holding an opinion other than one that aligned with Elizabeth's own.

India was just as hard-headed, though she lacked her mother's kinder attributes. She lived in a black and white world without room for compromise or softness, and had always been determined to forge her own path, regardless of the consequences. It often seemed as if Indigo's twin deliberately chose paths that would provoke their mother's temper.

It had made for a difficult childhood on all sides.

Indigo pushed the door to her mother's room open and stepped quietly inside. Elizabeth lay on the hospital bed situated in the middle of the room, Indigo's brother held to her breast. His twin occupied a rolling glass cradle between the bed and the opposite wall. Pictures flashed across a television mounted to the far corner, the sound muted. Flowers, stuffed animals, and gifts covered nearly every inch of the institutional furniture decorating the room.

"Mámá." Indigo kept her voice soft as she closed the door behind herself.

"Darling." Elizabeth smiled and held her hand out. "I'm sorry to have missed you last night."

Indigo bent and pressed a kiss to her mother's smooth cheek. "You were a little busy having babies."

"True." Elizabeth ran a gentle hand over her son's head. "I would wish this for you, Daughter."

Indigo placed the gift she'd brought on the chest of drawers, then sat in the room's only chair. "Perhaps next year."

Elizabeth's gaze sharpened. "You've taken a lover?"

"A mate," Indigo said. "Bobby Upton, though we haven't sorted out all the details yet."

"Well, well, well. That's quite a step up."

Indigo rolled her eyes skyward. Why did everyone keep saying that? "I'm not that low on the social ladder."

"That's not what I meant. Here, take Joey, will you?"

Indigo stood and took her brother, cradling him gently. His delicate eyelids were closed in sleep, his mouth puckered as if it still suckled his mother's breast. A wave of tenderness swept through her. "So this is Joey."

"Joseph, after Glen's father." Elizabeth cleaned her breast and righted her gown. "And your sister, Beth, bless her heart. I couldn't bear to saddle her with my mother's name."

Indigo's lips twitched. "Uriana is a bit unusual."

Elizabeth laughed softly. "Poor Mother. She always hated her name, but refused to change it, even after she married. Stubborn woman."

Like mother, like daughter. Indigo wisely kept that thought to herself.

"Would you like Joey back?"

"No, you hold him for a while." Elizabeth pushed herself up in the bed until she sat straighter. "I want to talk about Bobby Upton."

Indigo sat down, using Joey as an excuse to avoid her mother's curious gaze. "You'll be up to a formal presentation this weekend, won't you?"

"If that's what you want."

"It's traditional."

"And you were always so bound by duty and tradition." Elizabeth sighed. "Have you submitted to him?"

"No." Joey's face scrunched up. Indigo shifted him to her shoulder and rubbed his tiny back. "He bears my *aenkanien.*"

Elizabeth's eyebrows rose. "I heard he carried a dove on his shoulder, though I thought that could only be rumor. Rebecca would never allow her son to be forsaken."

"Believe me, she extracted a hefty fine."

"So you knew about it."

"Not until last night. Apparently, he got it on his twenty-first birthday after getting really drunk."

"And she still penalized you?" Elizabeth blew out a disgusted breath. "The old biddy."

Indigo laughed. "Mámá, really."

"Well, it's true."

"She made a very reasonable offer, all things considered."

Elizabeth snorted. "Not before putting the screws to you."

"Well, there is that. But it's all settled, except for the formalities. Bobby's moving in with me tonight and we'll likely be married next year." Indigo rose and placed Joey in his own cradle, then took a moment to admire Beth. "If I have children within three years, she's promised to waive part of the fine."

"That bitch." Elizabeth drew in a sharp breath. "You should've taken someone with you to help you negotiate."

"I handled it fine." Indigo moved to her mother's side and sat gingerly on the edge of the bed. "Besides, Bobby and I were planning on having children anyway, so that provision is less harsh than it sounds."

"You were always too accepting, darling. Why didn't you fight for a better deal?"

"What makes you think I didn't?"

Elizabeth's expression turned skeptical. "Because I know you."

"Honestly, this is what I want. If I didn't, I would never have approached her with a formal claim."

"Be careful, darling." Elizabeth grasped Indigo's hand. "Rebecca Upton is devious and cunning. I can't believe she let you off that lightly."

"Not too lightly, I promise. The fine alone is significant enough to affect my investments."

"Do you need money? Your grandmother's funds…"

"No, really, Mámá. I'm fine." And even if she weren't, she wouldn't accept the money. A Daughter who couldn't care for her own mate was sorry indeed. Indigo had enough pride to want to care for Bobby on her own. Thank the Goddess she was frugal. "Can we come by on Sunday?"

Elizabeth hesitated, worry lingering on her face. "Of course. You're welcome anytime."

"Good." Indigo leaned forward to brush a kiss along her mother's cheek. "I have to get back to work now. Bobby's expecting me."

"Come by again, if you can. We're going home tomorrow."

"I will."

Exhaustion followed Indigo from her mother's hospital room to her car, all the way to BDH. Dealing with two strong-willed women in one day was not something she wanted to do again anytime soon.

On the way up the elevator, she remembered the traditional ceremonies, and slumped against the elevator's wall with a weary sigh. Her mother and Rebecca Upton in the same room, staring each other down, on top of the downright embarrassing rituals the traditional claiming demanded? No way.

Maybe they could just elope. Las Vegas was nice this time of year.

The elevator dinged, its doors opened, and Indigo stepped out. She made her way through the reception area to Bobby's office. Laura walked out and closed the door behind herself, and gave Indigo a thin smile that seemed a tad too self-satisfied. Indigo veered off, following the young girl. Whatever Laura was up to, she intended to nip it in the bud once and for all.

In fact, she'd be more than happy to set Laura straight on a number of items, starting with Bobby's availability.

Indigo stalked after the other woman, her fatigue forgotten, replaced by a stony determination that would've made her mother proud.

THE HOURS DRAGGED BY. Bobby tried to focus on work, knew he needed to, but his mind drifted and his eyes wandered to his watch. How long could it possibly take for two women to hash out a marital contract?

He checked the time again and pushed sharply back from his desk with a muttered curse. Only five minutes had passed since the last time he'd looked.

Indigo had texted him with the time of her meeting with his mother. Even with traffic, she should've been here by now.

He glared at the paperwork on his desk, picked up a pen, and tapped it in rapid beats against the top of his desk. *Patience.* She had to deal with this on her own, and he needed to let her.

He focused on the paperwork and forced himself to go through it point by point. Half an hour passed and then another one. Margaret poked her head in requesting a meeting. Drew stopped by with an update on one of their field teams. Laura came in needing his signature, and after that, Bobby gave up trying to work. He grabbed his empty coffee mug and headed for the break room. If Indigo hadn't made it back by the time he finished another cup, he was going after her, tradition be damned.

He left his office door open and stalked down the hallway, trying not to snap at the people he passed. They didn't deserve the lash of his temper, though it wouldn't be there if Indigo was around to soothe it away.

What could possibly be taking her so long?

He slapped the door to the break room open. Margaret stood at the coffee pot, filling her own mug.

"That better not be the last of the coffee," he said.

"There's a little more." She placed the pot back into the machine and moved aside. "Sounds like you don't need any more caffeine, though."

"Hunh. You're one to talk."

"I'm not the one walking around with a thundercloud hanging over my head."

"I'm not..." He let out a sigh. Yes, he was. "Forget it. What did you need a meeting for?"

"I have some interesting info for you on the manhunt you're doing for Mom." She eyed him levelly. "It can probably wait until you're in a better mood."

He grimaced and rubbed a hand across his nape. "Yeah. Sorry about that."

"Want to talk about it?"

And give her ammunition for sisterly blackmail? He wasn't that stupid, no matter what his sisters thought. A man couldn't get away with anything around that bunch. "Maybe later."

"Is it about Indigo?"

He returned her cool stare evenly. "Why would it be?"

"Because you've been groping her for the past few weeks, and mooning over her for a lot longer." Her mouth curled into a smug smirk. "I hear congratulations are in order."

Bobby opened his mouth to retort and was interrupted by Indigo, marching through the door to the break room, dressed in khakis and a BDH shirt with her coal black hair pulled into a ponytail. Her eyes glittered and red spots of color graced her cheeks. She looked ready to crush someone under her heel, if she hadn't already.

"Uh oh," Margaret muttered.

Bobby set his mug down on the counter.

Indigo's gaze zeroed in on him. "I need to speak with you."

"Sure. What's up?"

"Alone." Indigo stepped back, holding the door for him. "In your office, if you don't mind."

His heart took a nosedive and landed somewhere south of Peru. She'd changed her mind. *Dammit.* He knew he should've gone with her to see his mom, knew he should've gone after her sooner. Nausea rolled through him and a cold sweat popped out on his skin.

He was going to lose her.

"All right," he said, and barely stifled a wince at the crack in his voice.

He ignored Margaret's look of sympathy and followed Indigo out of the room. She stalked ahead of him to his office, ponytail swishing with her steps, her body taut and angry. Her ass twitched under her khakis and his body hardened with need, even as he steeled himself for rejection.

At least you had one night. His heart tightened painfully in his chest. One night and thousands more to endure without her, alone with the memory of her scent clogging his head, her soft skin under his hands, the ecstasy on her face when he filled her.

As soon as she entered the room, she moved to pull the blinds shut. He closed the door quietly and watched her. Her hands were shaking. Did she think he was going to hurt her when she let him down? Is that why she was closing the blinds, because she didn't want anyone to see his reaction after she let him go?

He rubbed a finger across his brow. Was he really that much of a bastard? *No.* He'd been good to her, given her his best, except for the night before, and she'd seemed to like that. Surely she didn't think he would hurt her. Maybe she just wanted privacy.

"We can do this somewhere else," he said.

Her laugh was as shaky as her hands. "I can't wait that long."

He flinched.

"Lock the door," she said, and her words were a sucker punch to his gut.

It was going to be bad.

He pinched the bridge of his nose, trying to breath through the agony building in his chest. One night. Sweet Goddess, he'd wanted more than one night.

She finished shutting the blinds and turned, facing him. Her mouth was set in a thin line and her chest rose and fell so rapidly, he thought she might be on the verge of hyperventilating.

"Did you lock the door?" she said.

"Yeah. Why don't we..."

Before he could finish, she crossed the room, fisted her hands in his shirt, and yanked him into a scorching kiss. He stumbled while his mind reeled and his body shouted, *Hell, yeah.* Her tongue pushed against his lips, so he opened for her, and groaned when she made sweet little forays into his mouth, teasing the corners of his lips and his tongue and shooting fire straight down to his groin.

She pushed him back and pulled her top off, then her bra. "Shirt off," she said, and her voice wasn't shaky anymore, it was hot and heavy and needy.

He pulled his shirt off and dropped it onto the chair, and helped her strip down until she stood nude under the harsh, fluorescent lighting. He reached for the waistband of his khakis, and she pushed his hands away and took his mouth in a greedy kiss. Her hands worked the fastening of his pants, dipping under his clothes in heated strokes while she edged him backward, and he went, eager to see what she'd do next, ready to meet her halfway. When the back of his legs hit the couch, she shoved his pants and briefs down to his ankles and pushed at his chest until he plopped onto the couch.

She straddled him and took him into her body in one long, heated stroke, engulfing him until he wasn't sure where he stopped and she began.

"So good," she gasped, and threw her head back with a low groan when he thrust up into her. Her hips began a slow, undulating rhythm, pulling him deeper into her wet heat, and her sex clenched around him with her movements, and his control slipped and shattered, and he didn't care because she was there and she was his and he wanted her so much, wanted whatever she would give him.

He wrapped an arm around her back and pulled her closer, and sucked her nipple into his mouth, laving it with his tongue, and put his other hand on her hip to urge her into a harder, quicker rhythm. He rocked up into her as her hands roamed over him, clutching his head to her breast, stroking his back and shoulders, digging into his skin, and he was so thankful she wanted him, *Goddess, yes,* but all he could think was *love her, love her* and his chest filled with it, filled with emotion and the beauty of their passion until he fell down, down, down into Indigo.

Her hips were a frenzy of movement, sharp thrusts that stoked the heat higher and higher until he was ready to burst, and her breaths came in pants. She pulled his mouth away from her breast and claimed it, moaning her pleasure against his lips, and braced her hands against the back of the couch. Her hips worked against his body, faster, faster, until she cried out and her body shuddered and her sex clamped down on his erection in hard throbs that sent him over the edge, and he thrust into her so that he was fully sheathed and his seed spurted into her in hot waves that pulsed through him again and again until he was spent.

She collapsed against him, gasping for breath, and nuzzled her face into his neck. He cradled her head and smoothed a hand down the sweat soaked skin of her back, and felt her shaky laugh caress him inside and out.

"Sorry." Her breath puffed across his neck and her hands curled into fists against his chest. "I shouldn't have done that here."

"Here was fine. Great, even. In fact, I vote we do this at least once a day until we're both gray headed." He brushed her hair back, dragged in a shuddering breath around his rocketing heartbeat. "I thought you were leaving me."

"What?" She jerked upright, her eyes wide with shock. "Why would you think that?"

"You were late." He shrugged as casually as he could. "Mom acted like she was gonna be difficult, and I thought you might've changed your mind."

"You talked to her?"

"This morning when I picked up some clothes." He pulled her down, tucked her against his chest, enjoyed the weight of her body draped over his. "Was she really bad?"

She cupped the nape of his neck and relaxed. "She was...merciful."

Merciful? *Shit.* That did not sound good at all. "What did she say?"

"Forget it, Bobby, I'm not telling you. She got what she wanted and now we can be together. That's the important thing, right?"

Not so much. What had his mother done to drive Indigo into sex in a semi-public place? Awesome hot monkey sex that had his dick hardening just thinking about it, but still. Not very Indigo-like behavior. He'd bet his bottom dollar his mother's *fun* had stepped over a line or two or, more likely, ignored those lines completely.

Indigo nipped at his neck with sharp teeth.

A familiar heat worked its way downward. "What was that for?"

"For doubting me. I can't believe you thought I changed my mind."

"This isn't exactly a love match, sweetheart."

She grew eerily still against him. "You don't love me?"

"I do, so much it hurts." His hand tightened in her hair. "I know you don't love me, though."

"I care about you, a lot." She sat up and met his gaze openly. "I know that's not enough."

"No, it's not."

Her lips turned up into a shy smile. "I'm working on it."

"Really?" The emotion welled up again, threatening to spill out. She was working on it, huh? Maybe even trying to take him into her heart. He didn't deserve her, never would, but he couldn't refuse her either, couldn't live without her gentle understanding and seductive heat. "How hard?"

"Pretty hard." Her face lit with humor. "So hard I'm pretty sure everybody knows it now."

"You weren't that loud."

"Not me, the couch. It squeaks."

He ran a hand over her back and didn't even try to hold back the satisfied smile. "I'll get that fixed."

"Mmm. I doubt it. I think you liked it."

"I did," he admitted. "And now, I want to take you home so I can feed you and we can do this all over again."

Her smile was sweet and tender and beautiful. "I can handle that."

They helped each other dress and straightened up as much as they could. He laughed with her and played and felt relief sag through him every time her shy gaze met his, but his mind kept drifting back to what she'd said. *Merciful.* As soon as he could, he was going to figure out exactly what had happened at that meeting, even if it meant standing against his mother, one of the People's most formidable warriors.

THAT NIGHT, Indigo woke him, screaming for her mother, her body jerking in hard spasms. He shook her, trying to wake her, and panicked when she scrambled away from him, slipping out of his reach and over the edge of the bed before he could catch her. Her head clipped the edge of the nightstand as she fell in a graceless heap onto the floor. He leaped around the bed and heaved a sigh of relief when she groaned and pushed herself up.

Sweet Goddess, what had she been dreaming about?

He helped her into bed, flipped on the light, tended the shallow wound. A slow, burning dread hit him when he asked her what had made her scream and her eyes fogged in confusion.

She slept peacefully in the nights after that, but he didn't forget that one nightmare.

Over the next few days, they began to learn one another, to work around each other's habits and shortcomings and develop a deeper bond. Indigo had a hard time waking in the morning, so Bobby cooked breakfast and then came back to bed and woke her with sweet kisses and long strokes along her sleep-warmed skin. He coddled her so much, she retaliated by ramping up their sparring matches and kicked his tail on a regular basis, a pointed reminder that she was a Daughter and not one to be trifled with.

In the evenings, they took slow walks around the neighborhood after supper or cuddled on the couch with a movie, but their nights always ended with him inside her, taking her as high as he could before they both shattered and fell.

Every day, she took a little more of his heart.

Before she'd claimed him, that would've worried him. Now, he held on to the hope that she really could learn to love him, that he was taking a little bit of her heart in return.

THIRTEEN

THE FIRST SUNDAY after Bobby moved in with Indigo, they went to her mother's house for the formal presentation. It was a modern structure made of rock and wood, and smaller than the older homes located near Tellowee's center, though still big enough to accommodate a large family. Indigo watched Bobby assess the two acre lots with a critical eye, likely noting the layout of the streets and the distance between homes, and knew exactly when he put it on his mental list of potential house sites.

Elizabeth met them at the door of her home, beautifully rounded beneath a loose, white peasant top and faded jeans, carrying her youngest daughter in the crook of her arm.

"Indigo." She leaned in to brush her lips across Indigo's cheek, though her coldly appraising gaze rested on Bobby. "Come in, darling."

They followed her inside and took off their coats, shaking off the cold November rain.

Indigo hung their coats on pegs next to the door. "Where's Glen? He'll be here for the presentation, won't he?"

"Of course, though he seems a bit baffled by the custom." Elizabeth led them into the living room and sat on a plush couch upholstered in earthy plaids. "He's upstairs changing Joey."

Indigo relaxed onto a matching chair and settled in for a good conversation while they waited. Bobby stood behind her with his right hand on her left shoulder, a silent guard in the manner this tradition demanded.

Moments later, Glen came down the stairs carrying Joey. He stood slightly taller than his wife and was whip thin with shoulder-length hair the color of gold, pulled into a ponytail at the base of his neck. His chambray shirt was untucked over jeans and his socked feet whispered against the hardwood floor. "Sorry. Joey was a little fussy."

"It's ok, dear." Elizabeth took the hand he held out to her and kissed the back of his fingers before rubbing her cheek over them. "Let me scoot up and we can begin."

When Elizabeth was settled, Glen stood beside her and watched with avid eyes.

"Indigo, daughter of my heart and my body, I give you leave to begin."

"Maetyrm." Indigo slid forward in the chair and bowed slightly. "I have come before you with a gift to your line, a Son of a reputable family who will bring much honor to our People."

"What is this Son's name?"

"Robert Lake Upton, the second of that name."

"Who is this Son's mother?"

"Rebecca, known as the Blade, a strong and skilled warrior and a Daughter of the line of Abragni."

"Who is this Son's father?"

"Robert Lake Upton, the first of that name, who has no kin among the People."

"Why should I acknowledge this gift?"

Bobby squeezed Indigo's shoulder when she hesitated. "I have claimed him as my mate."

Elizabeth nodded. "I would hear this from the Son's lips."

Bobby stepped forward and bowed. "Maetyrm."

"Robert Lake Upton, the second of that name, a Son of the People and a child of the Blade. Have you accepted my daughter as your mate?"

"I have."

"Why should I accept this mating?"

"I love her as no other ever will."

Elizabeth's eyes glittered in her pale face. "Pretty words from a man with such a violent reputation."

Indigo hissed in a breath. Trust her mother to bring up the past, and in a manner designed to illicit the sharpest response.

"I do what I must to protect my own," Bobby said, his voice as hard as her mother's.

"And should the day come when she grows weary of your attentions?"

"She may leave with no penalty or harm, though my heart will go with her."

Elizabeth nodded. "A rumor has come to my attention, that you bear the mark of a dove on your shoulder, and have since your twenty-first birthday. Whose mark is this?"

"It is the mark of Indigo Dupree."

"Was this mark taken with her knowledge?"

"It was not."

"Have you been faithful to her since taking her mark?"

Indigo froze. She hadn't anticipated that question, hadn't even discussed it with Bobby. If he'd taken lovers after taking her *aenkanien*, she wouldn't hold it against him, but her mother would. Elizabeth would refuse the claiming, sending them into a spiral of reprisals against Rebecca and her kin, and possibly leading to a vengeance war.

Rebecca's first act would be to claim Retribution.

Indigo flinched. Her body disfigured, Bobby lost to her forever. His hand tightened on her shoulder, comforting her.

"Answer the question," Elizabeth snapped.

Indigo heard Bobby's inhaled breath. "I have."

Elizabeth gaped. Indigo's head snapped around and she said, "What?" at the same time her mother did.

"Eh," Glen said. "Can I ask a question?"

Elizabeth nodded faintly. "As the second father of my daughter, I give you leave to ask what you will."

"How old are you?"

"I turned thirty last month," Bobby said.

Glen's eyes grew round. "You didn't have sex for nine years? Are you friggin' kidding me?"

"Ah," Bobby said. "I'm not kidding."

"Man." Glen looked down at his wife. "Don't ask me to do that."

Elizabeth patted his arm. "I would never dream of it."

Indigo caught his eye and mouthed *I owe you* before turning back to her mother.

Elizabeth cleared her throat. "Indigo, daughter of my heart and my body, I give you leave to join your life to this man's, the Son of Rebecca, known as the Blade, and Robert Lake Upton, the first of that name, and to bring him into our line with honor and love."

Indigo rose and bowed. "Thank you, Maetyrm."

"Can we eat now?" Glen said.

Elizabeth smiled. "Yes, I think we should."

SUPPER WAS A SIMPLE AFFAIR of roast pork and vegetables. Bobby listened more than he spoke, caught Indigo's gaze slipping to his at odd moments. She was wondering if he'd told the truth about not having sex after taking her *aenkanien*. It was plain on her face.

His brow furrowed. If she hadn't believed him under the duress of the presentation, when a lie could mean death, how would she ever believe him outside of it?

It's not that he hadn't wanted sex and, he was ashamed to admit, hadn't attempted it a time or two. It had never gone beyond a steamy dance and a completely passionless kiss, not for lack of trying, and he'd finally given up.

Of course, he'd had plenty of sex before he'd taken her mark, all futile attempts to erase her from his heart. He'd never tell her, not if he could help it. Her knowing would only widen the influence of his past on their future, and it might hurt her at a time when she was so close to trusting him, maybe even a step or two away from loving him.

The babies rested in a double cradle to the side of the table, sleeping peacefully until the meal was nearly eaten. Beth mewed and shifted, threatening to wake her brother. Bobby placed his napkin on the table beside his plate. "May I?"

Elizabeth's gaze rested on his with the heavy weight of a protective mother. "Of course."

He stood and moved to the cradle, and gently scooped Beth into his arms, holding her carefully. It had been a long time since he'd held a newborn, not since Charlotte's next youngest had been born. He'd missed the birth of the youngest while out of town on a business trip and had regretted it ever since. There was nothing like a baby cuddled up against you, trusting and sweet. He ran a finger over Beth's cheek and smiled when she turned her head toward it.

He looked up to find them all watching him, Glen with the proud look of a new father, Elizabeth wearing a dispassionate mask. Indigo's gaze held a longing that took his breath. She wanted this, wanted to hold a child of her heart and his. He would give her as many children as she wanted, as often as she wanted them. She would be a good mother, and he would watch over her and their children with all of the strength he'd inherited from the Sisters through his mother.

"She looks like you," he told her.

Glen folded his arms across his chest. "Well, there goes your special dispensation."

Bobby grinned. "Hey, it's the truth."

"She's probably wet," Elizabeth said.

"Oh." Indigo pushed her chair back and stood. "Let me. I've been dying to get my hands on her."

Bobby handed the baby over and watched Indigo walk from the room cooing to her little sister. Elizabeth and Glen rose, clearing dishes from the table, and Bobby decided that it was now or never.

"May I speak with you alone?" he said to Elizabeth.

"Of course. Glen, dear, if you'll get started, I'll finish up."

Glen pressed a kiss to his wife's cheek. "Fair enough."

Elizabeth led Bobby to a library containing two leather sofas placed facing one another over a coffee table. Windows lined one wall, with book-laden shelves filling the others. She sat on one end of the far sofa and gestured for him to sit next to her.

Bobby sat down and turned to face her, leaving a cushion between them to preserve some formality. Elizabeth was, in her own way, as formidable as his own mother, if centuries younger. He knew little about her life other than what he'd gleaned from Indigo. That put him at a distinct disadvantage when dealing with her, considering his mother's notoriety, and his own.

He studied her while they settled, and marveled at how alike in looks she and Indigo were, close enough to pass for sisters, with hair as deep as midnight and sapphire eyes tilted up at the corners in heart-shaped faces. Elizabeth's features were sharper, harder, and her eyes pierced where Indigo's merely observed. He'd heard Elizabeth was a fighter, a no-nonsense woman who wasn't afraid to take charge or get her hands dirty, and while Indigo shared those traits, they were tempered by her softer nature. She was the dove to her sister India's hawk, and their mother was an eagle with sharp beak and claws and eyes fixed on her prey.

"What is it you wish to discuss?" Elizabeth asked.

"Indigo." Bobby hooked an ankle over his knee and held it there with both of his hands. "Has she ever had nightmares before?"

"Not in a very long time." Elizabeth's brow furrowed. "Why do you ask?"

"She had one a couple of nights ago. Woke screaming and fell off the bed trying to get away from me." He leveled a hard stare at her. "She wouldn't tell me what it was about, but I'm guessing you probably know."

"I might." Elizabeth curled her legs up onto the couch and rested a hand on her ankle. "When the girls were little, they were mischievous children. India led." She laughed. "Well, you know what India's like. Back then, though, Indigo was a willing participant. The two of them would get into all sorts of trouble together."

Bobby tried to imagine Indigo as a mischievous child and failed. Until the day she'd brought her suit before his mother, she'd always been tentative, almost shy, a student of duty and obligation.

He'd been on the receiving end of that duty often enough to understand how deeply ingrained in her it was.

"They were born in England, but I wanted to travel a little. Restless feet." The smile lifting her lips held a touch of sadness. "So I took a job for the People investigating a slave owner here in the States, a man who had ties to the Shadow Enemy, though he didn't appear to be a member himself. I brought the girls with me, of course. There was no harm, or shouldn't have been, since I was going in as an independent woman, a widow, and not a member of the household."

Bobby nodded. It wasn't an uncommon scenario.

She sighed and shifted on the couch. "We were visiting this man's plantation down near Charleston and the girls got away from me. I never really pieced together everything that happened. From what I can tell, they were spying on some of the slave boys who were bathing in the river. The overseer caught them. He had his whip with him and used it on Indigo. India slipped out of his grasp and managed to claw the man hard enough to send him running, but the damage was done."

A slow burn of horror seeped into him. *Blessed Mother.* "I hope you killed him."

"Oh, I did. Skinned him from stem to stern while his heart beat and fed him his own entrails until he choked. He got India with his back swings while she was trying to stop him. Considering some of the scrapes that one got into, the wounds were relatively minor, but the overseer got in at least a dozen hits to Indigo. The damage was..." She sucked in a breath and let it out slowly. "Her skin healed and the scars faded, but she was never the same. No more running after India, chasing trouble. No more daredevil adventures. Her childhood was essentially over and she was only ten."

Bobby pushed down the hatred and horror. "And she had nightmares after that?"

"Every night for a while. They gradually tapered off. I can't think what would have triggered her recent nightmare. Are you certain nothing else has happened?"

"We're hunting down India and she's helping." He shrugged. "We've gone furniture shopping."

"Well, that's a nightmare on its own," she said with a laugh. "Indigo hates shopping."

"Hmm." She'd seemed to enjoy their trips together. "We went shopping a lot the first week or so after she came back. Other than that, I can't think of anything except her meeting with Mom."

Elizabeth's eyes narrowed. "Your mother imposed a heavy fine on her for your mistake."

"I don't consider it a mistake," he said evenly. "And whatever that fine was, my personal wealth is enough to make up for it."

"Like your mother would allow that," she scoffed.

"My mother has no say in how I spend my own money." He drew himself back before the argument escalated. "I told Mom to go easy on her."

"And you really think she listened? You don't know Rebecca very well."

"Well enough. She wants me to be happy. Surely she wouldn't have done anything to hurt Indigo."

"Maybe not," Elizabeth conceded, "but she might threaten it, if she needed leverage."

Bobby rocked his foot, considering that. "I told Mom flat out that I would protect Indigo if she came after her."

"You would defy the Blade for Indigo?" Elizabeth's lips, so like Indigo's, twisted into a disdainful sneer. "I have a hard time believing that."

He leaned forward and pinned her with a cold stare. "Believe it. Anyone who harms Indigo will learn exactly how vicious I can be."

She sat back, her expression nonplussed. "You're serious."

"I am. Mom knows that, too."

Elizabeth's face blossomed with a smile. "Well, well, well. I do believe that old biddy's met her match."

She slid off the couch and he rose to face her. She reached up, cupping his face with both of her elegant hands. "Robert Lake Upton, the second of that name, I accept you as my daughter's mate. Love her always. Harm her never."

"I shall protect her with my life," he murmured.

She pulled him down, pressed a kiss to his mouth and then his forehead. "Welcome to the family, Bobby."

He grinned and let her take his arm and lead him back to the kitchen where their two hearts waited.

FOURTEEN

TWO DAYS PASSED before Indigo had time to take a breath. News of her and Bobby's engagement seeped out, and before she knew it, her phone rang nearly constantly with people calling to congratulate her on making such a spectacular match.

She was polite, really she was, when what she wanted to do was say, *What am I, chopped liver?*

Ok, so Bobby was the only son of a powerful Daughter, allied closely with a member of the Council of Seven, and Indigo was a wallflower, but that didn't mean she was a nobody. Her grandmother had served on the Council of Seven representing their line through the Sister Lilleni before the current councilwoman, Gwendolyn, had taken the position. Elizabeth was relatively young, but she'd earned a certain notoriety as well and might have gone much farther if she hadn't become mortal.

Which was in itself a notable feat. Not every Daughter was born with a trusting heart. If they were, it was usually beaten out of them by the sheer difficulty of their lives. To submit one's will to a man and become mortal was an honorable action, marking such women as the wisest among the People.

Indigo had accomplished things in her time, too, so why did everyone treat her as if she were Cinderella to Bobby's Prince Charming?

She wrinkled her brow at the comparison and sighed. Bobby's stature as a Son, particularly when combined with his maternal lineage, very nearly made him a prince of sorts. The way people fawned over the match still rankled, as if snagging him was her biggest accomplishment to date.

In truth, he'd done all the snagging. She'd just stopped running.

Margaret poked her head into Bobby's office, startling Indigo out of her reverie.

"Hey," Indigo said. "Bobby's out running errands."

Margaret closed the door. "I can talk to you."

"Ok." Indigo scooped up her work and dropped it onto the coffee table in front of the couch, her favorite work station. "Want to sit?"

"I'll take a chair," Margaret said, and did just that, turning one of the chairs in front of Bobby's desk around before dropping into it. "I've been trying to run Bobby down for about a week now."

Indigo plucked at the seam in her khakis. Not everyone approved of her match with Bobby. She had a feeling Margaret would fall into that category. "It's been a busy time."

"So I hear. Congratulations on the engagement."

"Thank you."

"I'm sure Mom's making your life hell."

Indigo allowed a small smile to curve her lips upward. "Only a little."

Margaret snorted. "She must be getting soft in her old age."

"I dare you to say that to her face," Indigo said with a laugh.

"What am I, stupid?" Margaret shook her head. "She can still kick my ass around the block and back."

"Mmm." That was probably true. It was one reason Rebecca had retained her power long after becoming a mortal. She was a Daughter with whom one did not tangle. "We're thinking of having a party this weekend, maybe at The Omega."

"That's the other reason I came by. Jerusha's coming into town this weekend. She heard about the engagement all the way in London."

"Oh?"

"Yeah. We want to take you out, have a little girl time."

"By *we* you mean...?"

"Me and Moira, Jerusha, Dani and Charlotte, maybe Mom and a couple of other gals." Margaret shrugged. "You know. Girls' night out."

"Um." Indigo tried to imagine spending an entire night with the women in Bobby's family and making it through in one piece. Nope. That wasn't going to happen, but what could she say and still keep the peace? "Sure."

Margaret's smile seemed a tad too knowing, as if she'd seen right into Indigo's head and witnessed every single doubt. "It'll be fun. We can hire some strippers."

"I'll pass on the strippers, but maybe we could do pizza and pool."

"Ok. I'll arrange everything."

Indigo sighed her relief. One less thing for her to worry over. "What was the other thing you wanted to talk about?"

"Right, almost forgot." Margaret dug a folded sheet of paper out of the back pocket of her jeans. "I've been doing a little digging on my own and came up with a few ideas on solving the problem with traitors among the People. I was supposed to talk to Bobby about it last week, but..."

"He's been busy."

Indigo took the paper and unfolded it, and tried to push down the guilt that nagged at her. She'd had to let her own forays into Margaret's past go to concentrate on everything else, though a little niggle in her gut insisted the other Daughter knew more than she was letting on.

Indigo smoothed the paper across one thigh, pushing out the creases, and studied it, surprised that it contained not raw information but a chart showing relationships between people and events. She sat straight up and grasped the paper in tense fingers. "By the Goddess, Margaret. Why didn't you come forward with this sooner?"

"It's been busy."

"Yes, I know, but this is..." With one finger, Indigo traced the intricate connections outlined on the paper, studying them. "It's enough to break the whole thing wide open in a week, maybe less if we move hard and fast. How did you put this together? I mean, who could possibly know all of this?"

She clamped her jaws together and met Margaret's hard stare evenly. Hadn't she wondered if Margaret was a member of the High Guard, that mythical branch of Daughters bent solely on countering the Eternal Order? And if she was...

No. The more important question was, *What would Margaret do to protect her secret?*

"Never mind," Indigo said. "I don't need to know, and that's what I'll tell Bobby when he asks."

Margaret rose and bowed. "Use this information wisely. It cannot be traced back to me."

"I understand." Indigo stood and returned the bow. "Zenalisa and Laura are clever women."

"Yes," Margaret said with a careful nod.

"Hiro and Drew love intrigue. In fact, they're quite good at figuring out who did what and when."

"They are."

"Bobby's built up quite a business here, you know." Indigo folded the paper and placed it with her work. "I've been very impressed with the efficient way they operate."

Margaret's grin held an unholy mischief. "I think I'm going to like having you around."

Indigo returned her smile, sure for the first time that she had an ally in Bobby's family outside of Dani. "The feeling's mutual."

Margaret left, shutting the door quietly behind her, and Indigo settled down with the list to study and plan.

BOBBY STOOD in front of the bathroom mirror, hands tangled up in a tie. Why he had to wear one to eat with his own parents escaped him. It was just a dinner, but no. Indigo had insisted he wear real slacks instead of khakis, a button-down shirt, and a tie.

She was wearing a dress, a loose flowy thing that slid around her body when she walked, clinging to the swell of her breasts and the lush curves of her ass and stopping short enough that every time he followed her, his eyes fell to the bare sensitive skin behind her knees and made him want to drop to the floor and lick there, and keep going until she was naked and writhing beneath his mouth.

And she thought her dress was demure enough for a visit with his parents.

He grunted out a laugh. Goddess help him, he was going to have a hard time keeping his dick under control with all that beautiful flesh shifting around under her dress every time she moved. Dad would understand. Mom? Probably not.

The sharp clack of heels against wood sounded in the bedroom moments before Indigo rushed into the bathroom, her heart-shaped face flushed pink.

"You're not ready." She brushed his hands aside and lifted the two ends of his tie, folding and tucking until it was presentable. "There. Your parents will be here any minute."

"It's not like they're royalty or something." He dropped his hands to her hips and drew her in, stroking her through the silky fabric of the dress. "You didn't have to go to so much trouble."

She breathed out a faint laugh. "It's the final step before we can get married."

"As far as I'm concerned, it's a done deal." He pressed a chaste kiss to her lipsticked mouth and let her fuss over the smudge that transferred to his lower lip. "And it's just my folks. We'll be doing this a lot over the next few decades."

"Yes," she agreed as she stepped back. "But there's only one first dinner."

He rolled his eyes skyward and followed her into the apartment's main living area.

Indigo had spent the entire weekend polishing and scrubbing and fussing over every room in the apartment. If a cobweb or speck of dust had survived her laser gaze, he'd be surprised, but he had to admit the apartment looked nice. He'd finally talked her into taking the bookcases. They took up an entire wall in the living room and were filled with the books she'd collected over the years along with pictures of her family and his. Flowers decorated every surface, sprouting out of vases in shades of orange, red, and gold. The mission-style coffee and end tables he'd given her surrounded the leather couch and recliner she'd bought, and the TV rested safely behind the doors of an entertainment center, facing the couch.

She'd gone all out with the dining area. He'd scooted the table out for her and helped her drape it in layers of tablecloths. She'd dug out pewter candlesticks and made him polish them, and then filled them with pale yellow candles and placed them on either side of a low flower centerpiece.

The one thing he'd insisted on was having the meal catered. Otherwise, she would've worn herself into a frazzled wreck trying to please his mom. So he'd put his foot down. Frankly, he wanted her to have energy to spend on him after his folks were gone.

He was just crazy like that.

The doorbell rang and she jumped. He barely refrained from rolling his eyes again. It was going to be a long night. "Would you relax?"

She slid her hand into his and took a shaky breath. "I don't think I can."

"It'll be fine."

"Easy for you to say. They're your parents."

He gave her an exasperated look and opened the door for his parents, and suppressed an irritated grimace at their clothing. Mom wore a dress, for cripes' sake, and Dad had on a tie. Bobby shared a sympathetic look with his father as the two entered the apartment.

"Hello, dear." Rebecca tilted her cheek for his kiss. She slid her coat off and handed it to him. "What a lovely little place this is."

"Thank you," Indigo said. She stood solicitously at his dad's elbow, waiting patiently while he took his jacket off around his hand crutches. "We're pleased you could come."

"We appreciate the invitation," Rebecca said.

Bobby had never heard her sound so stiff and formal outside of a business meeting. The two women circled one another awkwardly, coming in for a brief brush of lips to air at the other's cheek before moving apart. The silence stretched thin between them.

He rubbed a finger across his forehead. Yup, it was gonna be a long one. "Dinner's warming in the oven. Why don't we sit down and talk before we eat?"

Indigo's expression held such relief, he had to bite back a smile. "Oh, yes. That would be lovely."

He settled Rebecca onto the couch next to his father, who dropped down with a sigh, and perched on the arm of the recliner to Indigo's left.

"Thanksgiving's just around the corner." Rebecca folded her hands in her lap. "Have you made plans yet?"

Indigo shot a glance at Bobby before answering. "We haven't really decided on anything."

"Jerusha will be in," Rebecca said. "She's staying for a while, so I thought we'd get the whole family together. What does your mother do?"

Rebecca touched a hand to the locket at her throat, and it dawned on Bobby that she was as nervous as Indigo. What a pair.

"We're usually never in one spot all at one time," Indigo admitted.

"We always have room, if she wants to join us," Robert said. "I need to talk with Glen about his family anyway."

"Dad, geez. Not the genealogy thing again." Bobby draped a hand on Indigo's shoulder and felt her muscles relax under his touch. "Don't get him started, Indi. He'll drive you nuts asking questions about your family tree, especially if there are gaps."

Indigo turned to give him a sweet smile. "I don't mind."

"There, now. A girl after my own heart." Robert leaned forward, bracing himself against the edge of the sofa. "Any chance you've got nobility in your father's line?"

"Oh, well." Indigo stuttered to a stop. "No idea."

"Robert, really. Don't put her on the spot." Rebecca patted his arm. "I hate to bring up business, but I need to borrow Indigo for a moment so we can go over the marital contract."

"I don't think so," Bobby said mildly. "In fact, I want to review it before Indigo signs anything."

"Well, really," Rebecca said.

He cut her off. "I have that right."

"Bobby, please." Indigo touched a hand to his knee. "I told you I took care of this."

"You told me you gave her what she wanted so we could be together," he said, and ignored the flicker of guilt when Indigo paled and looked away. "I want to read that contract."

Rebecca's posture stiffened. "Do you not trust me to deal fairly?"

"Not for this, no." Bobby pinned her with a hard stare. "Especially if you have something to gain."

Robert's eyebrows shot up and he coughed into his hand. "Get him the contract, dear."

"Oh, all right." Rebecca pulled her purse into her lap and extracted an envelope. "I'm sure you'll find it very favorable to both of you."

Bobby rose and took the envelope from her, pulled the contract out, and read it standing. He didn't miss the way Indigo's shoulders tensed, the white-knuckled grip of her hands in her lap, or the way her eyes fell to the floor; nor did he miss his mother's haughty gaze as she stared out the window and the way she twisted the locket between her fingers.

Most of it was legalese. He cut straight through that and hit the high spots. In lieu of physical Retribution, Indigo would create a trust for children born of her union with him, in which she would place a fine for forsaking a Son. Bobby whistled at the amount. Elizabeth had been right there. It was a hefty sum, but no larger than he'd expected. He read down, did a slow burn at the provisions for children, and noted the blank space under the section titled, "Son's Gift." When he finished, he started at the beginning and read the whole thing again, item by item, and wanted to strangle his mother at the noose she'd slipped around Indigo's neck.

In lieu of physical Retribution.

He'd heard of such things, harsh punishment doled out when a Daughter didn't treat the precious Son as his mother thought he should be treated. He cursed under his breath. No wonder Indigo clung to him so fiercely. She thought Rebecca was going to have her beaten to within an inch of her life if things didn't work out with him.

A wave of dizziness washed over him and he pinched the bridge of his nose.

"Bobby, what is it?" Indigo said.

He shook his head at the alarm in her voice.

Physical Retribution. Often meted out with a whip on bare flesh until the skin was raw. He bent over, bracing his hands against his knees, and sucked in a harsh breath as nausea roiled in his stomach. By the Lady Goddess. His mother had threatened her with a whipping.

Indigo's screams echoed through his mind and his gut clenched. He stood slowly and threw the contract down on the coffee table. "I told you."

Rebecca flinched.

Indigo looked between them, confusion replacing her alarm. "What?"

He ignored her and speared his mother with a cold gaze. "I told you that if you tried to harm her, I would stand in front of her. Did you think I was kidding?"

"No," Rebecca said, her voice barely audible.

"But you threatened her anyway." He stabbed a finger at the contract. "Physical Retribution. Do you think I don't know what that is, what it would do to her?" He yanked a hand through his hair. "For something that wasn't even her fault? How could you, Mom?"

"I..." Rebecca cleared her throat. "I did what I had to do to make certain you were cared for."

He laughed, a harsh, bitter sound that made her flinch. "And if she left me and you went after her, what do you think I would do? Do you think I'd let you whip her because I wear her mark, a mark she had no hand in placing?"

"Bobby, please," Indigo said.

He hushed her with a sharp wave of his hand. "I would stand in front of her and take Retribution in her place. You know I would."

"No!" Indigo said. The word held a horror so deep it startled him.

Rebecca sucked in a breath and the color drained from her face. "That would kill you."

"What's going on here?" Robert said. "I thought that was standard language in the contract."

"It's not." Bobby nodded at his mother. "She put it in there to keep Indigo tied to me, to make her have my children whether she wanted them or not. This is low, Mom, even for you."

Indigo stood abruptly. "Bobby, I'd like a word with you please."

"I think we need to..."

She cut him off. "In the bedroom. Now."

She turned on her heel and marched out of the living room. Bobby shelved his argument and followed her, ignoring the whispered conversation his parents were having on the couch. He shut the door behind himself and stood facing her.

She sucked in a breath. "How could you embarrass me like that?"

What the hell. "She was gonna have you beaten."

"She was going to do no such thing." Indigo crossed her arms over her chest. "And even if she were, do you think I'd let her bully me around like that? I'm not a child. It was my decision to claim you, *mine*, and my decision to bring a suit before your mother. I wouldn't do that if I didn't want you. I'm not some weakling that I can be pushed into doing something I don't want."

"Indi, honey, I didn't mean..."

"Don't you *Indi, honey* me." She dropped her arms and faced him with such a sad expression he reached for her, and flinched when she stepped away from him. "When are you going to trust that I'm strong enough to take care of myself?"

"I do. I know you're strong enough."

"Do you?" Her gaze went flat and cold. "Do you really?"

She brushed past him and left the bedroom. He yanked at his tie, loosening it, and undid the top button of his shirt.

Well, that wasn't how he'd expected that to go. For one, he'd hoped she'd be grateful he'd challenged that damned lopsided contract. Two children in three years? Ridiculous. He wanted kids, sure, but not like that, not rushed because his mom had set a timetable to it. And he sure as hell would never let the physical Retribution clause stand, even if he thought Indigo would never love him.

Why didn't she understand his need to protect her, to keep her safe and hold her to him and say to hell with the rest of the world? He'd wanted to since the first moment he'd seen her, when she'd walked into the classroom his tenth grade year and stolen his heart with the gentle smile in her sapphire eyes.

He folded his hands behind his head and ran through his options one by one. A triumphant grin twisted his lips when he hit on a way to even out the contract and force Rebecca to leave them alone once and for all.

FIFTEEN

A FIRE DANCED MERRILY behind the tempered glass doors of the fireplace insert. Rebecca stared at it and drew her legs tighter into the curve of her body. She took a sip of the wine she'd poured earlier, a nice red grown locally. The fruity undertones were lost to her, overwhelmed by the dismay ricocheting through her mind.

She'd severely misplayed her hand where Indigo was concerned.

The fire popped and sizzled, throwing warmth into the library. It was her favorite place, this room, with its overstuffed couches and walls of books. She and Robert had spent hours here together, and the children, too, when Bobby was younger. This was where she came to relax and think.

And sometimes to brood over her mistakes.

A woman of her age and experience should have grown out of strategic errors. Her son's life wasn't a battlefield, though, where the sides and issues were clear cut, where she wasn't so close to the action that she couldn't direct it as she had countless times over the centuries.

Perhaps if she loved him less, she'd have dealt with it more rationally, but that was asking too much from a mother, to erase the love she felt for her only son, and with it her heart.

When he'd learned the exact terms of the marital contract, he'd been so angry, and then he'd turned the tables on her nicely.

She hid the proud smile that rose behind a sip of wine. Yes, he was his mother's son.

A house and land. That's what he'd demanded as the Son's gift to his wife, not to enrich his new bride's pockets so much as to punish his mother for overstepping her bounds. She'd done what she had for the best, but of course he wouldn't see it that way. All he saw was the harm that could come to Indigo, not the harm that would come to him when she left him heartbroken and alone for the second time in his young life.

The pain of that memory still burned. Losing Bobby to the Army was one thing. Knowing what Indigo's rejection had pushed him to was another. All those years spent in a system that had channeled his rage to its own calculated purpose. He'd been wrong to think she wouldn't learn exactly what he'd done during that time, and wrong to be afraid when she'd invoked the Enforcer and pushed him into contact with the woman he'd lost.

That had been done for the best as well. It was far past time for Bobby's heart to find solace. Gentle Indigo was the perfect woman to help him find it.

Rebecca had never intended to enact the Retribution clause, regardless of what Bobby thought. It was there simply for leverage, to force Indigo to carefully consider her options should she ever wish to abandon him again.

Of course, if they had children, it wouldn't come to that. Indigo would never leave her children and Bobby would never allow them to be taken from him. If they were stuck in a loveless union until then, so be it.

Somehow, though, Rebecca didn't think it would be loveless. Bobby loved Indigo fiercely, of that there was no question, and Rebecca had noticed the shy glances Indigo had sent him, the way she'd relaxed under Bobby's hand, the soft blush that rose to her face when he gazed down at her, all the love and pride and joy shining from him. The love was there, or would be soon, and after that, surely it was only a matter of time before Indigo submitted her will to Bobby and became mortal, cementing their relationship.

The door creaked open. Rebecca allowed a small sigh to escape as Robert made his way slowly across the room on his hand crutches. Her beloved husband hadn't been happy with her either the night before.

She turned to watch his progress with a tenderness that surprised her, even now, decades after she'd fallen in love with her handsome Yankee scholar. They weren't quite into old age yet, and wouldn't be for a while, but they were getting there. She didn't regret it, not one bit. Here was the man who had given her purpose and reason, and a love deeper than she'd ever before known, even for her children, as much as she loved them. They had their share of troubles, true, but nothing they couldn't overcome together.

And his heart would always be hers.

"How was the doctor's appointment?"

He dropped onto the other end of the couch facing her and set his crutches aside. "It went well. Doc said what he always does. Take my medicine, eat well, get plenty of exercise and rest."

"And your progress?"

"Oh, that's just peachy." He settled into the back of the couch with a contented smile. "Says I'm gradually improving. If I'm lucky, I can get rid of the crutches soon, for short periods, anyway."

"That's wonderful." She put down her wine and slid over to him. He placed his arm around her shoulders, drawing her in, and kissed the top of her head when she rested it on his chest. "I wish you'd let me go with you."

"You were supposed to go to work," he chided. "I came home expecting an empty house and found you playing hooky."

"I needed a little time to think things over."

"Bobby?"

She'd never been able to fool him. Seeing through to her inner self was his best trait, and his worst. "Among other things."

"He was right to be angry."

"I was doing what I thought best for him." She toyed with a button on his shirt, just above his heart. "Besides, Indigo agreed to those terms on her own. I didn't force her into it."

He coughed to hide a laugh that she still heard. "Yes, you did. At least be honest about it."

She huffed, making his laugh deepen and rumble through his chest under her ear. "It's settled now, at any rate."

"Only because Bobby forced your hand." His arm tightened around her shoulders. "You heard him. Indigo gave you what you wanted so they could get married. That has to mean something."

It did. Hadn't her own thoughts drifted along similar lines? "We'll see."

"No more interfering, Becca. I want to live out my retirement in peace without my son and wife being at loggerheads."

"It won't come to that. I promise," she said when he gave a disbelieving *hmph*. "You'll see."

She stared into the flickering flames and pushed aside the worry in her heart. Bobby would come around, Indigo would learn to love him, and life would settle down as it should.

It just had to.

INDIGO BARELY had time to breathe the next day. As if the disastrous meeting of the night before were a spur goading him into action, Bobby charged into the office snapping orders and prodded everyone into working twice as hard as they usually did, Indigo included. It didn't leave them a lot of room to talk. Maybe that's why he'd done it.

She'd certainly left him wanting on that score after that awful dinner with his parents. Confronting his mother over the contract, distrusting his lover's strength and resolve. The heat of humiliation burned her cheeks. Their little talk in the bedroom hadn't helped at all. He'd marched back into the living room, demanded a Son's gift worth nearly four times the value of the fine Rebecca had imposed on her, and completely stricken the language regarding Retribution.

And then he'd shocked them all by looking his mother straight in the eye and telling her, flat out, that they would have children when they were ready and *he* would pay any fines imposed in the contract for the lack thereof.

It had warmed her through and through, even as his lack of faith clawed at her.

On the other hand, the look on Rebecca's face might've been worth Indigo's own discomfort over Bobby's actions. She chuckled to herself and imagined the director's stricken expression, the slump of her shoulders when she'd initialed the changes Bobby insisted on, and the small flash of pride.

It was the latter that kept Indigo's spite in check and gave her hope that someday, far in the future, she and Rebecca might meet as equals, united in their concern for Bobby.

If she could just get him to see her as something other than a shy, retiring dove, as a woman who needed his heart, not his protection...

Later, after a bemused Robert led his suspiciously silent wife home, Bobby had cajoled Indigo out of her anger and into bed where he'd loved her for hours, bringing them both to release after beautiful release with his whispered words and soft touches.

She could love him. It was there in the quiet longing of her heart, perched on the verge of falling, but still fearful of the long cartwheel over the edge into love.

Near the end of the workday, she cornered him in his office, after he'd spent hours evading her, pleading work whenever she tried to get him alone.

"Don't forget our dinner tonight with Dani and her sweetheart," she said.

He groaned and threw his pen down on his desk. "Dave Winstead," he spat, as if the words alone left a foul taste in his mouth. "Can't you go without me?"

She gave him a stern look. "If I have to go out with your sisters this weekend, then you can sit through one dinner with a former FBI agent."

He hefted a sigh and rubbed tired hands through his hair. "At least promise me this is the last one we have to do for a while."

She rose from the couch and came around the desk. He opened for her and pulled her onto his lap, and she nestled there, content for the first time that day. "I wish I could," she said softly. "Even after we're officially married, it'll take a while for people to quit dragging us out to celebrate."

"Kiss me, then, and let me forget about it for a while."

She did, drawing his head down so their mouths could meet in a gentle kiss. She loved this, the way his lips clung to hers and his tongue flicked and stroked, teasing her while his hands roamed until she squirmed under his touch with a need that ricocheted through her body, taking her heart with it.

She broke the embrace before it could get out of hand and talked him into coming home. When they arrived there an hour later, she stripped him down and led him to the shower and let him press her against the tiled wall while he rocked into her and drove them both to a sweet release.

They were toweling off when his phone beeped with a text. He flipped it open, typed out a quick return message, and dropped it back down on the counter. "Something's come up at work."

She rolled her eyes skyward. "Sure it has."

"Really." He hung his towel up and reached around her for his brush. "Laura has some paperwork she needs signed tonight so it can go out first thing tomorrow."

She refused to call the gnawing in her chest jealousy. Suspicion, maybe, but not the green-eyed monster. "And why didn't she ask you to do that before we left?"

"I don't know." He lifted one shoulder in a careless shrug. "Maybe she just got it finished."

"Right. Laura, who is normally so efficient you can't tell she has any work, has just now decided that, *whoops*, she's going to wait until the last minute to finish something time-sensitive."

Bobby's grin was knowing and a little too self-satisfied for Indigo's peace of mind. "You're jealous."

She gaped at him. "I can't believe you said that."

"It's just Laura."

"Oh, yeah. It's *just* Laura who moons over you and follows you around like a puppy begging for a good petting."

His grin slipped. "Are we talking about the same woman? Laura, the ice queen, whose middle name is formality, the same woman who wouldn't touch a man at work with a ten foot pole?"

"That would be her." Indigo turned on her heel and marched out of the bathroom. "She's got a major crush on you."

"C'mon, Indi. Don't be ridiculous."

She whirled on him and skewered him with a look that sent him stepping back, hands raised. "Trust me, Bobby. She's crushing on you."

"Ok, fine." He dropped his hands and retreated to the bed where he dropped down to watch her rummage through her clothes. "I'll talk to her, sort it out, but I still need to go in and sign those papers."

"You do that." She slammed her underwear drawer shut. "I'll be having dinner with Dani and her reputedly gorgeous hunk of a man. Who knows? Maybe I'll find another one of my own."

His eyes narrowed. "Don't push it, Indigo. It's all I can do to let you leave the apartment every day."

"Let me!" She huffed, saw that he was serious, and crossed her arms over her still-naked chest. "The day you *let* me do anything is the day I hand in my Daughter card."

His lips twitched. "Your Daughter card?"

She bit her lip to stifle a giggle, and loosed it when he collapsed against the bed, laughing so hard he rolled along the comforter. She pounced on him and rolled with him until their bodies were joined and he was inside her, exactly where she wanted him to be, always.

SIXTEEN

M UCH LATER, Indigo raced flustered and flushed into The Omega, Tellowee's one and only bar. She spotted Dani at a corner table sitting with a massive brute of a man and rushed over.

"Sorry," she said and pressed a hand to her racing heart. "I hope you've not been waiting long."

"Not at all." Dani stood to hug Indigo, a tight squeeze that let them both know everything was ok. "We haven't been here too long."

"Oh, well. I won't worry then." Indigo turned to take in Dani's companion, the famed Dave Winstead who, rumor had it, had left his job with the FBI to be with Dani. She nodded to him, determined to be polite to the man who had saved her friend's life, and her heart, no matter what Bobby thought. "I'm Indigo and you must be Dave."

He stood in a slow move that seemed to last forever as his long body rose and rose until he towered over her. "Nice to meet you."

"Wow," Indigo said, and knew her eyes were popping out of her head at his sheer bulk. "You're, ah..."

"Humongous," Dani said with a pleased sigh. "You can say it. I certainly think it enough."

Dave shot a disgusted glance at Dani as a slow flush climbed his cheeks.

"Farm boy here's a little shy," Dani said with a waggle of her thumb.

"Oh, well." Indigo took a deep breath and let it out on a shaky laugh. Her heart was still galloping from her race into the bar. "That's sweet."

Dani sat down, then Dave. Indigo pulled a chair out and sank into it gratefully.

"Where's Bobby?" Dani said.

Indigo rolled her eyes. "*Laura* called him back to work to sign some papers."

"And he went?" Dani arched a questioning eyebrow. "That's playing with fire. Doesn't he know she's got a crush on him?"

"He does now," Indigo said.

Will Corbin walked up to stand between Indigo and Dani, and rested a hand on each of their backs. "Who's playing with fire?"

Indigo turned to greet the bartender with a smile. His lean build reminded her of

Bobby, though his features and coloring were different. He had the easy grace and charming manner of a cherished Son. Indigo recalled uncomfortably that his grandmother, Anya, sat on the Council of Seven and was Bobby's aunt through his mother, making the two men cousins, close in age and lineage.

Will ran the bar for his parents, who preferred to travel, and kept the clientele in line with a flirtatious smile and a wooden bat tucked snug behind the bar.

"Bobby," Dani said. "He's ditched us to go to work and flirt with his secretary."

"Office manager," Indigo corrected, "and he's hardly flirting with her."

"Want me to handle him for you?" Will flipped the fourth chair at the table around and straddled it. "Better yet, why don't you forget about Bobby and run away with me."

Indigo pretended to consider it. "It's tempting."

"I saw you first, you know, back in school." He put his hands on the back of the chair and leaned forward, a boyish smile dimpling his cheeks. "But that rat snatched you out from under my nose before I could grow up and claim you myself."

They all laughed, though Indigo thought Will's was a tad wistful. Poor man. The life of a Son wasn't all it was cracked up to be.

He chatted with them a while longer, his casual friendliness drawing even the stoic Dave out of his shell, before he rose and flipped the chair back around. "Gotta get back to work before Moira destroys my bar."

Dani peered over her shoulder at her older adoptive sister and snorted. Indigo turned to find Moira at the bar going toe to toe with another Daughter in a heated argument over who knew what. She shook her head and turned back around. Moira's temper ran high, but she was a good person. Mostly.

Indigo caught Will's arm before he could leave. "We're planning a formal wedding ceremony for the spring. Would you be willing to stand with Bobby?"

"Of course." He braced one hand against the table and another against the back of her chair. "And since he's not here to save you..."

He pressed his lips to hers and took his time learning her, slanting his mouth over hers in a masterful display of sensuality. His hand crept up to tangle in her hair, tugging gently. Indigo sat there like a lump, unsure whether to pull away or kiss him back or bite the tongue that flicked out, testing the seam of her lips.

Dani cleared her throat loudly. "Cut it out, Will."

He drew back and tweaked Indigo's nose. "Serves him right for not being here."

She couldn't argue with that.

He moved away, earning a protest from Dani. "Hey, where's mine?"

Will flipped his towel at Dave before slinging it over his shoulder. "I like being in one piece, cousin. Catch you later."

When he'd gone, Dani fixed Indigo with a laser-bright stare. "I noticed you didn't struggle to get away from him there."

"Oh, well. I didn't know whether to punch him or kiss him back."

"Kiss him back," Dani said in a *well, duh* voice, and yelped when Dave punched her arm lightly as a reprimand.

"He's certainly got the moves." Indigo snuck a glance toward the bar where Will was pouring drinks. She fanned her face as discreetly as she could. *Moves* might be an understatement. "And I bet he'll make some woman very happy one day."

"Just not you," Dani said.

"No, I'm quite content where I'm at."

"Ditto," Dani said with a grin.

They waited for Bobby for over an hour, chatting and sharing gossip. Dave filled them in on what he could of the Shadow Enemy's movements, including what appeared to be a growing division in the Alexiou family over the organization's direction.

Indigo checked her watch for the umpteenth time and shifted on the wooden chair. Bobby should've been there to hear that, given the work they were doing for the IECS. Where was he? Surely it didn't take that long to sign papers.

Dani pressed a hand to her abdomen and grimaced. Dave placed a massive hand on her back and rubbed in slow, soothing circles.

"What is it?" Indigo said. "Are you pregnant?"

Dani gave her a disgusted look. "Why does everybody keep asking me that? No, it's this bad feeling. Ever since..."

She shook her head and the sadness in her expression touched Indigo's heart. Dani didn't have to say anything for Indigo to know where the younger Daughter's thoughts rested, on the recent events leading to her mother's death by her own hand.

"My instincts are getting stronger," Dani continued. "Right now, they're screaming at me that something's wrong."

"Can you pinpoint it?" Indigo said, but she already knew, because her gut was pinging with it, too. Something was wrong with Bobby.

No, Indigo. You're being irrational.

Just because he's running behind after visiting work late in the evening, spending time with a woman who has a big time crush on him. What could possibly go wrong?

Dani shook her head. "Not really. Something about a hawk carrying a dove in its claws. Dammit, why do these visions have to be so metaphorical?"

Indigo watched Dani continue speaking as if from a great distance. Her friend's mouth moved in animated slashes across her face, words tumbled out, she was certain, but Indigo couldn't hear them.

A hawk and a dove.

Bobby's *aenkanien*, a symbol for the weaker sibling, and her sister, the hawk, on the opposing side in their battle over the Prophecy of Light.

Indigo stood abruptly, knocking back her chair.

Dani stopped speaking in mid-word to stare at her. "What is it?"

"Bobby." Dizziness swept over Indigo. She leaned against the table until it passed. "He's in trouble."

Dani opened her mouth, but was cut short by the beep of Indigo's phone. She pulled it out with the mantra *Not Bobby, not Bobby, please, let him be ok* running through her head, and read a text sent by Hiro: *Bobby's been taken. BDH now.*

The breath froze in her lungs and she sat down as suddenly as she'd stood. Dani took the phone from Indigo's limp fingers, read the message, and flipped it shut. They looked at one another for long moments as a silent understanding passed between them. Someone had dared to take a protected son, their kin, a man who filled an important role in each of their lives.

Indigo's strength flooded back, braced by the slow anger bubbling up in her gut, and with it the steely will of a Daughter whose mate had been threatened. Bobby was in trouble. Goddess help the ones who'd taken him.

BOBBY DROVE between home and work with half his mind on the road and the other half on Indigo.

She was pissed at him.

It was bound to happen to any couple. He wasn't stupid enough to believe they were the exception, but man, her anger killed him almost as much as her tears did.

The image of Indigo huddled on the floor, sobbing after her nightmare, hit him full force and he shuddered. Nope. Didn't want to see that again.

Note to self: Keep Indigo happy. No exceptions.

Only, he wasn't going to bow to his mother the way Indigo did. Hell with that. Mom would weasel her nose in on everything if they let her. The only reason she didn't have more control over his life now was because he'd drawn those lines with her when he'd left home at sixteen. Goddess, he loved her to the bottom of his heart, but he didn't need her telling him how to run his marriage.

And Indigo didn't need his mother telling her how to treat him. His soon-to-be wife did that very well on her own.

His wife. Sweet Lady, he loved calling her that and it was true, or close enough now that Indigo had claimed him and both mothers had given their blessings. The ceremony was a formality, nothing more, a ritual that didn't mean dick compared to the love he held for her. He would hold on to her as long as she would let him, hold her, cherish her, give her the babies she longed for.

Earlier, she'd thrown Laura at him as if he could possibly care about another woman. Indigo *knew* she was the only one for him. Hadn't he shown her in every way he could? Yet she'd been jealous over his office manager, for cripes' sake.

He shook his head, bemused. So what if Laura had a little crush on him, which he didn't believe for a second. How could that possibly affect his heart, when it held only Indigo?

Anyway, Laura had never shown the slightest interest in him. Ok, so she'd given Indigo a hard time when she'd first joined them, but that was to be expected. BDH ran like a well-oiled machine most days. No one liked having a major player coming in to rock the boat. Surely once Laura got to know Indigo, the tension between them would ease into friendship.

He parked his truck in the parking deck, gave the aging dashboard a fond pat, and made his way to the elevators, bypassing security by using the private elevator. When he reached BDH's floor, it was quiet, the main lights dimmed during the off hours. He dropped by his own office, jotted a note on his calendar to talk to Margaret, then went to Laura's office. The lights were off in there as well, so he searched through the common areas until he found her in the break room.

She was sitting at a small round table in the corner, staring out the window at the night, with her hands folded demurely in her lap and her ankles crossed in that way elegant women had. He chuckled to himself at Indigo's ridiculous jealousy. Laura was pretty enough, true, but she was too staid and, frankly, too much like his mother for him to be attracted. Friendly, yes. She was a nice young woman, but she would never hold a candle to Indigo.

She looked up and gave him a faint smile, her lips tilted so slightly only someone who knew her well could distinguish the pleased expression from her normal business-like mask.

He dropped down in a chair across from her. "You shouldn't work so late."

"It's what you pay me for." She touched the fingers of one hand lightly to the pulse point at the bottom of her throat. "I appreciate your coming all the way back."

"Hey, business before pleasure, right?"

She blinked and looked away.

His heart sank. *Shit.* Maybe Indigo was right about the whole crush thing. He chafed his palms down his thighs and searched for a tactful way to test the idea.

"As a matter of fact, I was on my way to dinner with my sister and her new boyfriend. Indigo went ahead so I could come in and get those papers signed for you."

She turned her gaze back to his, solemn brown eyes wide in her face. "May I ask you a personal question?"

Uh oh. Here it comes. "Sure."

"Are you really going to marry her?"

"Yes." He met her gaze evenly and couldn't miss the slight furrow in her brow. "I've loved her for a long time, since I was a kid really."

"I see." She stood and stared down at him, a flurry of emotion running through her expression, changing it in tiny increments. "We should toast to a long and happy marriage. Would you share a soda with me?"

What harm could there be? Besides, he'd noticed her flinch. Indigo had been right. Laura *did* have a crush on him. Least he could do was let her know they would always be friends. "I'd like that."

She gave him that almost smile again and walked toward the refrigerator to pull out a coke. He took the time to observe her while she divided the soft drink between two glasses, to really see her, from the severe bun she kept her dark blonde hair in to the straight set of her shoulders to the curve of her ass. Which was nice, he admitted, but looking at it made him feel like a perv. She was a co-worker and she trusted him and, hell, half the time she felt like his kid sister. Nothing for Indigo to be jealous over. He'd be sure to tell her that asap.

Laura's hand appeared in front of him holding a half-full glass. When he'd taken it, she held hers out and said, "To the people we love."

"I'll drink to that." He tapped his glass against hers and took a sip, grimacing at the saccharine taste. There was a reason he stuck to coffee. "And I'd like to offer a toast, too. To family and friends."

"Of course," she said.

They tapped glasses again and sipped, and then she made a toast and they drank some more, and he thought of another one, and by the time they'd run out of things to toast, his glass was empty and he was pleasantly loose. That was what friendship was. Sharing a coke after work and celebrating life's moments.

"Well, I suppose I need to sign those papers, get back to Indigo before she gets worried." He tried to stand and his legs wobbled. "Whoa." He grabbed the edge of the table and laughed at his own clumsiness. "Guess I had a little too much coke, huh?"

Her features remained neutral, calm. The first inkling that something might not be right pinched at him.

He pushed up off the table, trying to stand again, and his head spun, taking him down with it until he collapsed bonelessly to the floor. The edges of his vision blurred and shrank, and the room slowly disappeared. Laura's face appeared in the pinpoint of light left, looking down at him so dispassionately, his mind flinched from it, doing what his numb body couldn't.

"You picked the wrong woman, Bobby," she said.

As the blackness took him, he thought, *Indigo's gonna kill me for this.*

SEVENTEEN

STREETLIGHTS FLICKERED BY outside the car as Indigo, Dani, and Dave sped toward BDH. Dave drove Dani's Jeep, his hands competent and firm on the wheel. Dani had taken the front seat and Indigo the rear, but their hands clenched together in the gap between the front seats, holding tight to comfort one another, staving off the worry until they knew more.

Dani had called Rebecca as soon as they'd hit the highway and even from several feet away, Indigo had felt the icy anger seeping through the phone when the Blade learned her only son had been kidnapped.

They arrived at the office fifteen minutes sooner than Indigo would've reached it on her own, even in the relatively light evening traffic. She used her keycard to enter the building at the front, and was grateful the security guards manning the lobby passed them through without question.

When they stepped out of the elevator, the entire floor was flooded with light. A man she didn't know, one of the people who worked for BDH, sat at the reception desk and pointed them to Zena's office. They rushed back and found her office crowded with people around the mass of technology the young woman had assembled.

Indigo had never been inside Zena's work area, and now she gawked at the row of monitors along one wall, the tables laden with keyboards and other equipment she barely recognized, all organized precisely under the strict hands of the tech expert.

Hiro stepped forward and pulled Indigo through to where Zena sat in a chair, rapidly tapping at a keyboard while images flashed across one of the monitors. The others showed stationary points around the building. Security feeds, maybe. One screen in particular caught Indigo's eye. She leaned forward, studying it, and recognized the break room. Laura sat at one of the tables, an ice pack pressed to her cheek, and was surrounded by a small cadre of BDH personnel.

Indigo focused on Zena and the rapid clack of her fingers on the keyboard. She faintly heard Dani introduce Dave to Hiro, Drew, and Margaret, but she ignored it to press a gentle hand to Zena's shoulder. "Have you found anything?" she said softly.

Zena nodded, shaking the multitude of thin, ebony braids hanging loose around her shoulders. "Got the whole thing, from the time Bobby entered the building to the time he left it. I'm looking for possible exits, maybe a direction we can follow so I can pick up feed from other security cameras in the area." Her soft Southern twang shifted to a pointed one as she raised her voice loud enough to be heard beyond Indigo. "Of course, I would *never* tap into those feeds without getting permission first 'cause that would be *illegal.*"

Hiro snorted. "Cut the crap, Zena."

She ignored him and lowered her voice. "Hold on. I'm gonna skip straight to the good stuff. Here, look at this."

Zena pointed to one of the monitors where an image of Bobby and Laura, seated at a table in the break room, popped onto the screen and then moved forward.

"Sound?" Indigo said.

"Nope, not in there. Sorry."

They were talking, a short conversation. Laura stood and walked to the fridge, pulled out a soft drink, and divided it between two glasses. She appeared to hesitate for a moment, and then turned and brought the drinks back, giving one to Bobby. Over the next few minutes of footage, they talked and drank as if they were toasting something. Then Bobby put down his glass, tried to stand, and slid to the floor, landing with an inaudible thump. Laura crossed to him, checked his pulse, then pulled out her phone.

A slow burn ate its way outward from Indigo's heart. She'd told Bobby to be careful with Laura. She'd *told* him. Sweet Goddess, when would he learn to listen to her?

"Ok, that was one thing, but here's where it gets interesting."

Zena typed commands and the feed skipped ahead. Another person entered the room and Indigo's heart froze in her chest. *India.* Her sister stalked over to Laura, barely sparing a glance for Bobby lying passed out on the floor. The two women talked, seemed to argue even. India pulled out the knife she kept strapped to her thigh and raised it to strike a cowering Laura. At the last minute, she pulled her blow and landed a pop to the mortal's cheek hard enough to send her sprawling. India dug a sheet of paper out of her pocket and pinned it to the table with the point of her knife before hauling Bobby up into a fireman's carry. On her way out the door, she turned and grinned smugly into the security camera.

Indigo sagged backward and bumped into Hiro. He draped an arm around her shoulders and rubbed his hand up and down her arm.

"I'm sorry," he said, so low Indigo could barely hear him.

"For what?"

"I should've known she was up to something."

She huffed out a surprised breath. "How could you possibly have known that?"

"Long story," he said, and moved away.

Indigo stared at the image of India with Bobby over her shoulder, fixing her gaze there as Margaret took the spot Hiro had vacated.

"Mom's gonna have a shit fit over this."

That was putting it mildly. "Don't worry. She'll find a way to blame me for it."

Margaret shifted her balance, crossed her arms over her chest. "Doubt that."

Right. India had kidnapped Bobby. Not a big leap to go from there to blaming Indigo. "What was on the paper?"

"And I quote, 'The Son of the Blade for the Oracle,' end quote. Woman's got balls."

"True." Metaphorically, anyway, though Indigo tended to agree with Betty White's thinking on that score.

"Hiro and Drew have already organized crews to do a search and retrieval." Margaret tapped a finger against one bicep. "That information you have might come in handy now."

Indigo whipped her head around to stare at the other Daughter. "It would expose you."

Margaret lifted one shoulder, dropped it. "Pass it off as your own. If nobody believes you, so what? It's not like they're gonna argue, not when Bobby's out there in the hands of...someone who'll probably harm him."

Indigo let the slip pass, filling in the gap in her mind. *The Eternal Order.* So her sister really was searching for a way to stop the Prophecy from happening. Why hadn't she taken that threat more seriously, especially knowing India's single-minded focus?

Indigo pressed a cool hand to her eyes, trying to find her own focus. If she could just think around the panic and worry.

"The more information they have, the easier he'll be to find," Margaret said.

Indigo rubbed a finger across her forehead, realized she'd picked up the habit from Bobby. A swell of sorrow rose within her, pushing its way upward until it hit her like a wave and threatened to drown her under its heavy weight.

"And the quicker he's found the less likely Mom is to get involved." Margaret leaned in and said in a low voice, "Do you really want her charging in here?"

"You're trying to blackmail me," Indigo said around the knot in her throat. How could she stand Rebecca peering over her shoulder while they hustled to find Bobby? "It's working."

Margaret winked. "Knew it would."

"She won't stay away, not for long, no matter what we're doing."

"No, but you won't need long. We know what India wants. All we have to do is wait for her to give us a location."

A quiet fear cut through the sorrow. India could do a lot of damage between now and then depending on how pissed off she was and whether or not she felt the need to prove something. There was a lot here for her to prove. Her superiority over their mother, who had submitted to a man and become mortal. Her diligence in chasing after a goal that would keep her from ever having to submit herself. Her worth as a Daughter and her cunning as a warrior, and the eternal struggle between one sibling and another over who got to play with the best toys.

Bobby was a valuable toy. India would want to play, and that was what worried Indigo the most.

INDIA FLEXED THE KNOTS securing Bobby to a sturdy, wooden chair, testing their strength. She'd searched him before bringing him to one of the empty houses the Order used and dropped the contents of his pockets into a trash bin outside BDH where they would be easily found. He needed to be weaponless in the off chance of an escape, though one wasn't likely. Too many eyes surrounded this house. The recent housing bubble had left them plenty of places like this, foreclosed homes held by banks that didn't watch them too carefully. This one was less than half an hour from BDH Security, nestled among several other houses also taken over by the Order, and was fully furnished to boot. Some of the Order's members even slept here.

India firmed her lips against a soft smile. She'd found a more comfortable bed not too long back. It had come with its own accessory, a sexy man with a nubile body and an endless imagination, plus as many monster movies as she could stomach, which was a lot.

Happy times.

Someone had cleared a space in the living room where they'd situated Bobby, away from the doors and windows, in part to keep him from being seen from the outside, and in part to give the Order room to maneuver in and out of the house without him knowing who, exactly, they were.

Olivia the Good stepped into the room carrying a glass and a pitcher, each full of water. Her bright copper hair was pulled into a braid that fell down her back over the leather vest she wore, a precaution every member of the Order had taken in case this whole thing blew up in their faces and ended in a ruckus. Like all of them, Olivia was a trained fighter, though she was one of the younger members, having just reached her fifth decade. Her value lay chiefly in her strategic placement within the inner circle of the Council of Seven, where she acted as an aide to one of the Seven.

"When will he wake up?"

India pushed herself into a stand and checked the clock on the mantle. "Probably not long."

"Do you think he's ok?" Olivia set the water down beside Bobby's chair before grasping his hair and gently easing his head back. She checked his pulse, pulled up one of his eyelids. "What did that girl give him?"

"No idea," India said with a shrug. "Don't care, either. He's here, right where we need him to be. That's what's important."

"Not if he dies from an overdose."

India snorted. "He's a Son."

"Yes, exactly." Olivia let Bobby's head drop and stepped back. "He might be more resilient than other mortals, but if something happens to him, it will bring the fury of the Blade down upon us all."

"Rebecca Upton," India said evenly through gritted teeth, "will do anything we ask to get her son back. She's the only one who can give us the Oracle. That's why we took him."

"Ok, ok." Olivia shook her head. "I know the plan as well as you."

"Then why are you questioning it?"

"Because it doesn't feel right to take a Son."

India stifled a curse at Olivia's naïveté. The preference Sons were accorded was one of the reasons the Eternal Order existed in the first place. No Daughter liked to be supplanted in her mother's heart by a mere mortal male.

Bobby grunted softly. His muscles tensed. India motioned for Olivia to move back, out of his line of sight.

She reached forward and slapped his cheek lightly, hard enough to help him wake up, not hard enough to leave a bruise. India had no qualms about using Bobby as a hostage, but she didn't want to rile his mother any more than was necessary by sending back a damaged Son.

He jerked away from her hand and shook his head, then winced. "Holy shit. What was in that coke?"

"No idea," India said.

He managed to open one eye enough to give her a *go to hell* look. "Couldn't you have given her something that didn't leave a headache the size of Wisconsin?"

"We'll get you something for that." India jerked her chin at Olivia, who scampered out of the room to look for aspirin. "Want some water?"

He laughed weakly. "You put something in that, too?"

"Of course not," she snapped, then inhaled sharply through her nose. Hiro kept warning her about her temper. It shamed her to admit she was working on handling it better because of him.

Changing to please a man. If anyone else knew, she'd be laughed out of the Order.

"Why did you take me?" He grimaced, shifted in the chair testing the limits of the rope. "Is it because of Indigo?"

"What does she have to do with anything?"

Bobby spared her a glance. "We're engaged."

Something ugly pushed its way up from deep inside her, shooting through her muscles until her lungs ached and her heart raced and her muscles trembled with it. "No," she said on a low growl.

"Yup. Elizabeth approved and everything." His steady hazel gaze held an odd mix of pity and triumph. "Figured you'd heard by now."

Fury. That's what was running through her. A twisted, bitter fury that her sister had chosen to mingle her life with this Son and risk submitting. Her sister, who had shared a womb with her and been her other half until that stupid man had unfurled his whip over a prank, a nothing, and Indigo had left her, retreating into a shell and abandoning India to a world that would never love her half as well as her twin had.

India swung out and backhanded Bobby in a powerful blow that jerked his head around and sent the chair teetering. "You're *lying.*"

"Nope." His gaze settled on her as he spat onto the carpet, sending bloody spittle through the air. "We're getting married in the spring."

She hit him again, so numb the sting of the blow was lost to her. The satisfaction of seeing his head pop around was not. "I'll kill you before I let her marry you."

He laughed, a hard sound that stoked her anger higher. "Too late. I already wear her *aenkanien.*"

India gasped. He was lying, in spite of everything. Men. You could never trust them. She yanked out her spare knife and walked around the back of the chair. A quick downward slash and the knit fabric of his shirt tore down the middle. She ripped it away and felt the air squeeze from her lungs at the sight of the tattoo imprinted into the skin covering his left shoulder blade. A dove. The rings symbolizing eternal devotion. Sweet Goddess, it was true. Indigo had taken him not just as a lover, but as her mate.

"Is she..." India cleared her throat, opened her lungs, searching for air. "Did she submit?"

"No." The softly spoken word fell between them like a wall dropping. "She

456

claimed me anyway."

Her palm itched against the knife's leather-bound hilt.

She could cut it off.

The idea sprang into her mind fully formed. If she cut off the *aenkanien*, Indigo would be free of him.

India's fingers tightened on the knife.

They could be sisters again, the way they once had. Working together, sharing everything.

Her last night with Hiro shuddered through her.

Well, maybe not everything, but he was just a man, nothing compared to the love one felt for a sister.

"I don't know what you're doing back there, but think hard on it." Bobby twisted around to peer at her over his shoulder. "Forget for a minute that my mom is gonna come after you. Indigo's the one you need to worry about."

"My sister will never harm me." Guilt twisted in her gut. No, Indigo wasn't the sister who lashed out and hurt her family. "And she won't miss you, once you're gone and this stupid prophecy is stopped."

"She wants my children." He turned around and slumped against the chair's low, rigid back. "Do you really want to get in her way on that?"

Indigo pressed the tip of the knife to the dove's forward wing, hard enough to draw blood. "She'll find another lover."

"Not like me."

Indigo twisted the knife, working it upward under the skin. Bobby yanked away from her with a hiss, far enough that the blade slipped out, leaving a thin line of blood. If Olivia had secured his torso to the chair, he wouldn't have been able to pull away. *Stupid girl.* Always secure a Son thoroughly, otherwise they could break free. That was the problem with having compassion for a mere mortal male. They never stayed where you put them.

India reached out to haul him back and was seized from behind by strong arms.

"Leave him," Olivia hissed, and squeezed until India dropped her hand. "No harm must come to the Son and you know it. What were you thinking?"

India drew in a shaky breath. Rational thought trickled in through the miasma of hatred and anger, and she closed her eyes at her own stupidity. She'd almost blown the whole thing because she hadn't controlled her emotions.

Hiro would be so ashamed of her.

Of course, he would be really pissed when he saw the security footage of her carrying Bobby off.

Not that she cared.

The sick roil in her gut said otherwise. She shuddered out a breath and clamped down on her emotions. Now was not the time to go all gooey over a man.

Olivia gradually let India go. "Give me the knife or you'll have to leave."

"Watch it, kid," India said as she handed her knife over. She didn't need it to have fun with Bobby. "You're not nearly as tough as you think you are."

"Try me," Olivia said. She slapped a bottle of aspirin into India's hand and stalked out.

"The fuck did you think you were doing?" Bobby said. "Maiming me isn't gonna keep Indigo from loving me."

"So now she loves you, huh." India set the bottle down and stalked around the chair to face him. "We'll see how much she loves you when I send you back to her in pieces."

She raised her fist and, with a familiar, malicious glee, rained the wrath of a scorned sister down upon him.

EIGHTEEN

THROUGH THE GLASS WALL between the hall and the break room, Laura appeared fragile, human. Her shoulders slumped, fine wisps of her hair spilled around her face, loosened from Laura's habitual bun, and a bruise bloomed across her jaw.

Fragile or not, this girl had betrayed Bobby. Temper lashed at Indigo in tandem with the cold chill creeping up her spine. India held Bobby in her tender mercies and they needed to find him. They needed information, and though Laura refused to talk, she was the best source they had.

Indigo pushed back the emotion, the urgency and fear, and reached for control. Laura would talk. Indigo would see to it.

She pushed the door open and stalked into the room, nodding politely to the one man Drew had left behind as a guard. Laura's eyes met hers then skittered away. Satisfaction shot through Indigo. The younger woman was right to be frightened.

She stopped three feet away, pulled out a chair, sat down to look at the woman who had betrayed Bobby in the worst possible way. She kept her gaze steady and direct, and waited.

After a few moments, Laura crossed her arms over her chest. "I have nothing to say to you."

"That's fine," Indigo said. "The police will be here soon. They'll be very interested to see the security footage of this room."

Laura blanched. "You can't prove I did anything, footage or not."

"Oh, but we can. No doubt your fingerprints are on the glass Bobby drank from and the residue of whatever you gave him is still inside." Indigo shrugged and tried not to enjoy herself too much. "Whether you'll be charged with kidnapping or being an accessory doesn't matter. I'll see to it you spend a long time behind bars atoning for what you did tonight."

"I'll never go to jail. My lawyer will get me off with probation, maybe community service."

"Really? Hmm." Indigo leaned forward and speared Laura with a deadly stare. "Do you think I'll let you off that easily?"

459

Laura laughed, a breathy sound that barely made it past her lips. "You can't touch me without bringing the police down on your head."

"Can't I?"

Indigo met the guard's eyes. He left with a nod and assumed a position on the other side of the break room's doors, out in the hallway with his back to them. Indigo slipped her jacket off, folded it, and laid it on the next table over.

"The thing about betraying a friend is that a lot of people are willing to look the other way to see justice done." Indigo slipped the rings from her fingers, unfastened the charm bracelet and matching necklace Elizabeth had given her for her birthday last year, and set them aside. "Zena, for instance. She was rather upset when she watched Bobby's kidnapping through the security feed. Apparently, she stays late most nights, monitoring the premises, tinkering with her gadgets. Did you know?"

Laura shook her head faintly, her brown eyes large and round in her ashen face. "What are you doing?"

"Getting comfortable. I had a long chat with Zena tonight." Indigo slipped off her flats and nudged them out of the way. An ancient Italian gentleman had hand-crafted them for her on her last visit there and they would be impossible to replace. "Now, Drew insists she's tight-lipped, won't spill a thing to him about her past, but I had no problem getting her to tell me how a job with BDH saved her and her family, lifting them out of poverty and a harsh life in one of Atlanta's worst neighborhoods. When she came to work here, she bought her mother a house in a nice subdivision out in the suburbs and now she's putting her little brother through school. Such a sweet girl."

Laura choked on a breath. Zena was many things. Intelligent and sharp, in more ways than one, but sweet was stretching it a bit. Indigo slipped the top button free from her blouse.

"What are you doing?" Laura said again in a voice shaky with the first threads of fear.

"Taking my shirt off. It's pure silk, quite delicate, and I really want to be able to wear it again after tonight." Another button and another. "Zena was so upset about Bobby, she agreed to cut the security feed to this room during our chat."

Laura stood suddenly and Indigo shoved her back into the chair one-handed.

"Try to leave again and I'll make it twice as hard on you," she warned.

Laura clutched the chair's arms. "What are you going to do to me?"

"Whatever I see fit." The last button slid free. Indigo pulled the shirt off and draped it over the back of a chair, then undid the fastening of her slacks. "The thing is, you drugged my husband."

"You're not married yet," Laura said in a thin, choked voice. "Bobby said so."

"We haven't had a formal ceremony, true," Indigo acknowledged. She slid her slacks off, folded them, and placed them on top of her jacket, and stood in front of Laura in the matching lace bra and panty set she'd worn to tease Bobby with later, before this woman had drugged him and allowed India to carry him away. A thin shaft of rage penetrated the icy calm. "But in the eyes of our People, the deed's been done, and was long before you came into Bobby's life."

"I don't know what you're talking about."

"You wouldn't because you're an outsider, a mortal human, and no matter what you think, you were never good enough for him. He would never have chosen you because he'd already given his heart to me." Indigo leaned forward and grasped the other woman's jaw in a firm grip. "How old do you think I am?"

"Urm." Laura's breath rasped out of her. "Twenty-five?"

Indigo laughed coldly. "One hundred and sixty two. Do you know how much you can learn about pain in a century and a half, even when you're not trying to?"

"You're crazy."

"I assure you that I'm quite sane. Pissed, yes." Indigo squeezed Laura's jaw until she cried out before letting go. "You harmed my husband. Another Daughter would've killed you by now. Me, I want to see you suffer a bit before you die."

A tear leaked from the corner of Laura's eye as she leaned as far away from Indigo as she could. "You'll never get away with killing me."

Indigo lashed out with her fist, popping Laura hard enough to break her nose. The other woman screamed and bent over, hands clasped to her face, blood dripping between her fingers onto the carpeted floor. Indigo walked behind her, dug her fingers into the remnants of Laura's bun, and yanked.

"When I was a little girl, my mother skinned a man while he was still living, merely for daring to strike her children." Indigo ran a fingernail down the long, slender column of Laura's neck, and let the shudder of fear that ran through the other woman stoke her own resolve. "How long do you think you would last, once I start peeling your flesh away?"

"Please." Laura's tears turned to quiet sobs. "Let me go. I promise I'll leave. You'll never see me again."

"I'm afraid that's not possible." Indigo released Laura's hair and brought her hand down in a hard chop that bruised Laura's back, drawing a high-pitched mewl from her. "No matter what I do to you, Bobby's mother and sisters will insist on coming after you. They'll go easy on you if Bobby's returned to us undamaged, but if he's harmed in some way, well. There's no telling what they'll do to you, little girl."

Indigo stalked around the chair to face the sobbing woman and casually backhanded her hard enough to snap her head around. "The women of his family have led interesting lives." A punch to the upper arm, followed by a loud cry of pain. "They call his mother Rebecca the Blade for her skill with the sword, earned in battle centuries ago when she was still little more than a child." A swift rib shot snuck in under Laura's raised hands, dealt hard enough to crack the bone and elicit another screaming sob. "I wonder if she's sharpening her blade now?"

"No," a steely voice said.

Indigo whirled. Rebecca stood at the entrance to the break room wearing a threadbare plaid shirt and worn jeans, calmly examining Laura slumped over in the chair, moaning, and Indigo in her lingerie with Laura's blood spattered along her hands. Bobby's sisters, all save Jerusha, and several other Daughters were ranged out along the glass wall in the hallway, backs to the break room in an unbreakable chain. No one was trying to get in, though several BDH personnel snuck peeks over and through the wall of Daughters.

Rebecca walked forward, grasped Laura's jaw, and raised the young woman's face to assess the damage.

"Please help me." Laura's voice wheezed out of her throat and her eyes were wild. "Please."

"No, child." Rebecca dropped Laura's jaw and leaned in until their faces were inches apart. "Do you know who I am?"

Laura shook her head slightly.

"I'm Bobby's mother. Whatever Indigo has done to you is a mere trifle compared to what awaits you at the end of my hand." Rebecca stood. "Where did India take my son?"

"I don't know. I swear." Laura sniffed once, winced and placed a delicate hand to her broken nose. "She said she would exchange him for something important and he would never be hurt. That's all I know."

"Pray India told you the truth and no harm comes to my son." Rebecca stepped back and gave Laura a final dispassionate look before turning to Indigo. "The police are on their way up. Hiro's delaying them as long as he can, but they'll be here soon. We need to get you cleaned up."

"Yes, Maetyrm." Indigo bowed solemnly. "There's a shower in the gym one floor up. It should be empty."

Rebecca gathered Indigo's clothes into her arms. "We'll take the stairs."

Indigo turned her back on Laura and followed Rebecca out of the room, ignoring the furtive stares from the mortal men and women clustered around the break room's door. Rebecca didn't speak on their way upstairs, through the gym, and into the women's locker room, leaving Indigo alone with the security feed playing in her head. Bobby falling to the floor, given into India's care by a woman he trusted. Her sweet Bobby, who held her in the night and loved her as no man had ever done. Temper leaked abruptly out of her, leaving a cold, tight fear. If something happened to him...

Her lungs froze in her chest. No, nothing would happen. She would find him and bring him home and he would be ok. They would both be ok.

The footage looped around and restarted, and her fingers curled into fists.

Laura, on the other hand, hadn't suffered nearly enough.

In the shower room, Indigo stripped off her bra and panties and placed them in Rebecca's outstretched hand.

"I'll check these for blood while you clean up." Rebecca set the underwear aside before tugging out the clip holding her own hair back. "Turn around and I'll pull your hair up so you can keep it dry."

"Thank you." Indigo turned, bending down enough so that Rebecca could bundle her hair up out of the way. "I'm fine here if you want to go back downstairs."

"I'll stay, if it's all the same to you. We can chat while you shower."

Indigo's heart slipped a notch. "Yes, Maetyrm." She stepped into the shower, left the curtain open so they could talk, and turned the water on, waiting for it to warm before she stepped under the steady spray and squirted soap from the container mounted in the stall into her hand. "How's Robert?"

"Oh, he's fine." Rebecca picked up Indigo's bra and ran it through her fingers, examining the fabric for blood spatter. "Miffed because I made him stay home. He's in no shape to traipse all over this building. He only agreed to stay after I pointed out that someone might call our home with a ransom demand."

Indigo bit the corner of her mouth as she scrubbed her skin. That someone would probably be her sister, which had to cut at Rebecca. How right Bobby's mother had been to bring India into the marital negotiations. Of course, if Indigo had known India's plan to kidnap Bobby, she would've nipped it in the bud before he could be taken.

"This is very nice lingerie." Rebecca shifted the bra in her hand and focused on the other cup. "Where did you get it?"

"A little boutique in Buckhead." Indigo squirted more soap into her hand and began to work on the beds of her nails, where tiny spatters of blood had already dried and caked. "Very exclusive. A lot of their inventory is handmade."

"It's too bad you didn't buy this in dark blue to match your eyes. The lavender is lovely, but the blue would've made your eyes pop."

Indigo wasn't sure what to say, so she held her tongue. How often did a woman have a conversation about underwear with her soon-to-be mother-in-law, especially if that underwear had been bought to entice said mother-in-law's son? Rebecca probably didn't need to know that, though.

"I bet Bobby went wild over this," Rebecca said.

Indigo snorted out an embarrassed laugh.

"Watch your hair, dear. It wouldn't do to get it wet." Rebecca raised a knowing eyebrow. "Do you think I don't know what the two of you do when you're alone? Child, I learned about the birds and the bees well before your mother was born."

Indigo turned her face carefully into the water, using it as an excuse to hide her flaming cheeks. Of all the things for them to talk about, this was the one Rebecca had to pick. Anything else would've been a more comfortable topic, even her rogue twin.

When Indigo was as clean as she reasonably could be, she turned the water off and accepted the towel Rebecca handed her.

"Besides, I want grandchildren."

Indigo blinked, suppressing the urge to roll her eyes. "I had no idea."

"Sarcasm is unbefitting a woman of your status," Rebecca said, though her voice held no bite. She handed the lingerie to Indigo. "I think these are safe to put back on."

"Thanks."

Indigo folded her wet towel and set it on the counter before shimmying into her underwear and pulling her clothes on over top. She pulled the clip out of her hair and handed it to Rebecca, who twisted her own blonde locks up into her customary chignon.

"Ok, let me look at you." Rebecca ran her hands over Indigo's hair, smoothing wayward strands, and straightened her shirt until it hung properly. "Yes, I think you'll do. No one will be the wiser unless one of Bobby's crew reports us to the police."

"I doubt that." Indigo slipped her jewelry back into place and stood patiently while Rebecca adjusted the necklace. "They're a loyal bunch."

"Not as loyal as some. I had no idea you could be so vicious."

Indigo ignored the odd note of pride in the older Daughter's voice with a casual shrug. "She hurt Bobby. I couldn't let her get away with that."

"Tell me something, Indigo." Rebecca paused, seeming to weigh her words before continuing. "Were you beating her out of duty or because you have feelings for my son?"

"Both. I would never have claimed him if I didn't care for him."

"You seemed so unfeeling. I have a hard time believing you were doing it because your heart was involved."

Indigo's temper spiked and she bit it back. "I was plenty pissed. Still am, but I went in there to gather information. Mortal humans are frail. If I'd let the anger take over, I would've killed her before learning anything."

"I see." A smile bloomed across Rebecca's even features. "Cold-hearted logic. Your sister could take a few lessons from you on that score."

"We're different people," Indigo said, and knew she'd failed to hold back the exasperation when Rebecca's smile widened. "People always assume that I'm weak because I'm quieter and sometimes more gentle, but I'm still a Daughter. The blood of the Sisters runs as swiftly through my veins as it does through hers."

"Yes, it does." Rebecca threaded her arm through Indigo's. "When Bobby told me you'd claimed him, I had my doubts, but now I can see how unfounded they were. I couldn't be more pleased at being wrong about you."

"Oh, well." Indigo cleared her throat. "I'm not sure how to take that."

"As a compliment. Now, come along, dear. We have work to do."

Indigo allowed Rebecca to lead her back through the gym, stopping long enough to throw her towel into the laundry before they went back downstairs to see if India had called.

IT TOOK HOURS to organize. In that time, no one called with a place to meet and exchange Bobby for the Oracle.

Rebecca had no intention of giving her up, not even for the life of her own son, but it wouldn't come to that. Bobby's people, his friends Hiro and Drew and all the others who worked with them, were scanning video feeds, tracking down leads from a sheet of paper Indigo had given them, and gearing up for surveillance and a rescue attempt when they had a location. Rebecca held back from the fray, observing the way they worked together as a near-seamless unit, tightly focused on their mission.

It brought back memories, some fond and others not, of her own days in the field, first as a squire, then as a soldier, and finally as a leader.

Indigo worked well with the others, slipping in wherever she was needed, and caring for everyone else when she wasn't. She and Hiro seemed particularly close, bending their heads together to confer more than once, seemingly reaching for an odd sort of comfort from one another. Once, Hiro drew her in for a hug and Indigo's shoulders trembled under his steady embrace. They seemed to be caught somewhere between friendship and something deeper, though what that might be puzzled Rebecca. There could be no doubt who held Indigo's heart after the little scene with Laura, none at all. This friendship, or whatever it was that had developed between Indigo and Hiro, was no threat to Bobby, and so didn't worry Rebecca.

What did worry her were the quiet looks passing from Margaret to Indigo and back again, except for the moment when Indigo had presented that paper with the miraculously appropriate leads they needed to track down India and her little gang in the Order. Then, Indigo had studiously kept her attention on the group, not once sliding her gaze to Margaret's.

That paper illuminated intricate connections only a handful of people could make. Indigo was not among those, but Margaret, with her particular duties to the

People, was. If others found out where Indigo had obtained that information, both their lives were forfeit.

Rebecca studied the pair as they worked apart toward the same end.

She hoped they knew what they were doing.

HOURS PASSED, dragging Indigo with them through the long night while they waited for word from anyone on Bobby. She stayed at BDH, helping where she could. The next day dawned and still no news. Her nerves stretched thin and taut as the hands on the clock in Bobby's office inched around its face, marking off the time until the sun fell again behind the mountains.

She missed him so much.

It had been easy to stay strong when the police arrested Laura and during the mini-interrogation Indigo and everyone else had endured.

No, she hadn't spoken to Laura since Bobby's kidnapping, though she'd heard the other woman had tried to escape a couple of times and gotten beat up pretty badly in the process. Such a shame, she'd said, and her expression had been so sincere, the police woman questioning her had let it drop.

Strength had come easily when Nicodemus Hutley, the Special Agent in Charge of the local FBI field office, had come in with his slow drawl and quick mind, asking nosey questions about the kidnapping that had taken him perilously close to learning about the People. Dave had taken care of it, but Indigo suspected Hutley would be back. Next time, he might not be put off so easily.

She made a note to remind Bobby to instruct Zena on better procedures. The next time someone was kidnapped, Goddess forbid, keep the police out of it. They only ever got in the way.

Her energy had gradually flagged, worn down one tiny incident at a time, from Rebecca's watchful gaze, darting between Indigo and Margaret as if she knew what the two of them were doing, to helping with efforts to track down India and Bobby, to Hiro's mournful apology.

Damn him, he'd finally let it slip that he and India had been, as he put it, *watching a lot of Godzilla*, which Indigo took as code for *having wild and dirty monkey sex*. She'd wanted to ask what had possessed him to take up with a rogue Daughter, but it had been plain on his face. Hiro was falling in love with India, Goddess help him. India wasn't known for her kindness toward men, though Indigo hadn't the heart to share that with Bobby's friend. In the past, her sister had never stayed with a man longer than one night. That she'd chosen to hang around Hiro long enough to *watch a lot of Godzilla* might be a good sign.

Indigo wanted to be happy for them. Maybe if things were different she could be, but until Bobby came back to them, it was hard for her to dredge up anything outside of exasperation for Hiro and a cold fury at her twin.

Now, twenty-four hours after Bobby's kidnapping, Indigo's energy had fled and her mind was gritty and numb. Everyone else had taken the time to rest, even Rebecca, who had gone out with Charlotte to tend Robert and her younger daughter's family.

Indigo had tried, by settling in on the couch in Bobby's office for a short nap. As soon as her eyes closed, she saw Bobby, trying to stand and then falling to the floor, and India lifting him easily and carrying him out, away from Indigo and the people who loved him. Over and over again, it played through her head until she'd finally gotten up and plowed back into the rescue efforts.

An hour later, Dani caught Indigo in the break room making the umpteenth pot of coffee and yanked her mug away.

"Forget it," Dani said flatly. "We're taking you home."

Indigo pressed tired fingers to her eyes. "I'm needed here."

"No, Indi," Dani said, and tears welled up so suddenly at the nickname that one escaped and slid down Indigo's cheek. "You're no good to Bobby like this."

It was the only thing anyone could've said to get her to leave. Indigo gathered her things, checked in with Hiro to let him know where she was going, and let Dani and Dave take her home. Indigo sat in the back, watching the lights flash past along the highway and listening to their softly voiced their conversation, a soothing murmur of comfort.

Dave parked Dani's Jeep and they walked up with her, making sure she was safely in the apartment. Dani hugged her hard before they left. The quiet support nearly broke the thin thread of Indigo's control.

She locked up and wandered, trying to pin down why the apartment felt so wrong before her tired brain put it together. Bobby wasn't there. It was too big without him, the rooms hollow and lonely. The yearning to have him close washed up so suddenly, she swayed and nearly toppled under its weight.

They would find him and bring him back. She repeated those words over and over again to herself, using them to block the images from the security feed that perpetually looped through her mind as she undressed, slipped on one of Bobby's t-shirts, and crawled into bed. She pulled his pillow close, holding it with a desperation born of fear and sinking hope. His scent washed over her, the spicy cologne he used mingling with the sharp fragrance of his shampoo, and under it all, Bobby's unique masculinity. She breathed it in, taking it into herself, and clung to it as tears leaked out and her heart throbbed in her chest and turned over in surrender.

She loved him.

A sob mingled with a half-laugh. What perfect timing, to figure it out now.

Another sob escaped and on its heels came the emptiness. Goddess, she missed him, missed him so much it hurt. She turned her face into the pillow and let go, let the hurt and the anger and the worried fear out in great, heaving sobs into Bobby's pillow, and when she was spent, finally fell into a restless sleep.

Intermittent beeps woke her. She peered at the clock, tried to bring the digital numbers on its face into focus and failed. Bleary eyed, she flopped onto her back and checked the light seeping in through the closed blinds. Sunrise, she guessed, and searched for the beeps.

She finally found the source in her cell phone. Someone had sent her half a dozen texts while she slept. She opened one and read the message. *Come now.* The next one said the same thing and the next. Neurons fired in her brain hard enough to bring her fully awake while she hurriedly scrolled through all of them. *Come now.* She checked the phone number, didn't recognize it, and sent back a message.

Where?

The answer was an address that Indigo immediately forwarded to Hiro, Drew, and Margaret. She bounced out of the bed and threw on clothes, and called a taxi to drive her to BDH.

It was time to get Bobby back from India.

Nineteen

BDH WAS A MADHOUSE of activity by the time Indigo arrived. Drew barked out orders from his office toward the back of the floor. Indigo weaved through the people rushing back and forth, saw Hiro conferring with a team already half geared up, and finally found Rebecca and her daughters holed up in Bobby's office.

She pushed the door open in time to hear Margaret say, "Forget it, Mom. You're not going."

"She's right," Indigo said.

Heads snapped around, Moira's, Charlotte's, even Rebecca's, who regarded Indigo with a flat stare meant to intimidate her into submission.

It wouldn't work this time.

Margaret gave her an amused look, but the person Indigo wanted to see was Bobby's next youngest sister, seated on the far side of the couch past Moira, slumped down with her eyes closed, and Charlotte, who smiled prettily at Indigo in greeting, and Rebecca, whose gaze never wavered.

Indigo and Jerusha were only two years apart in age and had attended school together at the IECS during the turbulent war years of the 1860s. They'd been fast friends until Bobby's failed play for Indigo had placed a harsh strain on her relationship with his family. It was the one regret Indigo had about leaving Tellowee and avoiding the women in his family. She'd missed her friendship with his sister. Now that the embarrassing *incident* of fourteen years past had been resolved, it would be nice if she and Jerusha could renew their friendship.

"Jerusha, it's so good to see you." Indigo picked her way over legs and knees and furniture until she could hug her favorite of Bobby's natural siblings. "When did you get in?"

"Couple of hours ago." Jerusha pulled back from the hug and touched her forehead to Indigo's. "Mom called as soon as she heard about Bobby. I packed a bag and started hopping flights to get here."

"I'm so glad. We could really use your help." Indigo moved away and settled into the empty chair in front of Bobby's desk beside Margaret, who had taken the other one. "Has Margaret filled you in?"

"Yeah. Hiro's got this idea about spreading us out between teams, with Mom here at command to oversee us and Charlotte back home with Dad to head off any calls there."

"Sounds like a good idea," Indigo said. "What's the problem?"

Margaret snorted. "Mom wants to go with us."

"Absolutely not," Indigo said. "You're mortal. You stay."

Rebecca narrowed an icy gaze at her. "I've been taking care of my own hide for nearly a millennium."

"That's not the issue here." Indigo leaned forward and met Rebecca's gaze with a steely one of her own. "You're a more valuable asset than Bobby. If for some reason you were to be captured, we would have no choice but to hand over the Oracle."

"That won't happen," Rebecca said.

"You're right, it won't," Indigo snapped, "because you're staying here to coordinate the teams and guard Zena."

"Wow, this is better than a tennis match," Charlotte said. "Maybe we should televise it. You know. Do the pay-per-view thing and make some money."

"I'd pay to see it again," Moira said. "Maybe after the sun's fully up. Don't know why you Yanks can't sleep to a decent hour."

Indigo ignored them. "It's settled then. Charlotte, check in with Hiro, make sure he doesn't need anything else, and then you can head to the Upton home. We'll call as soon as we have word."

"I'll make a good, solid breakfast and have it waiting for y'all," Charlotte said, and slid out of Bobby's office in search of Hiro.

"Is there a place I can get cleaned up?" Jerusha stood and pulled her lean body into a full, bone-cracking stretch. "Don't have time for a shower, but I'd love to brush my teeth."

"Oh, here." Indigo rose to rummage in Bobby's desk. "He keeps spare toothbrushes and toiletry items in here. I always wondered why before."

"Now you know," Jerusha said with a wink. "Which way?"

Rebecca rose as well. "I'll show you. It will give us time to catch up a little."

Moira went with them, mumbling about coffee and rubbing her eyes like a child pulled from her bed too soon.

When they were gone, Margaret swiveled her chair around to face Indigo. "Didn't know you had it in you to stand up to her."

Indigo huffed out a laugh, caught somewhere between insult and pride. "I'm learning to draw a few lines."

"Atta girl."

They hunkered down over a copy of the intel coming in from the team Drew had placed around the residence where Bobby was being held and strategized as time ticked quietly by.

THEY TIMED THEIR STRIKE for just after nine a.m., when nearly everyone in the neighborhood around where Bobby was being held would have gone to school or work. Hiro divided their groups into units containing two immortal Daughters and two mortal BDH personnel each, with extra teams standing by in case they were needed. The Daughters who weren't trained in BDH tactics were to take rear positions and allow the others to lead.

They parked a block away from the residence where Bobby was being held and walked in through back yards, up and over or around fences when needed, moving quietly in the morning's stillness. Hiro led one team with Indigo, Jerusha, and a young BDH man Indigo knew only as Sanchez. Margaret, Moira, Drew, and another BDH man comprised the other team.

They held their weapons at the ready, each according to preference, and eased around the sides of the house, Hiro's group to the front, Margaret's to the rear, avoiding windows and shrubbery as they moved into position. Hiro took the door, gently tested the handle, and mouthed *unlocked.* Sanchez peered carefully around the sill of the front window, frowned, and shrugged.

He couldn't see in.

Hiro nodded and mouthed a countdown, and then pushed the door open, allowing it to swing wide before they rushed in one by one, Hiro first, then Sanchez, with Jerusha and Indigo close behind. From the back of the house, sounds filtered forward of Margaret and Drew's team entering.

The first thing Indigo saw when she came in was Bobby slumped over in a chair with his back to them, his shirt torn completely off and a bandage wrapped around his ribs. India stood over him with her hands on his head. She looked up, her eyes round with surprise, and then she was gone in an agile sprint that carried her out of the room and into the hallway, away from the back of the house.

"Got her," Hiro said as he broke into a run.

Indigo caught Jerusha's gaze. "Go after him. I've got Bobby."

Jerusha nodded and shot out the front door.

Indigo raced to Bobby and dropped her sword behind his chair. The damage done to his beautiful body had her heart stuttering in her chest and a slow, crawling dread creeping up her spine. Ropes dug into his forearms, holding him to the chair. Probably the only thing keeping him upright. His eyes were swollen and bruised a dark purple, his nose bloodied, his lips split and cracked. More bruises blossomed along his jaw, down his neck, and over his arms and torso, running under the bandages before peeking out below them.

She inhaled sharply through her nose as a slow and steady heat rose in her, burning through her until her vision blurred red and her blood boiled.

Someone had beaten him, torn at him while he was helpless to defend himself.

Her fists clenched as the anger became so big, so hard, that it threatened to burst from her. She swallowed it back, and with it the bile that had gathered in her mouth on seeing her beloved husband's beautiful body treated like a punching bag.

No, Laura hadn't suffered nearly enough, but she would.

Indigo palmed her knife, used it to carefully slice away the ropes, and caught him when he slid from the chair. Hands pushed in, helping her settle him on the floor. She gently prodded his injuries, stripped his pants and boots off to check his legs and feet, and was relieved to find the bruises confined to his upper body and the breaks to his ribs.

She closed her eyes, steeling herself for what else needed to be done, and pulled down his briefs to check his penis and testicles, the first place a Daughter usually struck on an enemy male. And sank down with a small prayer of thanks to the Lady

Goddess that he was hale and whole there.

Whoever had beaten him hadn't wanted to maim him permanently.

Not whoever. *India*. No one else would've dared to treat such a valuable hostage so poorly.

Damn her twin's temper and complete lack of respect, for Indigo, for the strength of Bobby's family, for Bobby himself.

Hiro came back in puffing and dropped to his knees beside Bobby, his gaze steady in spite of his heaving breaths. Jerusha followed and stood behind him, and Indigo's heart sank at the hard set of the other Daughter's expression.

India had gotten away. For once, Indigo wished her sister wasn't such slippery prey.

Margaret came in from the back. "Checked the whole house. Nobody else is here."

Drew settled down beside Indigo. "Let us get him. He needs a hospital."

"I can help," she said.

"No, we've got him," Hiro said. "Won't be the first time."

"Probably not the last either," Drew added with a grin.

"Good times," Hiro agreed.

Indigo moved out of the way to let them care for her lover, and tried not to ponder what trouble the three men had gotten into before Bobby had walked back into her life.

BOBBY CAME TO with a groan amid the beeps and wheezes of machinery. His body was one big ache from his waist up and his eyes felt like they were frozen shut. He lifted a hand and felt a gentle touch on his arm, holding him back.

Indigo.

He turned his head toward the soft sounds of her breathing and said her name. A rusty, unintelligible grunt came out instead.

"Shh. I'm here. Everything's ok now." Her hand stroked his hair back, a cool brush along his skin. "Water?"

He opened his mouth, tried not to flinch when the cuts on his lips cracked apart, and felt the touch of a straw there. He sipped, let the water dribble down the back of his throat, and fell back against the pillow with a sigh. Questions sped through his mind, pushing their way through the fogginess of whatever drugs were in his IV. He cleared his throat and managed to grate out, "Long?"

"It's been three days since you were taken." Clothing rustled, a chair scraped back. "We came in and got you as soon as we could."

He nodded once.

"They were trying to exchange you for the Oracle. Did you know? Rebecca refused, of course, but there was no question about that. We were coming for you." Her hand fluttered across his thigh, landed there, a warm, solid comfort. "I hope you know we would never have left you."

Strain thinned her voice. He patted awkwardly around the bed, searching for her until she twined her fingers with his. It had never occurred to him that she wouldn't come for him, not once. Why would she even bring it up? Even if she never loved him, she would always come for him. He wanted to tell her he knew that, tell her he loved her enough for both of them. The words faltered in his throat, caught by the pain or the meds seeping through his blood or a parched and injured mouth. He heaved in a frustrated breath and gasped it back out when pain shot through his torso where his ribs had cracked under the hail of India's rage.

"Stop trying to talk," Indigo said. Her fingers tightened on his. "Get some rest. We can talk later."

He wanted to talk *now*, needed to tell her, and struggled with it until someone came in and adjusted the medicine in his drip, sending him into a numb void where Indigo couldn't follow.

BOBBY DRIFTED THROUGH THE NIGHT, waking more times than he could keep track of. *Indigo.* He had to find her, tell her something, *do* something. Every time he remembered what it was, *where* he was and what had happened, someone hit the pain meds on his drip and he fell back into the darkness.

At long last, light drifted across his eyes, piercing his subconscious. He followed it up into full wakefulness and inhaled, searching for air and hissing out a sharp breath when pain throbbed through his torso.

"Bobby, darling, can you open your eyes for me?"

"Mom?" He rubbed a sore hand across his eyes and pulled back when his fingers found a sticky gel slathered thickly over his eyelids. "The hell?"

"Dr. Phillips used a salve to keep the wounds around your eyes from sticking to the bandages." Cool fingers trapped his hand and pulled it gently away from his face. "Stop fiddling with it."

He tried to lift his eyelids, earned a thin shaft of light and a stab of pain for his troubles, and shut them again. "Get it off."

"Don't be a baby," Rebecca said.

"It's uncomfortable." He winced at the whine in his voice. "Where's Indigo?"

"Talking to the nurses. Here, hold still."

Something soft rubbed across his eyes, taking some of the sticky goo with it.

"Why were my eyes bandaged?" he said.

"Because you kept trying to open them. Dr. Phillips said they'd never heal like that. There now. Try again."

He slitted his eyelids open, let his pupils adjust. Rebecca moved away, out of his line of sight, and the room dimmed into blessed darkness.

"Thanks." He blinked, trying to focus. "Time is it?"

"Eight thirty four a.m., nearly a full day since Indigo and your friends rescued you." Something moved near him, a lightness against the darker shadows, and finally resolved into the blurry figure of his mother. "You've been under nearly that whole time, although that wouldn't have been necessary if you hadn't fought against your IV every time you woke."

He ignored the gentle chide. "Was trying to find Indigo."

"She's barely left your side. Poor thing." Rebecca sighed. "She's trying to assume responsibility for your kidnapping."

His heart sank. Indigo and her damn sense of duty. "Wasn't her fault."

"We all know that, darling." Her fingers grasped his gently, comforting him. "She feels guilty anyway."

He closed his eyes, tired of fighting to keep them open. "Did they get India?"

"She slipped away, though I suspect she hasn't gone far."

The door squeaked open and soft footsteps sounded on the tile floor. A hand stroked his forehead, then a light kiss pressed there.

"Indi?" he said and reached for her with his good hand.

"You're awake." Her voice held that soft lilt she used when she was happy. Her fingers found his and squeezed. "I was starting to worry."

"Don't." He tried to open his eyes again, needed to make sure she was really there and not another dream. "Missed you."

"Stop trying to open your eyes." Her lips touched his briefly before she let his hand go and moved away. "You're healing quickly, but they need a few more hours, ok?"

"Sure." He turned, trying to find her in the room by the sounds she made moving through it. "We were just talking about how my kidnapping was not your fault."

"Try being a little more subtle, Bobby," Rebecca said with a wry twist in her voice. "Else you'll bludgeon us all with your bluntness."

Better bluntness than Indigo on the run again, trying to outpace the guilt. "The truth is harsh sometimes."

"Yes, but it's not a hammer." A shoe hit the tiled floor. Cloth shifted as someone stood. "Now that you're awake, I'm going to go home and catch a nap. I'll be back in a couple of hours with your father so Indigo can take a break." Rebecca pressed a kiss to his cheek, then whispered, "Try to talk her into going home for a while when we return. She won't leave you and it's wearing her down."

Air brushed across his skin as she moved away. The door squeaked open, shut softly, and then Indigo was there next to him.

He felt for the edge of the bed and gingerly scooted over as far as he could to make room for her, holding a hand to his ribs to keep from jostling them. "Sit with me."

"Oh, no, I couldn't. Your ribs..."

"I'll heal better if you're close."

Her laugh held as much relief as it did humor. "Nice try, but no. You've had enough damage done to you to last us all a while."

"I've been through a lot worse than that, honey." He reached for her, found an arm, and tugged. "This is just scrapes and bruises."

"And busted ribs and burst blood vessels in your eyes and internal bleeding and bruising. You're lucky you didn't puncture a lung." She sat on the edge of the bed so that their hips touched, and placed his arm on her lap. "She punched your beautiful mouth."

He grinned. "Out of all the cuts and bruises, that's what bothered you?"

She huffed out a sigh. "No."

"So it didn't bother you at all to see me beaten up and wounded."

"Of course it did, you oaf." She squeezed his hand. "She did a number on your face, though. When I saw you, I thought she'd broken your jaw."

"Nope. Just the ribs." He ran his tongue over his teeth, testing them. "Loosened a couple of teeth, maybe."

"I could just kill her for this. What was she thinking to hurt you?"

"Ah, well." He cleared his throat, winced when even that tweaked his ribs. "I might've goaded her just a little."

"You *what?*" Her voice was sharp enough to make him wince again. "Why would you do that?"

"She tried to cut my *aenkanien* off and I got pissed."

"She..." A long sigh. "By the Goddess, I should take her down for that alone."

"Don't even think it. I know you. If something happens to her, it'll kill you."

"Not this time. It was one thing to kidnap you, and something all together different for her to tie you to a chair and beat you unconscious. Stop trying to open your eyes."

"I want to see you." He lifted his eyelids cautiously, found it easier to keep them open than before, and focused carefully on Indigo, sitting on the bed beside him. He drank her in, running his gaze over her hair hanging in a loose cascade down her back and the paleness of her face. "Is that my t-shirt?"

"Oh, ah. Yes." She fluttered a hand at it. "I hope you don't mind."

"Not at all." He tried to pull his hand free and gave up when she easily overpowered him. Damn drugs. "Are you wearing a bra?"

"Really, Bobby. This is no time for a question like that."

"It's always the perfect time to know if you have a bra on or not." He shifted and cursed under his breath at the stabbing pain radiating from his ribs. "Does this thing have a switch on it so I can sit up?"

"Hold on." She slid off the bed and searched, and a moment later the top half tilted upward, taking him with it. "Better?"

It stopped before he was sitting all the way up, but since it was easier to breathe, he didn't complain. "When can I go home?"

"Forget it," she said, and though her expression was stern, a quiet laugh tinged her words. "You're staying here until Dr. Phillips says it's ok, even if I have to sit on you to keep you here."

Interest stirred in his loins. "That sounds promising."

"Do you think of anything other than sex?"

"Yes, all the time, but right now, sex seems like a good topic."

"Sex is a horrible topic right now." She sat at the far end of the bed next to his legs. "What with those busted ribs and all."

Bobby winced. She just had to remind him. "How many did she get?"

"Three and that's plenty. Now, close your eyes and get some rest."

"Bossy." But he closed his eyes, content now that he'd found her. "It'd be better if you were up here."

"Maybe tomorrow," she murmured as he drifted into sleep, comforted by her nearness.

TWENTY

THE HOSPITAL was silent by the time India arrived. Visiting hours were over. The night shift nurses had clocked in and were quietly making their rounds. It was easier to sneak in and do what needed to be done in the still of the night.

If she hadn't been betrayed, the Oracle would already be in the hands of the Eternal Order, but no. That bitch Olivia had gotten cold feet and texted Bobby's location to Indigo. The safe house had been overrun by BDH personnel and Bobby's sisters before they could make the switch, Bobby for the Oracle. India wouldn't have made it out if Hiro were a Son. As it was, she'd barely managed to elude him.

He'd probably make her pay for that later, if he'd even speak to her again.

She bit back a sigh and checked the corridor before sliding into it.

That feeling in her gut wasn't disappointment. Couldn't be. She'd never needed a man before, never intended to in the future. It just wasn't in her make up.

Goddess, she missed him.

She closed her eyes and leaned her head against the wall as a massive ache lodged itself in her chest. What a fool she was. All this time, she thought she'd been so clever using Hiro for sex and an in with Bobby's company, but in the end, she was the one who'd been played. He'd snuck into her heart, taken over, and now, she felt so lost, so alone. It wasn't love, not yet, but she was getting there, and with a man who would probably never forgive her for kidnapping and beating his best friend.

He wasn't the only one pissed at her. Indigo would be after her for trying to peel the *aenkanien* from Bobby's skin, and Bobby's sisters, well. They would simply follow their mother's lead.

India beat her head against the wall, cursing her own stupidity. She'd known better than to take her anger out on Bobby and had done it anyway, in a fit of jealous rage over his place in her sister's heart.

Hiro was right. Her temper would get her in trouble one day. Looked like that time had come.

Once she'd left the safe house, she'd doubled back, watched Bobby being carted away, seen Indigo's heartbreak and felt its echo inside her own heart.

And then she'd found the traitor Olivia and taken great pleasure in beating a confession out of the sniveling Daughter.

Voices sounded at the other end of the hall, forcing India to move. She ducked into the stairwell and went up another flight. The Oracle was here, somewhere. The mission could still be salvaged. If India got caught killing her, it would be no loss, and at least the People would be rid of a possible key to the Prophecy of Light.

INDIGO WAITED WITH REBECCA in the hallway while Dr. Phillips examined Bobby. She and Bobby's mother hadn't spoken much since his return, not about his kidnapping or about the shape he'd been in when they'd found him. People had been streaming in and out since he'd been admitted, paying their respects, angling for gossip. She hadn't been alone with Rebecca long enough for them to really talk.

Indigo was glad to put it off. With everything else going on, the last thing she wanted was a conflict with Rebecca. Bobby needed them both right now, cooperating, not sniping at each other.

She smoothed a hand over her shirt, straightening it more out of habit than concern. Nurses came and went, their tread softened by rubber-soled shoes. Visitors filed out of rooms to head home for the night. The steady rhythm of the hospital ground its way through her frayed nerves. How long did a checkup take?

When she was on the verge of barging in to see what was wrong, Dr. Phillips came out of Bobby's room wearing a rueful grin. "He's asking to go home."

"You told him no, didn't you?" Indigo said. "Surely he's not well enough yet."

"Truth is, he could've gone home last night if I'd thought he'd rest," Ethan said. "I only kept him this long because I know what he's like."

Rebecca inclined her head in a graceful nod. "What excuse did you give him this time?"

"The two of you, and those are my last excuses. Tomorrow morning, he goes home and you'll have to find a way to make him rest once he gets there." A friendly smile stretched across his handsome face, crinkling the corners of his eyes. "Try to keep your children out of trouble, Director. This is the second one I've treated here in as many months."

"I shall do my best, Dr. Phillips," Rebecca said with a rueful smile of her own.

"Not much chance of that, is there?" Indigo asked softly when Dr. Phillips left.

"I'm afraid not." Rebecca pierced Indigo with a penetrating look. "When was the last time you took a break?"

"Not long ago. Um." Indigo flipped her wrist over and checked her watch, and was stunned to see how late it really was. "Around lunch, I think?"

"And it's after supper now." Rebecca placed her hands on Indigo's shoulders and squeezed. "Go take a walk, a nice long one. I'll hold down the fort here for a little while, try to keep Bobby from going stir crazy.'

A nice solitary stroll through the quiet hospital corridors, alone with her thoughts. What a lovely idea. No one to entertain while they visited Bobby, none of the noise of people trooping in and out nonstop. Being with Bobby was easy by comparison, even with his restlessness. They'd spent the day talking during the few moments they'd been alone and he'd been awake, simply chatting about whatever came up. But having all those people there, pressing in, their words friendly but their expressions questioning. It had been difficult to bear, on top of everything else.

Guilt cut in and Indigo bit her lip as fear quickly followed it. The last time they'd been apart...

She pushed the thought back and the flutter of panic with it. Begging trouble wouldn't do any good. Being prepared by carrying a weapon wherever she went, that was smart, but lingering on what might have been was pure foolishness. "It's my place to take care of him now," she reminded Rebecca.

"Go," Rebecca said firmly. "Robert's expecting me home soon, and when I'm gone, you won't have another chance for a break until tomorrow morning."

Indigo hesitated, torn between protecting Bobby and the need for space.

Rebecca leaned in close to her ear and said in a barely audible whisper, "The Oracle's on the next floor up."

The Oracle. Here? What was she doing...? Indigo searched her memory. Right. The Oracle had awakened during a visit by Maya Bellegarde and her fiancé, James Terhune, less than two months before. She'd been moved out of her special room near the IECS Archives to receive better care, though Indigo hadn't heard that the Oracle was still in Tellowee.

"Will you stay with him?" Indigo said.

"For a while," Rebecca promised. "He'll be fine if I have to leave."

Indigo wasn't so certain. There was always the worry that Bobby would get up and walk out of the hospital on his own, though surely he would wait for her.

"I'll be quick," she said, and waited until Rebecca went into Bobby's room before heading for the elevator.

BOBBY WAITED PATIENTLY while Ethan Phillips flicked a light across his eyes, checking to see if they reacted properly. Ethan was a couple of years older than him. They'd gone to school together at Tellowee before Ethan graduated and went on to study medicine. In the way of Sons in all of the People's settlements, they'd banded together with the other Sons both in school and out, to train, to make mischief, and to have friends who understood what it was like to be the protected child.

It was hell growing up among a bunch of kick ass girls who tolerated zero sass, but it could also be a lot of fun. Panty raids at the dorms brought all-out wars on the campus' quads in the middle of the night, to the exasperation of the dorm parents, but what could they do? When you trained kids from birth to fight and spy, it was pretty hard to stop them from sneaking out and wreaking havoc on their fellow students, all in the name of fun.

The Sons had always gotten their asses handed to them because they were always outnumbered, but they'd had a hell of a time doing it.

Bobby grinned. "You remember that time Darren Stovall got stuck in the AC vent trying to raid his girlfriend's dorm?"

Ethan clicked his pen light off and put it away. "Haven't thought about that in ages. What ever happened to him?"

"Heard he got married, moved to the California branch to be with his wife a couple years ago."

"Who in their right mind would take him?" Ethan said with a grin. "I guess you and Indigo'll tie the knot soon."

"Officially, yeah. Unofficially, it's a done deed."

"Congratulations, man. She's a good woman." Ethan leaned against the side of the bed and crossed his arms over his chest. "If you play your cards right, I'll let you go home with her tomorrow morning."

Another night stuck in this hospital bed, with Indigo sleeping in the chair? Not if he could help it. "Any chance I can leave now?"

"Nice try, but no dice. Your mom would kill me."

"Come on, be a pal." Bobby dropped his voice to a whisper. Indigo was out in the hall with Rebecca. If he was quiet, maybe their supersensitive Daughter ears wouldn't catch him begging. "I'm a newlywed, for cripes' sake. Do you know how long I waited for her?"

"Sorry, man." Ethan snagged Bobby's chart and scratched notes onto the top page. "Indigo's already threatened to put the hurt on me if I release you any sooner than I have to."

Bobby dropped his head back against the pillow. He'd wanted Indigo to find her courage, really he had. He just hadn't wanted her to use it against him. "Don't be a wuss."

Ethan narrowed his eyes. "If you weren't lying in that bed, I'd show you what a wuss I'm not."

"Bring it, man. I could use a diversion."

"Concentrate on getting better so you can go home to your wife." Ethan tucked the chart away and moved to the door. "See you tomorrow, bright and early. Get some rest."

"Yeah, thanks."

When Ethan was safely out in the hall, Bobby sat up carefully in the bed. His ribs still ached and made breathing a little hard, but the rest of him was healing rapidly. This time tomorrow night, he'd be back in Indigo's arms, showing her how much he loved her, as often as his body would let him.

Damn India's hide.

He shook the thought off and placed his feet flat on the cold tile floor. It wouldn't hurt to walk a little, move around to ease the stiffness. Since his wife and mother were out in the hallway being distracted by the good doctor, now was as good a time as any to try his legs out.

He gripped the edge of the mattress and was leaning forward to ease off of it when his mother came in. She took one look at him and frowned as she shut the door behind herself.

Busted. *Dammit.* He'd hoped to at least make it to the bathroom on his own.

"What do you think you're doing, young man?" Rebecca said.

"Getting up. What does it look like?"

"Getting into trouble." She sat down in the chair at his bedside. "You're lucky Indigo took a walk to stretch her legs or she'd have you back in that bed quickly enough to make your head spin."

He rolled his eyes skyward. Oh, if only she would. He snuck a glance over his shoulder to find his mother pinning him with a glare. "Gimme a break, Mom. I've been stuck in this bed for more than a day now."

She inhaled a sharp breath. "You're lucky that's all you'll spend there. When we find India..."

"Don't start." With a sigh, he shifted back onto the bed so he could talk to her face to face. "She's Indigo's sister and as far as I'm concerned, that makes her off limits."

"Off... Are you out of your mind? Look at what she did to you. If I don't go after her, it sets a horrible precedent."

He gave a half laugh. "Yeah, right. Leave off, Mom. I'm not gonna have an all-out war with Indigo's family over a couple of cracked ribs."

Rebecca's mouth thinned into a harsh line. "Elizabeth agrees with me on this. She's done everything but banish India."

"Well, she can just unbanish her." He cut her off with a wave of his hand. "When we find India, she'll take responsibility for her actions, but I don't want it to go beyond that. No revenge killings. No harsh fines. I mean it, Mom."

She considered him for a moment before tucking her feet under herself. "Indigo's already influencing your judgment."

"No. We haven't even talked about this." He clutched his thighs, willing his patience to win out over the exasperation. "Are you ever going to accept her in my life?"

"Oh, Bobby. I didn't mean it like that." She reached forward and grasped his hand, squeezing it gently. "It's a good thing, her influence. You're happier now. A blind man could see how much better your life is with her here. I'm very glad the two of you have finally found each other."

He covered her hand with his, felt it warm against his skin. "I love her so much."

"I know." She turned her hand over and threaded her fingers through his. "I know you do. She loves you, too, you know."

He shook his head and let his hand slide away, afraid to hold on to any hope where Indigo's feelings were concerned. "No, but it's ok. Someday she will."

"What a pair the two of you are. You're afraid to look into her heart and she's worried she's not good enough for you. Honestly, what am I going to do with you?" She sat back with a smile that made him nervous. That was her devious smile, the one she wore when she was up to something, and it sent a chill of unease down his spine. "Do you know where she is right now?"

"Walking the halls, trying to find some peace, if she's got any sense in her," he retorted.

"The Oracle."

He sat straight up and grimaced at the tug in his ribs. "You're kidding."

"It shouldn't be a difficult walk for you." She stood and gathered her purse and coat together. "Your father's expecting me at home. I'll have a nice lunch waiting for the two of you when Dr. Phillips releases you tomorrow."

He held his cheek up for a kiss and said goodbye while a quiet buzz grew in his head and his heart beat double-time in his chest.

Indigo had gone to see the Oracle.

Daughters went to see the Oracle all the time, to read to her, to bring her gifts, but there were two times when the sleeping woman was always visited: When a Daughter submitted her will to a man and became mortal, and when she married.

Usually, those two occasions happened at the same time.

His heart sank. Of course. Indigo was only visiting to tell the Oracle she'd married. Dammit, she still could've waited for him, even if she didn't love him. It was traditional for the couple to present themselves together. He ignored the stab of hurt to his heart and focused on the irritation instead. What was she thinking, doing an end run around him and making such an important visit without him?

He scooted off the bed and eased onto his feet. Indigo might not love him, but she needed to understand that they were in this together. His wife needed an object lesson on that score. There was no better time than the present to give her one.

TWENTY-ONE

I
T WAS A QUICK TRIP to the next floor. Indigo used the time to clear her mind. Traditionally, couples approached the Oracle with news of a happy event, but from time to time, Daughters went there alone for counsel.

The Oracle never spoke, save when she'd awakened the previous month. It was the solitude, the time for reflection in the presence of a woman who was thought to be one of their oldest Daughters that drew people to her. It was for this that she'd allowed Rebecca to persuade her to leave Bobby. Indigo was in dire need of time to sort her mind out.

She hadn't had the nerve to tell Bobby of her love. He would accept it, not as his due but as the natural course of their relationship, and he would be happy. She just wasn't ready yet to share it with him. As deep as her feelings ran, they were still new, fragile. She wanted to hold on to them a little longer, treasure the love for the rarity it was.

She could tell him tonight, she thought, and immediately reconsidered. No, not while he was still in hospital. It had been hard enough to resist him when it was his heart alone involved. Now that hers was, too, she had a feeling he would try to charm her right out of her clothes and into the hospital bed with him, where they would do many things other than rest.

She smoothed her ponytail back and firmed her lips against a smile. If she told him she loved him, he would want to... How had Hiro put it? Oh, yes. *Watch a lot of Godzilla.*

A laugh left her before she could stop it. She put a hand to her mouth and looked around before remembering that she was alone. No one had seen her being silly.

The elevator dinged and Indigo stepped out into the silence. The ICU was on this floor, though she doubted a long-term care patient like the Oracle would be there. Maybe in a private room?

She followed the signs to the nurse's desk and found it empty. Odd. Weren't there always supposed to be nurses on duty, especially here?

She tapped her fingers against the laminated countertop, racking her brain for another solution. The Oracle never went anywhere without at least two Handmaidens guarding her. *Find the Handmaidens, find the Oracle*, she thought, and set out to do just that.

The soft clack of her shoes against the floor echoed eerily in the empty hallways. Indigo bypassed the ICU, searching for a private room instead, but after circling the floor and encountering not one living soul, her sense of wrong blossomed into unease. She slipped her shoes off and hid them behind the desk, then pulled her Keltec from its holster at her ankle. It wasn't much and she probably wouldn't need it, but better out and unnecessary than holstered and needed.

She checked the ICU first and found only one patient, an elderly gentleman who was very much alive, judging by the beeps and whirs of all the machinery he was hooked up to. She checked the other rooms one by one, easing each door open and peeking in before clearing it. The first two rooms were empty, so she moved to the next one down the hall.

She pushed the door to the third room open and scanned it. Unlike the other two rooms, this one's bathroom door was closed. She checked the handle, turned it easily, and opened it on three nurses sitting in the tiny space, bound and gagged. Two were out cold, and had been put that way with a hard right hook, if the bruises on their jaws were any indication. The third, a young brunette, eyed Indigo warily above her gag.

"Indigo Dupree," she whispered. "I'll cut you loose if you promise not to try anything."

The other woman nodded. Indigo placed the Keltec on the floor outside the bathroom's entrance, pulled out her pocket knife, and gently sawed through the gauze wrapped around the nurse's head and across her mouth.

"Thanks," the nurse whispered when Indigo was finished pulling it away. She wiggled around and offered her bound hands to Indigo, and rubbed her wrists when they were loose. "Are you the cavalry?"

"Hardly." Indigo set her pocket knife to the bindings around the nurse's ankles, then carefully began cutting through the gauze securing the other two nurses. "My fiancé's downstairs, waiting out some busted ribs. I decided to take a break and come up here to visit someone special. Who did this to you?"

"You did, I thought," the nurse said. "And then it hit me that if you'd done this, you wouldn't come back for us, not to set us free."

Indigo rubbed the back of her wrist against her forehead. India. *Sweet Goddess.* There was only one thing her sister would want on this floor. "Can you walk?"

"Sure. What do you need?"

"Call down to the next floor and tell Rebecca Upton that India Furia is after the Oracle."

"I know Director Upton." The nurse shrugged at Indigo's curious look. "You work here long enough, you get to know the regulars."

Indigo bit the inside of her cheek to stifle a laugh. Regulars, indeed. "Will you be ok?"

"Yeah, I know what to do. Thanks."

"Anytime."

Indigo retrieved her gun and padded out of the room into the hallway, peering up and down it before she entered, then resumed her search for the Oracle.

After checking several empty rooms, she pushed open the last door at the end of the hallway and found India standing over the Oracle, a sharp, long-bladed knife in her hand. Indigo propped the door open and cursed under her breath. The Handmaidens were nowhere in sight. What had her sister done with them?

"She's beautiful," India said without looking up. "I didn't think she would be."

"Step away, India. Please." Indigo raised her gun with one hand and aimed the barrel at her sister's chest. "I don't want to hurt you."

"Don't you?" India flipped the knife in her hand, tapped the blade against her thigh. "I tried to kill Bobby."

"You did a piss poor job." Indigo inhaled sharply, barely reining in her growing anger. "You should never have taken him."

"It was the perfect plan. Bobby for the Oracle. The Son for the woman whose death might ensure that no more Sons would be born. What could go wrong?" The last words were said so softly they were barely audible. India reached out a hand and gently smoothed it across the Oracle's forehead. "I told her about Hiro."

Indigo's grip on the gun faltered. "You've submitted?"

India's laugh held equal parts humor and bitterness. "No."

"Then what?"

"I realized I could love him someday, if things were different. If I had less of a duty and more of a heart."

"You have plenty of heart, India," Indigo said gently. "It's just not always in the right place."

"Is it not, kaetyrm?" India turned to face Indigo, her face twisted with anger. "Did I not love you enough?"

"Of course. I know you love me."

"Is that why you turned on me, when that man hit you?" India reared back and hit the headboard of the Oracle's bed with enough force to crack it, jarring the comatose woman. "Is that why you left me?"

Indigo shook her head, confused. "What are you talking about?"

"He whipped you and I couldn't stop him. Over and over again he hit you. I tried to get him to quit, to make him stop, and I failed." India threw her head back and screamed her rage into the empty air. When she stopped, her chest heaved with more emotion than Indigo ever remembered seeing her sister demonstrate. "You *left* me that day, Indigo, left me alone with Mámá, and she hated me for not stopping him."

"No, India. No," Indigo said as shock hit her. "That's not what happened. It was nothing, a few hits from a whip. I healed."

India shook her head. The tears streaking down her face glinted in the light spilling from the hallway. "You don't remember what it was like before, how close we were. Like two halves of one person. After, you were never the same and I was lost. I *needed* you."

"I was always there, India." Indigo dropped the hand holding the gun, numb. All that rage, building for a century and a half inside her sister's heart, and she could've stopped it, if she'd only known. "Tell me what to do to make it right."

"Leave him." India stepped forward, her hand raised in a silent plea. "Come away with me, tonight, and we can leave all of this behind us. It'll be just like it was when we were kids, you and me, together like sisters should be."

"I can't," Indigo whispered. "He's my heart, India. You don't know what you're asking."

"Your heart. A man is more important to you than your own sister?" India sneered as her hand dropped. "I should've killed him when I had the chance."

"Don't push me on this," Indigo warned. "I'll defend him to the death if I have to."

"You and your duty." India stepped back, moving slowly until she stood at the Oracle's side again. "I have my duty as well, kaetyrm."

She raised the knife high above her head. Indigo brought the Keltec up and squeezed hard against the trigger, firing into the wall above India's head.

"Step back, India." Indigo lowered the gun, pointing it at her twin's torso. "Next time, I won't aim for the wall."

India frowned with visible disbelief, though she held the knife steady. "You would really kill me over this?"

Indigo met her sister's gaze calmly. "If you force me to."

"Sister." Emotion flickered across India's face, softening it. "I won't blame you for it."

She raised the knife and bore down on it, and Indigo fired just as strong arms came around her, knocking her aim off. India cried out and clutched at her arm, her eyes wide in a face that had gone pale.

Indigo noticed her sister's wound and reaction only peripherally as she struggled to regain control of the Keltec and wrest herself away from whoever was holding her. She jabbed an elbow back, connected solidly, and froze when a low male hiss sounded in her ear.

"Bobby?" she asked and pivoted her head toward him.

"Easy with the elbow there, Indi." He shifted to hold her arms in a firm grip. "Give me the gun, sweetheart, and I'll let you go."

Indigo shrugged to loosen his hold. "She's trying to kill the Oracle."

"I can see that. Now give me the gun."

"No. She's crossed the line this time, Bobby." Indigo squirmed in his embrace, searching for a weakness in his hold outside of his ribs. "If I don't kill her, she'll keep trying and eventually, she'll really hurt someone."

"You're not killing her. Indigo, listen to me." He squeezed his arms until she stopped struggling and lost her breath. "If you kill her, you'll never be the same. I can't let you do that. Please, Indi. I know how much you love her."

Indigo hauled in a breath as emotion welled up, love for her sister and for the man beside her; regret over the past and the many wounds that could never be healed; and sorrow for the hand she'd had in turning her sister into the angry, bitter woman she'd become.

A tear slipped from the corner of her eye and then another, and she sniffed them back before they overwhelmed her. Her arms went limp and she let Bobby take the Keltec from her hand. He was right. She couldn't kill India, even knowing what her sister would do if left unchecked. In spite of all their differences, the love between them was too great. Bobby had known that, reminding her over and over, and had understood their bond much better than anyone else, even their mother.

Indigo turned her back on India and clung to Bobby, intending to tell him how very much she loved him. A sudden dizziness filled her head and her vision dimmed. She gasped as a huge, invisible weight pressed upon her, threatening to crush her and then lifted just as quickly, leaving her shaken. From a distance, she heard India call her name. Bobby caught her close to him and cupped her face with one hand. His lips moved, though she couldn't make out his words, and then her eyes rolled back in her head, sparks flashed through her brain, and her body jerked so hard she slipped from Bobby's grip and dropped with a hard thud to the cold, tile floor.

BOBBY DROPPED INTO A CROUCH beside Indigo and patted her face gently, trying to rouse her. India scrambled across the room and skidded to a stop, kneeling on her sister's other side.

"Is she ok?" she said in a tight voice. "What happened?"

"I don't know." Bobby checked Indigo's pulse and sagged with relief at the steady beat. Color had bled from her skin, turning it a shade paler than the floor, and she was as cold as ice under his fingers. "One minute I was trying to convince her not to kill you and the next she passed out."

India dropped onto her bottom and covered her eyes with her hands. "She's submitted."

Bobby did a double take. "No, can't be. She doesn't love me, not yet."

"Oh, please. You think I don't recognize the signs?" India dropped her hands and shot a withering glare at him. "Besides, she as good as told me she loved you not five minutes ago. It was just a matter of time before you broke her will."

"You have a really warped vision of love."

Bobby shook his head and turned his attention back to Indigo. She should've woken already, if she really had submitted to him. Hope blossomed in his chest. Did she really love him? He took a shaky breath, brushed her hair back, and tried it out in his mind.

Indigo loves me.

That sounded stupid, like a kid reciting a Sunday School verse, but he didn't care. Indigo loved him and she'd submitted, and she would never leave him again. He leaned down and pressed a tender kiss to her lips, pulling back when India hooted out a laugh.

"She's not Sleeping Beauty, you oaf."

"Shut up," he said, though he couldn't keep his lips from twitching into a smile. "You're bleeding."

"Yeah, flesh wound," India said with a shrug. "I would say thanks for saving me, but she was shooting a Keltec. Can't hit the side of a barn with that thing if you're not up close and personal."

"She didn't want to kill you."

India snorted. "Could've fooled me."

Bobby gave her a flat look. "She had a duty to protect the Oracle."

India returned his stare with one of her own. "I have a duty to protect the People, too."

"How is killing an innocent woman protecting the People?"

"Figure it out, Bobby. You're not dumb." She rolled her shoulders and winced before raising her arm to look at the bleeding gash bisecting it. "Doesn't matter anymore. Now that I've bungled this mission, the guard on the Oracle will double and we'll never get another chance at her."

"I don't want to know," he said in a hard voice. "But if you ever make Indigo choose between doing the right thing and saving your hide again, I'll come after you myself."

"It's not the first time it's happened. Can't promise it won't be the last."

"Try."

India grinned. "You know, I kinda like you."

"Yeah, I can tell. Next time, leave my ribs alone."

"Next time, don't pissed me off." She slapped his shoulder, then pushed herself into a stand. "She's coming 'round. Let's get her downstairs so the two of you can make goo-goo eyes at each other in private."

Bobby stared up at her, nonplussed. "You go down there, you'll get arrested."

"Hunh. Doubt it. I'm too slippery for that." She hefted him up. "I haven't forgiven you for taking her heart."

"Get over it."

She looked away, tapped her fingers against her thigh. "She was mine first."

"For cripes' sake, she's not a damn toy."

"I know," she said softly, and grabbed his arm when he made to bend. "I'll get her. You'll puncture a lung or something if you try to lift her."

India leaned down and pulled Indigo up. When she was halfway to standing, Bobby grabbed an arm and draped it over his shoulder while India took the other one.

"Bobby?" Indigo said in a slurred voice. "What happened?"

"You passed out," he said. "Can you walk?"

"Think so." She peered at him owlishly before turning her gaze on her twin. "Did you kill her?"

"No, now stop talking and start walking," India said. "I need to leave soon."

"Probably too late," Indigo said, and she sagged to one side. "Sorry. Still a little dizzy. One of the nurses called Rebecca."

India cursed under her breath and leaned forward to look at Bobby. "I'll help you as far as the elevator and then I gotta go."

They hobbled out into the hallway at a slow pace and made it only a few feet before Rebecca stepped into their path, her bare feet silent on the floor.

Bobby took one look at his mother's set expression and sighed. "Get out now, India," he murmured.

She carefully pulled Indigo's arm over her head and stepped back away from them. A booted footstep rang against the floor behind them. Bobby glanced over his shoulder. His gut clenched when he saw Margaret blocking the hallway to their rear.

"Get her out of here." India met his gaze calmly. "If I don't make it, tell her I love her. Tell her..."

"You can tell her yourself," he said. "They won't kill you."

She barked out a harsh laugh. "For what I've done, I deserve to die."

He shook his head, but it was too late. She'd already pivoted around on quick feet and made a running charge at his sister. Indigo tried to pull away from him and he gripped her harder.

"Forget it, Indi," he said and began hauling her down the hallway toward his mother, ignoring the twinge in his ribs. "You're not helping her this time."

"She's my sister."

Her voice held a kind of hopelessness that ate at him. Damn India for doing that to her.

When they reached his mom, he said, "Make sure Margaret doesn't kill her."

"Oh, we don't want her dead," Rebecca assured him. "She's too valuable for that."

A shiver of dread ran down his spine. "You're not talking about her being Indigo's sister, are you?"

"No, dear." She patted his arm. "But I'll keep that in mind."

"You do that."

Indigo shifted in his embrace, her eyes fixed on India and Margaret's fight. Bobby followed her gaze. Moira had joined Margaret, and though India was holding her own, she wouldn't be able to keep it up forever, especially if Rebecca entered the fray.

Indigo didn't need to see her sister being beaten into submission.

"Come on, love." He pressed gently against her waist until she turned with him. They leaned on each other as they walked down the hallway. The sounds of the fight receded behind them, the thuds of blows and grunts fading until the elevator doors closed them off completely.

BY THREE P.M. THE NEXT DAY, Indigo had had more than enough of other people. The night before, they'd waited an eternity before Rebecca came in with news. Margaret and Moira had subdued India and turned her over to the local police on charges of kidnapping and attempted murder. After Rebecca left, Indigo had allowed Bobby to coax her into the narrow hospital bed where he'd held her until the sun crested the horizon. She'd done her best not to disgrace herself by crying all over him.

When Dr. Phillips released Bobby, they'd gone straight to his parents' house and eaten lunch with his family, his mother and father, his sisters, Charlotte's family, and even Dani's new beau, Dave, who Bobby had scowled at until Rebecca sent them out to the basketball court behind the house to settle their differences.

Indigo had worried the entire time about Bobby's ribs, but apparently the two men hadn't played basketball or fought either one. They'd come back in looking less hostile, if not exactly friendly. It was a start, a foundation to what she hoped would become a lifelong friendship.

She and he had finally managed to sneak away half an hour before. Indigo opened the door to their apartment and heaved a sigh. It was good to be home.

Bobby came in behind her and closed the door before wrapping his arms around her. "Alone at last."

Indigo turned in his embrace and rested her head against the broad plane of his chest. It had been so long since they'd been here together. A lifetime seemed to've passed since then. "What shall we do?"

"I have ideas, lots and lots of ideas." He nuzzled her hair, bent to nip at her ear.

"Days worth, maybe. Let's lock the door and work our way through them one at a time."

"Mmm." She tilted her head to one side, giving him better access as he moved from her ear to her throat. Pleasure rippled through her at each touch of his mouth until a throbbing ache settled between her thighs. She untucked his shirt and ran her hands gently along the firm skin at his waist, mindful of the tender bruises lingering there, and reveled in the way his breath hitched with every stroke of her fingers. "It's the middle of the day."

"So? We're adults. Who's gonna stop us?"

"How are your ribs?"

"Still a little twingey."

She dropped her head to his chest. "Maybe we shouldn't do anything."

"Oh, we're gonna do something all right." He wrapped her ponytail around his hand, tugged her head back until their eyes met, and said in a soft, low voice, "I need you, Indi."

"Bobby," she whispered, and stood on tiptoe to press her lips to his. "Make love to me."

She led him into their bedroom where they undressed each other and fell into the bed, skin brushing against warm skin, their mouths locked in a desperate, needy kiss. When Bobby slid into her, she gasped and arched against him, and they moved together, letting passion build slowly until it overwhelmed them in a soundless wave that swept them into sweet release.

Afterward, Bobby rolled onto his side and pulled her to him. She rested her head on his bicep and slid a leg over his to keep him close, half afraid he'd slip away from her again.

"I love you," she said. "So much."

He leaned back and caught her gaze with his. "Yeah?"

"I do." She snuggled into him and let his heat warm her, as it always had. "I'm mortal now."

His arms tightened around her. "That's what India said. Didn't believe her, though."

"You talked to her?"

"While you were out." He ran his chin over the top of her head, pressed a kiss there. "She was worried about you and none too happy we'd mated."

"I know. Will you ever forgive her, do you think?" She sighed, regret filling her. Playing the *what might've been* game would do no good, but the possibilities roiled through her mind anyway. The what-ifs stretched from her childhood right up through India taking her rage out on Bobby and the Oracle. "I won't blame you if you can't."

"I'm not important here, sweetheart. She's your sister. If you can forgive her, I'll support that."

"This is why I love you," she said and laughed when he reared back, disbelief written across his face.

"You love me because of your sister? That's kinda kinky."

She curled her fingers into his chest, careful not to scratch. "Stop it. I meant, I love you because you understand, because you love me enough to want me to work it out with her."

"Is that all?"

She smiled at the humor in his voice. "No. You're the best man I've ever known."

"Hunh. I've done a lot of things you don't know about."

His words from the first time they'd made love drifted through her mind, all the things he'd done in the Army, and with it came the guilt. She'd pushed him into doing that through her own inability to deal with his young heart, through her own fear of his love. "I know enough to tell you it doesn't matter. We've both done things we regret."

"I don't want you to regret anything." He bent to take her lips with his in a tender touch that brought an ache to her heart. "Not a thing."

He slid his hand down her back and cupped her bottom, pulling her up until her hips pressed against his erection.

Her breath caught in her chest and the heat of desire throbbed through her. "Already?"

"I'm pretty sure always," he said with a laugh.

"What about when...?" She bit her tongue to hold the question back. "No, never mind."

He propped up on his elbow above her, his other hand a gentle caress on her hip. "What?"

"When you were in the Army." She shook her head slightly. "I don't think I want to know."

"You mean, how did I get through nine years without having sex," he said flatly. "I tried not to."

She flinched away. "I told you I didn't want to know."

"You need to hear this." His hand tightened on her hip. "I tried to have sex with other women after I took your mark, tried to love somebody else, and it never took, not once. You've had my heart since the first time I saw you."

"Oh, Bobby." Tears pricked at her eyes and she sniffed them back. Of all the things she'd ever done in her life, this is the one she'd do over if she could. "I'm so sorry for the way I treated you then, for running out on you and breaking your heart."

"Don't be. You were right the first time. I was too young." He rolled onto his back, taking her with him. "But now you're here and it's enough."

She straddled him and rested her hands on his lean stomach. "Tell me you love me."

"I do, baby. I love you." He squeezed her hips as his eyes went soft. "With all my heart until the day I die."

"Marry me." She lifted her hips and brought them down, sheathing him fully within her, stretching herself with his hard length. "My needing time is soon. I want to be married before we have children."

His wide mouth tilted into a wicked smile, lighting his hazel eyes from within. "Elizabeth already blessed us. We're married, sweetheart, have been for a while."

"Why didn't you tell me?" she said, and let happiness pull a laugh from her. Of course he'd already secured her mother's permission, not the grudging acceptance of a mother for her Daughter's mate that Elizabeth had given in the formal presentation, but a true blessing. In the eyes of the People, that final permission was more binding than anything mortal law required them to do. He would want them to be bound as tightly as they could be. Now that she'd found her heart and him in it, she wanted that, too, just as deeply.

"I've been telling everybody who'd listen." He took her hands and kissed the tips of her fingers. "Thought you'd figured it out already."

"No, but now that I have, it's too late for you. I'll never let you slip away again."

He pulled her forward and thrust up into her with slow, lazy strokes. "Just try and get rid of me."

"Not a chance," she said, and took her time giving him all the love in her heart.

EPILOGUE

INDIA WOKE SLOWLY, climbing her way carefully through the dense fog in her head. With every breath, her lungs burned and her ribs pinched. Aches blossomed across her face, down her torso, along her arms and legs, and memory hit.

Indigo shooting her to protect the Oracle.

Bobby throwing off Indigo's aim and Indigo losing her immortality to him.

Shuffling down the hallway with them. Rebecca stepping into their path.

Trying to get past Margaret, and then Moira, and the hits that kept coming, even after she'd fallen to the floor and curled into a ball to protect her internal organs and head.

And then nothing.

She tried to open her eyes and winced when light pierced through her. She lifted a hand to shield herself from it and heard the *shink* of metal on metal as her hand came up short, stopped by a cold grip on her wrist.

She lost her breath as dread crept through her. They'd chained her, probably had her in a cage somewhere. Her heart tripped, stalling in her chest, and raced hard and fast when it found its beat again. A cold sweat broke out on her skin and her lungs heaved, trying to catch air.

Locked up in a tiny cell surrounded by concrete and the hopeless stench of the enslaved. Her worst fear, come to life.

She struggled against whatever was holding her, trying to break free, and screamed when a hand came down on her arm.

"Hush now. You're safe."

She turned her head toward the gentle male voice. "Hiro?"

Her own voice sounded oddly broken as it rasped out of her throat. What had they done to her?

"Don't speak." A hand brushed hair off of her forehead. "If I unlock the handcuffs, will you promise not to try an escape?"

She nodded carefully, sighed when the metal bands slid away from her. "Where?" she whispered.

A long silence followed, so long she thought he'd left. "Somewhere safe. It's better if you don't know the details."

She nodded again, not sure why she was agreeing, and curled onto her side. The ground gave next to her. No, not the ground, a bed. Hiro had sat down close enough for his heat to radiate onto her. A shiver ran through her and then another one until her body shook from head to toe with it. She bit her lip, trying to quell the tears, and felt them streak hotly down her face anyway. Something soft fell against her, covering her, and then he was behind her, holding her gently.

"You're safe now. I've got you."

After an eternity, the tears quieted and her body warmed. Questions ran through her mind too fast for her to hold on to them, except for one. How had he gotten her away from Rebecca and her daughters? She struggled to form a question and finally managed a single, "How?"

"You want to know what happened. I get that, but it's too complicated to talk about now." Something brushed against her hair, his face maybe, and then his mouth found her neck, pressing a kiss there. "I'll tell you all about it later, when you're awake enough to understand. For now, try to focus on getting better. Dr. Phillips said you'll be fine, but you took a beating."

She winced. That part, she remembered. It was everything else that was fuzzy.

"Look, I'm still kinda pissed at you, so pissed I almost let them lock you up, but you don't have to worry about that anymore. You're safe. Your record's been wiped clean. As far as the law's concerned, you never existed." His sigh blew across the back of her neck. "I can't believe I'm telling you this now. You're not gonna remember."

"Will." She coughed to clear her throat, groaned as pain stabbed through her so hard her vision dimmed. She waited it out, clinging to his silent strength, using it to claw her way back to reality. "Thanks," she managed at last, and let his chuckle bring an answering humor from her.

"Stubborn. Thank God for that. I thought I'd lost you."

She shook her head, careful not to jostle it too much. There was so much she wanted to tell him, so many things bottled up in her heart. How she'd thought of him when she'd fallen under Margaret's sledgehammer-like blows, and how she'd wanted to live then, wanted so badly to live long enough to tell him how much he meant to her. She might never be able to love him, not the way a woman was supposed to love a man. Her heart was too damaged for that, but what was left of it, she wanted him to have.

Even if it could never be love.

"Shh, baby. Go to sleep now. I'll be here when you wake up, promise."

Dizziness washed over her. She let it take her down until she fell into a deep, healing sleep, secure in the embrace of the only man she'd ever trusted.

ACKNOWLEDGMENTS

So many people have helped me get to this point.

Richard E. Hopkins, Jr., has worn nearly as many hats as I have over the past eighteen months, including alpha reader, developmental editor, and cheerleader. He's provided paper and a copier, internet access, meals when I'm too tired to cook, and my daily ration of two caffeinated soft drinks to keep me going.

My father has consistently supported my writing career and has done as much to promote the Daughters of the People Series as I have. I have been blessed to be a part of this man's life and hope to have him in mine for many years to come.

L.J. Anderson of Mayhem Cover Creations has been a dream to work with. It's thanks to her that the individual books in the Daughters of the People Series have such a beautifully distinct appearance.

A growing number of readers serve as early reviewers, and for that, you have my eternal gratitude. In particular, Linnea Bassin, Tracy Ehlers of *Paranormal, Magic and Mischief,* Jackie Elkins, Marisa Gaither of *Reading to Distraction,* Ceit Kelly, Yvonne Mashburn-Schmidt, Philip Strickland, and Jessica Walenka have not only reviewed these books, they've provided valuable feedback on the stories and characters.

I am also blessed to be a tiny part of a huge community of family and friends who have graciously provided cover critiques, research help, good wishes, and a pat on the back (or a kick in the rear) when I needed it.

That community extends to fellow authors and the large network of affiliated individuals supporting independent writers. I have benefitted greatly from the wealth of knowledge on the self-publishing industry shared by members of the kboards writing forum, posted both there and on their writing blogs. There are way too many of you to name. If you've taken the time to participate on kboards and/or have detailed your journey through the self-publishing process on your blog, chances are good I've read it, absorbed it, and applied at least some of your lessons to my own journey.

Finally, my son has served as a sounding board, a source of much-needed comedic relief, a late-night driving partner, my music advisor, and my cohort in mischief making. There are no words to describe the depth of my love or of my pride for the young man he's become.

Thank you all for your continued support and encouragement. You have no idea how much it means to me to be part of such a great community.

About the Author

Lucy Varna lives in the Blue Ridge Mountains of northeast Georgia, surrounded by her large, extended family.

www.lucyvarna.com
www.daughtersofthepeople.com

Ready for More?

BOOK 3.5, *TEMPERED*. For Hawthorne the Chronicler, a strong arm and a sharp blade have always been her primary recourses against a cold and callous world. When her untrusting heart is tempted by handsome comic book illustrator Aaron Kesselman, Hawthorne learns that those may not be the best weapons in her arsenal, particularly when her family is targeted by a member of the Eternal Order.

Available in December 2014

BOOK 4, *IN ALL THINGS, BALANCE*. Moira Firebrand is intrigued by Tom Fairfax, the man her mother tasked with sorting through the IECS Archives for clues to the near-mythical Sanctuary. Nothing is ever as easy as it should be. The Archives is in disarray, odd artifacts show up in the strangest places, and Moira's own past wedges its way between her and Tom, the one man she believes may have the strength to capture her heart.

Available in February 2015.

BOOK 5, *SANCTUARY*. Jerusha Mankiller and Drew Martin continue the search for Sanctuary and the Bones of the Just.

Available in August 2015.